MIDNIGHTS

By Sarah J. Poulsen

Published by Sarah J. Stephenson

The story, all names, characters, and incidents portrayed in this production are fictitious. No identification with actual persons (living or deceased), places, buildings, and products is intended or should be inferred.

Editors: SJ Stephenson and Rachel Hermansen

Contributors: Anianne Owens; Brette Cody; Amanda Thompson

Cover Design: Asterielly Designs **Interior Formatting:** RH Designs

Stock Art Acknowledgements: https://www.instagram.com/ShotbyIreland; Adobe Stock

ISBN: 979-89927005-1-0 **Printed in:** United States **First Edition:** 2025

This is for all of you who run headfirst into the unknown...
If it doesn't scare you, it won't change you. Fear isn't the enemy; it's the spark that ignites the fire, shaping you into the storm no one saw coming.
This is for the wild hearts, the stubborn souls, the ones who refuse to be caged. For those who question everything, who carve their own path, even when the world tells them they shouldn't.
And to those who know that power isn't given—it's taken, earned, and built from the ashes of everything that tried to break you.
This one's for you.

Spotify Playlist

If I listed every song that inspired this book, we'd be here forever. I LOVE music. These are just *some* of my favorites. If you want the full experience go check out the full playlist. *(Swifties, you already know you're in for it.)*

Vicious - Tate McRae
Enchanted - Taylor Swift
When You Say My Name - Chandler Leighton
Sweet & Dark - Miles Hardt
Alkaline - Sleep Token
The Prophecy - Taylor Swift
Night Vision - Francis Doom
Lose Control - Teddy Swims
Close To You - Gracie Abrams
So It Goes - Taylor Swift
Problem - Natalia Kills
Cruel Summer - Taylor Swift
The Death Of Peace Of Mind - Bad Omens
State of Grace - Taylor Swift
Just The Same - Charlotte Lawrence
Little Girl Gone - CHINCHILLA
Greedy - Tate McRae
Middle Of The Night - Elley Duhe
Run For The Hills - Tate McRae
I Can Do It With A Broken Heart - Taylor Swift
Guilty As Sin - Taylor Swift
Let It Happen - Gracie Abrams
Glitch - Taylor Swift

"I don't start shit, but I can tell you how it ends."
-Taylor Swift

When I sat down to write this story, I didn't just want to create a world—I wanted to build something you could get lost in. A place that felt alive, where danger isn't just possible—it's inevitable. A story where survival isn't promised, where strength isn't about power, but about what breaks you and how you rise from it. I've always been drawn to books that drag you under, kicking and screaming, refusing to let go. The kind that shatter their characters, only to watch them claw their way back from the ashes. That's what I wanted for this. Something raw. Something real. Something that lingers.

At its core, this book is about fate, resilience, and the power of choice. About what happens when the world demands you break, but you refuse. Raven isn't perfect—she's reckless, headstrong, and reluctant to face the truth about herself. But she fights. She falls. She gets back up. Because strength isn't about never losing—it's about who you become in the process.

This isn't just a story about magic and war—it's about destiny and defiance. About a woman who isn't just running from her past, but hurtling toward a future she doesn't yet understand. And in the midst of curses, power struggles, and secrets that could tear everything apart—there's still room for passion, for connection, for a love that doesn't just consume but changes you.

This book is for those who crave magic, fae, witches, curses, slow-burn tension, and the undeniable pull of fate. For those who love adventure, impossible choices, and characters who challenge each other at every turn. If you love a heroine who is fierce, stubborn, and unknowingly powerful, and a bad boy who is possessive, intense, and torn between duty and desire, then this book is for you. Thank you for being part of this journey. I hope you lose yourself in it the way I have.

And remember—"Never be so polite, you forget your power."
With love and all the magic in the world,

Sarah J. Poulsen

Prologue

T his has been the longest week of my life.

Yesterday, I buried my grandfather, and the reality of it still refuses to settle in. It doesn't seem real. It just seems like some cruel joke where I'll wake up and he'll still be here, calling me 'Bird' and asking why I look like I haven't slept in days.

But he isn't.

One moment, he was here. Solid and real, and then *bam*. Gone. Just like that.

I keep expecting to hear his voice, to find him sitting in his chair, reading like he always did. Maybe it's the grief talking. Maybe it's just that I can't accept that someone who was part of my life every single day is suddenly *nowhere*.

It was the same when I lost my grandmother a few years ago. I thought I understood heartbreak back then, but this feels like a hollowing, like part of me was carved out, and I'm just supposed to keep moving like nothing's changed.

It's worse because they weren't just my grandparents. They *raised* me. My grandfather was my dad in every way that mattered.

The details of how I lost my parents are a little vague. I was only two when it happened, too young to remember anything. My grandparents called it a tragic accident, but that's all they ever said. Whenever I asked, grief clouded their faces, heavy and suffocating, so I stopped pushing. Some wounds, even time can't touch.

Still, they told me about my parents and the way they met, the things we did as a family, the sound of my mother's laugh, the color of my father's eyes. I don't remember them, not really, but I know them through those stories,

1

through the love that still lingered in my grandparents' voices whenever they spoke about them.

My grandparents moved to the States from Scotland after I was born, wanting to be close since I was their only grandchild. My grandfather used to say that in the first few years after my parents died, all I wanted was to be outside. I would talk to the flowers, sing to the trees, whisper to the wind like I was telling secrets.

Whenever I was upset, outside was the first place he would look. He said he could always hear my voice somewhere in the yard. Maybe I thought I was singing to my parents. Maybe, I thought that somehow, they could hear me.

Then I was homeschooled at some point during grade school. It wasn't the plan, but it became necessary after the teasing got to be too much. My wild hair that couldn't be tamed was always covered in dirt from playing outside, and no product and no amount of brushing could make it manageable. I could handle the names, but my grandparents were the ones who had to help me pick things out of it when I got home. One day, after they had to untangle gum for the third time in a week, my grandmother had enough. That was the last day I set foot in a public classroom.

She became my teacher, filling my days with more than just math and English. She taught me about plants, herbs, and flowers. What their uses were, along with their meanings. She told me the earth speaks to those who know how to listen, that nature has a rhythm, a pulse, a whisper of its own.

She also read to me every night. Her stories were always about magic, witches, dragons, fairies, and forgotten realms. Dark fairytales with no guaranteed happy endings. I loved those the most. They felt honest and real. Life wasn't a perfect fairytale; it was messy, unpredictable, and laced with shadows.

My grandfather was the opposite. Where my grandmother nurtured, he prepared. He taught me how to defend myself, how to throw a punch without breaking my wrist, how to plant my feet so I wouldn't be knocked off balance. He never said where he learned these things, and I never asked.

"There's always time for a lady to learn how to defend herself," he'd say with a wink. Then, quieter, like a secret, *"If you ever find yourself in a place you don't want to be, you'll know how to get out."*

2

They both insisted on daily meditation, something I wasn't allowed to skip, no matter how restless I felt. *"A sharp mind is as important as a sharp blade,"* Grandpa would say. I didn't understand then. I do now.

When I turned fifteen, my grandmother decided I needed to be around kids my own age. A week later, I was enrolled in high school. It was fine, I guess. I made friends, lived as normal a life as I could. But I never forgot the lessons my grandparents taught me. I never had to use them, but I'd like to think they're still in me, waiting for the day I might need them.

And now, standing in this empty house, surrounded by ghosts and memories, I don't know what to do.

My grandparents were my world. They raised me, shaped me, and taught me everything I know, even if some of it felt old-fashioned. When I dropped out of college to forge my own path, they supported me. When I started my own company, my grandfather helped me navigate business deals. And when I admitted I wasn't happy running it, he was the first to tell me to sell it.

"Do it scared," he'd say, *"because it's better than doing nothing."*

Right before he passed, we were supposed to take a trip to Scotland together. He never told me why the timing had to be *just right*, only that it wasn't ever right before. But now?

I didn't even know he was sick. One minute, he was fine. The next, he was in a hospital bed, and everything unraveled too fast for me to catch it.

Regret claws at me. I should have been here more. I should have called more, visited more, but life got busy. And then I met Chance.

He took up so much of my time, and I let him.

For months, I barely saw my grandpa. It wasn't until recently that I made a point to visit every week. Now, it doesn't feel like enough.

"Fuck you, Grandpa." The words slip out in a whisper, cracking at the edges. "Why did you have to leave me?"

Silence presses around me, thick and heavy.

I don't want to do this. Not now. Not ever. Sorting through his things feels like erasing him, piece by piece.

When my grandmother died, he barely touched her things. Now, I understand why.

He left everything to me, but I have no idea what I'm supposed to do with it all. We sorted through some of Marjorie's things after she passed, donated some of her clothes, and packed away little trinkets. But most of it stayed exactly where she left it. Like he couldn't bear to let her go completely.

And now... *I get it*. More than I ever wanted to.

I know there's no way I'll get through all of this in one day. Honestly, I'd be lucky to make a dent even if I spent every day here for a month. But I have the next two weeks off, so I'll figure it out, or at least come up with some kind of plan.

That's a start. Right?

Chance and I got into a fight right before I came, which is why I'm here alone. *Again*.

Apparently, he couldn't make it to the funeral. He was *"too busy with work."* Said it was *"too short of notice"* for him to take the time off.

I guess I can understand that. Not everyone has a flexible schedule. But still... funerals aren't exactly planned in advance.

Chance and my grandpa barely knew each other. He was always *too busy* to come with me when I visited. *Too busy*—that's always his excuse. And maybe it's valid, but how long do I pretend it doesn't hurt?

I don't need someone to solve my problems, but *damn*. Just showing up would be nice.

We got into it last night, which I hated, especially after the day I had. The storm outside seemed to echo my mood. Every crack of thunder felt like an extension of my own rage. The sky howled, gray clouds rolling like an ocean ready to swallow everything whole. It rained in torrents, thick and endless, as if the world were mourning with me.

When I got here after the funeral, I was a mess, barely holding myself together.

I tried calling Chance. No answer.

I called again.

And again.

By the time he finally picked up, desperation had settled into my bones. He sounded annoyed. Like he had already checked out of the conversation before it even started.

He rattled off how *busy* he was, how *sorry* he was, but he just *couldn't talk right now.*

And then there was, *"Not everyone can put their life on hold."*

That was the exact second something in me snapped and I almost broke up with his ass right then and there.

I knew he'd been stressed. Starting a business isn't easy. But I wasn't asking him to fix anything or move any mountains. I just *needed him here.*

A few hours later, he texted, apologizing. Said he was tired. That he *didn't mean it* and promised he'd talk to his boss and see if he could take the day off and come down in the morning.

This morning, however, I got another text.

> Chance: Headed into the office early. I'll call you after my meeting.

I didn't even reply.

At least I have Rachel. She's my best friend, and the closest thing I have to a sister. If she weren't out of town, I know without question she'd be here right now, forcing me into some ridiculous distraction, determined to make me laugh.

But she isn't. And I'm alone.

A loud growl from my stomach reminds me that I haven't eaten since before the funeral. I force myself into the kitchen, reaching for a glass of water. But when I look up, I freeze.

A photo sits on the counter.

Three figures with their arms wrapped around each other, smiling on the porch.

Me. Grandpa. Grandma.

The grief slams into me like a tidal wave before I can brace for it. The weight on my chest crushes down, and suddenly, the air is too thick, like the walls are pressing in. My vision blurs, a lump forming in my throat as hot tears sting my eyes. I try to shove it back down and lock it up tight where it can't reach me. But it's too late. The dam cracks wide open, and before I know it, I'm *sobbing.*

I sink to the floor, curling in on myself as the grief rips through me, raw and uncontrollable. Ugly, heaving cries tear out of my chest, shaking my whole body.

"Fuck," I whisper, voice breaking. "What am I supposed to do with all this stuff?"

My eyes burn as I stare at the endless sea of memories left behind.

"What am I supposed to do, period?"

Suddenly, a crash echoes from the other room and my sobs vanish, as instincts kick in. I push the fear down, letting it shift into something else.

Survival.

I grab a knife off the counter, and move slowly toward the noise, heart hammering in my chest. The house is suddenly too quiet.

I peek around the corner and come face-to-face with... a cat.

We both jump.

"Holy shit you scared me!" I exhale, pressing a hand to my chest as Fat Louie lll blinks up at me, utterly unbothered. Then, proceeds to sit and casually lick his paw like he didn't just almost send me into cardiac arrest.

Of course. How could I forget about the cat?

Grandpa got him a couple of years ago. Or rather, he just showed up at the front door one day and decided to stay. Naturally, Grandpa let him.

"Lou Lou, what the hell? You could've scared me half to death." I pause, "too soon. I know. But *fuck*."

Louie lets out a soft meow, rubbing against my leg, and something in my chest clenches.

"I know, I miss him too." My voice comes out quieter than I mean for it to. I crouch down, scratching behind his ears. "I guess it's just you and me now, pal."

Great. Now I'm talking to the cat like he can actually understand me.

I push up from the floor and force myself into movement. I need a distraction; I need something to do.

I ping-pong around the house, tidying up, taking out the trash, doing dishes. Tasks that offer a small, fleeting sense of normalcy. If I keep my hands busy, maybe my mind will quiet for a while.

By the time I make it to the office, my arms are full of mail I've gathered from around the house. I drop the stack onto the desk, but as I do, something catches my eye.

A black envelope with my name written across the front in familiar handwriting. My heart skips a beat, and I rush forward, shoving the rest of the mail aside. My fingers tremble as I tear it open, careful not to damage whatever's inside.

The moment I unfold the letter, goosebumps spread across my skin.

Yep. Here comes the waterworks.

I press the paper to my chest, squeezing my eyes shut, trying to hold it together.

All I can do is breathe through the flood of emotion as silent tears stream down my face.

This sucks.

I draw a shaky breath before finally looking down to read.

Dearest Raven,

I'm going to miss you the most, Bird.

I know you're going to do what you want anyway, but don't let yourself be sad for too long. It was time for me to go.

There's so much I wanted to tell you, and so many times I wanted to take you back, but it wasn't the right time. The time is coming, and you'll know when it's right. Trust that.

I am so proud of you, and the woman you've become. Remember that you're always in control. As long as you trust yourself, you'll know the way.

Oh, and I have something I want to give you.

I love you.

I read the letter six more times, crying harder each time. I flip it over, searching for more, but it's just as blank as it was the first time.

A pang of selfish disappointment hits me. *That's it?* He always had more to say, always had one last story to tell, one last lesson to sneak in when I wasn't paying attention.

Why couldn't he have written more?

I rush back to the desk, tearing through the envelope, fingers fumbling as I check again.

Empty.

My mind races. *Something I want to give you?*

Then it hits me. Louie.

Of course.

I glance at the cat, who's currently sprawled on the floor, licking his paw like he has zero concerns in the world.

"You wouldn't last a day out there on your own." He doesn't even look up. Probably because he knows I'm right. Spoiled little shit wouldn't make it past breakfast.

With a sigh, I turn back to the desk, planning to clear off the rest of the papers, but something catches my eye beneath the stack.

I lift the mess of envelopes and bills, and I freeze.

It's a gold key with a thin black ribbon tied around it.

Umm... okay?

The metal is old, worn with age, the edges are dulled from years of handling. I frown, turning it over in my fingers. *What am I supposed to do with this? What does this even go to?* I glance back at the letter, hoping for some kind of clue, but it's silent as ever.

I huff out a breath. "You're kidding me, right, Grandpa? Is this some kind of joke?"

No answer, of course.

Louie, however, meows loudly behind me, making me jump. I whirl around. "LOUIE. What did I *just* say about sneaking up on people?"

My pulse is still hammering in my ears, but the cat just stares at me with his unblinking, *I-know-you're-an-idiot* look before rubbing against my leg like I'm the one who scared *him*.

He is *so* lucky he's cute.

I sigh, rubbing a hand down my face. "I'm all you've got now, so you better start acting right."

Unbothered, he sits back down and resumes licking his paw.

With another deep breath, I refocus on the desk, clearing off more papers, searching for anything that might tell me what the key is for. *Or if there's something else I've missed.*

Before I get too far into my search, my phone vibrates in my pocket.

I pull it out, glance at the screen, it's Chance. And I already know what the message will say before I open it.

8

Chance: Hey babe, boss is losing his shit, and I'm stuck in this meeting. No way I can leave. We've got a deadline. I'll make it up to you later or something. You got this. Love ya.

I shove my phone back in my pocket, his words feeling like a hollow reassurance.

Of course.

I let out a slow, frustrated breath, though deep down, I'm not even surprised anymore. He's been buried in this project for what feels like forever, and I'm always the one left waiting.

I don't have the time or energy to unpack the emotional back-and-forth with him right now. I've cried enough for today. I'm sure he'll tell me *when* he's planning on coming later. *Hopefully.*

I swallow the lump in my throat and shove the thought aside. I'll deal with it when the time comes. Whenever *that* is. Until then, I'm on my own.

Again.

I finish clearing off the desk, tossing aside the last few loose papers and picking up a few books that need to go back on the shelf.

As I carry them to the bookshelf, something catches my eye. It's a deep mahogany cover, with hints of gold lettering etched into the spine. The book stands out from the others because I'm *one thousand percent* sure I've never seen this book before. The edges are scuffed, the binding worn, and the gold nearly faded from years of handling.

I carefully pull it from the shelf, my fingers brushing over the unreadable title. The leather is smooth but aged, carrying the weight of something long forgotten. It feels *ancient*. The spine cracks as I open it and the sound is sharp in the quiet room.

The first several pages are blank, nothing but faded paper staring back at me. I flip through more, my brows pulling together. Page after page. *Empty.*

Just as I'm about to give up and shove it back in its place, something shifts. This page has words scrawled in delicate slants of ink that stand out against the aged paper. It looks like my grandmother's handwriting.

My pulse stumbles.

Her stories. Witches and warriors, Fae and shadows, magic hidden in the world's forgotten corners. I always wondered where she got them, if they were borrowed from old books or something she made up. Sometimes, she made it sound like they weren't stories at all. *More like memories.*

I turn another page, fingers trembling.

More handwritten notes.

Before I can make sense of it, my phone rings. The sharp noise shatters the moment, yanking me back. I exhale, setting the book down with an almost reluctant hesitation before reaching for my phone.

A part of me expects it to be Chance. But when I glance at the screen, my stomach sinks.

Rachel.

A wave of disappointment crashes over me that it's not Chance, harder than I care to admit. I *shouldn't* be surprised. I *shouldn't* be upset. And yet, I am.

Shoving the feeling aside, I swipe to answer.

"Hey," I say, forcing some semblance of normalcy into my tone. But she doesn't buy it.

We chat for a few minutes keeping the conversation light but careful. Catching up on the small things that somehow feel much bigger now. She listens, offers comfort without pushing too hard, and doesn't hang up until she's convinced I'm actually *okay.*

Before we say goodbye, she makes me promise to text her regular updates, so she doesn't have to call every hour to make sure I'm not crying on the couch again.

Three more days until she's back.

When the call ends, I focus on tidying up, hoping the mundane act of putting things in order might help settle the storm inside me. Despite the hours spent sorting through memories, I still haven't found anything that hints at what the key might open.

And Chance still hasn't called back.

Exhaustion sinks deep in my bones, but oddly enough, the chaos feels lighter. Not gone, but *manageable.* As if organizing the clutter around me has somehow made the mess inside me *less suffocating.*

The steady rhythm of the song fills the kitchen, pulling me into its beat as I move through the motions of cracking eggs, buttering toast, flipping bacon. It's almost enough to push back the weight of yesterday.

Almost.

A knock at the door cuts through the music and I freeze, spatula hovering over the pan. I reach over to turn the music down, grabbing a towel. I dry my hands and make my way to the door, and when I open it, my breath catches.

A package sits on the doorstep with my name scrawled across the top. Whoever left it is already gone.

A nervous, electric kind of anticipation that I don't quite understand floods my system and my fingers itch to open it. I scoop it up and nudge the door closed with my foot.

I set the package on the counter and grab a knife. My pulse quickens as I slide the blade through the tape, cutting through the seal. The cardboard flaps spring open, revealing a smaller, polished wooden case.

I pause, breath catching in my throat.

The wood is smooth and dark, the edges slightly worn, but it's the carvings that hold my attention. Intricate patterns swirl and weave across the surface, the designs almost seem to shift under the light. The craftsmanship is impeccable.

I run my fingers lightly over the surface, tracing the grooves, half-expecting to feel something click into place.

"What are you?" I mutter under my breath.

The box opens and I go still, I stare at what's inside. My attention is immediately drawn to two things in particular. A white crystal and a black stone. Both are raw and unpolished. The crystal shines with a soft, ethereal light, almost humming with a quiet energy. The stone is the opposite, absorbing the light around it, dark and mysterious.

I reach out hesitantly, brushing my fingertips against the crystal first. The moment I make contact, a gentle warmth spreads through me, like sunlight melting into my skin. It's comforting. Familiar, even.

Then, I pick up the stone.

A sharp jolt shoots through my palm. The energy is instant, coiling up my arm like a current of electricity. It's not warm. Not gentle. It feels powerful and demanding. My breath shudders, a chill running down my spine as I yank my hand back.

What the hell was that?

I shake off the lingering sensation, flexing my fingers, but the phantom energy still hums beneath my skin. Forcing myself to refocus, I glance back into the box, trying to make sense of everything inside.

My eyes catch on something else. It's a braided rope, with three differently colored ribbons. I don't know what it is, but it's beautiful. I reach for it, lifting it carefully out of the box. The texture is impossibly soft, yet strong, like time itself couldn't fray it. Vines are intertwined with the braid, growing through the ribbons like they were always meant to be there.

The three ribbons tell their own story. One is a deep, earthy green. It's rich, vibrant, and pulsing with life. The second is a soft ivory one, its edges slightly aged, but still intact. But it's the last one that steals my breath.

A gold ribbon. Not fabric, not silk, but something else entirely. It shimmers, shifting like captured sunlight.

I swallow hard, running my fingers over the length of the braid, finding a crescent moon pendant at the end, its golden surface is smooth and cool beneath my touch.

Intricate carvings etch along the curve of it, delicate yet mesmerizing. They mean *something*, I just don't know *what*. At the other end of the rope, I notice a jagged edge, where it looks like a star once hung.

I wonder if it's hidden somewhere at the bottom of the box.

I glance back into the box and freeze.

Umm, what?

At the bottom, is a dagger, unlike anything I've ever seen. The blade catches the light, daring me to pick it up. But it's the hilt that really pulls me in, the details so precise, so deliberate, that my fingers itch to trace them.

A moonstone is embedded into the handle, its iridescent shimmer shifting with every tilt. Soft blues, purples, and greens dance beneath the surface, as if the stone holds the sky inside it. The contrast against the dark metal makes it stand out even more.

My fingers brush the cool hilt before wrapping around it completely. The dagger is solid and cold. But beneath the surface, something pulses, almost like a heartbeat.

My breath slows, my grip tightening as I turn it over, running my fingers along the details. It's deadly and beautiful, and something about it feels *familiar*. Like I've held it before, even though I know I haven't.

The blade itself is just as stunning. Ancient runes are etched into the steel, each delicate mark seamlessly blending into the next.

A slow exhale escapes my lips. *This is mine.* The realization sends a shiver down my spine, settling deep in my bones. I force myself to set the dagger aside, my pulse thrumming as my mind races.

My eyes land on something else, tucked neatly into the corner of the box. A small velvet bag. I pick it up, opening it to find a necklace. I lift it out carefully, turning it over in my palm. The design is as striking as the dagger.

At its center, a crystal flickers like bottled lightning, pulsing with an energy that hums against my skin. Twisting vines and intricate metal filigree weave around it. There's a snake that coils through the design, its scales etched with precision, gleaming like a silent warning. Like nature and something else have been fused together.

It's exquisite.

And like everything else in this box, it hums with energy.

I swallow hard. *Well. This is weird, but cool as hell.*

I glance back inside and my stomach flips when I spot two more things. A white envelope and a second key.

It's the envelope that has my breath stalling. Everything else fades as I press my thumb along the seal, the edges of the paper are soft and worn with time.

"Seriously?" I mutter, rolling my eyes with a small, breathless laugh. *More secrets. Of course.*

With a flick of my fingers, I tear open the envelope. My pulse quickens as I unfold the letter. I take a slow breath and begin to read.

13

Raven,

I knew this would keep your mind off of being sad. I know
how much you love adventures how much you need them.
But this one is different. This adventure has more
than just answers.

I've been waiting for the right moment to give these
to you, and I guess this is it.

The crystal and stone, they are for balance and protection.
Keep them on you at all times. No matter what. They will
be your companions as you navigate what lies ahead.

The dagger may seem strange, out of place, but it's more
than a weapon. It's both a shield and a key. Trust yourself
when the time comes. You'll know when to use it.

The key, my dear, will reveal its true purpose when you're
ready. Trust your instincts, trust the gifts you've been given.
You are stronger and more capable than you know.

And finally, our tickets.

I'm sorry I couldn't go with you, Bird. I wanted to. But I have
no doubt Rachel will go in my place and make it unforgettable.
There's no rush, use them when you're ready. They're
one-way tickets, but I've added enough to your account
for a return trip.

I knew you'd never buy them yourself, so now, you're
doing it scared, with your best friend.

Go have fun

Keep these things close. Always.

Love you kid.
Grandpa

CHAPTER 1

When in Rome... or in This Case, Scotland

RAVEN

1 year later

When I discovered romance novels, everything about relationships and happily ever after changed for me.

No man I met ever measured up. Not really anyway.

I constantly compared them to the characters in my books. Is asking for a man who would burn the world down for the woman he loved really that much of an ask? Reality, in comparison, was always an anticlimactic let down.

I blame my grandmother for that.

I've been in plenty of relationships, or rather, plenty of *lessons*, she would have called them.

There were the ones who were *too nice*, the kind of men who agreed with everything I said, who bent over backward with no spine of their own. *Doormats,* we called them. Instant turn-off.

And then, there were the others.

The ones who knew exactly how to play the game. Who saw girls who wanted love, who wanted to believe in something real, and used it against them.

In case you didn't pick up on that, it's me. *I'm that girl.*

Things always started out perfect. They pull you in with the whole nice-and-sweet routine, sprinkled with just enough of that bad-boy edge to keep you intrigued. They make you feel special. Chosen. And by the time their mask slips, by the time you see the cracks, it's already too late.

You're hooked.

By then, you're knee-deep in feelings and shit, with no clear direction.

Who shit in my Cheerios, you ask?

My Ex. That's who.

And look, I'll never claim to be perfect, but at least I'm working on it. Obviously.

This last year has been brutal, to say the least. Losing my grandfather was hard enough. Losing myself in the aftermath? Worse. Add a breakup on top of it, and you've got yourself the perfect disaster.

But here I am, fresh out of the slammer, so to speak. Or at least, that's what it feels like. I just clawed my way out of the worst relationship in the history of relationships.

It's like I have some twisted savior complex I never asked for and sure as hell didn't sign up for.

But now I'm indifferent. Grateful, even. Consider that lesson learned. *And then some.*

I never want to feel that small, that lost, that unseen again.

Ever.

I had to crawl my way out of that hole. Piece by piece, I put myself back together because I finally realized that no one was coming to save me.

This trip is one of those pieces. A way to take something back for myself. A way to breathe again.

I realized that I clearly have a pattern.

I fall for guys who seem perfect at first. They're nice, charming, saying all the right things, only to end up used and discarded the second I'm no longer *useful.*

It took weeks to find my footing again after Chance and I broke up. I'd wanted out of our relationship for a long time, but every time I tried, the douche canoe had a way of twisting things, making me feel like I was the problem. Made me believe that if I just tried harder, gave more, fixed whatever was broken in me, then maybe I'd finally be enough.

And that's never happening again.

The relationship finally ended the day I found out he was cheating on me. While I was at his house, scrubbing the counters and making us a romantic dinner, no less.

Long day at work, my ass.

Turns out "working late" meant screwing the girl next door. It wasn't a total loss, though. At least our two-year circus of a relationship was finally over.

I could go into all the details, but honestly? That's an entire library full of unsolved mysteries mankind will never crack. Which is why I now have a closet full of trauma I have zero intention of unpacking.

The point is, I've sworn off men.

Forever.

For good.

Well... at least until I decide otherwise. But I don't anticipate changing my status anytime soon.

I'm on this whole journey of self-discovery because, clearly, my radar for decent men is beyond repair. So yeah, I'm convinced there are no *right* men for me right now.

I know they exist because... books. *Obviously.*

But until then? NO men. Zero. Nada.

I just turned twenty-five, so it's not like I'm at risk of dying alone. I've still got time. Which is why I'm focusing on me, and this time I mean it. No distractions. No getting sucked into someone else's drama.

Rachel and I have traveled a lot together. Florida? Core memory. The Keys? Absolute magic. I *may* have fallen in love a little there. Those Keys, man...

Okay, I need to stop thinking about that trip.

Especially the part where I *definitely didn't* get free drinks all weekend from the bartender who *definitely wasn't* professing his undying love for me by day two. And Rachel and I *absolutely* didn't pretend we were together to avoid any further advances.

And then there was the real highlight. After the bartender tried to feel me up, Rachel, who's five feet of pure menace on a good day, slapped him clean across the bar. His *own* bar.

And in true Rachel fashion, she calmly leaned over his stunned form and threatened to haunt his dreams if he ever spoke to me again.

Still one of the best moments of my life. The look on his face was *priceless.*

Then there was the Oregon/Washington coast trip. Two weeks of absolute freedom. The kind of trip that makes you forget real life exists.

And yes, Jacob Black's house was involved.

Was I secretly hoping he actually lived there and would come outside to say hi? Absolutely. A girl can dream, right?

We've been on so many adventures together. Some big, some small, some so wildly questionable that, in hindsight, it's a miracle we survived them.

Honestly, what man would sign up for all of that? Probably none. Maybe this *no men* thing really is the way to go. Just me, Rachel, and Fat Louie, traveling the world and leaving chaos in our wake.

And speaking of adventures... did I mention we're finally in Scotland? I can hardly believe we're here.

After getting those tickets, I never expected it to take this long to finally make the trip. But things with Chance... well, they spiraled. Hard.

Like I said, I got lost in that relationship for longer than I care to admit. *Spoiler alert:* It wasn't for the best. Far from it, actually.

What started out as something thrilling quickly unraveled into a shitshow I never saw coming. Maybe it was toxic from the start, or maybe I just ignored the red flags because I *wanted* it to work. Because I wanted him to be who I thought he could be.

Either way, I found myself stuck in a never-ending loop of fight, making up, repeat.

It was like trying to patch a sinking ship with duct tape. Messy, exhausting, and completely pointless.

But now that things have finally settled and our schedules lined up, we made it.

Packing for two weeks had been a challenge since I wasn't sure how long I wanted to stay and Rachel could only stay for two weeks, so that seemed like a good starting point. I still don't really know what kind of answers I'm looking for here, or how long it'll take to find them.

I do have to work a little while I'm here. Just a single meeting with a potential client, which means checking my email occasionally to stay on top of things. Personally, I don't think we even need this guy, but it's not my decision. So I'll play nice for now.

Rachel and I also happened to buy tickets to a masquerade ball at a castle. She found them online one day, and honestly, she had me at "*ball.*"

Now, it's the main event of the trip.

We arrived last night, grabbed a bite to eat, and came straight to our place. Since then, we've been sleeping off the jetlag.

Our little cottage isn't a castle, but it's cozy, and I can almost picture some brooding aristocrat who once lived here, pacing the halls, whiskey in hand, waiting for a long-lost lover to return.

At least, that's the story I'm sticking with.

The cottage has two bedrooms, each decorated to match exactly what you'd imagine a Scottish hideaway to look like. It's rugged, yet modern. Minimalist, yet somehow still edgy. The room I'm in is straight out of a gothic fairytale. It's dark, dramatic, and ridiculously luxurious.

The walls are a deep, stormy charcoal, shifting in the light like rolling clouds. Black crown molding frames the ceiling, the kind of detail you don't see anymore, but it's stunning.

The furniture is sleek but imposing. Most of it is black and modern, with sharp edges softened by dim lighting. A massive fireplace sits along one wall, its carved stone mantel wrapped in twisting ivy patterns.

The artwork scattered across the walls is haunting figures frozen in time. The scenes tell stories I'd love to know. One painting in particular catches my eye, it's a woman standing on the edge of a stormy cliff. The wind ripping through her dark gown, her face turned toward something unseen.

Then there are the deer heads, watching over the space. It should feel creepy, but somehow, it just... fits. Dark aristocratic manor vibes, fully intact.

And this bed?

I sink deeper into the four-poster king bed, which probably isn't even a king. It's obnoxiously oversized, draped in sheets that feel like they belong to an actual goddess. I'm certain they have no less than a three-million thread count.

I reach blindly for my phone on the black marble nightstand, feeling the weight of exhaustion settle in my bones.

Two things hit me at once. One, I did *not* do this place proper justice when we got here. I should've been examining every inch, not passing out the second my head hit the pillow.

And two, I have absolutely no idea what time it is.

I hate jet lag.

It's like your period showing up unannounced, relieved you're not pregnant, but exhausted and completely useless to the world.

"Finally, you're awake!" Rachel practically yells, bouncing like a caffeinated toddler, while I nearly roll off the side of the giant mattress.

I steady myself, groaning, then turn and attempt to shove her off the bed. Only to realize she's too far away.

This bed is *huge*.

I pause, staring at the ridiculous expanse of pillows and silk sheets.

Wait. Do beds this size even exist in the U.S.? Whatever it is, I need it in my life. Immediately.

"Oh my God, why are we yelling?" I groan, dragging the blanket over my head.

"There's *no way* you've been awake for hours," I mumble. "If that were the case, we wouldn't still be in bed, and you would've woken me up ages ago."

I yawn, poking my head out from under the blankets for air, already regretting it.

"Who knows. I'm just relieved you're finally awake." She dramatically clutches her stomach. "I was about to die of starvation. Oh, and by the way, I'd like you to know that I like your room better than mine."

I open my mouth to respond, but she throws up a hand, stopping me mid-breath.

"Before you ask, *nothing's* wrong with it. It's gorgeous. I mean, obviously, we have taste." She flips her hair, which only makes me want to laugh even more. "But it's just *way* too far away from your room, and honestly? Spooky as hell. First night in a foreign country? Alone? No thanks."

I snort because I already know where this is going.

She crosses her arms like she's preparing for a fight. "Look, I don't want to be in my room alone. And who knows if some *Peeping Tom* could be lurking outside my window. You'd be all the way over here, fast asleep, totally unaware that I was getting kidnapped."

"Fine!" I say through my laughter. "You can stay in here, I guess."

Rachel grins triumphantly, already pulling the blankets around her like she's won something. I shake my head, unable to stop smiling.

She's an absolute lunatic. Love her to death, but she's definitely watched way too many true crime shows alone in the dark.

22

Sitting on the plane next to her was an experience. I *should've* put her in the middle seat between two strangers. Maybe she would've held it together a little better.

Rachel is *terrified* of flying. Keep in mind *she* wanted to come on this trip, fully aware how long the flight was. And yet, there she was, holding onto my hand with a death grip, cutting off my circulation the entire way.

And the movie she chose to watch?

Taken.

Of all movies to watch when traveling internationally, she picked the one about international kidnappings.

I told her she was making things worse for herself. And what was her response?

"I'm just preparing myself for the worst, so I know how to react."

See what I mean? Absolute lunatic.

She waves me off like it's no big deal. "Okay, okay. What's the plan? What time is it?"

I roll my eyes. "Well, I was *about* to check before you startled me awake like a demon-possessed toddler. I nearly had an out-of-body experience and fell off the bed."

She snorts, finally breaking into laughter, and I can't help but grin. Classic Rachel. Chaos first, questions later.

I push myself up, stretching out the jet lag from my limbs. "Do you want to go out tonight?" I glance at her. "Maybe a pub? I'd rather avoid anything too... touristy. Not my scene."

She arches an eyebrow. "And you think it's *mine*?"

I shrug. "Touché."

Finally checking my phone for real, I blink. "It's 6 p.m." My voice comes out in pure disbelief. "We slept that long?"

"*You* slept that long," Rachel announces, pulling out her phone with an exaggerated sigh. "*I've* been awake for hours."

I stretch, trying to shake off the weight in my limbs, but the exhaustion lingers. Lately, I've been sleeping more than usual. It feels like the kind of tired that sleep doesn't seem to fix. I've just been blaming it on the breakup, the stress, and the fact that I'm finally catching up on rest after months of feeling on edge.

She rolls over onto her side, scrolling through her phone, fingers tapping against the screen. Hopefully, she's actually looking for places to eat because I *hate* being the one who has to pick.

"Thank *God* you woke up. Seriously." Her eyes are still on her phone. "I was seriously about to jump on top of you and announce that I was dying of starvation, and if you loved me at all, you'd wake up."

Right on cue, my stomach growls, making Rachel smirk.

"Alright, alright. At this point, I'd go *anywhere*. Just please let it be somewhere with decent food."

Rachel's eyes light up as she wiggles her phone at me. "Good news, there's a pub just a short walk from here. Cozy, not too touristy. Perfect, right?"

Rachel's been relentless in trying to get me to drink for *years*. Especially post-breakup. I told her that on this trip, I'd *consider* trying a drink or two. Not that I've ever had much interest in alcohol.

She thinks it's about time I *lived a little* since I didn't party in my teen years like a *normal person*.

Whatever that means.

It doesn't help that several of the douchebags I dated conveniently also had alcohol problems. So yeah, drinking's never really been my thing.

He-*who-shall-not-ever-be-talked-about...* also an alcoholic. Shocker.

"Let's just hope this place has more charm than guys with whiskey breath," I mutter.

Rachel raises an eyebrow. "You know that's half the appeal of a pub, right?"

I groan, already bracing myself for whatever madness awaits.

I finally force myself to roll out of bed, and head straight to the fridge for our emergency stash of snacks.

"Let me get an outfit together, something pub-appropriate." I attempted my best Scottish accent. Which ends up sounding more British, but who am I kidding? I definitely just sounded like an American trying way too hard.

Rachel grabs her stomach, doubling over in laughter, her entire body shaking as she gasps for air.

"It couldn't have been *that* funny," I mutter, already fighting back a grin.

She wheezes between laughs, tears in her eyes. "No... it *really* was."

I roll my eyes. "Well, clearly, I need to practice more. I'd hate to stick out like a sore American thumb. After all, my family *is* from here."

Rachel finally catches her breath, wiping her eyes, but the moment she looks at me, her face twists in mock horror.

"If you talk like *that* while we're out, you will absolutely scare all the men away." Then, her lips curve into a devious grin. "Which is exactly why you *should* do it. Because then I'll pee my pants laughing, and it'll be the best day of my life."

This is why we can't have nice things.

I shake my head, laughing even harder. Maybe I've got it all wrong, as long as I let *her* talk first then no one will notice me.

Now we're both in tears, and I already know I'll be sore tomorrow from laughing so hard. I make my way to the closet, and I nearly trip over my suitcase lying in the middle of the floor.

Rachel, on the other hand, has already made herself right at home. Her clothes are perfectly hung, her suitcase neatly tucked away. Bless that organized bitch that I call my best friend. My stuff has magically been unpacked and put away like I have some invisible personal assistant.

Guess she wasn't kidding about being awake for hours.

I start rummaging through the closet for something that's not *too* extra, but still hot, when Rachel grabs her phone, and Taylor Swift starts playing through the speaker.

Call me a Swiftie, call me whatever you want, but *Enchanted* will forever be one of my favorites.

I eye my outfit options.

A little black mini dress? *Tempting.*

Jean shorts and a tank? *Basically, Rachel's entire personality.*

Leggings with a cropped hoodie? *The ultimate I'm casual but still hot energy.*

After all the traveling, I'm not going to lie, I'm seriously leaning toward the leggings. I'm not trying to impress anyone, and honestly I'm still groggy from just waking up, so comfy is calling my name.

Rachel catches the look on my face and immediately steps in like I just personally offended her.

"Nope. Absolutely not."

Before I can protest, she snatches the leggings and hoodie right out of my hands and dramatically tosses them onto the floor like they're toxic.

"Dress or shorts?" She demands, hands on her hips. "And remember, if there's music, you're going to be dancing with me, so choose accordingly."

As if I hadn't already thought of that.

I narrow my eyes, half-amused. "You act like I'm new here."

Rachel grins. "Just making sure."

After a lot of convincing on my part, I settle on my leather leggings, despite them *not* being in the official options pile. I top it off with my new cream lace corset from our pre-trip shopping spree. It's comfortable and sexy. The perfect middle ground. Which seems to make Rachel happy.

We snack while we finish getting ready because nothing says girls night out quite like a solid *girl dinner* to kick off a night of questionable decisions and good vibes.

For a two-bedroom, this bathroom is massive. It could probably count as a whole extra room. Rachel sits on the counter doing her makeup, when she suddenly pauses, meeting my stare in the mirror.

"Ummm, *hi*, we're in Scotland! *Finally!*"

She practically bounces, the thrill hitting her all over again. "We're going to have so much fun! I can't wait to dance and meet all the hot Scottish men. And before you go off on me, I *know*, I have Bobby."

She knows exactly what I was about to say.

Bobby.

Rachel's *situationship.* I refuse to call him her boyfriend, because he won't even commit to acknowledging their relationship. It's a disaster waiting to happen. Every title they have? *All courtesy of Rachel.*

She deserves better. And she knows it... I think.

She sits up straighter, adjusting her red cropped tank in the mirror before giving her boobs an extra push for good measure. Her expression sharpens, going completely serious. "Do I need to change into something *sluttier*?"

I slap my hand over my mouth, trying to smother the laugh threatening to escape.

"Oh, you *definitely* don't need to try harder. Pretty sure anyone within a two-mile radius will see the giant neon arrow pointing your way."

I wave my hand toward her like a game-show host. "Trust me, we look hot. We've got this."

Rachel's gaze drops to my pants, her expression shifting into something skeptical. She's probably debating if my outfit meets her ridiculous standards. I brace myself, expecting a critique, but after a long pause, she finally nods in approval.

"Okay, fine." She sighs dramatically, adjusting her top one last time. "You're right, those leggings *are* hot. Your ass looks amazing."

I smile, putting on my lip gloss. "Duh."

With both of us finally ready, I rush around tidying up, tossing snack wrappers, organizing the makeup that's been scattered across the counter, and grabbing last minute essentials.

Phone? Check. Lip gloss? Check. Sanity? Questionable.

Rachel stands by the door, bag in hand, bouncing impatiently on her toes.

"Got everything?" I ask, already knowing the answer.

"Yes," she huffs, shoving me out the door. "And if we *did* forget something, it's three blocks away. We can survive the trek back."

At least she picked somewhere close, so we don't end up on some *missing persons* documentary.

CHAPTER 2

Me vs. Darts

RAVEN

L inking arms with Rachel as we stroll down the street, I take a slow breath, soaking it all in. The charming stone buildings, the uneven cobblestone paths, the way the streetlamps cast a golden glow over everything. It's like I've stepped into a storybook.

I could seriously live here.

"So could I," Rachel replies with a grin. "That would be magical. Let's sell everything and move here."

I blink, startled. "Did I just say that out loud?"

She laughs, squeezing my arm. "Yeah. And honestly? I'm with you. Scotland feels like a dream we didn't know we needed."

A walk was exactly what I needed after sleeping for what felt like an eternity. The boutique shops and cafés lining the street glow warmly through their windows, spilling golden light onto the cobblestones.

We pause at a few shop windows, peering in at the displays of handwoven scarves, souvenir trinkets, and vintage books. I make a mental note to come back tomorrow, when we can actually go inside.

As we continue down the sidewalk, a couple with a fluffy brown dog turns onto our path. Before I can stop myself, I drop down to pet it, my fingers sinking into its thick coat. The dog's tail wags so enthusiastically it's a wonder it doesn't lift off the ground.

Rachel chuckles, crossing her arms. "And there it is. You lasted, what? Twelve seconds before finding a dog?"

The couple laughs, and before we know it, we're deep in conversation. They offer food recommendations, their favorite local spots, and a place called *The Realm*.

"You have to go," the woman insists, eyes shining. "Your trip will be tragically incomplete if you don't."

Rachel and I exchange a look, mentally adding it to our ever-growing list.

With one last round of goodbyes, we part ways with the couple, their dog's tail wagging happily as they disappear into the night. The air feels cooler now, the distant sound of laughter drifting from nearby cafés.

Rachel loops her arm through mine again, sighing. "I've missed this. Walking around, talking about everything and nothing at the same time."

Before this trip, we hadn't seen each other in months. Which is practically an eternity for us. Most of our walk is spent catching up, filling in the gaps that texts and FaceTime never quite cover.

I tell her about the massive work project that's been consuming my life, and her eyes widen when I casually mention the potential client I'm supposed to meet here.

"In Scotland?" she asks, intrigued. "Work *followed* you across the Atlantic?"

I shrug, smiling. "Apparently, my charm is in high demand."

Rachel laughs, linking her arm tighter with mine. "It *should* be. You're a badass."

I roll my eyes. "I don't really think we need a PR guy, but what do I know?"

The truth is, I've never met him in person. Our conversations have been strictly business. Emails, phone calls, endless back-and-forth. Now, we finally have a face-to-face meeting lined up to finalize everything.

Rachel shifts the conversation to her own work drama and the latest mess with Bobby. I nod along, doing my best to just listen. My opinions sit sharp on the tip of my tongue, unfiltered thoughts that I shove down before they escape. She doesn't need a lecture. Not tonight.

We turn the corner, and she points ahead. "I think that's it... and it already looks packed."

I take in the sight and nod. *I guess that's a good sign.*

The royal blue trim against the weathered brick makes the pub stand out, even though it's tucked snugly between neighboring buildings. It has that *old charm* to it, and it's clearly well-loved, like everything else in this town. Even the oldest spots look like they've been lovingly preserved.

Outside, clusters of people gather at the small iron tables, drinks in hand, their conversations blending into a pleasant hum. Others lean against the wooden railing, laughter spilling into the night air. It's the kind of scene that makes you want to stay just a little longer.

What really catches my eye, though, are the lush green ferns hanging above the carved wooden sign. They sway lightly in the breeze, a contrast to the deep blues and dark wood. I already know I'm going to love this place.

Stepping through the front door is the only moment I almost regret choosing this place. Almost. The space is smaller than expected, and packed. The murmur of voices rolls like waves, filling every inch.

But then comes the clink of glasses, the flickering candlelight on wooden tables, the way the low hum of music threads itself between conversations.

I let out a slow breath, letting it all sink in.

Despite the crowd, there's a warmth here. A welcoming kind of chaos. It smells like a mix of beer, musk, and a surprising hint of mint. Which is a random yet fitting addition. Somehow the scent suits this place perfectly.

The moment we step inside, my eyes flick around, unsure where to land first. To the right, a massive bar stretches along the entire side of the room. On the opposite side, wooden tables are packed with people, glasses clinking as lively conversations rise and fall. In the center, whiskey barrels repurposed as tables add the perfect touch of rustic charm. It's exactly the kind of detail you'd hope for in a pub like this.

In the farthest corner, a heated game of darts is underway, complete with gritted teeth, cocky grins, and an explosion of shouts. Just to the left of that, an open space sits almost forgotten, clearly meant for dancing. Which is exactly what we needed.

There's something oddly comforting about this place. It feels familiar, like we've stumbled into the perfect hideaway without even trying.

I look at Rachel, suspicion creeping in, noting the very distinct absence of food. "Why do I get the feeling you knew this place didn't have food?"

She shrugs, completely unbothered, and tugs me further into the pub. "Come on, let's go! Besides, you ate *tons* of snacks. You'll be fine. Who needs dinner when you can have a drink?"

Her carefree energy is infectious, the kind of recklessness that makes it really hard to argue even when I know I should.

I roll my eyes. "I said I'd *think* about having a drink on this trip, not that I'd get trashed the first night we're here."

31

Rachel smiles. "No time like the present. One drink isn't going to kill you. Live a little!"

I glance around, spotting an open barrel table with two stools in the middle of the room. It's the only unclaimed spot left, positioned right in the heart of all the action, and perfect for people watching.

A burst of cheers erupts into laughter, one of the guys stepping forward to yank the dart from the board, grinning like he just won the lottery. Their energy is magnetic, drawing my focus even as I try to act like I'm not blatantly staring.

I never really understood the appeal of darts. Seems like a stupid game. Throw things at a board, keep score, repeat. What's the big deal? But judging by the sheer intensity of this match, there's obviously something I'm missing.

An added bonus is that every single one of these guys is ridiculously good-looking.

I don't realize I'm still staring until Rachel's voice cuts through my thoughts.

"Careful, love, you're drooling," she teases, slipping into her dramatically perfected British accent.

I blink, feeling my cheeks heat slightly, my own body is selling me out.

"I am *not*," I protest, swatting her away.

She's still grinning, holding out a napkin as if she's doing me a favor. Her eyes practically sparkle with amusement, and I know, without a doubt, that she's not going to let this go anytime soon.

"Uh huh." She tosses me a wink. "Better take this before you make a puddle."

I snatch the napkin from her with a dramatic sigh. "Oh, come on." I smile, despite myself. "I was zoning out while listening to their accents. Honestly, I couldn't even tell you anything about them. That's how little I was paying attention."

Lie.

Okay, *maybe not a complete lie.* I had, in fact, been listening to their accents. But I'd also been watching, casually, of course. Admiring the muscles, their easy confidence, and the way their laughter rolled through the room. Appreciation, that's all. *Not interest.*

Rachel laughs, clearly not buying my excuse for a second. "Oh, well then, in that case, shut up so I can hear. It looks like the guy in the yellow is winning."

I blink. "There's no guy in yellow."

The second the words leave my mouth; I realize my mistake.

Rachel's grin spreads, victorious. "HA! I knew you were watching!" She practically shrieks, laughing so hard she has to grip my arm for support.

"Rave, you might fool anyone else, but don't act like you didn't notice how gorgeous all those guys were, *while* listening to their accents. You're an excellent multitasker."

I groan, attempting to turn her away before she draws even more attention to us, but it's too late. Her cackling has already caught the eye of one of the men.

A guy with dark hair and sharp cheekbones lifts his glass in our direction, a slow, amused smirk tugging at his lips. Shit.

Just great. That's exactly what we needed. To attract the attention of a bunch of men we don't know.

Rachel, of course, is delighted.

"Well, of course I noticed, I'm not blind," I admit with a grin, leaning in slightly so my voice doesn't carry across the room. "I'm just not available. So I settled for their accents."

Rachel laughs, clearly unconcerned about my life choices, and turns back to the table. Without missing a beat, she slides a drink in my direction, her smile is downright mischievous.

"Here. Drink this! You're going to love it."

I narrow my eyes, inspecting the glass with suspicion. "Are you *sure* about that?" My eyes shift to the two shot glasses on the table.

Oh, hell no.

"I'm really hoping those are both for you," I add, already preparing my exit strategy.

Rachel snorts. "Keep dreaming." She pushes the drinks toward me. "This one's yours, babe. Bottoms up."

I stare at the tiny glass of impending regret, hesitation creeping in. I've never done a shot before. And the longer I look at it, the more I want to back out.

Rachel notices immediately.

"Oh, don't even think about it," she warns.

I swallow hard, fingers curling around the glass. *Screw it.* Before I can talk myself out of it, I grab the shot and toss it back.

The second it hits my throat, I realize I've made a terrible mistake. It burns like hellfire, a slow, creeping warmth that erupts into a full-blown inferno. I choke, desperately fumbling for my other drink.

Rachel, the absolute ass that she is, is laughing so hard she nearly falls out of her chair.

I glare at her through watery eyes, still gasping. "People actually *enjoy* this?" My voice comes out hoarse, rasping like I just swallowed molten lava.

"You're a natural," she teases, raising her own shot in a toast before throwing it back like an absolute pro. Show-off.

I'm still recovering when I see someone move past us toward the bar.

Okay. Hi. He's more than good-looking from what I can see. He's tall, but that's not saying much considering I'm barely taller than Rachel. He's close enough that I catch the freckles scattered across his arms.

And those arms? Yeah. They're solid. *Not that I'm into that.*

Lies.

I'm absolutely into that.

He's wearing a button-up with the sleeves rolled to his elbows, revealing a tattoo on his forearm. I can't make out the design in the dim lighting, but it only adds to the intrigue.

The golden glow of the pub catches in his dark hair, and I can see the faintest traces of auburn in his dark hair. It's pulled into a bun—just messy enough to be effortless, and just tight enough to make my fingers itch to pull it loose. His lean muscle stretching under the fabric of his shirt like a damn invitation. Even from behind, he looks like the kind of man who could ruin a person without even trying.

Really? The universe is definitely testing me.

I roll my eyes, but let's be real, there's something irritatingly attractive about a man bun. The way it pulls everything together, making a sharp jawline look even sharper. Adds that edge that makes me want to start fights I have no business winning.

I try not to stare too obviously, but I didn't quite get my fill of those broad shoulders before Rachel steps right into my line of sight, waving a napkin in my face.

"Really? Twice?" She laughs, holding it out like an offering.

I blink, caught red-handed, and snatch the napkin from her, feeling my face heat. "Okay, fine. That time I *was* drooling. Not even going to lie."

Rachel smirks, clearly pleased, and shoves my drink back toward me before raising her glass of who-knows-what for a toast. "To drooling over hot men, even though you're *foolishly* choosing this vacation to swear them off."

I laugh, clicking my glass against hers. "To hot men."

I should've asked Rachel what to expect from drinking before I dove straight into the deep end. It might've been wise to know what I was getting myself into.

The man at the bar chooses that exact moment to turn around.

And, oh *fuck*.

Rachel's toast wasn't just accurate. It was prophetic.

Because he looks like my next mistake.

I've seen handsome men before, but him? Yeah, he's something else entirely. He's the kind of gorgeous that makes smart people do very, very dumb things. The first thing I see is his chiseled jaw, and lips—*Gods above, those lips*—full and sharp-edged like they were sculpted for sin. His dark eyes sweep over the room like he owns it, and I'm not even exaggerating when I say he was *born* to be worshiped. And honestly? Who am I to argue? Because d*amn*. The bastard is all hard lines and predatory grace, wrapped in the kind of beauty that make logic an afterthought. A *very* distant afterthought.

I'm lucky I didn't start choking again, because that would've been the cherry on top of this already awkward moment.

Everything around me goes quiet. A sharp, piercing ring cuts through my right ear, slicing through the noise. It's been happening more and more lately, or maybe I just started to notice it.

Before I can linger on it, just like that, it's gone.

But something feels off. I push the thought away, forcing my attention back to *him*.

He's walking right toward us. Paralysis creeps through my body like wildfire. A burning spread of tension that licks up my spine. My hands start to tingle and heat blooms beneath my skin, seeping into every nerve, every inch of me tightening under the sudden weight of his attention.

Shit.

Those deep brown eyes pin me in place like a blade pressed to my throat. Eye contact. *ABORT. ABORT.*

Before the moment can spiral into something I *know* I won't recover from, I whip my gaze away, pretending to be deeply, profoundly interested in absolutely *nothing* on the other side of the bar.

But two seconds was enough to sear the details into my brain. The freckles dusting his face, the rich brown of his eyes, and the flash of perfect teeth when he smiled.

I can only hope I'm radiating a solid *don't speak to me* vibe, because right now, I'm not sure if I'm capable of forming actual words.

Just keep walking. Just keep walking. Do NOT stop and talk to me, I chant silently.

And thank God, he doesn't.

He doesn't look at me again, doesn't acknowledge me, just keeps walking straight back to the dart game behind us.

Relief floods my system, though I have zero reason to feel relieved. It's not like I was in danger of throwing myself at him, but I also don't have the willpower of a saint here. I'm more like a little baby chipmunk out in the wild for the first time. Spooked.

The music swells or maybe it never stopped. It's like someone hit mute for a second, then cranked the volume back up to full blast. The noise of the pub rushes back in all at once, and the loudest sound is coming from the crazy brunette I call my best friend.

Rachel is standing in front of me, wide-eyed, waving her hands.

"HELLOOOO!" she practically shouts.

Oh, great. She saw that.

"Welcome to Scotland," I mutter, raising my glass and sinking a little further into my chair.

You'd think I'd never seen a good-looking man before with that grand display. I shake my head, tap my glass against hers, and sigh.

This night is either going to be an adventure... or a complete bust when I inevitably embarrass myself.

Perhaps tonight wasn't the night to try drinking for the first time. Far too late for that now.

We lose track of time, falling into easy conversation. We talk about all the things we want to do on this trip and laugh about my near-death experience via the handsome stranger.

There's so much we want to see and explore, but we refuse to be tied down by strict planning. We're taking it day by day. Which, honestly, is *exactly* my kind of vacation.

"Holy shit, it's ten already? How long did it take you to get ready?"

Rachel laughs, dodging the napkin I send her way.

"It's *your* fault for sleeping the day away," she teases. "However, we are not going to focus on that."

She winks, then nods toward the open space in the back of the room. "What we *should* do is go over there and dance!"

I follow her gaze and immediately regret it.

Because the dance floor is conveniently located right next to the group of men playing darts.

The same group of men that the gorgeous idiot happens to be a part of.

I groan, briefly consider faking exhaustion, but Rachel would see through that in two seconds. And then drag me over there anyway.

Before I can object, she's already up, grabbing my arm, and pulling me toward the dance floor.

Well, here goes nothing.

I down the rest of whatever concoction she handed me, and it burns like hell on the way down. I cough, wincing. *Are all drinks supposed to taste like this?*

As we weave our way through the crowd, I start giving myself a little pep talk.

Who cares if they're hot? I literally just reminded Rachel that I'm not blind. But that doesn't mean I need to fall apart just because a few attractive men are nearby.

They don't get a say in my trip, my mood, or my night.

With that thought locked in place, I step onto the dance floor, determined to have fun.

That's the spirit. Now let's get our ass on that dance floor. Shake it like a saltshaker. Go big or go home, right?

All lingering doubts scatter like leaves in the wind when the next song fills the room. I don't recognize it, but it pulls me in instantly. The beat is rich and soulful. It's the kind of folky tune that feels like it's stitched into your bones.

My body starts swaying before I even realize it, moving to the rhythm like I don't have a choice in the matter.

I swear the volume cranks up another notch, and suddenly, the energy in the room shifts. The beat pulses through my body, vibrating my chest and lighting me up from the inside out.

I let myself get completely lost and carried away by the rhythm. My hips sway and my arms move without a second thought. There's nothing quite like the feeling of dancing for me. It's pure freedom.

It's the moment where everything else falls away, where I feel completely alive. No doubts. No worries. No one holding me back. Just the music, my body, and the rush of being *here.*

You know what else is magical? The freedom of not being tied down by a relationship. I don't care how many times I have to remind myself. I'm sticking to my *no-men* rule.

And this moment just solidified it for me. Right here, dancing with my best friend, living my best life. I can't even remember the last time I had this much fun.

The song fades, another quickly taking its place. The music pulses, wrapping around me like a heartbeat. The songs start to blur together, some are familiar, most of them I've never heard before.

I know I've only been here a day, but if this is what Scotland feels like every day, I can't help but wonder why my parents ever left. Why didn't they just raise me here to begin with?

It feels like we've been dancing for hours, lost in our own little bubble, without a care in the world. It's a feeling I want to bottle up and keep forever.

When I finally stop moving to catch my breath, a realization hits me. *I've had my first drink of alcohol!*

I don't think it's something I'll be doing every day, but there's no denying that it's kind of fun.

For years, I had all these complicated thoughts about drinking. After waiting so long, it just felt pointless to start. I'd already made it this far, so... why bother?

I didn't really notice the effects while I was dancing, but now that I have stopped, there's a strange buzzing under my skin. And I feel a little dizzy.

My worries feel like they're a million miles away, and the only thing that matters right now is having fun. Not chasing answers about my family. Definitely not stressing over the interview I have scheduled.

For once, I'm just *living* in this moment.

I start making my way back to our table because, at this point, I desperately need some water. But as soon as I take a few steps, I feel myself swaying a little.

Oh no.

I quickly glance around, hoping no one notices, and do my best to act... sober.

Is that even a thing? Can you act sober? Or do you just end up looking suspiciously like a drunk person trying not to look drunk?

The thought makes me snicker under my breath, which probably isn't helping. I start walking again, a little slower this time, focusing on keeping my balance. Rachel is still on the dance floor, swaying like her life depends on it.

I take the opportunity to check my phone and catch my breath.

I must've been gone for too long, because suddenly, she appears out of nowhere and smacks my ass.

"I'm having the best time ever!" she shouts over the music, face glowing with excitement. Before I can even respond, she finishes the rest of her drink in one gulp, grins at me, and disappears back into the crowd like a whirlwind.

I laugh to myself as I head toward the bar for some water. But as I turn around, I walk straight into a wall of muscle.

Literally.

I bounce off him hard enough that I probably would've toppled over completely if two strong hands hadn't wrapped around my shoulders, steadying me.

And if I'm being honest, he's doing a lot more than just holding me up right now.

His grip is firm, and... *incredibly* effective at keeping me upright. Which, to be fair, is probably for the best, considering I was struggling to walk in a straight line earlier.

I try to look up, hoping to get a glimpse of his face, only to realize that I've run into an actual human brick wall. My heart skips a beat as I take in just how *solid* he is. The kind of effortless strength that makes my stomach dip unexpectedly.

He's still holding onto me, his hands firm but careful, and trying to get a good look at his face is proving difficult.

Mostly because—holy hell—he's tall. Up close, it's even more obvious. He has a strong build, the kind of effortless confidence that comes with knowing exactly how good he looks. Not that I care. But still...

I tilt my head back slightly, realizing I might need a damn step stool if I want a proper view. And then, he speaks.

"Excuse me, lass," his tone low and playful, amusement dancing in his voice. "Good thing I was here to catch ye, eh?"

Then, he winks.

The accent alone makes the whole moment so much worse, in the best possible way.

Heat floods my face, betraying me instantly. I let out a nervous laugh, completely aware of how ridiculous I must look staring up at him like some kind of idiot.

Luckily, I recover quickly. *Mostly.*

"Well, to be fair, if you hadn't been standing there when I turned around, I wouldn't have needed catching." I keep my tone playful, despite the fact that my heart is hammering against my ribs like it's trying to escape.

His grin widens, and I become hyper-aware of the fact that his hand is still lightly resting on my arm. A slow burn starts at the point of contact, seeping into my skin, making it incredibly difficult to think.

"However," I add quickly, trying not to sound breathless, "I do appreciate it. I'd really hate to face-plant in front of a room full of strangers."

He throws his head back and laughs, a deep, rich sound that seems to fill the whole room, and relief floods through me.

"What are you two doing in a place like this?" His eyes are bright with curiosity. "Are you on holiday, or are ya here for work?"

I let out a soft chuckle, finally feeling a little steadier on my feet. "We're here for anything and everything. Adventure. Exploring. Some family stuff." I scrunch my nose at the thought of working, a reminder I'd rather ignore. "And, unfortunately, I do have to work a little bit."

His gaze lingers, something unreadable flickering behind it. The low lighting casts shadows over his features, and I can't tell if it's that or the sudden heat creeping up my neck, but I suddenly feel very warm under his stare.

I shift, forcing a casual tone. "What about you?"

His chuckle is quiet, effortless. And that's when I notice his dimple. A single, devastating little dip on one side of his mouth.

Okay, he's not the *beautiful man bun guy* from earlier by any means, but he's still very attractive. And that accent is enough to make any rational thought evaporate.

I realize that he's still talking. My brain scrambles to catch up, praying I don't look as dazed as I feel.

"... and yes, most of us live in the area. We're actually out celebrating." He finishes, his voice still casual, his expression still easy.

Meanwhile, I'm standing here, barely holding onto my last two brain cells.

"Well, now I have to know," I say, tilting my head, curiosity piqued. "What kind of celebration involves a dart game?"

He huffs a quiet laugh, his lips twitching like I've just asked him something ridiculous. And maybe I have. But really, when I think *celebration,* I don't immediately picture a bunch of grown men yelling over darts like their lives depend on it.

"To be fair," he laughs, amusement flickering in his eyes, "it started with drinks, then someone made a bet, and now..." he gestures toward the commotion behind him, where accusations and victorious shouts fly across the bar. "Now it's a full-on war."

I raise an eyebrow, lips curving. "Sounds serious."

It's surprising how easy he is to talk to. No hovering. No lingering stares that make my skin crawl. No obnoxious pick-up lines designed to get me to leave with him.

He's just... normal. Friendly, even.

And maybe it's the alcohol warming my blood, but I feel myself relax, the tension that had been buzzing under my skin since we walked into this bar *finally* starting to fade.

"One of the guys is celebrating his engagement," he nods toward the man in question.

I follow his gaze and spot the blonde guy laughing mid-throw, locked in what appears to be a brutal match against... Oh.

The stunning God from earlier.

The man bun.

I quickly school my features, keeping my expression neutral, but something must flicker across my face. Because when I glance back, he's watching me. Closely.

His lips curve, slow and knowing. "Not big on engagement parties?"

I blink, heat crawling up my neck.

"What? No! That's—" I flounder, scrambling for something to say that doesn't sound stupid. "That's exciting for him! So... who's winning?"

The way his lips twitch tells me he knows exactly what just happened, but mercifully, he lets it slide.

Instead, he throws another glance toward the game, amusement gleaming in his eyes. "You know, I'm not really sure."

I laugh, but he continues, shaking his head. "That's why there's so much yelling, they're trying to decide who's actually winning."

I open my mouth to respond, to say literally anything, but no words come out. Oh my God. Surely, he's going to assume I'm drunk. Which, honestly? He wouldn't even be wrong.

I try again, determined to salvage what's left of my dignity, but before I can embarrass myself any further, I'm saved by the bell.

And by bell, I mean Rachel.

She appears out of nowhere, grabs my arm, and without so much as a pause, announces, "Hi, I'm Rachel. I'm so glad you met my friend. She's sworn off men, so don't waste your time, *but* this is our song, so if you'll excuse us..."

And just like that, I'm being dragged away. I barely manage to throw him an apologetic look over my shoulder, but all I get in return is that damn smirk.

"Raven, come *on! This is our song!*"

I stumble after her, laughing, because only Rachel could bulldoze through a conversation like that and make it look effortless.

"You *would* say that! But to be clear, it wasn't a rescue mission!" I protest, failing miserably at sounding convincing. "I wasn't even swooning over the accent..."

I pause, then snort. "Okay, *maybe* a little. But he was really hot!"

Rachel lifts an eyebrow, her grin stretching wider. "Exactly. And you were gone for too long. Our song is on, so, priorities."

She starts swaying effortlessly to the beat, her movements fluid, hips rolling with the kind of ease that makes me wonder if she was an exotic dancer in her past life. Or maybe in her current one, and I just don't know about it.

"We can always go talk to them after," she adds, throwing me a mischievous look. "Or better yet, maybe we should challenge them to a game of darts. Show them how it's *really* done."

I bark out a laugh, shaking my head. "Rachel, we don't even know how to *play* darts."

"Minor detail." She waves me off like I'm the ridiculous one.

The song ends, and for a brief second, the bar stills. Conversations hum, glasses clink, the low buzz of laughter and movement filling the space between beats.

I'm still catching my breath when Rachel grabs my arm again, already dragging me toward the bar.

"We need more drinks. You're way too sober for this time of night!" She declares, cutting through the crowd with me in tow. I stumble after her, laughing, because honestly? At this point, resistance is futile.

I think I'm doing pretty well after the few drinks I've had. Then again... maybe I should just get it all out of my system now. One epic crash course in bad decisions, and if I end up sick, I'll never want to touch alcohol again. *Sound logic.*

I stop at the table while she bounces off to the bar, weaving through the crowd like she owns the place.

A few minutes later, she appears with a grin plastered across her face, drinks in one hand, and another round of shots in the other.

Uh-oh.

I narrow my eyes. That look *never* means anything good. "Alright, what is it?"

She practically vibrates with excitement, like a kid on Christmas morning. "Nothing too fancy, just some vodka with cranberry juice and a lemon drop shot. So basically, it's healthy. You're welcome."

I snort, shaking my head. "Healthy, huh?"

She plops the drinks down triumphantly. "Oh, and bonus? They were already paid for."

I blink. "Wait, what?"

She winks. "Apparently the dart dudes picked up the tab."

Lovely. Now they're buying us drinks.

Maybe we *should* go over there. Be social. Say thanks. Who knows? We might even have fun.

I'm in no way a dart expert, but the guy I was talking to earlier seemed nice enough... and, let's be honest, this gives me a chance to get a closer look at the Brooding God over there.

Then, when I go home tonight, at least I'll have a very attractive face to think about as I fall asleep alone. *Small victories.*

Decision made, I grab Rachel's arm, and this time *I'm* the one dragging *her* toward the dart game.

"That's my girl!" She cheers, laughing as we push through the crowd.

CHAPTER 3

Long Live

RAVEN

"Hello, *boys*!" She calls, loud enough for everyone in the bar to hear. "Who's winning?"

If they weren't looking at us before, they definitely are now. The whole group pauses their game, turning toward us.

The guy I talked to earlier is the first to speak, flashing that familiar grin.

"Well, well, well. Look who decided to join us," he teases, the Scottish lilt of his voice making the words entirely too smooth. "If it's not the American girls who've taken over our pub."

He winks.

Sarcasm is practically my love language, so I fire back without missing a beat. "*Taken over*? If it was commandeered that quickly, then you're lucky we decided to show up to liven the place up. *You're welcome*."

A ripple of laughter spreads through the group, and I can't help but giggle a little because, really, *who even says commandeered*?

Well, I guess the list now includes Jack Sparrow and me.

I'm going to blame it on vodka-cran running wild through my system.

"Yup, you ladies will fit right in here," the guy says, his attention completely locked onto Rachel like they're the only two people in the room. "How long are ye staying for?"

Yeah. That question is clearly meant just for her. I arch an eyebrow, smirking to myself. *Well, well, well...*

Rachel, to her credit, barely misses a beat. "We're here for a few weeks, but we don't really have anything specific planned. Just want to explore and do whatever." She flashes a bright smile.

Which is hilarious, considering this is the same girl constantly worried about being trafficked, taken, or peeped on. But introduce a hot guy into the equation and suddenly, she's very approachable.

The man looks seconds away from heart eyes, like he might actually need the napkin I used earlier.

"Why don't you ladies bring your stuff over here and watch us play darts?" Tall, dark, and entirely too handsome says, resting his hands on Rachel's shoulders, steering her toward a prime viewing spot. Then he gestures toward the table for me with an easy smile.

I trail behind, amused. Honestly, I'm kind of glad he's more focused on her. If anyone can finally make her ditch that loser Bobby, it's probably a hot Scottish man who looks like he wants to worship her.

Still, I'm not about to sit here and be eye candy while they show off.

"No offense," I arch a brow, "but we didn't come over here just to watch you play darts."

The men exchange glances.

"We came to challenge you to a game," I continue, flashing a grin. "*And kick your ass*. Boys against girls. We're here to show you how it's *really* done."

Laughter erupts, and Rachel claps her hands together. "You heard her. Prepare to be humbled."

A sharp snort to my right cuts through the laughter. I glance over, already knowing exactly who it is. *The man of the hour himself.*

Of course, it came from him. I was doing a perfectly fine job of pretending he didn't exist.

No, we weren't, my brain betrays me as a swarm of butterflies take flight in my stomach. I try to shut it down, but nope, they're having a full-on parade.

He leans back against the table, arms folded, exuding the kind of effortless confidence that makes my teeth grind. "Sorry, but have you ever even played darts before?" His smirk is infuriatingly perfect. "Wouldn't want to ruin your manicure. Maybe you should sit this one out and just watch."

Um, excuse me?

As if I'm about to let this motherfucker tell me what I can and can't do.

Heat flares in my chest, a wildfire licking its way up my spine. My fingers twitch at my sides, tingling again with that same strange sensation. A pulse of warmth floods my fingertips, like a warning signal, but impossible to ignore.

Have I ever played darts before? *No.* But is that any of his business? *Absolutely fucking not.*

The nerve of him, assuming I'd ruin my nails. I curl my hands into fists, forcing a slow inhale. *He's not worth it.*

But, God, how satisfying would it be to wipe that smug smirk off his face?

Rachel's eyes flicker to me, her expression shifting as she takes in my clenched fists. She knows me too well and can feel the shift in my energy. She's probably already debating whether she needs to step in.

The bastard chuckles, completely unfazed, as he pushes off his chair and strides toward the dart board.

Okay, Raven, let's be honest, we don't actually know how to play darts.

I take a slow, steady breath. *Calm down. Let's think rationally.*

But then he glances back over his shoulder, that infuriatingly cocky look still in place, and my temper snaps.

"Aw, well, that's super nice and thoughtful of you," my voice is all sugar and venom. "Are you the one celebrating his engagement?"

He stops mid-step, his head tilting slightly. One brow lifts, and the amusement in his eyes is quickly replaced by intrigue.

"It's likely going to be short-lived if your fiancé finds out that you think that just because she's a girl with a manicure, she should sit down and look pretty."

Rachel stifles a laugh behind her hand, her shoulders shaking with the effort. I catch the quick flicker of his eyes widening before a low, surprised chuckle rumbles from his chest.

Okay, was that a little too far? Maybe.

Maybe Rachel's right. Maybe I do have a little unresolved trauma from Chance bubbling under the surface. But over my dead body am I going to sit back and let someone talk down to me like being *just a girl* is some sort of disadvantage.

I'm already gearing up to throw another verbal dagger, one I probably would regret in the morning. Mr. Tall, dark, and handsome throws his head back and starts laughing. Not just a chuckle, but a full, unapologetic laugh.

Even his friends join in, the entire group erupting into laughter like I just delivered the punchline of the year.

Rachel is staring at me, wide-eyed and open-mouthed, completely stunned.

49

Honestly? So am I.

How much of tonight can I blame on the drinks?

"Well, if that isn't the funniest thing that's happened all night. Hell might even be the funniest thing I've heard all year," the man drooling over Rachel says, grinning as he leans forward, offering his hand. "I'm Cam, and that one there that you so hilariously put in his place is Kane."

I glance over just in time to see Kane shake his head.

Cam gestures to the rest of the group, introductions flowing smoothly. "That's Brandon, the engaged one, then there's Tyler, and James."

I give them all a polite nod, but my focus keeps getting pulled back to the man whose ego I apparently bruised. Kane is still watching me, studying me like I'm a puzzle he hadn't planned on solving tonight.

Tyler claps him on the back with a bark of laughter. "Don't mind him, his ego just took a hit. He'll take a moment to recover, but he'll be fine."

I almost apologize, the instinct so ingrained it nearly slips out, but I catch myself just in time. *Nope. Not apologizing for that.*

Kane shakes off whatever lingering surprise he had and leans in just enough that I can feel the shift in the air between us. His smirk turns razor-sharp, a slow burn of amusement and something else flickering behind his eyes.

"Why don't you put your money where your mouth is...?" He trails off, waiting for me to snap back.

The challenge is unmistakable, his tone a deliberate dare wrapped in smooth confidence.

Oh, he's good.

I know he expects me to back down. That much is clear. This is probably going to be the easiest win of his life, considering I *definitely* don't know how to play darts. My money is *certainly* not going where my mouth is.

In fact, maybe I'd have room to put money in there if my foot wasn't already lodged firmly in my mouth.

I hum, tilting my head, pretending to consider my options when, really, I'm just stalling long enough to set the stakes in a way that won't sting too badly when I inevitably lose. "Hmm... how about this. If you win, I'll tell you my name."

Seems like a safe enough bet, considering I'm almost guaranteed to lose.

Kane crosses his arms, his expression unreadable, but the hint of amusement in his eyes tells me he sees right through my weak attempt at strategy. "And if *you* win?"

Well, great. Didn't think of that. Obviously, I didn't think that far ahead because I know I won't win.

"If I win, then I guess you don't get to know my name, *and* you have to buy us a drink. *Plus*, I'll have all the bragging rights that you lost to a girl." I keep my voice light, like this isn't a completely ridiculous, unfair challenge.

Fake it till you make it, right?

Rachel, clearly catching onto the game, bursts out laughing. "Well, boys, do we have a deal? Our names and phone numbers, or you're buying drinks."

I glance at her, wondering if she remembers that she already gave Cam her name. But he doesn't mention it, his grin says he's more than happy to play along.

"Deal," Kane's tone is final.

The way he's looking at me makes it crystal clear that he fully expects to win.

Cam and Kane exchange a quick glance before turning back to us, their friends already settling in like they're about to watch the best entertainment of the night. The two of them against the two of us.

This should be a quick game.

The good news is I'm last to go. Which means I have time to mentally prepare... or more time to panic.

Cam steps up first. He throws with an effortless flick of his wrist. Dart on the board, inner ring.

Ten points for Gryffindor... or however the hell this game works.

Rachel's next. She barely makes it, but it sticks. I have no idea how many points that gives us, but it's something.

Then it's Kane's turn.

I already know how this is going to go.

And sure enough. Bullseye.

"Wow," I deadpan. "I never saw that coming."

Kane shoots me a look, smirk tugging at his lips. "Careful, your jealousy is showing."

I snort. "Jealous? Of what? Your... dart-throwing skills?" I gesture dramatically at the board. "Yeah, you're so impressive. What a talent. Truly inspiring."

Rachel nearly chokes on her drink, covering her mouth to keep from laughing outright.

Kane just shakes his head, exhaling through his nose like I'm some kind of impossible child. "Are you going to talk or throw?"

"Oh, I can do both," I say sweetly, taking my place at the line. "It's called multitasking. You should try it sometime."

"Impressive," he muses. "Is that what they're teaching these days?"

I flash him a smug smile. "Yep. Right after we master sarcasm and humbling cocky men."

That gets me a full laugh from the group. Kane just smirks, unshaken, like he enjoys the challenge.

I grit my teeth, feeling the competitive fire flare back to life. I can't tell if it's the drink or just me, but I'm instantly annoyed at how good he is. Annoyed, impressed, and okay, slightly turned on.

Of course they're going to not just win. They're going to mop the floor with us. But losing isn't the problem. It's losing to him that's the real issue.

Now, the moment of truth. My turn.

Whichever way you want to look at it, I know I'm about to make a fool of myself. But weirdly enough? I don't think I care. My only goal is to get the dart *somewhere* on the board. *Anywhere.*

I grab my drink and down the rest, hoping it'll either sharpen my focus or at least soften the blow of embarrassment.

It's just the dart and me. *We are ONE.*

I take a breath, trying to tune out the music, the chatter, the low rumble of laughter. I roll my shoulders back, mimicking what the other guys did, even though I know I'm working with pure delusion at this point.

Kane shifts slightly in my peripheral, watching, waiting. I refuse to let him be the reason I mess this up.

Ignoring him, I grip the dart lifting my arm, pulling it back. Right before I let it fly; I say a silent prayer to the Dart Gods.

Please, just let me hit the board. That's all I ask.

The dart leaves my fingers in what feels like a decent throw. For half a second, I hold my breath. The little traitor flies straight, hitting the board dead center. Bullseye.

And then, in an act of utter betrayal, it bounces off the board and lands dramatically on the floor.

The silence that follows is deafening.

I stare.

Rachel makes a strangled sound. Kane lets out a low chuckle, running a hand over his jaw as he looks between me and the fallen dart.

"Well," he drawls, titling his head, "you certainly made a statement."

I exhale sharply, ignoring the heat rising to my face. "Oh, go ahead. Say it. Rub it in."

His smirk deepens. "You know... I could. But honestly?" He glances at the dart again, shaking his head. "I don't think I need to."

I stare at the dart on the floor, half tempted to throw another one purely out of spite.

Somewhere behind me, someone stifles a laugh, and I fight the urge to groan.

Rachel, however, does *not* hold back. Oh, no. She howls, doubling over like this is the funniest thing she's ever witnessed.

I shoot her a glare. Traitor.

At least her cackling is distracting enough that the guys focus on her instead of me. The poor, unfortunate soul who just managed to defy the laws of physics in the most humiliating way possible.

Kane, naturally, is still watching me. Clearly enjoying every second of my downfall.

"Cam, you're up," he says, his voice smooth, laced with amusement.

He gives me a look, like he can see right through me, like he knows exactly how much I want to crawl into the floorboards. And damn it, my face is burning. I know it's bright red.

Cam steps up, effortless as ever, sending his dart flying. It lands with a satisfying thunk, right on the board. Of course.

And just like that, we're back to our regular scheduled programming.

Halfway through the game, Brandon, I think it was, insists on a round of shots. At this point, another shot can't hurt. So why not?

I throw it back with zero hesitation, feeling the warmth bloom in my chest, loosening some of my residual frustration.

Shockingly, the game is actually pretty fun, despite the fact that I've only managed to make *one* dart stick. And even that felt like pure luck. It's a hell of a lot more enjoyable when you go into it with zero expectations. Especially about things like scoring points.

I'll admit it, though. These guys are stupidly good-looking. And, unfortunately, fun to be around. But no matter how beautiful they all are, I remind myself why I'm here.

I've sworn off men. Not interested.

Kane, in particular, seems like the exact type of guy who's fully aware of his effect on people. He's smug, cocky, and too good at everything he does.

Annoyingly, he's been throwing bullseyes like it's second nature, every dart landing dead center with infuriating ease.

Hopefully, this is his only skill and he's not obnoxiously good at everything.

"Do you just come here every night and play darts?" I ask, narrowing my eyes as he nails another bullseye like it's nothing. "No one is *actually* this good at darts."

I roll my eyes as he retrieves the dart, stepping back with a smirk that makes me want to throw something. Preferably right at him.

"I didn't peg you for a sore loser," he says, his tone dripping with amusement.

My mouth practically drops open.

Okay, ouch. He's not wrong.

I hate losing. And I really hate being bad at something, which means I officially hate darts.

"You clearly need to be more observant," I giggle despite myself. "I'm absolutely terrible at this stupid game, so of course I'm going to be a sore loser."

I gesture toward the board, "Like, how does one just get good at darts? Do you just wake up one day and decide, 'Yup, today's the day I become a dart-throwing legend'?"

I throw my hands up for emphasis. "Is this even a real game?"

Rachel snorts behind me. "You're asking the real questions now, Rave."

Kane just shakes his head, chuckling like he actually finds me amusing, which somehow only fuels my irritation. And then he smirks. That slow, devastating curve of his lips that has to be illegal.

There's no way he doesn't know the effect that smile has on people. And if he knows it? That makes him *enemy number one*. The exact kind of guy I need to stay far, far away from.

"Clearly, it's natural talent," he says, his voice laced with pure, undiluted smugness.

Oh, for the love of...

"Who would've guessed you were all talk?" Kane muses, eyes gleaming. "Looks like you don't get that drink after all."

And then the bastard winks. Oh, he's enjoying this way too much.

I huff out a dramatic sigh, though I can't stop the grin tugging at my lips. "Okay, fine, full transparency? I've never played darts in my life."

He raises an eyebrow, giving me a look that practically screams *you don't say.*

"Which I am sure you've gathered by now," I add, flashing him a sheepish grin. "I am, without a doubt, all talk. Guilty as charged. Thank God I didn't bet anything worthwhile."

His smirk deepens, and I swear, for half a second, I catch something flicker in his eyes. Amusement?

Which, frankly, is rude, considering I'm the one who should be amused at *his* expense, not the other way around.

Then he moves toward me. My entire body is suddenly hyper-aware of how close he is, how his presence seems to eat up every inch of space between us.

I know the pub is small. But it sure as hell feels like he's doing it on purpose.

He holds out his hand. For a second, my brain completely short-circuits. *Why is he holding out his hand?* Is he trying to—

Oh.

Heat creeps up my neck as I quickly recover, with a forced laugh before I can dwell on whatever the hell that moment of stupidity was.

"Here you go, *Princess*." His tone is dripping with playful smugness.

I nearly drop the dart. Princess? Where the hell did that come from?

I blink up at him, searching for any sign of teasing, or reason he just decided to call me that. But he just stands there, watching me with that infuriatingly unreadable expression.

Okay. Sure. We're just handing out pet names now.

Snapping out of it as quickly as the moment came, I snatch the dart from his hand, narrowing my eyes. "I wonder how accurate my aim is when I'm aiming it at *your* head. Maybe you should go stand over there with an apple on top and see if I miss."

Kane chuckles, completely unfazed. "You can try. But this is your last turn, and I wouldn't want you to waste it."

Then he leans in slightly, his voice dropping just enough to make my stomach flip.

"Take your turn. I'm ready to collect my prize."

Oh, absolutely not.

I don't even want to acknowledge the little traitorous butterflies that decided to stir at that.

Collect my prize? Like, okay, Mr. Scottish man, reel it in.

I roll my eyes at myself, furious at the ridiculous commentary running rampant in my head. Kane's smirk hasn't faded, not even a little, and it's wreaking havoc on my already fragile composure.

The pub's warm light catches on the gold flecks in his eyes, and it's infuriating how much it adds to the already-too-smug expression he's wearing. Like he knows I'm going to choke again.

Well, fuck that.

Backing down isn't an option. Not when he's looking at me like that. Not when everyone's watching. I take another deep breath, centering myself. It's not like it really matters. One throw won't change the fact that we're about to lose. But still... I refuse to go down without a fight.

Cam looks way too pleased with himself, like he's already won. Or like he wants to drag Rachel to a dark corner and devour her. Meanwhile, Rachel looks like she's about two seconds away from decking him.

And Kane? He's watching me with an expression I can't read. Assessing. A hint of amusement laced with something else.

None of that matters.

Right now, I need to reclaim a shred of my dignity. If I can just get the dart to stick, anywhere near the inner circle, I'll walk out of here satisfied.

Okay, Raven, get your shit together.

I almost laugh at myself, because this is where my night has led. Psyching myself up over a dart like my life depends on it.

Rachel is shouting something about how I better get a bullseye. Cam and Tyler are standing off to the side, whispering like they're plotting my downfall. The rest of their friends are hurling encouragement, their voices a hum in the background as I step up to the line.

I inhale deeply, exhaling slow.

You know what's absolutely *stupid*? I can throw knives better than this. And yet, I cannot, for the life of me, get a stupid dart to stick. I adjust my grip. Roll my shoulders and picture Kane's smug face right in the center of the board.

And I let it fly.

The dart soars through the air, a blur against the dim light. It collides with the board, embedding deep into the center.

Silence.

For a second, I don't even register what happened.

"Oh my God," Rachel shrieks. "You did it!"

I blink. The dart is still there. Stuck. Dead center. I actually did it. And judging by the look on Kane's face, he wasn't expecting that either.

Rachel is screaming, jumping up and down like we just won the damn lottery. "Raven, you did it!!! *WE WON!*"

We're both bouncing like maniacs, clutching each other in triumph as the pub erupts in cheers. Cam is laughing, clapping Kane on the back.

Tyler strolls up, patting me on the back. "Good job, *Bird*," he chuckles, heading toward the bar.

I freeze mid-step.

Bird.

My stomach flips, the sound of the pub fading to a distant hum. No one has ever called me that, but my grandparents.

The moment unravels before I can grasp it. Kane strides toward me, his smirk annoyingly smug.

"Now where was that skill the entire game?" His voice is thick with amusement, his eyes gleaming as he winks.

He raises his hand to give me a high-five and the moment his palm meets mine, a jolt shoots up my arm like an electric current, sharp and unmistakable.

I smirk, trying to drown out the way my body is suddenly very aware of his. "We didn't *really* win, did we?"

He lets out a full laugh, shaking his head. "Not even close."

Didn't think so.

Well, at least I've learned something valuable tonight. That picturing his smug face on the dartboard might actually be the key to winning.

Rachel, naturally, gets right in Kane's face. "We *won* fair and square because we got a bullseye!"

Cam steps in, still laughing, as he starts explaining how darts actually works and how, technically, we lost by a landslide.

Honestly? Don't care. I got a bullseye, and that's all that matters.

I turn back to Kane with a grin, crossing my arms. "I guess that means you get to know my name after all."

But before I can get another word out, Kane's smirk deepens. "Good game, Raven." His voice dips as he says my name, like he's savoring it.

Raven.

I lose all sense of time, the pub noise fading as the way he says it slams into me like a fist to the gut.

Like it means something. Like *I* mean something.

I shake it off, plastering on a smirk. "Well, now you know," I say, tilting my head. "And you can finally sleep like a baby, knowing you're the reigning champion of darts. A skill most people don't possess because, you know, they have better things to do with their time."

There's that look again. The one I can't quite decipher, but my body *loves* it all the same.

Kane leans in slightly, eyes twinkling with mischief. "Looks like you *are* a sore loser after all, *Princess*."

All right. That's it. I'm *never* drinking again. Clearly, this is not working in my favor.

I roll my eyes, masking the fact that my body is entirely too happy about his teasing. His smartass comments, despite my best efforts, make me want to bite back.

Actually, his teasing is almost enough to make me want to throw another dart, this time right at his head.

"Just so you know," I toss my hair over my shoulder. "I was picturing your face on my last throw."

I turn on my heel, sauntering toward the bathroom, leaving him to sit with that.

When I glance back, he's shaking his head like he can't quite believe me.

Good. Let him wonder.

CHAPTER 4

Knowing When to Quit

KANE

This is one of the few places where I can actually breathe. No tourists, no whispers about my name, no unwanted eyes tracking my every move. Just a low hum of conversation, the scent of aged whiskey, and the kind of anonymity that's hard to come by.

That's why I come here.

But tonight, the air feels different. And I know exactly why.

From the second she walked in, the entire atmosphere shifted.

It wasn't just her looks. Though, fuck me, she's beautiful. The kind of natural, effortless beauty that isn't drowned in pretense. Long, dark, wild hair that looks too soft for its own good. A body that could make a man stupid, all curves and confidence wrapped in something entirely untouchable.

Then she walked by, and I nearly fucking lost it.

Those leggings? A goddamn crime.

Her perfect curves were impossible to ignore, and trust me, I tried.

But it was more than that. She had this energy, an unshakable presence, the kind that sent a warning down my spine even as it pulled me in. She was trouble. The kind of trouble I should stay far away from.

They settled a few tables over, close enough for me to hear bits of their conversation. Close enough for me to catch her name.

Her friend must've shouted it five times already, making sure it burned itself into my brain.

I'd spent most of the night trying not to look at her, but it was fucking impossible. She commanded attention without even trying, like the whole place was drawn to her without understanding why.

And she sure as hell didn't seem concerned that this wasn't the kind of bar where people come to dance.

No, she danced anyway. Like she belonged and she couldn't care less if anyone was watching.

And that? That was dangerous.

Normally, we don't pay much mind to tourists. When they do come in, they keep to themselves, grab a drink, maybe snap a few photos before they move on. We've seen it a hundred times. But these two were different.

When I walked away from the bar and our eyes locked, it was like time slowed.

Freckles dusted the bridge of her nose, softening the sharp edges of her exotic beauty. She wasn't trying to be anything other than exactly what she was, that much was obvious. And that damn hair. Thick, unruly strands were clinging to her flushed cheeks like they had a right to touch her. Framing her face like a fucking halo, though there was nothing angelic about her. No, she looked like temptation itself—like sin in its purest form. Full lips, high cheekbones, and eyes that made a man forget why he should stay away.

She was a goddamn contradiction. Beautifully and completely undone, a mess of laughter, and energy, and I've never seen anyone look so fucking hot and unbothered at the same time.

My body responded before my brain even had a chance to process what was happening. Heat surged through me, blood rushing south as my dick stirred, pressing hard against the seam of my jeans like it had a mind of its own.

Shit.

I shifted my stance, trying to get my body under control, but my mind was already useless, spinning with nothing but images of her with her hands in her hair. Stirring at the way her body moved with the music, how she looked when she laughed, completely lost in the moment.

I hadn't even *spoken* to this woman, and my cock was acting like she was already coming home with us.

I needed to get a grip.

This wasn't what I'd planned for tonight. Hell, I came here to unwind, not to lose my mind over some stunning, messy-haired American. It had been years since I'd met someone at a bar and decided to bring them home. Years. But apparently, my body had decided tonight was a great time to fuck with me.

I did everything I could to avoid looking at her while she danced, focused on my drink, the game, anything but the way her hips moved, the way her head tilted back when she laughed, the glow of her skin under the lights.

Eventually, I couldn't take it anymore, and neither could the pressure straining against my zipper.

In a desperate move, I downed the rest of my whiskey in one go and ordered another. I'm not the kind of guy who gets drunk at the pub, but desperate times and all. It was shaping up to be a long fucking night.

They weren't doing the usual tourist routine, either. They weren't drinking to fill the time before heading to their next stop. No, they were settled in, like they had no plans of leaving anytime soon.

I run a hand down my face, groaning under my breath. I need to get my shit together. She's just a woman. One drink, one night, and then it's back to normal.

Just as I'm about to regroup, Cam saunters up with his usual shit-eating grin, looking far too entertained by whatever the hell was about to come out of his mouth.

"If ya stare any harder, they're gonna think ye're a creep. And then they won't come over here." His grin is infuriating. "I already went over there to warm them up a bit."

Of course he did.

By now, I'd pieced together that the one Cam was practically drooling over was Rachel. Dark brown hair, tattoos on her arms, the kind of boldness that made it clear she had no problem taking up space. Her energy mirrors Raven's.

Honestly? They could be sisters.

But Raven...Just watching her dance is enough to tighten my grip on my glass. There's something about the way she moves, like she owns the room. A girl like that doesn't beg for attention. She simply exists, and the world bends around her.

Let your imagination run wild for half a second, and you'd know exactly how she'd move in bed.

And if you know what you're doing...

Fuck.

My lower half stirs again at the thought, and I down another gulp of my drink, willing my body to behave. I don't have time for this.

Setting my glass down, I step forward and take my turn at the board, forcing myself to focus on *anything* other than the two women closing the distance between us.

Then she pops off, throwing down a challenge like she actually thinks she can win.

Adorable.

I lean against the table, watching her with a mix of amusement and something much darker. She has no idea what she's just walked into. The fire in her eyes, that sharp edge in her voice, it all makes me want to test just how much of that attitude she can back up.

And beneath it all, there's this wild urge in me to grab her, pin her against the wall, and tell her exactly what she'd get if she won.

The image hits me like a wrecking ball, raw and unrelenting, and for half a second, I actually choke on my drink.

Fuck.

Now she's looking right at me, hazel eyes locked onto mine like she can sense the shift in my thoughts.

She has no idea what's running through my head right now. No idea what I'd do to her if I got her alone. And that's the problem.

I need to stop looking at her like this.

I fire off the first thing that comes to mind. The one thing I know will get under her skin, just so I can see that fire in her eyes again.

If I win, I get her name and number.

I don't even hesitate before agreeing, keeping my face neutral, my voice smooth. *Like I don't already know her name.*

We start the game, and I know from the first throw that she doesn't stand a fucking chance. But I'll give her credit, she's stubborn as hell.

She bites her lip when she focuses, and the way she scowls at the board like it personally offended her. Is not doing anything good for me.

And when she finally lands that bullseye? The way her face lights up, it's the kind of shit that makes men weak. Makes them stupid.

But I'm not that kind of man.

I let her have the moment. Let her bask in it. Let her think she won something. Because in the end, the game was never actually about winning.

Cam, of course, has been laying it on thick all night, flirting like it's a damn sport. As if no one can see exactly what he's doing. The man doesn't even try to hide it. I've known him my whole life. I can spot his moves from a mile away.

I don't make time for distractions. And I don't care to.

Everyone around here already knows who I am. Every woman within a fifty-mile radius has already tried, and failed, to hold my interest.

I've gone on dates. Had some *fun.*

It's all fun and games until the next day, when they start calling. Maybe that makes me a dick, but I don't really give a fuck.

It's hard to find someone who can actually hold a decent conversation without an agenda. So I don't bother anymore.

I focus on work. Keep to myself. Handle my shit.

It's easier that way. Honestly, this is the first time I've been out with everyone in months.

As the game wraps up, the noise dulls to a low hum, the kind that signals the night is winding down. That's when Cam stumbles over, clapping me on the back, grinning like a fucking idiot.

"Aye, I think I'm in love," he declares, nearly tipping over. I catch him just in time, gripping his arm before he face-plants.

"Nah, yer just drunk," I reply, shaking my head as I steady him.

I've dealt with enough nights like this to know exactly how they end. But tonight feels... different.

My attention shifts back to Raven, I know I should look away, forget about her. But I don't. I just watch as she leans in, laughing at something Rachel says.

CHAPTER 5

The Vodka is Talking...

RAVEN

I spot the guys lingering by the bar as we come out of the bathroom, their presence impossible to miss.

"Your bill's taken care of." Says the most infuriating man of the night, his tone leaving no room for argument.

I arch a brow, annoyed. "Thank you, but you didn't have to do that."

The bite in my voice is sharper than I intended, but he remains completely unfazed. Not even a flicker of reaction. Just smug confidence.

He just shrugs. "Aye, I did have to. You're in the Highlands."

Whatever the hell that means.

I roll my eyes but smile anyway. "Well then, thank you, kind *sir*." I exaggerate a curtsy for good measure, my smile widening as I slide past him toward the exit. I can feel his eyes on my back the entire way.

Walking outside is like a breath of fresh air.

Literally.

The cool night air nips at my skin, it's refreshing.

I inhale deeply, savoring the crispness of the night compared to the heat that seemed to crawl up my neck every time Kane got too close.

That thought alone makes me pause.

I look up and the sky is impossibly clear, the moon casts a silver glow over everything, making the whole world feel different. Like the air itself is humming with something just out of reach.

Rachel's off to the side, deep in conversation with Cam, and for the first time tonight, I have a rare second to myself.

I close my eyes and let the breeze wash over me, drinking in the stillness and the sharp bite of the Highland air.

At the base of my neck, I start to feel a tingling sensation, like the faintest whisper of a breeze brushing against my skin. Except... it's not windy. And I go completely still.

A chill races down my spine, like fingers tracing along my skin. For a heartbeat, it feels like someone just walked right through me.

My pulse kicks up, and my eyes snap open.

The street lights flicker overhead, stuttering erratically and a rush of déjà vu slams into me so hard I have to steady myself.

What the fuck was that?

Ever since my grandfather passed, strange things have been happening. Small things, subtle shifts in the air, little moments that felt... off.

This was something else though. Before I can chase that thought any further, someone crashes into me.

Strong hands grip my waist, steadying me as I stumble back.

"Are you okay?"

His voice is rough in a way that sends something hot curling through my stomach.

I look up, and *damn it,* Kane, is looking right at me.

"I'm sorry! I just stopped right in the way. And yes, I'm okay." I laugh a little too quickly, desperate to shake the sudden heat creeping up my neck. "Thank you for not letting me fall. That would have sucked."

I cut myself off, cringing internally.

Normally, I'm not this chatty with men I've just met. And yet, here I am, word vomiting all over him. *These drinks are getting real chatty.*

At least it's not *actual* vomiting. *Now that would be worse.*

The reality of what happened is... the second his hands wrapped around my waist; my body *caved.* And that startled me enough to actually stumble for real. I pray he doesn't notice. *He probably did.*

"Anyway," I jerk my thumb toward Rachel. "They're still over there chatting, but you can wait here with me if you want."

I can't tell if Rachel wants saving... or if she's the one causing all the trouble.

He shifts, sliding his hands into his pockets. "I give it about eight minutes before she decides whether she's going to ditch him or give him her number."

I huff out a laugh. "Nah, more like two." I glance toward Rachel, who's flipping her hair. "Either way, we'll be calling it a night soon."

"Are you two sisters?"

There it is again, that damn smirk. The one that's been driving me insane all night, like he's in on a joke I haven't figured out yet.

I scoff, shaking my head. "Do we look like sisters?"

He tilts his head, meeting his eyes, then they slowly roll down my body and back. "Not particularly."

I roll my eyes. "Then why'd you ask?"

He shrugs.

"Well... technically, no, we're not sisters. But we might as well be." Like that explanation makes perfect sense.

His brows lift slightly. "That was... unnecessarily complicated."

I open my mouth, then immediately shut it.

Oh wow. *Hi, I'm the problem, it's me. Again.*

He lets out a genuine laugh, the kind that vibrates through his chest before trailing off into a half-cough. It does dangerous things to my resolve.

"Well... that's *cool*," he says, like my stammering only amused him more.

That's it?

I wait a beat, expecting him to say something else, but he doesn't. He just stands there, looking at me like he's waiting for something.

"We've known each other for years. We do a lot together, so we're practically sisters. Like... twin-flame level friends. Ya know?"

His eyes drop to my lips before looking back up and I swallow hard, forcing myself to ignore the way my pulse spikes, and the way my body betrays me with every single move he makes.

As if I needed *any* more reasons to be humiliated tonight.

"Why did you come to Scotland?" He asks, sounding genuine.

I hesitate. "I was supposed to come here with my grandpa, actually. But... he couldn't be here. Rachel came with me instead, so we're here to have a little fun."

I offer a small smile, hoping to steer the conversation back to safer ground. I don't know why that was the first thing that came to mind, it slipped out before I could stop it.

He nods, but a flicker of something unreadable flashes in his eyes. "Yeah, I get that. That's Cam, for me. Family."

He glances past me at his so-called family. The same guy he's been talking shit to all night.

"So, what you're saying is... if I asked Cam for dirt, I'd get a hell of a story?"

Kane's attention snaps back to me, his cocky grin spreading like I just made another bet. "Aye, I'm sure Rachel's got *years* of dirt on you too."

I scoff, folding my arms. "Bold of you to assume I have anything to be embarrassed about."

My pulse flickers wildly in response. And judging by the way his eyes darken just slightly, he knows it too.

He shifts closer, his voice dipping as he looks behind me. "They're definitely blowing past your two-minute mark. You lost, Princess. Are you okay?"

I snort, look over at Rachel and Cam, who are locked in conversation, oblivious to anything but each other. "There's still time for her to change her mind."

"Doubt it." His eyes flick back to mine, softer now, the teasing edge fading. "I'm sorry your grandfather couldn't be here."

For all his cocky remarks and smug little grins, the unexpected kindness catches me off guard.

I look at him, surprised. "Thanks," I say, my voice quieter than before. I turn my attention back to Rachel, watching her closely. Cam's pulling out all the stops, his charm is dialed in. And judging by the way she's leaning in, and tilting her head, she's loving every second of it.

"She's a goner, he's getting her number." Kane murmurs, amusement lacing his tone.

I shake my head. If there was no Bobby, he would be completely right.

"She'll walk away."

He huffs out a low laugh. "Not a chance, or she wouldn't have offered."

I study Rachel again, watching the way her fingers graze Cam's arm, the way she angles herself just enough to brush up against him.

Damn. He's right.

I roll my eyes and exhale dramatically. "Fine. Maybe she's charmed by him. But don't get all cocky about it. It's not cute."

"Too late." His smirk is instant.

I narrow my eyes, fighting the urge to roll them right out of my skull. But the truth is, he's right. Rachel isn't about to pull the plug. She's fully caught up in Cam's pull, and I've officially lost.

I, on the other hand, am currently dealing with a different kind of problem. The kind that involves Kane standing too damn close, his presence wrapping around me like a goddamn noose.

I really don't appreciate my body reacting without my consent. Every time I look at this infuriating asshole, something inside me snaps to attention. Like my body is caught in some cruel game, it refuses to let me win.

And I'm *not* interested.

Not even a little. Despite what my pulse is doing, and despite the warmth curling low in my stomach.

I force myself to shake off the thought, but before I can make my escape, Kane breaks my concentration, his voice cutting through my spiraling thoughts.

"It's been thirteen minutes. You lose," he murmurs, eyes locked onto mine. "Too bad we didn't make another bet."

"Damn. And here I was, just *dying* to lose more imaginary things to you," I say, flashing him a smile as I turn around to take a step toward Rachel, nearly taking a table with me, but I don't get far.

A hand closes around mine.

I whip my head back toward him, ready to throw out a smartass comment, but the second we make eye contact. The words catch in my throat.

"So when are you going to give me your phone number?"

I swear the temperature spikes at least twenty degrees and for the first time in my life, I wish I was cold. Instead, I'm overheating in places that have no business reacting.

My pulse is out of control. My body is at war with my brain, and I pray to every God listening that he doesn't notice the way I'm unraveling right in front of him.

Wouldn't be the first time tonight.

Clearly, men are not good for my hygiene, or my mental health.

And this one? He's the poster boy for *bad decisions.*

I take a slow, deep breath, trying to rein myself in. My voice is light when I force out a laugh. "Oh, I guess that would be okay. Hopefully, you're not a crazy person that's going to murder us. I'd hate for Rachel to be right. Although, I guess if I do get murdered, at least I can say I checked someth—"

I don't get to finish my sentence.

His mouth crashes into mine, obliterating whatever ridiculous thought was about to spill out.

I don't even have time to react before his hands are threading through my hair, gripping the back of my head, tilting me up to meet his demanding kiss.

My thoughts? Gone.

Every coherent string of logic I had left? Shattered.

His lips are soft, nothing like I imagined, yet exactly what I should've expected.

Of *course* he kisses like he owns the very air I breathe. And of *course,* my body betrays me, responding on instinct. My mouth parts, my hands grip his shirt, *pulling* him closer instead of shoving him away like I should be.

I really need to work on my self-control. Because, clearly, I don't possess a damn ounce of it right now. One hot guy pays attention to me, and suddenly, I'm *melting* in his arms?

Absolutely not.

Except that's exactly what's happening.

I should be furious. I should be shoving him off, throwing out some stupid comment to put distance between us, but instead, *I'm sinking into him.*

The seconds my lips part, his tongue sweeps into my mouth, claiming every inch like he's starving for me.

A low, satisfied groan rumbles from his chest, vibrating against my skin, and that's it. I'm done for.

I meet his intensity with my own, my fingers twisting into his hair, dragging him closer.

His grip tightens at my waist, his palm spanning the small of my back as he pulls me against him. The heat of his body is *everywhere*, consuming and setting fire to every nerve ending I have left.

He tilts my head back, deepening the kiss, *taking*.

God help me, do *I let him*.

Because right now, I don't care about logic. I don't care that Kane is probably nothing but trouble.

All I care about is how he tastes. Whiskey, and something *dark*, something that makes me ache in a way I don't want to think about.

His teeth graze my bottom lip, sharp enough to send a shockwave of heat straight through me. A broken gasp escapes, and that must be all the permission he needs, because his hand slides lower, gripping my hips, anchoring me to him.

I'm so fucked.

I'm never drinking again. I know I'll regret this, but right now I don't give a damn about anything except the way his mouth moves against mine.

His kiss is relentless, and *damn*, he's good at it.

A tiny voice in the back of my mind whispers that I should be mildly embarrassed by how easily I caved. But I'm not.

One little kiss won't hurt. His grip tightens at the nape of my neck, fingers threading into my hair as he tilts my head, holding me still.

Every nerve in my body ignites, heat pouring through me like wildfire. My hands slide up his chest and my body presses into his. I swear I hear a low, dangerous growl vibrating against my lips like a promise. Before I can even process what's happening, he pulls away.

He steps back so suddenly, I almost stumble forward, like my body physically refuses to let him go.

And then he has the audacity to smirk at me. What felt like an eternity was probably only a few seconds, but fuck. I'm left standing there, completely untethered.

I blink, trying to regain control of my traitorous, weak-willed body, as my mind scrambles to process what the hell just happened.

Because no one who kisses me after this will stand a chance. And that was *nothing*.

I steel my spine, schooling my features into something vaguely resembling composure, even though every cell in my body is currently rioting against me.

This is *not* how I imagined my grand exit would go.

I'm frozen, standing here like an idiot. He's watching me like he knows I have no goddamn clue what to do with myself right now. I need to get out of here before I do something I *will* regret.

Like kiss him again. Or worse, *want* to kiss him again.

Summoning whatever shred of dignity I have left, I extend my hand, palm up. "Phone," I demand, my voice blessedly steady.

His brows lift slightly, a flicker of amusement dancing in those sharp, assessing eyes. Without hesitation, he slips his phone into my palm, his fingers grazing mine just long enough to be *annoyingly* intentional.

The smirk on his lips tells me he wanted me to notice.

I narrow my eyes but say nothing, focusing on entering my number adding *Your Royal Highness* as my contact name, before handing it back. Petty is a personality trait at this point.

"If you turn out to be a creep, I'm going to be *really* pissed," I warn, crossing my arms.

His smirk deepens, like I just handed him my resignation letter and he's already planning my downfall.

"Oh, don't worry, Princess," his voice dragging over the word. "If I were a creep, you'd already know it."

My brows shoot up. "Wow. That's... comforting."

He winks.

I scoff, shaking my head. "Thanks again for not letting me fall," I force a breezy tone even though my skin *still* tingles where he touched me.

His smile widens just a touch, like I'm entertaining him.

Perfect. That's exactly what I need, *him* thinking I'm cute while I'm over here desperately trying not to combust.

And in typical, infuriating Kane fashion, he adds, "Anytime. Maybe you should go practice some darts, so that next time you actually stand a chance at winning."

Mouth open, I *stare* at him for a moment, completely thrown.

Seriously?

He kisses me like that, practically melts my brain, and now he's going back to this? I quickly recover, snapping my mouth shut before the words *I'll likely never see you again* slip out.

Instead, I punch him. Apparently, I woke up from my nap today choosing *violence*.

His deep, rich laughter follows me as I turn away, and I know that sound is going to haunt me later but over my dead body am I letting him have the last word.

CHAPTER 6

So Long

RAVEN

Rachel picks that exact moment to come over, likely saving me from my own self-destruction. We can dive deep into *that* mind-fuck *later*. Maybe if I'm lucky, she didn't notice.

But the second I look at her, I know with absolute certainty, that she *definitely* noticed. And, judging by the barely-contained grin stretching across her face, she's ready to talk about it right now.

I shoot her a pleading look that screams *NOT RIGHT NOW!*

She clears her throat dramatically. "Okay, time for us to go home. It's late, and we have a big day ahead of us tomorrow with our friends."

We don't.

We don't have any plans tomorrow. And we *definitely* don't have any friends here. *They* don't know that, though.

But before I can fully detach myself from this moment, Cam speaks up. "Why don't you let us give you a ride?"

I freeze, glancing at Rachel, hoping she's about to bail us out of this. But she tilts her head, looking intrigued. *Of course she is.* I brace myself for whatever is about to come out of her mouth.

"Thank you, but we're fine," Rachel tells them. "Our place isn't too far, just a few blocks."

Kane just stares at me, not saying a word.

"What?" I frown. "Why are you looking at us like that?"

He huffs a quiet laugh, shaking his head. "A few blocks? You can't seriously think we're going to let you just walk home. Especially when you're drunk in a foreign country."

His tone is final, like this is not up for debate.

I fold my arms, trying to ignore the way he's looking at me. Like he's already decided how this is going to go.

"I appreciate the concern," keeping my voice level. "But it's really not necessary. Plus, it's a nice night."

Rachel shifts beside me, her eyes flicking between Kane and me like she's debating whether or not she should step in or let me dig my own grave.

Before I can say anything else, Cam grins and shakes his head. "For real, what kind of men do you think we are? Letting two beautiful women walk home alone in the dark? That's how horror movies start. Next thing you know, you'll turn into pumpkins."

I snort. *What?*

Rachel, on the other hand, thrives in moments like these and doesn't miss a beat. "First of all, it was just the *carriage* that turned into a pumpkin, *not* Cinderella," she corrects, hands on her hips. "And second, we're not even remotely Cinderellas. We don't need saving."

She flashes a wicked grin. "But hey, close enough. *Anyway, bye!*"

Before they can argue, she grabs my arm and starts to drag me down the sidewalk.

Kane clears his throat, his deep voice smooth and commanding. "We insist. Excuse me, ladies. Right this way."

His hand touches the small of my back for just a second longer than necessary, guiding us down the street like he's completely unbothered by the fact that we already said no.

I spin around, placing a hand over my heart like I'm genuinely concerned. "Goodness," I say, pretending to be shocked. "You really should work on your people skills."

His lips twitch.

Kane exhales sharply, shaking his head like we're both insufferable. "Okay. But don't think for a second that we're letting you walk just because you're determined to be stubborn." His smirk is lazy, but no less confident. "Consider it my good deed for the evening."

I arch a brow. "A good deed? Wow, how selfless of you."

Rachel hums thoughtfully. "We wouldn't want you to ruin your fancy shoes."

Cam bursts into laughter. "Fuck, I like you two."

Kane's eyes gleam with amusement as he watches me, like he enjoys getting under my skin.

"Fine," I mutter, cutting my losses. "You can walk us home. But you're not driving us anywhere."

Rachel leans in, grinning. "We're not about to give you an opportunity to kidnap us with your car."

Kane scoffs, shaking his head. "Christ, you two are exhausting."

I flash him a satisfied smile. "Not even sorry. You're the ones insisting on walking us home.

Rachel leans closer, whispering just loud enough for me to hear, "You know, you really do have a way of making things interesting wherever we go. Maybe Scotland during your *No Boys* era should be reconsidered."

I roll my eyes, but a smile tugs at my lips. "Yeah, well, let's just hope the rest of the trip doesn't involve more unexpected makeouts."

Rachel laughs, her eyes sparkling with amusement. "I wouldn't hold your breath, and I still want the details later."

"You coming?" I ask over my shoulder, walking with a little extra sway to my hips. What can I say? A girl's gotta use what she's got, even if nothing's coming of it.

Kane catches up in two strides, effortlessly matching my pace. "You realize it's a little odd to assume *everyone* is out to kidnap you, right?"

I laugh, shaking my head. "True. Better safe than sorry, though."

I mean, he does have a point. For how worried we are about being kidnapped, we caved in less than two seconds when they offered to walk us home.

"I wouldn't say you're walking *with* us," I add with a smirk. "You're walking us home, then turning right back around, getting in your car, and driving home. There's a difference."

I glance over at him, and sure enough, he's raising an eyebrow.

I sigh dramatically. "Okay, fine. I know. If you really were a killer, it wouldn't matter. Yeah, yeah, we get it."

Then again, with the books we read, who's to say we wouldn't secretly enjoy being kidnapped by two hot men in the middle of Scotland? Like, *yes please, take me into the woods.*

"Okay, Princess. Whatever you say."

I blink, my brows lifting. "There you go again, with that *Princess* thing."
I side-eye him, refusing to let him see how much it gets to me.

He grins, the corner of his mouth twitching with amusement. "You don't seem to mind."

I roll my eyes but can't help the little smile tugging at my lips. "Sure, keep telling yourself that."

We fall into comfortable silence as we walk, the cool night air settling between us and I start to wonder just how far our place really is.

As if reading my mind, he says, "I thought you said it was only a couple of blocks?"

"I'm sure we're almost there. Don't you worry your pretty little face about it," I shoot back, flashing him a sweet smile. "Are you in a hurry to get rid of us?"

His gaze sharpens, the playful glint in his eyes shifting into something that makes my pulse stutter.

I instantly regret the teasing. Not because I don't mean it, but because I have the sinking feeling he's about to flip this whole conversation on me.

"You know," I continue, desperate to regain control, "I heard once that if you make a face too much, it'll stick like that forever." I shoot him a grin, the best defense I have. "Which would be a shame."

Kane smirks, not missing a beat. "Oh yeah? And why's that, *Princess*? Because you think I'm pretty?"

I groan internally. Walked right into that one. Rookie mistake. His grin deepens as he leans in slightly.

"You know you're not unattractive." I aim for nonchalant and fail miserably. "Don't get all shy now. I'm not blind. So yes, you're a pretty boy. It would be a shame if your face got stuck like that though."

Oh my God. Why would I say that?

Of all the possible responses, that is what I went with? I mentally smack myself. Clearly, I drank too much. Who needs advanced interrogation tactics when a couple drinks or three can turn you into an open book?

Then he laughs, a low, rich sound that I absolutely shouldn't enjoy as much as I do.

"Pretty boy, huh?" He repeats, amused.

Using his own words against him, I glance sideways and smirk. "You don't seem to mind."

His chuckle is warm. "Well, I guess I'll take the compliments where I can get them."

"Good idea," I reply, matching his energy. "Or I might just have to call you something else next time."

His brow lifts. "Oh? And what would that be?"

I shrug, keeping my expression perfectly unreadable. "Guess you'll just have to wait and see, won't you?"

His smirk deepens, but he says nothing. He just watches me, eyes flickering with something unreadable of his own. I mentally curse my inability to quit while I'm ahead. *Seriously, Raven. Learn when to shut up.* My smart mouth is going to get me in trouble one of these days.

"You are something else." His voice is softer, the teasing edge momentarily gone. "It's actually quite refreshing."

The words slip out like he hadn't planned on saying them, and the second they do, he looks like he wants to take them back.

Interesting.

Before I can push, he swiftly changes the subject. "So what else do you have planned while you are here?"

I let him have the out, but his comment lingers, poking at me in a way I don't entirely understand. I have to think for a second, realizing I've completely zoned out. Damn that accent. He could be reciting the ingredients on the back of a cereal box, and I'd still be standing here, mesmerized.

Focus, Raven.

"Well, I know we want to do some hikes. Hopefully, they won't be too crowded with tourists... but, knowing our luck, they absolutely will be, and I'll hate it," I grumble.

His expression shifts slightly, like he's already wishing me luck because I'm doomed.

"I know, I know," I sigh. "We probably won't get that lucky, but still. I love being outside." I hesitate before adding, "If it wasn't frowned upon, I probably wouldn't even wear shoes."

As soon as the words are out, I cringe internally. Another overshare. *Why am I like this?* I can practically hear my brain keeping score: *Vodka-6, Raven-0.*

His lips twitch like he's holding back a laugh. "No shoes, huh?"

"Not in a weird way," I clarify, suddenly needing to defend my stance on foot freedom. "Just, I don't know... I like feeling connected."

The second it leaves my mouth, I wince. *Jesus, Raven.* Might as well start juggling crystals, burning sage, and howling at the moon.

To my surprise, he doesn't laugh. He just tilts his head slightly, studying me.

"I'm sure the trails will be a bit busy," he finally responds. "Hopefully not too bad, though. Are you planning on doing anything around town?" His voice is casual, but there's a flicker of curiosity beneath it. "If you want, we could show you guys around. Take you to a castle or two, show you the places that aren't packed with tourists."

I arch a brow, tilting my head slightly. "What's the catch?"

He shrugs, casual as ever. "No catch. Just thought I'd do my duty as a Scottish gentleman and give you ladies a proper tour."

"A private tour guide?" I nudge him playfully with my elbow. "How much would that cost? Because just so you know, we're *definitely* on a budget."

Kane chuckles, shaking his head. "Don't worry, Princess. First tour's on the house. Consider it a favor."

"A favor?" I arch a brow. "What exactly are we going to owe you?"

His smile deepens, "Guess you'll have to wait and see."

I scoff, nudging him again, this time with a little more force. "If that's your way of scamming tourists, I gotta say, I'm not impressed. You should work on your pitch."

His gaze drips to where my elbow brushed against him, then back up to my face, amusement dancing in his expression. "You're saying no to a free, exclusive tour of Scotland? I don't know, sounds like a missed opportunity."

I narrow my eyes, pretending to weigh my options. "I don't know... I feel like this is how those true crime stories start. *She was last seen accepting a favor from a charming Scottish man...*"

Kane's laughter is effortless. "Charming, huh? I'll take that too."

"Not the part you should be focusing on."

His grin doesn't falter, but there's something unreadable that flashes through his eyes.

I laugh, shaking my head. "You'll have to let us know. We'll be expecting the *royal treatment,* of course."

Rachel suddenly turns and yells over her shoulder, "How far away is our place? I swear we should be there by now."

She's right. It feels like we've been walking forever. We definitely should've been there already.

Good news: my phone has three percent.

Bad news: my phone has *three percent battery.*

This would *not* be an ideal night to be kidnapped by strange men in a foreign country while my phone gasps its last breath.

"Rach, how much battery does your phone have?" I call out, trying to sound casual despite the sinking feeling in my stomach.

She spins around, grinning like we're having the time of our lives. "Oh, I'm sure it's fully charged... back on the charger, in our room."

Of course.

I blink at her, stunned by her carefree attitude. I let out a slow breath, leveling her with a look. "Oh my God, Rachel. Who doesn't bring their phone out? What if you *did* get kidnapped? How would you call for help?"

Rachel bursts into laughter, doubling over as she clutches her side. "Well, Cam here has a phone." She giggles. "So worst case, I'd use his to call for help. You're supposed to be the responsible one! Where's *your* phone?"

Her teasing sets all of us off, and soon we're all laughing, including Kane. I glance over at him, momentarily caught off guard by how the sound of his laughter makes my chest flutter. I shake it off and shoot Rachel a glare, but it has no real bite.

"You two are something else." Cam says, shaking his head with a grin. "I think we'll show you around after all, if only for the entertainment value."

Rachel nudges me playfully. "See? At least one of us is prepared for anything."

Honestly, sometimes I think we shouldn't be left alone together.

"Okay, well, I think I remember this part of town," I say, forcing confidence into my tone. "Let's just keep walking for a bit. I can try to look up the address while we walk and *hopefully* my phone won't die."

Kane leans in, unimpressed. "So let me get this straight, you won't let us give you a ride home, but you were going to walk home without knowing where you were going?"

I exhale sharply. "Yes, actually. And I'd appreciate it if you'd stop judging my entire existence."

He hums, completely *not* stopping his judgement.

Rachel laughs and says, "We're bound to find it eventually. And if not, I'm sure we could find some charming gentlemen who can help us out."

Not funny. I glance at Kane and Cam, who both seem more *amused* than concerned. They're definitely trouble, but hopefully not the kind we need to worry about.

Kane walks beside me, keeping to the side closest to the road. A car passes, and before I can react, I feel his hand gently press against the small of my back.

It's a casual touch, except it does something to my body. A slow treacherous warmth spreads from the spot where his fingers linger, curling low in my stomach before I can stop it.

I should move.

But I don't.

Instead, I keep walking, trying to ignore the way my pulse picks up and how, despite everything I know to be true about men like him... I feel safer than I should.

It's only midnight, but honestly, I'm relieved they're here. The thought of wandering these unfamiliar streets, in the dark, slightly buzzed and running on questionable decision-making skills? Yeah, not my brightest idea.

"Do you remember what your place was by?" Kane asks, pulling me out of my thoughts. "If you can remember any landmarks, I can probably figure out where it is."

I glance over at him, appreciating that he's actually trying to help instead of just making fun of me.

"A couple more emails, and I should be able to find the right one. *We're not lost*," I say with way more confidence than I actually feel.

My phone screen blinks at me like it knows I'm lying.

One percent left.

I open my email, silently begging it to hold on a little longer. *Please don't die. Please, please, ple—*

The screen goes dark.

"Noooo!" I yell as my phone finally dies, leaving me stranded with nothing but my panicked thoughts and a useless piece of metal.

Rachel stops mid-laugh and turns to me, eyes wide. "Oh my God, did your phone just die?"

"No, Rach, I'm just dramatically mourning my fully charged battery." I snap, shaking my dead phone like that'll bring it back to life. "Yes, it died. It's dead. Deceased. Gone forever."

Rachel cackles like this is hilarious.

Cam, just smirks. "Should we light a candle for the vigil, or..."

Kane, on the other hand, just watches me, arms crossed like he's debating whether to find this amusing or concerning.

Meanwhile, my heart is racing because *holy shit, we are actually lost.* The once comforting quiet of the streets now feels heavier. The wind whispers through the alleyways, carrying a chill I hadn't noticed before. The street lights flicker, casting long, shifting shadows against the cobblestones. The night that previously felt alive, now feels too still.

This is *not* how I die.

"I'm pretty sure we're right around this corner and down the street a little," I grip onto blind faith like it's my lifeline. "We are *not* lost."

Rachel's blissfully unaware of my impending breakdown and is still laughing at something Cam said. *At least she's having the time of her life.* Meanwhile, I'm about five seconds away from activating *full-blown* survival mode.

Kane's voice cuts through my panic. "So, to recap, your phone is dead, you don't know where you're going, and you're relying on guessing?"

His smirk is firmly back in place, and I immediately regret everything.

"I'm not guessing," I argue, lifting my chin. "I *mostly* know where we are."

His brows lift. "Mostly?"

I open my mouth, ready to fire something back, but before I can, a blacked-out SUV slows to a stop beside us.

Every muscle in my body locks up.

My pulse spikes, my breath catching in my throat. This is it. This is how we die. If it weren't for the solid heat of Kane's hand resting low on my back anchoring me, I'd be convinced that this is the moment we get kidnapped and murdered.

Cam hauls Rachel toward the SUV like it's his personal getaway vehicle. He's literally hauling her over his shoulder as her laughter echoes down the street. For a split second, I'm about to freak out.

She's giggling like a maniac, and I'm about to kick Cam in the shins and drag her ass straight to the nearest police station.

Before I can fully spiral, Kane's voice cuts through the growing tension.

"It's fine. He's a friend." His tone is maddeningly calm. "We needed a ride, and a charger so you can figure out where your place is."

I blink.

I didn't even see him pull out his phone. His smirk doesn't fade, but there's something in his eyes, like he's waiting for my reaction.

Then he adds, way too casually, "Unless of course you want to come back with us and drive around in my car to try to find your place?"

The look I give him says *absolutely not*. He just laughs, shaking his head. "That's why our ride is here, Princess. You can plug your phone in, figure out where you're going, and we'll get you home. You're safe."

You're safe.

Two simple words, and yet the tension in my shoulders melts like ice under a flame.

How the hell does this man know exactly what to say? How does he do it so easily, like it's second nature? Or maybe this is just what decent men do. Either way, hearing him say it makes me feel a little better.

Not that I fully trust him. But something about the way he says things with such certainty, makes me want to.

I could stand here and argue, or I could just get in the damn car, charge my phone, and figure out how to get home from there.

I exhale slowly, giving in to the inevitable.

"Okay," I murmur, the word slipping out before I can second-guess it.

The night around us seems to settle, the tension easing as Kane gently guides me toward the SUV. His touch is grounding in a way that quiets the chaos in my mind. I don't know why, but the moment he reassures me, everything stops spinning. It's strange how easily he does that.

As we approach, the tinted windows catch the streetlights, and out of the corner of my eye, I catch a flicker of movement. I pause, turning, but there's nothing there.

A strange sensation curls at the nape of my neck, like something is pressing on my skin. I swallow hard, pushing the thought away. Kane is already leaning forward, talking easily with the driver like they're old friends, just like he said.

It should put me at ease, but it doesn't.

Rachel, however, looks completely unbothered, throwing me a shrug as she climbs inside like she's stepping into a damn limo. I hesitate for only a second before following.

Kane slides in beside me, his voice as smooth as ever. "Would you rather drive around for a bit, or just sit here and wait?"

I blink, thrown by the question.

Why would he even ask that? It's such a random thing to offer, and yet something about it puts me at ease.

"If we can just sit here and wait, that'd be great." I make my voice as confident as possible. "I promise we're close. No point in driving around just to end up back here."

His gaze lingers for a second longer than necessary, then he nods, satisfied.

"Okay. We'll wait." He settles back into his seat.

No teasing. No smug grin. Just calm, steady acceptance.

The shift is unexpected. I take a moment to really look at him and the relaxed way he drapes his arm along the back of the seat, the way his expression has softened. It's a stark contrast to the cocky, sharp-witted man I've been dealing with all night. And somehow, this version of him is even more dangerous.

Because there's no arrogance here. No attempt to impress me.

Just Kane.

The realization makes my stomach twist in ways I don't have the energy to unpack. I force myself to focus on my phone, watching the screen slowly flicker to life as it charges. The tension from earlier still lingers, woven into my muscles like knots I can't untangle.

Rachel, on the other hand, is still deep in conversation with Cam, her laughter is easy and light. It's almost funny how she's fully enjoying herself while I'm sitting here overanalyzing everything.

I exhale slowly and close my eyes, running through a few breathing exercises my grandmother taught me. Focus on the inhale, count the exhale. Let everything else fade.

The SUV hums softly beneath me, the faint scent of leather and cologne settling in the air. I focus on that instead, letting it steady me. When I open my eyes, I find Kane watching me.

His gaze is steady, but there's something there, something quieter than before. A small knowing smile tugs at the corner of his mouth.

"You alright?"

"Yeah." I say automatically, but even I can hear the lie in my voice.

He raises a brow, waiting.

I sigh, rubbing a hand over my face. "Okay... I *hate* being lost."

The words come out before I can stop them. And surprisingly, saying it out loud actually helps. Like admitting it makes the weight a little lighter.

The screen of my phone lights up, buzzing faintly in my palm, and I nearly groan in relief. I quickly scroll through my email, finding the booking confirmation. My stomach untwists the second I see the address. *Finally.*

I turn the screen toward Kane, and his eyes flicker over the address, something unreadable flashing across his face before he smooths it out. Without hesitation, he leans forward, says something to the driver, and just like that, the SUV starts moving.

A prickle of unease skates down my spine. I lean back into the seat, exhaling slowly, trying to shake the gnawing feeling creeping in like an unwelcome shadow.

Maybe I'm just being paranoid. Spiraling because of the kiss, the drinks, the entire night spinning faster than I can process. Or maybe I've been too trusting.

I don't actually know this guy. I haven't asked him anything real, haven't even covered the basics. What does he do for work? Does he even have a job? Does he have someone waiting up for him? A wife? A girlfriend?

And why the hell didn't I ask any of this before I let him steal that damn kiss?

The worst part isn't just the kiss. It's *this*. The way he makes me feel safe even when I know I shouldn't. It terrifies me more than anything. I'm always the one with backup plans, with an escape route mapped out before I even walk into a room.

But here I am, sitting in the back of a strangers SUV, fighting the undeniable pull between us, while my instincts scream at me to *wake the hell up.*

A thousand little red flags I hadn't noticed earlier now wave wildly in my mind, warning me that I've made a mistake. But I push it all aside. Right now, the only thing that matters is getting out of this car, making it inside, and sorting my own head out before I let this go any further.

The SUV rolls smoothly down the street, and finally, things start looking familiar. Relief floods through me as the tension in my shoulders unwinds.

I glance at Rachel, half-expecting her to be looking out the window, worried about where we are going, but no. She's perfectly at ease, whispering to Cam like none of this is messing with her the way it's messing with me.

Which, honestly? Only makes it worse.

The nagging voice in the back of my mind refuses to shut up, quietly questioning every choice I've made tonight.

"Here we are." Kane says as we slow to a stop, giving a quick nod to the driver.

I reach for the door handle, eager to put some space between us, but as I shift, my leg brushes against his. The contact is instant. A live wire of heat shooting through my entire body. I jerk away so fast, you'd think I'd been burned.

I make a break for it, gripping the handle and pushing the door open, only to nearly fall out.

Smooth, Raven. Real graceful.

Rachel's laughter rings out behind me, Cam saying something equally obnoxious, but I barely register them. I need to get inside. I need to get control over whatever *this* is.

It's probably just the vodka talking.

Well, the vodka can shut the hell up. And so can my body, for that matter. No men, remember?! Now I'm officially the crazy person, arguing with myself.

"Thank you guys so much…" I hop out, and Rachel follows close behind, echoing her own thanks.

"Thanks, guys! See ya later. *Enjoy the blue balls!*" she calls out, laughing like a maniac.

I freeze.

My jaw drops. *Did she seriously just say that?*

I whip around, eyes wide, but Rachel just winks at me.

"Rachel," I hiss, my voice barely above a whisper as we make our way to the door. "I cannot believe that you said that! You can't just say things like that."

She bursts into another fit of laughter, practically doubling over. "Oh, come on, you know it's true!"

I groan, shaking my head as I type in the code on the door, willing my face to cool. They're *still* sitting there, waiting.

I don't dare turn around again. Instead, I shove open the door, stepping inside as quickly as possible.

Rachel makes her way to the bedroom and immediately flops face-first onto the bed like a ragdoll. "Uggg, I'm so *tired*. Let's go to bed. We'll talk about *smart choices* tomorrow."

"Yeah… smart choices," I mutter, slipping off my shoes before collapsing onto the bed.

My brain is still running laps, replaying the night's events in vivid detail. Kane's smirk, the way his hand felt at my back, that stupid, perfect kiss. I let out a slow breath, pressing my fingertips against my lips.

I should be analyzing this more. I should be going over all the reasons that this was a terrible idea. But despite the whirlwind of weirdness, despite every reason I should be running in the opposite direction… it was fun.

Confusing, electrifying, and utterly bizarre. But fun.

A small, reluctant smile tugs at my lips.

As exhaustion settles in, a faint hum echoes in my ears. Heat blooms beneath my skin, radiating outward. I exhale slowly, my thoughts growing hazy, tangled in the space between waking and dreaming.

Then the air shifts.

A ripple moves through my consciousness. The world distorts, bending at the edges, stretching and shifting like something is pulling me deeper.

Flashes of unfamiliar places flicker in my mind, misty landscapes, endless corridors lit by a dim glow. The sensation of being *watched* tugs at the edges of my awareness, a presence lingering just beyond what I can see.

I can sense eyes on me.

Not threatening. But *familiar.*

Faintly glowing orbs hover in the distance, their light pulsating with the rhythm of my breath. Shadowy figures slip through my vision, dissolving before I can focus on them, as if they're not meant to be seen.

A weight settles in the air, wrapping around me. The darkness isn't empty, it's alive.

"Raven."

A voice reverberates through my mind, smooth as silk yet laced with something deeper.

I turn and see Kane standing there, his figure illuminated by the shifting silver mist. His eyes glow faintly, but the mist curls around his frame, thick and restless. He reaches for me and when my fingers brush against his, the world shatters.

A ripple spreads outward, the force of it sending energy pulsing through the ground beneath us. The air hums, and suddenly everything shifts. The forest thrums, and the trees arch toward the sky. Leaves whisper overhead, their hushed voices carrying secrets. The mist surges, swirling in intricate patterns, weaving threads of light and shadow around us.

The whispers grow louder.

A chorus of voices, hundreds overlapping in a forgotten language. A language I shouldn't understand, and yet...

Then, like a flame flickering out, the vision begins to blur at the edges. The warmth vanishes. The whispers retreat. And I slip further into sleep.

CHAPTER 7

Currently NOT Enjoying Blue Balls

KANE

R aven.

The name suits her. She fires shots like she's been waiting her whole life to sink her teeth into someone, and I'll be damned if she doesn't hit the mark every time. And here I am, willingly walking right into her line of fire, not even *trying* to dodge.

And no, it's not helping my current case of blue balls. *Not even a little.*

I meant what I said when I told her that talking to her was refreshing. She's chaos wrapped in something I can't seem to tear my eyes away from.

Most of the women I've dealt with have no personality. No depth. Sure, some seemed interesting at first, until they weren't. Give it a few dates, and they're dull as hell. No spark. No challenge.

Lost in my thoughts, I almost forgot that Cam is still in the car until he says, "Are we staying in town?"

I drag a hand over my face, shaking off the lingering pull of the night. "Yeah," I nod to the driver, who's already making his way toward the townhouse. "Are you going to be able to keep it in your pants around Rachel? She seems into you, but that's probably the alcohol talking, you're not *that* good looking."

Cam just laughs, shaking his head. "Of course she's into me." His grin turns cocky, but there's a flicker of something else there. "Look, Rachel's fun. She's got a boyfriend but I'm not exactly losing sleep over it. If it gets freaky, it's because *she* wants it to." His voice dips, smooth and smug. "That's on her, not me."

I chuckle despite myself, shaking my head. Same Cam, same bullshit.

Then he turns the tables, giving me a pointed look.

"The real question is," he stretches in his seat like he's got all the time in the world, "are *you* going to scare Raven away with your moody, smartass comments? Girls like to be charmed, not glared into a corner, bro."

I huff out a laugh, "Real funny."

Cam lifts a brow, daring me to deny it.

I don't. Instead, I smirk, leaning back against the seat. "Charming's overrated."

Doesn't matter, though. Women like Raven don't stick around. They set fires just to watch them burn.

We stroll to a stop in front of the townhouse.

Cam has his own place, several, actually. But he crashes here whenever he's in town. Sometimes I think he thinks I need constant company.

Once inside, he heads down the hall, kicking off his shoes as he goes. "I'm heading to bed."

"Night."

I reach for the glass of whiskey waiting on the side table, swirling the amber liquid before downing it in one long pull.

One night.

One night, and she's already under my skin.

I set the empty glass down with a quiet clink, my jaw tightening.

When I started my first business, Cam was right there with me. I offered him a partnership, but he said didn't want to be *tied down.* Which I get.

I don't sit around all day either. I do go out in the field sometimes. Lately it's been more behind the desk shit. Build. Expand. Repeat.

When I made my first million, I did the usual—traveled, bought a few cars, you name it. I reinvested, built something bigger. Now, everything runs like a well-oiled machine, and a huge part of that is thanks to Cam. He works out the kinks and makes shit happen. He thrives on getting his hands dirty.

Real estate, high-end security, discreet personal protection, and occasionally dealing with the people who don't play by the rules. Everything I do caters to people who have something to lose. People who need someone like me to keep it from slipping through their fingers.

Over the years, I've pulled strings, gotten people out of trouble, and out of the headlines. I know how to dig up dirt, how to erase it, and how to make sure people don't come asking questions.

It's all part of the game. That's what keeps me in business.

I drag my hand down my face with a quiet growl. *What the fuck am I doing?*

Vanilla and amber still cling to my skin. I can still feel the press of her body against mine, the heat that pulsed between us every time she looked at me like she was daring me to make a move.

Rachel's smartass blue balls comment? Yeah, that hit too fucking close to home.

I exhale slowly, rolling the tension out of my shoulders. She's beautiful, stunning, actually. And that sharp tongue of hers? It's going to get her in trouble. She talks a big game, throws out challenges like she's waiting for someone to call her bluff.

And fuck, do I want to.

I run a hand through my hair, jaw tightening as I head to the bathroom. Looks like I'm gonna need that cold shower after all.

I crank the water to freezing, strip, and step under the spray. The shock slams into me instantly, but it does nothing to drown out the thoughts racing through my head.

What I wouldn't give to run my hands down her body, to grip those smooth thighs and hear exactly what kind of sounds she makes when she's got no more comebacks left.

Fuck.

"What the hell am I doing?" I mutter to myself.

My fingers curl into fists, water sluicing down my back as my mind spins in circles, with every dirty thought I shouldn't be having about her. Her long, wild hair tangled around my fist. Her soft, breathy gasps as I press my mouth against her throat, dragging my teeth over her perfect skin. Her smooth, toned little body pinned beneath mine, writhing, begging...

This is a problem.

All night, I had to fight the urge to channel that sharp little attitude of hers into something much more satisfying. I wanted to push her, to see just how far that fire in her eyes would go before it burned out completely.

Being close to her had me hard as a fucking rock faster than I could say, *Welcome to Scotland.*

Provoking her just to see the sparks flash across her face is going to be my new favorite addiction. *If I ever see her again.*

Watching her at war with herself, trying to hold back, pretending she wasn't affected was intoxicating.

It was fascinating to watch her effort to stay polite and composed while her real thoughts bubble just beneath the surface. That raw, unapologetic part of her that broke through when she finally let go? That's what's got me hooked.

No one talks to me like that. Not in a way that makes me want to press them against the nearest wall just to see what sound they'd make next. The way her breath hitched when I told her I wanted her number. It was sharp enough to cut the resolve of a weaker man.

And right now, I'm gripping the shower wall, fist tight around my cock, because that woman is burned into my fucking brain.

She doesn't even realize the power she holds, and that might be the most dangerous thing about her. Watching her get flustered over a simple command was a high I hadn't expected. I wanted to see how she'd react, and her stumbling over her words was worth every damn second. But when she licked her bottom lip, and bit down. *Fuck me.*

I barely managed to keep it together after that.

I pump my hand up and down, vision going white as I picture how I could push her. How she'd sound moaning my name. How her body would tremble beneath my touch.

It doesn't take long. The sharp pull of release rushes through me, my groan swallowed by the hiss of the shower as white ropes of cum disappear down the drain. But the tension in my chest doesn't ease, not even close.

That wasn't enough. I barely scratched the surface of how much I want her. I crank the water hotter, trying to shake her loose from my head as I scrub a hand over my face. No good can come from this.

Sleep refuses to come. My mind replays the night with painful clarity...

The relief on her face when I told her she was safe did something to me. I could see the way she fidgeted with her phone, trying to stay calm when it died. How her whole posture shifted. She was still guarded, but slightly more open when she realized I wasn't going to push her.

And then there was that weird rush when our legs brushed in the car.

Maybe I need another cold shower.

I exhale sharply, dragging a hand down my face as I check the time. 5 a.m. Not even a full night's rest, and I already know sleep isn't in the cards for me. Not today.

Cam's probably still dead to the world, sleeping off last night, which means I have a couple of hours to burn.

I push up from the bed, shoving Raven out of my head where she doesn't belong, and head straight to the gym. If I don't do something with this restless energy, it's going to eat me alive.

I crank up the music, letting the pounding bass drown out my thoughts as I load the bar. Bench press. Squats. Deadlifts. Anything to push my body to the brink, to force myself into exhaustion. With every rep, I push out the tension and the frustration. Small victories.

I switch to cardio, hitting the treadmill at a punishing speed, my legs pounding in a rhythm as sharp as my thoughts. This should be where my mind clears, where I lock in and find my focus.

I crank the speed higher. My pulse pounds in my ears. She's a distraction I don't need. I've kept my distance from women for a reason.

I try to focus on the job I should be wrapping up in less than forty-eight hours. A high-profile client who needs a delicate situation *handled*. The money's good. The target's worse.

And yet, instead of replaying how I'm going to execute the extraction perfectly, and how there is going to be one less piece of shit running around out there, I'm here, running myself into the ground over a woman I met less than a day ago.

I slow to a stop, wiping sweat from my face, and consider waking Cam up and dragging his ass down here for a round in the ring. A good fight might be the only thing that shakes this shit loose.

"Fuck."

I mutter the word to myself, dragging the towel across my face.

This is going to be a long fucking day.

CHAPTER 8

Calm Before the Storm

RAVEN

Is this what a hangover feels like? I don't feel completely awful, just... sluggish. My body's heavier than it should be my thoughts tangled in a haze.

But that could just as easily be because of the dream. I close my eyes, trying to piece together the fragments. Misty trees. A dense forest humming with energy. And Kane.

I remember his face, the way his hand reached for mine, the air crackling between us as if the world itself was holding its breath. The mist swirled around us, weaving through the trees like it had a will of its own.

I shiver, rubbing my arms as I force my eyes open, the details slipping away like smoke through my fingers. The more I try to grasp them, the faster they vanish.

I find Rachel sprawled across the bed, half-dressed and half-buried under the blankets. Her hair is a wild mess, one arm flopped over the edge of the bed like she passed out mid-sentence.

Yeah, that checks out.

She'll be out for at least a few more hours.

I reach for my phone, squinting at the screen. *6:13 A.M.* Ugh. Maybe I could go back to sleep, but I already know I won't. I'm not used to sleeping in and my mind is too restless to even try.

Rolling out of bed as quietly as possible, I grab a hoodie and slip outside to the front porch. The morning air is crisp, biting at my skin just enough to wake me up. It smells different here. I inhale deeply, letting it ground me as I settle into one of the chairs, tucking my legs beneath me.

Pulling out my phone, I flip through a few emails. There's only one pressing thing on my list, one last work-related task I've allowed myself on this trip. *I'm determined to keep it that way.*

I fire off a quick message to my assistant, double-checking that she's got everything handled. More importantly, I make sure Louie, and all my plants are still alive. That's the real priority here. The rest can wait.

Honestly, I'm basically an old lady trapped in the body of a stripper. Just give me my cat, my plants, and some tea, and I'll happily avoid human interaction for days.

A small smile tugs at my lips as I picture Louie sprawled in his usual sunspot, likely plotting his next dramatic display of disdain for my absence. I miss that furry little creature.

I lean back against the chair, letting the cool breeze chase away the last remnants of sleep.

I start to open the email I was looking for when it hits me like a ton of bricks. I went to a pub last night. I got drunk. And made out with a hot Scottish man. An *infuriatingly* hot Scottish man, who drove us home because we got lost when my phone died.

And because I seem to be on a roll with questionable life choices, I also gave said *annoying* man my *phone number*.

"*UGGHHH.*" I groan into my hands as my body decides that *now* is the perfect time to flood with warmth. Seriously? Now?

Maybe he forgot I gave it to him. I mean, he was probably just as drunk as I was... *right*? And besides, he might not be able to find it in his contacts. That'll teach him to call me *Princess*.

I roll my eyes at myself. *Yeah, sure.* Like a man that smug wouldn't be able to scroll through his contacts and figure out which one was mine.

Deep down, though, I know better. He probably remembers *everything*.

But for now, I'll cling to the *very* slim hope that he was too distracted, or too drunk, to put the pieces together.

I sigh and force my focus back on my phone, attempting to drown myself in the one thing that always helps. Work. Prioritizing tasks. Review deadlines. Confirm Louie's care.

Yet, no matter how hard I try, my thoughts *keep* drifting back to Kane. His hands. His voice. The way he kissed me.

Damn it.

Nope. Not doing this.

My stomach growls, loud enough to shake me back into reality. Right. We didn't really eat dinner last night. Low blood sugar, not Kane-induced hysteria.

I toss my phone onto the table, email completely forgotten, and stand. If Rachel's going to sleep in, the least I can do is grab us something to eat. I need to walk off some of this restless energy anyway.

I pull on some leggings and slip into my Converse, giving myself a once-over in the mirror. *Presentable enough to step outside without scaring small children.*

Good enough.

If I'm lucky, Rachel will be awake by the time I get back, and we can figure out our plans for the day. *Preferably, plans that don't involve men.*

I grab a notepad off the nightstand and scribble a quick note, leaving it on her phone.

Gone to get breakfast. Don't freak out. Call me if you wake up early.

With that, I slip outside. I double check that the door is locked before heading down the quiet street.

There's something oddly satisfying about being out while the world is still waking up. The usual chaos hasn't settled in yet, and the hush of early morning feels like it belongs to me alone. The hum of distant voices, the rhythmic sweep of a broom against cobblestone, the occasional bark of a dog. It's a different kind of music; one I didn't realize I missed.

As I walk, I recall the quaint little café we passed on our way to the pub last night. The streets are bathed in morning light, filtering through the buildings, making everything look softer. And for a moment, I wonder if I could be happy here.

I get it now. I get why my grandparents loved this place so much. The scent of pine and damp earth lingers in the air, the distinct after-rain freshness that feels like home in a way I can't explain.

I'm admiring the architecture of a particularly charming townhouse, when I collide with someone.

"Oh! Excuse me! I'm so sorry, I wasn't watching where I was going. Are you okay?" I stammer, looking up at an older gentleman.

The man chuckles, his warm, rich accent instantly soothing. "That's quite alright, lass." He winks, a mischievous glint in his eye. "Now, if I'd fallen, I might've cursed ye for knockin' me down. Only because I'd need a crane to get back up."

A laugh bubbles out of me despite myself. His humor is disarming, and the crinkles around his eyes deepen as he smiles.

"Ye looked miles away. Lost in thought, were ya?"

I brush a stray curl behind my ear, nodding sheepishly. "Yeah... something like that."

He hums knowingly, "Aye, happens to the best of us. This place has a way of sweepin' people up. It calls to ye. Especially if ye've got old ties here."

Something shifts in my chest, an invisible thread pulling tight. *Old ties?* The way he says it makes my stomach flip, like he knows something I don't.

Before I can ask what he means, he shifts the conversation smoothly, like he wasn't just on the verge of saying something important.

"So how are you likin' Scotland so far?"

I chuckle, trying to shake off the strange weight of his words. "I just can't get enough of how beautiful it is here."

His eyes glint with something unreadable. "Oh, that she is... Scotland is indeed beautiful." His voice is soft, yet threaded with something deeper, something I can't quite place. "She's full of magic and mystery. Enjoy your stay... and be mindful of those Highlanders."

I nearly choke. "Wait, what?" I stammer, eyes wide. "Are the men here *dangerous*?"

His brow furrows for a split second, but then he chuckles. "No, lass, not dangerous... just *determined*."

Something about the way he says it makes my skin prickle.

"A beautiful woman like yourself won't stay unclaimed for long," he continues, like it's the most obvious thing in the world. "No need to go lookin' for him. He'll find ye."

His words settle over me like a whisper carried on the wind, light and impossible to ignore. I open my mouth to object; to tell him I'm *definitely* not looking for a man. But before I can, he nods at me with a warm smile and continues down the sidewalk, humming softly.

I exhale sharply, rolling my eyes at the entire encounter. First the cryptic *old ties* comment, and now this?

I shake my head, pushing it to the back of my mind as I reach into my pocket for my phone, only to come up empty. *Seriously?*

I could've sworn I grabbed it before I left.

With an annoyed sigh, I shove my hands into my hoodie. Whatever. I'll just grab breakfast and head back to the house.

The café comes into view, a cozy little spot with flower boxes bursting with vibrant blooms lining the windows. The sight is inviting, like a hidden world tucked away from the rest of the street.

As I push open the door, the rich aroma of fresh coffee and baked goods wraps around me. Inside, the atmosphere is calm, only a handful of people scattered at the tables, sipping their drinks and chatting softly. The décor is charming. Rustic wood accents, soft lighting, the kind of place that feels like a secret worth keeping.

I head toward the counter to place my order, but something in the corner catches my eye. I see a small bookshelf tucked beneath the window. I walk over, and sitting on one of the shelves is a weathered book, its spine cracked, its pages worn with age.

Scottish Folklore and Legends.

The title alone sends a shiver through me. Its faded cover has intricate symbols curling across the leather like vines. The moment I see it, my breath catches because it reminds me of the book I found after my grandpa's funeral.

That familiar pang tugs at my heart, a mixture of nostalgia and something heavier. I exhale sharply, forcing my feet toward the counter. *Food first. Weird, magical book later.*

I glance up just as a tall man shifts at the counter, his dark hair catching in the soft light. My body stills as a rush of either panic or excitement hits me all at once. I swallow, pulse spiking as he turns slightly.

Not him.

Relief crashes through me so quickly it leaves behind something I refuse to name. I shake my head at myself, mentally forcing my heart to calm the hell down. The last thing I need is to run into *him* this morning, especially after last night.

Just the memory makes my skin warm.

I drag my gaze back to the menu and end up ordering a little bit of everything. Tea, coffee, pastries, my inability to make a decision now disguised as a breakfast feast.

The girl behind the counter takes my order, but the second I say my name, her eyes flick to mine and widen. Just for a fraction of a second. Then, just as quickly, she masks it, smoothing her features into a polite but tight-lipped smile.

"Thank you. I'll let you know when it's ready." She tells me, before hurrying into the back.

Weird.

Maybe she's just surprised by the amount of food I ordered. *That, or she thinks I'm about to eat my feelings.* And honestly? She wouldn't be wrong.

I shake it off and wander over to the shelf where the book waits, drawn in despite myself. The second my fingers brush the worn leather, opening the book, a strange sensation ripples through me, like a current beneath my skin.

My stomach tightens as I flip through the pages. The bindings creak in protest, the scent of aged parchment filling the air. The pages are delicate and frayed at the edges, but something feels off.

I skim a random section; my eyes catch on a single word that makes my breath stutter. I see *my name.*

My pulse quickens, a strange rush of anticipation flooding through me. But when I lean in, the rush deflates just as quickly. It's not my name at all. It's *a* raven. Literally. A hand-drawn sketch of the bird, its wings outstretched in flight, inked in intricate, almost delicate strokes at the bottom of the page.

I exhale, a small laugh slipping past my lips, more out of relief than amusement. *Seriously, Raven?* Get a grip. I shake my head at myself, willing away the ridiculousness. But as my eyes linger on the drawing, something tugs at the edges of my mind, a distant familiarity, like a word on the tip of my tongue that refuses to take shape.

I close the book, and the lights flicker.

My breath catches as the bulbs overhead dim, a faint hum vibrating through the air. I glance up, scanning the café, but no one seems to react. No one but me.

Another flicker. Stronger this time. A pulse of something shifts through the room, crackling against my skin like static. The air turns crisp.

Goosebumps rise along my arms, and I rub them instinctively, trying to shake off the sudden chill crawling down my spine.

Then, just as fast as it started, the lights steady. And my name is called. I blink, shaking off the unease as I step toward the counter. The girl behind it hands me my order, but her gaze flickers upward toward the ceiling before settling on me.

"Were the lights just flickering?" She asks, her voice quiet.

My heartbeat stumbles. *So it wasn't just me.*

I force a casual nod. "Yeah... I thought it was just my imagination."

She doesn't respond right away, her expression unreadable as she glances around the café. "It was and wasn't," she murmurs, like she wants to say more but holds back. The silence between us stretches, thick and heavy, until she busies herself behind the counter.

Something about the moment sticks, latching onto me in a way I can't quite shake. I swallow the unease, offer a smile and turn to leave.

I step outside; the cool breeze carries the faint scent of rain. But something is different now. Something presses at the edges of my senses, like I've brushed against something I wasn't mean to.

And I can't tell if it's a warning or a whisper. There's definitely something about Scotland.

I start to walk back toward our place, but the feeling doesn't fade. It lingers, weaving itself into the air, pressing in from all sides. A shiver runs down my spine. The hairs at the nape of my neck prickle. *Remain calm.* I tell myself, but the unease is impossible to ignore. That distinct sensation of being watched creeps in.

I stop mid-step, my breath catching as I turn, sweeping my gaze across the street behind me. A few early risers walk their dogs. A man waters the flowers on his stoop. A cyclist speeds past, the faint hum of his tires whispering against the pavement.

No one's watching. And yet, I can't shake it.

There are more people out now than earlier, but the feeling clings to me like a shadow I can't outrun. My pulse quickens, and the instinct urges me to move faster. *It's probably just my imagination,* I try to convince myself, but my body disagrees, the tension coiling tight in my chest.

By the time I reach the front porch, I exhale slowly, but the weight in my chest doesn't fully ease. I check the porch again, hoping my phone will magically appear. *Nothing.* A frustrated sigh escapes me as I step inside and shut the door behind me.

The house is quiet, no signs of life, which means Rachel is still dead to the world.

I drop the bag of pastries onto the counter and start retracing my steps, scanning every usual spot. The couch? Nothing. The side table? Empty. The bathroom counter? Nope. *Weird.* I know I had it this morning, I was literally scrolling through emails.

My heart sinks as I sweep the house again, a nagging discomfort creeping up my spine. *Where could it have gone?*

Shaking it off for now, I focus on the one thing I can control, food. I start unpacking the breakfast, deliberately making as much noise as possible in the hopes of waking Rachel.

Sure enough, there's a loud groan, followed by a very dramatic, very grumbled, "Please tell me you have coffee and food. In that order."

I stifle a laugh as I hear what sounds like an elephant tumbling out of bed, followed by sluggish, uneven stomps. A few seconds later, Rachel drags herself into the kitchen, her hair an absolute disaster, looking like she's been through an exorcism.

Her bloodshot eyes land on the coffee and pastries, and she gasps like I just handed her the cure to every problem in existence. "Oh my God, bless your heart. *This* is why we're friends," she declares, snatching the coffee like a lifeline before immediately tearing into the food.

I smirk as she shoves half a croissant in her mouth like she hasn't eaten in weeks. "You're welcome, how are you feeling?"

She mumbles something incoherent around her bite, gives a lazy thumbs-up, and plops into a chair like moving was already too much effort for the day.

I take a sip of my tea before filling her in on my strange morning. The odd conversation with the old man, the unsettling moment at the café, and, most annoyingly, the fact that my phone has somehow vanished. "I still have no idea where it is, which is mildly irritating," I add, frustration creeping into my voice.

Rachel, still half asleep, blinks slowly as she processes my words, nursing her coffee like it's the only thing tethering her to reality. Finally, she sets the cup down, leans forward, and gives me a look that's equal parts curiosity and mischief. "Okay, so let me get this straight," she pauses for dramatic effect. "I leave you alone for an *hour*, and in that time, you've nearly knocked over a fortune-telling old man, had some kind of *haunted café* experience, and *lost your phone?*"

Her lips twitch, and then she completely loses it. She throws her head back, clutching her stomach as she cackles like this is the funniest thing she's ever heard.

I roll my eyes, but a reluctant smile tugs at my lips. Trust Rachel to turn my morning into a comedy special. "It's really not that funny." I shoot her a flat look.

"Oh, but it *is*," she gasps between fits of laughter. "This is literally your life, Raven. Weird shit follows you around like a lost puppy." She wipes at her eyes dramatically. "Honestly, I don't know why you're even surprised anymore."

I groan, throwing a pastry at her in retaliation. "You're annoying."

She grins, taking another sip of coffee. "You love me."

"Debatable."

Still chuckling, she waves a hand toward the bedroom. "Just call your phone. Maybe it fell between the couch cushions or something."

I nod, pushing up from my seat, going to get her phone.

Straight to voicemail.

I frown, hitting redial. Same thing.

"That's weird," I mutter, more to myself than her. "I was literally just using it this morning, and it definitely wasn't dead."

Rachel lifts a brow. "You sure you didn't drop it on your way in?" She asks, stepping outside without waiting for an answer. A second later, she pops her head back in. "Nope. Not out here."

I exhale slowly, forcing myself to brush off the unease creeping beneath my skin. Either way, there's nothing I can do about it right now.

"Let's just get ready." She stretches her arms over her head. "It'll turn up."

I nod, sipping my tea in an attempt to shove the growing tension aside.

Getting ready is easy enough since I'm already dressed. A quick brush of my teeth, a splash of cold water to shake off the lingering fog, and I'm good to go. Our plan is to wander Edinburgh without a real destination in mind, just seeing where the day takes us. But one thing is certain, castles are definitely on the agenda at some point.

While Rachel finishes getting ready, I sit at the edge of the bed, my mind still racing, but I can't hold it in any longer.

"Okay," I say, exhaling sharply. "We need to talk about last night. What the *fuck* happened?"

Rachel pauses mid-mascara swipe, then shrugs. "Look, I *didn't* plan for last night to go the way it did either," she says it like she's already rehearsed this defense in her head more than once. "Those guys just happened to be in the same place at the same time. And they were *fun.*"

Uh-huh. That's the story she's sticking to?

I arch a brow, smirking. "Oh yeah. *So much fun.*" I lean back, arms crossed, waiting for the *real* talk to begin. "That's the official version? Have you been texting Cam?"

The way she freezes for half a second before schooling her expression tells me everything I need to know.

"Maybe." She sighs in surrender. "Yes. He texted me last night."

A grin spreads across her face, her eyes lighting up in a way that tells me exactly *how* those texts have been going.

She bites her lip, trying and failing to suppress a smile. "Look, he's really nice."

I raise a brow.

"And fun to look at," she adds, caving instantly.

I burst out laughing. "Oh, *that* you made abundantly clear. Multiple times."

Rachel huffs, but her smirk is pure mischief. "Listen, I'm *allowed* to appreciate a pretty man, okay?"

I shake my head, laughing. "And isn't that *lovely* for you? We've been here, what? *Forty-eight hours* and you're already soaked over a guy you just met?" I toss my hands in the air. "And before you get all defensive, *same.* UGH. What are we even doing?"

Rachel opens her mouth like she's about to argue, but then her face shifts. She exhales, shrugging. "Okay, fine. You're right. I'm totally *wet* just thinking about him. But that doesn't mean anything."

Her voice is lighter, but there's something else beneath it. She pauses, chewing on her bottom lip before finally saying what I knew was coming.

"I have Bobby."

And just like that, the mood shifts. The undercurrent of guilt she's been pushing down finally breaks the surface. I don't say anything right away. Because *yeah,* we do know. And it's more than just a mess.

Then she tilts her head, giving me a pointed look. "You, on the other hand, could actually do something about it if you wanted to. You're just choosing *not* to." She grins, leaning back with a satisfied smirk. "Good luck, girl. You're gonna need it. I've *seen* that man."

I laugh, shaking my head, but her words sit heavier than I'd like. Because she's right. I'm actively avoiding something I *can't* ignore forever.

"I'm only going to indulge in *looking,*" I declare, more for my own benefit than hers. "No more touching."

"And now that my phone is lost, that part's easy," I add.

Rachel arches an eyebrow, crossing her arms. "Ummm... I *saw* you last night. Don't act like you're swearing off men when you were practically climbing him like a damn tree."

Heat rushes up my neck. *Busted.*

"I was *not* climbing him like a tree," I protest, though I'm already laughing. "That would've required *having enough feeling in my legs to climb.*"

Rachel loses it, doubling over as she cackles. "Rave, I don't know what to tell you. You're *screwed.*"

She sighs dramatically, twirling a lock of her hair. "As for Cam? He's so funny. I thought he was hilarious last night, but I wasn't sure if that was just the alcohol talking." Her grin widens. "I mean, it's *not* like we're getting married or anything. Since there's *Bobby, obviously.*" She waves a hand like that's a footnote rather than the main issue. "It's not like that."

She pauses, sighing. "But he's just so damn beautiful to look at. And that accent?"

I snort. "Umm, Rach? I hate to break it to you, but you have said that about *every* man you've climbed. "

Her mouth drops open in exaggerated offense. "That is completely *untrue*. I've *never* called another man *beautiful*." She shakes her head, still caught up in whatever fantasy world she's living in. "Cam is beautiful in a *manly* way. These Scottish men are something else."

I can't help but laugh. She's not wrong. And *that* is exactly why I'm on a hiatus from men. *All men*. Scottish, American, mermen. Every last one of them.

By the time we're ready to head out, I do one last walkthrough, scanning the place for my missing phone. Still no sign of it, but I refuse to let it ruin my day.

Rachel's already tapping away on her phone. "Let me just send off a quick text, and we're good to go."

"Wait, who are you texting?" I ask, though I have a feeling I *already* know.

She glances at me, her face too smug to be anything but trouble. With a shrug, she tries to play it cool. "He asked what we were up to, so I told him we're hunting for your phone." She pauses, biting her lip to suppress a laugh. "To which he replied, 'I bet a raven took it.'"

I groan. "You've got to be kidding me."

Her phone starts ringing and I glance over her shoulder, sure enough, *Cam the Man* flashes across the screen. Along with a candid photo Rachel clearly snapped of him at the pub. Judging by the confused look on his face, he wasn't exactly ready for his close-up.

Yup, sounds about right. Rachel has a habit of taking the most unflattering yet hilarious photos of people for their contact pictures.

She answers with a dramatic eye roll. "Hey, loser."

A pause. Then a chuckle. "Yeah?" Another pause. "No, we looked and can't find it... of course I'm sure."

She listens for a second, and then her brows pull together. "Wait... what do you mean *you* have it? Why do you have it?"

Her eyes narrow as Cam says something on the other end. Then, she pulls the phone away from her ear with an exaggerated huff. "*Rude*! He *hung up* on me!"

Right on cue, there's a knock at the door.

Rachel strides over, swings it open, and standing there is *Cam the Man* himself, holding my phone with a smug grin plastered across his face.

"Hey! Where did you find that? Wait, why are you *here*?" I ask, caught between relief and complete confusion.

Rachel jumps in before Cam can answer. *Oh no.*

"I told them to come get us so we could sightsee in style," She announces, doing a little celebratory dance.

I whip my head toward her. "Rachel!"

She beams. "What?"

I shoot her a look. "Can we talk for a second?"

She just grins, already grabbing my wrist and steering me toward the bedroom. "We'll be out in a minute!" She calls over her shoulder.

The second the door clicks shut behind us, I turn on her. "You told them to come get us?"

Rachel flops onto the bed like this is the best idea she's ever had. "Listen, it'll be fun, I promise. If you hate it, we can bail. But they've got a car, and we don't. And I'm still feeling a *little* hungover, and—"

I hold up a hand. "I get it, it's fine. I'm sure it'll be fun."

I *do* think it'll be fun. But that's not what I'm afraid of.

"Stevie Nicks?" I ask, raising an eyebrow.

Rachel doesn't even hesitate. "Always."

Our safe word. A failsafe from our first trip together, when I needed rescuing from a guy who wasn't getting the hint. It took her way too long to catch on, but once she did? She swooped in, dramatic as ever. The guy ended up getting kicked out, ego bruised, but otherwise harmless. So now we use it whenever we want out of something.

We walk back out, and I immediately notice Cam isn't in the house anymore. Grabbing our things, we step outside to find a blacked-out Range Rover parked in the driveway.

Cam leans casually against it, spinning my phone between his fingers like a prize. The cocky grin he wears is nothing short of infuriating.

"It was under the coffee table on your porch," he announces before I can even ask. "Maybe next time, try looking."

I blink, "Wait. What? I swear I checked there."

Cam just shrugs, giving me a knowing look. I narrow my eyes. *Weird. But whatever.* I have it now, and that's all that matters.

As I step toward the car, Kane moves around to open my door. Cam does the same for Rachel, and they both hop in together.

Kane crosses in front of me, rounding the car to his side, and despite every single warning bell in my head telling me not to, my eyes betray me.

Oh, for fuck's sake.

The way he moves is effortless, confident, and completely unbothered. It pulls my attention in a way I *wish* I could ignore.

It's going to be the death of me, pretending like I don't notice.

"Hi."

That's it. Just one word. His voice is low and casual, like he has no idea how easily he's throwing me off balance.

"Uh, hi."

Kill me. My voice comes out way too airy, and to make it even worse, I wave at him.

Kane's lips twitch, like he's holding back a smirk.

I scramble for any sense of normalcy, but it's impossible when he looks like that. All he's wearing is jeans and a t-shirt, but they look like they were made just for him. My eyes flick to his arms.

Jesus.

Does he *live* in the gym? Could his arms get any bigger? How is it that, without even touching him, I already feel guilty for the things I'm picturing him doing with those things.

I'm fine. It's nothing.

"Phone mystery solved?" He asks as the car smoothly pulls away from the curb.

"Yup," still a little thrown off. "I thought I lost it. I *swear* I looked everywhere. It went straight to voicemail when I called, which is weird because it was fully charged when I was using it this morning. Apparently, it was on the porch the whole time."

We stop at a red light, and Kane glances over, his gaze locking onto mine.

It lingers longer than necessary. Long enough that my lungs suddenly forget how to function properly. Then, just as smoothly, he shifts his attention back to the road.

"Do you have a password on it?"

I hesitate, catching the twitch of a smirk at the corner of his mouth.

"Um, yes?" I drawl, suspiciously. "If you're planning on stealing it, I should warn you, you won't be able to get in."

His eyes flick back to me, and for a second, I swear I see a smile creeping in.

But then he rolls his eyes, shaking his head. "I'm not interested in your secrets, Princess."

"Uh-huh. Sure." I smirk, crossing my arms.

His lips twitch, but he doesn't take the bait.

"So, where are we going?" I ask instead, eager to break the tension swirling between us.

"You'll see." Cam chimes in from the backseat, his tone dripping with mystery.

CHAPTER 9

Tour-Guide-Kane

C ould I have someone drive us around? Yeah, easily. But I actually *like* driving, it keeps my mind busy. Besides, I didn't want to be *that guy*.

When she walked out of the house, I was grateful I was already sitting down.

Lord, have mercy.

She's got on a green hoodie, black leggings, and hiking boots with fluffy socks peeking out of the top. It's not anything special. Not anything designed to grab attention.

And yet, here I am, gripping the wheel like it's the only thing keeping me from completely losing my damn mind.

How the hell does she make hiking gear look like something straight out of a photoshoot? She could probably wear a paper bag and still look hot as fuck.

I make the grave mistake of letting my mind wander, picturing her bent over the hood of the car in just that damn hoodie.

I shift in my seat, praying no one notices.

What the hell am I supposed to do all day if just knowing she exists makes my body react like this? I'm not fifteen, for fuck's sake.

I exhale slowly, forcing myself to focus on the road.

I point out a few landmarks, throwing in bits of history. Cam, never one to pass up the chance to add a little flair, jumps in with tales of ancient curses, mischievous Fae, and dark legends. It's the kind of thing that holds their attention far more than a rundown of historical battles ever could.

Raven soaks up every word. She leans forward, hanging onto every detail, and *fuck*, I hate how much I like watching her like this.

When we finally pull up to our first stop, a small, weathered bookstore tucked between stone buildings, I catch the way her eyes linger on it, wide-eyed and curious.

The place has been around for as long as I can remember, and the owner is a good friend. I park the car, and the second Raven steps out, she exhales a quiet, "Wow."

I don't even try to hide my smirk. "Thought you might like this place," I watch the way her fingers flex, like she's already itching to get inside. "There's a pretty impressive section on mastering darts you should check out."

She barely hears me. She's already moving, taking it all in like she's trying to commit every detail to memory.

"This place is perfect," she murmurs, voice full of awe.

I wasn't sure just how deep her love for books ran, but if she loves this place? She'd lose her mind over the library at the estate.

Cam strolls up beside me, his hands in his pockets, grinning like an idiot. "Mind out of the gutter, mate."

I shoot him a sharp look, but he just smirks and saunters off.

Inside, the scent of aged parchment and polished wood fills the air. Raven heads straight for the folklore section, fingers trailing along the spines of books like they're secrets meant only for her. I pretend to browse nearby, but let's be honest, my attention is completely on her.

She's fascinating to watch. The way she tilts her head when something catches her eye, the way her lips part slightly as she skims a page like she's trying to drink in every word.

Rachel and Cam are off doing their own thing, talking and laughing somewhere in the back. I hear a sharp inhale and look over just as she pulls a book from the shelf, her eyes wide with excitement.

Scottish Folklore and Legends.

I read the title aloud, and the grin she gives me is enough to knock the air right out of my lungs.

"Rachel, look at this!" Raven calls out, waving the book in the air like she's just discovered treasure.

Rachel, already balancing a ridiculous stack of books, grins. "Obviously, you need to buy that."

"I could stay here all day," Raven admits, clutching the book to her chest like it's something precious. A strange tug pulls in my chest, but I shove it down before I can make sense of it.

Rachel wanders off, disappearing deeper into the store, leaving us alone in a quiet aisle.

Raven steps closer, stopping right next to me at the bookshelf I'm leaning against. Her shoulder is just inches away, close enough to feel the warmth of her body.

"Thanks for bringing us here." Her voice is soft, as she pulls another book off the shelf.

"My pleasure, *Your Highness*," I murmur, letting the teasing edge curl through my voice.

Raven bursts out laughing.

Without realizing it, I lean in just enough for her to feel the shift. My hand hovers near the shelf, so damn close that if I moved even an inch, I'd brush against her shoulder.

I watch as her breath catches for the briefest second, but it's enough to make my pulse kick up a notch.

"You're dangerous in a bookstore," I murmur, my voice lower than before.

She tilts her head up, eyes flickering with a heat she tries to hide.

"If you're thinking this is the part where I rip your clothes off between the romance and folklore section—" she pauses, lips twitching into a smile. "*It's not.*"

I blink, caught between surprise and amusement.

Then, slowly, I grin taking a deliberate step back, just enough to give her space, but not enough to erase the heat still lingering between us.

"Good to know," I say smoothly, voice dropping a little lower. "I'd hate for us to traumatize the customers."

Her eyes flash with something unreadable, but a slow smile tugs at her lips.

This woman is going to be the death of me.

She rolls her eyes, brushing past me, her shoulder grazing mine. It's the lightest touch, but fuck.

She hugs the book to her chest like a shield and throws over her shoulder, *"Just keeping things realistic."*

"Realistic? That's what we're calling it?" I murmur, stepping closer. Close enough to let my breath tease against the shell of her ear. She tenses just slightly, and I smirk. "That's interesting, because the way you reacted just now? Didn't seem like it was nothing to me."

She exhales sharply but recovers fast. Spinning on her heel, she meets my gaze head-on.

"Oh please," she drawls, lifting her chin. "Not everyone wants you, Kane. Maybe I just have a thing for bookshelves."

I arch a brow, enjoying this far too much. "Is that so? Because if you're into wood and leather bindings, I could think of a few things that might interest you."

Her mouth parts slightly, but she clamps it shut.

She narrows her eyes, but I can see the fight to suppress whatever is on the tip of her tongue. "You're annoying."

"And yet," I say, leaning against the shelf beside her, "you're still standing here, looking at me like you're two seconds away from proving me wrong."

She huffs a laugh, shaking her head as if trying to rid herself of whatever *this* is between us. But she doesn't walk away.

Instead, she plucks a book off the shelf, flipping it open with forced nonchalance. Her breathing is heavy, and she's pretending like the book in her hands is the most interesting thing she's seen all day.

"For the record," she mutters, "the only thing I'd do between these bookshelves is read."

"Pity."

Her head snaps up, eyes locking onto mine. And before I can push her further, she flips to a new page, her expression shifting, softening just slightly.

"You know," she begins, fingers tracing the edges of the worn pages, "I actually love books. Growing up, it wasn't always the *cool* thing to love, but my grandmother used to read to me every night, telling me stories about magic, curses, witches, shadows, and angry kings." Her eyes shimmer as she chuckles softly. "I would always ask her how I could find these places so I could run away there."

I lean slightly against the shelf, watching her. "And what did she say?"

Raven smiles, something warm flickering across her expression.

"She'd say, *'You can never find it, but it will always find you.'*"

I tilt my head, letting her words settle.

"Smart woman."

She nods, absentmindedly running her fingers over the book in her hands.

"She really was."

I hesitate a second, then say, "My mum's the same way. She loves reading, she can't get enough of it. She always says books are her escape."

Something shifts in her expression.

"Yeah," she murmurs, meeting my gaze. "Smart woman."

For a moment, we just... stand there. The air between us isn't playful anymore, it's something heavier. And just like that, it's gone as soon as Rachel's voice breaks through the moment.

"Raven, stop flirting and come look at this!"

Raven startles, blinking like she's shaking herself out of whatever spell we've fallen into.

She rolls her eyes, muttering, "As if I'd ever flirt with him."

I smirk, crossing my arms, tilting my head slightly as I watch her try to walk away. "Careful, Your Highness. Lies have consequences."

She pauses, glancing over her shoulder with a slow, sweet smile. "So does an ego too big for its own good."

I let out a low chuckle, stepping forward just enough that she has to tip her head back to meet my eyes. "And yet, here you are, feeding it."

Her lips part, and I can see the battle in her eyes. The sharp retort she wants to throw at me warring with whatever else is lingering beneath the surface. But instead of indulging me, she scoffs and turns back toward Rachel.

"I'd say keep dreaming, but I'd hate to feed into whatever delusion you've got going."

"Not a delusion, Princess, more like an observation."

She exhales sharply, flipping her hair over her shoulder as she walks away, but not before I catch the way her fingers tighten around her book. I watch her go, my smirk widening.

Yeah. I definitely hit a nerve.

She makes her way toward Rachel, tossing out some comment that earns a laugh, but even as they talk, I watch her fingers drift absently over the book's cover. It's subtle, like it's pulling her in more than she'll admit.

As soon as the conversation fades, she flips it open.

Her laughter quiets, her posture shifting as her focus sharpens. Page after page, her brow furrows, her lips parting slightly in concentration. It's like the rest of us disappear, swallowed up by the pull of whatever she's reading.

I lean against a nearby shelf, watching. She's lost to the world, oblivious to anything outside those pages, and for some reason I can't look away. There's something so sexy about her right now. But I've lingered long enough.

I push off the shelf just as Rachel drags her toward the counter. Cam appears beside me, "She's got you all kinds of fucked up, doesn't she?" he muses, his tone just low enough for only me to hear.

"Fuck off," I mutter, grabbing a book of a nearby shelf like I'm going to throw it at him.

Cam just chuckles. "Never seen you this distracted before. It's almost cute."

I shoot him a glare, but he's unfazed, scrolling through something on his phone. Then, just like that, he shifts gears. His voice dips low, almost cold.

"Hey, since we're here—" he flicks his screen up with his thumb, eyes locked on whatever intel he's got pulled up, "got a sec to talk about the Owens job?"

That gets my attention.

I glance at him, keeping my expression neutral. "Didn't we already turn that one down?"

Cam hums, tilting his head slightly. "Yeah. But they came back. Doubled the offer."

That *definitely* gets my attention.

I exhale slowly. "Dead?"

Cam shakes his head. "Not confirmed. But the client's panicking."

My jaw tightens. "Find out who the last person to have eyes on him was?"

Cam taps his screen a few times, his expression unreadable. "Still digging, but from what I've got, someone lost track of him two nights ago."

Which is a polite way of saying he's probably dead.

This is why I don't have time for distractions. Because there's too many people needing their hands held as it is.

I glance toward the counter where Raven is still chatting with the shopkeeper, completely oblivious. She leans on the counter, her body relaxed, like they've known each other for years.

The shopkeeper's face softens, clearly charmed by her. She tilts her head, listening to his story about the book. How she can be so open and engaging with complete strangers is beyond me, but it's also exactly why I can't look away.

She's the kind of person who draws people in without even trying. And that's dangerous in more ways than one. I run my hand down my face, exhaling slowly before refocusing. Not the time.

"Ready for the next stop?" I ask, holding my arm towards the front of the store.

She nods, clutching her new book like a treasure. "Lead the way."

We've been walking around long enough that I know they've got to be hungry. What they don't know is that we're heading to a restaurant that happens to be Cam's pride and joy.

He's been obsessed with cooking for as long as I've known him. And, annoyingly, he's damn good at it too. I host most of my work events here and people never shut up about the food. For good reason. He loves making the occasional appearance in the kitchen when he's bored, just to shake things up. The staff knows we're coming tonight, and they've been given strict orders *not to be weird*. His words.

This place was Cam's first big project, his baby, and it's done better than even he expected. Not that I'm remotely surprised. He's got a habit of turning things to gold, whether he means to or not.

As we round the corner, I slow the car to a stop in front of the restaurant.

"Alright, we're here," Cam announces, pushing his door open. "This is the place we wanted to take you for dinner."

"Thank *God*, I'm starving," Raven exclaims, her voice dripping with dramatic desperation.

"SAME!" Rachel groans, clutching her stomach. "I was about to eat the next cow we passed."

Raven gasps like Rachel just suggested treason. "Oh my gosh, we can't be friends. *Not* the Highland cows!"

Her eyes are wide, hand over her heart like this is a personal betrayal. I bite back a smirk. The look on her face? Instant fucking boner. A girl getting defensive over cows should not be this hot. And yet, here I am. Hard as a rock.

We step inside, and Cam leads us to a round corner booth in the back. The waitress barely sets the menu's down before Rachel and Raven dive in like their lives depend on it.

Rachel's eyes flick across the options, overwhelmed with possibilities, muttering under her breath about needing at least five things to truly experience the menu.

Meanwhile, Raven looks like she's staring down a life-or-death decision. Turns out, she's terrified of trying new food.

Cam is *not* having it. He's throwing out recommendations like a damn salesman. Raven, meanwhile, is staring at him like he's asking her to drink poison.

" —you made me try coffee that one day for breakfast, remember?" She accuses, eyes narrowing in betrayal. "It tasted like burnt toast. You guys all need to get your tongues checked, 'cause that stuff is *nasty*!"

I can't stop myself from jumping in. "If your coffee tasted like burnt toast, then you didn't have the right kind."

Her eyes snap to me, all fire and defiance, like she's debating whether to be polite or double down just to be difficult. I swear, if she chooses to let the brat out, I'm going to have a real fucking problem keeping my self-control intact.

She leans forward, resting her elbows on the table. "There's nothing you can do to convince me to drink coffee. Sorry, but *yuck*." She scrunches her nose in disgust, looking way too adorable for someone slandering one of life's greatest necessities.

Cam tries to cut in, but she's already on a roll. "So no, Cam, I will *not* be trying haggis." Her tone is final, and stubborn as hell. "I promise, I believe you that it's the chef's specialty, but I'll just stick with my salad, thanks."

She folds her arms, leans back against the booth, and meets my gaze with the kind of determination that makes me itch to mess with her.

I smirk, shifting slightly so my shoulder brushes against hers, keeping my voice low, like I'm making an offer she can't refuse.

"Alright, how about this—" I lean in. "You try this coffee, or one bite of something."

She scoffs, but I catch the flicker of heat in her eyes.

"Pass." Her voice is unimpressed, but the smile she's fighting back betrays her.

Her gaze snaps to mine, and she chews on her bottom lip. She doesn't answer right away, but the tension between us tightens. I can *feel* her resistance, but it only makes me more amused.

She wants to push back, to win whatever silent war she thinks she's fighting. But she's so easy to read. She's already lost; she just doesn't realize it yet.

She exhales through her nose, then crosses her arms. "You promise it's not disgusting?"

I lift a brow. "Do I look like I would lie to you?"

Her eyes narrow instantly. "Without hesitation."

I bark out a laugh. "Alright, fair. But I don't break my promises, Princess." I let the last word roll off my tongue slowly, watching the way her jaw tenses.

She likes it.

She shifts in her seat, clearly trying to act unaffected. "What if I say no?"

I lean forward, closing the space between us just enough for her to feel the shift in the air, to make her aware of how close I am. "Then I'll just have to find another way to make you say yes."

She blinks, inhaling a little too sharply before covering it with a scoff. "You really think you can just charm me into eating something weird?"

I drag my tongue along my bottom lip, letting my smirk turn downright dangerous. "I think we both know I could charm you to do a lot more than that."

123

Her breath hitches, and I feel the way her body tenses at the challenge. Her fingers tighten around the edge of the table, and for a split second, I think she's going to tell me to go to hell.

Instead, she tilts her chin up, "You sure think highly of yourself."

"Observant, as always." I mirror her tone, my smirk unwavering.

She lets out a huff, rolling her eyes, but I don't miss the way her breath falters. She's close to giving in, closer than she wants to admit.

Then, just when I think she might throw her napkin at me and call it a night, she leans in slightly, her expression shifting into something darker. "Deal. But if it *is* gross, I'm never trusting you again." Then, with that wicked little smirk, she adds, "And you couldn't, by the way."

There she is.

Oh, sweetheart, you have no idea.

The second the words leave her mouth, heat rolls through me, and my body reacts in ways I really don't need right now. My mind? Fully in the gutter. My self-control is hanging by a thread.

It's a good thing I've mastered the art of looking unaffected because if she glanced down, she'd figure out exactly where my thoughts just went.

The waitress returns, and Cam orders for both himself and Rachel, because, as she put it, she wanted him to *surprise her.* Raven orders her salad, all calm and confident. Predictable.

When it's my turn, I give the waitress my order, barely getting the words out before I feel her gaze drilling into me. A sharp smack lands on my arm. I blink, looking at her and she's glaring daggers.

"You *would.*"

Her tone is dripping with accusation. Violent little thing. It's honestly adorable how she's ready to fight at the drop of a hat. And fuck if I don't enjoy every second of it.

"Something wrong, Princess?" Like I don't already know.

Her eyes narrow. "You did that on purpose."

I lean back, arms crossing over my chest. "Did what?"

She throws her hands up, looking personally offended. "You know what."

I smirk, thoroughly entertained. "Enlighten me."

The waitress walks away, and that's when she loses it. I settle in, watching the way the pink in her cheeks deepens. She grabs her glass, taking a big gulp of water.

I lean in just enough to make her breath hitch, holding her gaze with an easy, teasing smirk. "One bite isn't going to kill you, Princess. All you have to do is put it in your mouth."

Her lips part slightly, and the color on her cheeks deepens. I swear to God, if she bites that lip one more time, I might just have to reconsider my plans.

I catch the flicker of curiosity in her eyes, that playful challenge I'm quickly becoming addicted to. She's caught between fighting me and giving in, balancing on the edge, unsure whether to snap at me, or accept it.

I see it the second she makes her choice.

Her shoulders drop, the tension melting away, but her attitude is still on full display.

"Fine." Her voice drips with defiance. "But what do I get out of this deal?" She tilts her chin up, all sass and stubbornness, but there's hesitation beneath it. Like she's not entirely sure if she wants to play this game.

I lean in closer, voice low, meant only for her. "Whatever you want."

Her eyes narrow, but the corner of her mouth twitches, betraying her. She likes this.

She likes me getting under her skin.

"You're annoying," she mutters, but it holds zero weight.

I grin. "And you're stalling."

Her glare sharpens, full of fire, but she grabs her fork like a weapon.

Yeah. I want to fuck her.

Not even an option right now, but my body has other plans. The way she fights me, the way she pretends to be unaffected, only to give in at the last second is addictive.

I shift in my seat, again. And of course, Cam catches it from across the table, letting out a knowing chuckle.

I shoot him a glare. *Don't even fucking start.*

Raven doesn't notice. She's too busy psyching herself up, trying to convince herself she's still in control.

She's not.

125

I watch her drain the rest of her water, fidgeting in her seat. She's thinking about backing out, but she won't. That would mean I win. And there's no way in hell she's letting that happen.

I lean back, stretching my arm along the back of the booth, watching her squirm.

Her fingers tighten around her fork, but the tension in her body shifts. She nods once.

Cam tosses out random questions that send the girls into a battle of ridiculous retellings. They argue over details, each version more absurd than the last, voices overlapping as they fight for the *real version*.

Rachel is waving her hands around like a dramatic reenactment is necessary. Raven, on the other hand, is all razor-sharp wit until she gets into it, and suddenly she's fully invested, defending whatever point she was trying to make like it's a blood sport.

My cock is really straining to make a reappearance. So I shift in my seat, grateful that so far, my struggle has gone unnoticed. I'd rather not have to explain that over dinner.

But listening to them, I can't ignore the thought creeping into my head. They're wild. Unpredictable. And they attract chaos like it's second nature.

The second the food hits the table, the energy shifts. Everyone digs in, everyone except Raven. She hesitates, her usual confidence cracking just enough for me to notice. It's amusing, and I'll admit, kind of cute.

But if I so much as chuckle right now, she'll definitely back out. And I'm not about to let that happen.

Let's see how this plays out.

Rachel's already pulled out her phone, her camera aimed like she's about to document history.

"It's not that bad. You're being a big baby," Rachel teases, her grin stretching ear to ear.

Raven shoots her a glare, then flicks her gaze back to me. I grab my fork, loading a decent bite, but not enough to make her panic. If I hand it to her, she'll refuse or stab me with it. And honestly? I wouldn't bet against either possibility.

So I don't give her the chance. I raise the fork toward her, watching for her reaction.

Her eyes narrow, fire flashing behind them. She's stubborn as hell. But she doesn't back down.

A smirk pulls at my lips. And then she leans in. The second her lips wrap around the fork, her eyes lock onto mine.

Daring.

My pulse thickens, heat slamming through me as I drag the fork back slowly. Yeah. This was a fucking terrible idea. Because now I'm thinking about those lips wrapped around something else entirely.

I tighten my grip on the fork, clenching my jaw to keep from reacting, because the thoughts running through my head are not safe for dinner conversation.

I can't stop picturing her on her knees, can't stop wondering if she'd keep eye contact then, too.

Little shit.

The moment vanishes as quickly as it came. Her expression shifts, bracing for impact, afraid to let the taste spread across her tongue. It's almost comical how invested I am in this, but I can't look away.

I see the exact moment the flavor hits. Her brows pull together, concentration flickering in her eyes. She chews slowly, analyzing it like she's mentally breaking it apart, layer by layer.

And then there's a flicker or something else. Curiosity? Maybe even the smallest hint of approval.

I press my lips together to keep from grinning, bracing for whatever bullshit she's about to come up with.

"Oh, my hell, just swallow it, you know you've had worse things in your mouth," Rachel chimes in, while Cam laughs beside her.

I barely hear them, because watching Raven swallow is now the top of the fucking list of my favorite things she's ever done.

And my body reacts immediately.

Hard. Again.

This night is going to be a damn challenge. No question about that.

She stares down at her plate like it's personally betrayed her. Then, her eyes finally lock onto mine, her expression pained like this confession might actually kill her.

"Okay, fine," she mutters, rolling her eyes. "It's not that bad. Don't let it go to your head, though."

Too late. She shoots me a look meant to wound, but the fire burning behind her eyes has already gone straight to my head. *Both* of them.

There she is again, fighting a losing battle with her pride. She clearly hates losing, and that's an interesting little fact I'm tucking away for later.

I lean back in my seat, arms draped lazily across the back of the booth, enjoying every second of watching her suffer.

Cam and Rachel erupt into laughter, instantly breaking the tension, and Rachel launches into a series of dramatic reenactments of all the times she's tried, and failed, to get Raven to try new things. Each story is more ridiculous than the last, and suddenly, Raven's stubbornness is the night's main entertainment.

I should be listening. But I'm not. I'm too busy thinking about how much I want her.

When dinner winds down, Cam and I push to our feet, motioning for the girls to do the same. Raven doesn't even argue.

That alone feels like a victory.

We step out of the restaurant, Cam pausing to whisper something to the hostess before falling in beside me, leading the girls toward the car.

My properties aren't publicly listed. In fact, they're only available through an internal network, reserved for specific referrals. Rachel? Maybe. But my gut tells me otherwise.

Raven is connected or, at the very least, she's connected to someone who is.

And I want to know who.

I glance at her in the passenger seat, watching as she stares out the window, completely unaware of the questions stacking up in my head.

It would take me less than an hour to get answers. One call and a few keystrokes. But I'd rather see how much she's willing to give.

Cam slips easily into tour guide mode. "Thank you for a charming day, ladies," he announces smoothly, pulling up to their house. "We hope you enjoyed your exclusive VIP experience with Cam's Highland Adventures. Five-star service, guaranteed. Tips encouraged."

Raven laughs, her smile widening, opening the door like she can't get out fast enough, then turning back to say, "Someone actually recommended that place to us the other day, and they weren't wrong, it was amazing. Night, guys."

Rachel chimes in, just as bubbly, opening her door, "It really was! Maybe a cold shower will do the trick. See you guys later!" She hops out, closing the door.

Cam's already slouched in one of the chairs, looking downright miserable. His usual energy is nowhere to be found, and he's staring off like his mind's miles away.

I grab a bottle off the shelf, twisting the cap off with one hand. "You doing all right over there?" I ask, pouring myself a glass. His whole demeanor's off, and I don't like it.

Cam exhales sharply, rubbing his hand over his face. "Of course, why wouldn't I be?"

Ah. So that's where we are tonight. I don't push. We both know some things are better left unsaid.

A beat of silence. Then, "Sorry, I'm fine. Just... thinking."

The laugh I let out is dry and humorless. "That's the problem."

Cam doesn't answer, just glances at me with a look that says he knows damn well I'm in the same boat.

Touché.

I pour us both a drink because we clearly need it. Getting my head on straight is proving to be harder than I anticipated. No matter how much I try to focus, all I can think about is Raven, and it's starting to piss me off. Standing around drinking isn't going to fix this.

I drain my glass glancing at him. "Want to go a couple rounds?"

His head snaps up. He studies me for a second, then a slow, knowing grin spreads across his face.

"Thought you'd never ask."

We head to the elevator, taking it down to the basement. The second the doors slide open, the lights flicker on automatically, illuminating the hall as we step inside.

The basement is more than just a gym, it's my own personal training center.

One side is dedicated to the boxing ring, surrounded by weights and enough training gear to keep me occupied for hours. The other side is all hand-to-hand combat. A stretch of mats beneath racks of gear, along with dummies.

Cam and I move like we've done this a thousand times, because we have. He shrugs out of his jacket, stretching his arms, rolling his neck.

I do the same, rolling out my wrists, letting my muscles loosen. My body's still coiled too damn tight, but this is what I needed.

There was a time when he wasn't the guy standing across from me now. When he was the one getting knocked down instead of throwing the punches.

He used to come over with bruises and scrapes like they were badges of honor he never asked for. And one night, one bad fucking night, I wasn't there when I should've been.

I remember the way my stomach dropped, the way my hands curled into fists at the sight of him. That feeling still sits in my gut all these years later, making my blood boil.

But that night he was a fucking mess. Bruised, bloody, and barely standing.

I got him back to my place, patched him up myself because he refused to see a doctor. Stubborn bastard.

We were inseparable after that. I taught him how to fight, and damn, was he a quick learner.

There's nothing that clears my head quite like this. I go through the motions of wrapping my hands and stepping into the ring, my mind zeroing in on the routine. The scent of sweat and canvas steadies me. And still, she creeps in. Slipping past my defenses like she's got a damn key.

I was on my best behavior today, keeping my distance. Even though it took every ounce of control not to close the gap and touch her. The temptation was there, with every glance and every laugh. And my dick was a relentless reminder of everything I couldn't have.

Before I can sink any deeper into that mess of thoughts, Cam lands a sharp jab to the side of my face.

The impact snaps my head to the side, snapping me out of it.

"Fucking hell, man," I mutter, shaking it off.

Cam just grins, his eyes lighting with a familiar challenge. "Where's your head at?"

He knows *exactly* where my head's at.

I exhale slowly, rolling out my shoulders as I step further into the ring. "You know you'd never land a blow like that unless I was distracted," I taunt, stepping in and throwing a punch of my own.

This time, Cam doesn't dodge. The hit lands solidly, and while he laughs it off, I know that one stung.

"Just because Rachel isn't into you, doesn't mean you two can't be friends," I circle him, aiming another swing.

Cam wipes at his mouth, spits out blood, and flashes that cocky grin like he didn't just take a solid hit to the jaw. "Yes, I'm aware," he says dryly. "Ow, that hurt."

He's not taking it personally, he never does. Cam knows what this is. We've always settled things like this. No holding back, no sugarcoating. Just fists, sweat, and a chance to clear the air.

"Cry me a fucking river," I mutter, stepping back into the fight.

Cam's laughter echoes off the walls as we clash, fists meeting flesh, the familiar rhythm of violence, and shaking the tension loose.

I just needed to hit someone a few times, and already the fire burning in my gut is beginning to settle.

"You know," Cam says, slipping past my guard with frustrating ease. "You can just be friends with Raven, too."

I freeze for half a second, just enough time for him to land a shot to my ribs that forces a sharp exhale from my lungs.

He grins. "Doesn't have to be all or nothing. Just think of her more like a sister. Then maybe you won't want to bend her over the nearest surface every time she fucking smiles at you."

Wrong move.

131

The second the words leave his mouth, I swing, fast and hard. Cam dodges, barely, his grin only widening.

"Interesting." he taunts, sidestepping another punch.

I narrow my eyes. "Stop talking."

"Or what?" He dodges again, still bouncing off his feet like this is all just a game. "You gonna hit me harder? Shit, I should've brought popcorn."

I lunge and finally land a clean shot to his shoulder. His smirk falters, just for a second.

"See?" He coughs, rolling out his neck. "I'm practically doing you a favor."

I grit my teeth, the irritation rolling through me in waves. Not because he's wrong, but because he's right.

As we trade blows, my focus sharpens, forcing me out of my own fucking head. One slip and I'll take a right hook to the jaw. Cam's not holding back, and that's exactly what I need right now.

The rounds blur together, our bodies moving on instinct, but my muscles are screaming. I haven't done this in a while, and I can feel it.

"All right, fuck it," I finally pant, rolling back on my heels, sweat dripping down my back. "It's a tie."

Cam's barely winded, the bastard. "Getting soft on me?" He taunts, wiping the blood from his lip.

I shake my head, smirking despite myself. "No, just don't feel like walking around looking like I got the shit beat out of me."

Cam chuckles, tossing his gloves down. "Unless you think Raven will nurse you back to health?"

I still, my grip tightening around the ropes.

That little fucker.

Cam spits out more blood, shaking his head with a smirk as he heads toward the fridge. He knows exactly what he's doing.

I shoot him a glare but can't hide the smirk tugging at my lips. "You're really trying to die today, aren't you?"

Cam raises his water bottle in a toast. "Just keeping you honest, man."

"Yeah, keep talking," I mutter, grabbing a towel. I toss a water bottle at him, then drop on the bench, rubbing the towel over my face.

Cam takes a long swig before speaking. "So how do you want me to handle the job?" His tone shifts, no more taunting, no more games. Just all business.

I sigh, rolling out my shoulders. "What's the latest?"

Cam leans against the wall, arms crossed. "Client's still panicking. They want an update. Says they can add more money if they need to. They're getting desperate."

I exhale through my nose. "Still no confirmation?"

He shakes his head. "No body, no proof. But they're certain something's off."

That's the problem with these types of jobs; there's never a clear answer until it's too late.

I lean forward, resting my elbow on my knees. "We need more intel before we commit. I'm not walking into this blind."

Cam nods, jaw tightening. "Already on it. We should have something soon."

I tilt my head, studying him. "And you? What's your take?"

He drags a hand through his hair, his expression unreadable. "Something's not right. Feels like we're only getting half the story."

That's what I was afraid of.

Silence stretches between us, both of us lost in our own thoughts. Cam and I have been doing this long enough to know when something doesn't add up. And this smells like a set up.

Cam exhales sharply, shaking his head as he tips half his water over his face. "What are we going to do?" His voice is edged with frustration, but there's something darker.

I let the question hang between us for a beat, rolling my shoulders, my mind already moving ten steps ahead.

Then I stand, tossing my towel aside.

"Invite the boys over." My voice is calm. "Time to get some answers."

CHAPTER 10

Deranged

RAVEN

"O kay, spill. You've got that look. What is it?"

I peek at her from under my arm, playing dumb. "What look?"

Her eyebrows lift. She looks thoroughly unimpressed. "The one that screams, '*I'm spiraling and overthinking.*'"

I sigh dramatically and roll onto my back, staring at the ceiling like it owes me an explanation. "It's not like that. Kane's existence is pissing me off."

Rachel's mouth twitches, amusement flickering in her eyes, but she wisely stays quiet as I sit up, rubbing my temples.

"He's annoying," I continue, words spilling out like I've ripped open a dam. "He's never serious about anything. He's bossy, smug, and thinks he knows everything."

I let out a breath and roll off the bed, pacing the room like a caged animal. The energy needs to go somewhere, and apparently, lying down isn't cutting it.

Rachel watches me like she's watching her favorite TV show. "Yeah, why don't you tell me how you *really* feel?"

I stop, whipping around. "I just did."

Rachel hums, full of judgement and not an ounce of subtlety. "Mmm. Sure. I happen to know you also think he's gorgeous. I know you get all hot and bothered every single time he looks at you. And I *definitely* know you're in denial about your feelings for him."

I scoff. Loudly. "Excuse me?"

But she's already smirking.

She leans in, eyes glinting with pure evil.

"All you've done is think about sucking his face off. Or maybe..." She pauses for effect. "... you're wishing to suck something else off."

135

Heat rushes up my neck like I've been set on fire, and I gape at her, choking on my own air. "Rachel!"

She just grins, looking way too pleased with herself. "Just saying, babe. Own it."

"Oh, absolutely not." I throw my hands up like I'm warding off a curse. "Nope. We are not going there. Delete that thought from your brain. Burn it. Bury it. Immediately, no."

Rachel smirks, her eyes full of menace. "Too late."

Groaning, I grab a pillow and hurl it at her head. She dodges like a damn ninja, cackling.

"You could not be further from the truth."

"And you're in *so much denial,*" she sings, tossing the pillow right back at me.

I don't catch it so much as it smacks me in the face.

The thing is, she's not wrong.

These are feelings I haven't really examined, nor do I want to. I like things the way they are. The moment that line is crossed, everything changes.

And that's not an option.

Besides, we're in another country. I'm going home eventually. And Kane? He's the kind of man who leaves a mark. I'd rather not find out firsthand just how hard he'd be to forget.

So I pivot.

"Oookay, *Miss Perfect,* let's talk about how you have a boyfriend at home who refuses to commit, and you're over here with an equally gorgeous man willing to commit to at least one good orgasm." I give her a pointed look, crossing my arms. "Are we going to dive into *that* while we're at it?"

Rachel's smug expression vanishes, and her mouth opens, then closes. Like a fish gasping for air.

She exhales sharply, visibly regrouping. "We're just friends. And you're right about one thing, it's definitely complicated." She hesitates, fingers absently playing with the edge of her coffee cup. "Bobby's great, and he's going to propose... eventually. He just has a few..." She pauses. "Commitment issues."

I tilt my head, arching a brow. "A *few* commitment issues?"

Bobby is a fucking joke. He's been stringing her along for years. It's the same story every time she brings up taking the next step, he pulls away. Goes radio silent for days, sometimes weeks. Then, like clockwork, he shows back up, acting like nothing happened. And Rachel forgives him. Again.

She groans, throwing up a hand. "Okay, fine. More than a few. But it's not all bad."

Her tone shifts, softer now, like she's trying to convince herself.

"And yeah, I know Cam's hot. We've been over this. I'm not blind." She gestures vaguely, her voice picking up speed. "I love knowing that I don't have to worry about him making a move or reading into things. I can actually breathe around him. I'm not into Cam like that."

I stare at her for a beat.

Then I deadpan, "You're so full of shit."

With a sigh, I place a hand on her arm, squeezing gently. "For what it's worth? You don't have to decide anything right now. Just... do what's best for you. Not what anyone else expects. And don't waste your time feeling guilty about it."

Because honestly? I've been there.

I get it. I really do.

I was stuck in my own hell for years before the universe practically had to drag me out of it. And once I was finally free, I could breathe again. I saw things for what they really were, not the watered-down version I convinced myself was okay.

I hate seeing her go through the same thing.

I meet her gaze. "I just don't want you to waste your time on someone who's never going to give you what you deserve." I pause, letting the words settle. "Whether Cam's in the picture or not."

Rachel's expression shifts, her defenses faltering just a little. "I know you're right. I do." She swallows hard. "But it's... hard. And as much as I hate to admit it, I'm scared."

Her voice drops, quieter now. "What if things end badly? What if someone gets hurt because I walk away? I wouldn't be able to live with myself. And what if I leave Bobby and end up with nothing?" She hesitates. "We still have good days, ya know?"

I do know.

I lived in that limbo for too long, clinging to the good days, pretending they outweighed the bad. Pretending it was worth staying. It never is.

I exhale, nodding. "Yeah, I get it."

She looks relieved, like she expected me to push harder, but I know better. You don't walk away until you're ready. No one can make that choice for you.

I give her a small, knowing smile. "I feel the same about Kane."

Rachel's head whips toward me so fast, I think she might get whiplash.

"Oh, we're talking about Kane now?" She smirks.

I roll my eyes. "I just mean... I really enjoy being friends with him. He's obviously hot and fun, but at the same time, I promised myself I wouldn't date anyone. I didn't come here to find a man. I came to spend time with my best friend, explore the countryside, and to find out whatever I can about my family."

Rachel nods, watching me closely.

Then, like a switch flipping, she grins. "So... let's go out tonight. No boys, no complications. Just fun."

I smirk, tilting my head. "What are you thinking?"

Rachel's smile turns downright wicked. "Let's just say... I know a place."

I grab my phone and type out a text to Kane to thank him, before I forget.

> Me: Heyyy. Thanks for the tour, I had a lot of fun! Even though you made me eat haggis. I'm still a little sweaty just thinking about it.

I see the dots pop up, only for them to disappear. Just as I'm about to put my phone down, his reply comes through.

> Kane: You're welcome. I knew you'd like it. But I also wouldn't make you eat something that was gross... I'm a little wounded.

I roll my eyes, biting back a smile. Wounded. Please.

> Me: Do your feelings always get hurt so easily? I think there's something that should be able to fix that.

His reply comes through almost immediately.

> Kane: I thought I smelled something funny at dinner. You might want to shower before you decide to do anything else. ... & enlighten me, what could fix me, Princess?

My mouth drops open. RUDE.

> Me: EXCUSE ME?! I do not smell. You have NO idea how much I hate trying new food... I know, I know, it's stupid. But I still hate it. ... I'm a child, I know. Stop laughing.

> Kane: Who said I was laughing

I can feel the smugness dripping off that text.

> Me: You're laughing. I can hear it.

He leaves me on read. I stare at my phone, waiting, watching the screen like an idiot. The little bubbles pop up again... then disappear.

And then nothing. Annoying, insufferable man.

I drop my phone onto the bed with an exasperated groan, rolling onto my stomach. If I'm being honest, I was sweating when he was trying to talk me into eating that. I don't know why I have such a fear of trying new food, but I do. Another mystery to add to *The Book of Raven: Unsolved and Mildly Embarrassing Edition.*

Although... he did manage to talk me into it faster than anyone has. Rachel included. Maybe it was the accent. Or the voice. Or the way he said my name.

I groan, pressing my face into the pillow. Nope. Not going there. I probably should've just said thanks and left it at that. But no. Every time I talk to him, I apparently forget how to function. Even forming sentences is a struggle because that damn voice of his scrambles my brain.

And don't get me started on his smartass comments. Those *really* push my buttons. Then there's the fact that every time he opens his mouth and tells me what to do, I want to punch him in the face. And maybe also kiss him.

Yup, this is exactly why I'm not dating. If we stay friends, he can be like an annoying older brother. *A much older brother...* I don't even know how old he is, anyway.

While we're adding to the list of things I don't know about him, let's go ahead and tack on why the hell he gets under my skin so badly. If I didn't know any better, I'd think that he was doing it on purpose.

Usually, people don't get to me this easily. But Kane slowly becoming the exception to every rule.

I sigh, debating if I have the energy to go out tonight. If we don't make plans soon, I'm clocking out.

"Rach, are you going to shower?" I yell from the bed, too lazy to get up and find her. I think she's in the kitchen, but who knows.

Rachel sprints into the room like she's being chased. "Yes! Just a quick rinse, I promise! Not even washing my hair. I'll be fast, and then we can leave. And... calm your tits, it's only seven!"

At least she knows the clock is ticking before I officially tap out.

I groan, sitting up as my phone buzzes just as I get one on.

> Kane: Okay, I won't make fun of you too badly. I'd still recommend a shower, though.

> For hygienic purposes, obviously.

140

Did he really just—?

Then another text comes through.

> *Kane: And maybe I like the smell of sweat??...*

I blink. Is this guy for real?

A laugh bursts out of me before I can stop it. Half the time, I genuinely can't tell if he's joking or dead serious. It's infuriating. And yet, I can't figure out if that's a good or a bad thing. He keeps me on my toes, which is probably dangerous.

And then, again with the *Princess* thing.

I roll my eyes, but my body, the traitorous whore that she is, doesn't get the memo.

My pulse kicks up a notch. There's that stupid flutter in my stomach every time his name pops up. It's like my body and my brain aren't on speaking terms anymore.

> *Me: Okay, you did NOT just say that.*

> *That explains so much about why you're struggling to find women…*

> *But don't worry, I'm an excellent wingwoman.*

> *Ask Rachel!*

I smirk as I hit send.

> *Kane: Who says I'm struggling?...*

Of course, he'd say that.

> Me: How rude of me.

> You probably have a girlfriend tied up in your basement right now. Just waiting until she's ripe from all that stressing. Is that when you go down and have your way with her???

> ... honestly, everyone has their kink. It's okay! Don't be shy!

There's a pause. Then...

> Kane: Wow, that was...

> ...Everyone??? What's yours?

I snort, biting my lip as I stare at the screen. Shit. I didn't mean to go *there!*

I can already feel my face heating up.

What is with this guy? One second, he acts like I exist just to test his patience, and the next... he's flirting?

Sure, we shared an earth-shattering, time-stopping, universe-altering kiss? The kind of kiss you write about in your journal and tell your best friend in mortifying detail. But maybe he was just drunk. Maybe '*kiss an American*' was something he wanted to cross off his bucket list.

Emotional whiplash. That's what this is.

I don't know why I even care. Men can fuck all the way off... unless I say otherwise.

I take a deep breath.

> Me: You're out of control.

> Kane: Oh, I assure you, Princess, I'm very much in control.

Right.

My eyes roll so hard I nearly give myself a headache.

I toss my phone on the bed and grab my shoes. If I don't get them on now, I'll never hear the end of it from Rachel.

> Me: Yeah, sure you are, Mr. Perfect.

> Kane: Well, perfection comes naturally to some of us.

> Me: Naturally insufferable, more like it.

> Kane: Insufferably charming, you mean?

> Me: Is that what you call it?

> I'd for sure describe it a little differently...

> Kane: I'm intrigued, go on...

> Me: We don't have time to unpack those control issues, sir.

> We're headed out for the night, so that might have to wait for another day. Don't worry. I'm sure you'll survive.

> Kane: You're right,

> 'Tour Guide Kane' is exhausted after working so hard today.

> Me: You can't be that tired… you didn't even finish the itinerary we paid good money for.

> We were promised a castle.

> Kane: Does the Princess always get what she wants?

> Me: Usually.

> Kane: Noted

> Kane: Don't worry, I always keep my promises.

> Me: Just keep your weird food away from me, and we'll be fine.

> Kane: Can't make any promises about that. I like them sweaty, remember?

> Me: UGH, you're impossible…

> Kane: Don't forget charming!

I burst out laughing, clutching my phone, still grinning like an idiot.

Rachel walks back into the room, eyebrows raised. "What did he say?"

I read her the messages between giggles, and her eyes widen. By the time I finish, she's shaking her head, lips twitching.

"He's a deranged weirdo," She laughs. "But, like… kinda charming in a messed-up way."

I shake my head, still smiling. "Yeah, well, I'm not falling for it." A pause. "Still funny, though."

Rachel smirks, disappearing into the closet. "Mmm-hmm. Keep telling yourself that. Now, get your ass up. We're going out."

I sit up, reaching for the shoes I never put on. What even was that conversation? Kane is funny, in an infuriating sort of way.

Rachel strides past me toward the door, grabbing her phone off the table. "Are you ready? Waiting on you."

"I'm coming!" I grab my phone and follow after her.

I pause, glancing toward the couch. "You know, we could just stayyy." I drag the word out dramatically, attempting to lure her back inside. "Sit on the porch, have some wine, talk about life. You *love* that kind of stuff."

Rachel stops mid-step, turns, and levels me with a look. "Bitch, we are going *out*. Let's go!"

I groan but let her drag me toward the door. As we step outside, I punch in the code to lock it, only to hear a sharp beep of rejection.

I frown. "That's weird."

Rachel crosses her arms, unimpressed. "It's six numbers. What's the hold up?"

"Fine," I huff, stepping aside. "Go ahead, Einstein."

CHAPTER 11

Poker Night

KANE

I look down at my phone and frown. It's not late, but no one calls me at this hour unless it's important.

"Mr. Robertson?"

"Yes." My tone is clipped, already bracing for whatever bullshit is going on now.

"It's Ren. There was a security issue, and the access code had to be changed about thirty minutes ago."

I sit up a little straighter. "Why?"

Ren explains there was a problem with the door, the access code wouldn't work, so they reset it as a precaution. Seems harmless enough.

Still, something about it doesn't sit right.

"Understood. Keep an eye on the system logs. If anything seems off, I want to know immediately."

"You got it, sir."

I hang up, jaw tight.

Glitches happen. Sure. But not with *our* system. Cam and I built it from the ground up. Well, mostly Cam, he's the tech genius. I had the vision for what I wanted, and he made it happen. There's no reason for an error like this.

I exhale through my nose, running a hand through my hair. Maybe I'm overthinking. Wouldn't be the first time. Comes with the job, what can I say, paranoia pays the bills. But the last few days have been anything but predictable, and I don't like the variables I can't control.

Still, I let it go. For now.

The guys are over for poker night, which should be a decent enough distraction. And if I'm being honest, I could use the space. The conversation

147

with Raven earlier was a mistake. Not because I didn't enjoy it. The problem was my dick was hard the entire time.

She spent half the time insulting me, and yet every smartass comment had me picturing the look on her face as she delivered each blow, waiting to see if I'd bite.

I'm not entirely sure something isn't wrong with me with how much I loved it.

I stand, rolling my shoulders before heading for the bar. Time for a drink. Anything to get my head back where it needs to be.

I've always been good at reading people, it's second nature. And Raven? She walks around like a little princess who always gets her way.

The truth is, I don't think she could handle me. The things I'm into alone would probably send her running. Fast. I don't do careful. And if she got a real glimpse into my life, she'd probably decide this little game we've been playing wasn't worth it.

Doesn't stop me from thinking about her, though. She's in my head, taking up space she has no business occupying.

I glance down at my dwindling pile of chips. I've already lost £10,000, distracted as hell, even though my hand was a winning one.

The guys are eating it up. I never lose, and they know it.

"Listen, whatever's going on, keep doing it. I finally made back some of the money I lost last time. Brittany will be thrilled, and maybe she'll stop harassing me now." Brandon grins as he leans back in his chair.

Looks like his engagement is going well if she's already getting after him for losing our last game. Not that I blame her. He told her he was going golfing. If she finds out he's been lying about poker, he's fucked.

"Are we not going to hang out with our two favorite girls tonight?" Tyler asks, casually tossing chips into the pot.

"No, Tyler. We are *not* going to hang out with them tonight," I say flatly, giving him a pointed look. "There are far more pressing things than women, and right now, we're busy. Besides, I plan on taking all your money tonight and winning mine back in the process."

My phone buzzes in my pocket, and I think about ignoring it. But then I wonder if it's another message about the house. With a sigh, I pull it out to check.

It's Raven.

I stare at the screen for a second, debating whether to reply. A smarter man would let it go. But then again, I like messing with her. And if I get the chance, I'm taking it.

If only she knew the kinds of things I was thinking about doing to her, she'd probably never text me again.

> **Your Royal Highness:** What are you up to tonight?

> **Me:** Just cleaning house… What did you guys end up deciding to do?

So much for not replying.

> **Your Royal Highness:** We're dancing. Just getting a few drinks. I may or may not have already had one. Okay, maybe three.

> **Your Royal Highness:** … wait, you're cleaning?? Forgive me, but that's not something I can imagine. Do I get proof?

I chuckle at her response. God, she's something else when she's had a few drinks. I can only imagine the trouble they're getting into. And of course, she's demanding proof.

> **Me:** You want me to send you a photo of my clean kitchen?

> **Me:** Or are you wanting a dirty photo of me cleaning?

> *Your Royal Highness: Ew. You're gross.*

> *I hope your kitchen is a mess and it takes you hours to clean it.*

I laugh out loud, drawing a few curious glances from the guys. Cam doesn't even bother looking up, just rolls his eyes.

But that first part of her message hits me.

They're dancing.

She's probably out in the middle of some dimly lit bar, moving her body like a damn invitation. Practically fucking the air around her.

My grip tightens around my phone before I can stop it, something hot curling in my chest. I have no right to be possessive of her. She's not mine. That reminder loops in my head, but it doesn't stop the way my pulse hammers harder.

Raven's not the kind of woman who needs saving. I know that. If some asshole tried something, she'd probably break his fingers before he even got close. It's everyone else I don't trust. Drunk idiots who don't know when to back the fuck off.

The urge to send a message telling them to be careful creeps up on me, but before I can type it out, I miss a play that would have won me some money. Instead, I flop.

"Head up in the clouds again?" Cam smirks, leaning back like he's already won the game.

I grab the bowl of pretzels and launch it at him. Pretzels flying. "Fuck you."

The guys burst out laughing, and Cam just grins, catching the bowl before it can crash on the floor.

I shake off whatever the fuck that was and type out a reply.

> *Me: I'm not cleaning my house. I'm playing poker.*

Your Royal Highness: Interesting.

I want to play!

Are you winning or losing?

Actually... I hope you don't win!

Me: Ouch.

Fuck, that smartass mouth is tempting enough to ruin me.

Every time she opens it; I'm torn between wanting to argue and wanting to shove my cock so far down her throat she has no choice but to surrender. To show her exactly what I think about that mouth.

She has no idea who she's playing with. No idea who she's inviting in. She's messing with fire, and when she finally gets burned, she'll learn. I don't do halfway.

Your Royal Highness: Well, I'm going back to dancing.Enjoy losing.

Your Royal Highness: ... Don't worry, if you're short on cash, I might pay you extra for a castle tour. Depending on how good a job you do ;)

If I need some money?

I huff out a laugh, shaking my head. This woman.

If only she knew.

I can just picture her body arching against mine, my hands gripping her hips, moving her exactly how I want. The echo of her moans filling every space.

The idea alone almost makes me tell the guys we're going out after all. I roll my eyes, locking my phone before I do something stupid.

Because there's nothing I could text her right now that wouldn't scare her off. Every response swirling in my head is filthy and depraved.

When I finally say something, it'll be in person. I need to see her face and watch her reaction.

It takes several minutes for my brain to regain control over my cock. Once I wrangled my thoughts back in, I manage to win back most of my money, much to everyone else's disappointment.

But I know one thing for damn sure.

Next time I see her, she won't be walking away so easily.

Probably for the best that she didn't see us tonight. Cam and I still look a little roughed up from earlier. The bruises would've raised questions. Questions I wouldn't have answered.

After the guy's head out, my phone buzzes on the table. I glance over. Probably the adorable little American, drunk texting her way into trouble.

Cam walks in, tossing some trash in the bin as his phone vibrates. He checks it, then laughs. "Those girls are wild. Maybe they did need a chaperone, after all."

He holds up his phone, and it's a photo of Raven standing on the bar at the pub with a drink in each hand.

And just like that, my dick makes its grand entrance. Again.

Every time her name comes up? Boner. Seeing her? *Boner*. Breathing in her general direction? A fucking boner.

This is starting to feel like slow, painful torture.

I drag a hand down my face, exhaling sharply as I reach for my phone, to see a message from my sister.

Thank God.

> *Khloe: Hey, do you have everything ready for this weekend?*

> *Me: All I have to do is show up...? Right?*

> *Besides, it's still days away!*

152

Khloe: Well, yeah... but are you ready?

Me: Mentally? No.

Is there anything you need me to do?

Khloe: Nope!

Just don't be a loser and actually show up.

She can be a real pain in the ass sometimes, but she's my sister, so I deal with it. Of course, I'm going to show up, she knows that.

Despite my better judgement, I decide to respond to Raven.

Me: Maybe I'll take you up on that offer, get in some extra tour hours.

Your Royal Highness: Okay! Deal.

Wait... are castles open on Sundays?

Me: Consider it done.

Your Royal Highness: Okay, Mr. Scottish man,

who thinks he can do whatever he wants and waltz into castles whenever he pleases.

Do you have keys to all of Scotland or something?

Me: I'm glad you're catching on...

Your Royal Highness: Whatever

Your Royal Highness: What are you doing?

Your Royal Highness: Are you home?

Are you in your basement… with your girl?

Me: Yes, Princess, I'm home.

Your Royal Highness: There you go with the 'Princess' thing again…

Me: Observant as always, I see.

Your Royal Highness: Whatever. I didn't want to come over, anyway.

That would've gone nowhere good. Not with the shit running through my head from earlier.

Me: You have a busy day tomorrow. Get some sleep.

Your Royal Highness: YOU get some sleep.

I roll my eyes, a quiet laugh escaping before I can stop it.

Of course, she has to have the last word. It's almost impossible not to engage.

I stare at my phone for a second longer, my fingers hovering over the screen, tempted to fire back just to keep her talking. But I know better.

She's dangerous for my self-control.

I set the phone down, muttering under my breath, "Goodnight, Princess."

CHAPTER 12

Castles

RAVEN

R achel's giggling about something I've already forgotten as we wait by the curb. The street is quieter than I expected, the hum of distant traffic is the only thing breaking the silence. The air smells cool and a little earthy, that crisp nighttime scent I've always loved.

But something about the stillness feels off. My skin prickles as the sensation creeps up my spine like a warning.

I glance around, and that's when I see him.

A man, standing just across the street, barely visible in the shadows. The red glow of his cigarette flares every few seconds, the embers burning bright before dimming again. But he isn't moving. He's just standing there. Watching.

Unease tightens in my chest. Especially after what happened earlier.

"Do you think that guy is staring at us?" I whisper, nudging Rachel.

Rachel, of course, *immediately* turns around. Subtlety? Never heard of her.

His silhouette remains frozen, carved into the night like a statue. No shifting, no reaction. Just that steady, unnerving stare.

"I *know* he's staring at us," Rachel says breezily. "We're the only ones out here, and we're hot."

I bite the inside of my cheek, trying not to laugh at her confidence despite the eerie vibes crawling up my spine. "Yeah, that's exactly what I was worried about," I mutter under my breath.

Still, my pulse kicks up a notch. The air feels heavier now, thick with something I can't explain. Instinct claws at me, telling me to pay attention.

The wind picks up, cutting through my jacket and sending a shiver skittering across my skin. I sneak another glance his way and my stomach drops.

He takes a step forward, his gaze locked on us. My breath catches as my body goes still.

A sharp beam of lights cuts through the darkness, and I exhale hard as the Uber's headlights wash over us. Without hesitation, I grab Rachel's arm and practically drag her toward the Uber.

"Okay, okay," she laughs, stumbling a little as I all but shove her into the car, oblivious to why I'm in such a rush.

Just before sliding into the backseat, I risk one glance over my shoulder, but the man is gone. No sign of him at all.

The street is empty, shadows swallowing the spot where he stood like he was never there. I swallow hard, trying to steady my nerves. *Maybe* it was nothing. *Maybe* I'm just being paranoid.

But as the car pulls away, and the street disappears behind us, I can't shake the feeling that we're still being watched, and that whoever he was, he wasn't some random guy out for a smoke.

By the time we get back to the house, the night's events feel like a fever dream. We change into comfy clothes, ditching the heels and tight outfits for oversized sweats, and collapse onto the couch. Neither of us wanted to stay out too late anyway, since we've got a big day tomorrow.

We're going to a freaking castle!

I'm way more excited than I probably should be. Then again, who wouldn't be excited?

Rachel glances over at me, one eyebrow raised. "Why do you look like a kid on Christmas morning?"

"Texting Cam?" I ask, giving her a knowing look.

Her lips twitch like she's trying not to smile. "Maybe." Her grin widens. "And I *may* have mentioned that we wanted to see a castle." She holds up her phone. "He responded with, '*We already are.*'"

I grin, unable to help myself. "I told Kane that we wanted to go tour a castle, too."

The thought of spending the day at a castle tomorrow should be enough to push every weird interaction from tonight out of my mind. But when Rachel sets her phone down, I can tell she's thinking the same thing I am.

"Dude," I exhale, rubbing my arms. "That guy at the bar tonight was an *absolute* creep."

A shiver runs down my spine at the memory.

Rachel's smile fades as she tucks her legs under herself. "Yeah," she agrees, her tone more serious now. "I mean, I know he was drunk, but something about him really freaked me out. It wasn't the usual *drunk guy being a little too persistent* thing either, you know?"

"Yeah, he was weird, but nothing we couldn't handle."

Rachel nods, but her expression darkens. *She's still pissed.* "Honestly, I was this close to throwing down and beating his ass. Like, what the actual fuck?" Her tone is biting. And Rachel isn't just talk. *She's got the bark and the bite.*

I laugh, shaking my head. "It was Florida all over again."

Her eyes widen before she groans dramatically, covering her face with her hands. "Don't remind me." She peeks through her fingers, smirking. "Except this time, I wasn't wearing anything I could use as a weapon."

I snort at the memory, but it does the trick. It shakes off the last of the tension in the air. Or at least, most of it.

The moment he grabbed my arm, there was this feeling. A flicker of something. I don't know how to explain it, and honestly? I don't feel like trying.

I shake it off, chalking it up to paranoia or maybe just the fact that his grip was too tight. No use dwelling on it now.

Rachel yawns and stretches before grabbing my arm, tugging me toward the bedroom. "Come on, let's crash."

I let her pull me along, forcing my mind to focus on tomorrow. Not some drunk idiot with grabby hands. Not the strange man outside. Not the feeling still crawling beneath my skin.

That night, I have another dream.

I'm back in the bar, standing face to face with the guy who grabbed me. His grip is still firmly around my arm. Only this time, I'm not empty-handed.

159

The dagger my grandpa gave me is in my grip. The stone embedded in the hilt glows faintly, casting eerie shadows between us.

His eyes widen the second he sees it. "How?" He whispers, voice barely audible but thick with something close to panic. He drops my arm like it had burned him and bolts for the door.

Before I can react, everything shifts.

The bar dissolves around me, melting into darkness. Twisting trees emerge in its place, their gnarled branches stretching overhead, cracking against a wind that wasn't there before. The air is thick with something I can't name. The shadows between the trees seem deeper than they should be, like they're watching.

A sharp gust whips through, tangling my hair, sending a chill skittering down my spine. My heart kicks up, the unease curling in my stomach like a warning. I see a raven sitting on a branch nearby.

"Raven, trust your instincts. If something feels off, it probably is."

I whip around when I hear my grandpa's voice, but no one is there.

But his words settle over me like a comforting weight. I squeeze my eyes shut, taking a slow breath.

At first, there's nothing. Just the rush of the wind, the racing of my pulse. But then the air shifts. The chaotic gusts seem to bend, adjusting to the steady rhythm of my breath. My heartbeat evens out, and for a second, the tension unravels.

Another beat, and pain slices through my arm.

I gasp, clutching the spot where the guy grabbed me, looking down to see black veins spreading down my arm. My fingers press against a bruise that shouldn't be there, the ache throbs like it's real. My other hand tightens around the dagger, and the glow from the stone pulses around me.

The wind howls louder, almost deafening. I try to open my eyes, but the force of it shoves against me, whipping my hair across my face, blinding me.

"Grandpa?" My voice is barely above a whisper against the storm. "Where did you go?"

No answer. Just the trees. The wind. The shadows pressing in.

My pulse pounds against my ribs. Faces flash through my mind in a blur. Rachel. Cam. Kane. The man from the bar.

"Feel the energy around you, Raven. It's always guiding you."

My grandpa's voice echoes again, wrapping around me like a lifeline.

I jolt awake, breathing heavily. The ghost of his words still lingers. The dream clings to me like static. It's there but slipping away the harder I try to grasp it. The only thing that sticks is a memory of training with my grandpa.

I stare up at the ceiling, my mind pulling me backward, back to the backyard where he first made me do it.

How am I supposed to fight without seeing? I'd ask him, frustration boiling over. *When would I ever need to fight blindfolded?*

The thought of it still makes me laugh quietly to myself. It drove me crazy back then, but looking back, maybe he had a point.

The memory unfurls in sharp clarity, the warmth of the sun filtering through the trees, the scent of wildflowers thick in the air. I can almost feel the steady weight of my grandpa's hands as he tied the blindfold securely over my eyes.

"Raven, your eyes lie to you. Trust your instincts."

"Grandpa, how am I supposed to see without my eyes?"

He never wavered. Just took a step back, his voice resolute as ever. "Find me."

I remember the frustration, the way I wanted to rip the damn thing off. But then, slowly, I'd start to notice things I hadn't before.

It was always the birds first, their song cutting through the quiet. The rustle of the wind shifting the leaves. The way the earth felt beneath my feet, alive and humming with something steady and grounding.

Rachel stirs beside me, then immediately jolts upright.

"Ahhhh wake up, wake up, wake up! It's castle day!"

A pillow collides with my face before I can react. If I'd actually been asleep, that would've been the worst way to start today.

I push it away, groaning as I rub the sleep from my eyes. "Alright, alright! I'm up," I mumble, stretching. I roll over, blindly feeling around for Rachel so I can land a well-deserved punch. "We never told them what time, so technically, we can sleep in."

I burrow deeper into the blankets. "Go back to bed."

Rachel does not go back to bed.

"I can't sleep, I'm too excited." She yanks the blanket down, leaving me exposed to the cold morning air. "I had the *best* dream. We were at a castle, and a prince came out. He told me I was the most beautiful creature he'd ever seen and asked me to marry him, making me a princess!"

I bite my lip, barely holding back my laugh. I can picture it so clearly, Rachel in an extravagant princess gown, her prince groveling at her feet like she's the sole reason he breathes.

Rachel sighs dramatically, flopping back onto the mattress. "And after the ceremony, he went under my dress and—"

"Nope!" I cut her off, launching another pillow at her. "How are you going to marry a prince when you're *clearly* still in a Bobby situation?"

She just grins, unbothered. "You're just jealous." She rolls onto her stomach, kicking her feet behind her. "And I'll tell you this once, so listen up. If a prince proposes and wants to whisk me away to a castle, I'm not about to decline. You only get *one* hall pass in life, and Bobby would *definitely* understand."

I arch an eyebrow, smiling. "Yes, I'm sure if a prince came knocking to make Bobby *his* princess, he'd be just as accepting."

Rachel gasps, clutching her chest like I've personally offended her honor. Then she hops off the bed, snatching her phone with a dramatic huff.

"Testy this morning, are we?" I tease. "So, how is good old Bobby?"

The shift is subtle, but I don't miss the flicker of something in her expression before she schools her face into something unreadable.

"He's... Bobby." She mutters like that's supposed to be an answer, but it's not.

I wait.

She exhales, fingers gripping her phone a little tighter. "He's mad at me, so we're not speaking." She says it like it's not a big deal. "I told him about the trip and made sure he knew not to worry if I wasn't texting back right away. That I'd call him when we got back to the house."

She hesitates.

And then, quieter. "He told me not to bother."

She tries to brush it off, tucking the hurt away behind a forced shrug. But I see it. The tightness in her jaw. The way she won't quite meet my eyes.

What really gets me, though? That flicker of something else just before she looked away. Not just hurt. Not just frustration.

Fear.

It's gone as fast as it came, but my stomach still knots. *No. That can't be right. What the hell would she be scared of?*

A slow, simmering heat rises in my chest, the kind that makes me want to drive straight to his place and tell him exactly how I feel about him. *God, I hate that she looks like this because of him.*

I force my voice to stay light. "Sounds like he's being a jealous, insecure little bitch. Again." I tilt my head to study her. "I also want you to know that I'm about one comment away from burning his house down."

Her lips twitch, but the smile doesn't quite reach her eyes. "No need for arson... yet."

We spend the next hour lounging in bed, dismantling every flaw, every disappointment Bobby has thrown her way. And yet, despite the venting, she still defends him. It's like she's stuck in this loop, but unwilling to break it.

But what gets me the most is, a guy she *just met* and isn't even dating, treats her better than Bobby ever has.

I shake my head. "Look, as long as you're happy, I'm happy. I just don't want you to be sad because Bobby is being a douche." My voice softens as I meet her gaze. "And if you *aren't* happy... you don't have to wait for the universe to intervene. You're allowed to make that call yourself."

She blinks at me, something unreadable flickering in her eyes before she sighs, flipping backward onto the bed. "Ugh. Why are you so wise in the mornings? I hate it."

I grin, nudging her with my foot. "It's a gift."

"Okay, let's get up! We need to start getting ready, they could be here any minute!" She injects enough urgency to get my ass out of bed.

I freeze mid-stretch, eyes snapping open. "Wait. Do you *know* when they're coming? Are they almost here? *Good hell*, why didn't you tell me?" I scramble up, practically tripping over everything in sight as I hunt for something to wear.

"Well, no, they're not coming *right now*," she admits, way too smug, "but I *do* know that if I said that, you'd get your ass in gear."

I whip around, gaping at her. "YOU WOULD!"

"Hey, whatever works!" She giggles, disappearing down the hall.

I huff dramatically and stomp toward the bathroom, gathering my things for a shower. Honestly, that's a process in itself. Regardless of when they're coming, I'd better shower *now* so my hair has a decent chance of drying before midnight. Hair wash days are a *ritual* you simply *cannot* skimp on.

The second I step under the hot spray, Kane sneaks right back in. I groan, dragging my hands down my face. *Ugghhh.*

Do cold showers work for girls too? Because good hell, *I might have blue-something.*

Princess? Seriously? He probably calls everyone that. Or he just thinks I'm a spoiled brat. Whatever he can think what he wants.

I mean, I've had boyfriends, one-night stands that I'm not exactly *proud* of, just like any normal person. But *that kiss...* it was something else entirely, and I can't stop thinking about it. My toes curl against the tile as the memory floods back in vivid, dangerous detail.

Kane kissed me like a man on a mission. Like he *knew* exactly what he wanted and wasn't afraid to take it.

And then he backed away like I was on fire. Epic kiss, followed by an epic failure. I still can't figure out what that's supposed to mean. It doesn't matter what has his panties in a twist. Whatever he dishes out, I will give right back, because I'm not here to impress him.

The only downside to not being in a relationship is, there's *no one* around to handle my *needs.* Sure, I can take care of myself, especially if it means avoiding assholes. But the problem with Kane is that I can't *stop thinking about him.*

Which means I've been turned on, way too much. And right now? It's inconvenient as hell. I groan, tilting my head back against the shower wall, willing the intrusive thoughts away, but it doesn't work. Because all I can think about is *him.*

The way his hands felt when they gripped my face. The way his lips molded to mine like they belonged there. The way his voice, seductive as sin, said my name like he was tasting it.

It's a problem that leads me to *one* inevitable conclusion. If I'm going to get through today, I need to take matters into my own hands. I reach for the showerhead, adjusting the angle as I let the hot spray hit exactly where I need it.

I shouldn't be thinking about him like this, but it's impossible not to. And just imagining what that man could do if given the chance? The thought alone is enough to unravel me.

It's not quite the release I was hoping for, but it'll have to do for now.

I barely have time to recover before Rachel bursts into the bathroom, music blasting from her phone.

I jump, quickly shoving the showerhead back into place like I wasn't just defiling myself in the sacred waters of our rental. If she suspects anything, she doesn't say a word. Bless this woman I call my best friend. I grab a towel and get out of the shower.

She turns up the music while I go through the motions of getting ready, but really I'm just trying to wrangle my brain while towel-drying my curls into controlled chaos.

Rachel bounces out of the room, shutting the door behind her, and I slip back into my pajamas, while I finish my hair.

When I'm done, I wander into the kitchen, scrolling through my phone as I go. My heart sinks just a touch when I don't see anything from Kane. Just work stuff and the usual garbage texts from Chance.

Ugh.

I don't even bother opening them. The last five are the same regurgitated *I still love you, please call me* nonsense. Not diving into *that* mess right now. We are never getting back together. I should honestly just block him, now that I'm thinking about it.

I'm so distracted, I barely register stepping into the kitchen until I hear a cough. A very male cough. I freeze, my pulse stuttering as my head snaps up.

And that's when I see Kane. Sitting casually on the couch like he owns the damn place. And of course, this would be the moment I choose to parade around in the least amount of clothing possible.

Internally, I scream.

Externally, I remain frozen, staring at him like an idiot.

He licks his lips. *Licks. His. Fucking. Lips.* Then coughs again, like he knows exactly what's going through my head.

I despise him... and I really wish I was wearing a snowsuit.

I scramble to recover, forcing my spine straight, plastering on a forced, unimpressed smile. "You really should get that cough checked out."

His eyes flick back to mine, like I just snapped him out of something. His expression shifts so quickly that, for a split second, I wonder if I imagined the whole thing.

"Morning, Princess."

Deep. Rough. And entirely too smug for my liking.

I hate that my body reacts before my brain does. My stomach dips, my pulse kicks up, and I swear I feel heat bloom across my skin. I'm wet instantly.

I force an awkward wave. "Uhh, hi."

Real smooth, Raven. ABORT.

I turn to go flee back into the bedroom, because clearly, I need to put on some damn clothes and take another cold shower. But before I can take another step, his voice stops me.

"What happened to your arm?"

I pause mid-step.

Something in his tone makes me turn back. Not the same lazy rasp from a second ago. This is different. It's edged with something cold.

I glance down, suddenly hyper-aware of the dull ache in my arm. When I twist it to look, my stomach drops.

A dark and oddly shaped bruise. *What the hell?*

"Oh, that's nothing." I quickly force out a laugh, letting my arm fall back to my side like it's no big deal. Because it's not. And the last thing I want to do is make a big deal out of nothing.

But my luck sucks, so naturally, that's the exact moment Rachel and Cam walk into the room.

Rachel's eyes *immediately* lock onto me, and then my arm.

"Is that from last night? *Holy shit,*" she blurts, walking over and grabbing my wrist before I can move. She turns my arm gently, looking at the bruise.

I shrug. "It's not a big deal."

Wrong choice of words.

Everything happens at once. Kane steps closer, his voice demanding. "What exactly happened?"

Rachel starts pacing, muttering about hunting someone down and making them pay. Cam glances between all of us, assessing how close we are to a full-scale eruption. And the tension in the room suddenly thickens, pressing down like a brewing storm.

I glance at Kane again, and it's unsettling how calm he *looks* while also radiating something dangerous. His body language is deceptively relaxed, but his eyes are *lethal.* Like he's five seconds away from losing it.

I swallow, forcing a breezy, unconcerned tone. "It really is nothing." Their stares burn into me, and I shift under the weight of it. "It didn't hurt that badly."

That was the wrong thing to say.

Kane steps closer, his jaw locking tight. "What. Happened?"

Each word clipped, dripping with barely-contained anger. I meet his stare, leveling him with the best unimpressed look I can manage while half-naked in my damn pajamas.

"For the record, I can take care of myself," I say, my voice steady, daring him to argue. "I appreciate the concern, really, but everyone needs to calm down."

If anything, Rachel looks even more ready to throw hands. Kane? Still too quiet. He doesn't need to know *everything*. I'm a big girl. We handled it and made it home safe.

No harm, no foul. Except, well... the bruise.

"I bruise easily," I add casually. "And honestly, I practically tripped. He already had a hold of my arm, so it wasn't intentional." I shrug, hoping that will be the end of it.

But Kane's expression barely shifts. His jaw flexes, his shoulders tighten, and that intensity in his eyes doesn't waver.

"I'm going to go get dres—" I start, desperate to change the subject.

Rachel cuts me off.

"*You're being way too nice about this,*" she snaps, eyes blazing. "That guy was a creep. He stared at us all night, hitting on you, and wouldn't take no for an answer."

The temperature in the room drops. Kane's breathing slows. Cam drags a hand through his hair, already looking like he's mentally preparing for whatever comes next. Rachel, oblivious to the sudden *lethal* shift in energy, keeps going.

"Then, when we left, I swear he followed us outside. We got in the Uber fast, but—"

Kane moves, his head tilts slightly, assessing. "What do you mean, *followed you?*

I roll my eyes, throwing my hands up. "Okay, now you're both being dramatic."

Kane's voice slices through mine, "Did you see him again?"

I falter. His stare sharpens, pinning me to the spot. I cross my arms, shifting uncomfortably. "No," I admit. "I mean—"

Rachel snorts. "Tell that to your arm."

I wince. She's exaggerating. But also... she's not entirely wrong.

"To be fair," I hold up a hand, "he didn't *actually* make me fall." I glance around like there's an escape route, but Rachel's on a roll now, and there's no stopping her.

"I was drunk, so that's not fair. Honestly, if he didn't have a hold of me, I probably *would've* fallen over when I turned around."

Cam stays suspiciously quiet, but I see him. Phone out, typing something with quick precision. Like he's on some kind of mission.

Rachel mutters something under her breath that sounds suspiciously like, *"you're too nice,"* followed by something about still murdering the guy if she ever sees him again.

Kane, however, hasn't taken his eyes off me. Like he's trying to read between the lines. Lines that don't even exist.

"Did he touch you anywhere else?" Kane finally asks, unwavering.

My frustration bubbles up.

"No, that was it." I cross my arms tighter. "Honestly, we were drunk, and this whole thing was just a weird, harmless situation that wasn't intentional. And I'll decide who touches me, thank you."

I shoot Rachel a glare, even though I know she means well. Cam finally looks up from his phone, his expression unreadable, and I let out a slow breath, forcing my voice steady. "I'm not excusing what he did, okay? I'm just saying it's over, and I'm fine."

I shift my gaze back to Kane, who still doesn't look convinced. His jaw is tight, and his hands flex at his sides like he's itching to hit something.

"I don't need a rescue team, everyone can chill now, alright?"

That's mostly directed at Kane. Rachel raises an eyebrow but, for once, doesn't argue. Kane's jaw ticks, again, but he doesn't say a word. Cam gives me a small nod, but his fingers still linger on his phone.

They're not letting this go. Fucking great.

I huff, "I'm going to get dressed, so everyone calm your tits."

And with that, I spin on my heel and head for the bedroom. The second I'm behind the door, I let out a slow breath, shaking off the weight of the room.

I rifle through my clothes, tossing aside random pieces, mentally plotting to throw something at Rachel the second she walks in.

Why does Kane have to be so damn intense?

I yank a sweater off its hanger, irritation flickering through me. *I'm perfectly capable of handling creeps on my own.* Yet, no matter how hard I try to cling to that thought, the look in Kane's eyes sticks with me. That kind of anger that simmers beneath the surface.

Whatever. Not my problem.

Before I can shove those thoughts away completely, Rachel bursts into the room, practically vibrating with outrage.

"Dude, I can't believe you have a bruise from that fucker," she seethes, pacing like she's ready for round two. "I swear, if I ever see him again..."

"Rach!" I cut in, grabbing a shirt and tossing it at her head. "Settle down. It doesn't even hurt. I bruise easily; it's really no big deal. Can we please drop it and focus on exploring a freaking castle today?" I plead, hoping she'll finally let it go.

The truth is, it does hurt, but I don't even care about the stupid bruise anymore. I just want to enjoy my day.

Rachel catches the shirt with a dramatic sigh, tossing her hands up in surrender. "Okay, okay" But she's still visibly annoyed. "I'm just pissed. And clearly, the guys are too. It's not okay."

She pauses, her frustration softening slightly as she flops onto the bed.

"Also, I don't think castles work like that. We can't just go frolicking around like it's a movie set. There are rules, you know."

That finally gets a laugh out of me, the tension in the room easing. I hate when people make a fuss over me, especially when I'm clearly fine. If I was making a fuss? Sure. Let the dramatics fly. But I'm not. I can handle myself.

Not that anyone else seems to get that.

I reach for my necklace, fastening it around my neck before slipping my stones into my pocket, just in case.

The remnants of my dream still linger in the back of my mind, but I push them aside.

CHAPTER 13

Troubbble...

KANE

The girls disappear into the other room, and I meet Cam's gaze.

He nods once. *Already on it.*

Of course he is.

Tyler actually owns the pub, though he prefers to call himself a *silent partner*. The long-time regulars know the truth, but beyond that, it's not something he advertises. He's had the place for years now. He won it in a card game, of all things. One of those stories you'd never believe unless you were there to see it happen.

There aren't any cameras in the pub. A fact that's never bothered me until now.

My jaw tightens as the realization sinks in. *That's changing.* I don't give a fuck if it's overbearing. Men like that thrive in places where no one's watching. Where they think they can do whatever they want without consequences.

I don't take kindly to men putting their hands on women. I drag a hand down my face. She's not mine, but still. Raven might think this was nothing, but my gut says otherwise. She brushed it off too quickly, like she was working too hard to make it sound insignificant. Like she didn't want me to make a big deal out of it.

Which means there's a fucking reason for that.

Cam watches me, his expression unreadable, but he knows.

"It's handled," he mutters, like that will somehow settle the fire burning through my veins.

Not fucking likely.

"Good." I don't look up from my phone as I type out a message to Tyler.

Raven doesn't want a fuss, but that doesn't mean I'll let my guard down. If there's more to this, I *will* find out.

Just before the anger took over, before my focus shifted entirely to the bruise on her arm, there was something else. Something that completely blindsided me.

For three full seconds, my brain fucking short-circuited. Every rational thought in my head evaporated, leaving nothing but a singular, driving impulse to throw her over my shoulder, carry her straight back to her room, and lock the door behind us.

Fuck the bruise.

Fuck the conversation.

I wanted my hands on her. My mouth. My teeth.

She has no idea what she does to me. That sun-kissed skin of hers is practically begging to be touched.

I felt it in every inch of me, the pull to close the distance, to see her melt against me like she did the first time. My body responded instantly.

All I could think about was pulling her against me, pushing her up against the nearest surface, and pulling those hard nipples right in my mouth. My hands itched to pin her wrists above her head, to tear those flimsy little shorts off her body and see just how wet she was.

I was mid-fantasy, imagining the sounds she'd make, when she turned around and I saw the bruise.

Just like that, the heat in my veins shifted into something darker. We should call a fucking rain check on the castle. The whole plan suddenly feels like a very bad idea. I'm not sure I can be on my best behavior today. Not with my blood still boiling from knowing what happened to her and my mind stuck on all the filthy things I want to do.

Very bad things.

The kind I'm sure she'd enjoy.

But I'm not even going to let myself go there. Not today.

I shove those thoughts down, forcing them deep where they can't distract me. There's a reason I thrive in my line of work; I operate best when I'm in control. I anticipate every variable before it happens. It's how I've always been.

But she's fucking chaos. A wildflower that grows wherever the hell she pleases, unpredictable as hell, saying whatever comes to mind with that sharp tongue of hers. I don't know what she'll do next, and it's driving me insane.

But one thing's for damn sure.

I'm going to find out exactly who that guy is, and he's going to pay for putting his hands on her. At the very least, he'll be blacklisted from every pub in the area. No one touches a woman like that and walks away without consequences.

Cam and I move through the house quietly, checking every lock, every window. I don't know if they walked home last night or got a ride, but I'm not taking any fucking chances. My gut is still twisted, something gnawing at the edge of my thoughts that I can't quite place.

A few minutes later, they finally emerge, ready to go.

Those leggings are going to be the death of me.

I don't react. But I clock the way they hug every curve, the way they move with her as she walks. It takes everything in me to keep my eyes on her face.

With a single nod, we step outside to the waiting car. My eyes track the way Raven locks up the house, making sure she double-checks the door. Satisfied, I open the passenger side for her, watching as she slides in before shutting it behind her.

I don't know why I feel this unsettled.

I push the thought aside as we leave the city behind. The further we get into the countryside, the more the tension in my chest eases. I've always liked this drive. There's something about watching the land open up, shifting from stone and steel to endless rolling green. The road leading into the Highlands is a personal favorite. Hills rising like ancient sentinels, stretching toward the sky, silent and unmoving.

Maybe I should tell them to add it to their list if they haven't already. For now, I lean back, letting the view and the quiet hum of conversation calm my nerves.

The gates swing open as we approach. The car rumbles down the long driveway, gravel crunching beneath the tires. I barely reach for my door handle before Raven's already out, practically bouncing onto the path.

She doesn't even close her door.

Cam leans out his side, calling after her with a grin, "I'll get your door, don't worry!"

Raven doesn't even look back. "Thanks!" She calls over her shoulder.

I shake my head, stepping out more slowly. No urgency on my part, I already know exactly what we're walking into. She, on the other hand, looks like she's about to break into a full sprint. Like this is the first castle she's ever seen in her life.

Hell, maybe it is.

The estate is already prepped for this weekend's event. Everything's roped-off, added security, everything in place. Should be smooth sailing.

"Wait, where is everyone? How are we the only ones here?"

Raven fires off the questions barely pausing for a breath, her head snapping between us. I pause for half a second, like I don't have years of training in thinking on my feet. Simple questions shouldn't be this fucking difficult.

Before I can answer, Cam jumps in smoothly. "We got special permission from the owners. They kinda owed me a favor."

I glance at him. Technically true. *Nice save.*

Raven tilts her head, curiosity sparking, but lucky for us, excitement outweighs her need for details. She moves on, already distracted. Rachel, though, is not as easy to shake.

Her arms cross, her eyes narrowing. "Why do they owe you a favor?" Suspicion drips from every word.

Cam just chuckles, playing it off with a shrug. "Let them use my restaurant for a work party once.

Rachel eyes him like she's deciding whether or not to believe him. I don't hold my breath.

"Wait, *what*!?"

Rachel and Raven spin in unison, their curiosity locked onto a new target.

Cam, meet the interrogation squad.

"What do you mean, *your* restaurant?"

"You own a restaurant?"

"Where is it?"

"What's it called?"

Cam blinks, clearly not expecting the sudden ambush. His eyes dart between them like he's searching for an escape route.

I smirk, leaning against the car, arms crossed, enjoying the rare sight of Cam caught off guard. Usually, he's the smooth one, always two steps ahead. But right now? He looks like a deer staring down two very determined hunters.

He holds up his hands in surrender. "Woah, woah, woah, ladies. Patience."

Raven crosses her arms, unimpressed. "Oh, sorry, I forgot you're some high-profile mystery man with all these *secrets*."

Rachel taps her chin, eyes narrowing. "Mmm, yeah. First, we find out you know castle people, and now this? You better not be a hitman, Cam."

Cam grins, shaking his head. "If I were, I definitely wouldn't tell you."

"Uh-huh," Raven deadpans. "Suspicious."

"Extremely," Rachel agrees.

I shake my head, amused as hell. To his credit, he handles it well, recovering fast. He always does. That's part of why he's successful, he thrives under pressure. Meanwhile, I file away the fact that Raven's default setting is interrogation. Good to know.

"All right, first things first. Where would you ladies like to go?" Cam asks, smoothly diverting. "We've got the gardens, the wooded trails, or if you're cold, we can head inside."

They exchange a look before Raven looks over at me, as if waiting for my input.

Interesting.

A smirk tugs at my lips. She doesn't even realize she's instinctively looking to me, like she *wants* my opinion. Trouble. She's *trouble*. And if she knew what that did to me, she'd run. My cock stirs in response. *Fantastic.*

"Whatever you want, Princess," I say, keeping my tone casual, even though my thoughts are anything but.

She rolls her eyes but turns back to Cam, and at the same time, they both say, "The forest."

I blink. *Not what I expected.*

Cam straightens his jacket with exaggerated elegance and, in his best butler voice, says, "Right this way, ladies. It's a bit of a walk, so I'll regale you with the tale of the restaurant as we make our journey into the enchanted woods."

I shake my head, laughing under my breath. He's completely in his element, and they're eating it up. Watching them get sucked into his bullshit is honestly entertaining as hell.

As we fall into step, the forest opens around us, towering trees swaying in the breeze. The golden sunlight filters through in soft streaks, casting long shadows across the path. The scent of pine and damp earth lingers in the crisp air, grounding me in a way I hadn't realized I needed.

For the first time in a while, I feel like today might actually be *fun*.

Cam's voice breaks the moment. "It all started when I was a young lad," he begins dramatically, making Rachel grin. "My granny, who basically raised me, loved to cook. She taught me everything I know. We'd start every meal by picking fresh ingredients from the garden, according to her they had to be fresh. Then, we'd try making up our own dishes to add to the family recipe book."

He pauses, "Of course, there were plenty of disasters. Some of them so bad, even the dogs wouldn't touch 'em."

Rachel bursts into laughter, and even Raven giggles, shaking her head. Cam's good at spinning stories like he's been rehearsing them all his life.

Then Raven speaks, her voice is quiet, "I was raised by my grandparents, too."

I glance over at her. There's something different in her voice, it's softer. Almost like she's slipping into a memory. I've seen the sass, the sharp wit, the fire in her. But this? This is something else entirely.

Cam gives her a thoughtful nod. "Really? Guess we have that in common, then."

Rachel and Raven exchange a quick glance, their curiosity practically radiating off them, but they hold back from interrogating him again. Cam must pick up on it, too, because he keeps going, smoothly easing back into the story.

I stay a step behind, listening. I already know this story; I was there for half of it. We grew up together, running through these woods, raising hell.

"Anyway," Cam waves a hand dismissively, grinning, "that stuff is boring. Let's skip to the important part."

"*NO!*"

They say at the exact same time, their voices overlapping in perfect sync.

Cam raises an eyebrow; he's enjoying this way too much. I almost lose it myself, but somehow, I manage to keep a straight face. *Barely.*

"We want to hear *all* of it," Rachel insists, crossing her arms like she's daring him to try cutting the story short.

Cam pauses for a second, like he's debating, before finally sighing dramatically. "Alright, I'll give you the quick-ish version."

I shake my head, knowing full well the *quick-ish* is still a long-ass story. But there's no stopping him now.

"So, where was I? Ah, yes." He clears his throat dramatically. "When the dogs wouldn't eat my cooking, we'd pull out the fancy china, set the table like it was some five-star dining experience, and serve my granddad instead. Granny and I would hide in the kitchen, trying not to laugh as we timed how long he'd last before caving. He'd put on a good show, act like it was the best meal of his life. But then, after a few bites, he'd set down his fork, clear his throat, and announce that he was *full* and needed to *retire for the evening.*" Cam shakes his head, grinning. "She always made him a proper plate after, while I helped her clean up."

Raven's smile softens, and for a second, she looks... distant. Like the story hits closer to home than she expected.

Rachel, oblivious, bursts into laughter. "Poor granddad! The lengths men will go to, so they don't piss off a woman in the kitchen. That's actually adorable."

Cam winks. "Exactly. He was a smart man."

His eyes light up as he keeps going. "Fast forward about ten years. My favorite restaurant was going out of business, and I thought, *why not?* Bought the place, fixed it up, tweaked the menu, and the rest is history." He claps his hands together just as we reach the clearing. "Ahhh, here we are... the infamous forest."

I inhale, the familiar crispness of pine and earth filling my lungs. No matter how many times I've been in here, it never gets old. The towering trunks, the sunlight trickling through the canopy, it's the one place that's always felt *mine.*

177

And then Raven gasps, cutting through the quiet, all talk of restaurants forgotten.

Before I can say a damn word, she bolts into the trees.

"Oh. My. God," She spins in a slow circle, arms stretched out, taking in everything at once.

She looks like she *belongs* here, untouched by the world outside. The way her lips part in awe nearly knocks the breath from my lungs. *Fuck me.* That look alone makes me want to hand her the whole damn forest.

"Is there a certain time we need to be out of here, or can we stay a while?" She asks, turning to me, her excitement crackling in the air between us.

If only she knew, I'd let her stay here as long as she wanted.

Cam chuckles behind me, but I keep my voice even. "I don't think the trees are going anywhere anytime soon. But it depends, we planned on taking you guys to dinner at some point." I glance at Raven, who's already looking *way* too hopeful. "Totally up to you."

Her face lights up with a hopeful look, "Wait... what time does this place close? And can we go to your place for dinner?"

Cam laughs, shaking his head. "We'll head out around five so we can make it to dinner. And yeah, that's where we planned on going, unless you had something else in mind?"

Rachel practically *bounces* in place. "Nope! That sounds *perfect*. A private dinner at *your* restaurant? What more could a girl ask for?"

I glance at Raven, expecting her to roll her eyes at Rachel's enthusiasm, but she's already back to touching trees, brushing her fingers over the rough bark like she's memorizing the way it feels.

We spend another hour wandering through the woods, throwing out bits of history about the estate and answering their endless stream of questions. Their excitement is contagious, and for the first time in a long time, I catch myself seeing this place the way they do. Through fresh eyes.

Cam and Rachel walk ahead, locked in a heated debate over who's the better poker player, their laughter echoing through the trees. Meanwhile, Raven strolls beside me, her steps slow and thoughtful. The way she's absorbing everything around us, head tilted back, eyes fixed on the sky like she's seeing something the rest of us can't. It keeps me rooted in place, caught between admiration and temptation.

She's lost in her own world, and I can't decide if that's what makes her so damn captivating or so damn dangerous to me.

"That's a really great way to trip and fall on your ass," I tease, keeping my tone light, hoping to break the spell she's under or maybe it's the one I'm under.

She lowers her gaze, her eyes narrowing playfully. "Is that your professional opinion?"

"Absolutely. Maybe you should hold my hand?" I offer, extending my hand with a smirk. "I'd hate for you to fall, although I *will* have to charge you a rescue fee."

She lets out a scoff, lips twitching at the corners. "Oh really? And what's the fee for a forest rescue?"

I raise an eyebrow, leaning in just enough to make her breath hitch. "Priceless, I'm afraid."

Her cheeks flush just a little, and fuck if it doesn't make my fingers twitch with the need to touch her. But instead, I shove my hands into my pockets, hoping it'll keep them in check.

She tilts her head, giving me a slow once-over, then smirks like she's figured something out. "You *would* assume that I'd trip. Or is this just your terrible attempt at getting me to hold your hand?"

I chuckle, stepping just a little closer. "If I wanted to hold your hand, Princess, I wouldn't *ask*." My voice drops just enough to let the implication hang between us.

Her lips part, fire sparking in her eyes, and I know she's about to fire back something sharp, something that'll go straight to my dick and make me regret teasing her in the first place.

But before she can speak, a *yelp* echoes through the trees, cutting through the moment like a blade.

We both whip our heads toward the sound just in time to see Rachel go flying, arms flailing as she hits the ground with a loud *thud*. She's sprawled out on the forest floor, laughing hysterically despite the fall.

Raven's concern flickers across her face as she rushes forward. "Rachel!"

Cam is already kneeling beside her, eyes scanning her legs for damage. "Jesus, are you okay?"

Rachel waves him off, still giggling. "I'm fine! I just... forgot how to walk for a second."

I shake my head, amused. "Shocking."

Cam sighs, but there's something affectionate in the way he shakes his head before scooping her up effortlessly, like she weighs nothing.

"Oh my God, put me down! It's just a scrape; my leg isn't broken!" Rachel protests, squirming in his arms. "I'm not bleeding to death either, it just needs to be cleaned up a bit."

Raven crosses her arms, watching him with a grin. "See? *That's* how you rescue someone. No fees required."

I smirk, tilting my head toward her. "I don't know, Princess. I think you'd enjoy owing me."

Her breath hitches, but she recovers fast, narrowing her eyes. "In your dreams, Mr. I-Don't-Ask-To-Hold-Hands."

I grin. "More often than you'd think."

Her lips part slightly, her eyes widening for just a second before she catches herself. And just like that I know I've won.

Rachel groans from Cam's arms. "I *cannot* believe I just tripped, but at least I make it look graceful!"

Cam snorts. "Sure, if cartwheeling mid-air counts as graceful."

Despite her protests, he still carries her, and I have to admit, it's pretty damn entertaining. If it were Raven, I'd be doing the same thing, ignoring every demand to be put down. And something tells me she'd be even more stubborn than Rachel, which would only make it more fun.

We make our way back to the estate and through the back entrance, stepping into the mudroom. The playful banter still fills the air, laughter bouncing off the walls. I grab the first aid kit and head back, shaking my head as Cam sets Rachel on the counter.

"Alright, hold still," I say, crouching in front of her to clean the scrape. "Wouldn't want you to lose the leg over this."

Cam grins, shaking his head. "You might end up with a sick scar though."

Rachel scoffs. "That's the least of my problems."

Something about the way she says it makes my stomach tighten. It's offhanded, casual even, but there's something *under* it. I glance up at her, debating whether to push, but she quickly covers it with a bright smile.

Raven is already bouncing on her heels, completely oblivious to the shift in Rachel's tone. "Okay, now what?"

I toss the bandages back into the kit, arching a brow at her enthusiasm. "What do you mean *now*? Didn't we just spend an hour in the woods? I thought you'd be ready to sit down, catch your breath..."

She gasps like I just said something truly offensive. "Absolutely not. We haven't even seen the castle yet."

Cam chuckles. "Technically, we are in the castle."

"Okay, smartass, you know what I mean," Raven huffs, crossing her arms. "I want the full experience! I want to see the throne. Is there a throne? *Can I sit on it?* Are there secret rooms? Hidden passageways? Oh, wait! *Are there any ghosts?*"

I blink at the onslaught of questions, barely holding back a grin. "I'm sorry, am I supposed to answer those in real time, or—"

She waves a hand dismissively. "I expect you to answer all of them *eventually*. And if I think of more, I'll be adding to the list."

Rachel hums in agreement, hopping off the counter with a grin. "Honestly, I also want to know about the ghosts."

Cam groans. "Oh fantastic. Now we're ghost hunting."

Raven perks up even more. "Wait, *can* we ghost hunt?"

I smirk, leaning against the counter, arms crossed. "You planning on running screaming out of the front door the first time a shadow moves?"

She scoffs, tilting her chin up. "Excuse *you*, but that would never happen."

I raise a brow. "You sure about that?"

"Positive." She folds her arms. "I've seen all the horror movies. I know the rules. *You*, on the other hand, are exactly the type of guy who'd ignore all the obvious signs and end up possessed."

Cam snorts. "Yeah, Kane's the one who hears the weird noise and says, 'I'll check it out' right before he gets dragged into the woods."

Rachel grins. "Or worse, he'd be the skeptic who refuses to believe anything is happening until it's too late."

I shake my head, unimpressed. "If I hear a weird noise, I assume it's an intruder, not a damn ghost."

Raven waves a hand. "Classic denial. First stage of a haunting. Next thing you know, you're awake at 3 AM in a cold sweat, hearing whispers in this *very haunted* castle."

Cam laughs, clapping me on the shoulder. "Could explain why he's such a joy to be around."

I shoot him a glare, but Raven's already moving toward the door laughing. "Alright, *Tour Guide Kane,* let's go. Time to see this castle before we *conveniently* run out of time. "

She's smirking, but I can see in her eyes, she's *dying* to know more.

No, there's no throne here. But if there *was*, I'd be telling her to sit her pretty ass on it while I kneel in front of her, tongue tracing every inch. Worshipping her the way she *should* be.

I shove that thought far, far down before it turns into something I can't hide.

As for secret rooms? Yeah, there are a few. But I'm not telling her that. We move through the house, keeping to the main areas. The living room, the kitchen, places that won't raise too many questions. But when we step into the game room, Rachel's reaction is immediate.

"Whoa!" She exclaims; her eyes wide as she takes everything in. "This place is *insane*."

Raven steps past her, spinning slowly in place, her gaze sweeping across the room. She lingers, eyes trail over the sleek pool table, the leather seating, the vintage arcade games in the corner.

"Okay... now *this* is impressive." There's actual surprise in her voice.

Cam elbows me, smirking. "She's impressed."

I shoot him a look. "Yeah... I noticed."

Raven turns toward me. "These people have way too much free time."

I smirk. "Observant as always."

Rachel, already grabbing a cue stick, "Let's play! Kane, you're my partner."

Raven tilts her head, eying the table with mild suspicion. "Are we even *allowed* to play?"

Cam leans against the bar, flashing his signature grin. "Well, no one here is going to stop us."

I suppress an eye roll. He's really leaning into this whole *I-have-all-the-answers* act, and I'm definitely going to owe him for it. That's probably exactly what he's counting on. I should've just booked them a standard castle tour. This is turning into way more than I bargained for.

Rachel, already chalking up her cue, grins. "I'm in. Kane, let's go!"

I glance at Raven. "Do you know how to play?"

She lifts a brow, crossing her arms. "Oh, please. I may not have grown up playing darts, but I can handle a stick just fine."

Cam chokes. Rachel outright cackles.

Raven blinks, realization dawning. "Oh my God! *Not like that!*"

I lean in slightly, voice dropping just enough to watch her squirm. "It's okay, Princess. Everyone has their kink."

Her lips part, and for a second, I swear she stops breathing. Then she recovers, narrowing her eyes. "Please, if that were the case, I'd be way more into watching you struggle."

Cam groans. "Jesus Christ, just hit the damn ball before this turns into full-blown foreplay."

Rachel howls with laughter, and Raven gives me a triumphant smirk as she steps up to take her shot.

And I swear to *God*, this woman is going to ruin me.

She bends forward, lining up her shot, and the oversized hoodie she's wearing rides up just enough to give me an *unfiltered* view of the curve of her ass. My fingers twitch at my sides as I inhale sharply, trying to tear my gaze away before I do something stupid.

But not soon enough.

Cam notices, but he's smart enough to keep his mouth shut. Rachel, on the other hand? Not so much.

"Maybe if you take a picture, it'll last longer," she teases.

I drag a hand down my face, already regretting every choice that led to this moment. But before I can say anything, Raven straightens, rolling the cue stick between her hands as she saunters past me.

She leans in just slightly, her voice teasing.

"Excuse me, *sir*, it's not polite to stare."

Then she keeps walking, completely unbothered, and high-fives Rachel like she just scored a game-winning shot.

And me?

I'm standing here, gripping my cue stick way too fucking tight, caught between wanting to throw her onto table and making her *pay* for every single one of her smartass remarks... and pretending like none of this is getting to me.

I shake my head, trying to clear the haze of frustration and lust clouding my judgement. But then Cam leans in close, whispering something in Raven's ear, and she laughs, like she's enjoying this way too much.

I line up my shot, gripping the cue tightly, forcing my focus back on the game. Just as I'm about to take my shot, Raven casually strolls by and sits herself right on the edge of the table, directly in my line of sight.

I miss.

The grin tugging at her lips tells me *exactly* what she's doing. Playing dirty. And loving every damn second of it.

Cam whistles low under his breath. "She's got you wrapped, mate."

I glance at him, then back at Raven, who's doing a piss-poor job of pretending to be innocent. "Oh, you think this is funny?"

Raven tilts her head, the picture of innocence. "Got to use all my resources to win, and it looks like it's working."

She spins on her heel, walking past Cam and giving him a high-five like she just won the bloody Olympics. Cam practically doubles over laughing, shaking his head in admiration.

That little brat.

My cock twitches in response, and I *really* need to get a grip. This is getting ridiculous.

Cam smirks clearly entertained. "You have to hand it to her, man. That was a solid move. We're going to crush you."

Raven leans on her cue stick. "What does the winning team get?"

"What do you want? A gold star? Or maybe a cookie?" I deadpan, still annoyed that I fell for her stunt.

Her grin widens, eyes glinting with challenge. "I, for one, would like both a gold star *and* a cookie, since you asked so nicely."

Cam lines up his shot, and at this point, I almost hope he just puts me out of my misery and finishes the game. He could try to lose and still manage to pull off a win.

The sound of the final ball sinking is quickly followed by an ear-piercing scream.

"AHHH! We won!!"

She bolts toward Cam, jumping into his arms, and he catches her effortlessly, spinning her around.

A sharp, unwelcome pang of jealousy flares in my chest. I shove it down, telling myself it's just because I haven't been laid in a while. My body's just reacting, nothing more.

Raven brushes past me, her arm grazing mine, sending a jolt through me like a live wire. "I'll take my gold star now, if you don't mind. And as for my cookies, I like chocolate chip," she purrs, throwing a look over her shoulder.

She's teasing me, waiting for me to bite. "Are you sure you're going to be okay? I'm sure losing was hard for you."

Rachel snorts. Cam covers his laugh with a cough.

I take a slow step forward, closing the space between us just enough to watch the flicker of heat in her eyes. "Careful, Princess."

Her lips part, and her tongue darts out to wet her bottom lip. Then, in true Raven fashion, she scoffs, flicking her hair over her shoulder. "Whatever helps you sleep at night."

And just like that, she walks away. I watch her go, jaw tight, every muscle in my body wound like a fucking coil.

Cam claps a hand on my shoulder, shaking his head. "Yeah, you're so screwed."

I drag a hand down my face, forcing myself to exhale. She's a menace. A gorgeous, sharp-tongued menace who has no idea what kind of fire she's playing with. That cocky little smirk, the way she taunts me like she's untouchable is infuriating. And it's working.

I laugh because she thinks this is a game. That she's winning. She has no idea that I never start something unless I'm prepared to win.

I'll let her have her fun. For now.

I move to follow Cam, gesturing toward the door with a bow. "After you, your highness." She rolls her eyes but doesn't hide the way her lips twitch, like she enjoys pushing me just as much as I enjoy pushing her.

She narrows her eyes, but there's no real heat behind it. "Enjoying yourself?"

Oh, sweetheart, you have no idea.

We move through the halls, passing roped-off doors. Rachel slows, eying them with barely concealed mischief.

"I wonder what's in there," she muses, her fingers twitching like she's debating whether to push her luck. "Should we sneak in? What do you guys say?"

I huff a quiet laugh, already knowing where this is going.

"Don't even think about it, Rach," Raven warns, nudging her friend.

But I don't miss the flicker of interest in *her* eyes. Raven might not say it outright, but I can tell. The temptation is there. And fuck if that doesn't stir something dark and dangerous in me.

I can see it now. Raven sneaking through these halls at night, her body pressed against the stone as she listens for footsteps. Slipping past locked doors, her fingers trailing over surfaces she's not supposed to touch. Getting caught.

By *me.*

I swallow hard, shoving the image down before my thoughts go somewhere I won't be able to control.

She catches me watching her, curiosity flickering across her face.

"You thinking about breaking the rules, Princess?" I murmur, keeping my voice just low enough to make it feel like a challenge.

She lifts a shoulder in a lazy shrug. "No, I would never do something like that."

Liar.

I arch a brow. "Oh, so you only break rules when no one's looking?"

She flashes me a grin, and *fuck*, it's lethal. "I never said that."

I chuckle under my breath. I should stop provoking her. I should *definitely* stop imagining what she'd do if I caught her in one of these rooms.

Rachel interrupts, stopping in front of a massive portrait. "Look at her dress! Can you imagine if we had to wear that every day?"

"I'm sure you'd trip at least once a day if you had to wear that," Cam teases.

Rachel glares. "Rude."

Raven just shakes her head, laughing softly. "Hey, don't make fun of her baby deer ankles."

186

We keep moving until we reach a large room lined with glass cases. The second I see them; a curse burns the back of my throat. Their eyes light up as Raven practically presses her nose against the glass.

"What are these?" She asks, voice edged with curiosity.

I should've known she'd be drawn to them.

I clear my throat, forcing casual. "They're just... old things." My voice comes out a little too controlled. "Daggers, knives. Some artifacts." I hesitate for half a second, "I think they belonged to m—the original owners of the estate."

Fuck.

Her fingers skim the edge of the glass, tracing the outline of one of the daggers. A small, knowing smirk tugs at her lips, like she *knows* I'm holding something back.

Cam, sensing the tension, steps in. "It's wild how much history is packed into these places, huh? Who knows what kind of stories these things could tell."

Raven hums, nodding. But her attention stays locked on the display. Like she's trying to absorb every detail.

"Too bad you don't know more about them," she muses, tilting her head as if trying to puzzle something out. "They're actually pretty cool."

I force a casual shrug, my pulse steady even though I know she's digging, even if she doesn't realize it.

Rachel chimes in, clearly bored. "Yeah, shame."

"Maybe I'll look into it sometime for ye." Keeping my expression unreadable.

Raven's face lights up, and *fuck*, I wasn't expecting that reaction. "I would *love* that," she exclaims, her voice brimming with genuine excitement. "I've never seen anything like them before... I'd love to know..."

Her voice trails off, but I can already see her mind piecing together theories, crafting stories, reaching for answers no one else would think to ask.

I hesitate for half a second before turning to the girls. "Would you ladies care to sneak into the library or move on to the next room?" I ask, grinning.

Raven's eyes go wide, she practically bounces on her feet, hands clutched together.

"YES! Oh my God, *YES!*"

I chuckle, shaking my head. If I didn't open these doors, I swear she'd find a way to break in.

The doors swing open to reveal the library, and I don't miss the way Raven's entire expression shifts. Sunlight streams through the tall windows, casting a golden glow over the black shelves, the plush armchairs, the ladder that glides across the cases.

She steps forward, breath hitching. "This is incredible," she whispers, more to herself than anyone else.

She moves like she's in a trance, fingers trailing along the spines of the books just like she did in the bookstore. Something about the way she does it makes me pause.

She spins, looking over her shoulder at Rachel, and they both gasp at the size of the collection.

"This is insane!" Raven exclaims, turning back to me. "If I lived here, I'd *never* leave this room."

Something flickers inside me at those words. A dangerous, treacherous thought. Because the first thing that comes to mind is that my mother would love her. I shove the thought down so fast it nearly chokes me. *Absolutely not. No.*

Cam, oblivious to my internal debate, is laughing at something Rachel said, pointing to some of the taller shelves. Meanwhile, Raven continues moving through the space, running her fingertips over the weathered covers like they *mean* something to her.

It's been a long time since I've seen someone experience this kind of joy over something so simple. A *long* time. I exhale sharply, rolling my shoulders, forcing myself to refocus.

Head in the game, Kane.

But the more I watch her, the harder it is to remember where the lines are supposed to be.

CHAPTER 14

Castles Crumbling

RAVEN

R achel and I just stand there, rooted to the spot, eyes wide like a couple of idiots. The endless shelves, stretching to the ceiling, packed with more books than I can even begin to count is overwhelming in the best way. Like the walls themselves might actually stretch on forever.

It's like we've stumbled into a book lover's *wet* dream.

Off to the side, there's even a little dimly lit nook, lined with more books. I can't see where it leads, but my heart kicks at the thought. A secret passage, maybe? Or just more shelves. Either way, my pulse races.

I might have just died and gone to heaven and I'm never leaving.

At the center of the room, two massive, plush couches sit on a beautifully patterned rug, a low table between them. The set up is practically *begging* someone to curl up with a good book and disappear for hours. This space isn't ancient either, it's modern and inviting.

Nothing in here is roped off. There are no "Look, don't touch" signs. No suffocating rules that say this place is for *display*, not for use. And that makes my heart skip. This isn't some dusty, forgotten room meant for tourists to gawk at behind velvet ropes. *People actually use this place.*

My gaze drifts to the massive floor-to-ceiling windows on the west side of the room, where soft golden light spills in, illuminating every shelf, every book, casting the space in the perfect glow. It feels like the kind of place that warms your soul. That makes the rest of the world fade away.

Did I say I was in heaven?

Because *this* might actually be better.

I spin toward Cam, practically vibrating with excitement. "Can we walk around? We won't touch anything. I *promise*." My voice is embarrassingly eager, but I *need* to explore this place.

Cam's lips twitch, but he doesn't answer right away. Instead, he glances at Kane. And just like that, the two of them have one of those silent conversations men seem to have.

Kane finally gives a small nod, and Cam turns back to me, his voice all smooth and amused. "I think that would probably be okay."

Yes!

I don't even bother waiting, as I stride forward, already drawn to the towering shelves. I feel his eyes on me, tracking my every move.

Let him.

I have more important things to focus on. Like figure out if that nook actually leads to a secret passage.

I don't waste another second. My feet carry me straight to the nearest shelf, where row after row of worn leather spines and gold lettering glimmer in the sunlight. My fingers skim over the bindings, and my pulse kicks. *Where do I even start?* There are too many books, too many places to explore.

"Rachel! *Look* at all the books!" I blurt out like she isn't standing right next to me, seeing the exact same thing. But I can't help it. My excitement is practically vibrating out of my skin, and judging by the way Rachel's eyes are shining, she's right there with me.

"I *know*!" she practically squalls, and just like that, we dissolve into laughter.

This room is insane, straight up *Beauty and the Beast* vibes, only better, because *I'm* the one inside it. The walls are lined with floor-to-ceiling black shelves, packed with books of every size, color, and age. Some look old enough to have lost secrets of the universe, while others seem like they were added yesterday. The air is thick with the scent of aged paper, ink, and worn leather. It's an intoxicating mix that only book people can appreciate.

Above the center of the room, handing over the plush couches, is a massive crystal chandelier. The kind that belongs in a fairy tale.

Would that be too much in my bedroom? I'd make it work. Somehow.

I imagine how this place must look at sunrise, golden light pouring in through the massive windows, catching on the chandelier's crystals scattering tiny rainbows across the shelves. The thought alone makes me want to stay here forever.

The guys are lounging on the couches, deep in conversation about *who knows what,* while Rachel and I continue to wander. We're soaking in the sheer magic of this place when I spot a set of stairs, leading up to a loft.

Likely more books, maybe another seating area, a place where someone could escape for hours and be left alone with nothing but words and silence. My kind of heaven.

If this were my house? That loft would be my throne room. My private kingdom of books. My hideaway where no one could find me unless I *wanted* to be found.

And honestly?

I'd rarely come down.

My attention flickers to the little hallway I spotted earlier, that's practically calling my name. No idea where it leads, but there aren't any signs telling us not to explore. No ropes, no closed doors, nothing that suggests off-limits.

I lean toward Rachel, keeping my voice low. "The boys are busy. Should we see where it goes? Or maybe tell them and all go together?"

Rachel looks over at the guys, who are still deep in conversation, then back at the hallway. That mischievous grin flashes in her eyes before she shrugs, her grin widening. "Never ask for permission, that's my motto. They're busy being boys, totally oblivious. We're in this *beautiful* library, and obviously, we need to explore."

Without waiting for a response, she steps toward the hallway. Of course she's already decided.

I look back at the guys and she's right. They're completely unaware. Kane is leaned back on the couch, his expression unreadable, but he's too caught up in whatever Cam is saying to notice us slipping away.

Perfect.

"Alright, let's go," I whisper, feeling a rush of excitement thrumming through me as we step silently down the hallway.

The deeper we go, the more... *off* everything feels. A strange tingling spreads through my fingertips, like the air around us is charged. A faint, humming static that lingers against my skin as I brush my fingers against my arm. *It's nothing. Probably just old wiring.*

But then it shifts, that creeping sensation curling up my spine like a whisper, like something just outside my line of sight is watching.

I flick a glance at Rachel. She's totally unbothered, strolling like we're window-shopping instead of wandering into what is definitely the start of a horror movie. It is obviously just me.

We round a corner, and the walls shift, lined with old paintings with faded figures staring right at us.

The only thing that would make this moment perfect is if the paintings started moving. Hogwarts, here I come... and I swear to God... the eyes follow us as we pass. I tilt my head, squinting. *No way.*

The dim light overhead flickers slightly, casting warped shadows against the floor. The easy hum of life from the library fades into an eerie, stretched out silence.

A chill skates down my spine.

"You get the feeling we shouldn't be here?" I murmur.

Rachel hums thoughtfully. "Nope."

I arch a brow. "Even when the walls are literally watching us?"

She side-eyes the paintings, then shrugs. "Maybe they're just jealous."

I choke on a laugh. *Of course* that's her response.

She tosses me a smirk and keeps walking, her shoes barely making a sound against the ancient floors. Meanwhile, I keep my eyes on the paintings a little longer. *Just in case.*

We round another corner, and at the end of the hall, a door sits slightly open. Not wide enough to see inside, but open enough to be tempting. My steps slow as a prickling nervousness creeps up the back of my neck.

There's something about this place... something too *lived in.*

I tilt my head, taking in the space with fresh eyes. The vases lining the walls, the faint scent of something like aged wood and the barest trace of cologne. It's subtle, but unmistakable.

"Does this place not seem like someone actually *lives* here?" My whisper barely cutting through the stillness.

She glances around, her brow furrowing as she notices the same details. "Now that you mention it... yeah. It *does*. Maybe someone stays here part-time?"

She pauses, eyes narrowing slightly. "Cam *did* say they owed him a favor. Maybe that's why we're allowed to wander alone?"

Rachel pushes the door open, and the moment we step inside, I forget everything else.

I gasp.

It's a greenhouse. And not just any greenhouse, it's the most stunning one I've ever seen.

The air is thick with warmth, wrapping around us like a blanket, rich with the scent of fresh dirt and blooming flowers. The entire space is bathed in golden light, filtering through the towering glass walls and ceiling. Vines twist along the beams overhead, their leaves sprawling in lush, cascading waves. Vibrant flowers burst in wild colors from towering planters, and everywhere I look, the plants seem to be alive in a way that makes the whole space feel... untamed. Like stepping into another world.

Rachel lets out a low whistle. "Holy shit."

She wanders ahead, completely at ease, trailing her fingers along the leaves of a tall fern. Meanwhile, I stay rooted in place, overwhelmed in the best way.

I take a slow breath, inhaling the delicate scent of something floral. Jasmine, maybe? Or lavender? It blends with the earthiness of damp soil. It's perfect. Quiet. And yet... something about it feels different.

I can't explain it, but there's something to this place.

I glance at Rachel, who seems completely unbothered, strolling like she's looking for something. Maybe I'm just being weird, reading into things that aren't there. But I can't shake the feeling that we don't belong here.

Still, I can't help but smile.

"Someone *definitely* lives here if they have plants like this," I say, already feeling a strange connection to the space. My fingers trail along the cool edge of a stone planter, the leaves brushing back against my hand.

Rachel hums in agreement, running a hand along the leaves of another plant.

I glance at her, grinning. "Obviously, whoever lives here is basically *me* in another life. I mean, I love books, *they* love books. I love plants, *they* love plants." I pause, pretending to consider. "We need to meet this person so we can become best friends."

Rachel snorts, shaking her head. "You would."

"I *would*," I confirm, stepping deeper into the greenhouse. The energy here hums beneath my skin.

Rachel leans against a planter, smirking. "Wouldn't it be funny if the person who lives here is, like, some badass who just plays in the dirt for fun? You know, to wind down after... murdering someone?"

I lose it, bursting into laughter. "Rachel."

"What?" She grins. "I've read books like that. The guy is always secretly a killer with a weird hobby."

I roll my eyes, but... she's not wrong. The idea is both ridiculous and weirdly plausible in a setting like this.

I trail a hand over another set of leaves, the odd tingling sensation returning to my fingertips. It's stronger this time, like the plants are reaching for me.

"This place is huge," I say, still in awe. "I wonder if this leads outside?"

Rachel's eyes gleam with mischief. "Only one way to find out."

We weave through the winding stone paths, passing walls of greenery bursting with delicate white flowers. The deeper we go, the more the room feels like stepping into a secret world. Like we shouldn't be here, but I don't want to leave.

I hear a soft click of footsteps against stone. Rachel and I both freeze. The air shifts with silence. My pulse kicks up, fingers tightening at my sides. We flick wide-eyed glances at each other, hearts racing. But when we scan the room, there's no one in sight.

"Well, well, look who decided to go exploring."

Cam's voice cuts through the silence, and we both jump like we've been caught stealing the crown jewels.

"Holy shit!" I exclaim, pressing a hand to my chest. "You ever heard of giving a girl some warning before sneaking up like that?"

Cam smirks, all too pleased with himself. "If you weren't snooping, we wouldn't have snuck up on you."

And then there's Kane. His voice cuts through the humid air, dripping with that signature *Kane attitude.*

"If you weren't wandering into places you *shouldn't* be, you wouldn't *need* a warning."

196

I roll my eyes so hard they might get stuck. "The door was open. What were we supposed to do? *Not* look?"

Kane crosses his arms, his expression unreadable, but his eyes flicker with something I can't quite place. Annoyance? Amusement? *Something else?*

I straighten, refusing to let him get under my skin. "Besides," I add, lifting my chin. "We didn't touch anything."

Cam chuckles, shaking his head. "It's fine," he says, and unlike Kane, he actually *sounds* like he means it. "No harm done."

Rachel nudges me, giggling like we just won an argument. Before I can respond a crack of lightning illuminates the entire room, turning every plant, every shadow a contrast against the glass walls. The sharp flash is gone in an instant, but the thunder crashes through the space like a war drum, shaking the air, rattling the windows.

I barely have time to process it before—"Fuck."

Kane mutters it under his breath before turning on his heel and stalking out of the room.

I blink. Umm... what the hell just happened?

My eyes trail after him, my mind tries to piece together what that was all about. It wasn't just irritation. It was something else. Cam watches him go, shaking his head slightly before stepping forward. He flashes an easy smile, but there's a sharpness to it, like he's smoothing over something I should be questioning.

"You can keep looking around," his voice is too calm. "Don't worry about him. He's probably just making sure the windows are up on his car."

Bullshit.

Something in his tone makes me pause. He knows exactly what's up with Kane, but he's not about to spill it.

Rachel, either oblivious or just rolling with it, loops her arm through mine. "We should probably be heading back soon anyway, right?" She glances between us, brushing it off. "Especially if we're going to make it to dinner on time."

Then, with a bright smile, she turns to Cam. "I'm so excited to go to your place, Cam."

But my thoughts are still stuck on Kane, and the look in his eyes before he walked away.

Another rumble rolls overhead, deeper this time, closer. The storm is right on top of us now. I can't help but smile. I *love* thunderstorms and if we weren't about to leave, I'd be out there in a heartbeat, soaking it all in. *Literally.*

What I wouldn't give for this to be my house.

Correction, *my castle.*

The rain starts to patter against the glass, a steady rhythm that only adds to the moment. Every flash of lightning briefly illuminates the room, casting shifting shadows along the greenhouse walls. It should feel eerie, but it doesn't. It feels alive.

That strange energy hums in the air again, but stronger this time. And my fingertips won't stop tingling. What is going on with me? I flex my fingers, trying to shake off the sensation, but it's persistent. Maybe I should pull up WebMD and figure out what kind of rare disorder this is, because this can't be normal, right?

I clench my fists, forcing my attention back to the soothing rhythm of rain.

Then, lightning strikes, blinding for a split second. Thunder crashes right after, so loud I swear the glass rattles in its frame. I jump, my whole body jerking on instinct.

A loud crash echoes through the room and my heart slams against my ribs. I whip around, eyes wide, just in time to see an empty space on the shelf beside me where a pot *used* to be.

Now, it's shattered across the floor in a mess of broken ceramic and spilled soil.

I freeze, Rachel stares at the pot. Then at me. "Uh... did you just..."

"Did *I* do that?" I blurt, my pulse still hammering.

Cam steps forward, completely *unbothered* like the world around us isn't actively losing its mind. "It's just a wee pot," he says, lips twitching in amusement. "You okay?"

I let out a breath. "Yeah, just... startled." Which *isn't* a lie, but I don't know what the hell happened. I must've bumped the shelf.

Cam follows my gaze, but if he finds anything strange about this, he doesn't say it.

I look at the shattered mess again, guilt stirring. "What do we do about the pot?"

Cam just shrugs, that easy-going smirk still in place. "I'll make sure it's cleaned up. Come on, let's go."

I hesitate but eventually follow, Rachel at my side. As we step out, Cam quietly closes the door behind us. We pass through the library again; I don't want to leave. I could live in this castle, spend my days curled up in here, disappear into the greenhouse whenever I needed a break from reality. A girl can dream, right? This place is definitely going on my vision board.

We head back through the mudroom, but the moment I step into the doorway, my gaze snags on Kane outside. He's talking to someone, though, talking isn't the right word, his stance is too rigid. It doesn't look like just a casual conversation.

Rachel notices it, too, nudging me. "Why does that look like a tense business meeting instead of a friendly chat?"

Cam steps between us. "Hang on a second, let me see what's going on." His tone is smooth, but there's an edge to it that makes my stomach tighten. He glances between us. "You two stay here." Then, without a word, he heads toward Kane.

Rachel and I linger in the doorway, watching. The storm outside should be soothing. The kind of storm that usually makes me want to curl up with a book and let the world fade away. But not tonight. Every crack of thunder feels like a pulse of unease, every flicker of lightning sharpens the tension threading through the air.

Rachel shifts closer, lowering her voice. "You okay? You seem... off."

"I don't know," I murmur, my fingers clench at my sides. "I just feel weird. And bad about the pot... and the..." I trail off, searching for the right word.

Rachel tilts her head, watching me carefully. "Energy?" she suggests, her tone light but curious.

I exhale, relieved that she feels it. "Yeah," I admit.

She hums, considering. "What kind of energy are we talking? Like... chemistry? She wiggles her brows. "Or are we going straight to *this place is haunted* territory?"

I shoot her a look. "Not spooky ghost vibes." I struggle to describe the weird, electric hum beneath my skin. "And definitely not chemistry vibes."

She gives me an unconvinced side-eye. "Mmm-hmm. Well, if you suddenly start levitating or reading my mind, give me a heads-up, okay?"

I chuckle, trying to brush off the way my fingertips tingle again. "Yeah, I'll be sure to warn you."

Rachel locks her arm with mine and leans in. "I also saw a certain someone looking at a certain someone else."

I roll my eyes. "Yeah, Cam wasn't exactly subtle," I shoot back, keeping my voice low and playful. "Guess that means it's time to cut Bobby loose, huh?"

She snorts, crossing her arms. "Nice try." But the slight flush in her cheeks tells me I hit a nerve.

Before she can retaliate, Cam strides back toward us, hands tucked in his pockets. "Alright, we're heading back inside so we can regroup."

Rachel leans into me. "Regroup?" she whispers. "That's way too serious for *everything's fine.*"

I nod, glancing toward the storm again, my skin buzzing with unease. The tension outside hasn't eased, in fact, it's stretched tighter, wound like a coil ready to snap.

Rachel's grin tilts. "Whatever's going on, I hope it's dangerous or at least mildly illegal. We could use some excitement."

CHAPTER 15

State of Grace

RAVEN

W e step into the library, and Rachel squeezes my arm, snapping me out of my thoughts. Her gaze flicks toward Kane. *Where the hell did he come from?*

He stands near the window, his back to us, staring out at the storm like it's talking to him. The fire crackles behind him, casting a warm glow over the room, but it doesn't touch him. He's too still, his posture is too sharp.

He turns, his eyes sweeping the room before locking onto me. Just long enough for my breath to hitch. Then he moves, sinking into a chair with a slow, deliberate ease, like he's forcing himself to be relaxed.

Something's definitely off.

He doesn't waste any time. "There's been... a situation," he says smoothly, though there's an unmistakable edge beneath his calm.

Rachel shifts beside me, arms crossing like she's about to negotiate a business deal. "Well?" she prompts, like we're on a tight schedule and she's got places to be.

A smirk tugs at my lips before I can stop it, and Kane catches it. His eyes flick to Rachel, and for the briefest second, something almost amused flashes across his face. But it's gone just as fast, his expression hardening again.

"Alright, here's the deal." His voice drops slightly, his accent curling around the words like a slow caress. My thighs clench together, and I have to fight the urge to look away. Focus. Now is not the time to get turned on by his voice.

"There's a storm coming, which I'm sure you noticed," he continues, shifting his weight like he's already preparing for an argument. "We're far out from town, and it's supposed to hit hard and last a while." His gaze lands on me, pausing for a second longer than necessary before he continues. "If you want to head back, we'll need to leave now. I can take ye, if that's what ye want."

I barely register the next part, too caught up in the way his voice drags over every syllable. My body is reacting, heat pooling low in my stomach.

"... or we can stay here for the night and leave in the morning."

Rachel vibrates with excitement. She grabs my arm, her eyes wide. "We get to stay here?" She whispers, practically bouncing in her seat.

I glance at Kane, who's watching us with an unreadable expression, like he's waiting for my answer just as much as Rachel is.

I clear my throat, trying to force my brain to function. "Um, if you don't like driving in the rain, we can totally get an Uber."

His face goes blank. And not in a pleasantly neutral way.

"That wasn't on the list of options."

I blink. "Well, okay, but... how are we just supposed to stay the night here?" My brows knit together. "That's kinda weird. What if the owners come home?"

Kane leans back in his chair, his lips twitching like he's fighting a smirk. *Oh, he's enjoying this.* "Like we said, we know the owners." His voice is smooth as hell. "No one's coming here tonight."

My eyes narrow. "This feels like the perfect setup for a horror movie."

Rachel nudges me, grinning. "A horror movie where we get to live in luxury for the night? I'll happily be dragged into the forest in exchange for that."

Cam snorts, barely holding back his laughter. "What's with you guys and horror films?"

Kane ignores him and just watches me. *Like he's waiting for something.*

"Everything can be arranged either way." His voice is steady, though his gaze hasn't left mine. "I'm just asking if you could please decide what you'd like to do, so we can make said arrangements."

The *please* doesn't soften the command behind his words.

And there I go, wet again.

Fucking hell.

It's infuriating. No matter how hard I try to stay in control, one look, one word from him, and I'm *unraveling*. He's not even doing anything, and yet here I am, spiraling. I hate that he has this effect on me. I swallow, locking eyes with him, refusing to let him see how much he's getting to me.

I shift in my seat, willing the heat in my veins to settle, reminding myself that staying here is just practical. Nothing more. But with him around, everything feels like a test. A game neither of us will admit we're playing.

I lean in slightly, grinning. "Kane! I didn't realize you knew how to say *please.*"

His lips twitch, the flicker of amusement barely contained. "I guess I'm just full of surprises."

He stands and extends his hand toward me.

I blink, eyeing his outstretched palm like it's a trap. Because let's be honest, it probably is.

"What are you doing?" I raise a skeptical brow.

"Helping you up. You know, like a gentleman." His smirk is pure trouble, his eyes dark with something unreadable. And damn if he isn't the hottest man I've ever seen. My pulse betrays me, skittering like it's trying to keep up.

"Believe it or not, I'm quite well-mannered," he adds, voice laced with sarcasm.

I snort, crossing my arms. "Well, I'm not sure how I feel about this sudden display of chivalry. You're creeping me out."

Kane chuckles. "Get used to it, *Princess*. I have layers."

"Like Shrek!" Rachel chimes in, doubling over with laughter. "You know, like onions."

Cam groans, rubbing his forehead. "Please, no. Don't encourage her."

I giggle, shaking my head. When I glance back at Kane, he's watching me. Not just looking but *watching*. His expression still unreadable, but his eyes hold something else, something that makes my stomach flip.

Then softer this time, like he's trying to reassure me. "If you're not comfortable, we can head back to your place. It's up to you."

I shake my head, fighting the urge to smile. That shift in his tone does something to me. He's impossible to read, impossible to predict. And yet, for some reason, I believe him.

"Well," I say, dragging the moment out just because I can. "Since we're *so graciously* being given the option..." I turn to Rachel with a slow grin. "Might as well stay."

Kane's expression doesn't change, but something in his eyes flickers. *Challenge accepted.*

Rachel claps her hands together. "Oh, hell yes."

Cam chuckles, pushing off the counter. "All right then. Guess we're having a sleepover."

"We're staying in a castle and we're not changing our minds now." Rachel squeals.

Cam shakes his head with a chuckle. "Shrek? Really, Rach?"

Rachel crosses her arms with a huff. "Hey, don't act like you don't know all the words to *All Star*."

Cam points a finger at her. "First of all, that song is iconic."

"And second?" I ask, grinning?

"There is no second. That's the point," Cam replies, making everyone laugh.

I turn back to Kane. "Alright, so we have permission to stay here? Where exactly are we going to sleep?"

Kane chuckles, shaking his head. "Yes, we have permission. And as for sleeping arrangements, there are plenty of rooms for everyone." His voice is calm, but his eyes glint with something else, like he's holding back an inside joke.

Cam claps his hands together. "We can figure that out later. Food first. Unless anyone prefers to starve?"

Right on cue, my stomach growls loudly. "Okay, yes. Dinner first. I'm starving."

Rachel chuckles beside me, "That makes two of us. Let's eat before I have to go out and find a cow."

Kane's grin is pure mischief, a slow smile that spreads across his face as he nods toward the doorway. "Alright, follow me," he chuckles as his hand lands on the small of my back.

It's barely a touch, but it brands me all the same.

A slow flutter of anticipation curls low in my stomach the moment we step into the kitchen.

I stop dead in my tracks. *Holy fuck.*

It's massive. The kind of kitchen that shouldn't belong inside a castle and yet somehow fits perfectly. Earthy tones of rich brown and deep green

206

dominate the space, accented with just enough white to make everything pop. It's modern, but every detail speaks of warmth, of something *lived in*. Gold accents are scattered throughout the room. They're subtle but undeniably regal. Because, of course, we *are* in a castle.

The countertops are a polished dark granite, their glossy surface catches the ambient light. The deep green cabinets contrast beautifully against them. The whole space is designed with an effortless kind of sophistication. It's stunning. Clearly renovated, but whoever did it knew exactly what they were doing. The balance between classic and modern is seamless.

The floors are a dark wood, so rich and inviting, I almost want to walk barefoot just to feel it under my feet. Plush rugs soften the space, adding a cozy, almost intimate feel to a room that should be entirely too grand. And off to the side, a massive oak table sits near the windows, its surface worn and full of character. Marked by years of use.

Yep. Someone definitely lives here.

My gaze catches on the hanging planters overflowing with trailing vines, their leaves stretching toward the light, and the potted herbs lining the windowsill, their fresh scent filling the air. The greenery breathes life into the space, making it feel... real. Not just a castle, but a home. Whoever lives here is living their best fucking life.

I bite back the jealousy threatening to rise. If I had a place like this? I'd never leave.

I turn to Kane, arching an eyebrow. "Alright, what are we making, and what can we help with?"

He doesn't answer. Just stares, his eyes locked onto mine for a beat too long. *Is it getting hot in here for anyone else?*

Rachel's gaze flicks between us, a slow grin stretching across her face before she bursts out laughing.

"Oh, my God, can you two just fuck already?" She blurts.

Cam chokes so violently on his drink, I half expect him to drop dead on the spot. He sprays liquid all over the counter, coughing as he tries to recover, while Rachel just beams like she's cracked the world's biggest mystery.

"Holy shit, Rachel!" Cam sputters, wiping his mouth, still half laughing.

I gape at her, horror and mortification slamming through me in equal measure. "What the—"

207

Meanwhile Kane's not even fazed. He just cocks his head, his smirk deepening as he leans against the counter, watching me squirm like this is the best entertainment he's had in years. "Tempting, but no."

The bastard.

Heat floods my face. Instantly. I want to crawl into the nearest pantry and die. Meanwhile, Rachel is practically vibrating with joy, her smile wide and smug as she shoots me a wink.

"You're welcome," she mouths.

I level a glare at her that promises death.

"The answer is still no, Rachel," I mutter, barely resisting the urge to throw something at her.

She just laughs harder, flipping her hair over her shoulder like she's done me the biggest favor in the world. "What? The tension in here is going to fry all our brains, and I'm way too hot to die!" She declares dramatically.

Cam shakes his head, already done with this conversation. "Don't look at me." He says, hands raised in surrender. "I'm not getting involved."

Kane chuckles softly, still standing way too close for comfort, his presence pressing against my senses, making the heat in the room feel a little too real.

"Still?" he repeats, that cocky, infuriating smirk firmly in place.

I take a deep breath, trying to keep my composure, and step around him. "It's nothing personal. Don't you worry, I'm sure there's a lovely woman waiting for you in a basement somewhere."

Rachel snorts, barely containing her laughter, while Cam raises his brows, clearly enjoying the banter. Kane, on the other hand, just stares at me, his smirk unwavering, like he's already won some invisible game.

I glance around the room, making sure everyone knows I'm sticking to my story. "I am still swearing off all men. Nothing has changed. Everyone calm down."

Rachel bites her lip, looking like she's seconds away from cracking up. Cam leans casually against the counter, arms crossed, fully invested in the show. Meanwhile, my body is clearly having withdrawals from the lack of physical contact, reacting to the dumbest things, like Kane's stupid smirk or the way he says my name. It's honestly embarrassing how deprived I feel.

Although Cam has been calling most of the shots, I've noticed the subtle glances he sends in Kane's direction before making any decisions. And honestly? I get it. Kane commands attention without even trying.

Now that we're back to preparing dinner and not talking about my sex life, or the lack thereof, I don't exactly volunteer the fact that I hate cooking. Instead, I just follow their lead, grateful they're taking charge.

Cam assigns Rachel and me the task of washing, peeling and cutting potatoes for the fries or rather, the *chips*. Apparently, we're making homemade fish and chips.

Joke's on him, I love fish and chips.

Kane moves around the kitchen like he owns the place. It's hard not to sneak glances at him, though I try to keep it subtle. Every so often, despite the size of the kitchen, his shoulder brushes against mine as he walks by. And each time, a little spark rushes through me.

Thunder rumbles outside, flashes of lightning casting fleeting shadows across the room, adding to the cozy atmosphere. The sound of the rain would be soothing, if not for the ridiculous tension thickening in the air.

While Rachel and I handle the potatoes, the guys prep the fish and set out sauces on the table. I'm focused on cutting a lemon when Kane laughs at something Cam says. Instinctively, I pause, glancing at him.

That laugh hits me like a gut punch. My grip on the knife loosens, and before I know it, it clatters to the ground. *Deep breath.*

Every time I see him let his guard down, it's a direct hit to my self-control. Honestly, he's straight-up bad news for my lady parts.

I have zero complaints about being on prep duty if it means I get to watch these two fry up our dinner like they've been cooking their whole lives. Well, Cam actually has, which works out great for me and my lack of cooking skills. Kane, though? He hasn't really said much about his childhood. But right now, none of that matters, because watching his muscles flex while he works is... well, distracting enough. Unfairly so.

I bite my lip without realizing it.

Rachel nudges me with her elbow, a knowing smirk plastered across her face. "You doing okay there? Need another napkin?"

"Shut up," I mutter, trying, and failing, to hide the blush creeping up my neck.

Just then, Kane looks over and catches me staring. One brow lifts, and a slow, devastating smirk tugs at his lips.

"Enjoying the view?"

My face flames as I snap my attention back to the lemon in front of me. "Just making sure you're doing it right. I wouldn't want to get food poisoning." The words come out way too fast, and I curse internally. *FUCK. Of course, I'd get caught staring.*

Kane chuckles softly, his smirk widening like I'm the most amusing thing in the room.

Rachel loses it, cackling as Cam shakes his head, muttering through his laughter. "You're hopeless."

I shoot Cam a glare but can't help the smile tugging at my lips. "*NO BOYS!*" I declare over the laughter, attempting to reinforce my *very* shaky stance.

Rachel rolls her eyes playfully. "Yeah, yeah, we get it. *No boys.* Except... well, you know." She winks, and I want to crawl under the table.

Kane chuckles, his eyes twinkling with amusement. "Good thing I'm not a boy."

No, no he's not. *Boys don't look like that.* Or move like they were carved from temptation itself. And this man? He could ruin me with just a look, and I'd probably thank him for it.

Despite my resolve, my eyes betray me, flickering back to Kane. He's leaning against the counter now, arms crossed over his chest, watching me with a look that practically drips amusement.

The one that makes my pulse stutter and heat bloom across my skin.

I quickly drop my gaze, pretending to clean up my mess, but I can still feel him watching me. Like he's waiting for me to break first. Then, of course, he chuckles. Again.

Ass.

Cam walks over, probably to see if we're actually being helpful. "You ladies go take a seat; we'll get your drinks."

Just as I'm pulling out my chair, Kane's voice rumbles from behind me, husky enough to send an inconvenient shiver down my spine.

"Would you like some water, or can I get you something else?"

I clear my throat, snapping out of my wandering thoughts. "Water is great, but also... what exactly is *something else*?" I aim for light and playful, but my traitorous voice comes out softer than I intended.

Kane's smirk spreads. He doesn't even wait for me to respond, which is probably for the best, considering I'm momentarily speechless. My body, however, has zero shame, warmth unfurling in my chest and well, other places.

I silently curse him for being so damn good-looking. And worse? For knowing it.

Rachel, of course, catches the entire exchange. She snickers and nudges me hard enough to jolt me back to reality. "He's totally into you," she whispers, barely containing her grin.

I shoot her a desperate look, but she just winks, clearly enjoying my slow, inevitable unraveling. Meanwhile, Kane is still watching me, his eyes dark with something I can't quite name.

My throat tightens and I can't decide if I need water or a damn fire extinguisher.

"We're just friends, Rach." The words fall out, sharper than I meant.

She raises a brow, unconvinced. "Sure, keep telling yourself that." She leans in, voice dipping, "Friends don't look at each other like that."

I risk another glance at Kane, who's casually making our drinks like he didn't just reduce me to a puddle.

Staying here tonight was a bad idea.

A moment later, Kane returns with two glasses of water, setting them down in front of us without a word. He disappears and comes right back with two more drinks.

Rachel takes a sip, and her eyes widen in delight. "Okay, this is good," she says, raising her glass in a toast to him.

I follow suit, taking a cautious sip. Perfect. Not too sweet, but just enough bite to keep it interesting.

Kane leans against the counter, arms crossed, that infuriatingly smug look plastered across his face. "Glad you approve."

"Well, I had a lot of fun, and I'm genuinely shocked that you got Raven to cook," Rachel teases, nudging me again. She knows exactly how I feel about cooking. It's basically a running joke at this point. She's tried so many times to get me to make something, only for it to end in disaster. "I'm counting this trip as a win! Miracles do happen."

"Wait, are you telling me you don't like to cook either?" Cam looks horrified, maybe even a little offended. "I can tell you right now, if you hate cooking, it's because you've had the wrong teacher, or you're cooking the wrong dishes."

I giggle, unable to stop myself. Blaming the drink. It's just the right amount of strong, and I'm feeling a little more relaxed than usual

"Yeah, cooking has just never been my thing." I admit. "And hold on, let's be clear. I know how to cook some things. I'm not completely helpless. I've made it this far in life, so let's not get it twisted."

My gaze locks onto Kane, a challenge sparking in my eyes. "Do you know how to cook?"

Who am I kidding? He looks like he was bred for luxury, the way he moves, the way he carries himself, it all screams that he was raised with etiquette and fine dining lessons.

He's a mystery wrapped in control and sharp edges, and some reckless part of me wants to dive in. Kane looks like he was practically born to be a National Treasure with that body. Where's Nicholas Cage, and where do I sign up?

"I happen to know how to cook quite well, thank you very much," he murmurs, his voice low and confident. "I actually enjoy it. Although... I haven't really cooked like this in a long time."

I blink, slightly thrown off by how at ease he looks. This is the most relaxed I've seen him since we met. His usual guarded intensity has softened, and for some reason, that makes my heart skip.

Rachel smirks, crossing her arms as she throws me a teasing glance. "See? Even Kane can cook. Surely you can give it a whirl?"

Kane raises an eyebrow, leaning back in his chair. "What's that supposed to mean?" His voice dips, a hint of amusement lacing his words.

Rachel waves him off. "Oh nothing! Just, you know... pretty boy and all..."

I lose it, I can't help but laugh while Rachel grins proudly. And Kane just shakes his head, looking amused but not the least bit insulted.

212

We keep talking, keep laughing, learning bits and pieces about each other. When it's my turn to answer questions, I keep it vague while talking about my childhood, steering clear of the... unconventional details.

Like how other kids were probably playing tag or hide-and-seek, while I was learning how to punch and throw knives for fun. And honestly, how do you even bring that up?

"Hey, remember recess? Well, I was busy learning how to disarm someone in under ten seconds."

Yeah, not exactly casual conversation.

Kane's presence is both calming and stressful. An infuriating contradiction that leaves me teetering between fascination and frustration. Every time our eyes meet, a flutter of excitement rises in my chest, uninvited, but undeniable.

It's strange, being so drawn to someone I barely know while simultaneously being annoyed by him. Throughout dinner, I catch him stealing glances when he thinks I'm not looking, and every subtle brush of his knee against mine under the table feels loaded. I try to act unaffected, but it's impossible to ignore the heat creeping up my neck.

Every time I look up, he's watching me with that same infuriatingly amused look.

"So, what about you, Kane? What did you grow up doing?" Rachel asks.

"My family believed in being well-rounded, so I learned a bit of everything," he says, voice smooth and effortless.

The intensity in his gaze sends a chill through me, spreading slowly. His eyes flicker over my face like he's daring me to look away first.

I don't.

Instead, I hold his stare, there's something deeper there than the casual banter we've been tossing around all night.

My heart pounds against my ribs.

A small smirk pulls at the corner of his lips, but his gaze never wavers. The room could disappear, and I don't think I'd notice.

I can feel heat pooling between my legs, my nipples tightening beneath my shirt. I have to fight the urge to cross my arms over my chest, suddenly feeling way too exposed.

Why does my body betray me like this? Making me hyper-aware of every breath, every heartbeat, every inch of space between us. I swallow, trying to regain control, but the way he looks at me is like he knows. Like he's fully aware of how my body is responding to him. *Which I really hope isn't the case.*

Rachel's voice slices through the tension like a cold gust of air, snapping me out of the heated trance I was caught in with Kane.

I blink, forcing myself to breathe as she suddenly stands, phone in hand.

"Alright, I'm calling it a night. Got a migraine," she announces louder than necessary.

She glances between me and Kane, wearing a knowing smirk that I swear I'll kill her for later. Then she turns to me with a dramatic sigh. "Rave, I love you, but you snore, and tonight, I want my own room. If you get scared, be quiet when you sneak in, yeah?"

I shoot her a look that screams *what in the actual fuck,* but she conveniently pretends not to notice, turning her attention to Cam instead.

Cam rises from his seat, his tall frame dwarfing hers as he stretches. "Yeah, I'm beat too. *Tour Guide Cam* has done his duty for the day."

Then, as if on cue, he claps his hands together before placing his hand on the small of Rachel's back, guiding her toward the door.

"Better get going."

Rachel gets migraines a lot, and when they hit, she's out for days. If it's a bad one, I don't see her for weeks. Something always triggers it, and then she vanishes.

Tonight, I'd be suspicious and think she was just making excuses if she didn't actually look like she was suffering. Her face is pale, and I know that look all too well.

So as much as I want to investigate further, I hold back.

"I'll show her to her room, since we're going the same way." Cam quickly ushers her out of the kitchen.

Um... okay, that wasn't weird at all.

"Goodnight. Text me if you need anything... I guess. Love you," I call after her.

"Love you. Make good choices. Don't do anything I wouldn't do." Rachel calls over her shoulder before disappearing around the corner.

Which let's be real, that doesn't narrow it down much. There's not a lot she *wouldn't* do.

I sit there for a moment, thrown off by their sudden departure. The room feels smaller now. Quieter.

But still charged.

Kane raises a brow, clearly amused. "Well, I guess it's just us, then

He leans forward slightly, resting his elbow on the table. "Unless you're too chicken to be alone with me."

CHAPTER 16

The.One.

RAVEN

A s much as I want to bail and sprint to my room like the chicken I clearly am, there's just one small problem. I don't actually *know* where my room is.

I'd planned on going to bed at the same time as Rachel, assuming we'd turn in for the night together. But no. Of course, she had to pull the *I need my own room* card and leave me stranded. Now, I'm stuck.

Fuckity-fucking-fuck.

And of course, Kane would find this whole situation *hilarious.*

You're a big girl Raven. You can have a man walk you to your room without your mouth falling on his dick.

It's not that I don't trust myself. And it would just be rude if I didn't help clean up. That's why I'm staying. That's the only reason I stand up to start gathering dishes.

As I move around the table, I catch a glimpse of Kane out of the corner of my eye.

"What?" I pause, picking up a plate.

"Nothing." His voice is too casual, but there's a hesitation in it. Then he quickly adds, "Here, let me help with the food."

He looks like he was about to say something else, but he stays quiet.

I narrow my eyes. "What were you about to say?"

Kane doesn't strike me as the type to hold back, so whatever it was, I want to know.

"It's nothing, really."

Liar.

I hold his gaze for a moment, not buying it, but I let it slide for now. The sound of running water fills the silence as I rinse off a dish, my mind still turning over his reaction, when he laughs.

217

A low, unexpected chuckle, breaking through the quiet. The sound catches me off guard.

I glance at him. "Okay, what is it now"

His eyes are playful, but there's something else there, too. Something I can't place. But instead of answering, he just smirks. The same infuriating, ridiculously attractive smirk that's been driving me insane since the moment we met.

It's like the man has more layers than Fort Knox.

"I'm just surprised to see you getting your hands dirty," he shrugs, rolling up his sleeves. His tone is teasing, but the look on his face is still unreadable. "Doesn't seem like your thing."

I pause, momentarily distracted by the movement, because holy shit. Forearms.

I blink, caught off guard, my gaze locking onto the ink peeking from beneath his sleeve. Intricate and dark, it winds its way up his forearm like it's hiding a story I suddenly need to know.

Focus, Raven.

"Rude!" I recover quickly, snapping my eyes back to his. "I happen to know how to wash dishes, thank you very much. And I'd also like to point out that I'm not getting my hands dirty. I'm getting them *clean*."

I grin at my own joke, feeling a little too proud of myself. And before I can second-guess it, I scoop up a handful of bubbles and blow them straight at him.

Kane raises an eyebrow, and a slow devastating smile spreads across his face, and the corner of his mouth quirks up just enough to make me forget how to breathe.

He takes a step closer, and suddenly, the air shifts. The space between us feels dangerously small.

Heat rushes through me, straight to my core, and I'm praying he can't tell. I need to look away. Step back. Say something. Anything. But I don't.

I can't.

"Fair point," he murmurs, his voice dropping dangerously low. "And here I thought you were just a princess."

My pulse stutters.

I roll my eyes, ignoring the way my body reacts to the way he says *princess*.

"Well, this princess happens to know her way around a sink. Ever heard of Cinderella?"

For a split second, my brain supplies an entirely different kind of fairytale, one involving a very different kind of happy ending.

I shove that thought into a vault and throw away the key.

"I'm not sure if you were taught this," I continue, forcing my voice back to casual teasing, "But insulting people is generally frowned upon."

Kane tilts his head slightly, "Noted."

Then, because he's an ass, he leans in just enough that I swear I feel the heat radiating off him.

"I'll be on my best behavior from now on," he adds smoothly, his gaze flickering over my lips for half a second too long.

God help me.

I force myself to break eye contact and point at his arm, needing a distraction. "So, what's the story behind the tattoo?" I ask, hoping my voice sounds steadier than I feel.

Kane glances down at the ink, and for a brief moment, something shifts. The teasing vanishes, the cocky smirk eases, and it's replaced by something heavier. Like whatever memory is tied to that ink is important.

A small, smile tugs at his lips.

"It's a long story," he turns back to the dishes. "Maybe I'll tell it to you sometime."

That's it. That's all he gives me.

I wait a moment, half expecting him to elaborate, but he doesn't. He just keeps rinsing dishes like the conversation never happened.

I narrow my eyes. "Seriously? That's all I get?"

Kane shrugs, the corners of his mouth twitching. Instead of answering, he throws his own question at me.

"What's the story behind swearing off men?"

I roll my eyes but don't deflect. After a beat, I decide to just tell him the truth.

"You know when you give your entire soul to someone? When you love so hard, it almost consumes you?" I pause, collecting my thoughts before continuing.

"Well, I learned the hard way that when you love like that, you fall just as hard. And when it ends? You realize everyone was right, and you got played."

I keep washing the dishes, the weight of my words settling over the room like a quiet storm.

"It sucks realizing you were just used and tossed aside like a crumpled piece of paper." My voice softens as I add, "But the worst part is the guilt. Because deep down, you knew. You knew you had to get out, but you didn't have the guts to do it."

I meet his gaze, my voice stronger now.

"I refuse to believe that's what love is. I refuse to believe that real love doesn't exist. So until I find that love, I don't want any of it. I won't live in a relationship where love isn't real because I know it's out there. Somewhere."

Kane watches me like he's seeing me for the first time. Like something I said hit deeper than he expected. His mouth parts slightly, like he's about to respond but he doesn't say a word.

Finally, he breaks the silence, "It's just a reminder of where I come from." His tone is measured. "Family crest, the whole deal."

There's a steadiness to his voice, but beneath it, I catch something else. Something raw and guarded.

He's putting up a wall, his guarded mask slipping back into place. Like whatever the tattoo represents is a door he's not ready to open.

Now I really want to see it.

But the way he told me just enough then shut that conversation down tells me it's not happening. Not tonight.

Figures.

I'm in way over my head here. And all we're doing is washing dishes. Damn Rachel for leaving me alone to deal with this on my own. How the hell is a girl supposed to focus when his sleeves are rolled up, and I can see the veins in his forearms standing out like that? It's downright distracting.

And now, with the whole tattoo mystery, I can't help but wonder what else he's hiding.

Just what I need, another puzzle I have no business trying to solve.

Just seeing his body in *clothes* is enough to mess with me. But imagining him without the restrictions of fabric?

I quickly lick my suddenly dry lips and force myself to focus on the dishes, drowning my wandering thoughts in the suds.

Kane chuckles softly like he knows exactly what's going on in my head and the sound sends a shiver straight down my spine.

Of course, he finds this amusing.

"Touché," is all he says.

I glance at him out of the corner of my eye, and there it is. That damn self-satisfied smirk. Outside, the storm rumbles again, thunder rolling through the room like a warning. All I know is my heart is racing. I turn to grab a towel, but don't get far because Kane's right there, holding it just out of reach.

My breath catches, and for a moment, I forget what I was even doing. His eyes lock onto mine, and I feel the shift, the tension snapping tight, thick and unrelenting.

"Looking for this?" He asks, winding the towel up with a mischievous grin.

Oh, hell no.

"Don't. You. DARE," I warn, narrowing my eyes at him. But it's too late.

The flash in his eyes says it all. Gone is the composed, always-in-control Kane. What stands before me now is pure mischief. Like a predator ready to pounce.

He raises an eyebrow, and that's all the warning I get before the towel snaps through the air with a *sharp crack*.

I yelp, twisting out of the way, barely dodging it in time.

I scramble to the other side of the island, my heart pounding, adrenaline surging through me. My eyes dart around, searching for something to shield myself with or maybe even to throw at him.

"Kane, think about this," I say, trying to sound calm and reasonable, as if I'm talking him down from the ledge.

His grin widens.

"Oh, I'm thinking about it."

Shit.

"You *really* don't want to do this." I warn again, holding my hands up like I'm surrendering. My voice wavers slightly, betraying me.

He tilts his head, taking a slow, calculated step forward.

"I promise you'll regret it." I add, desperate now.

He hums, pretending to consider it.

"Really, Princess? Because I think that it's exactly what I want to do."

The way he says it. Dark and smooth. The kind of voice that digs under your skin, settling in places it has no business being.

My pulse spikes, the heat in his eyes is different this time. It's unfiltered and raw. Like he's finally tired of hiding it.

And suddenly, I'm one hundred percent certain I'm definitely out of my depth. If I don't get control of this situation fast, I'm going to do something stupid. Like... I don't know. Throw caution to the wind and climb him like a goddamn tree.

I fake left, eyes locked on his. The second Kane shifts to catch me, I dart right, to my utter delight, he actually falls for it. A small victory.

I make a break for the sink, my heart pounding like a war drum. The second I reach the sink, I grab the sprayer, twist the water on, and spin right as the towel snaps against my leg. At the same moment I blast him with ice-cold water.

I scream, laughing, as the cold spray hits both of us, soaking through my clothes. But he's too quick. He's on me in an instant.

Water flies everywhere, drenching the counters, the floor, *us*.

I twist, refusing to let go, but I never really stood a chance. I should've surrendered the second he came after me. But apparently, common sense has left the building, and I'm blaming *him* entirely for it.

His deep, rich laughter rolls through the kitchen, and damn him, it's contagious. I try to pivot, to regain some ground, but it's too late. He catches my wrist, yanking the sprayer out of my grip with ridiculous ease. He presses into me, his body solid as he traps me against the counter. A sharp inhale gets stuck in my throat.

The hard planes of his chest burn through my wet clothes, his strength effortlessly holding me in place.

"Let go, Princess," he purrs, voice dripping with a lethal mix of playfulness and something darker. His breath fans over my skin, trailing down the back of my neck like a slow burn, leaving goosebumps in its wake.

I should tell him to back off. At the very least push him away.

Instead, I do neither.

His grip tightens slightly, and it's enough to remind me how easily he's holding me in place. How effortlessly he could turn things if he wanted. I can feel every inch of him, his hard muscle pressed against me, his body all heat and strength and pure aggravating control.

Well, if I wasn't wet before, I sure as hell am now. In *every* possible way.

"No way," I manage, though my voice comes out breathier than I'd like.

Kane's lips graze the shell of my ear, his voice rougher. "You're playing a dangerous game."

The sensation sends a jolt of heat right to my core. I swear the air around us shifts once again, like something is building beneath the surface, pressing against the edges of reality, waiting to snap.

I push the thought aside, focusing on the words falling out of my mouth before I can stop them.

"Maybe I like danger," I whisper, though my voice wavers, betraying the calm I'm so desperately clinging to. "And I'm not scared of you."

A bold-faced lie.

Not because I think he'd hurt me. But because I have no idea what I'd let him do.

Because my pulse betrays me. Pounding, quickening, contradicting every word I say.

His low chuckle rumbles through me, sending another shiver coursing through my body.

"You have no idea what you're getting into," he murmurs, voice thick with warning.

I open my mouth to respond, but nothing comes out. Because he's right. I don't.

The air presses around me, the warmth in my fingertips flaring without warning.

Kane's grip stiffens slightly. Like he felt it too. His breath hitches, the smallest pause, gone so fast I almost think I imagined it. Almost.

Then his voice drops, rougher than before. "Raven." His lips brush my ear, "you're making it hard to be a gentleman."

I swear the temperature spikes. Heat pulses through my body, thick and unrelenting, and I can't tell anymore if it's from him or... something else. My hands flex involuntarily, a warmth coiling through my veins, pressing against my skin like static.

I should break this tension before it swallows me whole. But I don't move.

Then I realize we're in someone else's house, someone's castle, no less. And we've just made an epic mess. That thought hits me like a cold splash of water, and just like that, the spell shatters.

I exhale slowly, forcing myself to raise both hands in surrender. "Okay, okay, you win."

Kane stays pressed against me for a moment longer, just long enough to drive me absolutely insane. Then, he finally steps back.

The second he does, the absence of his warmth feels like stepping into the cold. And I'm already questioning everything. Why was I saying no, again?

I clear my throat, hoping it snaps me back to reality. I steal a glance at Kane, catching the way he drags a hand through his hair, looking just as shaken as I feel. His jaw ticks, his expression back to his usual unreadable mask. But there's something lingering in his eyes. Like he's also trying to shake off whatever the hell just happened.

"Smart choice," he tries to hide the smile creeping onto his face.

"I'll clean this up after I show you to your room. Come on," he adds, nodding toward the door.

"Um, no. I helped make the mess, so I'll help clean it up." I cross my arms, giving him a look.

He hesitates, his gaze flickering over my face like he's considering arguing, but instead, he gives a small shrug.

"Alright," he concedes, grabbing a towel.

We move around the kitchen, silently working to dry the countertops and floor.

Neither of us acknowledges the tension that seems to coil tighter with every accidental brush of our shoulders. Despite the lingering banter, there's something different in Kane's eyes now.

Something serious, like he's wrestling with his own thoughts. And oddly enough, it's comforting.

"Thanks."

It catches me off guard. I blink up at him, surprised by the unexpected softness in his voice.

"Why wouldn't I help?" I ask, genuinely taken aback by his gratitude.

His lips twitch, like he's about to say something more but thinks better of it. Instead, he just nods, tossing the damn towel over the sink.

I need to get to my room and deal with everything that just happened. My heart's still racing, and my body... well, let's just say relief isn't anywhere in sight unless I decide to take matters into my own hands.

Kane's voice cuts through my spiraling thoughts. "Alright, let's get you to your room. The host says to make yourself at home, I know there's a bathtub in there if you want a bath."

His gaze lingers a second too long on my lips. A shiver runs through me, and my skin prickles with awareness.

A hot bath sounds tempting, especially since my clothes are still damp, and my body is still on fire.

I don't trust myself to respond. Instead, I grab my bag from the corner and sling it over my shoulder, needing the distance as I follow him out of the kitchen.

We move through the castle's dimly lit hallways, the storm still raging outside. Rain pounds against the windows, the occasional rumble of thunder rolling through the stone walls like a distant heartbeat. The flickering candlelight casts long shadows, making everything feel impossibly cozy, but also electric.

My body still feels off, hyperaware, and charged. I keep my eyes ahead, but my mind is still spiraling with mixed emotions. Attraction, frustration, and that damn heat I can't seem to shake. My panties are soaked, and I didn't even bring a change of clothes.

I barely pay attention to where we're going, which is probably stupid. I should at least know where my room is in case I need to bolt later.

Kane walks beside me, his presence a force without even trying. I steal a glance at him, and he looks relaxed now. There's still an undercurrent of something beneath the surface, like he's holding something back.

Either way, I wish I knew what the hell he was thinking right now.

I clutch the strap of my bag tighter, trying to shake the thought. *I don't need to be wondering about Kane.*

He stops in front of a large wooden door, pushing it open to reveal a room bathed in the soft glow of firelight. The warmth hits me first, carrying the scent of aged wood and something faintly spiced. The fireplace crackles in the corner, casting flickering light across the walls, shadows dancing in the dim light.

A massive bed sits against the far wall, layered in plush fabrics and thick blankets that look almost too perfect to disturb. It's the kind of bed you could sink into and never leave.

Another door sits open off to the side, giving me a glimpse of what I can only assume is the bathroom and the infamous tub waiting to erase the entire night from my memory.

I step inside slowly, letting the warmth settle into my bones, letting myself breathe. Then, I make the mistake of looking at Kane.

I was going to say something. A *thank you*, maybe. Goodnight. Some type of acknowledgement. But the second my eyes land on him, the words vanish like smoke.

I'm no stranger to the male body, but Kane? He's another beast entirely. Sculpted muscle, raw power beneath controlled grace. If I didn't know better, I'd swear he spent every spare moment chiseling himself into perfection at some exclusive, underground, Greek-gods-only gym.

His muscles have muscles.

And it would be so much easier if that was all it was. Just a ridiculously unfair body, another frustratingly attractive man with nothing else to offer. But no.

Of course not.

It's everything else that's throwing me off balance.

I really hoped drenching him in water would make him look like a wet dog, so I could use it to fight off whatever this is. But no, that would be too convenient. He somehow pulls off drenched and disheveled like it's a damn fashion statement.

And because luck, apparently, is not on my side. Kane catches my lingering stare, and a slow, knowing smile tugs at the corner of his mouth.

"Do you need anything else?" he asks, amusement flickers behind his dark gaze.

I snap right out of my trance so fast I'm surprised I don't get whiplash.

"Nope, totally fine. Thanks." My voice is a little too forced, and I can only hope he doesn't hear how breathless it sounds.

"Well, if you need anything, just let me know," he finally says, his voice low and smooth. "I'll be right next door."

He pauses just long enough for my breath to catch. My eyes snap to his and he looks amused.

"Otherwise... goodnight."

For a second, I wonder if he has any idea what's running through my mind. Instead, he turns on his heel, heading out of my room. His unreadable mask firmly back in place.

"Thanks for the experience." And then he winks.

Before I can muster a single response, he's already disappearing through his door.

My mouth opens, but no words come out, again. I stand there for a beat, heat creeping up my cheeks, my brain still trying to catch up. His door clicks shut, and I finally let out a breath I hadn't realized I was holding.

Stellar performance. Maybe next time try using actual words.

I roll my eyes at myself.

The warmth from the fire wraps around me, but it does nothing to settle the restlessness thrumming beneath my skin. Every muscle still holds the tension of the night, like my body hasn't gotten the memo that the chaos is over.

If there's one thing I can do for myself right now, it's sink into scalding hot water and pretend I don't exist for at least an hour.

The tub fills quickly, steam curling into the air in soft tendrils. My gaze flicks over the neatly arranged bath salts on the shelf. Of course, the castle has every luxury bath essential a girl could ask for. This place is stocked like a damn five-star spa.

I sprinkle a generous handful into the water, watching as the scent blooms instantly, wrapping around me in a soothing, floral warmth that feels like slipping into a dream.

The second I step into the tub and sink down; a slow exhale leaves me. The heat works its way into my muscles, unwinding knots I didn't realize I had, coaxing my body into something resembling relaxation.

For a moment, I let myself get lost in the flickering candlelight, in the way the flames dance along the stone walls, their rhythm slow, hypnotic.

But beneath the calming warmth, there's something else.

An undercurrent of energy that hums just beneath the surface, like the air itself is charged.

It's subtle at first, like a whisper just out of reach. But the longer I sit there, the stronger it gets. My fingers tingle, the sensation creeping up my arms in slow, pulsing waves.

Not again.

I flex my hands beneath the water, watching as droplets roll off my fingertips, catching light before disappearing. The feeling doesn't go away.

Maybe I'm just overthinking.

Maybe my nerves are fried from everything that's happened tonight.

Or maybe, I should stop drinking alcohol, because clearly, my body is not built for this.

I sink lower, letting the water cover my shoulders, as if that alone could wash away the buzzing beneath my skin. I should be relaxing. I should be clearing my mind. Instead, my thoughts are circling back to him.

I curse myself immediately for letting Kane take up even one more second of my night. He's like a splinter I can't dig out.

Kane McWalking Distraction is not my problem.

I tilt my head back, inhaling deeply, letting the scent of lavender fill my lungs. I just need sleep. *A night in this castle has my head spinning in ways I don't want to analyze.*

But just as I start to let go of the day's chaos, a soft shimmering light flickers at the edge of my vision. I sit up, eyes snapping open, scanning the dimly lit room when I see my necklace on the nightstand, just barely catching the firelight.

But it's not just reflecting the glow. It looks like it's pulsing. A faint, silver-blue light flickers around the intricate metal, like it's breathing.

I blink, hard, wondering if the flickering candlelight is playing tricks on me. I let out a slow breath, shaking my head. But then it happens again. A faint, rhythmic pulse, like a heartbeat. And just like before, the tingling in my hands starts up again, stronger this time.

I reach for the towel, barely noticing the way my hands tremble.

By the time I cross the room, my pulse is a wild, frantic thing. I hesitate above the necklace, my fingers hovering inches from the metal. Something inside me warns against it. But curiosity has always been my greatest downfall.

I press my fingers to the pendant, and the moment my skin touches the cool metal, a rush of heat surges through me. Not warmth. Not comfort.

Fire.

The sensation floods my veins, crackling along my skin like an unseen force just waiting to be unleashed.

Every nerve sparks to life, my breath catching as my vision tilts.

"What the hell," I whisper, gripping the edge of the nightstand as the room sways beneath me.

A slow, hot pulse blooms in my chest, spreading outward, leaving a tingling wake in its path. My heartbeat slams against my ribs, erratic and unsteady.

I blink rapidly, trying to anchor myself, trying to breathe through the dizziness, but it's no use.

Then, like a lightning strike, a memory crashes through me, sharp and vivid.

I'm small again, curled in the tub, steam curling around me as my grandmother sits on the edge, her familiar scent of lavender and honey filling the room.

The air outside had been sharp as knives, the kind of cold that seeped into my bones and refused to leave. My muscles still ached, the lake's icy grip lingering even now, but I did it. I swam across and back, just like I was told.

She hums softly as she works the conditioner through my tangled curls, her fingers gliding with practiced care, the gentle rhythm of her touch lulling me into something safe.

I sink deeper, letting the warmth chase away the cold.

"What are you humming, Marjorie?" I murmur; my voice thick with exhaustion.

She pauses, before she smiles down at me, eyes crinkling at the corners.

"You know you can just call me Grandma, right?" she teases, her fingers resuming their careful path through my hair.

I shrug, leaning back against the tub's edge. "I know. But I love your name. It sounds special... so I want to say it as much as I can."

A soft chuckle rumbles through her chest, warm as the bathwater and rich as the stories she always wove around me.

"Do you remember the story I told you about the witch who could catch lightning in a bottle?"

I nod without hesitation.

This was her favorite story. I already know it by heart, but I stay quiet, letting her voice stitch the tale into the air once more, the melody of her hum lingering between her words, like a spell waiting to be cast.

"She only wanted to fall in love," my grandmother begins, her voice low.

"But she was cursed, you see, for she was powerful. Too powerful."

My breath slows, my eyes fluttering closed as I listen.

"They called her the Winter Queen, because her sadness lingered like the frost on the earth. She longed for love so desperately, but no matter how many men adored her, none truly saw her. They just saw her beauty and her power. The one who could melt the ice inside her heart never came."

Her fingers continue their slow, soothing path through my curls, but the story itself carries a chill.

"In her despair, she swore to the heavens," she continues, her voice dropping lower, like she's telling me a secret only meant for my ears.

"She pleaded with them. 'Who do I have to speak to?' she cried. 'How can I break this curse? Change this, please!'"

The words coiled around me, like something I was always meant to remember.

"No matter how many times she found herself on her knees in the woods, pleading with the moon, no matter how many letters she burned, sending her words into the night sky in hopes that the Goddess Clea would hear, nothing changed."

Her voice dips with sorrow.

"The years slipped by, one after another, and still... no sign of a soulmate. No promise of love."

"The longer she waited, the more she withdrew," my grandmother murmurs.

"Her duties, once her pride, slowly fell away as hope dimmed, fading like the winter sun."

A beat of silence.

"That's when they began to call her the Winter Queen, not for the season itself, but for the cold that settled around her. It was more than just the weather. It was her loneliness, her despair... and the unbearable weight of her longing."

A sudden flash of lightning splits the sky, bright and fierce. It rips me from the memory like a slap of cold air.

I gasp, my body jerking forward as my vision reels, my breath catching in my throat. My fingers go slack, and the necklace slips from my grasp, landing against the rug with a soft, final thud.

The vivid image of my grandmother fades, dissolving into the flickering candlelight like smoke curling into the night.

My heart hammers, disoriented by the sudden shift, the violent crash between past and present.

I squeeze my eyes shut, digging through my memory, trying to hold onto the rest of the story.

What came next? What did she say after that? All that remains is a lingering sense of urgency, like I've forgotten something vital. Something important enough to pull at the edges of my soul.

Chapter 17

Lucky Me

KANE

Fuck.

I drag a hand down my face, exhaling through clenched teeth. I've lost count of how many times I've muttered that word in the last twenty-four hours.

The second I shut my door, I just stand there, trying to get my head on straight.

Part of me wants to go upstairs to my actual room, lock the door, and put some fucking distance between us.

But then I remember what I told her, that I'm right next door if she needs anything.

Christ. That was a mistake.

I lean my head back against the door, staring up at the ceiling like it'll fix this problem I walked straight into.

Then I hear a faint noise. Her voice but muffled. I can't make out the words, but a small smile tugs at my lips, knowing she's talking to herself. I shouldn't find it fucking adorable, but I do.

A slow exhale leaves me as I rake a hand through my hair, willing myself to shut this shit down.

Too late to reel it back now.

My body's already reacting, the pressure straining against my jeans is unbearable. Still rock fucking hard.

I groan, shifting my stance, wishing I could get her out of my head for even a second. But it's impossible.

It took everything not to pin her against the counter and sink my teeth into her neck. The way she arched against me, pressing her ass back like she didn't know what it was doing to me. Yeah, I nearly lost it.

And when she whispered, *'I'm not afraid of you'...* I groan again.

Fuck.

I exhale sharply, rubbing my jaw, frustration crackling through every inch of me. She has no idea that she's been pulling a sleeping beast by the collar all fucking day.

I deserve a medal for holding back. Restraint of a saint here.

But the problem is, I don't want to hold back. The way she pushes my buttons, always with that infuriating, smug little smirk, has every cell in my body tuned in to her and nothing else. I've never felt this kind of raw, unrelenting lust for anyone before.

I start pacing the room, trying to shake this restless, blistering need, but it's fucking useless.

Today has been a complete mindfuck. Too many close calls. Too many moments where I almost came clean. When they wandered into the greenhouse? Yeah, that was definitely one of them.

I scrub a hand over my jaw, knowing I should've shut this down earlier. But by then, I was already in too deep.

I exhale, shaking the thought away.

I pull out my phone, typing out a quick message to Cam. Who, let's be real, is doing anything but sleeping.

Me: This was a bad idea. Still with Rachel?

Cam: Nope, watching Netflix. Might just crash.

I roll my eyes. Bullshit. I hesitate, thumb hovering over the screen before I type.

Me: Any news on the Owens' shit?

Cam: ... waiting on one thing to come back, then I'll have your answers.

Are you going to have some fun with Raven?

I stare at the text, my jaw clenching. I type out my response and hit send without another thought.

Me: No.

Cam: Right.

Cam: ... make good choices

As I move through the house, I make a conscious effort not to make too much noise.

Which is fucking ridiculous. Why the hell do I feel like a thief in my own house?

But here I am, tiptoeing around like an intruder, as if someone's about to catch me red-handed.

On my way upstairs, I check the security system, make sure everything's locked, running through the same routine I've had for years. It's muscle memory at this point. Especially after what happened earlier.

Once in my room, I grab my stuff and brush my teeth. Can't risk hauling too much downstairs and raising suspicion. The last thing I need is to out myself because I left a damn toothbrush in plain sight.

That would be next-level fucking idiotic. Security expert, exposed by a toothbrush.

Heading back down, I shake my head, chuckling quietly to myself. I really do feel like I'm sneaking around... what the hell has my life become?

Back in my *room for the night*, I sink into the chair by the window, the weight of the day settling in my chest.

I've learned a few things about Raven tonight. She's playful when she lets her guard down. And she's the single biggest test of my self-control I've ever fucking encountered.

Who would've guessed that washing dishes would be the thing to finally pull that side of her out? Certainly not me.

I exhale slowly, rubbing a hand over my jaw.

I wasn't planning on doing anything. I told myself I'd behave. But then she looked at me like that, all fire and defiance.

And then she ran.

And God help me, the thoughts that flashed through my head were not those of a man trying to keep his distance.

I'd like to think I'm a gentleman, but even I have my limits. This entire situation has my cock so hard it's almost painful. What I wouldn't give to just bend her over the counter. I groan, running a hand through my hair, forcing myself to shut it down.

But then my phone pings from the nightstand.

Saved by the fucking bell.

Another night of frustration, another raging case of blue balls. At this point, not even a cold shower can fix this.

I grab my phone, but then I see a notification from the security system. Why would the back door open?

My irritation sharpens, focus locking in. I pull up the live feed and scroll to the most recent footage.

"Well, well, well," I mutter under my breath, half-irritated.

The screen flickers, and I see Raven. Slipping out of the house. Clever girl. She didn't make a sound. Didn't set off a single alarm beyond the initial door trigger. What's even more impressive is that she used the greenhouse door to go outside. Not the most direct route, but it's discreet.

So, the little princess has a rebellious streak after all.

Very interesting.

The part that really gets me, though, is that I didn't fucking notice. I should've caught her. I should've known the second she moved. And why the *fuck* didn't the alarms go off?

I was too busy picturing all the ways I'd ruin her. Too busy imagining how she'd feel wrapped around me... thinking about what sounds she'd make when she screamed my name.

And the whole time I was busy doing that, she was slipping right out the back door. I grip my phone tighter, my jaw locking as I force myself to think past my own fucking distraction.

The real question is... where the hell is she going? Especially in this weather. Curiosity gnaws at me, a burning itch I can't ignore.

I exhale sharply, tension coiling tight in my chest. My security team mentioned that there was a breach when the storm rolled in, and I already knew tonight wasn't going to be a quiet one. Something happened, something we haven't quite figured out yet, and that has me on edge.

And now she's out in the dark, in the middle of a storm? Yeah, no. Not happening.

I grab my shoes without another thought. I'm trying to give her the benefit of the doubt, assuming she's at least got some sense not to wander too far. But rational thinking clearly went out the window the second she decided to sneak out in the middle of the goddamn night.

I know every twist and turn of this place like the back of my hand. I could navigate it blindfolded.

Raven, on the other hand, has no idea what she's walking into. Not because of the terrain, but because of what happened earlier. I doubt anyone's still out there, but I've also never had a security breach before.

I should've just taken them home, but I thought this was the safer option. Muttering a curse as I step outside, the cold air hits like a slap to the face.

Where would she go?

The only place that makes sense is the woods. She was obsessed with them earlier. She probably convinced herself she was just taking a harmless stroll

Stepping off the porch, my boots sink into a puddle of thick mud. I grit my teeth, already regretting this.

"When I find you..." I mutter under my breath, the sentence trailing off.

And then what? Yell at her? Drag her back inside?

No, I'll probably do nothing. Absolutely nothing, because the truth is, I'm not even mad. I'm fucking worried.

And maybe that's the real problem.

The wind rips my words away, barely a whisper beneath the rumble of distant thunder.

The rain's holding off for now, but the storm hasn't let up, lighting still splits the sky, and the air feels heavy, like it's holding its breath before everything breaks loose.

At least when I checked the cameras, she was wearing a hoodie, so that's something. If she heads back to the house, I'll know. For now, I know she's still out here.

I move deeper into the woods, the shadows stretching between the trees. Doubt creeps in, twisting in my gut. Did I miss her? I pause, forcing myself to stay still and listen.

The forest hums with the kind of silence that's never really silent. Leaves shift in the breeze, distant raindrops hitting branches, but underneath all that, there's something else. Some pull of a thread, that has me shifting directions. My boots sink into damp earth as I cut through the trees.

"Where are you, Princess?"

I'm halfway to the house when it hits me again. That same feeling, stubborn and unshakable. Like a pulse, tugging at me.

Instead of heading straight for the house, I veer left, angling toward the garden. The trees thin out and the faint outlines of stone pathways come into view.

Today's been a fucking roller coaster. And now she's out here, in the dead of night, with a storm at her back.

The frustration simmering inside me mixes with something else.

The rain picks up, heavier now, soaking through my shirt and dripping down my face. When I find her, we're definitely going to have some words.

It's been long enough that the knot of concern twisting in my gut feels like a fist. I can't believe she managed to sneak out of the house without me knowing, and what the fuck is going on with my system?

Just as I'm about to pull out my phone, something flickers to my right, over by the garden.

I freeze, instincts kicking in. I move closer, and there she is.

Sprawled out on the wet ground, arms spread wide, eyes fixed on the storm above like she doesn't have a single care in the world.

What the hell?

It's strange how completely at peace she looks with rain running down her face, clinging to her like she belongs there.

I pause, standing still, as thunder rolls overhead.

She doesn't hear me approach, completely lost in her world. Lightning splits the sky again, lighting up her face.

Fuck.

Ever since I met this woman, she's been a fucking enigma. The most unpredictable person I've ever met. Who in their right mind sneaks out of a castle in the middle of the night, during a raging storm, just to lay on the soaking wet ground like she belongs there?

Her hair fans around her like a wild halo, tangling with the earth beneath her. She's so still, so utterly unbothered by the storm raging above her. Like she isn't just witnessing the chaos, she's part of it.

I shake my head, a small, reluctant smirk tugging at the corners of my lips. This woman defies logic.

And they said I'm supposed to be the onion?

I take a slow step forward, scanning the sky, trying to see whatever the hell has her so mesmerized. But all I see are thick, rolling storm clouds. Not a single star in sight.

Then, lightning splits the sky. A violent, jagged streak of white-hot electricity, ripping through the dark. The thunder that follows, shakes the air with a sound so deep it feels like the earth itself is growling.

I look back down at Raven, and she's smiling.

Completely fucking absorbed.

I don't know what it is about the way she's laying there, so unshaken, so utterly in tune with the storm, but I can't take my eyes off her.

And here I am, standing in the shadows, watching her. *Well, now I just feel like a fucking creep.*

"If ye wanted to see the gardens, ye could've just said so earlier." My voice cuts through the silence. No point in just standing here like an idiot.

She lets out a startled yelp, scrambling to her feet. She raises her arm, and there's something clutched tightly in her hand, standing like she's ready for a fight.

Adrenaline spikes in my veins, instincts firing as I take a half-step forward. Fight or flight? Which is it, Princess?

But the second she sees me; her muscles relax.

"Oh, it's just you," she exhales, lowering her arm. Relief flickers over her face first. Then, instant irritation.

"Why are you sneaking up on people in the middle of the night? You're lucky I didn't stab you!"

I bite back a grin. "Stab me?" I raise an eyebrow, taking a slow step closer. "With what?"

Then I see it. She's holding a butter knife. The laugh bursts out of me before I can stop it.

"Princess," I say, between low, rumbling chuckles, "you're not going to be hurting anyone with that thing." I shake my head, still smirking. "You're better off throwing it, maybe buy yourself a few seconds to run."

She scowls, her grip tightening around the useless blade, and damn if it doesn't make me laugh harder. The visual alone is enough to make my dick instantly hard.

Soaking wet. Half-drenched clothes. Dripping hair. Standing in a thunderstorm like she's some kind of defiant goddess, armed with a butter knife.

Her expression flickers, but it's gone in an instant. Replaced by pure murder.

And I can see the exact moment she seriously considers my advice, and I swear to God, she's about to throw that fucking thing at my head.

"Why are you out here, Kane?" She demands, all sharp edges and suspicion.

I roll my shoulders, my smirk widening. "Because I li—"

CRACK.

The sky splits open, and lightning rips across the sky, so close it's blinding. Like the storm itself is cutting me off. I clamp my jaw shut, shoving the words back down. As much as I want to come clean, now is not the time.

I glance at her, hoping she didn't catch that.

Her eyes stay locked on mine, waiting. She doesn't miss a fucking thing. For a split second, I falter.

The way the storm lights up the wildness in her eyes has me completely fucking spellbound. I don't even try to hide it. There's no point. She already knows how much I want her. And it doesn't matter how much I pretend I've got a handle on it.

I don't.

She stands there, completely unbothered by the storm, staring at me like she isn't the most dangerous fucking thing in this moment. She tilts her head, eyes narrowing just slightly, something unreadable flashing across her face.

"Why are you looking at me like that?"

I blink, realizing she just said something. But my head is someplace else entirely. Fixated on how she looks right now.

Drenched and stunning.

"What?" I ask, my voice rougher than I intended, edged with something I don't want to name.

I take a step closer, the wet ground soft beneath my boots.

She doesn't move, doesn't step back. Just tilts her head up with every inch I close between us, and it hits me just how fucking small she is.

Why does that do something to me?

"I couldn't hear you," I murmur, as thunder rolls through the sky, rattling the air . The sound rumbles like a warning.

Or a fucking dare.

I lean in, watching the way her breath catches, watching the way her eyes stay locked on mine. Waiting.

"You know..." I say, voice dropping lower, "the thunder and all." The words slip out easily.

Because I can feel the tension crackling between us. Every rumble of thunder, every crack of lightning, is pulling us in.

Closer and closer.

Daring me to cross a line I know I can't come back from.

I don't know if it's the storm or if it's her, but standing here feels like standing on the edge of a cliff, and it's becoming more impossible to ignore.

My instincts scream at me to walk away. To step back, to keep the distance I've fought so hard to maintain.

And yet, every single nerve in my body is telling me to do the opposite.

She's drawing me in and it's fucking *obnoxious* how much I want to give in to it. One more step. The space between us disappears, and the shift is so subtle, so seamless.

The rain slides down her face, catching on her lips. Her eyes are still locked on mine.

I can't tell if she feels the same pull I do or if she's about to push me away.

All I know is that being this close to her, with the storm raging around us, feels like standing in the eye of the hurricane.

CHAPTER 18

In or Out of the Woods...?

RAVEN

T he storm rages around me, a steady drizzle soaking into my clothes, my skin, grounding me in a way nothing else has in years.

For once, there's nothing pulling at me. No expectations to meet. No ticking clock reminding me of what I'm supposed to be doing. Just me, wrapped in the untamed fury of the sky.

And I've never felt more alive.

I tip my head back, letting the rain slide over my face, my thoughts drifting to the necklace, to the memory of my grandmother's voice weaving through my mind.

I can almost hear it now, the way her voice would drop to a whisper during the magical parts, like we were the only two people in the world who knew the tale. Like it was meant only for us.

And yet, even as a kid, something about it frustrated me.

Why couldn't she find love? Why did she have to beg for it? The Winter Queen was powerful, capable of things most people couldn't even dream of, and yet, she was brought to her knees by the one thing she couldn't control. Her heart.

At this point in my life, though... I kind of get it.

Maybe she was better off without them.

Then again, if I'm being completely honest with myself, who's the one standing out here in the damn rain now? *Oh, hey... remember me. The problem.* There's been so many moments where I've wished for the same thing she did. That kind of real, all-consuming, soul-shaking love.

I haven't exactly had any luck in that department. But maybe that's for the best.

Still, something about the thought of having to beg the heavens for something as simple and profound as love... hits somewhere deep.

I picture her now, standing in the middle of the forest, arms stretched toward the sky, rain pouring down, mixing with her tears as she whispered her desperate prayers to the universe.

And maybe it's not so hard to imagine.

Because, in some strange way, I understand her longing. Her frustration. That deep, aching need to grasp onto something real. Something she couldn't conjure or create. Someone that would choose her back.

The wind surges around me, curling through my hair, the storm mirroring the thoughts tangling inside me.

But for the first time in a long time, I feel like I'm exactly where I'm supposed to be.

My hands slip into my pockets, fingers brushing against the smooth stones tucked away there. I've carried them around in my pockets, but I still don't know why. Now, more than ever, I really need answers.

What are they for? What do they do? Why do they sometimes feel warm, like a pulse beneath my fingertips?

I still myself, focusing on the sensation. It's stronger now, a low, steady vibration. Maybe it's because I'm outside surrounded by nature. Or maybe it's the storm.

And then there's the necklace. The memory. The stories. Why, out of nowhere, am I remembering them?

The more I think about it, the more the questions pile up, stacking like dominos with no clear answer in sight, ready to top over at any second. My chest tightens, and I feel a single tear roll down my cheek, mingling with the rain. I spread my arms out, sinking my hands into the mud.

They should be here.

My grandparents should be the ones explaining all of this to me. They always had the answers. Always knew what to say, what to do. So why did they keep me in the dark about this? Why wouldn't they tell me?

The ache in my chest spreads, a hollow, unbearable thing that twists deeper with every thought.

And then, out of nowhere, Kane's voice cuts through the storm.

Holy fuck.

The butter knife is clenched tight in my hand, but it's useless now. Nothing could've prepared me for the way he's looking at me.

His smirk is still there, but it's softened, his gaze dipping lower, taking in the sight of me standing in the rain, soaked to the bone. There's something different in his eyes. Something intentional.

"I said, why are you looking at me like that?" I snap, the words tumbling out before I can stop them. My voice is sharper than I meant it to be, edged with irritation, but I can't help it. I need the irritation, because the way my pulse is hammering isn't exactly helping my case.

Kane doesn't answer right away. His jaw tenses, his expression unreadable as ever, as he takes a step closer.

His eyes find mine, locking with an intensity that makes my stomach flip.

"I think the more important question is," he growls, the rough rasp of it cutting through the storm like a blade, "why did ye sneak out of the house and come to lay in the mud in the middle of a storm? What the hell were ye thinkin'?"

His accent is thicker now, the words gritted out, wrapping around each syllable like a warning. And it hits me hard.

The sound of his voice alone sends a shiver through me, heat coiling low in my stomach, tightening my nipples beneath my soaked clothes.

Damn him.

I shift my stance, crossing my arms over my chest as if that will somehow hide the effect he has on me. My thighs press together, and I silently curse my body for betraying me yet again.

"For your information, I didn't sneak out," I snap, my tone clipped. "You said we could *make ourselves at home*, did you not?"

I don't give him a chance to respond before the words spill out, fueled by frustration and the lingering adrenaline from thinking I was about to be attacked in the dark.

"I needed to clear my head, and I happen to love thunderstorms," I continue, lifting my chin, daring him to challenge me. The rain drips down my face, but I don't care. I'm not backing down.

"So I was doing just that. Making myself at home and enjoying nature." My breath quickens, my chest rising and falling. "If that wasn't allowed, then maybe you should have made that clear."

He doesn't say a word. Doesn't so much as blink.

247

His gaze stays locked with mine, unreadable, but I can feel the storm brewing, just as volatile as the one raging overhead.

Who does he think he is, acting like I need a babysitter? No one told me I couldn't come outside, and there sure as hell wasn't a sign warning against it. I checked.

I stood by the door, waiting, half-expecting some sort of alarm to blare the second I stepped outside. But nothing happened.

His broad frame looms over me, his presence is suffocating in a way that makes my pulse thunder in my ears. But I plant my feet, refusing to let him see how rattled I am.

The wind picks up, tossing strands of my hair into my face, and lightning splits the sky, drenching the world in white light for a heartbeat.

And still, he doesn't look away.

Finally, he exhales. The rise and fall of his shoulders almost imperceptible. "Aye, ye're right. There wasn't any rule about goin' outside, I just—"

He stops. His jaw clenches.

I don't jump into smooth things over, I don't fill the silence just because it's there. I stare him down, waiting for him to finish his damn sentence.

"I just didn't think that ye'd come outside, I guess," he mutters, like the words taste bitter on his tongue. His eyes flicker with hesitation.

My eyebrows lift, "Oh, so you didn't think I'd come outside because I'm a girl and might get dirty?"

I gesture down at myself, soaked through, mud streaking my legs, hair dripping, the very definition of a disaster.

"Hate to break it to you, but I think I've already crossed that bridge."

His gaze slowly drops down over my bare, muddy feet, slowly dragging his eyes back up.

A low, amused chuckle rumbles from his chest, he sound curling around me like a lazy flame. "Umm... no?" He almost sounds like he's questioning his own damn response.

His tone sounds unsure, but amused, and I hate that it makes my stomach flip.

I catch the flicker of a smile tugging at the corner of his lips, and damn him, because it's doing more damage to my resolve than anything else he could've said.

There's curiosity in his eyes now, like he's trying to figure me out.

"Probably because it's the middle of the night, in a place ye've never been, in a country ye're not from, and it's—" he gestures upward, his hands cutting through the air toward the storm-filled sky, "well, *this*."

His voice is dripping with frustration, but there's something else there, too, something quieter beneath the sharp edges.

He runs his hand through his hair, messy and wild from the rain, droplets clinging to the strands as they tumble over his forehead. The movement feels unguarded, yet entirely him.

And just when I think he's about to walk away, he stops mid-step. When he turns back, something shifts. His expression hardens, sharp and predatory in a way that steals the air from my lungs.

It's that look again, the one that sends a shiver racing down my spine, pooling low in my stomach.

His eyes pierce through me, but beneath it, restraint. And somehow, that's more dangerous than the storm around us.

The air crackles, with tension that has nothing to do with the lightning overhead.

His fists clench at his sides, then relax, then clench again. Like he's fighting something. The slow, deliberate breath he takes is measured, his chest rising and falling in a way that tells me exactly how hard he's working to stay in control. He doesn't speak, but his stare is relentless, dragging over me like a physical touch, unraveling something inside me that I don't fully understand.

My breath catches, my skin humming with awareness under the weight of it. And as much as I hate myself for it... it turns me on. It's like Niagara fucking Falls with him.

"I didn't think about any of those things, if you want to know the truth," I admit, my voice quieter than I intend, rolling my eyes to cover the unease creeping into my throat. My arms drop to my sides, no longer a defensive shield between us. I look away, trying to ignore the heat licking up my spine.

"I just needed to be outside." The words slip free, almost lost beneath the distant thunder.

The admission feels like a mistake the second it leaves my lips. It's too open. Too raw. And I hate that I feel the need to explain myself to him. But it's too late to take it back now.

I force myself to meet his gaze again, hoping my face doesn't betray the storm raging inside me. A storm he seems to have complete control over right now.

He runs his hand through his hair again, rain-soaked strands falling across his forehead, and I catch a flicker of something unguarded before he slips his mask back on.

Then he's right there, towering over me. Close enough to steal the air straight from my lungs.

He's too close. And not close enough.

His tension rolls off him in waves, crashing against me, mingling with the storm's wild electricity. My skin prickles, every nerve attuned to him. And I've never wanted anything more than I want him right now.

His hand brushes my face, his fingertips grazing my cheek so lightly I question whether he touched me at all.

"I am out here, Princess," he says, teasing me. "Because I was worried that you might be…" He pauses, his lips twitching like he's fighting a grin. "Out here, minding your own business, enjoying your holiday, and then, out of nowhere, the ground attacks you."

His voice drops lower, amusement glinting in his dark eyes. Oh, this cocky, smug bastard.

"You know, twist your ankle or something princess-like."

I arch a brow, refusing to let him have the upper hand. Kane, the ever brooding, infuriating Highlander, who always looks like he's one bad mood away from breaking someone's face, is rambling.

And it's adorable in a way that makes my stomach clench.

He keeps talking, his fingers still grazing my cheek, but I'm not listening anymore. His voice is a hum in the background now, drowned out by the heat of his touch.

"Then ye'd need help back to the castle," he mutters, his accent curling around each word, rich and extremely dangerous for all my lady parts.

"Can't have ye go missin' on my watch. It'll give us a bad name."

His thumb brushes my cheek.

I doubt he even realizes he's doing it. He's still too busy rambling about my ankle and imaginary distress.

But all I can focus on is his touch.

His presence is suffocating in a way that makes me want to drown in it. My body, on the other hand, has stopped giving a single damn about logic.

It doesn't care about castles, or storms, or even my self-control.

All it wants is him.

And I know *with humiliating certainty,* that if his hand drifted any lower, he'd feel exactly what he's doing to me.

The aching tension between my thighs and the pulse that refuses to be ignored. It's all-consuming. And I don't know how much longer I can fight it. My mind is losing ground to the pull of him, to the way his gaze darkens like he knows exactly how close I am to unraveling.

I glance up at him, trying to make sense of the shadows playing across his face, the intensity coiling in his muscles, but he's impossible to read.

His expression is carved from stone, and yet, his body is telling a different story. His fists clench and relax at his sides as if he's at war with himself.

"You were worried about me?" My voice is quiet the teasing edge slipping away before I can catch it.

His entire body stiffens.

The storm overhead is nothing compared to the one brewing in his eyes as they lock onto mine.

"And yer wee ankles," he mutters.

Before I can decide whether to laugh or shove him, his lips crash into mine.

It's not gentle. It's not sweet. It's ravenous and desperate.

The force of it knocks the breath from my lungs, a needy whimper escaping before I can stop it. The second it leaves my lips, he groans, like it's the only sound he's been waiting for.

His hands are everywhere at once, gripping, pulling, owning. The one cradling my face slides into my hair, his fingers tangling at the nape of my neck as he tilts my head back, claiming full control over the kiss.

His tongue teases and dominates. Shockwaves slam down my spine, every bit of resistance shattering under the weight of his touch.

And I fucking melt.

251

My fingers dig into his soaked shirt, desperate and hungry. There's no other way to handle him, to keep up with the storm he's unleashing between us.

He growls into my mouth, his teeth graze my bottom lip, his grip tightening, anchoring me in place.

My body presses into his, chasing the friction, needing more. A chuckle rumbles through his chest as his hands slip lower, gripping my waist with an ease that's both possessive and claiming.

His mouth trails along my jaw, his breath searing against my damp skin and then his lips hover at my ear. "Ye kiss like you've been waitin' for me," he murmurs.

Cocky bastard.

"Maybe I have," I whisper, but the words aren't a lie.

His hold on me tightens.

Fuck.

That was the wrong thing to say. Or was it the right thing?

Because his hands are suddenly gripping my ass, lifting me like I weigh nothing, pressing me flush against his body.

And I feel him. All of him. The hard, thick length pressing against my core, the only barrier is our soaked clothing.

A gasp tears from my throat as the friction sends a jolt of pleasure spiraling through me, making me arch into him.

"Christ," he mutters, his head dropping to my shoulder as he exhales a ragged breath. His grip tightens for a moment, as if he's on the verge of losing control.

My nails sink into his back, needing him to. He doesn't move, so instead, I slowly rock against him. His whole body stiffens, and then his teeth sink into my shoulder. Just enough to remind me exactly who I'm playing with.

A strangled moan slips from my lips, and his hands flex against me, like he's fighting every primal instinct clawing at his resolve.

For a second, I think he's going to give in. His lips brush my ear, hot and heavy with wanting. "Ye keep doin' that, and I won't stop."

I clench my thighs together and he must see it on my face, because his smirk sharpens into something lethal.

But then he pulls back. The loss of him is a shock to my system.

He releases me so fast my knees nearly buckle, and the bastard catches me before I can fall.

His smirk deepens, and I should be pissed. I should shove him, call him out, demand why he's always playing this game. But all I can think about is how fucking much I need him to touch me.

Despite the rain pouring down, my skin burns under his touch, every sensation magnified. I'm drowning in him, completely consumed.

He pulls back just enough to stare down at me, his eyes dark and unreadable, his breath uneven.

For a moment, I swear the shadows around us shift. Then just like that it's gone, and I shake off the thought.

Needing him closer, I pull him to me. My lips crash into his, fingers threading into his soaked hair, dragging him closer.

His hands are on me in an instant. Meeting me with the same raw hunger. My tongue tangles with his, chasing that fire he's igniting in every nerve of my body.

The thunder overhead blurs with the storm raging between us, the rain sliding over our bodies. Lightning strikes close by the flash is so blinding, it feels like the air itself shatters. The deafening boom that follows rips through me, snapping me back to reality.

I stumble back, gasping, my chest heaving and my pulse pounding in my ears.

"Come on!" He takes my hand. His voice is commanding, cutting through the chaos as we run for cover.

I don't hesitate.

The rain falls harder, but Kane doesn't let go. The canopy offers some relief, but it doesn't matter, we're soaked. My hoodie clings to me, the cold rain a cruel contrast to the heat still coursing through my veins.

I lean against a tree, catching my breath. A soft laugh escapes me, the sound spilling out before I can stop it.

Kane stands close, his chest rising and falling. Then, to my surprise, he laughs, too.

It's infuriating how good he looks right now. Loose, wild strands of hair frame his sharp jaw, dripping with rain.

The emotional whiplash from our rain-soaked dash, mixed with the way he kissed me, leaves me wrecked in every sense of the word.

This man is driving me absolutely insane.

Always pushing my buttons, getting under my skin, twisting me into knots. Successfully, I might add.

Yet, he was the one who kissed me. And fuck, what a kiss. For the first time in a long while, I feel... free.

I look up at him as he runs his hands through his hair, pushing the rain-soaked strands back from his face. My breath hitches, caught somewhere between awe and complete fucking destruction.

Without thinking, my gaze dips to his mouth, and I catch myself licking my lips.

Big mistake.

His eyes snap to my mouth, tracking the movement, lingering just long enough that my pussy throbs in response.

When his gaze drifts back to mine, the intensity in his expression is predatory.

My pulse is hammering as his jaw tightens. "*Princess.*"

Neither of us move.

His voice alone should be illegal.

But I straighten my spine, refusing to let him see how wrecked I already am. How much I want him to keep pushing me, pulling me into his orbit.

I roll my eyes, "What? What did I do now?"

His expression hardens, his frustration cutting through his usual amusement. He gestures broadly to the raging storm around us, his voice sharpening, low and irritated.

"This. This is why you bein' outside was a bad idea."

I blink at him. "Are you serious right now?"

Then, before I can think better of it, I take a step back, straight into the rain. Cold droplets instantly drench my skin, but the sensation is exhilarating.

His brows furrow. "What the hell are ye doin' now?"

I grin over my shoulder, rain streaming down my face.

"This doesn't feel like a bad idea at all."

Tilting my head back, I close my eyes and let the storm consume me.

"It feels more like everything is being washed away," I murmur. "A fresh start." My voice softens, barely audible over the thunder. "I can't think of a better place to be than right here, in the middle of a thunderstorm."

My fingers brush over the smooth stones in my pocket, they're warm again. That same faint buzz, pulsing against my fingertips, tugging at something deep inside me.

I snap my eyes open to find Kane watching me. His gaze, as always, is unreadable. A sliver of embarrassment flickers through me. I've said too much, let him see too much.

I shake it off, schooling my features back into playful confidence.

"Never mind," I mutter.

The flicker of confusion in his eyes is brief, but then his expression shifts. Almost concerned.

And for some reason, that makes my chest tighten. Needing to shift the conversation, I smirk and motion toward the rain.

"Come out here!"

He stares at me like I've lost my mind. Then he sighs, before stepping forward looking like a man walking into battle, not rain.

"I'm wet enough, thank you," he grumbles, but there's amusement laced through the words.

Even soaked to the bone, he moves with purpose and control.

"Don't be a baby, Kane," I taunt. "Get out here, already."

The storm surges around us, but all I can focus on is him. The way his shirt clings to his body, the way he carries himself, even now, like he's barely restraining something raw, and dangerous.

He steps closer, now towering over me, droplets of water sliding down his face, catching his lashes. His dark eyes narrow. "What for?"

I swallow, pulse spiking. "Because I want to stand out here longer," I grin up at him. "And I don't want to get struck by lightning!"

He blinks, looking confused, "What?"

I take a slow step closer, daring him. "You're practically a leprechaun, which means you're lucky! And I don't want to get struck by lightning."

His entire body goes still.

The look he gives me is priceless. Like he's genuinely debating whether I've officially lost my mind or if I've just confirmed all his suspicions about me.

Then, to my absolute surprise, he bursts out laughing. Like I just shook something loose inside him.

I don't think I've ever seen him laugh like this. And it's completely devastating. How is that even possible?

Mental note, *I need to start finding things wrong with Kane.*

"You know leprechauns are Irish, right?" He finally manages, running a hand through his soaked hair, still smirking.

"Doesn't Scotland have its own version of a leprechaun?"

I glance over my shoulder and catch him mirroring me with his shoulders squared to the rain. Arms crossed. Like this is perfectly normal.

I can't help but giggle.

His head tilts, just watching me.

"Why don't you try it? You don't have to do anything," I murmur. "Just feel."

I turn back to face the storm, closing my eyes, breathing in the rain. There's something about this place that feels alive. I've felt drawn here for years, always wanting to come because of my grandparents. But now that I'm here, everything about this place feels like magic.

"Sometimes I close my eyes, just to listen. Or I just take it all in. Every sound, every breath, every flicker of light."

I hesitate, then sneak a glance at him, peeking with one eye to gauge his reaction. This is usually where people start looking at me like I've lost my damn mind.

Maybe an internal *Is this woman completely coo-coo for cocoa puffs?...* or a *How do I back away without making it awkward?*

But Kane doesn't do either.

I pride myself on being able to read people. Their words might be polished, filtered bullshit. But faces don't lie, they always give something away.

Yet Kane's isn't giving anything away.

Then, without warning, he closes his eyes and tilts his face up toward the rain. Is he... actually doing it?

My jaw nearly drops, a stunned laugh bubbling up, but before it escapes, he cracks one eye open, his eyebrow raised in a playful challenge.

"What?" His voice is low and teasing. "Am I doing it wrong?"

I'm completely floored. My brain scrambles for words, "Uh... no. You're... doing great."

Fantastic recovery, Raven. Absolutely award-winning. Heat rushes to my face, and I whip my head back toward the storm.

Who cares if he's standing next to you? Or that his muscles are on full display, looking like every reckless decision I've ever wanted to make. Or that we just made out?

I take a slow breath, letting the storm anchor me. The low rumble of thunder rolls through the air, a perfect distraction from the man currently taking up far too much space in my brain.

I let myself feel all of it. The storm. The pull of this place. And even the beautiful, annoying man standing beside me.

Minutes pass or maybe it was just seconds. But my heart finally steadies. My thoughts are no longer spinning out of control.

I open my eyes, and of course, he's staring at me, again. My pulse skips. "What? How did it go? Did you feel anything?"

I'm half expecting him to shrug it off, to dodge with some sarcastic comment, but part of me wonders if he actually tried it. *Detective Raven is officially on the case.*

At first, he looks like he's going to brush it off, his eyes flicking to the trees. But then, something about his expression shifts. "I felt... weird at first," he admits, his voice quieter than I expect. "But then... I felt this buzzing in the air, like it was under my skin somehow. And the rain on my face, it was... refreshing."

I blink, and for a second, I don't even know what to say. *Did he actually mean that?* Kane, the man who treats emotions like a liability, just admitted something that sounded almost poetic.

Before I can process it fully, he surprises me again by continuing. "When I closed my eyes, it was like I could feel every drop of rain, every gust of wind. There was this energy in the air. The sound of the rain, the rumble of the thunder. It felt alive, like everything around me was breathing."

He pauses, his eyes meeting mine with a rare openness. "There's a lot you can feel about this place, but I can't say I've ever experienced that."

I stare at him, floored that he just said that. "Are you sure you didn't hit your head out here?"

He huffs out a laugh, shaking his head. "Why? Because I said something deeper than 'pass the salt'?"

"Basically." I smirk, tilting my head. "I don't know, Kane, you might have a poet's soul under all that broody intimidation."

He exhales sharply, like he's already regretting saying anything. "Or maybe I was just standing in the rain like an idiot and got caught up in the moment."

"Oh no, don't backtrack now," I tease, nudging his arm. "You were two seconds away from writing a sonnet about the storm."

He narrows his eyes, but his lips twitch. "Aye, well, don't let it go to yer head, Princess."

I can't stop the grin from forming, "Too late."

For a fleeting moment, he's not just the cocky, infuriating man who kisses like he owns the air I breathe. He's thoughtful, charming... maybe even a little funny.

But perfect or not, he's also a man. With a penis. A very nice one, probably. Not that I'm going to think about that.

Kane equals *friend zone* for life.

I fold my arms over my chest and let out a slow breath, trying to steady the mess of emotions swirling inside me. I need to remember the rules I've set for myself, even if this storm, and this man, seem hellbent on washing them away.

CHAPTER 19

CHAOS

KANE

I'm not going to make it.

This woman has me completely fucked.

First, I wanted to wring her neck for sneaking out in the middle of a goddam storm, making my heart nearly stop when I thought of something happening to her. Then, when I found her, the relief hit me so hard it knocked the fucking air out of my lungs. And I'm still trying to pretend that didn't happen.

And of course, she couldn't just leave it at that. No, she had to call me out for accusing her of sneaking out. And the worst part was, she was right. I'll give her that.

Then, she had me standing in the rain with my eyes closed, *feeling* the goddamn forest, like some lovesick fool.

And the worst fucking part is that it worked.

For the first time in years, I felt something. But it wasn't the storm that unraveled me, it was her.

My hands curl into fists at my sides, the urge to taste her again is strong. She's under my skin, twisting me up in ways I can't explain, and I don't like it. No matter how much I tell myself to back off, she keeps pulling me back in.

She's looking at me now like she's peeling back layers; dismantling walls I've spent years building. And it's fucking unnerving.

Hell, she's a lot of things. But the one thing she isn't? Mine.

And that makes her completely off-limits. I can't let her in any deeper than she already is.

Then, something flickers in her eyes. A vulnerability so fleeting I almost miss it. But just as fast, she buries it, slamming the door shut with that guarded mask she wears like armor. And it should be enough of a warning of exactly why I need to stay the hell away.

Because she's a master at keeping people out. And I can't afford to get tangled up in whatever she's hiding.

"Time to go back inside," I say, trying to put distance between us.

She tilts her head, pretending to look annoyed, but I catch the flicker of amusement in her eyes. "Are you just saying that so you can get out of the rain?"

My cock twitches in response, but the moment's passed, and I force my body to settle.

"No," I pause, watching her expression shift, softening just a fraction before I add, "It's late, and you've been out in the cold for a while."

Her mouth parts, and I can see the spark of defiance flaring in her eyes, the battle lines forming in her mind. She's seconds from arguing, already preparing her counter.

"Come on, Princess," I cut in, smirking before she can push back. "I'll make ye some hot chocolate."

Her eyes narrow slightly, and I swear I can see her brain process. Chocolate. That was the key.

A flicker of hesitation before her shoulders drop, just enough that I catch it.

"Fine. Lead the way," she mutters, crossing her arms but falling into step beside me.

I take a faster route back toward the castle, but she's watching me, her brows furrowing.

"How do you know where you're going?"

I stiffen, "This is the way I came." Technically, not a lie. But definitely not the full truth.

She studies me for a second longer, like she's trying to piece something together, but thankfully, she doesn't press further.

The silence between us grows heavy with things neither of us are willing to say. The storm is still there, but it feels distant now.

When we finally reach the back door, I push it open, letting the warmth of the kitchen spill over us. She steps inside without hesitation, and I trail after her, locking the door behind us.

She heads straight for the counter, practically bouncing into the seat like the cold never touched her. It's the most relaxed I've seen her, and for some reason, it makes me smile.

"You should get out of those wet clothes," I tell her. "Hang them in front of the fire in your room, there's a robe in the bathroom."

Her lips purse like she's considering arguing, but then she nods. "I can do that," she says, standing quickly.

And just like that, she's gone, bouncing down the hall like she didn't just spend the last hour in the rain, challenging the gods themselves.

I exhale a breath I didn't realize I was holding before stepping toward the stove. I got through the motions of making the hot chocolate, heating the milk, adding the cocoa powder, sugar, and a touch of vanilla. The scent fills the room, but my mind isn't on the damn drink.

Thinking about the moment in the rain, with her standing there, chin tipped up, fire flashing in her eyes as she stood her ground.

It was hot as fuck.

There aren't many people who dare to do that. Who would look me in the eye and call me out. And it only makes me want her more.

And what's worse is, she won't back down. Not that I'm trying to intimidate her, but let's be honest, I'm intimidating. That's the point. Yet this woman doesn't seem to have a back-down button.

I grip the counter, jaw clenching as I try to push the thought away. I'm trying to be respectful. Trying to keep my hands to myself. For her sake.

I know exactly what would've happened if we'd stayed out there a second longer. If the storm hadn't snapped me out of it. I would've had her against that tree, her legs wrapped around me, her nails digging into my back as I—

I cut that thought off before I lose the last shred of restraint I have left. My cock is already hard enough to break through steel, and I don't need to make it worse.

She chooses right then to walk in, damp and barefoot, wearing a robe.

The tie at her waist is cinched tight, but it doesn't fucking matter. My brain is already stripping it off, imagining how easy it would be to pull the knot loose, let it pool at her feet, and take what I've been craving since the moment she walked into my life.

263

"Here, sit down." I set the steaming mug in front of her. And because I'm already too far gone, I set a chocolate chip cookie next to it.

Her gaze lifts to mine, those big, dangerous eyes going wide with surprise and she fucking lights up.

"My cookie!!! You remembered!" She beams, suspicion flickering through her delight. "Wait, when did you have time to make cookies?"

I chuckle, leaning back against the counter, watching the way her whole body reacts to something so small. "Found them over there."

Technically true.

She doesn't need to know that I had someone make them earlier and bring them over. She doesn't need to know I would've made her fifty fucking cookies just to see that look again. And why the fuck do I feel like I need to shield her from the world? And at the same fucking time... why do I want to bend her over the counter?

I'm losing my goddamn mind.

She takes a bite of her cookies, and a satisfied moan slips out, and I swear to God, I almost black the fuck out.

I grip the counter hard enough to crack it. My fingers twitch with the need to grab her, to make her moan like that for something other than a goddamn cookie.

"Oh my God," she mumbles around a second bite. "This cookie is amazing."

She talks through a mouthful, completely oblivious to what she's doing to me.

I exhale slowly, forcing my body to stay in check. I want her. And yet, there's one massive, glaring issue. She has no fucking clue who I really am.

"Raven, there's something I—"

But before I can get the words out, Cam strolls into the kitchen, stretching and yawning like he just rolled out of bed.

Fucking perfect timing.

"I *knew* I smelled cookies!" He declares, making a beeline for the counter. His grin widens when he spots the cocoa. "Aw man, and cocoa too? You really *do* love me," he adds, patting his chest with exaggerated appreciation.

I grind my teeth. Not sure why the hell I'm irritated.

Raven shakes her head, still smiling. "Try one, they are amazing."

Cam narrows his eyes at me, gaze dipping to my still-damp clothes before shooting back up. His brows climb high, his expression shifting into exaggerated shock.

"Why are you wet?" His tone is loaded. Then he pauses, glancing between us with a slow, shit-eating grin. "Wait... you actually..." He gestures wildly, making the implication painfully obvious.

Raven reacts first. Her eyes widen for half a second before she turns on him, sharp as ever.

"Oh my God, *Cam*! No, we did not fuck," she rolls her eyes. "And for the record, none of your business."

Cam barks out a laugh, throwing his head back like this is the best entertainment he's had all week. I shake my head.

It's rare to see Cam caught off guard. But Raven knocks him off his pedestal like it's her personal mission. Watching his jaw drop as he looks between us is pure gold. A chuckle escapes me. His expression shifts from shock to amusement, and I know he's gearing up for something.

"You know," Cam starts, his grin returning in full force, "I don't know what's more surprising, Raven turning you down or the fact that you're laughing. Should I be concerned? Is the world ending?"

Raven smirks, leaning her elbows on the counter. "Relax, Cam. The world's safe. For now."

Cam let's out another laugh. "Alright, Kane, seriously. Did you slip and fall on the way here?"

I hold his gaze, "Yeah. Right over your pile of bullshit."

He laughs, swiping another cookie, taking a slow, exaggerated bite, groaning dramatically. "God, I've missed these."

My pulse stutters. My grip on the counter tightens.

Shit.

Rachel shuffles into the kitchen, looking half-asleep but fully ready for chaos. Her eyes dart straight to me, narrowing slightly as she takes in my still-drenched clothes. Then, she scans the room.

"I'm *so* glad everyone's awake," she says, dripping with sarcasm.

Without hesitation, she heads straight for Cam and snatches his cookie right out of his hand before plopping down on the stool beside Raven.

"Wait, we have hot chocolate, too?" Her eyes lighting up like this is the best thing that's ever happened to her.

Cam groans, "That was my cookie, woman!"

Rachel doesn't even blink. "Possession is nine-tenths of the law, Cameron." She takes a slow smug bite. "Mmmm, these are delightful."

Rachel is both a blessing and a goddamn problem. Because now, there's zero chance I'll get Raven alone again tonight. I grab another mug and slide it toward Rachel, who hums in satisfaction as she takes it.

Cam, still not over his loss, turns back to Raven. "So why were you outside in the first place?"

Before she can answer, Rachel cuts in without hesitation. "She was probably laying in the rain somewhere." She waves a hand like it's the most obvious thing in the world.

Cam raises a brow, staring between them like they've lost their minds. "Laying in the rain?" He repeats, like he's trying to understand the logic.

I lean against the counter, "Aye, but thank God her ankle survived."

Raven snorts, shooting me a glare that could flay skin. And fuck if that doesn't make me want to kiss her again.

"That's exactly why I was outside, actually. And it was epic," Raven fires back, rolling her eyes. "Kane here, thought I was sneaking out to snoop through the garden or meet up with some bandit in the night."

"A bandit in the night?" I bark out a laugh. *Where the fuck does this woman come up with this shit?*

But she plows forward like I never spoke. "So" she continues, her tone smug as hell, "he decided to follow me outside and *sneak up on me*. He's lucky I didn't stab him. It rained, we got soaked, and then we came back inside."

She's grinning now, clearly pleased with herself. She forgot to mention a few details, but I'll let it slide. Details like her moaning into my mouth. And the way she melted against me. Like the way her thighs clenched when I—

I force my grip to loosen on the counter, exhaling slowly. Not the time.

She also conveniently glossed over the part where she wanted more. But that's fine. Let her pretend.

She's not mine. That fact alone should be enough to kill whatever this is. But it's not doing anything other than make me want her more.

Cam chuckles, shaking his head, "Why is it you're always finding trouble?" His teasing grin makes her roll her eyes, but I don't miss the way her cheeks flush just a little.

Before she can say anything, Rachel cuts in. "Um... Kane, gross. We don't follow people into the woods. *Bad.*" She wags her finger at me like I'm a fucking golden retriever.

Cam bursts out laughing, slamming a hand on the counter. "Oh my God, you guys are fuckin' hilarious. How long are you staying again?" He turns to me, his eyes sharp with mischief. "Can we keep them?"

I shake my head, but his question lingers in my mind. *How long are they staying?*

Raven doesn't answer. She doesn't even look up. She just focuses on her cookie, pretending to be so intrigued by each chocolate chip. But I see the slight blush creeping up her neck. And that tiny, almost imperceptible smile tugging at the corner of her lips? It's a goddamn weapon.

Cam and I have a meeting tomorrow about a case, so we're having it in the ring. And after that kiss? I've got more than enough fucking steam to blow off. And I already know he's gonna give me hell for it.

Rachel stretches, letting out a dramatic sigh. "Well, thanks for the cookie and hot chocolate," she announces, already moving toward the door. "I still have a headache, so I'm going back to bed. See you in the morning."

She hands Cam her half-eaten cookie before disappearing down the hall and Raven jumps up like the building is on fire.

"Night," she mutters, trailing after Rachel without so much as a glance in my direction.

I watch her go, my smirk deepening. *You can run all you want, Princess.*

Once the girls are out of earshot, Cam elbows me hard, his grin downright infuriating.

"Sooo..." He drags the word out, leaning in. "What's going on with you two?"

His brows lift like he's been waiting all night to ask that question. I roll my eyes, no point in lying. "We didn't do anything."

Cam lets out a low whistle, leaning back in his chair with a grin. "Ahh, so the ring then, aye?"

"As soon as we drop them off, aye." I nod.

"And the breach?" His voice drops slightly. "Still nothing?"

Tension coils in my chest, but I shake my head. "Tomorrow."

His jaw tightens, but he nods.

I clap him on the back before pushing off my chair. "I'll see you in the ring."

Cam lets out a low chuckle, looking down the hall. "You're fucked, mate."

CHAPTER 20

Afterglow

RAVEN

5:35 A.M. Too early to function. Too late to force myself back to sleep.

With a sigh, I roll onto my back, already regretting my decision to work. I know I need to message... Jordan? No, maybe it was John?

Ugh whoever it is, I'm sure he's expecting a reply.

If I had an official title, I guess you could call me a marketing director. Translation, I'm really fucking good at having ideas and helping people.

It all started when my social media blew up, and suddenly, people wanted to hire me to teach them how to market their business. At first, it was fun getting creative, watching people grow. But then it became a full-time job with all the stress and none of the freedom I used to love.

So I sold the company, and it was the best decision I ever made. Now, I get to take on projects when I want to. On my own terms.

Which brings me to the pain in the ass currently filling my inbox.

The guy I'm meeting with... Josh? Jake? *Shit*. I really need to figure that out.

He's under the impression that he's interviewing me on behalf of my *boss* to see if they'd be interested in partnering with our company. From his emails, though, he's already coming across as a little too pushy for my taste.

Hopefully, he's less irritating in person.

Technically, my boss, Steven, wants me to meet with this guy, but he left the final call up to me.

"It's your company anyway." He'd said right before I got on the plane.

"If you keep saying shit like that, I'm going to help Ashley buy this company out from under you. It's your company for a reason, quit trying to give it back. But yes, I'll help you." I told him.

I groan internally, already annoyed that I volunteered for this. And honestly? I don't think we need this guy or his company at all, but it's no longer *my company*.

Opening my inbox, I spot them immediately. Three new messages from *Mike*.

Close enough.

The first email asks, *again*, which day we're meeting, even though I already told him two emails ago that I was free any of the next three days and asked him to choose.

The second email repeats, word for word, what he wants to discuss. Because apparently, saying it twice is going to make me care more.

But the third email? Oh, the third email is the real gem.

Apparently, he's *not thrilled* about being *left in the dark* since it has been more than *forty-eight* hours since he's heard from me and has kindly informed me that if I need to reschedule, I can do so through his secretary.

Oh, Mike.

Sweet, pushy, can't-read-an-email Mike.

I stare at the email for a long second, debating whether I should respond now or wait until I've had caffeine.

Better yet... maybe I just won't respond at all.

I'm so tempted to fire off a reply telling him there's no need to reschedule. But technically, that isn't my call. Even though Steven made it painfully clear that it actually is.

I sigh, cracking my knuckles before typing out a very professional, totally appropriate response to Meathead Mike.

> Good morning, Mike,
>
> As much as I would love to reschedule, I regret to inform you that after your inability to read all three emails where I explicitly gave you the dates you're looking for. And your remarkable lack of patience ...

I paused, smirking as I reread it.

Okay, so it's not the most professional move. But damn, does it feel good to type it out. I sit there for a second, reveling in my imaginary satisfaction, before rolling my eyes and deleting the entire thing.

Not my company anymore.

But I'm the one who's stuck dealing with him.

With a resigned sigh, I settle in and type out a much more professional, painfully polite email:

> Good morning,
>
> Thank you for your patience. I apologize for any
> confusion regarding the day and time of our meeting.
> As I mentioned, I'm available any time before
> Wednesday for our interview. Please let me know what
> works best for you.
>
> Best regards,
> R. Taylor

I hit send, feeling a wave of relief for handling it like a responsible adult, despite the very real temptation to tell him off.

I lean back against the pillow, letting out a long sigh. Ten minutes with Magic Mike, and I already feel drained.

The one silver lining is that after this meeting, I won't have to check my email for nearly a month. Small wins.

Sliding out of bed, I step into the bathroom and brace my hands on the sink, staring at my reflection. No visible evidence that we kissed last night. And yet, for a split second, I half-expected to see some subtle clue staring back at me, screaming *guilty*.

I splash some cold water on my face, but the thought lingers.

Rachel already knows, I'm sure of it. The second she sees me; she'll demand every last detail. And, God help me, I'm not even sure I want to tell her.

Drying my face with a towel, I wander over to the window. The view outside is breathtaking. The sun is just waking up, spilling a soft glow across the grounds, the faint sound of birds chirping filtering through the glass. Everything sparkles, still slick and dewy from last night's storm.

Without thinking, I step into the hallway. It's too early for anyone else to be up, and if I can just make it outside without running into *him*, I'll call it a win.

The thought of Kane has me biting back a groan.

Gorgeous, annoying Kane. The Highlander God I was more than willing to climb last night. Unfair doesn't even begin to cover it.

The castle is blissfully quiet as I tiptoe through the halls, the only sounds coming from the birds outside.

When I finally step into the garden, I pause, my breath catching at the sight before me. The space feels like a different world in the light of day. Last night, it was wild and stormy, now it's soft and serene. The flowers glisten with leftover rain, their petals glowing under the sun's warmth.

I catch sight of a lake, perfectly still in the early morning light, its surface shimmering like glass. Just off to the side, a massive old tree stands tall, its branches stretching wide. There's a tree swing swaying slightly in the breeze.

Naturally, I have to check it out.

I start toward the tree, when my phone buzzes in my pocket. Of course. I turned notifications back on for *dear old Mike,* so I wouldn't leave him waiting.

For a moment, I consider ignoring it. The swing is calling my name, but halfway there, I decide to stop.

I know if I make it to that swing, his email will be the last thing on my mind. And knowing Mike, I'll have eight more unread messages by then.

Not today, Satan.

Rolling my eyes, I pull out my phone and open the email, bracing for whatever he's conjured up this time.

I'm being petty, but I'll feel bad about it later.

Mike wants to meet *today.*

"*Of course* you do, Meathead Mike," I mutter under my breath, startling a squirrel.

"I bet *your* life isn't full of pushy emails," I add dryly as scurries up a tree, blissfully ignorant of my rant.

A soft cough sounds behind me, startling me.

Shit.

Turning, I find Kane standing there, arms crossed and looking entirely too amused.

"Are you following me? Again?" I give him my best unimpressed look. "You know what they say about stalkers..."

"Last night there was a storm, and your safety was in jeopardy." The smirk tugging at his lips is hard to miss. "Thought maybe you were sleepwalking or something." he adds with a cough.

"Well, *obviously*, I'm not sleepwalking," I snap back, the words spilling out before I can stop them. "I was sightseeing. Same as last night, in fact. Why on earth would I be sleepwalking at this hour? The sun's up, for heaven's sake!"

My voice rises slightly as I realize I'm rambling, and I clamp my mouth shut.

Kane raises an eyebrow, his lips twitching like he's fighting off a grin.

"Why are you out here with no pants, heading to the lake, then? Are ye goin' for a swim?"

Shit.

"I realized you were awake when ye pulled out your phone and cursed 'Meathead Mike' to hell."

His lips curve into a smirk.

"Quite the morning?"

My cheeks burn as I glance down at my bare legs, suddenly very aware of my lack of pants. I also wouldn't have called him *Meathead Mike* if I'd known someone was listening.

Woopsie.

"Oh, uhh..." I start, feeling a bit flustered as I try to gather my thoughts.

"Not that it's any of your business," I tease, lifting a brow. "But I saw how beautiful it looked outside and... sort of got distracted."

Totally normal behavior. Nothing to see here.

"I was headed to the swing when I got a work message."

The corner of his mouth tips up, humor dancing in his eyes as he struggles to hold back another laugh.

"From 'Meathead Mike'?"

I groan. "Yes."

Moving on.

"*And*? No backstory? Come on," he presses, nodding toward the house as he falls into step beside me. "Let's go have breakfast, and ye can tell me on the way."

The swing is all but forgotten the second he says breakfast. And the reminder that I have to sit across from Meathead Mike in a few hours seals the deal. With a sigh, I match his pace, shaking my head.

"I just have a meeting with him later. He seems like a total tool. Nothing crazy."

Kane chuckles, his eyes flashing with humor as he watches me. "Ah, so that's what's got you all wound up this morning." His amusement is palpable, and I swear I can feel him cataloging every little tick of irritation, filing it away for later use.

By the time we reach the house, he pulls the door open, stepping aside like the perfect gentleman. The universe is clearly playing favorites, how does he always look so good? I suck in a small breath, completely distracted by the sight of him. And naturally, I trip.

Not a full-on face plant, thank God, but enough that my balance wobbles, and heat rushes to my cheeks. I catch myself before any real damage is done, but when I glance up, Kane's already watching me, and I can tell he's trying not to laugh.

I point a warning finger at him. "Not. One. Word."

A laugh rumbles through the air, as he raises his hands in surrender.

The kitchen smells unreal. The kind of scent that shouldn't exist this early in the morning but somehow makes being awake worth it.

I take exactly one step in before freezing. Cam's wearing an apron. Flipping something on the stove with way too much confidence.

I shoot Kane a disbelieving look, barely holding back a laugh. "Who did you say was making breakfast again?"

Kane smirks, leaning against the counter like he planned this. "I was helping. But I don't like cooking with him. He's bossy".

I snort. "Poor thing, did you get in trouble?."

Cam doesn't even turn around. "Raven, darling, you get extra bacon for that. Thank you."

I huff out a laugh, "Thanks. Is Rachel awake yet?"

Cam shakes his head, stirring something that smells like it was handcrafted by angels. "Not yet. But this might lure her out."

I laugh under my breath. "Doubt it. She sleeps like the dead. I'll go wake her up," I say, already heading down the hall, bracing myself.

When I push open the door to Rachel's room, she's exactly as I expect. Tangled in a mess of blankets, her bleary eyes barely open.

She groans dramatically, dragging the covers over her head. "My headache is gone, thanks for asking."

"Thank God." I lean against the doorframe, crossing my arms. "Hate to be the bad guy here, but I have to meet with that guy I was telling you about. So we gotta leave soon. Unless you want to stay, and I'll meet you back home later?"

Rachel peeks out just enough to glare. "Why would I stay here without you?" Her head barely lifts before she groans, sinking back into her pillow.

I sigh, "Oh, I don't know, so you could do something fun."

Her hand emerges from the blanket cocoon just far enough to flip me off, and I burst out laughing.

"For your information, I could totally handle both of them at once," she huffs, stretching. "And I could tell you all the ways it would go down, but I have Bobby. Plus, one of them seems to only have eyes for you. "She gives me a pointed look. "So he wouldn't want to play. Which is truly a shame."

I snort, shaking my head as laughter spills between us.

"That means it's time to go. But not before we eat whatever Cam's whipped up."

The mention of food is all it takes. Rachel's sleepy demeanor vanishes instantly, her face lighting up.

"Say less." She tosses off the blanket, sitting up with newfound energy. Then her eyes narrow, arms folding as she tilts her head. "All right .Quick version now. Ten-minute version when we're alone."

My stomach knots.

"I did all the things I said I did last night in the kitchen," I start, feeling my pulse pick up. Then, before I can stop myself, the words tumble out. "... and we made out. Again."

Rachel's brows hit her hairline.

"But listen," I rush on, "before you say anything, I don't like him like that. It just happened. Caught up in the moment kinda thing. It is not happening, so there's nothing to talk about."

Rachel mimes zipping her lips, then throws away the key. But her expression is nothing short of entertained.

"Ooookay," she mouths, dragging it out with exaggerated skepticism. Then, holding up both hands, she grins. "So there's a *lot* to unpack there—"

"Breakfast," I blurt, already backing out of the room.

She laughs, throwing off the covers, and getting out of bed. "Oh wow, that was subtle."

I pretend not to hear her, but I can feel her grin burning into the back of my head.

Within a millisecond of the door latching behind us back at our place, Rachel pins me with a "*Ten-minute version. Now.*"

She marches to the couch, flopping down with purpose, arms crossed.

"And don't leave *anything* out."

I sigh, rolling my eyes. No escape then. I start with the basics, recapping everything she already knows. But the second I get to the part where Kane showed up, her eyes go wide, body snapping upright like she's watching her favorite movie.

"I *knew* it!" She squeals, practically vibrating.

"Would you let me finish?" I shoot her a look, but it only makes her grin wider.

"And... he kissed me, and we made out. That's it." The words leave me before I can overthink them.

Rachel's jaw drops.

"Okay, okay, go on! But, just so you know, I *knew* it!"

She grabs a pillow, hugging it tightly to her chest like she's physically bracing for the next part.

I take a steadying breath.

"Nothing to tell, we were standing there, arguing about why I was outside, and then..." I swallow, remembering the way his body felt against mine, how his mouth took control like he was starved for it. "... before I knew it, he was kissing me."

Rachel's grin turns feral.

"Then what?! What happened next?!"

I hesitate. Just thinking about it makes my skin tingle.

God, he's such a good kisser. I push the thought away, forcing myself back on track.

"We both... kinda got lost in it. It was... confusing, to say the least."

She grins, "Sounds like you two have some serious chemistry. What's confusing about that?"

I shrug, shaking my head, feeling more vulnerable than I expected. Which is saying a lot, considering I tell Rachel everything.

"I don't know. He's so hot and cold. Half the time, he's *beyond* annoying, and then, BAM, we're having this mind-blowing, spit-swapping sesh, and... here we are." I run a hand through my hair, trying to untangle my own emotions, feeling just as confused saying it out loud as I do in my own head.

Rachel nods, her face the perfect mix of sympathy and amusement. "Are you still swearing off men?"

I take a deep breath, gathering my thoughts, and nod. "There's... a little more I need to tell you."

Her eyes light up instantly.

"Oh my God, you *totally* fucked, didn't you? I *knew* it. I bet he was amazing. He *looks* like he knows how to use his dick." She gasps dramatically, practically vibrating with excitement. "Spill. All. The. Deets. Did he choke you or was he all sweet and gentle?"

"Ew, no! Well... it definitely wouldn't be *ew*, but no, Rachel. We are done talking about Kane. This is something else." I stumble over my words like an idiot, heat rising to my cheeks. How do I even begin?

I inhale sharply. "Ever since my grandfather died, strange things have been happening..."

Might as well rip off the Band-Aid.

Rachel's smirk vanishes as I start talking. I tell her about the letters, the box, the strange things inside it, the flickering lights, the memories resurfacing like whispers in the dark.

She sits there, wide-eyed, absorbing every word. At one point, her expression shifts. I can't quite read it. Is she mad I hadn't told her sooner? A knot forms in my stomach.

"Wow. That's... a lot." Her voice is thoughtful. Then, "So, basically, you're a witch?"

"What? No! *Bitch,* were you even listening to a word I said?" I grab a pillow and chuck it at her, half-expecting it to hit her square in the face.

She ducks, laughing even harder. "Of course I was listening! But come on, it's giving witch vibes, and I'm here for it." She wiggles her brows. "Sounds like we have a lot more to dig up and figure out."

Her grin widens as she shifts forward, her excitement radiating off her.

"And secondly," she adds, holding up a finger, "I want to see everything that was in the box!"

I exhale, relief flooding through me. She's not mad. Thank God.

"Okay, let me get everything." I stand, heading for the bag where I stashed it all.

"One more thing." Her tone stops me in my tracks.

She lifts a finger, eyes locking on mine. "I'm a little upset that you didn't think to tell me this goldmine of information sooner, but I'm choosing to look past it." She tilts her head. "Because, honestly? It sounds like this is why you were supposed to come here in the first place. To figure yourself out and to have fun. So fuck you for not saying anything sooner, but also..." she shrugs, her smirk returning, "I get it."

I laugh, shaking my head. This is exactly why I love her. Brutally honest.

"Oh, and I guess another *one more thing,*" she says, waving her hands dramatically around her head. "I hear you, but you're clearly the one who needs to hear yourself. Because *all* of this—" she gestures broadly, "—witchy shit, is a fucking sign. It's staring you right in the face."

Her expression sobers for a beat, her voice turning thoughtful. "With everything so ungodly abnormal about your life, Rave, I'd say this makes the most sense. So just humor me and consider it."

And because she's Rachel, her smirk returns in full force. "Honestly? Maybe you should've fucked Kane, because some post-orgasm clarity might help you figure out what the fuck is going on around here." She wiggles her brows again. "Now, show me your shit."

Her excitement is practically vibrating off her as I grab the items and lay them out on the bed. The necklace, the dagger, and my stones.

Rachel's energy shifts instantly. The teasing fades, replaced by something almost reverent as she picks up the necklace, turning it over in her hands.

"This is beautiful," she murmurs. "And it looks... ancient."

When she reaches for the dagger, the second her fingers close around the hilt, she jerks like she's been burned.

"Holy fucking fuck!" She yelps, dropping it back onto the bed.

She stares at me, eyes wide, hand flexing like she's trying to shake off whatever just happened.

"Rave, what the hell is that? And what does it do?"

I blink. "Are you okay? What does it do?" I roll my eyes. "I imagine it pokes holes in things? Have you never seen a dagger before?"

Rachel levels me a flat look before dramatically rolling her eyes. "Okay, so let me get this straight, we have an ancient necklace, a dagger, *and* some rocks? This is like a damn treasure hunt!"

Her excitement builds with every word. "Now all we have to do is figure out what they mean and what you're supposed to do with them."

I sigh, rubbing my temples. "Yeah, that's the problem. I have no idea where to start."

Rachel opens her mouth to reply, but before she can, I glance at my phone and see the time.

My stomach drops. "Shit! I have to go, or I'm going to be late!"

My heart kicks up at the thought of facing *Mr. Mike* and all his pushy nonsense. I dart into the bathroom, scrambling to pull myself together.

I look presentable enough. My phone is charged, my notes are ready, and the Uber is almost here.

This meeting isn't going to last too long, and with any luck, I'll be back in vacation mode in no time.

Rachel doesn't even look up from whatever she's scrolling through. "Maybe you should take the dagger, just in case!" Her smirk is wicked.

"Yeah, I think I'm good." I grab my bag. "I just need to survive this meeting. Find us something fun to do when I get back."

She waves me off with a lazy hand as I head out the door.

I've barely been on the road for two minutes when my phone buzzes.

> Rachel: Maybe when you get back, just for shits n' giggles, we try a little spell on Mr. Lover Boy. You distract him, I'll snip a piece of his hair, and we can voodoo your way into the best sex of your life. We can see just how witchy you really are.

I snort out a laugh, shaking my head at her insanity. Typical Rachel.

Although... I'm pretty sure I wouldn't need a spell for that.

Kane's barely done more than kiss me, and he's already blown every past experience out of the water.

The thought sends a flush creeping up my neck, heat pooling between my legs.

I mentally scold myself. I need to stay focused. The last thing I need to do is to leave a wet spot on the Uber's seat.

I groan under my breath, but the damage is done. My brain spirals straight into a highlight reel of last night.

The Uber driver catches my expression in the mirror. His brow lifts slightly, probably wondering why I look like a lunatic. Grinning one second, scowling the next.

CHAPTER 21

No Signs

KANE

T he coiled tension in my body is past the point of reason. My jaw is locked so tight it aches, and every muscle feels like it's primed to snap. Only one thing is going to take the edge off.

Violence.

I glance at Cam as he lounges on a barstool, his usual smirk firmly in place.

"Ready to lose?" I arch a brow, even though my blood thrums beneath my skin.

He lets out a sharp laugh, shaking his head. "You know damn well I'm going to kick your ass."

I smirk, rolling my shoulders. "We'll see about that."

But even a fight won't be enough to put out the fire burning through me. Raven's unraveling me, piece by fucking piece. Every part of my life, every calculated move, every carefully constructed plan, I've built on control. Always knowing the next step before anyone else does.

But with her, it's a goddamn freefall.

I can't predict what she's going to do, what sharp-witted response she's going to throw out, or what reckless thing she'll do just to prove a point. She's chaos, and I want to burn in it.

If she hadn't been rushing off to that damn meeting, I might have kept her in the car and laid it all out. But she slipped through my fingers again, leaving me holding back the truth.

I know I can't ignore it much longer.

Cam's already halfway down the hall, calling over his shoulder. "Let me get changed. Be right down."

The short walk gives me just enough time to wrestle with the part of me that's still back in that storm with her.

I'd kill to be a fly on the wall during that meeting of hers, watching her annihilate whatever fool had the audacity to overstep. She has no patience for men who don't listen.

And Meathead Mike is about to learn that the hard way. If I had more than just a nickname to go off, I'd already have his entire history laid out in front of me.

She doesn't need me to watch out for her. She's made that abundantly clear. But that doesn't mean I won't.

I inhale sharply, shoving the thought down before it can go any further. Not my problem. I have bigger things to worry about.

Cam finally emerges, stretching his arms over his head like he's on a goddamn vacation.

He takes one look at me and smirks. "You look like shit. You sure you don't want to just talk it out?"

I don't bother responding. Instead, I step into the ring making the message loud and clear. Talking isn't an option.

He laughs, shaking his head as he climbs in after me. Before he's even fully upright, I slam a right hook into his face.

He stumbles back, eyes wide for half a second before swiping at the blood trickling from his lip, then grins.

"Well, all right then. Guess we're skipping foreplay." He squares up, rolling his shoulders. "Holy shit, you got it bad, man."

He's not wrong, and that only pisses me off more.

"If you dodged half as much as you talked, maybe you wouldn't get hit as much." I snap, circling him, fists clenched and ready to burn off every last ounce of this frustration.

He barely dodges the next swing, his smirk turning razor-sharp as we fall into rhythm.

The first hit comes fast. A sharp jab to my ribs, but I don't react. He knows where to aim, when to push, and when to shut the fuck up. And right now, he's pushing me.

I counter hard, swinging for his head, but he ducks, landing an uppercut that rattles my jaw.

We keep going, the sound of fists meeting skin and the dull thud of impact filling the space. It's fast and brutal, every muscle straining under the weight of the fight.

But he's watching me. Waiting. And I know exactly what he's waiting for.

He dodges my next swing, then exhales sharply. "I have some information I think you'll find interesting."

I pause, a fraction too long. It's all the opening he needs. His fist slams into my ribs, pain exploding through my side. My vision flashes for a second before I shake it off.

"Go on." My voice is clipped.

Cam rolls his shoulders, staying light on his feet. "Security caught something near the east wing. Someone tried slipping past the outer gate, like they were trying to get out, not in. But they didn't get far. But we still don't know how they got in."

I throw a jab that he easily blocks, but the tension crawling up my spine has nothing to do with the fight.

"Who?"

"That's the thing." He shifts his stance, watching my reaction. "No ID, no clear motive. Just someone testing limits is my guess." His eyes narrow. "Could be tied to our new client. Could be something else."

I grind my teeth, dodging a sharp left hook before landing a brutal strike to his ribs.

"Tell me."

Cam winces, shaking it off. "Not much else to tell. Security handled it before anything happened, but the timing's suspicious, don't you think?"

I don't reply because he already knows the answer.

It's been *years* since I've had a real attempted breach, let alone someone actually breaking in, slashing my tires, and then trying to slip away unnoticed. What was the point?

Coincidence? Not a fucking chance. Clearly they know I'm distracted.

Each hit I throw is faster, sharper, my body moving on instinct while my mind fights for clarity. For control.

Cam staggers back, breathing hard, wiping sweat from his brow. "As much fun as I'm having kicking your ass," he mutters, rolling his shoulders, "I'm starting to think we could be using, you know... words."

I pause, chest heaving. He has a point. Doesn't mean I give a damn. "You might be right," I admit, smirking. Then I throw another punch.

Cam barely dodges, cursing under his breath. "You're a fucking asshole."

"Glad you're finally catching on."

Right now, this is the only thing stopping me from hunting down every lead until I know who the hell is poking around my house.

Cam's scowl deepens as he shifts his stance. "Besides," I taunt, sidestepping a jab, "You're just mad you're not winning."

Cam doesn't take the bait. Instead, he goes for an uppercut that I dodge. Which is exactly what he wanted. Fuck. His fist connects with my ribs. Again.

A sharp grunt escapes me, the ache already spreading. That's going to be a bruise by the end of the day.

"Care to talk yet?" He's relentless, barely giving me a second to breathe, landing hit after hit.

"I'm fine," I grit out, stepping back to shake off the sting of his last hit.

Cam circles me, eyes sharp. "Fine, huh? Then tell me what the fuck is going on." His voice lowers, but the weight behind it is heavier than any hit he's thrown. "You've been all over the damn place since she showed up. You're getting sloppy."

The words hit like a gut punch, and it does nothing but piss me off. I throw a punch, aiming to shut him up, but he deflects easily, proving his point.

He shakes his head. "That's what I thought. Get it together."

I'm dodging his hits as best I can, but for everyone I avoid, he lands two more. My arms are heavy, my breath comes in bursts, and he's not letting up. I swing wide and miss completely, cursing under my breath.

"Alright, alright," I bark out, holding up a hand.

Cam bends over, hands on his knees, chest heaving. For a second, I think he's going to take another swing. Instead, he straightens, raising a slow thumbs-up with a smug grin.

I chuckle, wiping sweat from my forehead. "You're lucky I'm tired."

"Yeah, keep telling yourself that." His grin widening as he stretches his neck like he's ready to go another round.

I drop onto the bench, leaning forward with my elbows on my knees. I need to breathe. To think.

"I assume we still have him?"

Cam's laughter cuts off instantly.

"Aye." He nods, stretching his arms before leaning back against the ropes. "He's in the basement. Security ran their tests, but nothing matches. He won't talk and hasn't asked for anything. Just sits there." His brows pinch. "You think he's connected to the new client?"

I exhale sharply, rubbing a hand over my jaw. "I don't know yet."

I don't believe in coincidences. The timing is too clean. No, there's something more going on here, and I don't like being in the dark.

I push off the bench, reaching for a towel and tossing it at Cam with a smirk. "Guess I'll have to make an appearance, do your job for you. Just make sure he stays put until I get there."

Cam groans, swatting the towel away. "You're the worst."

The time in the ring took the edge off, but not nearly enough. My body is loose, but my mind is still wired, caught between thoughts of everything I have to do, the dumb ass in my basement who thought he could sneak around, and Raven.

After a quick shower, I pull on a fresh shirt, rolling my shoulders as I grab my phone, deciding to check in.

Me: How's your meeting going?

A moment later, her response flashes across the screen.

> *Your Royal Highness: I'm not there yet, but I'm NOT looking forward to it at all.*

I smirk, picturing her, she's probably tapping her fingers, glaring at the clock, already over it before it's even started. Poor Meathead Mike doesn't stand a chance.

> *Me: How come?*

> *Your Royal Highness: Just a feeling I get from him.*

> *Me: Spidey senses just not vibin' with Meathead Mike?*

I wait for her response, but alarm bells are already ringing. I don't like this. Raven's sharp. She trusts her instincts, and if something feels off to her, it probably is.

> *Your Royal Highness: No, they're not.*

> *I'm sure he's fine.*

> *Me: Cancel then. Tell him today's meeting isn't happening.*

There's a longer pause this time, and I know she's weighing her options, probably chewing on her lip the way she does when she's deep in thought.

> *Your Royal Highness: If only it was that easy.*

I frown, irritation settling under my skin. Why the fuck not? If she's uncomfortable enough to even mention it to me, that's already a problem.

I type out a response, then delete it. She'll shut me out if she thinks I'm overstepping.

> Me: Well, just say the word, and I'll come get you. I have no issue telling Meathead Mike where he can go.

The three little dots appear, then disappear.
A moment later, her reply pops up.

> Your Royal Highness: Hahaha, you're out of control.

> Me: We've established this already, Princess, I'm very much in control.

> Would you like a demonstration?

I hit send, and satisfaction rolls though me. I'd give my right fucking nut to see her face when she reads that.

> Your Royal Highness: Well, Prince Charming, I'll let you know if I'm ever in need of rescuing.

> Unlikely, since I can handle it myself.

> BUT I'll keep you in mind if I need back up.

> Me: Did you bring your butter knife?

The image of her in the garden flashes through my mind with her clutching that dull-ass knife like she was ready to go full gladiator. I wouldn't mind seeing her grip something else with that same intensity.

I groan inwardly, shaking off the thought. Not fucking helpful.

> *Your Royal Highness: ... sure did!*

I chuckle.

> *Me: Should we take bets on if you can hit the bullseye with it?*

> *Your Royal Highness: Name your price...*

My pulse spikes. I lean back in my chair, staring at the screen. I'd happily give her anything she wanted. But considering her *darts skills*? Yeah, I'm not too concerned.

> *Me: A favor. No questions asked.*

> *Your Royal Highness: Deal.*

> *Me: And yours?*

> *Your Royal Highness: Any favor I want.*

> *Me: Done.*

I laugh at her response; fully aware she thinks she's winning this little game. Let her think it. I'll let her play along, let her feel like she's in control, because the truth is, I'm already five steps ahead. And if she actually manages to hit that bullseye? Even better.

My phone stays in my hand longer than it should. I assume she's made it to her meeting, and my fingers itch to dig into her background. Part of me resists, wanting things to unfold naturally. But let's be honest, that's not how I operate.

Before I can talk myself out of it, I pull up her social media. Nothing invasive. Just enough to get a better sense of who she is. But then I hit a wall, realizing I only know her first name.

This might take longer than expected.

Then it hits me that she's staying in one of my properties. I type her name into the booking system, and there it is: *Raven Taylor, staying with Rachel Allison Teller.*

Raven Taylor.

There she is.

Her profile's public, which makes this all too easy. The entire page looks like something out of a magazine. Polished but raw.

A photo catches my eye immediately. She's standing in front of a house, a box of things in one arm, a cat in the other. She's smiling, but it doesn't reach her eyes.

There's something off, something guarded about the photo.

The caption reads: *Never be so polite you forget your power.*

Something about that makes my jaw tighten. She looks stunning, her hair wild and loose, caught in the wind. The shot's taken at dusk, but she stands out, glowing in a white summer dress, barefoot.

The contrast draws you in, but it's the haunted look in her eyes that lingers, like she's carrying the weight of that moment alone.

I find myself leaning closer, studying the picture. What put that look on her face?

I scroll further, letting the pictures fill in the blanks. The cat's name is Fat Louie.

Of course it is. That checks out. She travels a lot, nearly always with Rachel. Her bio mentions marketing, which explains the professional polish on everything she posts.

Not a single food photo. Figures. I smirk, imagining her rolling her eyes at the thought of posting a picture of brunch.

I lean back in my chair, fingers tapping idly against the desk as I pull up my system and type in her name. Let's see what we're working with.

A quick glance tells me she's listed as a marketing manager, straightforward enough. But as I scan further, something pulls me up short.

She started her own company. Built it from the ground up, then sold it for three million dollars. *Impressive.* And yet... she stayed on as an employee, for a business she built. That doesn't track.

I sit forward, scanning for an explanation. Nothing. No board pressure, no legal clauses, no personal investments tying her there. So why stay?

She doesn't strike me as the kind of woman who lingers out of obligation. She's sharp. Calculated. There's a reason behind every move she makes. Yet this move doesn't make sense.

Then I find something even more interesting. Her original birth certificate is from Scotland, and it's been sealed. My focus sharpens as I dig deeper. There's several interesting things here, but no documented reasons for a sealed record.

People don't go to these lengths to hide something like that. There's a bigger story here, but that's not what makes my blood heat.

The police report does. Six months ago, she filed for a restraining order. It was dissolved not long after. Then, a couple months later, she petitioned for a protective order, that's still active.

I sit back, jaw tightening as I absorb the details.

Whoever put her in a position to need those orders better pray I never find them.

I roll my shoulders, pushing down the sudden surge of anger. I need to focus. The question still remains, who the hell is *Meathead Mike*, and why does he have her on edge?

A quick dive into her company doesn't connect her to any marketing firms here. If this trip was work-related, there's no record of it. Which only makes me more suspicious.

I flex my fingers against the desk, debating my next move. I know just the person who can find what I need a hell of a lot faster.

> Me: Need you to run a check.

> *Cam: That depends. Am I breaking any laws?*

> *Me: I'll let you know when I care.*

> *Cam: I love it when you talk dirty to me.*

> *Send me a name.*

I exhale, rolling my neck, letting the tension settle into something useful. Cam will find what I need, he always does.

A sharp knock on the door pulls me from my thoughts.

Carrie steps inside, moving with the same unshakable confidence she always does, a stack of papers balanced effortlessly in her hands. If she were any more capable, I'd be working for her.

"Hey, boss!" She chirps, flashing a knowing smile.

I lean back in my chair, taking a moment before responding. "What are you up to, Carrie?"

She narrows her eyes, tilting her head. "I'm great, Kane, thank you for asking. What do you want?"

I chuckle, shaking my head. "What I want is for my secretary to do her job and not act like my boss," I reply, a grin creeps into my voice. "And for the record, I do actually care about how you're doing."

Carrie snorts, clearly unimpressed. "Uh-huh. Sure, you do." But then, her expression softens. "Actually, I spent the weekend looking for a dog."

I straighten slightly. "Finally." A laugh rumbles in my chest as I shake my head. "I was about to go out and buy you one myself. I've only heard you talk about getting a dog for three years now? I was starting to think it was a cover."

She rolls her eyes but doesn't lose her grin. "Good things take time." She says smugly.

Carrie's one of the few people I trust completely. Over the past six years, she's more than proven herself. Handling everything from boardroom disasters to my worst hangovers with a kind of ruthless efficiency that would put most CEO's to shame. She's saved my ass more times that I can count and kept my schedule, and my life, running smoothly.

If she ever tries to quit, I *will* bribe her. Without shame. Which is why I make it a point to stay on her good side.

"I've got a favor to ask," I let a grin creep across my face. "But don't worry, I come bearing gifts."

Her eyes narrow, but the curiosity is already flickering in her expression. "Kane Robertson... this better be good."

"I just need you to finalize the guest list and send it to Khloe. Double-check that everything at the estate is sorted. The cleaning crew, security, all of it. Maybe check with Khloe to see if anything else is missing, then let me know if she needs anything else." I pause, watching her reaction as I add, "As for your present, it should arrive within the hour."

Carrie arches an eyebrow. Unimpressed. "Oh, well if that's *all...*" She rolls her eyes before laughing. "For your information, the guest list has been triple-checked, cross-referenced with ticket sales, and sent to Khloe." She lifts a single brow, challenging me. "She also wanted me to inform you that she's *deeply offended* you'd doubt she had everything under control."

"Of course she did," I mutter, lips twitching.

"And, yes," Carrie continues, "everyone with estate access has been contacted and confirmed, including security. Anyone new has had a background check done."

I lean back, letting out a slow breath as I watch her. It's almost unsettling how good she is at her job. Either that, or I'm becoming predictable, which is its own problem.

Before I can open my mouth, she holds up a hand. "Don't even *think* about saying it," she warns. "Otherwise, you'll owe me *another* raise."

I smirk. "You're already overpaid."

She scoffs. "And yet, I'm still underappreciated."

"Debatable," I counter, amused. Truth be told, I'd pay her whatever she wanted. "Thank you," I add, keeping my voice even. Can't let it get to her head, she'd tell everyone.

Once, I made a mistake of telling Carrie how much I appreciated her. The next day, she told the entire office I was a secret softy because I got teary-eyed while saying it. In my defense, a gust of wind blew dust in my eyes. Completely justified.

She turns to leave but hesitates, glancing over her shoulder, "Oh, and thanks for the dress, by the way. You know I could've bought my own."

I look up, caught off guard that she knew. "If ye didn't want to go, then buying your own dress would've just made ye mad at me." I smirk, watching her reaction. "And I can't be having that."

She tilts her head, studying me for a beat before laughing. "Smart man."

"I try."

Carrie shakes her head, amusement clear as she walks out. Leaning back in my chair I exhaling slowly as I roll the tension from my shoulders. Time to handle the rest of the shit on my plate.

I glance at my schedule, scanning the list of meetings, calls, and security briefings I still need to get through before this weekend.

I lean back, and a sharp wave of unease crashes over me, the sensation so sudden that my pulse skyrockets. My breath catches in my throat, muscles tensing as if preparing for a fight. And just like that, it's gone. What the fuck was that?

I blink, running a hand down my face, trying to shake the lingering edge of it. Maybe I need to get back in the ring with Cam sooner rather than later if my body's pulling this kind of shit.

CHAPTER 22

Long Story Short

RAVEN

E very instinct in me is screaming that this is a waste of my time. The facts I've gathered about him so far don't exactly scream *valuable business opportunity*. It's actually more like *walking red flag*.

Curse Steven for making me handle this. He could've dealt with it himself, but no, apparently *I'm* the picture of responsibility these days. Lucky me.

After giving myself a quick *be-a-responsible-adult* pep talk, I'm good to go. Maybe Mike-n-Ike just has terrible email etiquette. Maybe he had an off day when he sent those delightful passive-aggressive messages. Maybe his entire personality isn't actually insufferable, and his bad attitude is just the unfortunate byproduct of a bad mattress situation. Stranger things have happened.

Satisfied that I've sufficiently worked through my frustrations with Mike-n-Ike, my mind drifts to more... interesting matters.

Specifically, *that* kiss.

Epic kiss number two.

I thought maybe the first one was a fluke. A side effect of a little alcohol and the perfect storm of bad decisions. But nope. Turns out it wasn't just a lucky shot. It was *him*.

My stomach flips at the memory, and I have to resist the ridiculous urge to smile to myself like some lovesick fool. But, that kiss is definitely going to live rent-free in my mind forever. Definitely a core memory.

The thought of texting him flickers through my mind, something casual, just to see what he's up to tonight. But the second that thought forms, I shove it back down where it belongs.

Down girl.

As if the universe is testing my willpower, my phone buzzes on the seat beside me. I glance down, speak of the devil.

Kane.

Just his name on my screen is enough to send a little rush through me, which is stupid.

I swipe open the message. He's asking how my meeting is going. Yet, something about the fact that *he's checking in* sends my pulse skittering.

I reread his message, staring at my screen, trying to figure out what the responsible adult version of myself would say.

I inhale sharply, gripping my phone a little tighter as my brain stops working for a solid three seconds. *Would I like a demonstration?*

He thinks he's the hottest thing since sliced bread. Which, to be fair, he kind of is. And that's exactly why I need to get a grip.

This man is a disaster waiting to happen. And I refuse to be his next casualty. That would, without a doubt, become the disaster of the century.

Decision made. Kane is going under the *summer's epic fling* category. A perfect distraction, nothing more. I'll enjoy his company, have some fun, and keep things light. *No strings.* No mess. Just a little heat to brighten up my stay here.

I just need to keep my head in the game and my heart far, far away.

Now that he's thrown down the gauntlet with his bullseye bet, I can't help but smirk. There's nothing quite as satisfying as proving someone wrong. Especially when that someone has an ego the size of Scotland. Watching his face when he realizes he's underestimated me? *Oh, that's going to be so worth it.*

I might be able to ignore my feelings for Kane, but what I *can't* ignore, are all the strange things that keep happening to me lately. No matter how hard I try to write them off as coincidences, they just keep piling up. The tingling in my hands, for starters, like they're humming with static. Then there are the dreams. *Vivid, and way too real for comfort.* All those memories that suddenly feel like I'm live-streaming them in HD? Yeah, those are new too.

And let's not forget the flickering lights. *That's normal, right?* Probably just faulty wiring. Scotland is old, after all.

There's also the persistent feeling that I'm being watched. I keep telling myself it's paranoia, but deep down, I don't really believe in coincidences.

I sigh, shaking my head at Kane's text again. *If only bullseyes and inflated egos were the only things I had to deal with right now.*

The Uber pulls to a slow stop in front of the diner where I'm supposed to meet Mike *Wazowski*. The driver glances at me, eyebrows raised, clearly waiting for me to get out. But something makes me hesitate.

"Do you mind if we just sit here for a few minutes?" I shift my gaze back to the diner.

He shrugs, nodding easily. "Aye, take yer time."

I lean back against the seat, exhaling slowly as I scan the small restaurant through the window. It's probably just nerves, but I need a second to clear my head.

For someone who was so insistent on this meeting, *Big Mike* sure as hell didn't want to meet in his office. Oh no. He insisted on keeping it *casual*, claiming he didn't want things to feel too formal since I'm technically on vacation.

From the outside, the place looks like one of those small, locally-owned diners that probably serves the best damn pancakes in town. Too bad I'm not planning on eating a full meal, since I've already got dinner plans. The last thing I need is to be too stuffed to enjoy whatever place Rachel drags us to later.

My gaze drifts to the windows, scanning for anyone who looks like they might be *The Mike. And that's when it hits me.*

Oh my God.

I don't actually know what this guy looks like.

"UGGGHHH. *This* is why I meet people in their office," I mutter, fumbling for my phone.

Stress level: officially at DEFCON 1.

I roll my eyes at the thought, still scanning my phone, when a sharp *knock* on the window makes me jump.

My phone flies out of my hand, vanishing into the dark void between the seats as I clutch my chest like I've just been personally attacked.

Whipping around, I'm ready to cuss out whatever serial killer just *jump-scared* me, but instead, I freeze.

Outside my window stands a very ridiculously attractive man. His apologetic smile somehow softens the sharp angles of his face.

His dirty blonde hair is tousled just enough to look effortless, like he woke up looking like that. He has a strong jawline that's framed by just the right amount of stubble, the kind that says, *I know exactly what I'm doing, and yes, it works for me.*

And then there are his eyes.

Wow.

Deep, piercing blue, with a glint of amusement that makes it painfully clear he's enjoying this far more than I am.

His broad shoulders fill out his suit in a way that should be illegal, hinting at a build that probably *lives* at the gym, or maybe he just wrestles Highland cattle for fun. Either way, I don't hate it.

Lifting his hands, his grin widens, as if this is the funniest thing that's happened to him all day. *Can't say the same.*

"So sorry, love," his voice is effortlessly smooth, and laced with an accent that could charm a nun. "Didn't mean to scare you."

I blink. My brain still buffering. What the actual hell is happening right now?

The Uber driver glances at me in the mirror, his brow furrowing. "You alright? Do you know him?"

"Oh! I'm fine, sorry. Thank you!" I reply quickly, willing my voice to sound steadier than I feel. My heart is still hammering against my ribs, and I'm about two seconds away from dissolving into a puddle of embarrassment.

Rolling the window down, I hear him repeat himself. "So sorry, really. But are you, by chance, Raven?"

The sound of my name coming from his mouth sends a flicker of unease through me. *How does he know who I am?* My brain finally kicks into gear, the missing puzzle pieces snapping into place.

"Uh-yes, that's me," still working to catch up. "Sorry, you just caught me off guard... are you Mike?" I add, trying to compose myself before I make this moment any worse.

"Yes! Again, so sorry!" He flashes a sheepish but confident smile. "I saw ye sittin' here and thought it might be you, so I figured I'd come check."

The Uber driver raises a skeptical brow but keeps his thoughts to himself. *Same, buddy. Same.* I thank him for waiting and slip him a little extra money for the trouble. Finally stepping out of the car, I take a steadying breath as I follow Mike into the diner.

Inside, the cozy atmosphere does nothing to settle the odd mix of adrenaline and unease still buzzing in my veins. Mike leads us to a booth near the window, I set my bag down beside me, pulling out my phone to fire off a quick, preemptive text to Rachel.

> Me: If you get the bat signal, call immediately. Just in case.

Hitting send, I look up just in time as Mike offers a smooth smile. "I took the liberty of ordering you a glass of wine," he gestures toward the table. "I told the waiter to bring it once you arrived. Don't worry, you didn't keep me waiting long."

Umm. Excuse me? I was early, *but sure, let's go with that.* My brain flips between irritation and politeness. I was also about to mention I don't drink, but that's not *entirely* accurate anymore. Instead, I muster a polite, "Oh, thank you."

There's no way I'm drinking during an interview. I'm here to get through this meeting, not play along with whatever vibe Mike is throwing out.

When the waiter arrives, I ask for a glass of water as well. He nods and leaves us alone, while I shift my focus back to Mike, keeping my expression neutral.

"I'm still terribly sorry about scaring you earlier," he says, his voice perfectly smooth. But something about his tone doesn't match the words. He doesn't *actually* sound sorry. If anything, there's a subtle edge beneath his practiced charm, like he's watching me just a little too closely.

There's something a little intense about him, nothing outright creepy, but it's enough to send a quiet hum of warning through my gut.

"That's okay." I smile, keeping my tone light and easy. "So, where would you like to start?"

I'm not here to be rude, but I *am* on vacation. And between his emails and this meeting, I feel like I already have a solid read on him.

His smile stays tight, but his eyes narrow slightly. "Oh please, I insist we talk business *after* we order. That way, there won't be interruptions."

I nod, keeping my face pleasant, but internally, I'm rolling my eyes.

His type is so predictable. *Control freak, ego central, everything by-the-book, barf.* I'd bet good money he's calculated this down to the second, including a time limit for how long he thinks we should chat. My first impression of him was spot on.

The waiter returns, and we both place our orders. I opt for a side salad, because I am *not* about to sit through this while trying to enjoy an actual meal. I swear I catch the faintest flicker of irritation cross Mike's face at my choice. *Oh well, buddy. You'll live.* It's not like we're on a date.

He takes a deliberate sip of his wine; his movements are smooth and practiced. The way his eyes stay fixed on me over the rim of his glass makes me resist the urge to shift in my seat.

"So, tell me," he begins, setting the glass down with a little too much ease. "How has your trip been so far?"

His tone is casual, but the way he asks that feels *off*. Like he's less interested in my actual answer and more interested in *how* I answer.

"Actually, it's been really good so far," I offer a polite smile. "Scotland's beautiful. I've just been trying to soak it all in."

His smile widens slightly, but it doesn't quite reach his eyes.

"It is, isn't it?" he muses, swirling his wine slightly before taking another sip. "I imagine it must be quite the change of pace for you."

I tilt my head slightly, my own smile never faltering. "It is. But a good one."

I almost second-guess myself. There's an ease to his tone that doesn't quite match the controlled, calculated version of him I had pegged in my mind. His charm isn't over the top, it's subtle. The kind that sneaks up on you.

Maybe this won't be the stuffy work meeting I was dreading after all.

As we start talking about the places I've visited so far, any initial doubts I had about Mike start to fade. Naturally, I leave out any mention about the castle. And Kane. Especially Kane. Instead, I focus on how Rachel and I are excited about the ball, keeping things light.

The second I mention it, something shifts. Mike's whole expression changes, his interest sharpening in a way I wasn't expecting.

"Ah, the masquerade," he says, his smile finally reaching his eyes. "Now that's an event worth attending."

Okay, so this is what gets him excited? Noted.

I tilt my head slightly, curiosity piqued. "You sound like you've been before."

His lips quirk, almost like he's amused by my observation. "A time or two," he admits, swirling his wine lazily before finishing it off. "It's a very coveted event... a fundraiser, technically. Very exclusive."

That *technic*ally makes me want to ask more questions, but before I can he smoothly pivots the conversation.

He listens intently, nodding at the right moments, offering recommendations for places we should check out. Some of them are already on our list, but others sound intriguing enough to consider.

He actually *knows* what he's talking about, I'll give him that. His enthusiasm isn't forced, and the way he describes each spot is almost unexpected.

Still, my gut tells me to stay on guard. First impressions aren't always the full picture, but instincts don't lie.

Our food arrives, and he thanks the waiter with a polite nod before turning his attention back to me. "I'd love to share more places you should check out while you're here, but you're on vacation and I don't want to take up more of your time than necessary."

I nod, acknowledging the sentiment even if it feels slightly rehearsed. "I appreciate that," I offer a small, easy smile.

And to my own surprise, despite how weird this meeting started, I'm actually enjoying the conversation. He's polished, well-mannered, and there's something oddly deliberate about everything he does. It's not quite arrogance, but a blend of refinement and control, like he was born and bred to move through the world in a certain way.

I noticed how attractive he was the second he scared the shit out of me outside the car. But sitting across from him now, I notice something else. There's something just beneath the surface of all that careful composure. A flicker of unpredictability.

Interesting.

Still, good-looking or not, I'm not here for casual conversation. Time to get back to business.

Leaning back, I take a sip of water and shift gears. "Your company has a strong reputation," I keep my tone professional but friendly. "What I'd like to know is how you plan to tailor your approach specifically to our brand."

Mike leans in slightly, his eyes locking onto mine with an intensity that feels a little too heated. "Our team specializes in customizing strategies to fit the unique needs of each client."

It's the kind of voice that's not just selling a pitch. It's selling him.

And I can't quite decide if I find that impressive... or exhausting.

He launches into polished stories of past successes, every word flowing effortlessly. I'll give him credit, he's good at this. Flawless, even. But as his well-rehearsed spiel continues, I feel my attention start to drift.

I've heard these lines before. Everything is where it should be. The right buzzwords, the right tone, the right examples. And yet, there's something missing. There's no spark of genuine passion that would make it all feel real. His delivery is perfect, but perfection has a way of feeling hollow.

I pop a tomato off the top of my salad into my mouth, savoring the burst of flavor. "I'm sorry," I say, covering my mouth as I chew. "What did you just say?" I swallow quickly. "That tomato was amazing!"

He chuckles, his dark eyes meeting mine with a flicker of amusement. "I only said, why don't you tell me what you're hoping to get out of this?" His voice drops slightly, and I catch a brief flash of heat in his gaze before he masks it. *Interesting.* "That way, we can skip to the good stuff and make the most of our time," he adds, his smile lingering.

He's smoother than I expected, but I can't tell if that's a good thing or a red flag wrapped in a well-tailored suit.

"If I get into bed with you, so to speak," his tone dipping into something low. "What's in it for me? I know exactly what I'm bringing to the table, and I'm very clear on what I expect in return. I'm here to take full advantage of what you have to offer."

Wow.

He smirks, pausing just long enough to let his words sink in before adding, "Your expertise and your involvement."

I blink, processing the way he said that. His choice of words gives me pause, and I raise an eyebrow, unsure if I should feel flattered or wary. *Okay, so this just took a turn.*

It's bordering on flirtatious, and it doesn't fit the rigid personality he walked in with. Then again, maybe he's just trying to drive the pitch home a little harder. Or maybe there's more to *Meathead Mike* than meets the eye.

I lean forward, propping my elbows on the table and resting my chin on my hands, watching him like I'm considering his words. Then, with a slow, deliberate smirk, I deadpan, "Oh, absolutely. I'd be *thrilled* to offer my expertise. In fact, I'll even throw in a free tote bag, limited edition."

The second the words leave my mouth, he stills. Just for a second.

I can *feel* the way his brain misfires, the flicker of shock in his expression before he masks it.

Then, he laughs, low and smooth, shaking his head. "I like you," he muses, "you're sharp."

I tilt my head, amusement curling in my chest. *Bet you weren't expecting that, were you, Mike?*

"That's one way to put it."

His smirk lingers, but there's something else behind his gaze now. Time to see just how much he likes being on the receiving end of a curveball.

"Well," I begin, returning his sharp smile with one of my own, "what you see is pretty much what you get with us. Steven keeps a close eye on his internal team, making sure everyone is aligned and working toward the same goals. Communication is key with him."

I pause, letting the silence stretch just enough to get his attention. "I do have one question, though," I lean in slightly. "What's one decision you've made as a CEO that keeps you up at night, and how do you justify it to yourself?"

For the first time, something shifts in his expression.

A flicker of something unreadable.

His smirk twitches, just a fraction, but I catch it. A little crack in his polished mask. He leans back slightly, fingers tapping against his empty wine glass like he's considering his next move carefully.

"The only thing that keeps me up at night, Raven, is knowing every move is... handled. I don't second-guess. I execute."

He holds my gaze as he continues, his voice steady. "Every major decision comes with its fair share of sleepless nights. The key is making sure the wins outweigh the losses."

Classic. A non-answer wrapped up in a pretty bow.

I tilt my head, mirroring his smooth smile. *Oh, we're playing games?*

Clearing my throat, I plaster on a smirk of my own. "Well, as long as you're confident you can keep up, I guess I'll just have to take your word for it."

He just stares at me, pausing for a second.

"Well, as you know, true success comes from addressing the root of any problem," he says smoothly. "Once you eliminate that, and build from a solid foundation, you can achieve anything."

"Interesting," I nod, absorbing his words. They're polished, but there's something beneath them I can't quite put my finger on.

I pop another tomato in my mouth, savoring the fresh, tangy burst of flavor, letting my eyes briefly close before I catch myself. When I open them, he's watching me. His gaze lingers a little too long.

"If you'll excuse me, I need to use the restroom." he mutters, standing up with a tight smile before heading off.

I nod, waiting until he's out of sight before immediately glancing down at my phone. The screen lights up, and I quickly try to schedule a ride.

Nothing. Just the dreaded spinning wheel, while it's *searching for drivers...* fantastic.

If there are no drivers now, what are the odds I'll find one when we're actually done? The idea of lingering here after we wrap up doesn't exactly sound appealing. Not that Mike's giving off serial killer vibes, but I'd rather not test my luck.

A quick glance at the hallway confirms he's still gone. The coast is clear.

With a sigh, I decide it's time to swallow my pride. Kane said I could call if I needed anything, and while this isn't exactly an emergency, it feels like a solid enough reason.

Sure, I might regret this later, but waiting around isn't an option.

Me: You busy?

I hesitate, wondering if I sound too casual. Or worse, needy. But I hit send before I can overthink it.

A beat passes with no response, so I add another message.

> Me: No worries if you are! I'm at this diner, and my phone is being weird. I'd rather not wait around with Magic Mike after the meeting.

With a groan, I start to type again, a weak attempt to backpedal.

> Me: Never mind.

I lock my phone and slide it onto the table, determined not to obsess over Kane's response. My nerves are already frayed, and the last thing I need is to spiral over a text.

I'm a big girl. I can try checking the app later.

The thought barely finishes when my phone buzzes. I glance down at the screen, pulse kicking up a notch.

> Kane : Does this diner have a name?

My heart skips a beat. No hesitation, no questions. Typical Kane. *Thank God.*

Hearing movement, I glance up and see Mike heading back toward the table. I quickly send my location, locking my phone and setting it down before he slides back into his seat.

He leans back with a satisfied smile, confidence practically oozing across the table. "I think we've got everything covered here, don't you agree, love? Unless there's something else you'd like to discuss?"

I keep my expression neutral, returning his smile with polite professionalism. "No, I think that's everything."

Mike raises a hand to the approaching waiter, handing over his card with an effortless flick of his wrist. The waiter nods and disappears, while Mike turns back to me, smile still firmly in place.

"Thanks for fitting me in," he says, tacking on a wink that lands somewhere between smug and patronizing. "I know you've got a lot on your plate. But, really, don't skip out on Skye. It's stunning. Feel free to reach out if you need any other recommendations."

Oh, I bet you have all sorts of recommendations, don't you, Mike?

His tone is smooth, but there's a quiet arrogance behind it that's hard to ignore.

The waiter returns with his card, and as Mike tucks it away, he shifts his focus back to me, his gaze lingering a little longer.

"I don't want to rush things," his voice all easy charm, "but my car just pulled up. Would you like a lift back?"

It's subtle, but heat flashes in his expression before he masks it with another polished smile.

I match it with my own, keeping my tone light. "No. Thank you, though. My driver is almost here."

He stands, buttoning his jacket with fluid ease. "Well, we'll be in touch, Miss Taylor, that I assure you."

Then, after the slightest hesitation, he adds, "Would you like me to wait with you until your driver arrives?"

It's meant to sound polite, but there's something in the way he studies me that makes my instincts prickle.

I keep my expression easy, lifting my phone. "I'm sure that's him now. Thanks again, though."

He nods, extending a hand. I reach out to shake it, but instead of the quick, professional exchange, his grip is firm and lingers just a fraction too long.

And there it is.

I hold my ground, keeping my posture relaxed, but I don't miss the way his fingers tighten slightly before he finally lets go.

Yeah. Definitely not taking that ride.

"It was a pleasure," he chuckles, his smile lingering too long.

I nod, withdrawing my hand as smoothly as possible, then watch as he holds my gaze for a beat longer before finally turning and heading for the door.

The moment it swings shut behind him, I exhale, tension easing from my shoulders. I track his movement, watching as he slides into a sleek, black car. Tail lights glow red against the pavement as he pulls away, disappearing down the street.

I settle back against the seat and glance at my phone as it vibrates with a new message.

Kane: Four minutes away.

Sliding my phone into my bag, I stand and step out into the cool evening air. A shiver rolls down my spine as the breeze snakes around me, but it's not just the temperature, it's something else. The faint, unmistakable feeling of being watched.

I scan the quiet street, eyes flicking over parked cars and dim shop windows. Everything looks normal, just the muted hum of the city in the distance. But the feeling lingers, prickling at the back of my neck.

The light drizzle turns into a misting rain. I slide my hands into my pockets, my fingers curl around the stones I brought along. Normally, their warmth is steady, but tonight, they feel different.

I take a slow breath, forcing myself to focus on Kane. He'll be here any second. Nothing to stress about. Just an overactive imagination and a long day playing tricks on me.

Still, my muscles stay coiled, restless energy humming just beneath my skin. I pull my jacket tighter against the damp chill, scanning the road. My phone buzzes again, and I glance down.

Kane: Here.

A sleek Range Rover rolls up moments later, barely slowing before Kane steps out. His movements are controlled, like he's keeping something barely in check. When his eyes lock onto mine, tension coils around him like second skin.

I reach for the door handle, but his sharp look stops me cold.

"Don't touch that door." His voice is firm, leaving no room for argument.

In one fluid motion, he swings it open, stepping aside just enough to let me in. His face gives nothing away, but there's an urgency in the way he moves, a quiet demand in the way he watches me.

Sliding into the passenger seat, I glance over as he shuts the door behind me, then moves around to the driver's side.

The second he's in, his eyes cut to mine. "What happened?" His tone is level, but it's laced with restraint.

The flicker in his eyes catches me off guard, he looks ready to dismantle something with his bare hands if I give him a reason to.

"Nothing happened," I say, lifting a shoulder in a half-hearted shrug. "I just didn't feel like hanging around waiting for a ride with him. My phone was being weird, and I couldn't find a driver."

I pause, then smile. "Though, I think you've got some competition in the tour guide business. He offered to show me around."

Kane doesn't take the bait. He doesn't even glance at me. But his grip on the steering wheel tightens, knuckles flexing against the leather.

"Competition, huh?" His voice dips, dark amusement threading through it. "Doubt he could keep up with my tours."

I bite back a laugh, but I don't let him off the hook that easily. "Maybe I should see if his castle is better than yours," I tease, stealing a quick glance at him.

His jaw clenches, muscle ticking, and I swear the air in the car shifts. *Oh my God. He's jealous.*

"He was harmless," I add, though I can't help but enjoy this a little more. "It wasn't as terrible as I thought it'd be. He even offered to take me home, but I remembered you offering, so I figured it would be safer... considering I know you better."

I trail off, suddenly hyperaware of my own *rambling*.

Heat creeps up my neck, and I resist the urge to bury my face in my hands. If I keep talking, he's going to need his car detailed from all the word vomit I'm getting everywhere.

Silence stretches between us.

When he finally glances over, his expression is unreadable, but his dark eyes hold something intense. Like he's wrestling with a thought he refuses to say out loud.

He watches me for a beat too long for someone who's driving, and I swear my heart skips under the weight of his stare. Then, he shifts his attention back to the road, his grip flexing briefly against the wheel.

The corner of his mouth lifts slightly, a faint smirk that somehow feels both teasing and dangerous. "Good choice."

I roll my eyes but don't bother fighting the small smile tugging at my lips.

Then he exhales. "I guess you're lucky I was in the area then."

My curiosity flares. *What exactly were you doing in the area, Kane?* But before I can ask, my phone buzzes sharply.

Rachel's name flashes on the screen, and I swipe to answer, bracing for impact.

"Hey," I say, holding back a sigh. "Yeah, I'm okay. Uber was being weird, so I'm with Kane."

The moment I say his name, Rachel's rapid-fire questions come in hot. I pull the phone away slightly, wincing at her volume.

"Yes, we're still going. And, no, I'm not talking about that right now. Bye."

I hang up before she can argue, chuckling as I tuck my phone away.

When I glance over, Kane's watching me again, his expression unreadable, but something flashes across his face. Before I can place it, he shifts his gaze back to the road, but the question lingers between us.

"Wait," I blurt, the words slipping out. "What were you doing in the area? Hot date?"

The second it's out, I want to take it back. *A date? In the middle of the afternoon? Really?*

He raises an eyebrow, his smirk deepening ever so slightly. "I was working."

Well, okay then. Not exactly the *intriguing mystery* I was hoping for.

I chuckle, playing it off with a casual shrug. "Hey, you never know. Some people keep interesting schedules."

I let the conversation settle for a moment before glancing at him again, curiosity still pulling at the edges of my thoughts. Everything about Kane feels deliberate and intentional. *Carefully put together.*

Today, he's in a fitted black T-shirt, the fabric clinging to the defined lines of his chest and arms like it was made for him. But it's not just that, there's something about the way he carries himself.

My eyes catch on the tattoo curling up his forearm, dark ink twisting like shadows, alive with an energy that feels almost out of place on someone who otherwise looks so polished.

I force myself to look away, hoping he hasn't caught me staring.

But even as I turn my focus back to the road ahead, my thoughts linger on the contradictions he seems to embody.

His clothes, his presence, everything about him screams power and control. Like someone who either *has* money or wants to look like he does.

Either way, he pulls it off effortlessly.

Yet for all his polish, there's an edge to him. A rawness. Like he's spent just as much time in the dark.

And I can't decide which version of him intrigues me more.

God help me, my eyes dip lower, just a quick, totally harmless glance.

Big mistake.

Suddenly, my mouth is bone-dry, my thoughts absolutely *not* on business. Licking my lips, I whip my gaze toward the window, pretending I'm very, *very* interested in the rain-speckled glass. But the heat simmering between my legs betrays me, making it impossible to ignore the way my body reacts to him.

Taking a steady breath, I try to focus on the passing landscape, but my curiosity has a mind of its own. Against my better judgement, I sneak another glance.

Bigger mistake.

I shift in my seat, cheeks heating as I pray the car suddenly develops ejector seats. Then, just to make things worse, Kane glances over, catching me *not looking*. The corner of his mouth lifts, like he sees *exactly* where my head just went.

"Something on your mind, Princess?" His voice is a thread of dark amusement.

I clear my throat, gripping my water bottle, like it's going to save me. "Just enjoying the scenery." I keep my tone light, forcing my gaze back to the window, where I *absolutely* do not look at him again.

He chuckles, a deep, quiet sound that sends a fresh wave of heat through me. "I see that."

I roll my eyes, determined to shove my brain back into something resembling submission.

One thing is obvious, Kane doesn't look like a man who spends his days working outside. No suit, no tie, but there's still something *polished* about him. He's sharp, put together, but not in a way that screams desk job.

"What do you do for work?"

"Depends on the day," he replies. "But today? I was finalizing details with my secretary. She's trying to pick out a puppy. She's only been talking about it for the last three years, so that was top priority today." His lips twitch, amusement flickering in his eyes.

I blink. *A puppy?* That was not what I expected.

"Three years?" My curiosity fully engaged now. "What, was she waiting for, a sign from the universe? Were *you* the reason she didn't get one? And, more importantly, what kind of puppy is she getting?"

His laugh is deep and unguarded. "Alright, Princess, one question at a time," he shoots me a look. "We've got a bit of a drive, so no rush."

I press my lips together to keep from grinning as he continues.

"But aye, three years," he confirms, shaking his head like it still baffles him. "First, it was all the reasons why she *should* get a dog. Then, it was all the reasons she *shouldn't*. Then came the endless debates about which breed was smartest." He chuckles again. "So no, it wasn't my fault. Though, I *did* threaten to buy her one a few times just to put her out of her misery."

I laugh, imagining the scene. *Of course* he would resort to brute force.

"You sound like a fun boss," I smile.

The laugh he lets out is low. And it does something to me. It's not just his humor; it's the way he talks about the people in his life. A loyalty that runs deep, the kind that isn't loud, but it's there.

315

"Well, that's adorable," I tease, but the warmth curling in my chest is real. The idea of *him* being involved in something so normal, so... soft, tugs at something in me I don't want to name.

And that's when I make my next mistake.

I let my gaze linger. Too long.

I *feel* his voice more than hear it, each word curling around me like smoke, sinking in like a slow pull I can't escape. The space between us feels smaller, every breath charged with something unsaid.

And then my eyes drop to his mouth.

I desperately want to cross my legs, but I know if I move, he'll notice. And the last thing I need to give Kane is the satisfaction of knowing he's having any effect on me at all.

I try a few discreet Kegels, praying it'll ease the ache growing between my legs. But it doesn't.

In fact, it makes everything worse.

I keep my face neutral, but my pulse is *wrecked*. I need a distraction, now. Anything to ground me before I leave a mess on his seat.

Then, like some cruel joke from the universe, he glances over. His mouth tugs into a slow smile, and I swear he *knows*. He's so full of himself. I roll my eyes and decide to redirect this conversation *immediately*. I'm not about to let him get under my skin, or my clothes.

"What do you actually do for work?"

He chuckles, shaking his head slightly like we're sharing some private joke I'm not in on. "Quick version? I work in security."

That's it? That's all I get? I narrow my eyes. "That's suspiciously vague."

His smirk doesn't falter. If anything, he looks entertained. "It means I handle things," he replies, still evasive. "Each client's needs are different, so every job is unique."

He's being deliberately secretive, which only makes me want to push further. But focusing on his words is proving *very* difficult when my eyes keep tracking the way his lips move, the easy way his jaw flexes as he talks.

Get a grip, Raven.

I shake off the distraction, forcing my focus back where it belongs. "Oh so you're pretty important?"

He tilts his head slightly, considering me. Then, with a smirk that feels a little too dangerous, he says, "You tell me."

And just like that, my stomach *plummets*.

Then he raises an eyebrow, looking over to me. "But what I'd really like to know is what *you* do. And I'm dying to know how *Magic* Mike managed to redeem himself."

He's totally jealous. The flicker in his eyes says it all, and I *cannot* help but laugh.

"I promise you don't want me to get into that," I wave it off with a grin.

"What I do isn't really that exciting to most people." I give a small shrug, hoping to steer the conversation somewhere else.

Don't get me wrong, I love my job. But outside of work, it always feels like a slippery slope into a never-ending Q&A with people who just want to network or pick my brain like there's some secret formula.

"As for Mike," I continue, "he came off as a bit of a dick in our emails, but it turns out he's just... really formal and straight to the point. I guess that didn't translate well over email."

I chuckle softly at the memory of my initial impression of him, glancing over at Kane to gauge his reaction. His expression doesn't shift much, but there's something in the way his grip tightens on the steering wheel, like he's not thrilled to hear that my opinion of Mike improved.

"Well," his voice is laced with something that *definitely* isn't neutral, "Let's hope his formal and to the point style doesn't extend to his tour guide skills. I'd hate for you to get bored halfway through."

I laugh again, catching the shift in his tone. The realization sends a little thrill through me, one I do my best to ignore.

"So, where's your office?"

Kane chuckles, sparing me a glance before turning back to the road. "Nice try, I wouldn't ask if I didn't want to know. I'm sure your job is plenty exciting for *you*."

"Quick version, I'm in marketing," I shrug. "I actually love what I do, and I'd say I'm pretty good at it." I pause, trying to sum it up without diving into the boring details.

"The gist of today's meeting was that we're interviewing Mike for a partnership of sorts. He works in public relations and came under the impression *he* was interviewing *me*, which is exactly what my boss wanted him to believe."

Kane raises an eyebrow, his smirk deepening. "So you're playing it cool while he thinks he's calling the shots. *Smart move, Princess.*"

And for a second, I don't know what to say.

Most people, hell, most guys, don't get it. They either assume my job is easy, dismissing it like it's a hobby, or give me that patronizing nod and say something like *oh, marketing. That sounds fun!* Kane seems like he actually understands, and he's actually interested.

He doesn't seem to notice my momentary brain malfunction and keeps asking questions, ones that actually make me want to answer. It's rare for someone to have genuine interest. Most people nod politely and move on.

And, of course, that's doing things to my heart. Unexpected, inconvenient things.

I clear my throat, forcing my attention back to the moment. "Well, now that I've spilled my secrets, maybe you should finally tell me where *your* office is," I tease, raising an eyebrow.

He laughs, and *God help me,* the sound warms the space between us. "Nice try again. You'll just have to keep guessing."

CHAPTER 23

Question...?

KANE

A m I asking her questions I already know the answers to? Yeah. But I want to hear it from her.

The more she talks, the more I realize it's not just about confirming what I already know. It's the way she lights up when she talks about things, even when she tries to play it off like it's nothing. She feels everything deeply, that much is clear. Even when she doesn't want to.

And fuck if I don't want to keep pulling more of that out of her.

The second I saw her text, everything else became irrelevant. I may or may not have broken a few speed limits getting here. Good thing I know the cops. But for those few minutes, when I didn't know what the hell was happening, something in my gut twisted tight.

I don't know what I expected when I pulled up. But seeing her standing there, safe, was enough to pull me back from the edge.

This should've been the perfect moment to tell her. To put it all out there. Timing's everything, or so they say. But when *is* the right time? Because the longer I wait, the more this game we're playing twists into something else.

She keeps looking at me and licking her lips.

Fucking hell.

I grip the steering wheel tighter, keeping my gaze locked on the road, because if I look at her right now, I'll forget every reason I have not to touch her.

Before I can gather my thoughts, she suddenly gasps. "I *love* this song!"

And just like that, she leans over, cranking up the volume. Before I know it, she's singing, full volume, seatbelt be damned, completely lost in the moment.

I've seen her dance before, but this is something else.

My grip on the wheel tightens because it's either that or pulling over and doing something I *absolutely* shouldn't.

She has no idea I'm here, gripping the wheel so hard my knuckles go white, trying not to let the low hum of her voice and the way she moves make me lose what little restraint I have left.

Her laughter breaks through the moment as the song ends, an electric hum left in its wake. I drag in a slow breath, forcing my focus back onto the road.

We drift back into easy conversation, and I focus on the way she talks. The way she scrunches her nose when she's thinking, how she gestures when she's excited, the way her words come alive when she forgets to hold herself back.

She has no idea how easy she is to read.

I shift in my seat, adjusting against the *very real* problem I'm having, and thank *fuck* she's still looking out the window. If she knew, she'd never let me hear the end of it.

By the time we pull up to her place, I'm somehow both relaxed and more wound up than I've been in years.

I take a slow breath, forcing myself to pull it together before turning to her. "Hey, have a great day, kid," I smirk, flashing her a grin, hoping the reminder of how young she is will calm me the fuck down.

Her head snaps to me so fast I barely hold back a laugh.

She glares at me, arms folding, her expression darkening into something deadly.

And *fuck me* if that look alone doesn't undo me all over again.

She narrows her eyes, "Kid? How old are *you*, anyway?"

"That is a question for another day, Princess. I have to go back to work."

Her lips press together into the slightest pout, and I swear to God, I might actually lose my mind.

I smirk, "Guess that means you'll have to keep talking to me if you want to find out."

She huffs, glaring at me, but there's the faintest hint of a smile as she reaches for the door handle.

"Don't you dare touch that door," I snap, sharper than I intended.

She freezes, looking back at me, mouth parting slightly in surprise.

"Good—" *Fuck.* I cut myself off, jaw locking tight as I push open my own door and step out.

I need a second to breathe.

Praying she won't ask what I was about to say, I run a hand down my face, trying to collect myself. Every muscle in my body feels wound tighter than a spring as I walk around to her side, forcing myself to *just open the goddamn door and walk away.*

I pull the door open, extending a hand and our eyes lock as her fingers slip into mine. Her grip is firm but careful as she steps out, avoiding a puddle with effortless grace.

Her fingers linger just enough to test me.

"See ya later, *Princess.*" My voice steady even though everything in me is anything but.

She waves over her shoulder, that knowing little smile gracing her lips and I watch until the door closes behind her, exhaling sharply as I run a hand through my hair.

As soon as I step inside, the smell of food hits me. My stomach clenches, a not-so-subtle reminder that I skipped lunch today.

"Long day at work, honey?" Cam's voice carries from the kitchen, thick with amusement.

"Fuck you. But aye, it was." I drop my keys on the counter with a clatter.

He laughs, barely holding it together. "You've been trying to for years, but no means no, pal." He waves a spatula at me like a weapon, his grin downright smug.

I shake my head, chuckling as I head to my room. Spatula or not, Cam could probably kill a man with that thing and make it look easy. He's lethal in more ways than one. But right now, with a smudged apron tied around his waist and a streak of flour across his cheek? He looks more like someone's frustrated housewife than a trained operative.

"Nice apron," I call over my shoulder, smirking as I shut the door behind me.

His muffled retort follows, something about me being jealous of his culinary skills, but I'm already peeling off my shirt, craving a shower before I deal with him and whatever he's made.

I'm past cold showers at this point. That ship sailed long ago.

Stepping under the scalding water, I let the heat work into my muscles, rolling my shoulders as I exhale. The weight of the day slips down the train, but the tension knotting my stomach refuses to go anywhere.

My thoughts go straight to that smart mouth of hers and how she would look on her knees, looking up at me with her lips parted, breath shaky.

Before I can stop myself, my hand slides down, gripping tight. A sharp groan escapes me, muffled by the pounding water. I brace my other hand against the shower wall, jaw clenching as my strokes deepen, pace quickening.

She's probably never had a man actually give her exactly what she *needs*.

My muscles coil tighter. My control is a thread away from snapping with the image of her completely undone, moaning around me.

Fuck.

The release tears through me, my body locking up before everything finally unravels. I brace against the tiles, dragging in a breath, heart hammering in my chest.

I laugh dryly, shaking my head at the mess I've become.

It's probably for the best that I've got a mountain of work to prep for this weekend. Time to get my head back in the game, because this? *This* is a distraction I can't afford to indulge.

Throwing on fresh clothes, I head into the kitchen, relieved to see that dinner is ready. Cam is still in that ridiculous apron, and the sight immediately puts a grin on my face. I pull out my phone, ready to snap a blackmail photo, but he's faster than I give him credit for.

"Don't even think about it," he yanks the apron off before I can hit the button.

"You're no fun," I mutter, sliding my phone back into my pocket.

He smirks, leaning back against the counter. "You look like shit. Did you handle that job without me, or did you decide to walk home?"

I grab a plate and start dishing up, shaking my head. "No, dickhead, I didn't walk home. And yeah, it was an eventful day. I've got some interesting shit to share though and more info on the job I need you to do."

"Well, this should be good," he grins pausing mid-bite, his fork hovering in the air. "Do tell."

As I dig into my food, I lay it all out. By the time I finish, I lean back, waiting for his response.

Cam snorts, setting his fork down. "Let me get this straight, you're losing your shit over Raven's new work contact because he's got a questionable record, or because you can't stand the thought of her being around another man?"

I roll my eyes, unfazed. "Hilarious. What I found was enough to make me want to dig deeper. What's the point of having our skills if we aren't going to use them?"

Cam stares at me for a long beat, like he's weighing something. Then his lips twitch, and before I know it, laughter spills out.

"I'm just giving you shit," he grins. "But you're down bad for our girl Raven."

I shoot him a flat look, but he keeps going, shaking his head like I'm some kind of lost puppy. "Obviously, I'll do it. Anything else?"

I let out a slow exhale, pushing my plate away. "No. That's it."

The truth is, I know Cam won't leave a single fucking thing unturned. He'll find everything I did, and then some. He's got a way of pulling apart every thread until he has the full picture.

Cam grabs his plate again, stabbing a bite of food before pointing his fork at me.

"Good. Because if you keep digging, you're liable to go full caveman. I've seen that look in your eye before."

I huff out a short laugh, shaking my head as I stand with my plate. "Thanks for the analysis. Let me know when you've got something."

Cam salutes me with his fork, smirking. "Anything for you, darling."

"And I'm heading over to the estate later to deal with our friend. Meet me there in an hour."

The man sags forward, blood crusting at his temple, dried and cracking where Cam put him. He's been out cold for over an hour. Longer than I'd like. I don't have all fucking night.

The overhead bulb flickers, buzzing softly, casting fractured shadows against the stone walls. No cameras. No windows. The kind of room that was designed to swallow screams whole.

Cam leans against the door, arms crossed, looking amused. But I know better. He's waiting.

I plant a boot against the guy's shin and press hard, not enough to break it, but enough for it to wake him up. The body always fights pain before the mind does. A choked groan rasps from his throat as he jolts awake, eyes snapping open in confusion, fear crawling its way in. He scans the room, sees Cam, then me.

His eyes widen, and he tries to fight it. "I—I told you already, I don't know anything," he sputters, wrists jerking against the zip ties. Pathetic.

I crouch, tilting my head, studying him like I give a damn.

"That's not true, is it?" My voice is calm and controlled, despite how wound up I am right now.

He swallows hard.

Good. He should be afraid.

Cam exhales through his nose, stepping forward, voice edged with bored amusement. "We already know you weren't working alone." He shifts his weight lazily. "So save yourself the trouble and tell us who sent you."

The guy presses his lips together.

I nod, slowly, tapping two fingers against my knee. "Right. The hard way, then."

Before he even registers the threat, I strike. A fist to the face, fast and clean, his head snapping back. His grunt barely registers before I grab him by the throat.

Not hard enough to crush, not yet. But enough to cut off every precious breath he thinks he has left.

His eyes go wide, legs kicking against the chair, his body begging for air even if his pride won't. I hold him there, his pulse hammering under my palm, waiting for that first real flicker of panic.

His body jerks as his lungs scream.

Then, at the exact moment before he spirals into the void, I release him.

He gasps, his throat convulsing as he drags in air, coughing so hard it rattles the chair. "You... you don't understand," he wheezes.

I arch a brow, my patience thinner than fucking thread. "Then help me understand."

His gaze flicks to Cam. Like Cam's the reasonable one. If only he knew.

His lips part, hesitation written all over his face. There it is. A crack. But I don't give him time to decide.

I grab the front of his shirt and yank him forward, bringing us nose to nose. His breath is shallow, stale with fear.

"Who?" My voice is quiet. Lethal.

His eyes dart to Cam again, and I tighten my grip, teeth clenched. "Who?"

A breath, then, "The one with the bloodline. That's why we're here."

A muscle in my jaw ticks. What the fuck is he talking about? My pulse stays steady, but my instincts sharpen. That phrase should mean something, but it doesn't.

I shift my attention to Cam and see the tension in his shoulders, the slight shift in his stance. So fucking subtle that anyone else would've missed it.

Cam knows something.

I take a slow breath, letting the silence stretch. Letting this fucker realize that whatever thread of control he thought he had, is already gone.

Then I turn to Cam. "Take care of him."

And I walk out.

The words settle heavy in the air, and for a split second, the man's breath stutters, panic flashing across his face.

CHAPTER 24

Come Clean

RAVEN

R achel and I have our next couple of days mapped out and it's officially a boy-free zone. No distractions, no detours, just the reset I need to get my head straight again.

We're not about to act like stage-ten clingers.

Every steamy, deliciously sinful thought of Kane, and his sculpted body, those lips, that perfectly styled hair, is going to be shoved into a mental lockbox. For good measure, I toss in the memory of his arms, his stupidly perfect smirk, and the way he says my name like it's something worth holding onto. I slam it shut, padlock it, and throw it into the deepest, darkest recess of my mind.

Rachel comes into my room, waving her phone like she just won the lottery.

"Good thing you're ready, because the Uber will be here in four minutes. Thank God you agreed, because if you hadn't..." She pauses dramatically, tilting her head. "This would've gone a totally different direction."

By the time we step into *The Realm*, the energy slams into me like a shot straight to the veins. The place is alive with people. The music hums through the air, blending into the chatter, creating that perfect, effortless buzz.

It's way busier than last time.

A hostess leads us toward the back, sliding us into a cozy booth near the kitchen. The low lighting makes the whole space feel inviting.

Before I can even settle in, a woman bounces up to our table. She's practically glowing, her smile so warm and bubbly that I wouldn't be surprised to find out how much she loves this job.

"Hey ladies! What can I start you off with to drink tonight?"

"We'll just start with water for now, thank you!" I reply with a polite smile.

She spins on her heel and heads toward the bar, and I take a second to soak it all in. The energy. The laughter. The unmistakable vibe of this place.

Scotland has this way of getting under your skin, and making you feel like you belong to it. There's something here that feels right, like a piece of me fits here in a way I've never quite felt anywhere else.

The waitress returns, bouncing slightly on her toes like she's about to deliver the best news ever.

"You ladies picked the *perfect* night! Our owner is here, and he's everyone's favorite chef. Would you like me to tell you about tonight's special, or have you already decided?"

Rachel perks up, "Oh, that sounds exciting."

The waitress nods, her smile widening. "Aye! It's a treat for everyone when he's in, because he's the one cookin' the specials."

Rachel doesn't hesitate. She snaps her menu shut and hands it back with a grin. "Two specials, please!"

The waitress claps her hands together, practically glowing. "Oh perfect! You're going to love it!" She takes the menus before disappearing toward the kitchen.

Rachel watches her go, then shakes her head with a small smile. "I swear, this place is amazing. We really should think about moving out here. I'm down if you are."

I pause mid-sip, arching a brow. "Wait, you're serious? You want to move here?"

She leans forward; eyes gleaming. "Think about it. We'd have all the time in the world to look for your family. Plus, Scotland just... fits, you know? Maybe stay for a year, then reevaluate?"

I tilt my head, letting her words sink in. But before I can respond, she waves a dismissive hand.

"You'd thrive here. You don't need the money, so you could do whatever you wanted. And I'd find my groove, for sure. Just imagine the cozy pubs, friendly people, Highland cows in our backyard." She pauses dramatically, her smirk turning downright sinful. "Oh, and hot Highlanders..."

I roll my eyes, but the idea sticks.

"Just think about it," she adds, wiggling her eyebrows.

"Okay," I roll my eyes, fighting back a small smile. "I'll think about it."

She beams, and just like that, switches gears so fast I get mental whiplash.

"Do we need to hit the dress shop tomorrow and get that sorted? I mean, I'm sure they'll fit, but can you imagine waiting until the last second and something doesn't fit? *Total disaster.*"

"Yeah," I reply, pulling out my phone, trying to push the bomb she just dropped in my lap aside. "We'll head over there as soon as we eat breakfast."

I type out a quick message to the shop owner, confirming the time. I actually connected with him through social media. His designs instantly caught my eye, and I had to have one. They're stunning, but with a modern edge. One of the best perks of my job is meeting such talented people, and I can't wait to see the finished product.

Just as I'm about to hit send, a cold prickle runs down my spine. The hair on the back of my neck stands on end. The feeling of being watched coils low in my gut, tightening with each second.

I wait a beat, forcing myself to act casual, then slowly scan the room. Nothing. No one's looking my way. The feeling vanishes as fast as it came, leaving me uneasy.

Our waitress reappears, expertly balancing plates, glowing as she sets them down. My stomach flips. Haggis.

Rachel unfolds her napkin like she's about to start a five-star dining experience. "I didn't try yours last time," she says, eyeing my plate. "But if you liked it, this one should be fan-fucking-tastic."

"Enjoy, ladies!" The waitress chirps, giving a playful bow before bouncing back toward the kitchen.

Here goes nothing. I scoop up a small bite, mentally preparing myself. The second it hits my tongue, my eyes widen. Holy shit. This *is* better than last time.

"Oh my God," I mumble, covering my mouth, because *manners.* "This is amazing."

Rachel takes her first bite, but instead of responding, she freezes mid-chew, her eyes locked on something behind me.

"OH. MY. GOD!" She chokes, muffling the words with her hand.

I frown, confused. "I mean, it's good, but not *that* good."

331

Her gaze doesn't shift. She's somewhere between awe and panic. I follow her line of sight, turning just in time to see Cam walking across the dining area in a crisp white chef's coat.

Holy fuck.

There's something about a man in a uniform that just does it. And Cam? Cam looks good. I almost drop my fork. I thank every star in the sky that I swallowed my bite first because Rachel, however, is not so lucky. She's still mid-bite trying to compose herself.

Cam's sharp gaze lands on us, taking in the absolute mess that is Rachel choking on her food and me sitting here, fork frozen in the air like an idiot. He looks surprised, but only for a second before his mouth curves into a smug, knowing grin.

"Ladies!" His voice is warm. "What are ye doin' here?"

Rachel, still recovering from nearly choking to death, slaps a hand on the table, her voice a little too high-pitched. "WHAT ARE WE DOING HERE? Are you—*THIS IS YOUR RESTAURANT*?"

Her wide eyes dart between Cam and the plate, like he just admitted to running a black-market empire instead of a kitchen.

Cam chuckles, his grin widening. "Aye, it's mine."

Rachel points at her plate, scandalized. "DID YOU MAKE THIS?!"

"I have so many questions." I gesture wildly at the restaurant. "Sit down! Wait, can you? Are you busy?"

Rachel pats the seat beside her, all but vibrating with excitement. "Oh my God, this is amazing."

Cam leans against the edge of the table, clearly enjoying every second of this.

"Welcome to my place," he chuckles, with an easy shrug. "I was gonna tell ye, but then we got stuck at the castle."

I laugh, shaking my head. "You could've mentioned it when we ate here the first time. Not that I'm complaining, this is next-level."

Rachel grins, nudging my arm. "That's saying something, coming from her."

She turns to Cam, beaming. "I love that this place is yours. It fits you."

She touches his arm, a light, playful gesture. Cam's always had an easy charm, but there's something about him right now that feels... different.

He chuckles, nodding. "The kitchen's my happy place when I'm not dealin' with other chaos."

Rachel tilts her head, her eyes glinting with curiosity. "Other chaos? Like what?"

Cam winks, brushing off the question. "That's a story for another day."

Rachel and I exchange a look. Yeah, that means he's absolutely hiding something.

But before we can push, he stands. "Anyway, just came out to mingle with guests." He nods toward the dining room. "Need to make sure everyone's happy and full. I'll be back."

We watch as he moves through the restaurant, effortlessly charming everyone in his path. He's in his element, and it's honestly such an endearing thing. Not to mention he looks really good doing it.

Rachel and I refocus on our plans for the rest of the week, deciding how to tackle my family stuff, but just as I'm about to ask her something, that feeling creeps up again.

A slow, uncomfortable crawl up my spine like I'm being watched. I scan the room, keeping my movements casual. And all I'm met with is diners enjoying their meals, chatting and laughing.

I'm about to brush it off when movement catches my eye. Cam steps back into view, grinning as he approaches our table.

"How was the rest of your dinner, ladies?" He asks, his energy buzzing like he's on top of the world.

Honestly? If I could cook like this and have everyone adore me, I'd probably radiate smug satisfaction too.

"This place is amazing," I say, still grinning. "I'm still shocked, but somehow also not surprised at all."

He chuckles, then pulls us both into quick, warm hugs before stepping back.

"And before ye even try, don't bother payin'. It's on the house."

"Cam!" Rachel protests, already reaching for her bag.

But he's already waving us off, grinning like the absolute menace he is. There's no winning this one.

By the time we finally drag ourselves back to the house, we're full, exhausted, and on the verge of a food coma. No deep conversations, no planning, just bed.

Except I can't sleep, because my brain is an asshole. How can one person stir up so many emotions? One second, I'm annoyed as hell, the next? It's a full-on flooding of the Nile.

It's more than annoying.

I don't even want to admit how many times on this trip I've reached for the stupid toy Rachel gave me as a post breakup gift.

Joke's on me, apparently.

That thing has become a lifeline. Every heated exchange, every lingering look, every moment I catch myself thinking about his voice, his smile, his damn arms. All of it fuels my guilty little late-night routine.

Even now, just thinking about him sends a wave of warmth through my body, my skin too sensitive, and my mind too restless.

I groan, flipping onto my stomach, burying my face in the pillow like that'll stop my thoughts from spiraling. I try to focus, to breathe, to sleep. Really I do. But then... that feeling creeps in.

It tightens, sinking deep into my gut. Something feels... off and I hold my breath, listening. Waiting. But all I hear is silence.

And just like that, the feeling fades, slipping away like smoke, but it leaves a tightness in my chest behind. A lingering unease coiling low in my gut.

I exhale slowly, shaking my head. I'm spooking myself over nothing, but now I'm even more awake than I was a second ago. I force myself to relax, stretching out under the covers, my body is still warm, restless and aching.

I roll onto my side, pressing my face into the pillow with a muffled groan. I should be asleep, but instead my mind is stuck on him.

I press my thighs together, but it does absolutely nothing to relieve the heat pooling between them. So naturally, my hand starts drifting toward my nightstand.

Maybe just a quick—

"You're not as quiet as you think you are, take the night off. Give her a break." Rachel yells from the other room.

I freeze. Oh. My. God.

The mortification is immediate. Before I can even process a response, her voice floats in again, cheerful as ever.

"Goodnight."

Heat scorches up my neck. I slap a hand over my face, debating suffocation as a better alternative to living through this moment.

Woopsie.

CHAPTER 25

Enchanted

RAVEN

This bed is a literal cloud. I sink deeper, cocooned in layers of soft, luxurious sheets that practically hug me back. If someone told me the Egyptian gods wove this fabric themselves, I'd believe them. I could stay in this bed forever and die happy.

Unfortunately, Rachel has other plans.

"Today is the day!" She declares, launching herself onto the bed like a human cannonball. I grunt as the mattress absorbs the impact; my little bubble of bliss officially shattered.

I pry open one eye. "The day for what? My untimely death?"

"*The sky's awake, today's the day*," she sings.

I groan, shoving my face into my pillow. She's lucky I love her.

Rachel grabs my arm, tugging at me. "Come on, we need breakfast before we start getting ready for tonight."

That gets my attention. My stomach rumbles, loud enough to betray me.

"Fine." I stretch lazily, reluctant to leave my paradise but tempted by the idea of fresh pastries and hot tea. "Want to go to that little cafe down the street?"

Rachel grins. "That's exactly what I was hoping you'd say."

The second we step inside, warm cinnamon and fresh coffee wrap around me. The energy in here is bright, cozy, and buzzing with life. Conversations hum around us, the low clink of mugs against saucers filling the air. It's busy here this morning.

We grab a table by the window, and Rachel immediately dives into the menu. I glance around and then freeze.

Mike Wazowski.

He's at the counter, laughing with an older man, his posture completely relaxed. Not the polished formal businessman I met the other day, but someone else entirely.

I lean over and nudge Rachel, keeping my voice low. "That's Mike. The guy from work. The one in the white shirt."

Rachel glances up. And goes still. Her eyes narrow slightly as she leans toward me. "Wait, *that's* him?"

"Yup," I tilt my head. "Not too bad-looking, right?"

She raises an eyebrow, nodding slowly. "Oh, for sure." A pause. "So do we like him? Or...?"

I lean back in my chair. "Eh." I drag the sound out, debating. "He's definitely attractive, but he came off... very formal. But maybe that's just the job. Emails and suits aren't exactly thrilling."

I glance toward the counter again. He doesn't look like emails and suits right now though.

"Although..." I continue, tilting my head. "He was kinda sweet. And he did offer to show me around."

Rachel is watching me like a hawk. "He's totally flirting with you, is that even appropriate? Remember no men."

"Was. Past tense." I correct quickly.

The look she gives me says she doesn't believe me for a second.

Then, Mike turns and starts to head our way. He stops beside the table, flashing a charming smile. His eyes flick briefly to Rachel before locking back onto me. His confidence is effortless.

"Well, well... fancy meeting you here," he says smoothly. Then, his attention shifts entirely to Rachel. "Who's your lovely friend?"

Rachel extends a hand, all warmth but with a sharp, assessing edge.

"Rachel." She gives him that unreadable look she only gives men she's trying to figure out. "And what *I'd* like to know is more about you."

Mike chuckles, clearly intrigued, his gaze flicking over her before returning to me. "I'm just a work friend."

Rachel's eyebrow twitches slightly at that.

"What brings you two out this way?" He asks, his tone smooth. "A bit of sightseeing?"

"Pretty much," I shrug. "Needed breakfast before our big plans tonight." I pause, curiosity tugging at me. "Do you live around here?"

"Oh no," he replies, waving a hand casually. "Just in the area checking on a friend."

His tone is easy, but there's something about the way he says it, has me intrigued.

Mike straightens slightly, adjusting his watch. "Well, it was a pleasure meeting you, Rachel," he says smoothly, his gaze lingering on her just a little longer than necessary.

Then, he turns back to me. "Good seeing you again, Miss Taylor. Enjoy your breakfast... and your ball."

And just like that, he's gone.

Rachel and I exchange a look.

"He's kinda fun, don't you think?

She smirks, giving me a pointed glance. "Too bad we're on a no men kick."

The bathroom is a war zone of curling irons, mascara wands, and colorful chaos. Rachel and I share the vanity, elbows colliding as we attempt to work our magic. The air crackles with energy, our ridiculous commentary bouncing off the walls, making it impossible to focus.

Rachel's half-done curls are close to smacking me in the face as I carefully apply my lipstick. I pause mid-stroke, dodging another close call before snapping, "Oh my God, Rachel, if you whack me with your hair one more time, you're going to for sure get lipstick on it."

She snorts, completely unbothered. "Relax, you're about to look like a goddess, you'll survive."

I huff out a laugh, shaking my head as I finish. She's not wrong. The anticipation in the air is undeniable, a heady mix of nerves and excitement.

This isn't just some event.

It feels more like a celebration. It's the solstice, a full moon, and somehow, we've found ourselves going to a ball.

It's like the universe hand-delivered every childhood fairytale on a silver platter. Except the dresses are better, the men are hotter, and the stakes feel impossibly high.

Rachel spins dramatically, her gown catching the light as she strikes a pose.

"How do I look?" she asks, giving me a twirl that sends a few curls bouncing.

"Like you're about to ruin some poor bastard's life." I grin. "Damn, you look *good*. Now hurry up before we're late... and not in the cute way."

I pull on my dress and catch Rachel staring at me in the mirror, her eyes wide, mouth slightly open.

"Holy fuck," she whispers, her grin splitting wide.

I turn, looking in the mirror. I barely recognize myself. Nephi's designs were already stunning at our fitting, but under the soft glow of the vanity lights, they're next-level. The fabric hugs me in all the right places, flowing like liquid with every movement.

Rachel nudges me, giving herself one last once-over. "Yup, we look amazing."

She's right. We do.

But as I glance back at my reflection, something tugs at me.

My necklace. I wasn't planning to wear it tonight; it doesn't really match the aesthetic I was going for. But suddenly, that feels irrelevant.

Without thinking, I cross the room, slipping it from the pouch. The metal is cool against my fingertips, but the moment it touches my skin, warmth spreads through me.

Rachel watches, her expression unreadable. "Perfect touch."

The car pulls up outside, its engine cutting through the quiet. Right on time.

We grab our stuff, lock the door, and head out. Sliding into the back seat, I'm practically vibrating with excitement. The car hums along the road, the city slowly giving way to the countryside. Rachel sits beside me, uncharacteristically silent, her gaze fixed on the passing landscape.

The soft hum of the tires, the faint music from the speakers, it's all so soothing.

I blink and suddenly, a sharp bump jolts me upright. The world outside has changed.

I sit up straighter, my eyes narrowing as I take in the darkened road, the towering trees that loom on either side. Where are we?

"Wait," I murmur, the word slipping out before I can stop them. Recognition tugs at the edges of my mind.

Rachel barely reacts, still staring out the window, lost in her own thoughts.

The car takes another turn, the sound of gravel crunching beneath the tires filling the silence, and a large iron gate looms ahead. As the car rolls through the entrance, the castle comes into view.

My breath catches.

"This is the same castle."

Rachel snaps to attention, blinking as she finally registers where we are. "Wait, what?"

I can't take my eyes off the massive stone structure, lit like something out of a dream.

Rachel practically vibrates beside me, her excitement suddenly radiating off her in waves. "You mean... the same castle we were at with the guys?" Her voice climbs, eyes wide as she presses up against the window.

I huff out a small laugh, shaking my head. "Unless you've been sneaking off to castles behind my back, I'd say yes."

Rachel's lips curve into a wicked grin. "Damn."

As the car rolls up the long drive, the full scale of the event unfurls before us. A steady stream of vehicles moves toward the grand entrance, valets guiding guests in a rhythmic, effortless dance. The warm glow of chandeliers spills out onto the courtyard, flickering across the cobblestone path.

Music drifts from the entrance, soft and hypnotic, weaving through the night like a spell. The entire scene hums with anticipation, energy thick in the air.

I reach into my bag, "Let's hurry and put on our masks."

Rachel nods, shifting closer as we take turns fastening the delicate straps, fingers working quickly. There's something thrilling about the anonymity of it all, like slipping into another life, another version of ourselves.

A gloved hand appears in my periphery, and I glance up to find a valet, his smile polished, as he opens the door. "Good evening, beautiful," he says smoothly, offering his hand.

Rachel, already stepping out on the other side, laughs as her own escort assists her. "Well, this is already turning into a night to remember."

The valet straightens, expression polite. "Would you like to leave your things in the car, Miss? Your driver will stay here until you're ready to leave, I assure you, everything will be safe."

It's an easy choice. Nothing ruins a look like a clutch weighing you down all night.

"That's perfect, actually," I reply, glancing at Rachel. "I think I'll leave my phone too. Let's just keep an eye on each other."

Rachel nods, already slipping her phone into her bag and setting it inside the car. "Deal."

And with that, we step into another world.

The castle at dusk is breathtaking. Its towering stone walls glowing under the last traces of fading sunlight, the gold hues softening the imposing exterior. The last time we were here, storm clouds clawed at the sky, twisting the castle into something out of a gothic nightmare. But tonight, it's something else entirely.

The courtyard thrums with life.

Guests move in clusters, their gowns sweeping across the stone, the soft candlelight catching on intricate masks and shimmering fabrics. Laughter and conversation intertwine with the music, an intoxicating blend of excitement.

No names. No pasts. Just the company of strangers, and the promise of a night where anything could happen.

Rachel loops her arm through mine, her voice hushed with awe. "I feel like this is going to be the best night ever."

Security is everywhere. Not obvious, but noticeable if you know what to look for. Men in sharp suits linger at the edges of the crowd, their earpieces barely visible beneath their polished exteriors.

They blend in. But they don't.

Two men in tuxedos stand on either side of the massive entrance, pulling the doors open in the perfect synchronization. They bow slightly as we pass.

"Ladies."

Rachel squeezes my arm, barely containing her excitement. "Shut up, shut up! I love this so much already."

I bite back a grin. Same.

Double doors swing open, revealing a short corridor lined with flickering sconces that cast golden light onto the walls. The anticipation thickens, humming in my chest like a second heartbeat.

Then, another set of doors swings wide. And I physically stop in my tracks.

The ballroom is massive, every inch of it is glittering with elegance. Chandeliers dangle from the high ceilings, casting a soft, golden glow over the spinning dancers and lavishly dressed guests. The gleaming floor reflects the twinkling lights above, and the musicians in the corner play a haunting melody.

Rachel lets out a breathless laugh.

"We definitely didn't see this when we were here before," I murmur, taking it all in.

Couples twirl in effortless synchronization, while others mingle in clusters, their laughter soft and smooth, blending seamlessly with the music. It's like stepping into a dream I never want to wake up from.

Rachel leans in, a smirk tugging at her lips. "Good thing we took those dance lessons. I'd rather not be the only ones here who can't do the waltz."

I laugh, adjusting my mask. "You're welcome for that brilliant idea. Though, no promises I won't twirl right into a wall."

We step off the last stair, blending into the throng of guests. The energy in the room is magnetic. Everything glows, from the extravagant table settings to the shimmering champagne pyramid, to the soft sway of skirts and whispers of silk.

A slower, more romantic tune begins, and couples flood the dance floor, twirling effortlessly. My gaze drifts toward the grand double doors leading to the gardens, their glass panes reflecting the full moon. The night is clear, and I already know I'm going to sneak out there before the night's over.

But before I can dwell on it, something catches my eye.

A tall man in a mask, gliding through the crowd with unmistakable ease. People turn as he passes, murmurs trailing in his wake. He moves like he belongs here.

And then, his steel-blue gaze locks onto mine. Something dark flickers behind his twisted smirk. It vanishes too quickly to name, smoothed by a look of intrigue. His eyes flick between me and Rachel, and then he strides straight for us.

Rachel stiffens beside me. Not obvious, but I feel it.

The man stops just short of invading my space, his smirk widening as he dips his head slightly.

His attention shifts toward Rachel. "You both look stunning tonight," he smiles. "Enjoying yourselves so far?"

Rachel tilts her chin up, offering him a polite but carefully measured smile. "Thank you, and yes, we are. What about you?"

Her tone is controlled. But I know her well enough to catch the unspoken edge. The man's predatory gaze drags over her before flicking back to me, the same unreadable glint in his blue eyes.

"Oh," he murmurs, voice like silk. "I have a feeling the night is just getting started."

I bet you do, buddy.

His unsettling smile doesn't waver, doesn't slip. But before I can respond, two more men step up beside him. Their attention is locked onto us, laser-focused, like they've just stumbled across their next conquest.

Friends? Bodyguards? Just more guys looking to chat?

One of them, another tall blonde, but with an easy, practiced grin that screams charmer, is the first to speak.

"Don't the two of you look absolutely dazzling tonight," his British accent smooth and rich with an effortless charm.

Rachel and I exchange a glance. I can already see the wheels turning in her head.

"Where are you gentlemen from?"

The playful blonde leans in slightly, grinning. "London," he answers. "And you?"

"Oooh, London boys! How positively dashing!" Rachel croons, her British accent damn near perfect. She even adds a ridiculous curtsy for good measure, drawing a low chuckle from the blonde.

I choke back a laugh. This girl is unhinged, and I love her for it.

"Not bad," he muses, eyes twinkling as he extends his hand. "For an American. Care to dance?"

Rachel doesn't hesitate. She flicks a glance my way, checking in. I roll my eyes, nudging her forward.

"Go."

"I'd love to," she grins letting him lead her onto the dance floor, vanishing into the sea of swirling gowns and masked strangers.

Which leaves me with the remaining two.

They both shift slightly, opening their mouths at the exact same time. "Would you—"

They freeze. Exchanging glances.

I burst into laughter, unable to contain myself.

"Rock, paper, scissors?" I suggest with a grin, tilting my head. "Winner gets the first dance."

Their expressions are priceless. A perfect mixture of amusement and disbelief. "You should see your faces right now." Another laugh slips out.

To my absolute delight, they recover quickly. Without hesitation, they go straight for it.

Rock. Paper. Scissors.

Mr. Mysterious lands on rock. His friend pulled out the scissors.

The friend stares at his defeated hand, shaking his head slightly before retreating with a small, amused smirk.

"Looks like I'm the lucky one." The mystery man says, stepping closer. He extends his hand, his steel-blue eyes gleaming behind his mask with the same twisted smile.

"Would you do me the honor, love?"

A ripple of anticipation skates through me as I place my hand in his, offering a polite but unreadable smile. "Lead the way."

The music swells, and my partner moves with precision and practiced ease. But beneath it all, an odd chill snakes down my spine, prickling my skin like invisible hands brushing too close.

That damn feeling again. *Can't I have one night with no weird shit?*

It's been happening more frequently now, an unseen presence just out of reach. But every time I turn, there isn't anyone there.

Still, it lingers. Tightening around my ribs.

I force my focus back on the dance, on the music, on the way my partner's hands guide me through each smooth step. But then everything shifts.

The sound around me dulls, the ballroom lights dim as a sharp, high-pitched ringing floods my ears, drowning out the laughter, the music, the murmuring voices. The world around me blurs, the colors fading, the movement slowing.

I blink hard.

My footing wavers, the floor beneath me is suddenly unsteady, like reality itself has tilted. My partner's lips move, but his voice doesn't reach me.

I shake my head, blinking again. The moment snaps like a rubber band, the ringing fades and the music filters back in.

His words finally cut through the fog. "... you alright, love?" His voice is careful, searching.

I exhale, forcing a reassuring smile, though my pulse is still thundering. "Yeah, just a little... distracted."

But he's not convinced, his brow furrows slightly. "Tell me," he muses, titling his head as if trying to read beyond my expression. "Do you ever feel like places like this are haunted with old memories?"

I blink. Not the question I was expecting.

"I suppose it's possible," I answer slowly, choosing my words carefully. "Especially places with so much history."

"Exactly." His voice dips lower, almost to a purr. "It's like certain people are more open to it, more attuned, you know?"

I shrug, "Could be."

"I get the sense you might be one of those people."

A shiver laces through me. I tilt my head, studying him. Trying to decide if I like this conversation or if I should be walking away already.

"Interesting observation," I let out a small laugh. "But I think I'd notice if I were... attuned."

The song winds down, and I step back, offering a polite smile.

"Thanks for the dance." My voice is smooth. "Have a great night."

I dip into a graceful curtsy, hoping to make my exit feel like a choice, not a retreat.

"If you'll excuse me, I promised my friend I'd find her after each dance."

I turn around and slam straight into a wall of solid muscle. A sharp inhale catches in my throat.

Warm hands find my waist. A touch that sears straight through me, sharp and sudden.

I look up and freeze.

His mask is dark and sharp edged. Beneath it, piercing eyes, flecked with gold, burning through the dim light like a wolf in the dark.

For a second, the entire room tilts. The music fades, the world narrows, and I'm caught in the weight of that stare.

They remind me of Kane's eyes. The thought hits fast and hard.

No. There's no way.

Before I can shake myself free, the next song starts. It's low and sultry, thrumming with something electric.

He steps closer, holding out a hand in a silent command, an invitation laced with something dangerous.

I hesitate, scanning his face for anything that might explain why every nerve in my body is suddenly on high alert.

Nothing. Just a smirk, and a low chuckle that rumbles from his chest.

And against my better judgement, I place my hand in his. The moment our fingers connect, the world shifts. A sharp jolt snaps through me. I gasp, nearly jerking away.

Every instinct I have screams at me to run. To fight. To do something. But I can't move. His grip is firm, his presence is an unshakable force, and his gaze locks onto mine like he's searching for something I can't see.

With a fluid motion, he spins me, pulling me into the rhythm of the music like he's done this a thousand times before. I barely have time to process

347

the heat surging through me, the strange electric pull tightening around my ribs.

I take in the man before me. All black, flawless tailoring. A suit that doesn't just fit, it commands.

Everything about him is deliberate. Like he knows exactly what kind of attention he draws and revels in it.

And damn it, it's working.

Is it just me, or is it getting hot in here? Heat rises up my chest, creeping up my neck, and I can't tell if it's from the dance or something else entirely.

I look up, and he's already looking at me, the look on his face is dark and intense. A shiver runs through me, sharp and unexpected, a stark contrast to the cool, composed air he carries.

Shit. My hands start to tingle and warm, energy curling beneath my skin, flickering to life in my palms.

I force myself to keep moving, to focus on the rhythm instead of whatever the hell this is. Why does this always happen at the worst times?

The music shifts, and we move closer. His grip is warm, and he's effortlessly in control of every move. I try to get a better look at him, but then he spins me and suddenly, he's gone. Just like that, I'm in the arms of a new partner.

The intensity of the moment lingers, leaving me breathless, like the cord was just cut between us, but the static remains. We didn't exchange a single word, yet it felt like something just passed between us. Like a match hovering over gasoline, waiting for the strike.

The music is a whirlwind, each new partner barely giving me time to catch my breath. Laughter spills from my lips, the sheer thrill of it sweeping me up. Every now and then, I catch Rachel's gaze across the room, and we exchange grins.

But the song fades and something shifts.

I step off the dance floor, pulse still racing, heading toward the spot Rachel and I agreed on earlier. I need a moment to breathe.

I don't get very far before the prickle at the back of my neck is back. Sharper this time.

I glance to my right and there he is. The brick wall.

My heart stutters. Those butterflies in my stomach lose their goddamn minds.

He leans against a column, all sharp lines and devastating precision, his dark suit and mask making him look like something out of a dream, or a nightmare, depending on the lighting.

A wicked, knowing smile tugs at his lips, like he's fully aware of the effect he has on me. And damn it, something about him feels achingly familiar.

I blink, and he's gone. Melted into the crowd, disappearing so seamlessly I almost question if he was even there at all.

Umm... okay? That wasn't weird at all.

Rachel appears out of nowhere, wrapping me in a tight hug, her energy pure excitement.

"This is so much fun!" She exclaims, vibrating with happiness. "Are you having fun? Dance with anyone exciting?"

I laugh, shaking off the lingering unease. "Yes!! I honestly can't remember the last time I had this much fun."

It's not a lie. The night is pure magic. And right now, in this dress, I feel like the Winter Queen herself, draped in stardust and mystery. Every single penny spent having this gown made was worth it.

The hum of conversation, the golden flicker of candlelight against the glass, the distant echo of laughter. Everything is spun in elegance, in a heady, intoxicating energy.

Rachel, of course, is already drawing attention like moths to a flame. Her dress is a deep, blood-red gown, the silk hugging her curves like sin itself. It's a weapon in its own right. The slit alone should be illegal. The neckline is even deeper. It's giving major Jessica Rabbit vibes, bold and unapologetically seductive.

And judging by the pack of men hanging onto her every word? Yeah, she knows it.

She waves me over, beaming. "Why have we never come to a ball before?"

Before I can answer, a tall man with a deep, accent I can't quite place, steps forward. His mask is adorned in shimmering blues and purples that compliment his eyes. "Your dance cards aren't full for his next song, I hope?"

Rachel curtsies, her voice dipping into dramatic elegance. "Of course not, good sir."

The man chuckles, offering his hand.

"I'll find you," she calls over her shoulder as he whisks her away, grinning wickedly. "Make good choices!"

I roll my eyes. Unlikely.

That's my cue. With the chaos of the ballroom swirling behind me, I slip toward the quieter hall, heading for the one place that's been pulling at me all night.

The library.

My steps slow as I approach the hallway leading there. Two security guards stand at attention, their sharp gazes scanning every movement.

I pause. Reconsidering. I didn't really think this through.

Then, one of them raises a hand to his earpiece. A brief moment of silence and they are exchanging glances. And just like that, they pivot. Moving briskly down the opposite hall.

My heart rate picks up. What luck.

I exhale slowly, steadying my breath, as I slip through the heavy doors. The shift is immediate. The music, the voices, the noise of the ball melting away.

Now, which way?

I close my eyes, piecing together my memory of the layout from our last visit. Before doubt has the chance to creep in, I head right, following an instinctive pull.

Each step echoes softly against the plush carpet. My heart races and I'm torn feeling both a thrill and unease.

After a few more steps, I stop. Found it. The library smells exactly like I remember. Old paper, polished wood, and something almost... charged.

"Thank you," I whisper to no one, relief and awe washing over me in equal measure.

Then, it happens again.

I all but roll my eyes at this point. A shiver ripples through me as that familiar, high-pitched ringing fills my ears. It's sharper this time, more insistent. I squeeze my eyes shut, willing it to stop. I don't have time for this.

The library is dimly lit, but scattered lamps cast a golden glow, illuminating the towering shelves and intricate details of the space.

I move quickly, following my memory to the large desk in the corner.

And then, I see it. The painting that stopped me in my tracks the last time.

A regal couple, frozen in time, dressed in clothing centuries old. My gaze locks onto the man first.

Tall. Broad-shouldered. Dark hair, chiseled features and piercing eyes that follow me through the canvas.

I swallow hard.

Even beneath the elaborate embroidery of his high-collard attire, there's something timeless about him. Something that tugs at the edges of my memory.

I step closer, drawn to his gaze, my fingers hovering just shy of the painting's surface. A flicker of déjà vu cuts through me, cold and sharp. My heartbeat pounds in my ears, as I take another step forward.

My focus shifts to the woman at his side. She's beautiful, her hair is styled in intricate waves, and her expression is soft yet mysterious. She looks at him with an intensity that mirrors his, like they're sharing a secret only they understand.

I can't shake the feeling that this painting holds something important, but what?

Then, I see it. The dagger.

Just like before, it catches my eye, and it's impossible to ignore.

Its hilt is embedded with stones eerily similar to mine, but not quite the same. These stones are black and void of depth, swallowing light instead of reflecting it. Just like the one stone I usually keep in my pocket. *I think back to the daggers in the display case we saw. I wonder if this one is in there. Maybe I can get a closer look.*

The rest of the painting is rich, vibrant, alive with color, yet the stones seem to pull everything into them, leaving only emptiness.

My mouth parts in disbelief.

There's no fucking way.

I lean in closer, breath shallow, studying every detail.

The dagger couldn't possibly be connected to mine, could it?

I tear my gaze from the weapon, looking back up at the man. His stare feels like it's anchoring me in place. The longer I study him, the stronger the pull grows, it's a recognition I can't name, that I can't explain.

351

Then, the scent of mint and pine hits me.

I inhale sharply, the crip, woodsy scent weaving through the warm, musty aroma of old books. My pulse skips as I scan the room, expecting to find someone nearby.

I'm still alone.

A shiver races down my spine, and my breath catches in my throat. I glance back at the painting, half-expecting something to have shifted.

Calm down, Raven. You're overthinking.

Exhaling slowly, I take a step back, forcing myself to steady my breathing.

My gaze drifts back to the woman beside him. A crown rests on her head that's both delicate yet strangely alive, like vines curling through her hair, with a serpent, poised to strike.

My brows furrow as I lean in, fascinated. There's an inscription beneath the painting, the words barely legible in the dim glow.

I squint, trying to make out what it says, when I hear a sound. A faint shuffle somewhere in the library.

I freeze. Shit. I can't get caught in here. The last thing I need is to get kicked out of a ball. How embarrassing would that be?

Straightening, my breath hitches. The shadows between the towering shelves seem to stretch wider, pressing in around me. The room is too still.

I scan the space, but I see nothing. Still, I feel it, the feeling that someone's watching me.

The weight of unseen eyes prickles against my skin, the air around me shifting, humming with something.

Well, guess that means it's time to go, and quickly.

Peering around the corner, I check for the coast to be clear. My muscles coil, ready to move, to slip back into the hall like I was never here.

I hear a low, urgent whisper that snakes down my body like ice.

"Raven."

I freeze. Every muscle locks as I spin, scanning the shadows behind me. Nothing. The library remains still, its silence stretching unnaturally, pressing in like a held breath.

"Raven, open your eyes."

My pulse pounds in my ears. The chill crawling over my skin isn't from the draft.

"Hello?" I keep my voice steady, but it barely carries beyond the shelves.

No answer, but the weight in my chest tightens, warning me to move.

I don't hesitate. Turning on my heel, I quickly retrace my steps, slipping back through the doors. The second I step into the ballroom, warmth crashes into me, and I realize just how cold the library was. The hum of conversation, the music, the flicker of candlelight, all of it is a jarring contrast to the quiet unease that still lingers in my bones.

My pulse slows as my eyes scan the room for Rachel.

I spot her near our meeting point, her dress catching the light like liquid fire, making her impossible to miss. Relief flutters in my chest, my steps quickening toward her, and then I see him.

A presence cutting through the room like a blade.

Every movement is effortless. The dark suit fits him like a second skin, the sharp lines of his mask only adding to the dangerous allure he wears so well. The crowds parts instinctively as he moves, their gazes flickering toward him, but he doesn't acknowledge them.

Because his eyes are on me.

And when they lock onto mine, everything else ceases to exist. The impact is instant, like the air has been knocked from my lungs.

Rachel sucks in a sharp breath coming up beside me, her jaw practically on the floor. She looks between us, back and forth, then jabs a finger at me, then the dance floor. Her wide-eyed expression screams one thing. *Go.*

Before I can even process her silent command, he's standing right in front of me.

The scent of pine coils around me, wrapping me in something both familiar and foreign. My lips part, but before I can summon a breath, let alone a reply, his hand takes mine in a single fluid motion.

No hesitation. No words.

He just pulls me into a spin, the world blurring as my dress flares around us, and before I can steady myself, we're swept into the rhythm of the music like we belong there.

His grip is inescapable, one hand pressed against the small of my back, the other keeping mine locked in his. He draws me so close that if I lifted my head, the space between us would vanish entirely. His breath is warm against my ear, sending a sharp, traitorous shiver down my spine.

"Has anyone told you tonight just how stunning you look?" His voice is like dark silk wrapping around me, weaving through my ribs, and pulling tight. "Because if any of those other gentlemen failed to mention it while they were touching you, I may have to have a word with them about how to properly treat a lady."

A rush of heat coils in my stomach. "Thank you," I manage, my voice betrays me, breathless and unsteady. Compliments have never been my strong suit, especially not from men. Men who wield words like weapons, cutting through resolve with nothing but a glance.

My instinct is to look away, to pretend that his presence doesn't unearth something I don't want to acknowledge. But before I can break free of his piercing gaze, his fingers brush my chin, tilting my face back toward him.

His eyes hold me captive, pulling me under. For a moment, he looks like he's about to say something else, but then his focus flickers over my shoulder. A fraction of a second. Barely noticeable.

And suddenly, something clicks.

The way he moves, the sharpness in his eyes, the sheer arrogance radiating off him like a damn beacon.

I narrow my eyes, my breath catching as the realization slams into me like a freight train.

"*Wait, Kane?*" My voice lands somewhere between disbelief and annoyance.

His smirk widens as his gaze sweeps down my body, deliberate and unapologetic, before trailing back up to meet mine. The heat in his eyes is unmistakable, and my treacherous heart stumbles over itself.

"This," he murmurs, his voice dropping lower, "my darling, will have to wait."

His words send a jolt through me, igniting the ever-growing problem that is Kane.

The moment stretches between us, the air thick with something heavier than it should be. But then he straightens, releasing my chin, but not my gaze. His presence is suffocating, but there's something else now.

A softness in his smile that wasn't there before.

A crack in his armor.

"I'm afraid I have to go take care of something," his voice drags over my skin like a whisper. "Please forgive me."

He steps back, giving me a graceful bow, but that smirk lingers, like he's leaving me with an unspoken promise I can't quite decipher.

"Wait, what?" The words slip out before I can stop them, the surprise impossible to hide.

For a heartbeat, something flickers in his eyes. Hesitation. Like he doesn't want to go. Then, his gaze shifts past me again.

Whatever he sees darkens his expression. His jaw ticks, his fingers curling into a fist at his side. A flash of something raw cuts through him so fast I almost wonder if I imagined it.

I want to turn around to see what pulled his focus and to understand what changed in that single instant.

But before I can move, his gaze snaps back to mine, and the shadow of something I wasn't supposed to see is gone. Replaced with warmth.

He lingers, just long enough that I feel the absence the moment he pulls away.

"Don't worry," he murmurs, his voice dipping into something almost intimate. "I'll be back to rescue you again. Excuse me."

And then, like a ghost, he's gone.

Vanishing into the sea of masks and gowns like he was never here. But I can still feel it. The last bit of air in the room leaving with him.

I inhale sharply, trying to shake the electricity still humming under my skin.

A part of me itches to follow him. To see what could possibly be so urgent that he'd leave so suddenly. I take a step to follow him, and Rachel is rushing toward me, pulling my focus, practically bouncing with excitement.

"You won't belie—"

We both stop short, breaking into a grin.

Rachel raises an eyebrow, her smile wicked. "You first."

"Actually, I think it's the same thing," I laugh, hardly able to contain my own excitement. "I swear I just danced with Kane."

Rachel bursts out laughing, nodding. "You did! I just talked to Cam, and the idiot really thought I wouldn't recognize him."

We dissolve into laughter, feeding off each other's own disbelief.

"I don't know where they went, but whatever," she says, grinning as she glances around the room. "Want to go out and see the gardens?"

"Yes, that would—" I stop mid-sentence as the first notes of *Enchanted* drifts through the room. The delicate chords fill the air, and I spin toward Rachel, my heart already racing.

"Ahh! My song!"

I grab her hand, practically dragging her back toward the dance floor. "We *have* to go dance right now!"

She lets out a laugh, nodding, but before we move any further toward the dance floor, I feel it.

That familiar pull that always seems to find me at the most unexpected moments.

A tap on the shoulder, followed by a small clearing of a throat. "Excuse me, Princess, would you like to dance?"

I turn, already smiling. Kane. The mystery man of the hour.

"I *knew* that was you!" I smile, unable to hide the excitement in my voice.

Cam steps up, his signature shit-eating grin firmly in place. He extends a hand to Rachel, his eyes twinkling with pure mischief. "My turn."

I glance between them, my curiosity impossible to hide. "What are you guys doing here?"

Kane raises an eyebrow, that infuriating mix of impatience and amusement already working its magic.

"Princess..." He extends his hand, his dark gaze locking onto mine.

"What?"

"Would you like to stand here asking questions," his voice soft yet insistent, "or dance to your favorite song?"

My heart stumbles, trips, then falls. The room shrinks, pulling me under.

He's right.

I'd much rather dance.

"Okay, yes!" I laugh, breaking into a grin as I place my hand in his.

CHAPTER 26

Blank Space

KANE

E verything's running like clockwork. Mics are live. Cameras are rolling. Every man's in position.

"Check, check, check," I mutter under my breath, scanning the final feed before stepping fully into the role I came here to play. The board is set. The pieces are moving. I don't need to micromanage anything tonight. I have people for that.

Khloe's satisfied with the arrangements, and I'll check in as needed, but for now?

It's time to blend in.

Carrie deserves more than a raise for the intel she brought me. Rides. Security. The whole fucking nine yards. I told her to make sure everything was seamless for them.

They've arrived, but I'm holding back. Cam and the others are already scattered across the ballroom, keeping their ears to the ground while blending into the crowd.

I step through the doors, and the shift is immediate. The energy, the pulse, the weight of a hundred conversations humming beneath the music.

Laughter rings out. Glasses clink. The guests move with the kind of grace and confidence that only money and power can buy.

The atmosphere is exactly the way I designed it.

My earpiece crackles with a final check-in, confirming what I already know, everything is under control.

I catch one of my men as he walks by. "I'm off the clock, don't bother me unless it's urgent." He nods, already disappearing into the crowd. Good. I don't need distractions.

I move with purpose, my gaze sweeping across the room until it lands on Tyler. He's in his element, laughing, surrounded by familiar faces and a cluster of women hanging on his every word. He catches my eye, grins. He's enjoying himself, even if he'll never admit it outright.

Then I hear her laugh.

Clear and unmistakable.

It cuts through the ballroom like a blade, sharp and impossible to ignore. Every other sound fades and my body moves before my mind can catch up.

There she is.

Fuck. Me.

My chest tightens and the air around me is suddenly too thick and too hot.

Her dress catches the light as she moves, her arm linked with another man. I don't even register him beyond his existence. All I see is her.

The way the corners of her mouth lift with that smile. Oh, my fucking God. I might actually have to worship this woman.

I stop dead in my tracks, my breath catching like she's just sucker-punched me from across the room.

She doesn't just look stunning, she looks untouchable. A goddess wrapped in a dress that could've been pulled straight from the night sky itself.

It clings to her in all the right ways, with slits high enough to make my throat go dry. The plunging neckline and intricate gold ropework? Jesus Christ. Whoever designed that dress must've had her in mind, because it's not just a gown, it's a weapon, and I'm about to be destroyed.

But it's not just the dress.

It's her.

The way she owns the space around her without even trying. That quiet, unshakable confidence. She has no idea she's stopped time itself.

Her shimmering gold and crimson mask frames her face like something carved from fire and mystery. It makes her eyes even more lethal.

Her dark hair falls in soft waves over one shoulder, and all I can think about is how badly I want to wrap it around my fist

The air shifts around her.

People don't just glance, they fucking stare. Some openly, and some are playing it off. She moves like she's daring the world to try. And I'll be damned if I let anyone close enough to even think about taking that dare.

Then I see his hand. Resting possessively at her back as he leads her onto the dance floor. A slow, hot surge of rage twists in my gut. My jaw tightens and my fingers flex at my sides.

"Easy, killer."

Cam's voice cuts through the storm behind me, his hand clapping down on my shoulder.

I school my expression, turning just enough to give him a measured look. My voice comes out clipped, the edge impossible to hide.

"Sneak up on me like that again, and you might be the one with the black eye."

Cam grins, completely unbothered. "Relax. The way you're staring, I'm more worried about *his* eyes."

My jaw flexes, but I don't bother arguing. My gaze cuts back to them.

"If he keeps looking at her like he's about to fucking devour her—" my voice lowers, razor-sharp, "I can't promise he'll walk out of here without a scratch."

Cam raises a brow, smirking like the infuriating bastard he is. "Oh, you mean the way *you're* looking at her? Glass houses, my friend."

I tear my eyes away just long enough to glare at him, but he's already laughing, the sound grating against my nerves. "Keep laughing, and you'll be next."

He smirks, slapping me on the back. "I'd say good luck, but maybe I should save it for the poor bastard trying to hold her attention." His tone is laced with the kind of amusement that only pisses me off more. "Just remember, no broken bones." With a chuckle, he strolls off, leaving me simmering.

My gaze locks back onto her, scanning for the smallest hint of discomfort. I watch the way she moves, the way she laughs, the slight tilt of her head.

And that idiot with his hands all over her will find out just how fast I can rearrange his fingers if he even thinks about stepping out of line.

Her dance partner looks unimpressed. His irritation is written all over his face. I should feel smug, but then I catch a flicker of something in her expression. Hesitation.

And just like that, every muscle in my body tightens.

I take a step forward, ready to close the distance, but then she shakes it off, saying something and his irritation deepens.

That's it. I'm done watching.

I cut through the crowd, my stride unhurried but deliberate. She turns at the last second, running right into me.

She's even more devastating up close.

The dress hugs her every curve and it's all I can do to keep my eyes on her face, to not map out every inch of her right here in the middle of the ballroom.

My body reacts before my brain does and I'm intently fighting a boner.

The music shifts, pulling me from the edge. Before she can say a word, I take her hand, spin her into the dance, and watch as her dress flares, revealing flashes of smooth golden skin.

She bites her lip.

I swallow a groan, my grip tightening slightly as I pull her close.

My hand settles at her waist, guiding her movements, hoping she doesn't notice my growing cock.

That familiar scent of vanilla wraps around me, and I know I'm already fucked.

I lean in, just enough to feel her breath against my skin. My fingers brush against the small of her back, drawing her even closer.

Her eyes snap to mine, fire flickering behind those eyes. She tries so hard to contain it, to pretend she's unaffected. But I see it.

And fuck, I want her to let it out.

When I finally settle her back into a dance, she's just as speechless as before, her hand hesitant in mine. I lean in, voice low, watching the way she reacts to every inch of space between us.

"Has anyone told you tonight just how stunning you look?"

Her eyes flick away, her discomfort clear. *Don't you fucking dare hide from me.* I catch her chin, tilting her face back toward mine.

I'm about to tell her exactly that when something over her shoulder catches my attention. Khloe.

She's standing near the east door, deep in conversation with a man.

"Wait, Kane?"

My earpiece crackles, someone's needed at the east door. The door where Khloe is standing.

Perfect fucking timing.

I hesitate long enough to feel that sharp tug of two worlds pulling me in opposite directions.

The job. And her.

I grit my teeth, step back, and let go.

"Excuse me."

I turn, heading for the east doors, irritation simmering beneath my skin. Whoever this guy is, he just ruined a perfectly good moment. And I might throw him out on principle alone.

I catch Khloe's expression, and the second guy spots me, he bolts in the opposite direction like he's just seen a ghost.

My sister sighs, turning with a shake of her head.

"I had that under control, you assholes."

I smirk, knowing every single person on comms just heard that. "And?"

She rolls her eyes. "If I catch anyone with eyes on him, you're all fired."

I let out a slow breath. "You okay?" I keep my tone casual hoping at least someone is smart enough to have eyes on him, despite her threat.

She crosses her arms, unimpressed. "I don't need my brother and all his men swooping in every time someone asks for a dance."

I say nothing, waiting.

She smirks, eyes flicking toward the ballroom. "besides, it looks like you've got your hands full anyway."

Then, with a wink, she turns on her heel and disappears into the crowd. I already know I'm going to regret letting her walk off that easily.

Cam's laughter crackles over the earpiece, full of that infuriating amusement only he can pull off. I ignore him, watching as he veers toward the girls, blending into the crowd.

Tapping my earpiece, I murmur, "Can you have the band play *Enchanted* by Taylor Swift? Thanks."

The moment the first notes of the waltz drift through the air, I cross the ballroom, my focus locked on her. Standing there, draped in midnight and gold, she looks every bit the queen of the night.

Her eyes meet mine, waiting. She doesn't fill the silence. Just watches, like she's waiting for me to talk first.

I exhale, jaw tightening. *Fuck it.* "Hey, Princess."

Smooth. *Real fucking smooth.*

Her brow arches, amusement sparking in her eyes. "*Hey, Princess?*" she echoes, lips twitching. "We are absolutely going to talk about this, just not during my song."

Then, like a switch flipping, she exhales slowly, closing her eyes. A slow smile curves her lips. "I'm having a magical evening, by the way," she adds, voice dipping into something playful. "Thank you for asking."

Oh, I fucking bet she is.

I tug her closer, pulling her into the rhythm of the dance, letting the music weave around us like a carefully laid trap. "Enchanted to meet you, by the way."

The smirk I wear is deliberate. I want her to catch it. The moment she does, her gaze sharpens, surprise flickering before it melts into something darker.

She tilts her head, slowly, like she's considering just how far she wants to take this. Then, her lips curve into a wicked grin.

"Why, thank you..." she trails off, her voice dipping into a low, sultry tone, running down my spine like a fucking caress. "*Sir.*"

Fucking hell.

I step back, just slightly, putting enough space between us to keep my dick from making its presence known. Doesn't fucking help. My body has zero intention of behaving tonight. Every move she makes, every teasing flicker of her gaze, has me teetering on the edge of control.

I keep my expression composed, but the tension coils between us, tight and electric. Her hands are warm in mind, and for a second, I swear her skin tingles against my palms.

I lean in slightly, lowering my voice. Just enough to pull her attention back to me.

"Am I allowed to tell you again just how absolutely stunning you look tonight?"

Her gaze snaps to mine, breath catching for a fraction of a second before she blinks it away.

"Thank you."

The corner of my mouth lifts. She's never been good at taking compliments. I don't miss the way her pulse flutters at her throat, the way she fights the urge to look away. I track the movement, catching the way her necklace flickers the light.

Before I can dwell on the thought, she clears her throat, shifting under my stare. "I'm up here."

I chuckle, shaking my head as I lean back slightly, giving her a deliberate once-over. "Princess, I've admired your body more times than I'll admit, but that wasn't one of those times."

The blush that rushes up her throat hits instantly. She stares at me, completely at a loss for words, before looking away.

I let her, for now.

She lets herself get swept into the dance, into the easy rhythm between us. When the song ends, her eyes flutter shut as she exhales. There's a contentment in simply watching her like this. A rare moment where she isn't overthinking, isn't second guessing. But the hum of voices around us pulls me back to reality.

I lean in, my voice low. "Can I show you something?"

Her lashes lift, curiosity sparking in her gaze, but she nods without hesitation.

Good girl.

I take her hand, threading my fingers through hers, leading her off the dance floor before she has a chance to second-guess herself. Her fingers tighten around mine, the smallest squeeze, but I feel it like a brand.

Her soft giggle echoes in the quiet hallway, and I glance at her, a rare, quiet smile tugs at her lips.

I lead her down the familiar path, knowing exactly where I want to take her. Right now, sharing that small, hidden part of my world feels like a good place to start with the truth.

"Are we going to the greenhouse?" She asks, excitement lighting up her eyes.

I glance at her, unable to hide the smirk tugging at my lips. "You'll see."

We move through the halls, the soft glow of the lanterns casting long shadows against the walls. As soon as we hit the greenhouse, the rich scent of earth and blooming jasmine clings to the air, mixing with the warm, familiar scent of her perfume.

She lets out a soft laugh as we weave through the plants.

"What?" I ask, catching the grin she's failing to hide.

"We're sneaking through a castle during a masquerade," she replies, her voice bubbling with amusement. "Doesn't that feel a little... ironic to you?"

Her laughter is contagious, and though I don't fully let it show, I can't deny the humor in the situation. "When you put it that way."

We're nearly at the door leading outside when her hand goes stiff in mine. I stop instantly.

Her entire posture shifts, her body locking up as her gaze locks onto something past me. I follow it, my eyes landing on a shattered clay pot near the entrance. The soil is still fresh, the shards scattered like someone dropped it in a hurry.

Her expression darkens as her brows furrow, her lips parting like she's about to say something but loses the words before they can come.

"Hey." I squeeze her hand, bringing her back to the present. "You still with me? We're almost there... sort of."

She blinks, her eyes snapping back to mine. Whatever held her in place fades, but not entirely. She tucks it away, before flashing a curious smile. "What does *almost there, sort of* mean?"

Before I can answer, she sees it, and her entire face lights up, all tension forgotten. "The swing!" She gasps, practically dragging me toward it.

The moment we reach it, she lets go of my hand and slips onto the swing without hesitation, her dress pooling around her like dark ink against the moonlit grass.

She's lost in the moment. The formality of the evening, the ball, the crowd, it's like none of it exists. This is where her focus is.

I place my hands on the ropes, giving the swing a gentle push.

She leans back slightly, the night breeze catching the waves in her hair. An unguarded smile spreads across her lips and her eyes flutter shut.

I watch the way her eyes flutter shut, the way she exhales like she's letting something heavy go, even if just for a moment. This is the most *real* I've seen her. No mask. No sharp edges. Just her.

A chuckle slips out before I can stop it, and her head turns, her eyes narrowing. "Don't you dare laugh at me," she warns, but there's no bite in it.

I smirk, keeping my voice steady. "Wouldn't dream of it."

Her lips twitch, fighting back a grin, and the shift between us is instant. If I let my mind wander too far into what this is turning into, I'll start thinking about all the things I should tell her. The things I can't tell her.

Not yet. Not here.

So I let her have this moment. And maybe, just for a second, I let myself have it too.

The swing slows, the world settling around us. She stands, drawn to the tree trunk like something is calling to her. Her fingers brush over the carving of the two *K's*, tracing the letters slowly, as if she's committing them to memory.

A sharp prickle runs down my spine, coiling tight in my chest. It's gone in an instant, but the weight it leaves behind lingers.

I clear my throat, stepping toward her, but when she turns to face me, I stop.

There's something different in her gaze. A depth that wasn't there before, curling behind those eyes, whispering beneath her skin. It's still her, but for the first time, it feels like she's looking straight through me.

The space between us is nothing but a heartbeat. I feel the rise and fall of her chest, her rhythm synching to mine, and for a second, I don't fucking move.

Her lips part, her voice barely more than a murmur. "A storm is coming."

The certainty in her tone roots me to the ground, sending another cold prickle down my spine.

I keep my voice controlled. "Do you want to go back inside?"

She glances toward the lake, something unreadable flickering across her expression.

"No," she says after a beat. "But I know we probably should. We've been out here for a while."

"We can always come back out later," I tell her, my voice steady, even as something in my chest tightens.

She studies me, head tilted slightly, eyes searching. "I would like that very much."

Her gaze locks onto mine, unwavering, her eyes wide and bright beneath the moonlight. Long, dark lashes brush against her cheeks as she blinks slowly, her lips parting slightly.

"Let's get you back to the castle, then," I murmur, my voice rougher than I meant it to be.

"Okay," she whispers, gaze flicking down to my mouth.

Every ounce of patience I have is obliterated.

My hand moves on its own before I can stop it, brushing a loose strand of hair from her face, my thumb grazing the smooth curve of her cheek. She doesn't pull away like I think she will, instead, she leans in biting her lip.

My restraint snaps.

I grip her jaw, tilting her head up as my mouth crashes onto hers, claiming her with a hunger I've been holding back since the moment she walked into the ballroom. She meets me with equal fire, her lips parting for me, soft and warm. Her body presses into mine like she belongs there.

My hand slips up her waist, fingers flexing as I pull her closer, desperate to feel her, to take whatever she'll give me. My control is a thread frayed to the breaking point, my pulse is a war drum pounding in my ears.

She gasps against my lips as my hand trails up the curve of her back, tracing the delicate fabric of her dress. I feel the way she shivers, how her body reacts to me. How every sharp breath, every shift of her hips, tells me exactly what she wants.

Then she pulls back just enough to smirk.

"That's all you got?" She taunts, voice full of smugness she has no business wielding right now.

Oh, sweetheart.

Heat scorches through me, my grip tightening at her waist as I press her back against the tree, my body caging hers in. My lips hover over hers, so close she can feel every breath I take.

"Careful, Princess." My voice is a quiet warning. "You might not be ready for what happens when I stop holding back."

Her eyes flash with something reckless, her fingers trailing slowly down my chest. Testing me.

And fuck, I let her.

Her fingers pause just above my belt, her touch featherlight, teasing. "That's funny," she murmurs, tilting her head just enough to bring our lips a breath apart. "Because from where I'm standing, it seems like you're all talk."

This woman.

A slow smile tugs at my lips, my grip tightening at her hip. My hand skims lower, while my fingers brush the slit of her dress, just enough to make her inhale sharply. I don't move further, I just let my knuckles graze against her bare skin as I watch her pulse jump at her throat.

"Don't mistake restraint for weakness, love." My voice is low, but I can tell she feels the weight behind it. "I could have you begging before you had time to think twice about using that attitude again."

Her breath hitches.

I lean in, trailing my lips along the curve of her jaw, just close enough that she can feel the heat of my breath. Her pulse is racing now, her hands gripping my shirt like she doesn't trust herself to stay upright.

Good.

Because I'm barely holding myself back from ruining every ounce of self-control she has left.

"Would you like that?" I murmur against her skin, pressing one slow, deliberate kiss just beneath her ear. "To be against this tree, breathless and wrecked, with my hands all over you?"

A soft, barely-there whimper slips past her lips before she bites it back, but I hear it. My smirk deepens.

I drag my palm up, cupping her breast, kneading slowly, my thumb rolling over the hardened peak. Her breath hitches, her back is arching just enough to push into my touch. "That's it," I rasp, my teeth grazing her jaw. "You want more don't you?"

Another whimper and my other hand slides lower, fingers skimming over her bare thigh. I hesitate, dragging slow circles over her skin and she's arching into me again. I dip my fingers beneath the fabric of her dress, and she isn't wearing anything.

A groan rumbles from my chest as I stroke her slick folds, teasing her clit with the lightest brush of my fingertips.

"You're already shaking for me," I growl, pressing my finger deeper, spreading her open just to feel how drenched she is. "So fucking needy."

Her breath shudders, hips shifting, chasing my touch, but I don't give her what she wants, not yet. I could have her right here, against this tree, wring her out until she's got nothing left to give me but my name on her tongue.

Instead, I straighten, forcing myself to take a slow breath, knowing that if I don't stop now, I won't.

Her eyes are darker, hazy with something she doesn't want to name, her body still pressed tight against mine. She sways slightly, her fingers flexing against my chest, like she's considering pulling me back in.

She won't.

Not because she doesn't want to, but because I won't let her.

I drag my thumb along the side of her neck, feeling her pulse hammer beneath my touch. Then, before she can react, I pull back completely, leaving her standing there in the cool night air, still burning for me.

Her brows furrow, like she's trying to catch up, like she can't quite believe I just stopped.

I bite back a smirk as I roll my shoulders and exhale hard, dragging a hand through my hair. "Aye," I say, my voice steady despite how hard my dick is right now. "We should head back inside."

I don't look back as I step away, grabbing her hand to lead us back toward the castle.

Her hand is in mine, but something feels off. Her hands are more than just warm, they're hot. And it sends a pulse up my arm, sharp and electric.

I glance over, about to ask if she's alright, but she suddenly jerks her hand away, eyes going wide with something I can't quite place.

CRASH.

Instinct kicks in and I move, pulling her against me, shielding her as glass from the nearest light fixtures shatter above us. Shards scatter across the stone path, plunging everything around us into darkness.

She covers her head, even though we're clear of the worst of it. Adrenaline surges, and my grip on her is firm as I press my earpiece twice, a silent call for backup. My body stays tense, my gaze scanning every shadow, but I don't let her go. I keep her close.

"What was that?" She looks up at me, her voice shaky.

"Not sure," I say, nodding toward the darkness. "But I could go ask that ghost over there."

Her breath hitches but she doesn't laugh. Doesn't even roll her eyes. Instead, she goes still, gaze flickering to the trees as if something is lurking in the shadows.

The subtle glow of her necklace catches my eye, pulsing faintly, almost too soft to notice.

She recovers fast, rolling her eyes like she wasn't just looking at something that wasn't there. "Of course something weird happens, and all you can do is crack jokes and stare at my tits. Real helpful, Kane."

Challenge accepted, Princess.

"Actually," I murmur, stepping closer, "I was admiring your necklace. Again." My fingers brush along the delicate chain at her throat, trailing down just enough to let my knuckles graze against her collarbone. Her pulse thrums beneath my touch. "But since I've been accused twice now, I suppose I might as well take a moment to appreciate the view."

I let my gaze drag deliberately down her body, mapping every curve, every inch of her that's wrapped in that sinfully perfect dress.

I don't rush it. I let her feel it.

Her chest rises, the fabric of her dress hugging her tight as she inhales just a little too sharply. When my eyes find hers again, her lips are parted, a breathless little hitch catching in her throat.

I take my time, knowing she won't move.

371

"You're right." I smirk, "your necklace is stunning." I let the silence stretch, watching the anticipation flicker in her eyes. "But your body is a much better view to occupy my thoughts."

Her eyes darken and she sways slightly toward me, as if she doesn't even realize it, and fuck, it would be so easy to pull her in. To drag my hands over every inch of that dress and see just how well she fits against me.

Then, she catches herself. The shift is instant, and the mask slides back into place. Her lips curving into something sharp and defiant.

"Flattery and ogling?" She muses, crossing her arms. "I'm surprised you didn't trip over your ego on the way here. Should I be concerned or flattered?"

A slow grin tugs at my lips. *There she is.*

"Flattered," I reply, holding her gaze. "Definitely flattered."

Before she can fire back, I grab her hand and pull her along, casting a quick glance at the shattered light fixtures. They should be here any second to check things out.

"This place is ancient," I keep my tone easy, almost bored. "Probably just got too hot and blew out. Old buildings. They've got minds of their own."

She makes a sound that's half disbelief, half annoyance, but I don't let her linger.

I feel her eyes on me, though.

Stealing a glance, I catch the annoyed little look she's trying to hide. The kind of irritation that's masking something else entirely. *Feisty little thing.*

She's still thinking about what I said and what we did. And she's still feeling every damn second of it.

Satisfaction rolls through me as I guide her back through the greenhouse, our steps quiet against the stone path, and for the second time since we stepped away from the ballroom, I feel her start to settle.

Cam and Rachel appear through the doorway. Just like that, we're yanked back into the present.

"There you are!" Rachel exclaims, hands on her hips but eyes full of mischief. "I thought Kane tried to kidnap you."

Cam shakes his head, chuckling under his breath. Always fucking amused.

Rachel's gaze sharpens as she looks between Cam and me. "Okay, before anything else happens, can someone please tell me what you two are doing here? And how did you even find us?"

Cam flashes his usually charming, smug-ass grin. "Well, considering this is one of the biggest events in the area and a fundraiser, we always attend." He throws me a look, one that makes my jaw tighten ever so slightly. "Call it... a write-off."

Raven's eyes lock onto mine. Demanding answers.

"Okay, but how did you know it was us?" Her tone cuts straight to the point.

I don't hesitate. My voice drops low, "A blind man would know it was you."

Her lips part slightly, and her expression falters, caught somewhere between surprise and disbelief. Her mouth opens like she wants to respond, but nothing comes out.

Rachel groans, rolling her eyes. "Still? Kane seriously? Do you have any game?"

Cam loses it, his whole damn body shaking with laughter as he leans against the door.

"Come on, ladies." He grins. "Let's get back to the dance floor before we get caught sneaking around." He offers his arm to Rachel, who takes it without hesitation.

I extend mine to Raven, and she hesitates. A heartbeat, maybe two, then she slips her hand into mine.

And fuck, if it doesn't go straight to my dick.

Her fingers are warm, but it's the way her breath catches, that does it for me. I lean in, my voice nothing but a low murmur, so she has to lean closer to hear me.

"Don't worry, I don't bite." A slow pause. Letting the tension coil between us."... hard."

Her entire body goes rigid.

A thrill shoots through me, sharp and satisfying. I let a low chuckle escape, letting her know I see every single reaction she's trying so hard to hide.

"You all right over there?" I ask, my tone deceptively light, like I'm not fully aware of how I'm affecting her.

Truthfully, I don't give a shit about her answer.

I care about the way her pulse flutters beneath my thumb. The way she sways closer to me. The way I know, without a doubt, she's fighting herself right now.

Knowing I can do this to her is intoxicating.

Before my cock gets any more bright ideas, I pull her through the doorway, guiding her back toward the ballroom.

The first notes of another song curl through the air and I don't hesitate, I don't even ask.

I pull her onto the dance floor. My hand finds her waist and I guide her into the rhythm, pulling her just close enough to feel every shift in her breath.

Her eyes flick up, her voice softer now. "I'm glad you guys are here."

The words hit me somewhere unexpected.

I don't answer immediately because, for once, I don't know how to.

"I meant to ask if you'd want to come," I admit. "But, truthfully, I kept forgetting." My gaze drops to where her hand fits perfectly in mine. And then, before I can stop myself, I add, "I'm glad you're here, too."

Her eyes snap to mine, like she wasn't expecting that.

For a second, one dangerous second, everything else fades.

The music slows, the crowd blurs into nothing, and it's just her.

Fuck, she's beautiful.

I lean in, my mouth brushing her ear, my voice dropping into something that's not quite a whisper.

"You really do look breathtaking tonight, Princess."

She tenses, and her breath hitches. Her lips part, and her tongue darts out, wetting them.

And there goes every single good intention I had left.

She coughs, a weak attempt to break whatever's brewing between us, but I catch the way her fingers twitch at my shoulder. That small smile of hers tugs at me, reeling me back just enough.

Her gaze flicks toward the crowd and I follow her line of sight. She watches another couple sway together, but I see what she's really looking at. Not them, but what they have.

She won't say it, but I recognize the shift. That moment of softness, a flicker of something raw before she buries it deep.

374

The woman leans into her partner, laughing lightly, while the man watches her like she's the only person in the room. Their heads tilt closer, sharing something private.

Raven's gaze lingers, unreadable at first. I study her, the way her fingers curl slightly against my shoulder, the way she sways just enough to keep from feeling like she's standing still. It's subtle, but I see it for what it is.

She doesn't just watch the world, she notices it. The little things. The things most people are too distracted to see.

And she doesn't even realize how fucking rare that is.

My fingers shift, tracing slow, lazy circles over her hip, testing the line she keeps drawing and redrawing between us.

Her body tenses when our eyes meet, there's something raw there, something pleading.

Then, in the next breath, it's gone.

That fire flares in her eyes, her defenses melting into something sultry and dangerous. *All teasing and bite.*

"Careful there, *sir*. Don't start something you can't finish."

Oh, sweetheart. *Wrong fucking move.*

Heat slams into me, sharp and immediate. The kind that makes it real fucking difficult to remember we're in the middle of a ballroom, surrounded by people.

I don't hesitate.

My grip tightens at her waist, pulling her in slowly, until there's no space left between us, until she has no choice but to feel exactly what she's doing to me.

My voice drops as my lips brush the shell of her ear.

"I never start something I don't plan on finishing."

She stills and inhales slowly. A flicker of something reckless in her gaze, then she shivers.

I lean in, my breath teasing her skin, my lips grazing the shell of her ear as I whisper, "Don't worry."

She opens her mouth, like she's ready to throw some smartass remark my way but hesitates. I wait, watching, every flicker of uncertainty, every battle waging behind those dark, defiant eyes.

But she doesn't speak.

Instead, the smallest, unsteady gasp escapes her lips as my fingers brush her bare skin.

A slow smirk tugs at my mouth.

I let the silence stretch, dragging this out just long enough for her to *feel* it. Every inch of space between us that no longer exists. Every breath she's struggling to take, I let her drown in it.

What the fuck am I doing?

Then the song ends, and my earpiece crackles.

I pick up just enough to know I'm needed. Cam's already looking my way, and the expression on his face tells me everything. There's a fight. And my sister's involved.

Perfect.

I exhale through my nose, forcing my instincts under control as I ease my hold, slightly.

I lean in close as I guide her toward where Rachel is chatting at the water table. My voice is steady. "We've got to handle something real quick. I'll find you when we're done."

Cam flashes Rachel a grin, adding with a wink, "Civil duties, pay our respects and all that. Be right back, love. Try not to break too many hearts while we're gone."

CHAPTER 27

I Know Places

"Wait," Rachel lowers her voice, her expression shifting. "Has anything weird happened since we've been here at the castle?"

My steps slow. The memory from the swing flickers back to life, uninvited. The way the air shifted. The sharp pull in my chest, like I'd seen it all before but through someone else's eyes. Yet, somehow, it felt like *mine*.

I hesitate, picking my words carefully. "I mean, yeah, actually." The admission leaves a strange weight in my chest. "It happened so fast. I touched the tree outside, and then it was like I got hit with this... I don't know, a vision? Like watching an old memory play out."

Rachel's eyebrows shoot up, leaning in with interest. "A *memory*?"

"Maybe?" I frown, trying to piece it together. "It felt like something I *should* know, but I couldn't quite reach it. Like waking up and knowing you had a dream, but no matter how hard you try, you can't remember the details." My voice drops slightly. "It reminded me of the stories my grandmother used to tell me."

She watches me carefully, sensing the shift in my tone. My mind is already dragging me back.

It was a fairytale, one I'd heard a hundred times, but suddenly, it wasn't just a story anymore. It wasn't just a memory. It was something more.

The grass had been impossibly green, vibrant in a way that felt *wrong*, like I was stepping into something not entirely real. The sky stretched above me, a deep, mesmerizing teal, its color shifting like water catching the light. Cold air bit at my skin, carrying the crisp scent of damp earth. Familiar, yet edged with something metallic and sharp.

Gold leaves swayed in the breeze, catching the sunlight like tiny flames, and for a moment, I could *hear* them. Not just the rustling, but something

379

else. A whisper of movement, as if they were alive. I wasn't just seeing it. *I was there.*

The damp grass pressed against my bare feet. The distant chirping of birds felt *too* close, as though they perched just over my shoulder. Every sense was heightened, stretched thin over something ancient and restless.

Then, just as suddenly, the memory jumped, like a dream yanked out of order.

A massive stone loomed ahead. It was dark and foreboding, its surface was carved with symbols that sent a shiver down my spine. Something about it seemed *off,* like I'd seen it a thousand times before but had never actually seen it.

I saw a crown, dark hair, a figure shrouded in power. It reminded me of the man from the portrait.

He held a dagger, the blade gleaming even through the thick smear of blood coating it.

My pulse pounded. A wave of ice crashed through my veins, locking my breath in my chest. The weight of it crushed me, freezing me in place. And then, just as quickly as it had begun... it was gone.

I blink, shaking my head, trying to shove the memory back into the dark corners of my mind. But Rachel is still watching me, waiting for something more.

And I don't have a single answer. Her voice jolts me fully back to the present.

"It happened so fast," I say, still piecing my thoughts together.

"Wait," Rachel cuts in, her eyes gleaming. "The tree's a metaphor for Kane's dick, isn't it?" She barely contains her laughter, and I immediately regret telling her anything.

I stop mid-thought, blinking at her in sheer disbelief. "Rachel," I hiss, before bursting into laughter despite myself. "No! Oh my God, *no*. It was not a metaphor for Kane's dick."

Her grin only widens as I drag her back toward the dance floor. "I'm just saying," she teases, "the timing's *suspicious*. A mysterious tree, and you've got *Sir Broods-a-lot* doing the whole dark and sexy protector thing. You sure this isn't the start of some kinky fantasy?"

I roll my eyes, though I can't help the laugh that slips out. "I hate you."

"Lies," she sings, linking her arm through mine.

"It wasn't like that," I say, shaking my head. "It just reminded me of this story my grandmother used to tell me when I was little. That's all."

Rachel narrows her eyes, unconvinced. "Uh-huh," she drags the sound out, like she's about two seconds from saying something else that'll make me regret every life choice I've ever made.

I glance away, the memory tugging at the edges of my thoughts again. And it wasn't just the tree. I remembered something else the other day too, in the bathroom. I hesitate, considering whether to tell her about it. "I guess I'm just remembering these stories all of a sudden because of Scotland. It's weird timing, but maybe that's all it is."

Rachel pauses mid-step, her expression shifting from playful to something more serious. "Okay, but *why now*?" she asks, her voice thoughtful. "Why is all this happening *here*? And to *you*?"

A flicker of heat ignites in my palms, that same strange warmth I felt earlier. It lingers just long enough for me to notice, before vanishing.

Rachel turns toward me, her eyes narrowing slightly. I open my mouth to say something, anything, but I don't get the chance.

A low voice dripping with confidence cuts in. "Why, *hello*, ladies."

Both of us turn at the same time.

A man steps forward, his presence commanding attention before he even fully reaches us. His voice is smooth, his accent thick and *velvety*, instantly drawing my focus. His gaze locks onto mine as a knowing smile tugs at his lips.

"I saw you from across the room and had to come over," he continues, his tone easy. "I'm here to humbly plead for a dance. *You*, in that dress, are nothing short of a vision, and I can't stand the thought of you hidden away, when everyone should appreciate the view."

He extends his hand toward me, the gesture all confidence. My pulse picks up under his scrutiny, and I *hate* that my body keeps having reactions without my consent.

Rachel's jaw drops, and for a second, I think she might intervene. But then she quickly recovers.

The bule-eyed mystery man I first danced with appears behind her, offering his hand.

I glance back at the stranger, inhaling slowly, and meet his gaze head-on. The heat crawling up my neck is entirely involuntary, but I refuse to let it show. "I'd love to," I say smoothly, sliding my hand into his with practiced ease.

His fingers curl around mine, firm but respectful. His charm is effortless, his presence disarming, and for a split second, I'm stunned by how easily the air shifts around him.

With practiced ease, he leads me onto the dance floor, twirling me once before pulling me close. His hands settle on my waist, light but intentional, and I *can't help* but notice the way he moves.

My pulse skips, though the rush is different from what I feel with Kane. Less charged, but more unexpected.

Leaning in, his breath warm against my ear, he murmurs, "I'm so very grateful you said yes. I'd *hate* for this to be a missed opportunity."

His voice sends a ripple of awareness through me.

I tilt my head slightly, letting the barest hint of challenge slip into my tone. "Do you?"

His chuckle is quiet, low. His gaze flickers, sharp and assessing. "*Very* much so." Then, after a beat, "I have to say, your dress is... *something else.* Whatever you set out to accomplish with it, you *succeeded.*"

A small smile tugs at my lips.

I'd chosen this dress to feel powerful, to feel beautiful, to feel like maybe, just for one night, I could be *untouchable.* Like I was in control of the attention I drew.

Mission accomplished, I suppose.

But I keep those thoughts to myself, letting out a soft, slightly nervous laugh instead.

His eyes linger, their intensity making me hyper-aware of *every single movement* as we glide across the floor.

His grip tightens just slightly.

And there it is again, the same faint pulse. A barely-there hum of energy where his hand connects with mine. It's subtle, but it's there.

A hum of something that shouldn't exist. Something that shouldn't be moving beneath my skin. It has to be a fluke. Some weird adrenaline response, nothing more.

I shove the thought aside, locking it down as refocus on matching his steps, refusing to let even a whisper of hesitation show.

"You dance beautifully, by the way." Pulling my attention back to him. His tone is rich with flattery. But underneath the charm, there's something else. Something calculated.

"Thanks," I say lightly, a little breathless. "I think you might be lying, though, because I've only had a handful of lessons." A grin tugs at my lips. "But you're not so bad yourself."

He chuckles, like I've just said something amusing. "I've got a lifetime of practice." His grip is steady, just enough to guide me without force. "You, however, certainly look like a queen tonight."

The compliment should feel harmless. Except... it doesn't.

"I wonder," he continues, voice dipping lower, "if anyone else here realizes the power that you carry. I can sense it, just looking at you."

My breath catches as his fingers press lightly against mine, his gaze steady.

"Don't forget to wait for the signal."

The words slip between us like a blade sliding into its sheath. My mind scrambles to catch up, but before I can form a single question, I'm suddenly spinning. I barely have time to register the shift before I land in someone else's arms.

My head whips slightly with the motion, my balance slipping for half a beat. Seriously, how's a girl supposed to know when it's switching time? They need a damn warning system.

My new partner's grip is firm, and he moves like he's unhurried. His energy is... different. Cooler. More laid-back, like he's entirely at ease with the chaos around him.

His eyes meet mine, flickering with curiosity.

And something about that look makes my skin prickle.

"You've done well," he muses, voice smooth but casual.

"Thanks?" My brows lift as I try to ignore the strange feeling creeping up my spine. "What's that supposed to mean? My dancing skills or my questionable taste in partners?"

He chuckles, the sound warm and easy. "All of the above," he admits, spinning me effortlessly before pulling me back in. "I'll give you a solid seven out of ten for form, but your habit of following mysterious men onto the dance floor? Bit reckless, Beautiful."

I roll my eyes but can't fight the grin tugging at my lips. "Says the guy who jumped in mid-spin like it was an Olympic relay."

"Fair point." His grin is all charm. "How's your night going?"

"Well, I haven't been propositioned or kidnapped yet, so I'd say things are looking good."

"Ah, a woman with high standards," he teases, his amusement evident. Then his tone shifts, just slightly. "Tell me... have you felt anything *unusual* tonight?"

I blink, taken off guard. "What do you mean?" My voice stays light, but my pulse picks up. *Why is every conversation I've had tonight so strange?* "Not really," I add after a beat, forcing a casual shrug. "Should I have?"

"Aye, you should," he murmurs, his expression shifting to something more knowing. "These are the Highlands, after all. A land of mystery, especially for those with a touch of magic in their veins."

He leans in, voice dropping as if sharing a secret. "And tonight? A full moon, and the solstice. *Perfect* conditions for the unexpected."

I huff out a laugh, shaking my head. "Yeah, I've heard that before," I flash him a grin. "And honestly? It just makes me love this place even more."

"Of course it does," he muses, spinning me again with an effortless precision. "You're one of those romantics, aren't you? Always dreaming of castles, magic, and a prince with a sword."

I scoff. "Castles, obviously. Magic? I wish. A prince?" I smirk. "Optional. The sword, however? Non-negotiable. You know... just in case the prince needs stabbing."

A laugh bursts from him, rich and unrestrained, vibrating through the space between us.

"Well," he chuckles, eyes gleaming, "remind me to stay on your good side."

Before I can reply, he spins me again.

And my breath catches.

Not because of the dance, but because my gaze lands on Kane, who's dancing with someone else. I can tell she's beautiful even from this far away.

384

She's tall and elegant, the kind of effortless grace that makes it impossible not to stare.

His hand rests easily on her back, their movements smooth and practiced. She leans in, saying something that makes him laugh. A warm, *genuine* laugh. One I've never seen from him before.

Not the sharp-edged amusement he usually throws my way. Not the half-smirk, and subtle taunts I've been trying to ignore

No, this is something else. He looks... *relaxed.*

Like that ever-present tension that coils around him has unraveled into something softer.

My chest tightens as I watch her hand slide up his arm, the touch deliberate. She lingers, tilting her head slightly, like she's *memorizing* him. Savoring every smile, every word. Like he's the only man in the room worth noticing.

And he doesn't seem to mind.

A sharp, foreign pang slices through me. Something I refuse to name, something I *definitely* refuse to call jealousy.

Why the hell should I care?

But I do. Because no matter how much I tell myself to look away, my eyes won't listen.

The smell of something faint, like smoke drifts to me while we dance, hinting at something burning nearby.

The thought breaks through the slow spiral, yanking me back to the present. I blink, scanning the room. Everything looks normal. No signs of a fire.

"Everything all right there beautiful?" His voice cuts through my alarm, but his voice has a hint of amusement behind it.

"Yeah," I say quickly, shaking it off. "I thought I saw a friend."

The song ends, and he releases me with a graceful bow, his gaze flicking downward, lingering a fraction too long on my cleavage before meeting my eyes with a smirk that's equal parts amused and knowing.

"Enjoy the rest of your evening, *Little Bird*," he murmurs, lifting my hand to brush a light kiss over my knuckles.

My brain short-circuits for half a second.

"Th-thank you," I stammer, caught off guard as he disappears into the crowd.

Little Bird?

I replay the words, still reeling, my pulse unsteady.

Who the hell was that?

I weave along the edge of the dance floor, my mind racing, replaying the exchange. His words. His look. That smirk like he knew something I didn't. And that feeling. The energy in his touch. Faint but undeniably there.

I shake it off, exhaling sharply as my gaze sweeps the room. I need to find Rachel.

That feeling hits again. The noise fades and my ears start to ring. I suddenly feel nauseous and dizzy like I'm going to fall over. I inhale deeply, willing my pulse to steady, before slipping toward the back of the ballroom.

The press of bodies, the heat, the *buzz* of conversation, it's all closing in, wrapping around my lungs like a vice. I need air. A second to think.

Right now, slipping outside feels like the best damn idea I've ever had, and the moment I step into the garden, the cool night air kisses my overheated skin, soothing the frayed edges of my nerves.

Moonlight spills across the leaves, painting everything in shades of silver and shadow, turning the world soft and still.

Finally. A moment of peace. A break from the chaos.

I find a secluded spot, tucked away from the main paths, and lean against a stone bench, letting the night wrap around me. The tension in my shoulders eases slightly, until movement snags the corner of my vision.

A figure, gliding through the garden, barely more than a silhouette against the moonlight.

I consider slipping away, minding my own business. But something makes me pause. Instead, I watch. Half-amused at the thought that he's sneaking off to meet someone under the cover of the trees.

Because let's be real, a castle garden at night? It's practically *begging* for a scandalous rendezvous. But there's something *off* about the way he moves.

His steps are too precise, his posture too rigid.

Instinct tightens my spine, my breath stilling as I melt deeper into the shadows. I don't move, don't even shift my weight, keeping myself *unseen.* Because suddenly, I'm not sure I *want* to be noticed.

He gets closer, and then our eyes meet.

A polite nod. A passing moment. I expect him to just walk by, for it to be nothing more to be a passing glance in his night. But as he steps past me, something shifts. A flash of movement.

That's all the warning I get.

A *sharp* crack shatters through my skull as his elbow slams into my face.

Pain detonates through me, white-hot and blinding. My head snaps back, my vision *bursts*, and for a terrifying second, all I hear is the sickening *ring* of impact echoing inside my skull.

What the fuck?

He just... *hit* me. On purpose. The sharp taste of copper floods my mouth, and a spike of rage drowns out the pain. That *wasn't* an accident. That was deliberate.

Muscle memory snaps into place before the shock can take hold. Years of training override the spinning in my head, and the pulsing throb in my cheek.

I whip around, fists already up, body moving before my mind fully catches up.

And then I see the smug *fucking* smirk curling on his lips.

He thinks this is *funny*.

I'm sure he thinks I'm just some girl caught off guard in a dress. *He thinks this is going to be easy. Yeah right if I'm going to let this be 'Taken' 3.0.*

Not tonight, *asshole*.

"Bet you thought I was just a pretty face, didn't you?" My voice is laced with venom, even as my jaw throbs. My eyes flick down, scanning for damage. "If you make me ruin this dress, we're *really* going to have a problem."

His smirk doesn't falter. If anything, his amusement deepens, like I'm the *entertainment* for the evening.

That's all the confirmation I need.

My fingers *tighten* into fists, adrenaline scorching through my veins.

"Pretty things break easily," he muses, his voice low and condescending, dripping with something dark and dangerous. "You really should've been more careful."

He steps closer, just enough for me to strike. I drive a sharp jab into his solar plexus, hard.

His breath *hitches*, and his body stiffens from the impact.

Where's that cocky smirk now, asshole?

"That's for the elbow," I snap, satisfaction curling through me as his eyes widen with surprise. "I looked amazing tonight."

His recovery is quick, but *mine is quicker.*

Before he can fully regain his footing, my knee slams into his groin with enough force to drop him.

A choked gasp escapes his lips, his body curling inward slightly as pain ripples through him.

"And that," I say coldly, glaring down at him as he stumbles back, "is for trying to ruin my night."

For a moment, all he does is *breathe.* The only thing I can hear is his harsh, ragged breaths as he straightens, his eyes dark and seething.

Then his expression twists as fury bleeds into something else. Something colder.

"You've got no idea what you're doing," he growls, hand clutching his side, his voice laced with warning. "*None of this belongs to you.*"

The words slide under my skin like a blade. Before I can react, he lunges. He's fast.

I *move*, but not fast enough. My dress catches on my foot, and his fist slams into my ribs.

Pain *explodes* through my side. The force knocks me back, my vision tunneling for a split second as I fight to stay upright.

A brutal reminder that this isn't a drunken bar fight. This is something else entirely. I stagger back, swallowing down the fire burning through my ribs. I will *not* show weakness. My breath hitches but my hands stay up.

"I wouldn't if I were you," I bite out, voice sharp despite the ache tearing through me.

Something flickers across his face, something I almost mistake for *hesitation.* But then his gaze drops to my chest and suddenly, he freezes.

"How?" he breathes, barely audible.

His posture shifts, his steps falter, and just like that, his bravado shatters.

His hands twitch like he's resisting the urge to reach for something. For a weapon? For *me?*

But then, he bolts. Vanishing into the shadows like a ghost.

Leaving me standing there, breathless, my ribs screaming and my face fucking hurts.

I press a hand against my side, wincing at the sharp throb. That's *definitely* going to bruise, if it's not broken. I might have even broken my nose too. *Great.*

But his words...

None of this belongs to you? What the actual fuck does that mean? Like no shit asshole, this isn't my house.

I exhale shakily, adrenaline still rattling through my veins. My reflection catches in a nearby window, and I wince.

My lip is definitely split. The dull ache in my cheek promises I'm going to be feeling this for days. But at least my nose is still intact. I shudder at the thought of it being broken. Because *that* would've ruined my night, and ben hard to explain.

The faint trickle of blood near my lip makes my stomach twist, but I swallow down the feeling, straighten my shoulders, and force my mind to *calm the hell down.*

I will *not* cry over this.

Tonight was supposed to be *magical.*

I refuse to let some deranged lunatic steal that from me.

A quiet thank you echoes in my mind to my grandfather. His words ring clear as ever.

'*Size doesn't win fights. Strategy does.*'

I inhale sharply, pushing away the lingering tremor in my hands. I *won't* let this ruin my night. Slipping back inside, I stick to the edges of the hall, eyes scanning for the nearest bathroom. The second I spot it, I duck in.

Empty. Thank God.

I brace my hands against the sink, finally taking in my reflection under the harsh fluorescent light.

Jesus.

The redness along my cheek is worse than I thought. My lip is definitely split, or at least it feels like it, but I can't tell with all the blood. And my nose? I *know* I took that hit hard. It's throbbing, swelling just enough that I expect it to be bruised. Maybe even broken.

I grab a paper tower, wetting it with cool water before dabbing at my mouth, wincing as the sting shoots through me. I clean it off expecting fresh blood. But there's nothing.

I blink, frowning.

My lip was split, wasn't it?

I *felt* it. The sting. The warmth of the blood trickling down. But now my skin is smooth, a little swollen, but *not broken*.

I swallow, pressing the paper towel against my mouth again, harder this time, like the pressure will confirm what I *know* I felt.

Still nothing.

The blood must've come from my nose. I *did* take that hit straight on, and I didn't exactly examine myself before wiping my face off. Maybe I panicked. Maybe I thought my lip was split.

I shake my head, exhaling hard. Clearly it's the shock.

I smooth my dress, trying to will away the faint tremor still lingering in my fingers. With one last glance at my reflection, I try to smooth out my hair and put on a smile.

Not perfect, but good enough.

Stepping out of the bathroom, my pulse is still too fast. I force deep, steady breaths, shaking off the lingering unease as I reenter the ballroom.

The second I step inside, my eyes find Cam by the edge of the dance floor.

Or maybe *he* finds me first.

His gaze sharpens, his entire demeanor shifting the moment he sees my face. I barely take two steps before he's in front of me, his hands firm on my shoulders as he leans in, his brows pulling together in concern.

"What happened?" His voice is low, almost demanding, his gaze already locked onto my lip.

I force a laugh, rolling my eyes as I gesture toward my thigh-high boots. "Oh, you know, I just tripped. Look at these things. A menace to society." I huff dramatically, lifting a foot. "I'm seriously considering ditching them."

His eyes flick down to my boots, unimpressed. His brow arches as he drags his gaze back to mine, voice flat.

"Tripped, huh?"

The disbelief is thick enough to *choke* on.

"Hey, these boots are dangerous territory," I insist, keeping my smile locked in place. "Trust me."

He doesn't move. Doesn't blink. His eyes search mine, peeling back the bullshit like it's his job.

"Raven." His voice dips lower. Quieter. "Don't bullshit me."

A flicker or something tightens in my chest, but I push past it. Before I can respond, his thumb brushes the edge of my lip, and I *flinch* at the slight sting. His jaw clenches, tension rolling off him in waves.

"Well," he says after a beat, his voice lighter, but forced. "Who am I to question a lady?" He grins, but his eyes don't match. Not even a little. "But seriously, you okay?"

I meet his gaze, steady and unwavering. "Yup. I'm fine. Just a little embarrassed, honestly."

He doesn't buy it.

His eyes stay locked on mine, waiting for anything that proves I'm lying. I fight the urge to shift my weight, knowing that I'm a terrible liar. After a beat, he exhales, letting go of my shoulders. But the look he gives me says this conversation isn't over. Not by a long shot.

"Dance with me."

It's not a question.

Before I can protest, he grabs my hand and pulls me into the music. His movements are effortless, twirling me with a confidence that forces a real laugh out of me. "If you insist," I tease, letting him lead.

His grin is sharp, but it doesn't reach his eyes. "If I find out something *actually* happened, and you didn't tell me, Raven..." His voice dips lower, his grip tightening slightly. "I'm gonna be *pissed*."

I arch a brow, my own smile turning sly as I meet his intensity head-on. "Oh, don't worry, Cameron. If I ever need a knight in shining armor, you'll be the first to know."

His hold tenses for a fraction of a second before he smirks. "You better. Because trust me, I don't play games when it comes to shit like this."

Something about the way he says it sends a slow ripple down my spine. But I refuse to let him see it.

Instead, I hold his gaze, "Noted. Now stop scowling, and dance with me."

He exhales a laugh, finally spinning me back out, but just before the song ends, his voice drops again, low enough for only me to hear.

"And don't worry. I won't tell Kane that you'd call *me* first."

I smirk, titling my head. "Oh, please. I'd call *you* first just to give Kane a reason to be pissed."

Cam's deep, amused laugh is the last thing I hear before the music swells louder, signaling the end of the song.

The night is winding down, but my thoughts are a tangled mess. One minute, I'm having the time of my life. The next I'm lying about getting *elbowed in the face* by some creep in the garden.

Why did we do that again? Too late to back out now.

The thought gnaws at me as Cam and I weave our way toward the back of the room.

The ballroom hums with life, a kaleidoscope of swirling gowns and polished suits under the glow of the chandeliers. My eyes sweep across the crowd, until they land on Kane, who's dancing with Rachel.

My stomach tightens, but I shove the feeling down as I watch Rachel grin up at him, lost in the moment. But the second Kane spots me, his expression changes.

His posture locks and his entire focus narrows in on me. They're both moving now, making their way toward us, but Kane gets to me first.

His presence alone is enough to suck the air from the room.

"What happened?"

The words aren't a question, they're a command. His eyes flick to my lip, narrowing slightly before snapping back to mine.

The weight of his concern is suffocating, but I refuse to let it shake me.

I force a laugh, adjusting my dress, keeping my tone light. "Nothing happened," I say breezily. "I tripped earlier, that's all. These boots might not have been made for walking after all."

Kane doesn't even blink.

His jaw tightens, his gaze burning through my flimsy excuse like it physically offends him.

"Tripped?" he repeats, the word dripping with dangerous skepticism. His voice stays calm, but there's a lethal edge beneath it.

Before he can press further, Cam lets out a snort, giving me a playful nudge.

"Great legs," he says, "but I'm not sure those boots are worth *risking your life* for." He shrugs, smirking. "Sorry, not sorry... still funny."

I force a chuckle, ignoring the way my heart is still racing, and cast a quick glance at Kane. His eyes haven't left mine, haven't moved, like he's peeling back every excuse I've thrown up, searching for the truth buried beneath it.

Rachel steps up beside me, giving me a once-over before shaking her head with a grin. "Of course you would fall," she laughs. "You've got the balance of a newborn giraffe in those boots."

I let out a dramatic sigh, relieved they seem to be buying it. My fingers toy with the hem of my dress, a nervous habit I force myself to suppress. The last thing I need is this suffocating scrutiny, and risk unraveling everything I've carefully tied together. Whatever happened in that garden, whatever *he* meant by *None of this belongs to you,* it's over. And I have no intention of dragging it into this night, of letting it bleed into something that was supposed to be magical.

At this point I'm banking on that creep being long gone. I've already flat-out lied, and I'm not about to unravel it now.

The music softens and a hush ripples through the ballroom as a woman steps forward, mic in hand.

It's Kane's dance partner from earlier.

Up close, she's even more stunning. The kind of beauty that doesn't require effort. She has short blonde hair that's styled to perfection, and she's wearing a deep emerald gown that hugs every inch of her. Her white mask has gold accents on it that make her look like some untouchable goddess, like she belongs on a throne rather than a dance floor. And the worst part is, she doesn't even have to try to command the room. Just lifting the mic is enough to silence everyone, like they're all waiting on her next word.

She might be small, but she radiates authority. *I like her already.*

"Thank you all for coming and supporting this event," she begins, her voice echoing through the room. "We always have so much fun putting this together every year. This is such a special night, and we couldn't do it without all of you."

She has the room hanging on her every word. Then her lips curve into something mischievous.

"And of course, I'd like to give a special thanks to my brother, *wherever he's hiding*, for all his help, even though he acted like lifting a finger might actually kill him."

A ripple of laughter spreads through the crowd, hers joining it, bright and unapologetic.

"Okay, I'm kidding," she continues, grinning. "He's the reason we all get to enjoy this beautiful space tonight. I hope you've all had a fantastic evening, and we can't wait to see you again next year. As things wind down, if you need a ride, just let security know on your way out."

A wave of applause sweeps through the room, cheers following as the finality of her words settles in.

I glance at Kane.

His expression softens slightly, but there's a flicker of something in his eyes as he watches her. Something *warm*.

It's stupid, really. Why should I care how he looks at her? She's clearly incredible, clearly beautiful, and the connection between them is obvious.

Still, no matter how much I tell myself it *shouldn't* matter, the flicker of jealousy snakes through me, unbidden and unwelcome.

Exactly what kind of history do they share?

The applause lingers, and she exits the way she came.

"So... does that mean it's over already?" I murmur to no one in particular, a hint of disappointment slipping into my tone.

Kane chuckles beside me.

"Aye, we're winding down," he says, his voice low. "But we've got another hour before they start ushering people out."

I glance at him, raising a brow, mildly impressed. *Guess he really does know how these events go.*

Just then, Rachel links her arm through Cam's, flashing him a grin that could melt stone.

"Cam, how about that private tour you promised?"

He arches a brow, flicking a glance toward Kane.

"Aye, I think I can manage that." He offers an exaggerated bow before guiding Rachel off into the crowd.

"Bye to you, too?!" I call after her, though I can't stop the laugh that slips out.

Rachel just waves over her shoulder, her laugh tangling with the music as she disappears with Cam.

I turn back to Kane, catching the soft chuckle that escapes him, then his gaze lands on my lip.

The laughter fades instantly.

I roll my eyes, slapping his arm lightly. "Oh, quit worrying," I tease. "I clearly survived."

His gaze flicks down to where I touched him, then back up, amusement curling the corner of his mouth like he already knows exactly where this is headed.

"Violent little thing, aren't you?"

His voice drops slightly lower, edged with something darker.

And suddenly, the air feels a *little too thin.*

I *laugh.* A real, unfiltered laugh, and suddenly, I can't stop. My body shakes with it, every last ounce of tension threatening to spill out in a ridiculous, breathless giggle. If only he *knew.*

Kane's brow lifts slightly, and I press a hand over my mouth, willing myself to get it together. Maybe this is the adrenaline crashing, or maybe my body just doesn't know how to handle the impossible heat rolling off him like a silent challenge.

He takes a slow step closer, just enough to steal my breath. "What do you want to do, *Princess*?" His voice is a weapon, designed to ruin. "Another dance? A private tour..." He pauses, his lips curving. "Or a trip back to the swing?"

His tone is laced with something far more sinful than a simple stroll under the stars.

I smirk, lifting my chin slightly, refusing to let him win whatever *this* is. "You wish," I say, voice smooth despite the riot in my chest. "Surprise me."

Something flickers in his expression, just for a second. A subtle shift. And then his smirk fades into something darker.

As if every last shred of morality between us has snapped, dissolving into something dangerous. My pulse pounds, a steady drum against my ribs, as my mind goes completely, utterly blank except for one singular thought...

I want him.

Here. Now. Against the wall, in the dark, hands gripping, mouths clashing. Heat licks up my spine, pooling low in my stomach.

I can see in his expression that he knows exactly what is racing through my mind, and exactly how far I've let myself fall into this moment.

His expression shifts again as his gaze drags over me, lingering just long enough to feel like a promise.

"Surprise you?" His voice is a rough murmur, the edge of it cutting through my already ragged composure. "You don't exactly strike me as someone who enjoys surprises."

His fingers brush against mine, just barely, but it's enough to send a jolt of something raw and consuming down my spine.

"And if you're not careful," he whispers, "I just might take you up on that."

God help me, I just might let him.

His words linger, heavy in the air, curling around my throat like silk and steel. My breath catches, pulse stuttering as something unravels between us, something neither of us is willing to name.

I try to speak, but my voice fails me. "I—"

He smirks.

I tear my gaze away, desperate for *anything* to break the moment before I do something stupid.

A slow smile tugs at my lips as I turn back to him. "The gardens."

A flicker of something crosses his face, but then he grins, offering his arm like he was expecting this all along.

"Right this way, my lady."

I slip my hand into his, letting him lead me toward the back doors. Except he veers left, heading down the hall instead.

I shoot him a look, about to ask if he even knows where he's going, but before I can speak, he glances back at me, lifting a brow with that infuriating smirk.

"Yes, I know where I'm going."

I bite back a laugh. Did I say that out loud?

The offense in his tone is almost too much, and I have to press my lips together to keep from losing it.

He narrows his eyes. "I can hear you thinking, Princess."

I snort. "Yeah? And what am I thinking?"

His grin sharpens. "That I'm making shit up as I go."

I *do* laugh at that, and he just shakes his head, muttering something under his breath as we continue down the dimly lit hallway.

Kane's movements change. Like he's suddenly more aware of our surroundings.

"We're just making a quick stop," he murmurs, voice low as his eyes sweep the corridor ahead, checking for any sign of security before tilting his chin, silently signaling for me to follow.

CHAPTER 28

It Hits Different

RAVEN

Kane quietly shuts the door behind us, the faint *click* echoing through the space.

I take a slow step forward, my breath is steady but my pulse is *anything but.*

He leads me deeper into the greenhouse, past curling vines and towering ferns, deeper into a space that feels untouched. Each step feels like slipping into something secret. The further we go, the wilder it becomes, the neat arrangements giving way to tangled greens and massive blooms.

Just ahead, half-hidden beneath the towering foliage, a small room comes into view. A room I wouldn't have noticed on my own. Nestled in a dense cluster of plants, it blends seamlessly into the chaos around it.

I follow behind him, gaze drifting despite myself.

The way his shoulders shift beneath his shirt, the easy confident stride is impossible *not* to admire.

His sleeves are rolled up, revealing those forearms that should be illegal, and I swear the absolute audacity of this man existing in my vicinity without a warning label should be a crime.

I try to keep my eyes where they should be. But they drift lower, tracing the lines of his back, the way his shirt pulls across his broad frame.

Damn it.

Heat simmers deep in my core, and I can feel how wet I'm getting. I drag my gaze back to the path ahead, determined not to actually trip.

One misstep and I'll not only eat shit, but I'll probably die from embarrassment.

We step into the hidden room, and I freeze. It's breathtaking. One entire wall is covered in wild thistles, their deep purple hues stark against the tangle

399

of rich green. Moonflowers bloom beside them, their silvery petals wide open, glowing faintly under the light.

Scattered across the ground, nestled among the roots and stones are tiny glass mushrooms that are glowing. Soft blues, deep violets, and eerie greens. Like tiny little lanterns.

I can't stop the soft gasp that escapes me.

"This..." My voice barely rises above a whisper. "This place is amazing."

My fingers brush over a moonflower, almost hesitant. A slow, knowing smile tugs at Kane's lips.

I swear to the Gods, because there's no way just *one* made him. He's a walking wet dream wrapped in bad decisions.

There *has* to be a flaw somewhere.

Maybe if I can get him to take his shirt off, *strictly for scientific purposes, of course,* I'll find something. No one should look this perfect.

He blinks, and the moment is gone.

"I brought you in here so you could pi—"

"How did you know this was here?"

His gaze flickers, something unreadable flashing through it before he steps forward, just enough to remind me we're alone.

"I've been here all day." he says, lowering his voice. "Pick anything you want"

I blink, trying to process his words. "What? Why? What are we doing?"

A slow smirk tugs at his lips as he closes the space between us. *Too close.* "Well, since it's solstice *and* a full moon, it's tradition to leave a small gift for the faeries. In return, they're said to leave one for you too," he explains. "Rumor has it, their gifts are full of magic."

He manages to keep a straight face, though a smirk is tugging at his lips as he watches me. "We used to do it as kids," he continues, shrugging. "Figured it was *just* strange enough that you'd be into it."

I cross my arms, tilting my head at him, unable to stop my grin.

"The only reason I'm *not* offended that you're judging my weirdness is because, for once, you're actually right," I say smoothly. "Only a tiny bit, though."

I shoot him a pointed look before quickly turning away, *because there's no way I'm letting him see me smile like an idiot.*

My eyes land on a beautiful, overgrown moonflower, its vines wrapping tightly around a tall thistle. White blooms curling around sharp, violet spikes.

Fitting.

"I want that one."

He follows my gaze, raising a brow. "This?" He gestures toward the plant, voice laced with amusement.

"Yes," I reply, my face neutral, though I can't stop the faint smile tugging at my lips. This is actually exciting, and the bastard wasn't wrong, I'm totally into this.

He exhales a quiet chuckle, shaking his head. "Only *you* would choose this one."

But he steps forward without hesitation, cutting the stem with precise, controlled movements. The air between us shifts slightly as he wraps twine around the lower part where the vines haven't tangled, securing a small handle before turning toward me.

He reaches out, handing me the bundle, his fingers brushing mine.

It's casual, nothing special. But the second our skin meets, I'm on fire.

A sharp jolt sears through me, head to toe, curling low in my stomach like a slow burn.

I jerk back, fingers tightening around the bundle like a lifeline. My eyes snap to his. *He felt it too.*

For a beat, neither of us moves.

His gaze locks onto mine, and a slow, lazy smirk tugs at his lips like he's waiting for me to acknowledge it. To admit what just happened.

His eyes drift lower, lingering. Not the first time tonight. Or the second.

My pulse pounds, my body betraying me in real time as the heat in his stare dares me to pretend I didn't notice.

"Have you heard of this solstice ritual?" He asks as if he didn't just eye fuck me like that.

I clear my throat, "No, can't say that I have." My voice comes out steady, but the heat creeping up my cheeks is impossible to hide.

He chuckles softly, the sound way too satisfying for my liking. "Well, there's not much to tell," he says smoothly. "Just that if you leave the Fae a gift, they'll leave one for you in return. The gift is tied to whatever intention you had when choosing it."

I glance down at the delicate bundle, fingers tightening around the twine. "And if I didn't have an intention?" I ask, desperately needing a distraction from the heat simmering between us.

His gaze darkens. "Oh, you definitely had an intention, Princess."

My breath catches, and heat spikes through me. I force a laugh, rolling my eyes to break the tension. "You're obnoxious, you know that?"

"Hm," he hums, unimpressed, stepping closer as he holds out his hand. "Ready?"

For a second, I hesitate. Why does it feel like this is a line I'm about to cross?

I place my hand in his, bracing myself.

A flicker of something flashes across his face as his fingers close around mine. The warmth is instant, the same heat pulsing up my arm like a whispered warning.

I silently beg him not to notice, but his thumb brushes over the back of my hand.

A spark ignites beneath my skin. His gaze lifts to mine, catching every reaction I'm trying so hard to bury.

We step into the gardens, and there he goes again, moving his thumb. Tracing slow, idle circles over my skin.

A tiny, meaningless touch, and yet, everything inside me tightens, and I can feel my nipples harden. *Who even gets turned on by hand contact?*

I pull my hand out of his, a little too fast.

It's just two people, under the stars, wandering through the gardens on a silly mission to leave gifts for the faeries.

Nothing remotely romantic about...

Shit.

I barely catch my breath as he turns toward a secluded spot, half-hidden beneath the low-hanging branches of an old oak.

His eyes dart from my face to the bundle of flowers in my hand, daring me to make the first move.

The quiet stretches between us, every second dragging just long enough to make my pulse skip.

"Alright, just pick a tree to put your offering under," he murmurs, nodding toward the base of the tree.

I hesitate, feeling oddly self-conscious under his watchful gaze, but I finally step forward and kneel to place the flowers at the base of the tree.

I hesitate, suddenly hyper-aware of how closely he's watching me. His patience feels like a trap I'm too willing to step into.

Gods. Since when did setting down a flower feel like a test?

"That's it?" I ask, glancing up at him.

He shrugs, heat flares in his eyes. That infuriating smirk pulls at his lips. I narrow my eyes, turning back to the flowers.

I reach to adjust them, only to prick my finger on one of the thorns. A sharp sting shoots through me, and I mutter a curse under my breath, pressing my fingertips to my mouth to stop the tiny bead of blood.

I arrange the flowers with more purpose this time.

As I smooth out my dress, I let out a quiet exhale, then just in case, I send a thought into the stillness.

I chose this because it just felt right. I don't expect anything in return for something you gave me first. Thank you.

The words linger, stretching into the night. For a brief second, I swear the air around us shifts.

A heartbeat later, Kane quietly offers his arm.

I hesitate again, because everything about this feels like a trap. But I slip my hand into his anyway. His arm is warm, solid, and unfairly steady as we start to move through the gardens.

Ugh, his arms are to die for.

The second I think I have the upper hand, he moves. It's not much, just a slight shift. But suddenly, the distance between us is gone. His fingers brush against mine, the contact so light I almost don't feel it. As we approach a beautifully detailed fountain, he pauses, glancing at me.

I look over at the fountain, captivated. The heat between my thighs is nearly forgotten. Under the full moon, the water glows softly, illuminating the intricate design. Vines and swirls are etched down the pillar, curling delicately around three tiers, each one cascading water into the next before it reaches the small pool at the base. Coins sparkle faintly beneath the surface, tiny hints of silver and copper catching the light. *Wishes. Hopes. Secrets left behind.*

I let out a soft breath, turning back to him with a smile.

He breaks the silence. "So, how was your first ball?"

"It's been... magical. Though, I have to admit, I'm shocked you're actually here. This doesn't exactly scream your scene."

I move toward the fountain, settling onto the ledge, letting my fingers skim through the cool water, swirling idle patterns over the surface.

He stands across from me, silent at first, watching. Then, finally, he tilts his head slightly.

"And what, exactly, would you say *is* my scene?" he challenges, voice smooth as sin.

My pulse kicks up a notch.

"Well..." I let out a laugh, shaking my head. "I don't know, maybe something a little more... mysterious." I flick water absently, watching ripples spread across the surface. "I can't picture you at a ball, mingling with people, pretending to enjoy yourself. No offense, but you seem more like the type to be off doing something a little more... *illegal*. Or at least, less refined."

His low, deep chuckle rolls through the quiet.

"So you've got me all figured out, do you?"

I flick a little more water in his direction. "Maybe I do," I tease, "But come on, you cannot tell me this is your crowd."

My laugh softens, and okay, *maybe* that was a little unfair. Especially since we're both here. He might think this is my comfort zone, but truthfully, I enjoy the quiet.

"Funny," he says smoothly, stepping closer. "I could say the same about *you*."

Touché. I guess I did walk right into that one.

I tilt my head up, locking onto his gaze. The way he watches me feels like a game I'm not entirely sure I know the rules to, but I don't back down.

"All right then," I cross my arms. "Why did you come tonight? Or is this secretly your thing after all?"

His chuckle is edged with something unreadable. *Shocker.*

"Just doing my duty, love."

Duty?

I narrow my eyes. "There go those vague answers again," I say, shaking my head. "You know, I'm going to let you in on a little secret, because that's what *friends* do." I emphasize *friends,* mostly for my own benefit. "Sharing is caring," I add with a grin.

"Alright," he says, the corner of his mouth quirking up. "Do you *really* want to know?"

I nod, anticipation buzzing in my veins. "Obviously."

Kane glances around, checking to make sure no one's listening, then leans in so close his breath brushes my cheek.

"I'm here because I was invited," he whispers. "But also... to keep an eye on certain people. Make sure they're safe."

He leans back, his gaze locking onto mine.

Oh. Right. Security. He's working.

"Safe from *what* exactly?" My voice is quieter than I intend. "Is this place not safe enough?"

He straightens, his smirk deepening into something more genuine. "You're close," he says, a twinkle of mischief flickering behind his eyes. "Mostly here to protect people from themselves." His gaze drops down to my boots, then back up. "Especially with the death traps these women are calling shoes tonight."

He winks. "Honestly, I'm impressed you haven't ended up headfirst in the fountain yet."

Without thinking, I flick a handful of water at him. This time, I don't miss. Water clings to the edge of his sleeve.

"Oh, you think you're hilarious, don't you?" I try to hide my smile.

I dare him to push his luck. But his laugh only deepens as he steps closer. I straighten slowly, edging away from the fountain. "Not funny."

His smirk doesn't fade for a second. "Oh, it was *hilarious*."

"Well, excuse me for being genuinely curious about who could possibly need that much protection at a party," I huff, crossing my arms.

His gaze is playful, but still sharp enough to pin me in place. "I know. That's exactly what made it so funny."

"Yeah, yeah," I mutter, attempting to brush him off. The light of the moon catches on him just right and I lose my train of thought entirely, my breath stalling.

He looks like he belongs out here, bathed in shadows.

Every sharp, angular feature carved in moonlight, shadows cutting across the ridges of his face, the mask still concealing just enough to make him untouchable.

I catch myself staring, my gaze traces every detail of him, knowing I should look away but finding it impossible. That infuriating pull between us only tightens, and it's beyond annoying, and I silently curse him for it.

The way he's just standing there, completely still, completely in control, while I'm completely undone.

No matter how impossibly frustrating he is, no matter how insufferable, I can't help but wish he'd reach out and touch me again. That he'd drag those rough hands down my body, claim me in a way that leaves no question about what's been simmering between us since the moment we met.

A dangerous ache curls deep, and it's not just heat pooling between my thighs anymore. It's a throb that's insistent, needy.

I squeeze my thighs together, like I can somehow smother the feeling, but it only makes me more aware of the steady pulse of want.

A slow smile tugs at the corner of his mouth. "You're staring."

"Maybe I'm just enjoying the view." My voice barely above a whisper. Shit. Did I really just say that out loud? The second it leaves my lips, my heart stutters, every nerve in my body going tight.

I have no reservations when it comes to him. Even when that honesty leaves me exposed.

His gaze darkens, hunger and amusement coiling together like he's thoroughly entertained by how easy this is for him. The look he gives me sends a shiver down my spine.

Because he's watching me unravel, and he's not even touching me. Part of me is *begging* me to retreat. To go back to the ballroom, to get out of this dangerous game while I still can.

But then there's the other part of me, the wild, reckless side. The side that wants to throw caution to the wind. The defiant, feminine part of me that wants to let him strip me down to nothing, unravel me piece by piece. To see exactly how far he could break me apart.

"We should head back."

His words cut through the haze like a cold blade, severing the moment so brutally it feels personal. My stomach drops so hard it's embarrassing.

I blink, dazed, feeling the tension rip away so fast I feel unsteady.

Because he's a man. He knows exactly what he's doing.

His expression remains unreadable as he extends his hand, and I hesitate, feeling the weight of the moment settle over me.

He doesn't move closer, doesn't pull me in, doesn't lean down, or brush his lips against my ear.

He doesn't do a damn thing.

And the pang of disappointment that hits me is sharp and unexpected, sinking deep into my stomach, twisting tighter than I care to admit.

I hate him for this.

For knowing exactly what he's doing and how wrecked I am right now and doing absolutely nothing about it.

But before I can spiral any further, I feel that same warmth creeping across my skin like a slow burn. A tingling, flickering sensation dancing over my palms.

Not now.

Panic claws up my throat, my breath hitching as I clench my fists, forcing it to stop, to fade, to go unnoticed. The ringing in my ears intensifies. And I try to focus on the cold night air, on the feel of Kane's hand in mine, willing it away.

Then I see a woman standing in the shadows, watching me.

My steps halt immediately, my stomach twists into knots as our eyes meet. For a fraction of a second, her expression shifts and a smile spreads across her face.

My grip on Kane tightens involuntarily, stopping him mid-step, but the second my gaze flickers back, she's gone. Vanished into the night like she was never there.

My pulse pounds, my breath catching as I scan the shadows, searching for any trace of her. Did she turn the corner?

Kane's voice cuts through my thoughts. "What's wrong?"

I force my eyes back to him, my heart hammering against my ribs. "Nothing," I say quickly, but the slight tremor in my voice betrays me. "I just thought I saw someone standing over there."

I nod toward the spot, still scanning the darkness, half-expecting her to reappear, half-terrified she actually will. Kane follows my line of sight, and I feel the shift before I even look at him. The relaxed amusement from earlier is gone, replaced with something colder. His eyes flicker across the area scanning every shadow, every possible movement, assessing the space with a lethal efficiency.

"Whoever it was, they're long gone," he says finally, though the weight in his tone tells me he isn't convinced.

Neither am I.

His eyes linger on me for a beat too long, like he's weighing his next words, deciding whether to push or let it slide. His voice drops slightly, quieter but no less intense. "You sure you're alright?"

I nod, even though my pulse is still hammering in my ears. Who the hell was she? And why did it feel like I should know her too?

We continue walking, and the silence between us stretches, thick with unspoken questions neither of us dares to ask. As we approach the door, something catches my attention, tugging me back into the moment.

The lights are all fixed. That was... fast.

I hesitate just slightly, my gaze flicking from the repaired fixture to Kane, suspicion curling in my chest.

He catches the look I give him, and of course, smiles.

The back-and-forth of emotions tonight is enough to make my head spin. One second, I'm fighting off the unease from the shadows outside. The next, I'm hyper-aware of Kane's presence, and the tension stretched so tight that it feels like one wrong move could snap it in two.

If only I could convince my body that all of this is exactly why we're steering clear of dating for the foreseeable future. That would be lovely. But no, my pulse refuses to listen. It refuses to do anything other than quicken every damn time he looks at me like that.

The heat of the greenhouse presses against my skin as we step inside, and suddenly, the tension from outside fades.

I let my fingers brush over the broad petals of a nearby plant, tracing the edges almost absently. There's something raw and untamed about it, something unapologetic, kind of like how this whole damn night has felt.

Kane's voice breaks the silence, low and almost too quiet to catch.

"You're fascinating, you know that?"

I blink, turning to him, my heart skipping exactly once before I shove the reaction down where it belongs.

I roll my eyes, a grin tugging at my lips as I lean into the sarcasm like the lifeline I desperately need. "What can I say? I'm an acquired taste."

I glance at him, all challenge and reckless defiance, and let my smirk widen. "If you don't like it, then I guess that means you should acquire some taste."

He chuckles, but there's something about the way his gaze lingers on me.

"So when do I get to see you throw a knife?" His brow lifts, the corner of his mouth tilting in amusement.

I blink.

"Oh, that's right! I can't wait for you to owe me a favor." I tilt my head, eyes gleaming. "Guess we'll play as soon as you're ready."

He huffs out a laugh, shaking his head like he thinks he's already won. "I'll find a knife right now if you're that confident."

"Do it," I challenge, stepping just close enough to let the air between us tighten. "Unless you're scared."

His smirk deepens, a glint of something deadly amused in his eyes, and I dare him to actually go find one. I could throw a knife in my sleep, and watching the look on his face when I prove it would be the perfect cherry on top of an already fantastic evening.

"Confident, aren't you?" He teases. That damn smile is doing exactly what it does best. Looking cocky, and sexy as hell.

"Well, you know what they say..." I trail off, my grin turning sharper.

Kane's eyebrow arches, that husky laugh rumbling from deep in his chest. "No, I don't. Care to enlighten me?"

I hesitate for half a second, just long enough to realize I don't actually have a follow-up for that.

I huff, rolling my eyes. "Honestly, I just figured you'd nod along and pretend you knew what I was talking about."

His laughter rumbles low and his eyes lock onto mine with a heat that feels entirely too dangerous, like it's wrapping around me.

"Who are you?" he murmurs, his voice a low ripple of curiosity, something unreadable beneath the words.

The way he says it feels like he's pulling me in, unraveling me without even trying.

"Who are *you*?" I fire back, tilting my chin up, letting the challenge slip into my voice like armor.

He doesn't look away and neither do I. "Touché."

The moment should end there, but it doesn't. The question lingers, heavier than it should be. Because the truth is, I don't even know how to answer him.

Ever since I lost my grandfather, it feels like pieces of me have been scattered, slipping through my fingers. Like the person I thought I was has been left behind somewhere, just an outline, blurred and incomplete.

Of course, I'm heartbroken that they're gone. But I'm left with so many questions.

I can't even answer the most basic things. Like how my parents died, where they were born, how old they were. And now, with that chest, those letters, and everything that's happening lately, it's like someone handed me a puzzle with half the pieces missing.

And there's no one left to ask. No one left to guide me. And that's the part that cuts the deepest.

The emotions coil tight in my chest, threatening to drag me under, and I don't want to drown in them. I need to move.

Rounding the corner, I let my hands graze over the edges of the leaves, the rough texture grounding me. That's when I see the broken pot still lying on the ground, shattered in jagged pieces.

I bend down, picking up one of the larger shards, and everything shifts.

Warmth wraps around me, the scent of lavender and old books filling my lungs, pulling me into something I shouldn't be able to step into.

CHAPTER 29

So It Goes...

RAVEN

"*What* story do you want to hear tonight, my Little Bird?"

Her voice is soft, warm like the blankets tucked beneath my chin.

"The magic poem!"

I sit up, excitement bubbling in my chest. But gentle hands ease me back down, fingers gliding through my hair, working through the tangles of the day.

"Shhh, lay back down," she murmurs, her presence as familiar as the stars outside my window.

She starts where she always does, voice dripping into the low whisper, as she tells the story. A secret just for the two of us.

"Once, there was a king who was always grumpy."

I giggle, just as I always do.

"Some say it was because he didn't have a woman to love," she continues, her tone playful.

I press my lips together, stifling another laugh.

"Others would even say he had a woman, and that's why he was grumpy."

She chuckles at her own words, her eyes crinkling, the magic of the story that belongs to me and me alone.

"One day, he met the most beautiful woman he'd ever seen," she lowers her voice, drawing me closer to the edge of the story. "She had hair like midnight. She was wild, and everything he found intolerable."

I peek out from the covers, wide-eyed, hanging onto every word.

"She spoke her mind. She never took things at face value. She always had to know the truth for herself. And that infuriated the king most of all. He never knew what she would say or do next. She was always causing trouble, and he wanted nothing to do with her."

She pauses, tilting her head, waiting.

I take the bait.

"And yet?" I whisper.

Her lips curve, her smile knowing, like she already has me right where she wants me.

"And yet," she continues, "try as he might, he couldn't stay away. He was infatuated. Obsessed, some would say. He knew that loving her would eventually cost him, but it was a price he was more than willing to pay, in the end."

My fingers clutch the blanket tighter. "Did the king stay away?"

She brushes a stray curl from my face, her expression soft, but her eyes... distant.

"Oh, no, my Little Bird. Kings are stubborn that way. He loved her beyond reason. He chose her, and with that choice, he sealed his fate. And hers."

The warmth in her voice fades, giving way to something heavier.

"He knew she carried a power as ancient as the stars. Magic that was as fierce as it was beautiful. He understood that if he bound himself to her, every child in his line would inherit her wildness, her fire... and her power."

Her fingers still in my hair.

"Every daughter. Every son. Would carry the mark and have her spark of something dangerous."

The air is charged with something I don't understand.

I almost think I imagined it, she speaks so softly, the words spoken more to the night than to me.

"It was never broken," she murmurs.

A heartbeat.

"You're running out of time."

I freeze.

Her eyes are distant, and unfocused, like she's seeing something I can't.

The words linger, and for the first time, I wonder if there's something more to this story?

"Raven?"

Kane's voice slices through the haze, grounding me too fast. I blink up at him, the memory, or whatever the hell that was, already slipping away.

And now I'm crouched on the floor holding a shard of broken pottery. Like a total lunatic.

"Yes. Sorry. What's up?" I quickly force my tone as casual as I can, like I wasn't just seconds away from mentally unraveling into the dirt.

He crosses his arms, tilting his head slightly as he studies me. His eyes, sweep over the broken pieces at my feet, then back to the way my fingers clutch one a little too tightly.

"I should be the one asking you that." His voice is low, but there's an edge to it, something unreadable lurking beneath. "You wandered over here, crouched down, and started picking up broken pottery. Care to explain what you're doing?"

I swallow, scrambling for an excuse that doesn't make me sound like I've lost my grip on reality.

"Oh, right. I just thought I'd pick up the broken pieces so no one else would cut themselves."

His gaze flicks down to my hand, landing on the tiny bead of blood forming on my palm. His expression shifts, the sharpness easing slightly.

"Seems like you're the only one who keeps getting hurt," he murmurs, stepping closer.

His voice is gentle, but it's laced with something else.

And that sends an odd thrill through me.

I straighten too quickly, brushing off my dress, waving it off before he can look at me like that again. "It's nothing," I say, but my body has other plans, because even as I dismiss it, my pulse refuses to slow the fuck down.

But Kane doesn't let shit slide.

Before I can fully escape the moment, his fingers catch my wrist.

"Let me see." His voice dips to that tone that says arguing is pointless. That he's already decided, and I'm just along for the ride.

I huff out a laugh, "Oh, what, are you suddenly a doctor now?"

Just the slightest tilt of his head, and somehow, it makes me think twice about saying no.

"Let me have a look."

Softer this time, but no less insistent.

I sigh dramatically, holding my hand. "Fine, Dr. Kane. Knock yourself out."

His scowl melts into a slow smirk, he looks far too amused. And then, he takes my hand. For a moment, I forget the sting entirely.

"It's not deep, *Princess*. No need for dramatics."

Then he winks. I swear this man is so insufferable.

Without any kind of warning, he drags me toward the sink like this is an emergency situation.

Of course this damn room has its own sink, why wouldn't it.

I open my mouth to argue as he pulls out a towel, wets it, and holds my hand under the stream of water.

The moment his fingers settle around mine, holding me in place, a shiver runs through me.

"You know," I murmur, desperate to focus on literally anything else, "I could've done this myself."

Kane makes a quiet noise, his thumb pressing slightly against my wrist, his grip steady. "Sure you could've."

I roll my eyes, but I can't ignore the way his touch sends tiny jolts of awareness through me, or the way his fingers, just slightly rough, seem to have way too much power over my breathing.

He glances up and the heat in his eyes is enough to make my pulse trip over itself.

I look away immediately, determined to keep my cool, but it's too late. Because when he pulls my hand from the water, and wraps it with the damp towel, his eyes are already trailing up my arm, pausing at my collar bone, and settling on my lips.

My grip tightens around the counter, but I catch myself too late. His gaze snaps back to mine. Something dark flickers across his face.

Then, with the slowest tilt of his head, "You're staring again."

"Still enjoying the view," I manage, forcing a shrug, but my voice is quieter than I want it to be.

His eyes narrow slightly, and whatever intensity was there before, doubles. His gaze devours me.

The terrifying part is how much I love it. Being pinned beneath the full weight of his attention is a thrill I shouldn't crave this much.

I'm caught in his pull, pulse hammering in my ears, hands tingling just enough to remind me how far gone I am. All I can do is stare back, completely captivated, the sensible part of my brain nowhere to be found.

He moves closer, lifting his hand as his fingers slowly brush against my cheek as he unties my mask, the silk unraveling effortlessly beneath his touch.

He slides it off, sets it down, and I forget how to breathe.

The world narrows to what little space is left between us, it takes every ounce of self-control I have not to close the damn distance and take what I want.

"You are a wild one, you know that?"

His voice sends a thrill pulsing through me so sharp, I swear I could come on the spot.

"Thank you." I manage, but it comes out shaky, more like a question.

His lips twitch, his fingers graze down my neck. Every inch of me he touches comes alive, tingling with a heat so sharp I feel it everywhere.

"You're also dangerous," his voice is rough and dark as his fingers trail down my arm, leaving a shiver in their wake.

I laugh, shaking my head even as my body leans toward him. "That's rich coming from you." Trying desperately to sound casual. But his touch scrambles every thought I have. "If anyone's dangerous here, it's you."

His lips crash into mine, stealing the breath right out of me, swallowing my gasp like he owns it. Thank. Fucking. God.

He tastes exactly like I remember, intoxicating with that faint woodsy bite that's unmistakably him.

This isn't like before. This isn't a kiss meant to tease. It's a goddamn war.

His tongue parts my lips, tangling with mine in a kiss so deep, so devastating, it burns right through me. A groan slips free, and the moment it does, his grip tightens, his hands slide into my hair, tilting my head back to take more.

The dress. The party. The world outside. All of it fades.

All that's left is him. His mouth, his hands, his body pressing into mine like he wants to bury himself so deep I'll never get him out again.

His hands roam lower, dragging down my sides, firm and possessive, like he's staking his claim inch by inch, and I feel every scorching second of it.

A small noise slips from me, a desperate sound that only makes him kiss me harder, like he's been starving for this.

His grip tightens at my hips, hauling me against him, and *oh, fuck*. The thick, hard length of him pressing against my stomach is undeniable, and it only fuels the fire raging inside me. My fingers knot into his shirt, yanking him closer, my nails digging in just to see if I can break that impossible control of his.

Because I want to see him lose it. I want him to snap.

I grind against him, and the sound he makes in response is filthy enough to send heat rolling straight between my thighs.

Fuck. Fuck. Fuck.

I'm drenched.

Aching.

Utterly wrecked.

He breaks the kiss, and I nearly whimper at the distance, but his hands are still on me, still digging into my hips, keeping me right where he wants me.

His gaze sears into mine, a promise and a warning all at once. "You drive me insane, you know that?"

His voice is a husky whisper, raw, drenched in need. His hands start to glide up my back, rough fingers skimming bare skin, leaving wreckage in their wake.

I swallow hard, my head spinning, my body screaming for more.

And just when I think I find my breath again, he takes it from me. His lips crash into mine, hungrier this time, no hesitation.

His fingers twist into my hair, tilting my head back, deepening the kiss, dragging me under with him. The dominance in his touch ignites something dark, something reckless inside me, and I gasp, arching into him.

His other hand slides upward, slow enough to be pure torture, his fingertips teasing along my ribs, brushing dangerously close to the edge of my breast. My breath stills.

He pauses, lingering.

His thumb traces lazy, devastating circles over my skin, each pass edging closer the tension builds, and I honestly wouldn't be surprised at this point if I was wet enough it was dripping down my legs.

"Please," I beg, but for what I'm not even sure.

"Tell me to stop."

The words rumble against my lips, dark and dangerous.

His mouth hovers just above mine, so close I can feel every ragged breath. My ears are ringing, my palms heat. I don't answer. I can't. The words won't come because they'd be a lie. I don't want him to stop, not tonight. Not when every touch feels like it's unraveling something inside me that I didn't even know was there.

Tomorrow, we can go back to pretending this doesn't exist. But tonight, I just want to get lost in him.

His thumb brushes higher, grazing my breast, and a shiver racks through me.

A growl rumbles low in his throat as his grip on my waist tightens.

"Princess," he growls, his voice edged with restraint. His lips hover just above mine, daring me to stop him.

Heat flares through me, and my hands move, sliding up his chest, tracing every sculpted inch of him, hungry to feel more.

Gods, I've thought about this so many times, but nothing compares to the real thing. The way his body feels beneath my fingertips, all control and chaos waiting to be unleashed.

I want more.

I push into him, and his hands snap around my wrists, catching them, pulling me back with a steady grip.

His gaze burns into me, entirely in control. The corner of his mouth curves, "You don't get to touch me, Princess."

His grip tightens slightly, dragging my hands back down, forcing me to stay right where he wants me. "Not yet."

A frustrated sound catches in my throat. I almost pout. My fingers ache to keep exploring, to test his control, to see how far I can push before he snaps.

His hand cradles my face, his thumb dragging slow, devastating circles along my cheek.

Then his mouth is at my throat, and the world ceases to exist. His lips press against my pulse, soft at first, a warning wrapped in velvet, his teeth graze my skin and then he bites down just enough to have me gasping. The sharp sting ripples through me, a perfect collision of pleasure and pain, and my fingers dig into his hips, clutching him like he's the only thing keeping me standing.

His grip tightens, and heat crashes through me, obliterating any thoughts I was having.

One second, I'm braced against him, rigid with anticipation. The next. I'm liquid in his hands, completely at his mercy.

His hands are the only thing keeping me upright as my knees threaten to buckle. Each breath I take is shallow, like I can't get enough air. The warmth in my hands flares, matching the electric heat coursing through my veins, leaving me shaking and completely undone.

His kiss is brutal. His tongue teases, demands, and coaxes me deeper into the fire. And I don't hesitate. I meet him halfway, pressing closer, tasting him like I'm starved for it.

A sharp nip at his bottom lip earns me a low growl, the sound reverberating through his chest and into me. His hands slide down my body, finding the slits in my dress. Fingers digging into the bare skin of my thighs, branding me with his touch. The way his hands squeeze, has me aching in all the places I wish he was touching.

I shift against him just to see how far he'll let me go and his control slips. I feel it in the way his grip tightens, in the way his tongue stutters for half a second, his breath catching.

And I smirk.

So I nip at his bottom lip again, harder this time, playing with the frayed edges of his restraint, and his answering growl sends a delicious thrill straight through me.

For one fleeting moment, I think I've gained the upper hand. Then his voice wrecks me.

"Careful, Princess." He warns. "You keep testing me like that, and we're not stopping here."

His gaze locks onto mine, daring me to call his bluff. The corner of my mouth lifts, my body acting before my brain can intervene. He might be fighting to keep control, but I see the cracks forming.

"Unless you don't care if someone walks in."

His hands slide up my sides, beneath the fabric, his rough fingers graze my nipple, and my brain short-circuits.

The shock of it sends me reeling, and when he pinches, a broken gasp leaves me. His smirk presses against my mouth, and I realize he was never the one unraveling. I was.

Every nerve feels exposed, as his hands explore me with devastating precision. I never stood a chance against this man. And I don't care, it's so fucking worth it.

But I'm not going down without a fight. My hand slides lower, grabbing the hard length pressing into me, he freezes.

"*Raven.*"

I lean back just enough to meet his eyes, batting my lashes like I'm feeling playful instead of completely undone.

"What's the matter, leprechaun?" I purr, arching a brow. "Let me guess... can't do that either?"

His jaw tenses, his grip on me tightens, but it's the chuckle that sends a sharp thrill racing straight to my clit. "Not unless you want to fuck around and find out."

Instantly soaked.

Heat flares through me, a wicked pulse between my thighs, and suddenly I'm fighting a losing battle against the storm crashing through me.

He chuckles, the sound vibrating through the air, and lord help me, I'm here for every torturous second of it.

The second my eyes flick to his lips, he's on me. His tongue teases mine, coaxing my lips apart. His hands are on my waist, his grip firm as he lifts me onto the counter, as I try to steady my breathing.

The only sign of my earlier incident is a slight jolt of pain. I wince slightly, but his mouth is on my ear, and I'm arching into him. His lips trail down my neck before his teeth bite down hard enough to have me gasping, my hand fisting his shirt.

"Kane, please." The ache between my thighs turns unbearable.

His teeth graze lower, and his hands gripping my thighs, spreading them just enough to make my breath catch.

Then he drops to his knees.

"Kane, wh—" My voice barely makes it past my lips before his mouth finds my knee, lips pressing a kiss so achingly slow that my pulse skips and finally gives up entirely. His lips trail higher, each kiss feels like a spark, his fingers slowly push my dress up inch by inch.

He kisses the sensitive skin there, lingering before his gaze locks onto mine. Waiting.

"Hmmm?" I barely manage, my voice a breathless whisper, my head already tilting back. I blink, trying to clear the haze.

"You were saying something?" His voice is low, and I can hear the smirk in it before I see it.

Smug bastard.

"Oh, umm…" I stammer, my mind a complete blur. Whatever I was going to say is long gone, obliterated, a casualty of his mouth.

My breath slows, every inhale dragging through my lungs like molten heat, as his mouth continues its torturous ascent, each kiss pulling me deeper under his control.

It's impossible to think.

Impossible to do anything but let him destroy me.

My head falls back, my hands gripping the counter, nails pressing into the surface, my thighs twitching, aching to press together. But his hands won't let them.

He pauses, his breath warm against my skin, his voice a dark rasp.

"Tell me to stop, Raven."

Like hell.

My breath stutters, my pulse a violent drum against my ribs, refusing to break under his stare. "What… what are you doing?"

His smirk is devastating, pure sin wrapped in arrogance, and he doesn't answer right away. Instead, his lips graze my inner thigh with his teeth, just enough to make me gasp again.

"You know exactly what I'm doing."

His hands press firmer against my legs, spreading them wider, his grip possessive. "You're supposed to kneel in front of a queen, aren't you?" His breath teasing against my skin. "So I'm exactly where I should be. On my knees."

Oh, fuck.

The cool air against my skin is the only warning I get before his hands slide beneath the fabric.

His eyes snap to mine, blazing with unfiltered hunger, but they don't stay there. They drop back down, his tongue flicking out as if he's already tasting me before he even touches me.

"Fuck."

The second his lips are on me, his tongue moves. My legs tremble, but his hands are there, keeping me exactly where he wants me.

"That's it, Princess," he murmurs against me, his breath hot. "Let me taste you."

He groans, the vibration sending a fresh wave of pleasure crashing through me, and I clutch at his hair, nails digging into his scalp.

"Is this what you wanted?" He taunts, voice dark. He drags his tongue achingly slow, teasing me with everything and nothing all at once.

"Or did you think I was going to leave you dripping and send you on your way again?"

His lips curve against me, and then he's devouring me. Each stroke calculated destruction, like he's learning every way to unravel me, testing how far he can push before I break.

My fingers tighten in his hair, pulling him closer, and his growl is pure sin, lighting up every nerve in my body.

"I said no touching," he warns, pulling back just enough to make my thighs tremble in protest.

I suck in a breath, glaring down at him, voice uneven. "Then stop making me want to."

He laughs, the sound pure arrogance.

"Careful, he drawls, his grip tightening, spreading my legs even wider. "Keep pushing, and you'll see exactly how well I keep my promises.

I'd do just about anything right now to relieve what's been building between my legs all day.

"No smart remarks?" His breath hovering against my aching heat, making me feel every second of exactly how in control he still is.

I could kill him.

I make a frustrated noise, my hips shifting forward.

He chuckles, "There she is." His mouth is on me again, his tongue moving with brutal precision. His grip tightens, his hands locking me in place, forcing me to take every slow, torturous stroke of his tongue.

423

My back arches, a sharp gasp tearing from my lips, my body straining toward him, desperate for more. The pressure builds, twisting into something unbearable, something that's going to shatter me completely.

The tingling in my hands spreads, the warmth expanding outward, creeping into every inch of my body, a wildfire I can't contain. The sensation coils at my core, ready to snap, but he's not done toying with me.

"Kane." His name slips out like a plea.

And he fucking answers.

He doubles down, his mouth relentless, each calculated stroke bringing me to the edge faster. My body tenses in his hands.

"Please," I gasp, my voice so wrecked, so desperate that if I had any shame left, I'd be mortified. But I don't. I just need him to finish what he started.

"Cum for me, Princess."

The command shatters me.

Pleasure crashes over me like a tidal wave, tearing through me with raw, violent intensity. I cry out, my body locking up as the release takes me, every nerve in my body on fire.

I don't even realize my fingers are tangled in his hair until I feel the silkiness against my skin, my grip tight enough to hold me together. My head falls back, my chest heaving as I try to remember how to breathe, how to think.

I don't know how long it takes for the world to settle again, but when I finally open my eyes, Kane is already standing, already watching me.

And that look? Pure, devastating satisfaction.

His fingers tug my dress back into place, his touch careful, a contrast to the absolute fucking destruction he just left in his wake.

And then, because he's a cocky bastard who was clearly made to ruin me, leans in and captures me in a slow, devastating kiss.

I can taste myself on him, and the power shift is so blatant, so intoxicating, that for a moment, I forget what just happened. His hands stay on my thighs, gripping firmly. A fresh wave of heat rolls through my body.

Then he pulls back, leaving me wanting.

He exhales a deep, steady breath, eyes flickering over me like he's making sure I'm still standing.

"We should stop."

My pulse still hasn't recovered, but my brain restarts at those words. I blink, trying to focus, trying to figure out if I misheard him.

His lips twitch, amusement curling at the corner as he watches me struggle. "Unless you want to be naked in here."

His eyes lock onto mine, and there's no mistaking that he means every word. And for one reckless second, I actually consider it.

His tongue flicks over his lips, and I swear to God, I almost cave.

The only thing stopping me is him stepping back. His head tilts, watching me like he knows exactly what I'm thinking.

"Can I show you something?" His voice is more controlled, like he's already moved on from whatever just happened.

The haze in my mind barely clears enough for me to process his words. "Oh, yeah. Sure," I manage, my voice still breathless, giving away just how far gone I still am.

I clear my throat, trying to calm my pulse, and my entire fucking existence, and force a shaky smile.

CHAPTER 30

Revelry

KANE

E very part of me is still wired, still on edge, still one breath away from dragging her into the nearest room and finishing what she started. My jaw ticks as I force down the urge, as I remind myself that before I take her, there are things she needs to know.

I at least owe her that much.

I glance down at her, and her big expressive eyes locked on me, waiting.

I can see that she doesn't understand why I'm pulling away, when every instinct in my body is screaming at me to sink my teeth into her soft, sensitive skin and make her remember exactly who had her falling apart moments ago.

I can see the flicker of confusion in her gaze. And something else. Something dangerously close to hurt.

Fuck.

"I can't stay in here with you," my voice is strained. "Because if I do, I'll ruin your dress."

Her brows shoot up, and her gaze darts away so fast I almost smirk.

The blush creeps in, blooming across her cheeks, and she bites her lip like she's already remembering the way I had her coming undone with my tongue.

"Besides," I add, holding out my hand. "There's something I want to show you. Something important."

She hesitates for half a second, eyes narrowing in suspicion, but that mouth curves into a slow grin. "Does the *no touching* rule apply if we're in a different room?" She pauses, tilting her head. "What's so important?"

I roll my eyes, smirking. She's relentless.

"If I told you, I'd ruin the surprise. And we both know you love surprises," I give her hand a slight tug. "Come on."

427

Even as she follows, I feel the hesitation in her steps, the weight of the questions stirring behind those calculating eyes of hers.

I shut the greenhouse door behind us, looking down the hallway, making sure no one's watching as I lead her deeper into the castle.

She's still searching my face for something I'm not ready to give her.

"Should we go find the others? The ball is probably over." There's a false lightness to her tone.

I shake my head. "Cam's got it handled."

Her lips part, like she's about to argue, but she stops herself. Instead, she lets out a soft laugh, though there's a thread of nerves beneath it.

"If I'm honest, I'm more worried about Cam."

"Are we not going to talk about what just happened?" My steps slow.

The words hit like the sharp crack of a whip across my already fraying restraint.

Because I *am* thinking about it. I haven't stopped thinking about it.

The way she moaned my name like a goddamn prayer. It took everything in me to stop. And I glance down at her, at the slight flush still lingering on her skin, the way she's biting her lip like she's still feeling me between her thighs.

"Not unless you want it to happen again," I whisper, edged with heat. "Right here. In the hallway."

Her eyes flash, that challenge sparking between us again. "You wouldn't dare." But I catch the way her pulse picks up, like that's exactly what she wants.

I tilt my head, closing the distance just enough for her to have to tilt her head up. "Wouldn't I?"

Her eyes flick to my mouth, and something inside me snaps.

I'm moving before I think, closing the space in seconds. Her back meets the wall with a soft thud, her breath catches as I tilt her chin up, forcing her to look at me.

Her lips are soft and flushed, and fucking begging to be ruined. The second my mouth claims hers, any pretense of restraint shatters.

She gasps into the kiss, her hands grip my shirt like she needs something to hold onto. I feel her surrender instantly.

And fuck, the soft, breathless moan that comes out of her. Gasoline on a fucking wildfire.

I need to stop. I need to tell her before this goes any further.

Instead, my grip tightens at her waist and my hands drag down, pinning her to the wall as I devour her. Until she's trembling, I can feel her nails dig into my shoulders like she's waiting for me to keep my promise.

My self-control is slipping. Fast.

So I break away, just enough to catch my breath, to force air into my lungs as I drag a hand through my hair. She's still looking at me with those wide eyes, her breath uneven and her lips swollen from my kiss.

"Don't start something *you're* not ready to finish." I warn.

Her throat bobs as she swallows, something unreadable flickers in her eyes. She's trying to gather herself, trying to pretend she's unaffected, but I see it. If I don't get us out of here, I *will* ruin that dress.

I grab her hand, guiding her quickly down the hallway. My office isn't far, but the sound of footsteps has me thinking twice. We need to stay out of sight. The last thing I need is for anyone to see us right now.

Without a word, I press her against the wall again, hand covering her mouth, as I tuck us into the shadows. Her breath quickens and I lean in, lips brushing the shell of her ear. "Scared?"

Her glare is instant. "No, I'm not scared. I just don't know why you insist on pinning me to walls like some kind of caged animal." She hisses against my palm.

She shifts slightly, stumbling in those ridiculously sexy boots of hers, and I raise a brow. I crouch down before she can stop me. "Let's make sure you don't trip again."

Her breath hitches as my hands slide around her calf, lifting her leg to unzip her boot.

"What are you doing?"

I drag the zipper down slowly, my fingers brushing against her skin as I slide her boot free. "Testing my sanity."

She opens her mouth, but nothing comes out. Her chest rises and falls quicker now, her lips parting slightly as I move to her other leg. I take my time, tracing along her smooth calf as I slip off the second boot.

When I stand, her eyes are locked on mine. "Better?" I watch the flush creep up her neck.

She doesn't answer. Doesn't move.

I smirk.

She huffs, looking away, but it's useless, her body betrays her. The way she shifts toward me, the way her pulse flutters at her throat, the way she licks her lips like she wants something but refuses to ask for it.

I'm so fucking hard, and holding back is a losing game. My hands slide to her hips, and her eyes snap back to mine, filled with that unmistakable hunger.

"Kane," she whispers, and just like that, I'm undone.

My mouth is on hers, needing to claim her again. One taste of her isn't enough.

Of all the things I've noticed about Raven, every single one just got bumped to the bottom of the list. Because now, my favorite thing is going to be making her cum.

I scoop her up easily, my arm locking around her waist, and her legs wrap around me without hesitation. Her arms go around my neck as I push open the door, stepping inside without missing a beat. Her body molds against mine, and I'm ready to take her against the nearest surface. That is, until a cough cuts through the air like a bucket of ice water.

"Good evening, sir. This was left for you."

Robert's voice falters as his eyes land on us.

Raven freezes in my arms.

Her head snaps toward him, her wide eyes betraying her shock. She squirms slightly, and with great fucking reluctance, I lower her to the floor. She steps away fast, smoothing her dress, her mask slipping right back into place. Going from wrecked to unreadable in seconds.

"Thank you, Robert."

"Is there anything else you need, sir?" He asks, already inching toward the door like he wants to live to see tomorrow.

"No, that will be all."

He practically sprints out, shutting the door behind him with more speed than grace.

The second we're alone, Raven turns on me, her eyes blazing. But it's not desire that's behind her eyes anymore. They're demanding answers I know I can't delay any longer.

I watch her, catching the confusion swirling behind her eyes as she backs away. Her fingers clutching her necklace.

Thunder rumbles faintly in the distance, a low warning, echoing the tension thickening in the room.

"Raven, listen—" I take a step toward her, but she keeps retreating.

She's putting distance between us. Physically and emotionally. Her eyes dart around the room, piecing it together faster than I'd like.

If I don't get ahead of this, she'll come to her own conclusions. And they'll be far worse than anything I could say.

I exhale, dragging a hand through my hair before meeting her stare head-on. "There are things you don't know."

A bitter laugh escapes her. "No shit."

She paces, jaw clenched, arms folded tightly across her chest like she's trying to shield herself. Lock up whatever this is between us before I can touch it again.

Then she stops, fixing me with a look that could flay a man alive.

"You have exactly two seconds to start explaining," she warns, and there's a deadly edge beneath it. "Because right now, it sounds a hell of a lot like you lied to me."

I didn't lie. But I'm sure it looks like I did to her.

I exhale, forcing my voice to sound calm. "I've got history, a life, a past—just like anyone else. At first, I didn't tell you because, honestly? You were just someone here on vacation. I didn't think it would matter." I pause, jaw tightening. "And because I didn't know how you would react."

Her arms stay locked over her chest, her expression stays unreadable. I'm sure she's waiting to see if she can catch me in something.

"I still don't understand what exactly you're trying to say." She's holding herself together by a thread. I see it in the flush on her cheeks, the way her fingers tighten against her sides.

I hold her gaze. "For starters... this is my estate."

Her lips part slightly, eyes widening.

431

But I don't give her the space to interrupt. "Technically, it's my family's. It was left to me as part of my inheritance. I did get invited to be here, yes, because it's my sister who put on the ball. It's something we host every year."

I watch the way her mind works through every interaction we've had, recalibrating *everything*. Her posture shifts, more rigid now, like she's bracing herself for the next hit.

"I should've told you sooner," I admit, irritation curling in my chest. "That's why I brought you here tonight, I was going to tell you."

Silence.

She's chewing her bottom lip, but she doesn't speak right away. Then, finally, she exhales, "That's... a lot."

I steel myself, waiting for the inevitable fallout, the questions, the accusations. But instead, she surprises me.

"I just have one question."

Her voice is quieter now, but no less irritated.

I nod, waiting.

She points to the desk. "Why is my name on that?"

Fuck.

My jaw clenches as my eyes find the envelope she's looking at. Of all the goddamn things to be sitting out.

I drag a hand through my hair, exhaling slowly. But there's no way out of this. No distraction, no well-timed smirk that's going to steer her away. She knows it. I know it. And by the way she's standing there, with her arms crossed and her chin lifted. She's daring me to try and talk my way out of this.

I hold her stare. "I told you I work in security. That's true. But after you mentioned feeling uneasy about meeting that guy for work, I wanted to make sure you were safe."

Her expression flickers. The shift is instant. Shock. Disbelief. Then something sharper before she locks it down.

She stares at me, unmoving. I'm sure she's trying to decide exactly which part of this to sink her teeth into first.

Finally, she speaks. "What did you find?" Then, almost immediately, "You know what? I don't even care."

Her tone is lethal, but she doesn't move.

"You could've just asked me, Kane. I would've told you whatever you wanted to know. I told you I can handle myself. I don't need a fucking babysitter."

And before I can stop her, she turns and starts to walk away. I grab her arm, just enough to stop her.

She freezes. When she turns back, the look she gives me is pure fire. "Don't touch me."

The cut of her voice is sharper than the glare she levels at me, and I drop my hand instantly. But I don't step back.

"Let me explain."

Her hands go to her hips, and her fury is a living thing. I can see it all over her face.

"Explain what?" She snaps. "That you're some rich, entitled asshole who couldn't just be upfront with me? That you didn't *technically* lie but conveniently left out the part where this is your fucking *castle*? That you decided to snoop into my life instead of just asking me like a normal person?"

Her words hit their mark. Aimed to wound. I inhale through my nose, jaw flexing as I will my temper to hold.

"I didn't lie to you."

Her laugh is sharp and bitter. "No? Just a selective truth, then?"

I take a step forward but she doesn't back up, doesn't flinch. She just glares daggers at me.

"I don't tell people things just for the sake of telling them." My voice is low. "You didn't need to know."

Her brows shoot up, disbelief flashing through her anger. "I didn't need to know?"

I exhale slowly, my patience hanging by a fucking thread.

"Would it have changed anything? If I told you the first night?" I let the words settle, let her sit with them. "I didn't lie to you, Raven. I just didn't give you something when you wanted it."

She shakes her head, letting out a slow, disbelieving breath. "Of course it changes things, Kane. I don't know if I can trust you. I don't even know you."

She throws her hands up in frustration, pacing a few steps before spinning back, her voice colder now. "I'm not interested in being with someone who thinks information is only shared when they want it."

She meets my gaze, her eyes blazing. "I know we're not talking about a relationship here, but lying? Deception? Selective sharing. They're all the same."

I take one step closer, my voice quiet but lethal. "I don't know anything about you either."

She spins around, her sarcasm biting. "Oh, I'm sorry, do you not have an envelope with *my* fucking name on it telling you exactly who I am?"

My hands flex at my sides, the restraint it takes not to grab her, and show her exactly how much her fire is turning me on is grating against my instincts.

"Look, you're great," she continues, "I've enjoyed spending time with you, I really have. But you lied to me, and you pried into my life just because you could."

She turns toward the door, and the lights flicker. Thunder rolls in the distance, deep and foreboding.

Her grip tightens on the handle.

"I'm going home now."

Her voice softens slightly, but she doesn't turn around and doesn't wait for a response. She just steps into the hall, leaving me standing there with the weight of everything unspoken pressing down like a fucking wrecking ball.

This is why I keep people at arm's length. Not because I don't get it. Not because I don't *understand* why she's pissed. But because this is exactly what happens when you let people close to you.

I catch up to her before she makes it to the main doors, my hand hovering just shy of her arm. "Raven, wait."

She stops, turning slowly. Her eyes are wild, frustration burning behind them, but there's something else, something unsettled.

"Look, Kane," she starts, "I'm not here to drag this into an argument. I don't really care that much. I just need to go home and... process everything."

I stay silent, watching her.

She exhales sharply. "Yeah, I'm pissed. And yeah, I know you probably think I have no right to be, but I am." Her jaw tightens. "So I'm just going to go home, sleep on it, and maybe then... I'll know what to say."

She takes a step, then stops abruptly. Like she wants to say something but won't let herself. The lights flick again, shadows stretching across her face, and whatever thought was lingering on her lips, she swallows it back.

Then, just like that, she's walking away.

I let her. For a second.

"Raven," I call after her, my voice cutting through the silence.

She slows, glancing back over her shoulder.

"Cam took Rachel home." I hold up my phone. "Let me at least give you a ride."

Her lips press into a thin line. "No, thank you." she says, looking down the hall.

That small detail gets under my skin. I'd prefer her to be angry. At least then, I know where I stand. "Well, I guess we'll talk in the morning, then. I'll take you to your room."

Thunder rumbles outside, the storm on the verge of breaking.

She turns, facing me fully. Fire and heat flashing in her eyes. "Yeah, that's not happening. I'll just grab an Uber."

I try my hardest to hide the smirk tugging at my lips. She's crazy if she thinks I'm going to let her get an Uber. "I'll have your driver out front, he'll take you home."

She hesitates, arms still wrapped around herself, waging some internal battle I can't read. Then, she finally exhales. "Fine."

The rain's coming down in sheets now, I grab an umbrella from the stand at the door and step outside, waiting.

She eyes me as she walks right past me, into the rain. "You think I'm afraid to get wet?"

Even now, she's still all fire. And it makes me want to drag her right back inside.

"Definitely not," I say smoothly, falling into step beside her, thinking of how wet she was for me. Something is seriously wrong with me. She's pissed as fuck at me, and I can't stop thinking of all the things I could do to her.

Her lips part like she wants to say something, but she just shakes her head, as I cover her with the umbrella. The faintest shiver rolls through her as our shoulders brush.

"I really did have fun tonight," she murmurs after a beat. "And your home is beautiful. I've thought that since the first time I saw it."

She reaches for the door handle. "Goodnight, Kane."

I reach out, fingering grazing her wrist, stopping here in her tracks. Her body stiffens slightly, but she doesn't pull away. Slowly, I take her chin between my fingers, tilting her face up to mine. Her gaze locks onto mine, layered with everything she's holding back. But beneath it, there's still something there.

Something I can work with.

"Don't touch that door handle."

My thumb brushes lightly against her jaw, savoring the feel of her. She hesitates for a second longer, then pulls away. "I'm sorry, Princess. I never meant to hurt you." I open the car door, but not enough for her to get in. "I hope you had a good night. I even added a few last-minute touches when I found out you were on the guest list."

Her lips part slightly, the faintest crack in her resolve. For just a second, the fire dims, something softer flickering in its place.

But she doesn't say anything, just slips into the car, as I close the door behind her.

As the driver pulls away, I step back, watching her go. And just before the car disappears down the long drive, I catch a glimpse of her through the window. She's holding her necklace, a faint smile playing on her lips.

Well, that went well.

I roll my eyes at myself, guess it could've been worse.

The rain picks up, turning into a full downpour. For a moment, I consider heading inside, but instead, I just stand there, rooted to the spot. The rain soaks through my shirt, cold and biting, but I barely feel it. I'm too busy replaying every damn moment of the night.

I shake it off and turn to head inside, but something catches my attention.

All the outdoor lights are out.

Every. Single. One.

I pause, glancing around the property, the hair on the back of my neck prickling. The air is too still, with the kind of silence that sets my instincts on edge.

CHAPTER 31

Something Bad

RAVEN

I *added a few last-minute things when I found out...*

When he found out? So he knew I was coming?

So you went out of your way for me knowing I was coming to your house? Your castle! For a ball you conveniently forgot to mention?

I blink hard, trying to fight the sting in my eyes, but it's pointless. The first tear slips free, hot and unwelcome, quickly followed by another. Before I know it, I'm full-on sobbing. Tears are streaming down my cheeks, and no matter how hard I try to pull myself together, they just keep coming.

And it's not just about Kane. It's not just the lies or the ball or the fact that his ridiculous *castle* somehow makes me feel even more out of place than I already do.

It's *everything*.

The months of uncertainty, the weight of trying to figure out who I even am. It's like every frustration, every bottled-up emotion I've been avoiding, picked tonight to break free.

I replay the night in my head, and even through the mess of my emotions, I can't ignore the magic of it all. The dress, the music, the way he looked at me like I was the only person in the room. *Well, aside from that beautiful blonde woman.* And that kiss... *God, that kiss.* It was more than I ever expected. More than I've allowed myself to want in a long time.

But now? Now it just feels like everything I've been trying so hard to do just unraveled at my feet.

I thought Kane was different. I thought... I don't know what I thought. And maybe that's the problem. Maybe I shouldn't have let myself *think* anything at all.

I swipe at my cheeks, the tears coming faster than I can wipe them away. The driver's probably watching me in the rearview mirror, thinking I've completely lost it. And honestly? Maybe I have.

A small, bitter laugh escapes me, surprising even myself.

I probably don't have the right to even be upset. I've known him for what, five minutes? And it's not like I've been completely honest with him either.

Hell, I didn't tell him the truth about my fat lip. I didn't tell him about the creep that was running around in the garden. At his *castle!*

The smell of rain drifts through the car vents, cutting through the frustration knotting in my chest. The steady hum of the rain against the windows, and the thunder rolling low in this distance, should be pulling me out of this tangled mess of emotions.

But it doesn't.

Lightning slices through the sky, flooding the dark countryside in a white-hot glow before disappearing just as quickly. The storm doesn't hesitate, it moves exactly the way it was meant to. Wild and refusing to apologize for its destruction.

Must be nice.

I hate that I'm hurt when I *know* I shouldn't be. We were having a great time, more than great, if I'm honest. And if we hadn't stopped when we did... God. I'd be spending the rest of my life replaying every second of it.

Maybe it's for the best we didn't cross that line.

But no matter how hard I try to stop thinking about him, he's right there.

The way he just knelt down, how his hands felt sliding up my thighs like they were his to claim.

My skin heats just thinking about it.

It was pure insanity. *And so fucking hot.*

Before we walked into his office, my mind was running wild with a thousand dirty things I wanted to let him do to me. And now I'm glad I didn't act on any of them, considering how pissed I am. Because if I had, I'd be even angrier at myself right now.

This is exactly why I swore off men in the first place. So I wouldn't end up here. Angry. Frustrated. And second-guessing every single decision that led to me letting him anywhere near my self-control. *And I wouldn't still be horny as fuck.*

The driver keeps glancing at me in the rearview mirror, probably trying to gauge if I'm about to start crying again. Poor guy looks like he'd rather launch himself out of the car than deal with that. I almost laugh but swallow it back.

Then out of nowhere, a strange wave of wrongness crashes over me.

My stomach flips, queasiness rolling through me like a sudden drop in altitude. My heart starts hammering like I just ran a mile and all I can hear is a sharp ringing in my ears. I press my fingers to my temple, squeezing my eyes shut.

Inhale. Exhale.

I try to shut it down, but a memory pushes through instead. The soft flick of my grandmother's knitting needles breaking the silence.

I can see her now, curled up in her chair, lost in her stories the way she always was. I'd stretch out by the fire, soaking in the warmth while her voice filled the room. Sometimes she got so carried away, she'd forget I was even there. More than once, I'd startle her when I got up for bed. Or when she tripped over me, realizing I'd fallen asleep on the rug.

And as I sit here, drenched in my own thoughts, that familiar ache settles deep in my chest.

"You know," she begins, her voice thoughtful. *"They really did find happiness. For a while, it seemed like they'd figured out how to make things work. No one could have guessed how it would all fall apart."*

I can't look away. I'm hooked.

"One day, out of the blue, he just stopped talking to her. No explanation. Nothing. She didn't understand why. The silence crushed her—devastated her. She didn't even know if she wanted to reach out, too afraid of what he might say."

The ache in her tone makes my chest go tight, and suddenly, I feel it like it's my own.

"What she didn't know," her voice dropping to a whisper, *"was that someone had discovered their secret. And whoever it was, they were terrified of what the two of them together could become."* Her eyes darken. *"So, they cursed him."*

The words send an eerie chill through me.

"Her sorrow consumed her," she continues, the edges of her voice slicing through the warmth of the room. "It twisted into bitterness and hate until she convinced herself that no one could ever truly love her like she needed. She believed that she would never have a soulmate. Storms chased her, but still her power grew, and yet..."

Her eyes find mine, pinning me in place.

"... the answer was always right there. If she just..."

I can't move. The book in her lap holds my stare like it knows something. Like it wants me to understand something that's slipping through my fingers.

She notices me staring and tilts her head. A slow, knowing smile plays at her lips.

"Wake up, child."

It's not a suggestion.

I frown, shaking my head slightly. "Grandma—?"

"WAKE UP, RAVEN!" Her voice cracks like thunder, sending a shudder through my bones. "You're running out of time."

I jerk awake, my chest heaving, my heart slamming into my ribs like it's trying to break free. The dream dissolves, leaving me disoriented, but even more nauseous.

What the hell was that?

Outside, the lights of passing buildings flicker against the car windows, ghostlike blurs that barely register. Another wave of nausea slams through me making my pulse spike.

I swallow hard, gripping the seat, trying to steady my breathing. But every inhale feels like I'm pulling in more than air.

We're almost there. I just need to get to the house. Maybe eat something. Maybe lie down. Just... anything to stop this awful spinning.

But the queasiness turns unbearable, and the air in the car suddenly feels suffocating. The ringing in my ears only gets louder. My skin prickles, and my chest tightens. There's not enough oxygen in here, I need fresh air. *Now.*

"Excuse me," I manage, catching the driver's gaze in the mirror. "Could you pull over? I'd like to walk the rest of the way. I need some fresh air."

His brow furrows slightly, his concern obvious as he glances at the rain streaking the windshield. "Are ye sure, lass?" His tone is hesitant as he pulls to the side of the road. "It's chilly out there, and it's late for wanderin' about."

I force a smile, though it feels about as steady as my stomach. "I promise, I'll be fine. It's not far." Then, I add, "If your boss gets mad, tell him I said he can shove it."

His eyes widen slightly, surprise flickering across his face before a smirk tugs at his lips. For a split second, the tension eases, and I catch the faintest twitch at the corner of his mouth.

"Okay, fine, maybe don't say that last part," I relent with a small laugh. "But I *wouldn't* hate it if you did."

He shakes his head, but after a second, he sighs, defeated. He unlocks the doors and steps out, circling around to open mine, nodding.

"Thank you." I smile, and climb out, meeting his gaze for just a second before he closes the door behind me. "Really, I'll be fine. No need to wait."

He looks slightly worried, but his voice is sincere. "Be careful, lass."

Thunder rolls in the distance, a low warning as the wind picks up, slicing through my dress like a blade.

The driver hesitates before finally getting back in the car and pulling away, the taillights fading into the rain. I'm half-surprised he doesn't circle back or watch from a distance to make sure I don't get lost.

The road ahead stretches into shadows, and with every step, unease coils tighter in my chest. My head is still pounding, and I can barely hear over the ringing. A shiver runs down my spine, and the hair on the back of my neck rises like something is brushing against me. I wrap my arms around myself, but the thin fabric of my dress does little to block the cold, or the sinking feeling that I'm not alone.

This was a *mistake*.

The fresh air, the walk, none of it is helping. My nerves are fried, my body's spiraling lower by the second, and I still feel like I'm about to puke. Even my usual comfort thoughts aren't enough to pull me out of my head right now.

I try to focus on *anything* else finding my mind circling back to the story. The king and his girlfriend. Or *not* girlfriend.

If she'd just gone after him, confronted him, demanded answers... maybe their story wouldn't have ended in tragedy. Maybe they could've had some sort of closure, or better yet, a happy ending.

But no. She let pride keep her from getting answers. So instead of fighting for something real, everything fell apart. Because why?

A fresh wave of bitterness settles in my chest. I shake my head at myself. Why am I even thinking about this? It's just some old story.

The tears crash into me again before I can stop them, trailing down my face.

The streetlights flicker and the rain falls harder, dripping down my face. Thunder snarls overhead, while lightning rips through the sky, painting the pavement in harsh, eerie flashes.

I make it a little further down the street when I feel the same tingling sensation from earlier. Only now, it's stronger, rippling across my skin like something is trying to pull at me. Goosebumps prick my arms, and my heartbeat thunders in my ears.

Okay, remain calm. Think.

My hands grow hot, uncomfortably so, the warmth is radiating from my palms like a fire I can't put out. Desperate to distract myself, I rub my hands against the wet fabric of my dress, trying to take in my surroundings.

But the heat won't stop.

"Fight."

A whisper, barely there, but clear as fucking day. What the hell?

Ice floods my veins and I stop dead. My breath catching as I whip my head around, scanning the rain-soaked street. *I don't see anything.* Just the empty road stretching ahead, the shifting shadows under the streetlights.

My pulse hammers against my ribs as I glance over my shoulder, the rain blurring my vision as thunder crashes above.

"Raven!"

The whisper slithers through the storm, closer this time.

Then I hear a cough, and ice spikes through my veins as something slams into the side of my face.

The impact is instant, a sickening crack as my head jerks back, pain splitting through my skull, radiating across my cheekbone. Stars burst behind

444

my eyes, my vision going momentarily dark. I barely manage to stay upright, as my boots slip against the slick pavement.

Really? Again?

The thought is quick but fueled by adrenaline as I force myself to focus, my breath ragged against the cold air. The storm rages around me, the wind whipping through my soaked dress, but all I can see is *him,* a shadow in the rain.

His stance is cocky, like he already knows how this is going to end.

I swipe the rain from my face, barely suppressing the white-hot anger unfurling in my chest. "What the *fuck*," I spit, voice sharp enough to cut through the downpour.

No answer. Just a slow tilt of his head, an almost amused flick of his fingers, like I'm nothing more than a passing inconvenience.

He moves.

I see the punch coming a second too late. My body reacts on instinct, twisting to the side just as his fist cuts through the empty air where my face was a second ago. The force of the swing makes him stagger slightly, and I backpedal fast, my heart slamming against my ribs.

"Honestly? That was embarrassing." Am I taunting a man that can kick my ass and probably kill me. Yeah, but I need to buy some time to figure out how the fuck I'm going to get out of this.

He laughs. A low, dark sound that sends a shiver rolling through my entire body.

Lightning flickers overhead, illuminating the jagged scar slicing across his cheek, and a cruel twist to his lips.

Yikes, he looks scary.

His stance is easy, almost lazy, but the way he's watching me, and the fact that he hasn't even bothered to speak yet is what puts me on edge.

He lunges.

I barely have time to process before he's on me again, he's fast for his size, his next punch is aimed straight for my ribs. I duck, but my boots slip on the wet ground. My damn dress tangles around my legs, slowing me down, but I stay upright.

His fist clips my side, not a full hit, but enough to make me grit my teeth against the pain. *Fuck that hurt.* If my ribs weren't already broken, they might be now.

Fucking dress.

I swing blindly, fueled by rage and desperation. My fist connects with his gut, solid and unexpected. The shock reverberates through my arm, sending a sharp jolt up to my shoulder.

He grunts, doubling over for just enough time for me to take a staggering step back, gasping for breath.

His head snaps up. His eyes burn with fury.

"Bitch," he snarls, his voice drenched in venom.

I scoff. "How original."

I'm still gasping for air, but I don't retreat. My hands clench into fists at my sides, and I can feel the heat in my palms pulsing again, only stronger now.

He's still watching me, his chest rising and falling in steady breaths, hands flinching like he's wondering how much it's going to take before I break.

The street lights flicker again.

Thunder cracks overhead, shaking the pavement beneath me. I swear, for half a second, the shadows around him shift, curling at the edges. Like something standing right behind him.

This isn't normal right?

I swallow hard and try to ignore the way my pulse is hammering wildly against my ribs. *Focus, Raven. Don't let him see you panic.* I keep my stance light, shifting on the balls of my feet. *Or trying to.*

Murderer? Probably not. But lunatic? Oh, absolutely.

This time, when he moves, it's more calculated.

I pivot, expecting another wild swing. But he turns at the last second, dodging my elbow and slamming his fist into my ribs with enough force to steal my breath from my lungs. A sharp blistering pain explodes through my side, and I stumble.

He doesn't give me time to recover.

A hand grabs my dress, jerking me back before I can find my footing, sending me sprawling onto the ground. I hit hard, rain splashing against my face as I gasp for breath, my vision darkening for a second. My ribs scream in protest, pain lancing up my side. Shit.

I'm certain they're broken now.

I need to move.

I roll just as his boot slams down where my ribs had been not a heartbeat before, the impact vibrating through the ground. My breath shudders as I push myself to my knees, blinking past the rain, my body protesting.

He crouches down, tilting his head as he watches me. His lip curls, and when he speaks, his voice is a whisper. "We've been watching you."

The words settle like a stone in my gut.

I push up to my feet, ignoring the way my ribs protest.

"That's creepy as hell," I mutter, my voice hoarse. "But hey, nice to have fans."

His smirk deepens, and I don't see his fist until it connects.

A blinding *crack* as my head snaps sideways, pain bursting through my jaw. My vision flashes for a second, stars flickering in the edges of my sight. My ears ring.

My knees give out, and I hit the pavement.

Not good. This is not good.

I lift my head, the taste of blood sharp on my tongue, and glare up at him. He stands over me, waiting.

"Get up," he taunts. "Let's see if you really have it."

Confusion lances through me, but I shove it aside. *Not now.*

I force myself up, my legs trembling slightly. Every breath sends a jolt of pain through my ribs, but I will not give him the satisfaction of staying down.

His eyes flick to my necklace and something shifts in his expression. A flicker of recognition. His fingers twitch like he wants to rip it off me.

I tighten my grip.

"You've got the wrong girl," I try to tell him. "Sorry to disappoint."

His smirk is slow. Patient, like he has all the time in the world to dismantle me piece by piece. *Okay, he might be a murderer after all.*

"You're exactly who we've been looking for."

A sick feeling rolls through my stomach, and it's almost too much.

"Look," I smile. "We don't have to do this. Save yourself the humiliation of getting your ass kicked by a girl in heels."

His lip curls, his expression shifts to something darker. "You won't get far," he snarls, "we know who you are now. You're reckless and we *can smell you.*"

"Ew," I blurt before I can stop myself. "Did you just say you can *smell* me? Gross."

The rain pounds harder, but the sound barely registers over the static filling my head.

Did he say *we?*

My pulse spikes, every instinct screams for me to *run*, to put as much distance as possible between me and whatever the hell this is.

Instead, I do what I always do, I dig my heels in, meeting his gaze with every ounce of defiance I can muster. "Seriously, wrong girl. So why don't you just…" I wave a dismissive hand. "Go back home and turn on some Netflix, try a different series man. Maybe Supernatural? It's really good. You'd love it."

He doesn't laugh. Doesn't react at all, except for the slow drop of his eyes right back to my chest.

His expression shifts, "You talk too much," he mutters.

The blade appears in his hand before I even register the movement. Ice floods my veins, my body locking up.

Fuck.

It's instinct that saves me. The second his arm jerks, I move. My feet stumble back, my arm flies up, enough to keep it from sinking into something vital.

The burn is instant. It feels like fire licking across my forearm. I bite down on a scream.

My grandpa's voice whispers through the chaos, a memory pressing against the pain.

"The first hit will tell you everything you need to know about your enemy."

"If they hesitate after they hurt you, they're inexperienced. If they smile? They'll enjoy it. But if they don't react at all? Then you're already in trouble."

I lift my chin, ignoring the blood dripping down my arm.

He's not smiling. He's waiting.

The rain slashes against my skin, and my breath comes faster. Alright. I'm not going down without a fight though.

His eyes widen, not with satisfaction, but with *pain?*

His body locks up like he's been struck by lightning. A raw, choked gasp rips from his throat, and then he *screams.*

His fingers claw at his chest, and his head tilts back, the streetlights overhead explode as glass rains down around us, like tiny fireworks.

I flinch, raising an arm to shield my face, and the moment I lower it, the world is black.

Darkness swallows the street whole.

He collapses to his knees, his body convulsing, his lips curling around strangled noises.

What. The. *Fuck.*

My chest rises and falls in frantic, shallow gasps. My ribs ache, my arm throbs, but my mind is moving too fast to care.

My hands *burn.*

I stagger back a step as he chokes out something I can't understand before his body slumps fully onto the pavement, unmoving.

I don't move.

I don't breathe.

I just stare at him.

What just happened?

The street is unnervingly silent except for the rain hammering the pavement and the distant growl of thunder rolling through the hills. My chest rises and falls in sharp, uneven breaths, the ache in my body is an afterthought compared to what just happened.

Then headlights slice through the storm, flooding the street with artificial light.

Relief surges through me. I whip my head around toward the approaching car ready to flag them down, and they turn going in a different direction. When I look back, he's gone.

I blink hard, rainwater blurring my vision, my heart lurching into my throat. I scan the shadows, searching for the silhouette that had been *right there,* but there's *nothing.* Just the empty street, the storm swallowing the space where he should be. *You've got to be kidding me.*

A shaky breath escapes me, my pulse thrumming against my ribs.

How is he just gone?

449

Every hair on my body stands on end, my senses screaming at me to move, but my legs won't cooperate.

I exhale sharply, forcing my muscles to unfreeze, to function. I need to get out of here. I stagger forward, my heels slipping against the wet pavement as I push into the downpour, every drop of rain feels like needles on my skin. Every breath feels like a knife to the ribs. My arm throbs, blood mixing with the rain as it drips down my fingers, but the physical pain barely registers over the chaos still wreaking havoc through my mind.

I keep moving, one foot in front of the other. My heartbeat still hasn't settled. And I bet if I took off my boots this nice evening stroll wouldn't be so bad.

The night is too still, too quiet.

I can feel something watching me, and I wonder if it's that same guy.

I shake the thought loose, focusing on the sound of my own footsteps, on the crunch of gravel beneath my boots. I'm almost there. Just a few more blocks, and I can collapse into bed and pretend none of this ever happened.

It's quiet at first, but then I hear the low rumble of an engine coming up behind me.

I tense, glancing over my shoulder just as headlights cut through the downpour. My stomach knots, dread crawling up my spine as the car slows beside me.

Shit. Can't a girl catch a break?

I brace myself, fingers curling into fists, until the window rolls down. "Miss Taylor! You forg—" The driver's words die in his throat as he squints, looking at me. "Are you all right?"

I blink, trying to pull my scattered thoughts together, but I can't. I don't even know what I look like right now, but thank God all the lights broke, so he can't really see me.

He's holding my phone, but I keep my arms folded tightly across my chest, hiding the cut and, honestly, my nerves. A few minutes ago, I was ready to beg for help. But right now I just need to get home as quickly as possible.

"I'm okay," I manage, taking the phone from his outstretched hand, and trying to avoid his gaze.

He doesn't look convinced.

"Are you sure?" His eyes flick to my trembling hands. "You look—"

"I said I'm fine." The words lash out before I can reel them back in. His brows shoot up, and I exhale, forcing a calmer tone. "Sorry, I just... it's been a long night."

He hesitates, clearly torn, then sighs. "Lass, I know you said you wanted to walk, but it's coming down proper now. Won't you let me take you the last bit? Please?"

For once, I listen to reason.

This might actually be the smartest thing I've done all day.

"Sure," I murmur, sliding into the back seat. The heat coming from the vents wrap around me, grounding me just enough to steady my heartbeat. The hum of the engine settles in my bones, but my hands won't stop trembling.

When I lift one to wipe my nose, I freeze.

The sight of blood smudged across my fingers sends a fresh wave of nausea rolling through me. Great. A bloody nose to go with my bloody arm.

I angle my body away, hoping the dim light and the driver's focus on the road will keep him from noticing.

Minutes stretch on, the drive impossibly slow. I try to replay the fight, try to understand what the hell just happened, but the moment I reach for the memory of him screaming, the lights shattering, my thoughts skitter away, a black void swallowing them whole.

We pull up to the house, the soft glow of the porch light flickering through the rain.

I don't wait for him to say anything else. The moment the car slows, I push the door open and step into the downpour, barely acknowledging his murmured "Stay safe" before shutting the door behind me. "Thank you."

I force my feet to move, making my way toward the house, my heels crunching against the wet gravel path. My dress clings to me, heavy and cold, every drop of rain only adding to the exhaustion dragging at my limbs. My arm aches, my head pounds, but none of it compares to the pain in my side right now. And then there's the sickening feeling still coiling in my gut.

So when I see movement out of the corner of my eye, I freeze.

It moves again and I huff out a laugh at myself. It's just a dog. Relief flutters through me, but it doesn't last. Every instinct I have is screaming. I just need to go inside. Then I can lay down.

Normally, I'd be the first to crouch down, to make some ridiculous noise, and try to coax it over. But after tonight? I'm not taking any chances, and if I don't get inside soon, Rachel will find me out here on the driveway in the morning.

I walk faster, even though every inhale and every step sends shooting pain through my body.

I look back over and the dog is gone.

Nothing stirs, but that feeling doesn't leave. It clings to me, an invisible weight pressing against my spine.

My fingers tremble as I wrap them around the door handle, twisting it with more force than necessary. The second I'm inside, I shut the door behind me, leaning back against it as if that thin barrier could keep all the chaos out.

I squeeze my eyes shut, inhaling deeply, trying to steady my pulse.

But as I press my hand to my chest, only one thought settles deep in my bones.

Someone is looking for me?

The thought burrows deep. I push off the door, my legs unsteady beneath me as I make my way down the dark hallway. Every step feels heavier, the weight of the night pressing harder with each passing second. A few more steps.

I reach my room and shut the door behind me, my body moving on auto pilot as I lock it. It's not enough to make me feel safe. Nothing feels safe anymore. But I don't want Rachel waking up and coming in here.

I let out a sharp breath and press my back against the door, then slide to the floor. My arms wrap around my knees, holding myself together even as the tremors rack through me. Everything hurts.

My dress clings to my skin, torn in some places. My arm throbs with every pulse of my heartbeat, and my insides feel like they're on fire. I don't think the cut is too deep, but it hurts like hell. Blood has already soaked into the fabric, and now that the adrenaline is wearing off, the pain is creeping in, sharp and insistent.

I drop my head to my knees, the exhaustion hitting me full force. The fight, the chase, the way he disappeared.

The lights. The screaming.

A violent shudder runs through me.

I don't understand what happened. I don't understand what's *happening*, period.

I should be dead. That guy should've killed me. My mind replays the way he writhed in agony, the way the streetlights shattered, the way his screams rang through the night like something had torn him apart from the inside.

The nausea returns, twisting my stomach into knots.

What the hell is happening to me?

I clutch my necklace, my fingers curling around the warm metal, hoping for some kind of comfort, but it offers nothing. The ache in my chest builds and before I can stop it, the tears come.

Not the quiet tears. The full, body-wracking, ugly kind. The kind that makes you feel like you're coming apart at the seams. *Which, right now, hurts like a bitch.*

I press my hand against my face, trying to muffle the sobs, but they just keep coming, spilling over faster than I can control.

Pull yourself together.

The words sound like my grandfather's. A memory surfaces, unbidden. His voice is patient, but unyielding.

"A fight isn't just about strength, Raven. It's about control. A warrior with no control is already dead."

I exhale shakily, gripping onto the words like a lifeline. Control.

I force myself to move, and I push to my feet. My body feels too heavy, my limbs protest. But I make my way to the bathroom, peeling off my dress, leaving a trail of my night behind me on the floor.

The moment I step into the shower, the steam surrounds me. The water is hot enough to scald my skin, and it stings as I step under the spray. But I don't care. This is a welcome heat.

I watch the blood swirl down the drain, the pink tendrils twisting through the water, and then vanishes. Gone. As if none of it happened.

I wish my thoughts would go with it.

I press my forehead against the cool tile, letting the water run over me, washing away the sweat, the rain, the blood. *The fear.*

By the time I step out, I feel more like myself. Not *fine,* but functional. I grab a towel wrapping it around me as I rummage through the first aid kit under the sink.

453

I clean the cut with shaky hands, sucking in a sharp breath when the antiseptic burns like hell.

The bandage wraps snugly around my arm, covering the wound. A temporary fix. There's nothing I can do about my ribs. The bruise already looks black and purple, and it takes up half my side.

I wipe the fog from the mirror, my own reflection staring back at me, eyes are still red-rimmed with dark circles beneath them.

I look like shit.

I let out a breath, forcing my shoulders to square. I'll deal with this tomorrow. Right now, I just need to sleep.

I drag myself to bed, collapsing onto the mattress with a heavy sigh. The wind howls outside, the storm still raging, but I focus on the steady rhythm of my breathing as I cry myself to sleep.

CHAPTER 32

Evermore

RAVEN

When I open my eyes, I'm no longer in bed. The air is heavy with the scent of rain. The ground beneath me is damp and spongy, against my skin.

I roll onto my elbows to see that I'm in a forest.

Above me, the sky stretches like an endless canvas, inky black streaked with swirling ribbons of deep purples and blues, shifting and pulsing like the sky itself is alive. Like it's breathing.

A chill prickles at my skin and I can tell I'm not alone.

A wolf moves in the distance, and its eyes glow faintly in the strange light, fixed on mine. It stalks toward me, like it's not in any hurry. Its steps soundless against the damp earth.

The silence is suffocating.

"Hey there," I murmur, voice barely a whisper, yet impossibly loud against the quiet. "You sure are beautiful, aren't you?"

The wolf doesn't react. There's a whisper in the wind, though the branches above remain still.

The hair on my arms rises, and the temperature drops.

The murmurs thread through the air like an echo of a long-forgotten memory brushing the edges of my mind. I strain to catch it, to make sense of the words, but the harder I try the more they scatter.

Then, I hear a voice cutting through the silence like a blade.

"Raven."

I whip my head around, searching for the source, only to find trees, and more shadows.

I look around, but the wolf hasn't moved, but its eyes still reflect the swirling lights above. It just stands there, staring. It's almost like he's waiting. But for what? I'm not sure.

The whispers get louder, wrapping around me like a warning. My breath quickens, and my pulse hammers in my ears. I press my hands to my head, desperate to drown it out, but the sound isn't coming from outside.

They're everywhere.

The wolf steps closer.

"You just stay where you are buddy."

The wolf tilts its head, watching. The whispers rattle through my skull like a rising tide.

Heat like I've never felt flares in my palms, spreading through my fingers, and slowly spreads through my whole body. Light flickers from my hands, glowing brighter with each erratic thud of my heartbeat. It radiates outward, forming a glow around me.

The whispers are there, just not as loud.

The wolf hesitates. Its glowing eyes widen slightly, watching the pulsing energy that flickers and shifts, symbols twisting through the air in an intricate, shifting pattern.

A shudder rips through me, breath catching in my throat. "What do you want?" My voice is hoarse, like I've been screaming.

The wolf tilts its head. I feel the answer more than I hear it. A single, unspoken command pressing into my thoughts.

Watch.

"Watch what?"

The voices call my name again, closer this time. My blood turns to ice.

I whirl around, heart in my throat, expecting to see someone looming over me.

But there's nothing. The only thing I can see are the shadows moving in the trees.

The symbols ripple faster, shifting and changing faster than I can track.

The wolf takes another step, its gaze locked on the glow. Its ears twitch, listening to something I can't hear. Then its eyes lift back to mine, and it's turning away.

"Wait," I call. It pauses, and looks back over its shoulder, meeting my gaze. Then, with a small nod, it disappears into the shadows.

The whispers retreat with it, fading into silence.

I turn in a frantic circle, searching, but my movements feel sluggish, my body feels all wrong, like I'm wading through thick mud.

Then, the ground shifts beneath me.

I lurch forward, my stomach twisting as if the world has been ripped from under my feet.

I'm falling.

Dizziness crashes over me, disorienting and violent. The sky distorts, warping like a shattered mirror.

And then I hear a familiar voice, "Princess."

I blink up at him, dazed, my heart hammering as I register the face above me. His usual confidence is there, but there's something different about him now. Something sharper.

"What are you doing on the ground?" His brow furrows, his head tilting slightly, like he's trying to decide if I'm worth the trouble.

My mouth opens, but before I can say anything, the dizziness surges again, pulling me under.

"Too soon." A whisper threads through my disoriented thoughts.

I squeeze my eyes shut, but the sensation doesn't stop.

And when I open them again, there's only silence.

CHAPTER 33

Daylight

RAVEN

I wake with a start, bolting upright, my chest heaving as my heart slams against my ribs. My breath comes in short, ragged gasps.

My hands shake as I rub my palms together, desperate to rid myself of the lingering tingling sensation. But it doesn't go away. It clings, pulsing beneath my skin like a second heartbeat.

The room is dark. My body is drenched in sweat, and for a moment, I'm completely disoriented.

The dream crashes back, sharp and vivid. The forest. The wolf. The whispers.

A shiver rolls through me as I scan the room, expecting shadows to shift in the corners. I look around and the furniture, the pile of my discarded clothes, the nightstand. Everything looks exactly the same.

Yet it doesn't *feel* the same.

I push the covers off and move toward the window. Pressing my palm to the cold glass, while I let the chill seep into my skin, willing it to clear the fog in my head.

In. Out. Deep breaths.

My fingers twitch. I feel so restless. I see movement and that's when I see a shape at the edge of the trees. My heart stutters until I see that it's the same dog. It doesn't move, just sits there. The hairs on the back of my neck rise, and a cold pickle races down my spine. Slowly, I step away from the window and yank the curtains shut. As if that will do anything.

Crawling back into bed, pull the covers up to my chin. I close my eyes and try to get some more sleep.

I hear voices drift through the closed door, followed by footsteps that are quick. A door closes and Rachel storms in like a hurricane, instantly shattering my fragile bubble of calm.

461

I thought I locked the door.

She freezes but recovers quickly. "How's my favorite dumbass?"

I groan, burying my face in my pillow. When I finally peel one eye open, she's standing there, hands on her hips, studying me like I'm a lab experiment gone wrong. And just like that, last night slams into me.

I shut my eyes again. *Nope. Not dealing with this yet.*

Rachel, as expected, does not give a single shit about my avoiding issues.

"I have a confession," she announces. Her tone hovering between guilty and smug.

That gets my attention. "What did you do?"

She shifts, like she's deciding what to say.

"Well…" she draws out the word, milking the suspense for all its worth. Then she rips off the Band-Aid. "When you didn't come home last night, I may have… well… I kinda texted Kane to ask where you were."

Both eyes snap open. I bolt upright. "You *what*?"

Rachel shrugs, utterly unapologetic. "You didn't text me back, and I was worried. Sue me. Just thought you should know."

I stare at her, half in horror, half in disbelief. "And what did he say?"

She hands me my phone, looking a little too pleased with herself. "You've got a few messages. I didn't tell him much, just that you got back and you're okay."

I flop back onto the bed with a groan. "Of course you did."

Rachel smirks, but her eyes hold something else.

I hesitate, thumb hovering over the screen. Before I can talk myself out of it, I unlock my phone.

> Kane: You get home alright?

When I look back up, Rachel is watching me. Suspiciously quiet. A small smirk tugs at the corner of her lips, and I narrow my eyes. "What?"

"Nothing," she says way too innocently, but the smirk doesn't budge. "Spit it out."

She lifts her hands in surrender. "Are you going to text him back?"

I scowl. "No, I'm going to go back to bed."

She leans against the doorway, arms crossed, eyebrows arched. "Keep lying to yourself, drama queen. You're already thinking about it."

I groan, but my gaze drops back to my phone, that small, traitorous flutter in my chest betraying me. My fingers hesitate for half a second, then I lock it and toss the phone onto the bed.

Not today.

Rachel doesn't comment, but she watches me like she's waiting for me to cave. I ignore her, stretching my arms over my head and pretending I'm not seconds away from spiraling into a full-on existential crisis.

She finally sighs, flopping onto the bed beside me. "Alright, fine. We'll just let *that* sit for now. I won't ask. Yet. But you came here for answers, and so far, all we've got is more questions. It's time to actually do something."

I groan dramatically, sinking back into my pillow and yanking the covers over my face. "I don't want to. Can't we just pretend we're normal people, on a normal vacation, doing normal vacation-y things? Like wine tours? Or I don't know, buy overpriced keychains?"

"Nope," she says immediately, her voice taking on that bossy edge she gets when she's about to drag me into something I *really* don't want to do. "We need a plan. And before you even think about trying to distract me, don't. I know you're holding out on me."

I peek out from under the covers, narrowing my eyes. "Excuse me?"

She crosses her arms, looking entirely too smug. "You're acting weird. You didn't text me back, you disappeared, and now you're doing that *thing* where you pretend nothing's wrong when I *know* something is."

I fight to keep my face neutral, forcing a yawn. "Maybe I'm just tired."

Her eyes narrow further, dangerously skeptical. "You're always *just* tired."

I shrug, rubbing my eyes like I couldn't care less, even though my pulse has kicked up a notch. "Sorry to disappoint."

She studies me, her gaze sharp, but after a moment, she exhales dramatically, rolling onto her stomach. "Fine. Be mysterious. But even if I don't get details about how you got dicked down, I'm still going to say *I told you so.*"

I snort. "Good to know you're so supportive in my time of need."

"Duh." She winks. "Now, want to get food? You slept forever."

"Deal." I mumble, dragging myself out of bed.

She practically skips out of the room, calling over her shoulder, "And for the record, it looks like we don't need a love spell for Lover Boy after all!"

I groan, rolling my eyes as I make my way to the bathroom. But despite everything, a small chuckle escapes me. She's impossible.

But as I catch my reflection in the mirror, my amusement fades.

My hair is a disaster, sticking up in every direction, my eyes are puffy from a night of too much crying and too little sleep. But it's the other thing that makes my stomach drop. My face doesn't look anything like it did yesterday. I pull off my hoodie so I can get a better look at my arm, and carefully peel back the bandage.

The cut, which I *swear* was deep last night, looks... smaller. Less angry. It's still there, but the raw, swollen redness has faded to a dull pink. The wound looks days old. Not hours. I look back up at my face, and you'd just think I just cried all night or was really tired. My lip is a little fat, but nothing crazy. My ribs are black and blue, but not quite as dark as it was last night. It still hurts like a bitch though.

I'm shocked that I don't look worse. I definitely feel worse than I look. I guess that's for the best. Less questions that way.

I press lightly against my skin, testing for pain. But it barely stings.

A mix of confusion and unease curls in my stomach. *I swear it looked worse last night. Am I crazy?*

Maybe it looked worse in the dark? Maybe I was overreacting.

Maybe nothing about last night was normal.

I swallow hard and reach for the first aid kit under the sink, methodically re-bandaging my arm.

One thing at a time.

By the time I make it into the kitchen, Rachel is perched on a stool, phone in her hand. She glances up briefly, and the worry etched into her face stops me in my tracks.

"What's wrong?" I know her well enough to call bullshit before she even tries.

"Nothing." She sets down her phone, and in an obvious attempt to change the subject, she grabs the teapot and pours me a cup like it's the most important thing she's ever done.

I don't even need to say anything. Just raise an eyebrow.

She sighs, her shoulders slumping as she leans against the counter. "Okay, fine. It's not *nothing*. It's Bobby."

I stay quiet, letting her talk. She doesn't need much prompting when he's the one on her mind.

She exhales sharply, fingers tapping absently against the counter. "He's just being himself. Throwing a fit about something. He's probably mad I'm not answering fast enough. You know how he gets."

My lips press together. I *do* know how he gets.

She waves a hand, brushing it off. "It's fine. He'll get over it. And I refuse to let him ruin this trip."

Her tone is casual, but the tension in her jaw gives her away. I take a slow sip of tea, considering my next words. I don't want to push if she's not ready to talk. But I also know her well enough to see the weight she's trying to hide.

I set my mug down, keeping my voice even. "You sure?"

Rachel meets my gaze, her mask slipping for just a second. There's a flicker of uncertainty in her eyes, and then it's gone. She forces a grin. "Yep! Now eat your damn toast. We have witchy business to attend to."

I snort, but the tension lingers in the air between us.

The next few days pass in a blur of research, frustration, and dead ends.

Rinse and repeat.

Rachel and I spend *hours* digging through books, online archives, and any scrap of information remotely connected to folklore, witchcraft, and my family's history. We keep slamming into the same wall of nothing.

The book I grabbed from the bookstore has been somewhat useful. We've learned a lot about crystals. Their meanings, their abilities. *Specifically,* the two I have and the one embedded in my dagger's hilt. But the biggest mystery is the stone in my necklace. We still can't find anything on that.

There were stories on fairies stealing babies, *Good fairies, bad fairies, but still nothing about witches.*

There was a decent section on wolves that I found. Something about how they're powerful symbols of sorts. There were only a few things on ancient rituals and how they're performed during the full moon. I did learn that the veil between worlds was at its thinnest during that time. And that certain blood rituals performed under the full moon could unlock hidden powers or connect one with the spirit world. And that wolves were often seen as protectors during those rituals.

But even with all this searching, we still don't have a single concrete answer. It's all stories and whispers of old magic. Some eerily close to what I've experienced, but nothing that *proves* what's happening.

And what's worse is, we can't find any records of my family.

Anywhere.

No trace of my grandparents. No lineage. No history in the usual places. It's like they never *existed*. The deeper we dig, the more frustrating it becomes.

Kane texted me once, asking how I was doing. I didn't reply.

I've just been too busy trying to figure this shit out. Too busy obsessing over answers I can't seem to find. And honestly, I don't really feel like talking to him right now.

But at least one thing is going my way.

My arm is healing fast. Faster than it should be, unless it truly wasn't as bad as I thought that first night. The bandage can probably come off soon, which is good news. My ribs are still pretty sore, but nowhere near as bad as they should be. I should be stiff, bruised, still wincing every time I breathe too deep. Instead, I feel... almost normal, and I have a pretty sick bruise. Thank God my nose wasn't actually broken, I wouldn't have been able to hide that under my clothes.

The last thing I need is Rachel asking questions that I don't have the answers to. By the time night rolls around, I'm too exhausted to overthink things. I pass out before my head even hits the pillow. No weird dreams. No creepy attacks. Just an *endless* loop of searching and finding nothing.

Until Rachel snaps.

"WHY IS THERE NOTHING?!"

The sound of a book slamming shut echoes through the room.

I glance up from my laptop to see Rachel pacing the living room, murder in her eyes. "It's like your family just *vanished* off the face of the earth. Like they don't want to be found."

I rub my temples. "I know." The words feel heavy. "It doesn't make any sense. There has to be something. A record. A name. *Anything.*"

Rachel abruptly stops. Her eyes go wide, practically buzzing with energy.

"Oh my God."

I sit up warily. "What?"

She turns to me, grinning like a lunatic. "If it's like they don't want to be found, then we need someone who's *really* good at finding things that don't want to be found."

I stare at her. "Let me guess... Kane?"

Her grin widens, all too pleased with herself. "Well, *yes*, Kane would be great, but I'm actually talking about *Cam.*" She wiggles her phone. "He's like Sherlock Holmes, but hotter. And *I have his number.* Convenient, right?"

I hesitate. The idea of involving either of them makes me uneasy. "I don't know, Rach." I shake my head. "This feels like something I should figure out on my own. Not... '*Hey Kane, remember that time you lied to me? Cool, now use those same sketchy skills to uncover my family secrets'.*"

Rachel's brows knit together as she watches me, her smirk fading slightly. "Okay, hold up, lied to you? What are you talking about? What did he lie about?"

Shit. I didn't mean to let that slip.

I shrug, trying for casual, but she isn't buying it. "It's nothing. Just..." I exhale, playing with my hair. "He didn't exactly tell me who he was at first."

Her eyes narrow. "What do you mean? Like... he has a wife and three kids? Or—"

"God, no." I groan, cutting her off. "It's not that. It's just—" I hesitate, "He owns the castle the ball was at."

Rachel blinks. "*The* castle?"

I shake my head.

Her lips part, realization dawning. Then her jaw drops. "Kane fucking lied about owning a whole-ass castle? Are you kidding me?!"

"Technically, he just... *left that part out.*"

Rachel stares at me like I've grown another head. "He casually left out that he's a literal duke or something?" She throws her hands up. "And you're just telling me this now? Jesus, Raven."

"It's not that important, I'm not doing *men* remember. So who cares."

She laughs, grabbing her stomach. "Well for starters, clearly you. Girl, that's need-to-know information. No wonder you're acting weird about asking him for help."

I roll my eyes. "I'm not acting weird."

Rachel crosses her arms, clearly unconvinced. "Mhm. Sure." Then her expression softens. "Real talk here for a second. What are you going to do?"

I exhale, my shoulders fall slightly, "I don't know," I admit. "I was pissed at first. But after everything else that's happened, it feels... small in comparison." I rub at my temple, the weight of it all pressing in again.

She watches me for a second before shaking her head. "Okay, well, you're not dragging him into this. Cam, on the other hand? He's a different story." She wiggles her phone again.

"Besides, we're running out of time. We're supposed to be going home and we have nothing. No leads, no records, no family history. We can't keep hitting dead ends."

A knot tightens in my chest. The thought of leaving this unfinished and walking away from this, feels wrong.

I sigh, running a hand over my face. "Fine," I relent. "We can ask Cam. But if he starts acting all cocky about it, I'm blaming you."

She beams, practically vibrating with satisfaction. "Deal."

CHAPTER 34

Delicate

KANE

The days pass in a restless blur of work and sleepless nights. Not hearing from Raven has been driving me insane. I've told myself I'd give her space and let her come to me. But every instinct in me screams to pull her back in.

I've sent her a few texts, but the silence on her end has been deafening. And it shouldn't bother me as much as it does. She's on vacation, enjoying time with her friend. She owes me nothing.

Work has been the only thing keeping me from losing my mind. Even that hasn't been enough to stop my thoughts from drifting back to her. I know she's safe, my security team is supposed to let me know when she leaves and returns to her house. *When the fuck did I become that guy?*

The thought leaves a bitter taste in my mouth, but that doesn't mean I'll stop. It's not like I'm the one watching. I just get updated when something does happen.

Knowing she's okay is the only thing that keeps me sane.

I walk into the office, head down, jaw tight, trying to stay focused. Carrie's laugh cuts through the silence as I pass her desk, her amused smirk impossible to miss.

"I don't want to hear it, Carrie," I mutter, heading straight for my office and slamming the door shut behind me.

I barely have time to sit before my phone buzzes. A text from my head of security. My brows furrow as I read the message.

471

Tension coils in my chest. I set my phone down, pulling up the footage on my computer. The screen flickers to life. At first, nothing unusual happens. Guests mingling about, sipping their drinks, thinking they're unseen in the hedges.

My eyes narrow as a group of men drift toward the outskirts of the gardens, lingering too close to where the lantern light fades. I know what this looks like.

My jaw tightens.

There are always the idiots who think no one's watching.

I lean back, fingers hovering over my phone before I fire off a reply.

The footage continues rolling at double speed, a familiar monotony of half-drunken conversations and stolen moments. I'm about to close the file when I see *her*.

In that fucking dress.

My phone buzzes in my hand, but I ignore it. I slow the playback, my focus locking onto the screen as she moves through the gardens.

What I see makes my blood go cold.

My fingers tighten around the arm of my chair, my jaw locked so tight I wouldn't be surprised if I cracked a tooth. The frame-by-frame replay is damning.

A slow exhale leaves me, but my hands have already curled into fists. I watch as she stumbles, her expression flickering with shock, and pain.

She rights herself, but she doesn't run. The moment his smug smirk flashes, she moves. Quick and precise. Her elbow slams into his stomach. Then, before he can recover, her knee drives up and hits him in the balls.

A sharp exhale leaves me, and the longer I watch the more rage I feel. I throw my glass across the room when I see her take another hit.

One thing I know for sure, is that she's *trained*.

There's something in the way she moves. She's fluid and practiced. I've seen fighters like her before. The ones who don't panic when they take a hit. The ones who don't flinch, because they've learned the hard way that showing pain gives their opponent leverage.

My violent little princess knows how to defend herself. And now I really want to know *why* she knows how.

I'm also realizing with painful clarity that she lied to me. Said she tripped. Looked me in the eye and fucking *lied. But why?*

Pride? Maybe. But that doesn't explain enough to make sense. *Who the fuck is she protecting?*

My grip tightens around the edge of my desk, fury simmering beneath my skin like a barely restrained beast. This happened in *my* house. Under *my* watch.

I push back abruptly, the chair nearly falling over as I stand. There's a difference between anger and rage. One flares hot and dies quick, and the other burns steady.

And right now?

I'm fucking livid.

The sharp ping of my phone pulls me back, reminding me I have an unread message.

Ren: I didn't watch those two getting it on. Gross. Should have clarified. There's a dude assaulting some chick. Thought you'd want to see it.

Me: Find out who the fuck he is.

Ren: Already on it boss. I'll send everything as soon as I've got it.

Without wasting another second, I pull up Raven's number, my thumb hovering over the call button. Enough waiting. She's going to tell me why she lied.

The door swings open, and Cam strides in like he owns the place.

"You'll never guess who just called asking for a favor," he announces, heading straight for the bar and pouring himself a drink without so much as a glance in my direction.

I glance up, patience wearing thin. "Who?"

He takes his time, dropping into the chair across from me with an ease that grates on my nerves. He swirls his glass, his grin sharp. "Rachel."

I figured.

"She texted me and asked if I could help her dig up some info. Apparently, they've hit a dead end on something, and lucky me, I came to mind." He takes a slow sip, waiting.

I lean forward, my voice flat. "And?"

Cam shrugs, like this whole thing is amusing to him. "She wasn't specific. Just said they were trying to track something down." He tilts his head, studying me like he already knows where this is going. "By the way, why do you look like you are about to rip someone's head off with your bare hands? What happened?"

My jaw clenches. "Remember when I asked you what happened to Raven's face at the ball?"

His smirk slips a little. "Yeah."

"And you said she tripped?"

He sets his drink down, his posture shifting slightly. "That's what she told me."

"She lied." My voice is ice.

His expression sharpens. "What?"

"I just watched it."

I pull up the footage, turning the screen toward him and pressing play.

The air in the room thickens as the scene unfolds. Cam watches silently, and when the clip ends, he lets out a slow breath.

"Well," his tone edged with something unreadable. "That's definitely not what I expected. But then again, I'm not shocked. She's feisty."

"She shouldn't have had to be," I bite out.

Cam nods, eyes still on the screen. "And what do you plan to do about it?"

My voice is cold. "Once we know who he is, I've got a few questions for him." My fingers tap against the desk. "After that I'll make sure he regrets ever laying a hand on her."

He doesn't hesitate. His gaze meets mine, and the flicker of agreement in his eyes is unmistakable.

"Let me know what you need."

"I was about to call Raven when you walked in."

He smirks, completely unfazed. "Relax. I'll handle it." He pulls out his phone, scrolling as he leans back, casual as ever.

He puts the call on speaker, the ringing filling the room. My fingers drum against the desk, my patience thinning by the second.

"Hey what's up?" Rachel's voice comes through, light and casual.

"Oh, nothing much." Cam replies smoothly, stretching his legs out like this is some social call.

I shoot him a look.

"Figured I'd call instead of texting, it's faster." He cuts to the chase. "So, what are you two trying to dig up?"

There's a slight pause before Rachel answers, her tone a little too neutral. "Oh, just some stuff about Raven's background. Who her family is. The basics. Can you do it?"

Cam raises a brow at me, confirming what I already suspected. She's being evasive.

Interesting. I roll my eyes, arms crossing as I lean back.

"Well, that happens to be really easy." He says, lounging in his chair with that lazy confidence that drives people insane. "Want me to call you when I find it, or should we just go over to Kane's?"

For a second there's silence. Then, "No, don't tell Kane. Shit!"

Rachel groans like she's just realized she's fucked up.

"Sorry, I wasn't supposed to say that." There's a beat of silence, then I can hear them talking quietly. "Raven doesn't want Kane to know because she's not ready to talk to him yet... for no other reason than she wants to be pissed at something."

A muffled scuffle.

"*Ow.* Sorry. Forget you heard that. *Ow.* Anyway, can you help us? We can go there, or you can come here."

Cam's smirk widens as he throws me a look, eyes alight with mischief. He's enjoying this far too much.

"We'll come to you," he replies easily. "That is, if Kane's invited. Otherwise, I'll come solo. Then again, maybe we *shouldn't* invite him. It'll give me a head start. He always thinks he's better than me."

Rachel snorts. "Umm... am I sensing some tension there?"

In the background, Raven's voice cuts through, sharp and unmistakably annoyed.

"That's because he's a dick!"

Rachel bursts out laughing, and Cam joins in, their amusement filling the office. I roll my eyes, unaffected, but the corners of my mouth twitch despite myself.

She's pissed. Of course she is. Between searching for answers, dealing with that bastard at the ball, and whatever this is, she has plenty of ammo.

Cam, still grinning, presses the phone back to his ear. "I'll head over. Don't worry, I'll keep Kane out of the loop."

Rachel hums. "Thanks, Cam, you're the best." Then, with far too much amusement, she adds, "Oh, and Kane, you *can* come, but you have to wait in the car. Okay, byeee."

The call disconnects.

"Well, she's got balls."

I exhale slowly, leveling him with a look. "You're enjoying this too much."

"Obviously."

We're driving down the road when Cam suddenly shifts in his seat, his frown deepening as he looks closely at the leather, and then looks around the backseat.

"You should detail your car after a job." His tone is casual, but there's a thread of curiosity laced with something sharper.

"What the hell are you talking about?"

Cam drags his finger over the seat, studying whatever the fuck he just found.

"Might not be blood," he muses, raising a brow. "But I'm pretty damn sure it is."

My jaw tightens. I sit up straighter, looking around the backseat. A slow, cold wave of unease rolls through me.

"Ren," I say, trying to keep the bite out of my voice. "What happened?"

Ren meets my gaze in the rearview mirror, shifting slightly in his seat. "She got out of the car, insisting that she walk the rest of the way home. Said she needed fresh air." A pause, then a frown. "She left her phone, so I turned back to give it to her."

Beside me, Cam leans forward, All amusement gone. "Was she upset?"

Ren hesitates, like he's sifting through his memory, then exhales. "Now that you mention it... she was crying. Looked like she'd had a rough night, but she didn't say why. Just wanted out of the car."

My fingers curl into fists against my thigh.

"When I caught up to her, it was too dark, and she was soaked from the rain. But she insisted she was fine." He chuckles faintly, but there's an edge to it. "Told me if you got upset about it, I should tell you to shove it. She's feisty, that one."

Cam snorts, but I don't react.

Feisty is one thing.

Crying and having blood in my car? That's another.

"It was only a block or so from the house," Ren continues, oblivious to the shift in the air. "She was still walking when I pulled up, so I insisted she let me take her the rest of the way."

Cam stays quiet, but I can feel his stare. Like he's expecting me to snap.

I'm not going to. At least, not yet.

I exhale slowly, keeping my voice even. "Did she say why she was crying?"

Ren shakes his head, looking almost apologetic. "No, and I didn't want to pry." His hands tighten on the wheel. "It was right after she got in the car at the estate."

My jaw locks. *The estate.*

Of course it fucking was.

The memory of the ball slams back into me. I should've known.

But there's more to this story. I know there is. She's keeping secrets and I want every single one of them.

I force a smirk, masking the frustration clawing at my chest. "That laptop gonna be enough?"

Cam finally looks away from me, rolling his eyes as he taps at the keys. "Don't be offensive," he scoffs, a smirk tugging at his lips. "This baby's never let me down."

I let out a small chuckle, but it's hollow. My mind is still racing. The unanswered questions taunting me like shadows just out of reach.

Whatever Raven's hiding, whatever she thinks she can keep from me, she's wrong.

One way or another. I'm going to get to the bottom of this.

CHAPTER 35

Don't Blame Me!

RAVEN

"I cannot believe you said that." I shake my head, laughing. "I hope he comes, and I hope he does wait in the car."

Rachel grins, unbothered. "It's no less than he deserves."

The mental image alone of Kane sitting in his car, stewing, while Cam smugly delivers updates, brightens my mood. Probably more than it should. He doesn't wait for anything, let alone sit on the sidelines while someone else does his work.

Which is why I know he won't stay in the car.

The thought alone makes my stomach twist in ways I don't want to analyze.

Rachel prattles on about how Cam is going to work his magic, but my mind drifts elsewhere. Her comment about going home has been gnawing at me ever since she said it.

Home.

The word feels... wrong.

Like a place I don't belong anymore.

Rachel has a life waiting for her back in the States. Messy and chaotic, but *hers*. I don't know what I have. Or where I'm supposed to be. The closer we get to answers, the more it feels like I'm standing at the edge of something impossible, something I'm not ready to name.

My ribs ache a little less today. My arm's actually healing nicely. I'm hoping in another few days, I'll be good as new. No one found out, no one asked questions, which is its own blessing.

A low rumble of thunder rolls in the distance, rattling the windows. *Fitting.*

As freaky as everything's been, I'm starting to expect it. The unease is still there, but beneath it, a sense of calm is there. Like my body knows something my mind hasn't caught up to yet. That alone should freak me out more than it does.

The doorbell rings, jolting me out of my thoughts.

Cam doesn't wait to be let in. I hear his voice carry down the hall, as I make my way to the living room. I don't see Kane, and a laugh escapes me before I can stop it.

Cam smirks, like he already knows exactly what I'm thinking. "Aye, he's waiting in the car. Probably for the best if we give him a minute."

Oh, that's rich.

Rachel snickers. "Coward."

I roll my eyes, crossing my arms as I glance out the window. The storm outside is getting worse, rain lashing against the glass. *Good, let him stay out there.*

I turn back to Cam. "Aright, Sherlock. What's the plan?"

His smirk widens. "First? We find out what the hell is so impossible to track about your family. Second? We drink. Because we're gonna need it.

Rachel sighs. "Sounds about right."

Cam moves toward the table, already setting up his laptop, but my focus drifts back outside.

I know Kane's not sitting in that car. He's too arrogant and far too stubborn. And the fact that he hasn't come in yet? That's because it's a game to him.

And I'm not playing.

After about thirty minutes, I push off the couch, ignoring Rachel's questioning look as I stride to the front door. When I swing it open, rain pelts down in sheets, soaking the stone path and the man leaning against the hood of his car.

Kane doesn't move.

He's standing there like the storm doesn't touch him. His arms are crossed, his expression unreadable, but there's something coiled beneath the surface. Something dangerous. For a split second, I *almost* shut the door and go back inside.

"You just gonna brood out here all night in the rain?"

He doesn't move, doesn't even look at me. He lets the silence stretch long enough to make me shift on my feet, his unreadable gaze locking onto mine like he's waiting for something.

His eyes slowly sweep over me, the kind of look that makes heat crawl up my neck despite the cold. "Wasn't sure I was invited," he finally says, but there's an edge to it.

I cross my arms, weight shifting to one hip. "You weren't."

That earns me a glare. "And yet, here you are."

My fingers curl against my arms, jaw clenching. Arrogant ass. I'm sure he loves that I came out here. That I opened the door at all.

I refuse to give him the satisfaction.

"Don't flatter yourself," I scoff. "Rachel said you could come in, and it's her house. *I* just figured I'd spare you the embarrassment of sulking in the rain like a kicked puppy."

I turn to go back inside, but his words cut through the rain like a blade. "You think I'd sit out here all night waiting on you, Princess?"

The way he says it, the way his voice dips, sends a thrill racing through me. Which is so stupid. I don't care what he does.

I arch a brow. "Well, you're the one standing in the rain, so you tell me."

Kane steps forward, just enough to make me notice. Just enough to make my pulse betray me. "Why are you out here, *Raven?*"

I roll my eyes, ignoring the way his voice wraps around my name. "Because some of us have the basic human decency not to leave guests standing in the rain."

"Decency," he repeats, like he's testing me. His eyes flick down my body. "That's what this is?"

I exhale sharply, the storm soaking through my hoodie, my patience thinning. "God, you're insufferable."

"And yet," he murmurs, stepping past me, his voice brushing against my skin like silk and steel, "here you are."

Before I can fire back, he moves. Like he owns the ground he walks on. His jacket brushes against my arm as he steps inside, dragging the scent of rain and something darker with him. He doesn't look at me as he passes.

But I can just feel his arrogant smirk.

And it infuriates me.

Rachel and I are devouring our food like we haven't eaten in days, while Kane and Cam's plates sit mostly untouched. Cam's laser-focused on his laptop, fingers flying over the keys, splitting his attention between the screen and the conversation.

Kane, on the other hand, looks like the poster child for brooding intensity, his gaze fixed on some invisible point just beyond the table. The moody, dark thing he's got going on is almost palpable, and despite everything, I find it a little funny in that *probably-losing-my-mind* kind of way. He hasn't said a word to anyone but little bits here and there to Cam.

Maybe it's the whole situation getting to me. Or maybe autopilot has kicked in again, leaving my reactions muted and detached. Either way, I'm starting to wonder if this is what a midlife crisis feels like. Except I'm not even thirty yet, so that's fantastic.

"All right, here's the deal," I say, breaking the silence and forcing a casual tone, even though the tension in the room feels like it could crush bone.

"I'm just trying to figure out who my family is. Without diving into the full sob story, my grandparents are gone, and no, I don't have anyone else. At least, not that I know of. My grandfather left me some things before he passed, and now I'm trying to find out what they mean, who they belonged to, and all that usual soul-searching crap people do after a loss."

I try to keep my tone light, but the room falls into an awkward silence. *Crickets.*

"Okay, tough crowd. I get it. But I'm fine," I force a smile that doesn't quite reach my eyes. I glance around the table, trying to gauge their reactions.

Kane's face is a *fortress* of unreadable intensity, his jaw tight and his gaze fixed like he's trying to not fly off the handle.

Cam, meanwhile, looks like he's only half-listening, his focus bouncing between me and whatever he's digging up on his laptop. He looks up, a small grin tugging at the corner of his mouth. "Never trust a fine."

I roll my eyes but can't stop the small smile that sneaks through. Rachel notices, and I catch her smirking behind her coffee.

"Seriously, though," I say, straightening in my seat, trying to shake off the tension. "I just want to figure this out, and I don't need everyone looking at me like I'm about to shatter into a million pieces. I'm not some fragile flower, okay?"

Cam chuckles, leaning back in his chair with that insufferable, easy confidence of his. "Fair enough," he says, his grin softening just enough to be disarming. "But don't expect us to just sit back and watch you stumble through this."

Before I can say anything, Kane speaks up, finally. "If you want us to help, we need the truth. *All of it.* No more *I'm fine* when you're clearly not."

The sharpness in his tone makes my spine lock up, irritation curling hot in my chest.

I exhale slowly, trying to ignore the way his tone makes me want to scream. The near-constant chaos, the bruises, and the things I haven't told anyone. I glance at Rachel, but even she doesn't know everything. No one does. And right now, the last person I want prying is Kane.

"All right," my voice is clipped. "I'll tell you what I can."

Kane doesn't react, but his gaze stays locked on me. He's reading me, dissecting my words before I've even said them and it pisses me off.

"When my grandfather passed, he left me a box of things he wanted me to have. Things I think he wanted me to figure out." I swallow, pushing through the sudden knot in my throat. "That's why I came here. I need answers about my family, and my past. Who my parents really were."

I hesitate, forcing my voice to stay even, while I take my damp hoodie off, and get comfy on the couch. "We were supposed to come here together, but he passed before we could."

The words sit heavy in the air. I don't look at Kane. I don't need to. His stare is a weight all on its own. But I can feel the moment his expression shifts, the subtle change in the air around him.

"This trip isn't just a vacation," I continue, my tone turning dry. "Though I'm sure that's what your research told you."

Kane doesn't flinch at the dig, but his gaze sharpens. Good. Let him stew in it.

I push forward before he can interject. "I've just been trying to piece everything together, but the more I dig, the more questions I uncover. And honestly at this point it's just getting annoying as hell."

A muscle in Kane's jaw ticks, but he stays silent.

Cam props his feet up on the coffee table, entirely too at ease. "Why do I feel like there's more?"

I roll my eyes but push on. "I did run into someone," I admit, choosing my words carefully. "They seemed to know more about me than I knew about him." My voice tightens, a thread of unease creeping in. "Only, nothing he said made any sense."

I brush my arm absently, fingers grazing over the spot where the knife cut me.

The memory is too vivid, like it's still imprinted under my skin. "As for what I'm looking for..." my words falter. "Just answers."

I meet their eyes briefly, then glance away, uneasy under their collective attention. Kane's gaze is unreadable, but it lingers too long, and I hate that it makes my skin prickle.

Cam, for once, looks like he's actually paying attention, his usual laid-back energy replaced with something razor-sharp. "Can we maybe start with what this *someone* told you?"

I shake my head, frustration bubbling to the surface. "It was just *odd*. He just said I was exactly who he was looking for. Honestly, he was probably having a little too much fun at the dance." I wave a hand dismissively.

I had something weird happen at both the dance and walking home, so it's not technically a lie. And yes, I'm going to justify that.

Rachel watches me closely. "You okay?"

I nod. Cam cracks his knuckles, leaning forward. "We need to figure out who this guy is. If he knows something about you that you don't? That's a problem. If he's willing to hurt you over it, that's an even bigger problem."

I shift uncomfortably, but Cam isn't finished. His usual humor is nowhere to be found as he locks eyes with me, his tone softening. "Let's start with the basics. What do you know about yourself?"

I clear my throat, suddenly feeling like I'm under a damn microscope. "Okay, well," I start, forcing a small smile. "My name is Raven Taylor. I'm twenty-five. My birthday is December thirty-first. My grandparents were

Anthony and Marjorie Taylor." I shrug, keeping my tone casual, even though the weight of it all is pressing in. "I was born in Utah, and I still live there."

"Good start," He nods, his fingers hovering over the keyboard. "Parents?"

I hesitate. "Not much to say. They died when I was young. My grandparents didn't like talking about them. I know they were from Scotland. I know their names. There's some photos of them back at my house, but..." I shrug like it's not a big deal, even though the ache I suddenly feel in my chest tells a different story. "They died in an accident. Some trip they were coming back from. That's all I've ever really known."

The silence stretches long.

Cam types something, his expression unreadable. Kane still hasn't said a damn word. The weight of the moment is making my skin itch. I push off the couch abruptly, needing to move, an escape from the awkward tension.

"Hold that thought," I mutter, already walking toward my room. "I need a new hoodie before I get hypothermia."

No one stops me.

I go into my room and grab a dry hoodie and take a moment to breathe. I'm on my way out of my room, but I don't make it very far because Kane's standing right there, blocking the hallway.

I scoff, shaking my head, crossing my arms. "Did you come to interrogate me?" I mimic his voice, dripping with sarcasm.

Kane's lips twitch, but his eyes darken, a slow smirk curving his mouth. "Trust me, *Princess*," he murmurs. "You wouldn't like my version of an interrogation."

Heat blooms, and my pussy starts throbbing. *Of course he'd turn this into something dirty.* I just wish my body would remember we're pissed.

I roll my eyes. "Oh, I'm sure I'd be fine. But hey, you seem to have a knack for keeping secrets. So, you could probably teach me a thing or two." My tone is all sugar and venom, daring him to take the bait.

His smirk doesn't falter, but something shifts beneath it. He leans forward slightly, hand resting on the wall above my head. His gaze locked with mine in a way that makes my pulse stutter. "That's rich, coming from someone who's been keeping secrets pretty damn well all night."

My jaw clenches. "Excuse me?"

He doesn't answer. Just watches, waiting for me to squirm.

Cam's voice cuts through the thick air from the other room. "Alright, we'll get this handled."

I take the distraction and slip out from under Kane's stare, moving toward the kitchen.

"It's getting late," Cam continues, tucking his phone into his pocket like this isn't a complete *shit show*. "You two should get some rest. Let the professionals take it from here."

I roll my eyes at his dramatics, but I can't help the faint smirk tugging at my lips. But it's Kane who pulls my focus. That usual brooding exterior softens just enough to make something catch in my chest.

"Raven," he says, looking at me. Which only annoys me more. "I've got something for you out in the car. Come with me?"

"Can't wait." I tease, trying to ignore the flutter that stirs in my chest. But I school my expression. "You're not luring me outside just to try and talk your way out of lying to me are you?"

His lips twitch, "Wouldn't dream of it."

I don't believe him. Not for a second.

I'm aware of everyone watching me. Kane's already moving toward the door, his stride effortless. I look over and Rachel's grin stretches wide as she whistles, followed by a giggle.

I shoot her a warning look.

Her smile only deepens. "Behave," I mutter under my breath, knowing damn well she won't.

The air outside is damp, thick with the scent of rain. At least it's only sprinkling now. Mist curls along the ground, swirling under the porch light, but my attention zeroes in on Kane.

He makes it impossible to look at anything else. The way he walks, tells me he's not in a rush. He wants me to have to wait on him, to feel every charged second of silence.

I cross my arms. "So, what is it? Some elaborate excuse to get me alone?"

Kane huffs a quiet laugh, shaking his head as he opens the passenger door, leaning in briefly. "You give me too much credit."

488

My pulse kicks up, heat prickling under my skin. Not from the cold, or the rain. But from *him*. When he straightens, turning back to face me, our eyes lock.

The storm rolls low overhead, and my mind flashes to the way his hands gripped my thighs. The way his breath teased against my lips before I stopped him.

Heat pools low and my breath catches as he steps closer. Close enough that I can feel the warmth of his body, the steady rise and fall of his breath.

I don't move.

Neither does he.

His gaze flicks to my lips, just for a second. Just long enough to make my heart slam against my ribs. I swear I see the moment he decides to close the gap. His hand brushes my hip, *testing me.*

I don't pull away.

The distance disappears, the tension stretches so tight I can barely breathe. And the sharp creak of the front door shatters the moment like glass.

Cam strolls outside, oblivious as ever. Kane's hand doesn't leave my hip. His other, I now notice, holds an envelope with my name scrawled across the front. The one from his office.

I blink, frustration slamming into me as I step away from him.

Kane extends it toward me. "Figured you'd want this."

The way he says it, makes something inside me twist. I snatch it from his grasp, forcing my voice to stay steady. "Thanks," I meet his gaze briefly before turning to Cam. "And thank *you*, Cam."

I know Kane's still watching me, but I ignore him, stepping toward Cam and pulling him into a quick hug.

He leans in, his voice low enough for only me to hear. "Remember what I said would happen if I found out you were lying?"

He knows.

I force myself to pull back, my expression neutral, but my heart is hammering against my ribs. I turn toward Kane, who's watching us closely, his brows faintly furrowed, catching everything.

Nope. Not doing this.

I step away waving awkwardly, "Talk to you guys soon. Thanks again." And then I turn and flee.

Rachel's curled up on the couch when I step inside, wrapped in a blanket like its armor against the growing tension. She pats the space beside her, and I drop down heavily.

"That wasn't so bad, was it?" she asks, adjusting her blanket. Her voice is light, but there's an edge to it. "If anyone can dig something up from the bits you gave them, it's those two."

Her smile is encouraging, but it doesn't reach her eyes.

I manage a small one in return, but my chest is still tight, my mind circling back to Cam's warning. *Does he really know? Does Kane?*

The idea makes my stomach twist uncomfortably. But before I can spiral too far, Rachel's voice pulls me back. "Rave," she says softly. "There's something I need to talk to you about."

The nervous edge in her voice is all the warning I need. Whatever she's about to say, I already know I'm not going to like it. My stomach drops as I brace myself.

"I need to go home."

The words hit harder than I expect, and I blink, caught off guard despite knowing, deep down, that this was coming.

"Are you sure you can't stay longer?" My voice is tighter than I'd like, betraying the ache already settling in my ribs.

She takes a deep breath, threading her fingers through mine. Her grip is warm, but it doesn't stop the tears that threaten to spill. "There's a few things I need to take care of," she sniffles. "Nothing crazy, but it has to be in person. But... I don't think you should come with me."

The words sink in, dragging my stomach down with them.

"I know you're not ready to move here yet, and you still need time to think about that. But you need to stay."

A lump forms in my throat. The tears come slowly at first, slipping down my cheeks in quiet betrayal. I knew this was coming. But hearing it out loud still sucks.

"You know I'm right." She squeezes my hand. "You keep looking, let them handle the hard stuff while you take care of yourself. Maybe even get a little dick on the side." She winks.

I huff a watery laugh, throwing her hand off me with half-hearted annoyance. "You're impossible."

"Besides," she adds, her voice softening again, "I can go to your grandparents' house and search through their things. I'll send you anything useful or mail over whatever you think you might need." Her smile is small, but sincere. "I'll be back in a few weeks. I promise."

Relief washes over me, but it's tangled with sadness, leaving a bittersweet ache lodged in my chest. I sniff, swiping my face. "I hate you."

Rachel pulls me into a hug, squeezing me tight. "Bitch, why are you crying? I'm coming back. You're a big girl, and you've got a really big, *hot* dude who's totally going to wine and dine you as soon as I'm out of the way."

I groan against her shoulder. "You're ridiculous."

She pulls back just enough to look me in the eyes, her expression is firm. "No matter what happens, just know, you can do this. You don't *need* anyone."

I swallow hard. She's wrong. I need her.

But I don't say it. Instead, I nod, dragging in a shaky breath as we both swipe at our tear-streaked faces.

Then she leans over, her sly smile creeping back in. "Alright, enough with the waterworks. Let's open that envelope and see what kind of mystery Kane dropped on your doorstep."

A nervous flutter replaces the ache in my chest. I pick up the envelope, my hands trembling slightly as I slide out the papers. My eyes skim the contents, my pulse quickening with every line. Then, I freeze, my chest tightens with every word I read.

"What?" I whisper, my voice barely audible over the pounding in my ears. My fingers tighten around the papers.

Rachel leans in, scanning over my shoulder. Her expression twists in confusion. "That doesn't make any sense."

My mouth goes dry. "I—I don't know..." My pulse is a hammer on my ribcage. "I've *seen* my birth certificate before. It had their names. I know it did." My voice rises slightly. "This... *this* can't be right. And why does this say I was born in *Scotland*?"

The confusion rises, fast and overwhelming. My hands start to tingle, I can feel the static creeping under my skin as my chest tightens further, making it hard to breathe. I grip the papers tighter, my voice barely above a whisper.

"Why don't I have parents?"

Rachel's hand brushes mine, "Rave... there's got to be more to it," she says gently, trying to anchor me before I completely spiral. "Remember, this was before the guys had the information you just gave them. Once they add the new details, I'm sure more will come to light."

Her voice is steady, but it doesn't stop my stomach from twisting.

Why wouldn't my grandparents have told me this? Why are there no answers? Just more fucking questions?

"Honestly, I'm not worried," I lie. "Like you said, if anyone can dig up more information, it's them."

I stretch, forcing a yawn past my lips, but exhaustion barely makes a dent in the chaos rattling inside my head. "But for now, I'm calling it a night. Let's focus on having some fun while you're still here, yeah? They can figure out the rest." I tack on a smile, hoping it masks everything I don't want her to see.

Rachel throws her arms around me, squeezing tight. "YES!" She all but yells, with an energy I wish I could match.

She pulls back slightly, her voice dipping softer. "Do you want company?"

I shake my head, managing another small smile. "Nah, I'm just gonna crash."

She nods, satisfied. "Okay, night. You know where to find me."

I wait until her door clicks shut before exhaling, shutting my own door behind me. The second I do, I collapse onto the bed, still clutching the envelope and all its damning contents.

I finally let myself feel it. The frustration, the confusion, the gnawing unease that hasn't left me since the second I opened that fucking envelope.

My gaze drops to the Scotland birth certificate. My name is on it, but below it, where parents should be, is a blank space.

I flip to the next document. My U.S. birth certificate. Same name. Same missing parents.

Frustration knots in my stomach, I'm about to toss it aside when my fingers catch on something stuck to the back of the U.S. copy.

Another birth certificate.

This one lists the same details, but with the names of the people I've always known as my parents. Relief washes through me for half a second before suspicion kicks in.

What in the actual fuck is going on?

My hands heat as I stare at the papers, my thoughts spinning too fast to keep up. The edges of my vision blur slightly, the room tilts in a way that makes my stomach hurt.

Then I hear a whisper. Soft, barely there, like a breeze curling against the edges of my mind. I jerk my head up, but shocker, it's empty. But the chill crawling up my spine says otherwise.

My eyes drift back to the Scotland certificate, and that's when I see my birthday.

6/31.

I blink, staring at the date like it's going to rearrange itself into something logical. Something *real*. But it doesn't. There's no such thing as June 31st.

My chest tightens, as I shuffle through the rest of the papers, each one sparking a different memory, a different surge of emotions.

My fingers flip through the pages and I skim over something else. A copy of my recent *run-in* with the law. My restraining order, and my protective order.

Heat rushes to my cheeks as I think about Kane or even Cam coming across these. *Wish I could've been a fly on that wall.*

When my eyes land on the papers about Mike, my curiosity gets the better of me.

I never would've guessed some of this about him. He's come a long way, turning his life around, building something for himself. I didn't expect to feel respect for him. *And yet.*

I set the papers aside, standing to turn off the lights. Crawling back into bed, I stare out the window, thoughts spiraling as I try to make sense of everything that I've just read.

This is getting out of hand.

The knot in my chest tightens, breath coming faster than I'd like. And here it comes again. A sharp, tingling sensation, spreading through my fingers, winding up my arms like a fuse lit too close to the bomb.

This has to be a sign of too much stress. Too much shit piling on at once, and too little sleep.

I don't even notice when the tears start, I squeeze my eyes shut, trying to breathe through it, but they just keep coming. I haven't cried this much in my entire life. *And yet here I am, unraveling at every turn.*

Everything I thought I knew, everything I believed about myself, feels like it's been built on half-truths and carefully constructed lies, and now that I've started pulling at the edges, the whole damn thing is unraveling faster than I can keep up.

I don't even know what to believe anymore.

The more I try to piece it together, the more untethered I feel, like I'm floating in the middle of a storm with nothing to hold onto. It's disorienting and no matter how much I tell myself to stop, it doesn't change anything.

Hopefully, Cam finds something because if he doesn't I don't know what the hell I'm supposed to do next.

For half a second, I wonder why I'm even doing this. Why I keep yanking threads when I could have just left them alone, let them sit here, neat and undisturbed, never questioning the life I already had.

I could just go home and pretend none of this ever happened.

It's not like my life was bad before this. It was *fine.*

I was happy... wasn't I?

I've spent my entire life not knowing who my parents were, and it never mattered before, so why should it now?

Except that's a lie, too. Because even as I try to convince myself that none of this should matter, that knowing or not knowing shouldn't change anything, I feel how wrong that is.

There's something here. Something telling me that if I leave now, if I walk away from this without seeing it through, I'll regret it for the rest of my life.

I can't leave.

I close my eyes, exhaustion pressing against my bones, my body sinking deeper into the mattress as silent tears slip down my cheeks. I don't bother wiping them away.

They don't change anything.

And just as sleep finally starts taking me under, a low bark echoes in the distance, followed by a long, slow howl.

CHAPTER 36

Change

KANE

S he drives me insane, and I'm not even sure she knows it. She's under my skin, and every second I'm near her, the urge to close the distance gets harder to resist.

Watching those tapes only drove it home.

Sleep feels like an impossible luxury, but I force myself to give in, knowing I need it if I'm going to make sense of this tangled mess. Or maybe I'll just find myself even deeper in it.

I'm in the forest. The air is thick with the scent of pine and damp earth, the kind of scent that clings to your skin. The sky above is endless and black, streaked with swirling blues that pulse in rhythm with my heartbeat.

Something's wrong. Everything feels off. The stillness isn't peaceful, it's suffocating. My instincts are on edge, and every step I take feels heavier than the last.

I know this place. Or at least, I thought I did. But tonight, it's different, drawing me deeper into the darkness.

A rustling sound shatters the silence, and I pivot, eyes narrowing as I track the movement flickering between the trees.

A massive wolf steps into the clearing, its fur is dark as midnight, its eyes steel-gray and glowing as they lock onto mine.

"I should've known it was you." My voice cuts through the stillness. The wolf lifts its head, sniffing the air like its searching for something then its eyes snap back to mine.

"Yeah, I smell it too," I mutter, keeping my voice low. The wolf's gaze sharpens, an unsettling intensity burning behind those steel eyes.

The air around me stirs, a breeze twisting through the trees, carrying whispers that brush against my skin like cold, invisible fingers. At first, they're faint, blending with the rustling leaves, but they grow louder, curling around me like a noose. "It's time," they whisper, their voices cold as ice.

"How is this possible?" I narrow my eyes at the wolf. "Go. Be careful," I command, my tone hard enough to cut through the rising whispers. The wolf dips its head in acknowledgment before melting into the shadows.

I exhale slowly, tension coiling in my chest as I look up. The swirling blues of the sky are streaked with a lavender haze that pulses with strange energy. It should be beautiful, calming even, but instead, it fills me with unease.

A scream slices through the air. My heart slams against my ribcage, and I move instinctively toward the sound. But before I get far, the scream cuts off, leaving only a suffocating silence in its wake.

"Raven?" Her name is a growl on my lips. She's on the ground, her face twisted in pain, and everything about this feels wrong. I move toward her, urgency spreading through me like wildfire.

But just as I reach out, her eyes meet mine, and she vanishes.

"Princess!" I shout, the word echoing into the emptiness as I spin around, searching the darkness. But she's nowhere. Gone.

I spin around again, and I'm in my office. Or at least, a version of it. The walls feel taller, and the energy in the room hums with something dark.

Cam's seated at the desk with a drink in hand, his expression infuriatingly calm.

"She was there," I snap, my voice a dangerous edge. "And then she was gone."

Cam's gaze lifts to mine, his face unreadable. "I know." He sets the glass down, the sound loud in the suffocating silence. "It's time. And I really hope everything's ready."

His words are meant to reassure, but they do the opposite. The detached calm in his voice only fuels the fire simmering in my veins, like a storm threatening to break.

A low growl rumbles in my chest, carrying the weight of everything spiraling out of my control. The windows rattle in their frames, the vibration echoing through the room like a warning. The sharp sound of shattering glass slices through the tension, and one of the panes fractures, shards scattering to the floor.

Cam doesn't even flinch. He leans back in his chair, rolling his eyes like this is an everyday occurrence. "You done?" he asks dryly, though there's a flicker of amusement in his eyes.

I wave a dismissive hand, jaw tightening. "Forget it." I don't have time for his sarcasm, and I sure as hell don't have time to figure out what the hell is happening in this nightmare.

I grab a drink from the desk, the glass cool against my palm, and drop into the chair across from him. My gaze falls on an open leather book in front of me. The pages are worn and yellowed, the ink is faded but legible. The handwriting is familiar, but I can't explain why.

My eyes shift to the shattered window behind him, except it's not shattered anymore. The glass is whole, not a single crack or shard out of place.

The hair on the back of my neck stands on end.

Suddenly I'm sitting upright in bed. Shadows stretch across the walls, the storm outside clawing at the windows, and the wind howls a haunting rhythm into the room. My hands tingle as a strange heat lingers in my fingertips, refusing to fade.

I drop back against the bed, eyes fixed on the ceiling, but sleep doesn't come.

Reaching for my phone, I tap the screen, the dim light casting a soft glow in the darkness. My eyes catch a message from Raven, and my pulse spikes.

> Your Royal Highness: If I can help, let me know.

> And please let me know what I owe you.

> I won't let you help if you don't at least let me pay for it.

I stare at the screen, rereading her words, my jaw tightening. *Stubborn little shit. What she owes me?* I should wait until morning to respond, but I'm annoyed enough to reply.

> Me: This stuff is basically a game. And you're not paying for anything. Ever. End of story. Also, you're not helping either. But if you need to talk, I'm here.

I hit send and toss my phone onto the nightstand, leaning back against the pillows. A ping that follows is immediate, pulling my attention right back to my phone.

> Your Royal Highness: You know, you're sweet when you aren't glaring at everyone.

> Why are you even awake right now?

> It's 3 in the morning.

I laugh at all her messages, shaking my head.

> Me: Sweet? Careful, Princess. You're going to ruin my reputation.

> Me: Why are you awake?

I hit send, as I settle back into the pillows, more alert than I've been all night, waiting for her reply. Another ping.

> Your Royal Highness: Couldn't sleep, so I finally gave up.

> I was about to head outside. I just have a lot on my mind.

The smirk fades from my lips, replaced by a frown.

> Me: Raven, if you need air, crack a window. Don't go wandering around outside in the middle of the night.

The silence stretches, and I can almost picture her sitting there, debating what to say. My phone vibrates again, her name lighting up the screen.

> Your Royal Highness: You're such a control freak.

> Do you ever sleep?

> Me: I sleep like a baby. You, on the other hand, clearly need more practice. Get some rest, Princess. If I hear about you going outside, I'll personally come over and lock you in.

> Your Royal Highness: You wouldn't dare.

> Me: Try me.

There's a pause, and I swear I can feel the shift in her mood before her next message comes through.

> Your Royal Highness: Want to know something funny?

> Turns out I wasn't even born where I thought I was.

> Not even sure my parents' names are real.

> *These birth certificates? Completely useless.*

> *One of them says my birthday is on a date that doesn't even exist.*

> *So yeah, might as well be searching for a needle in a haystack.*

> *Cheers to that, right?*

Fuck.

I stare at her message, the weight of her words hit me harder than I expected. She didn't know. I never even considered that to be a possibility. My grip on the phone tightens.

> *Me: Shit, Raven. I'm sorry.*

> *And hey, I know it feels impossible, but if anyone can figure this out, it's Cam. He's the best at this kind of thing...*

> *And if you tell him I said that, I'll deny it with my dying breath.*

I hit send, my jaw tightening as the thought of pulling her deeper into my world makes my chest ache. She doesn't belong in this chaos, but if it gets her the answers she needs, I'll make it happen. Hell, I'd burn down the whole damn haystack if it meant finding her needle.

And then there's this other part of me, the one that wants to do more than just protect her. This need to comfort her is almost maddening. I've never felt this before over someone I've barely known. It's unsettling as hell, and yet... I can't shake it.

> *Your Royal Highness: I'm absolutely telling Cam you said that. And you better believe I'm holding you to it.*

> *I thought you were in security?*

> *Me: I told you I don't make promises I don't keep. You might be stubborn as hell, but lucky for you, I'm worse. Try to relax for once.*

An hour later, after tossing and turning, I give up. Laying here is pointless when my mind is a shit storm I can't control. I throw on a shirt, heading downstairs with only one goal in mind, to burn off this energy before it turns into something reckless.

I find Cam already in the gym, leaning against the counter with a glass of water in his hand. He looks up, one brow lifting.

"You're awake," I state, my tone more bite than question.

"Couldn't sleep." His answer is casual, but the tension in his posture says otherwise. "I'll go a few rounds if you want, but after yesterday, I'm not really in the mood to coddle you."

I let out a low, humorless chuckle, cracking my neck. "Fair enough. I'm not feeling particularly restrained, so if you're worried about that pretty face of yours, I'll stick to a solo workout."

Cam's lips curl into a grin. "Nah, let's do this. Just don't cry when I make you eat the mat."

I smirk, rolling my shoulders. "No promises."

We face off on the mats, and the second I move, I know something's off. His form is solid, but there's a weight behind his punches that has nothing to do with physical exhaustion. He's holding back. And that pisses me off.

"Thought you weren't in the mood for gentle?" I taunt, as I dodge his next swing and land a sharp jab to his ribs.

He grunts, shaking his head. "You're not as good when you're cocky." He follows up with a right hook that snaps my head to the side, hard.

"Found something," he bites out, his tone cutting through the room like a blade.

I roll my jaw, tasting the sharp tang of blood. "You throw that punch like you're trying to prove a point," My tone is ice-cold, as I circle him. "Wanna tell me what it is?"

Cam's smirk is sharper than glass. "Even half-asleep, I can still kick your ass."

My eyes narrow, "You talk too much."

I move fast, and my next shot lands clean on his jaw. His head snaps to the side, and a low, satisfied rumble escapes me. *Payback.*

He rubs his jaw, laughing through the sting, his eyes cold with amusement. "Alright," He circles me, eyes locked on mine like he's got more to say. "Humor me for a second. I've got a question."

I stalk closer, keeping my stance loose, "A question? This should be good."

"Easy, Hulk," His grin sharpens as he sidesteps. "Think of it as bonding." He shifts his weight, eyes flicking over me with something calculating. "You notice anything... off lately?"

A low growl rises in my chest, and I force it down, keeping my tone even. "Define *off.*"

Cam shifts his weight, his movements controlled. "I don't know, anything weird? Out of place? You've been wound tighter than usual."

My fists tighten instinctively. "You know what would be more fun? Kicking your ass," I dodge his next swing and step in with a counter. "So either spill it, or stop wasting my time."

Cam laughs, dodging easily, his grin infuriating. "Patience is a virtue, man. Suspense is part of the game."

I roll my shoulders, stepping in closer, my tone a low, lethal growl. "You're not as funny as you think you are."

He sidesteps again, still grinning, but there's a sharpness behind his eyes. "I'm just saying, you've been... distracted. You want to tell me who's crawling under your skin?"

For a fraction of a second, I freeze, his words cutting closer than I'd like. "What is this? A therapy session?" I throw a jab that lands hard, forcing him back. "You want me to move to the couch, or are you finally going to hit me?"

He shakes it off, laughing. "Alright, alright," he says, raising his hands in surrender. "Just trying to keep it interesting. But if you'd rather get your ass beat—"

I don't let him finish. I step in, my next swing narrowly missing as he ducks under it. He retaliates with a hit that lands square on my ribs, sharp enough to sting.

"On a lighter note," he smirks, stepping back, "we found all the footage of our guy from the party."

My movements still, as I circle him. "And?"

"He was always near Raven, never too close, but never too far either." His tone is cold. "He was clearly watching her."

A muscle ticks in my jaw as I lunge forward, forcing him back with sheer presence alone. "Tell me you've got more than that."

He blocks my next punch, his grin sharp. "Relax. We've tracked him throughout the night. The bastard didn't make a move until the garden incident, but before that, he was always somewhere nearby. Staring. Whoever he is, he's not just some random asshole."

I exhale sharply, my fists lowering slightly. "Did you ID him?"

Cam's lip curls into something dark, sweat dripping down his brow. "Not yet. The footage isn't great, he knew what he was doing. No records, no identifiers, nothing." He ducks my next jab, his eyes flashing. "He went to a lot of trouble to avoid cameras."

Stepping in closer, I swing for the side of his face, "Well, figure it out."

He sidesteps, landing a hit to my jaw that makes me stumble. "If there's something to find, you know I'll find it."

I shake off the sting, the frustrating boiling beneath my skin. I step in closer, crowding his space, forcing him back. "You better find it fast," I growl. "Or I'll have to do your job for you."

He doesn't flinch, meeting my gaze with a flicker of amusement. "Relax, Kane. You're acting like someone's about to burn your house down."

A dark chuckle escapes me. "They already tried. Now it's my turn."

He smirks, wiping sweat off his brow. "Fair enough. I'll keep digging. But whatever's going on here? Might be bigger than a garden scuffle."

I exhale, my mind racing with too many of the same thoughts. "Keep me posted."

"Yeah," Cam says, rolling his neck. "But don't lose your head over it. Raven's clearly more capable than you think. She's not your damsel in distress."

The corner of my mouth lifts, "You think I don't know that?"

He laughs, stepping back with a loose, easy confidence. "Just checking, mate. Hate to see you lose your charm."

We move again, fists tightening as we circle each other, the energy still crackling. The fight's winding down, but neither of us is ready to back off just yet. I throw another jab, landing a clean hit on his shoulder that forces him to step back. His smirk doesn't falter.

I pause, lowering my fists slightly. "Have you found anything more on Raven?"

He huffs, rolling his eyes as he deflects my jab, his expression shifting into something darker. "Everything's been scrubbed. No babies named Raven Taylor were born in any hospital on her supposed birth date. Not here. Not there. Not anywhere." He steps back, his stance loose but coiled with energy.

The weight of his words sinks in, hitting harder than any punch. "Fuck."

"Exactly," Cam steps in, easily dodging my next swing. "Whoever did this knew what they were doing. That kind of thing doesn't happen by accident."

I exhale sharply, the frustration simmering beneath my skin. "But why?" My gaze is fixed on Cam like he's going to have more answers.

He raises a brow, his expression darkening. "Could be a number of reasons." He sidesteps me again, which is starting to piss me off. "... someone went to a lot of trouble to make sure no one could dig into her past. Or they thought *she* would never look into it."

The thought twists in my gut, my fists clenching at my sides. "What the fuck would hiding something like this even cover up, though?"

He tilts his head, unfazed by the tension radiating off me. "Look, I've got some leads I need to check on," he wipes his face with a towel. "Give me a couple of hours, and I'll see what else I can dig up. And try not to burn the whole place down before I get back, yeah?"

CHAPTER 37

Call it What You Want...

RAVEN

T he next few days pass in a blur, and for once, without incident. No strange dreams, no whispers brushing against the edges of my mind, and no one trying to knife me or elbow me in the face. Honestly, it's unsettling how normal everything feels.

The weather's been unusually perfect too, and Rachel's insisted on dragging me outside at every possible opportunity. She's convinced this is what vacations are supposed to feel like, and I almost believe her.

Rachel left for the airport this morning, and the emptiness hit me harder than I expected. Sleep has been a joke lately. Every night, I wake up restless and edgy, like there's something just beyond my reach, something I'm supposed to see. I've been awake since she left, watching the faint glow of sunrise creep over the horizon.

But sitting here now, with the morning sun spilling over the hills, it makes sense in a way I can't explain. This place feels like it knows me. Like it's pulling me in and refusing to let me go. The second Rachel mentioned going home, I knew, deep in my gut, that leaving wasn't an option for me. Not yet. Maybe not ever.

With Rachel gone, I decided to make some new friends. Or at least try. I've left food for the dog that's been hanging around the property, hoping to coax it closer. I glance toward the trees for any sign of movement.

The snap of a twig pulls me out of my thoughts. My eyes lock onto the edge of the woods, and there it is. The dog stands at the tree line, half-hidden in shadows. Its head tilts slightly, ears pricked forward, watching me with cautious curiosity.

There's something about it that makes me want it to come closer. Maybe it's the way we're both a little out of place, alone, circling something we don't understand. "Just in case you were hungry," I motion toward the food with a

509

shrug, feeling more than a little ridiculous talking to an animal that's clearly not ready to trust me. "It's not poisoned, promise."

The dog doesn't move, just keeps watching. "I'm Raven," I add, like the dog actually gives two shits about who I am. "And, honestly? I think we should be friends."

The dog's ears twitch, and for a second, it steps forward, closer to the light. My pulse quickens, though I couldn't say why. "I won't bite," I whisper. "Can't say the same for you, though."

A laugh escapes me, and I shake my head. "Alright, fine. Be that way." With one last glance over my shoulder, I head back inside, leaning against the door as it shuts behind me. "I need a hobby," I mutter, rubbing a hand over my face.

I grab my phone off the counter and collapse on the bed, tapping the screen and letting Kane's last message light up the screen.

> Kane: We've got some news to share.

That was yesterday morning. I should've answered then, but I didn't know what to say. Now, I'm just flat-out avoiding it. Whatever they found, it has to be big. I can feel it in the way he worded it, all formal and serious, like he's bracing for impact. And let's be real, I'm not exactly known for handling *big news* with grace.

> Me: Want to meet at The Realm?

I hit send before I can talk myself out of it, tossing the phone aside. But my phone buzzes almost immediately.

> Kane: I'll pick you up at four.

A smile tugs at my lips despite myself. Typical Kane, always so damn sure of himself. And damn him for the butterflies he stirs up, no matter how much I try to ignore them.

Me: See you then.

I drop my phone and stretch out on the bed, staring up at the ceiling as unease coils in my gut. There's a tension that claws at my chest that whispers something's coming. I can feel it.

I push myself up, deciding that a change of scenery might shake off the feeling creeping under my skin. I slip into my jacket, tugging it tighter around me as I step out into the crisp morning air. The cold bites at my cheeks, and I welcome the sting. The town is quiet this early, the streets painted in shades of gold and shadow, with only a few people drifting by.

As I turn a corner, my eyes catch an older woman standing at the edge of the street. She's bundled up in a long coat, her gloved hands clasped in front of her. When our eyes meet, she beams. My steps slow, a pulse of unease settling low in my gut as she lifts a hand and waves like she knows me.

I glance over my shoulder, half-certain that someone else must be behind me, but the street is empty. It's just us.

"Hello, beautiful," she calls out, her voice cutting through the morning air.

I hesitate, something about her energy makes the hair on the back of my neck stand on end. "Hi," I smile, forcing a casualness I don't feel. "I was just admiring your outfit, I love your jacket."

Her smile stretches wider, bright enough to light up her entire face. "Oh, thank you, dear. It's so nice to finally have someone so vibrant and full of life to talk to. You don't see that kind of spark very often these days."

A nervous chuckle slips out before I can stop it. "Well, I hope you have a great morning."

The woman's head tilts slightly, her expression shifting into something sharper. "Sweetheart, have you accepted it yet?"

A chill slides down my spine, "Accepted what?"

Her eyes lock onto mine, and there's something in her eyes. "Your gift. It's been calling to you." She steps closer, but it feels like the air thickens between us. "It's been waiting, you know. And you've been running for too long."

My pulse kicks up, heat pricking beneath my skin. "I'm not sure what you're talking about."

The woman lets out a soft, almost pitying laugh. "Oh, but I think you do. You can't hide, not here." Her eyes flick over me, "You carry something ancient, something that doesn't belong to you."

"Look, I don't know who you are, but I think you have the wrong person."

Her smile doesn't falter, but her eyes grow colder. "No, I've got the right person. You've been marked." She leans in, her voice dropping to a whisper. "You can feel it, can't you? The pull. The way it wraps around you."

My throat tightens, and I force myself to hold her gaze. "If you know something, then tell me what it is."

She laughs again, a sound that sends a shiver down my spine. "It's not my place, darling. But you'll find out soon enough. The question is, will you be ready?

The words hang in the air, heavy with a weight I can't shake. I swallow, struggling to keep my voice steady. "And what if I'm not?"

She shrugs, her smile turning faintly sad. "You've always been different, haven't you?"

A beat of silence stretches between us, and I hate how her words claw at something buried somewhere deep. "You don't know anything about me."

"Oh, but I do," she whispers, her eyes glinting with a strange light. "I've watched you for a long time, Little Bird. And they've finally found you. You must be careful."

The weight of my nickname on her lips hits me like a punch to the gut. "Who are you?" I demand, my voice coming out harder than I intended.

But before she can answer, another voice cuts in from behind me, shattering the tension like glass.

"What did you say, dear?"

I whirl around, my heart slamming against my ribs. A younger woman stands a few feet away, her expression polite but curious.

"Sorry, what?" I manage, my voice a little breathless.

"I thought you said something," she shrugs, tilting her head.

"Oh, no, I was—" I turn back, gesturing toward the old woman, but the words die in my throat. The corner is empty. She's gone. My pulse spikes as I scan the street, eyes darting over every shadow and space where she would've vanished. But there's nothing. No trace of her.

The other woman lifts a brow, shifting on her feet. "Well, have a nice morning," she says politely before quickly walking away.

"What the hell?" I mutter under my breath, my chest tightening with unease as I scan the street one last time. The absence of the woman gnaws at me, her words echoing in my mind like a ghostly whisper. She knew something and then she just vanished? My pulse thrums, each beat heavy with something I can't shake.

I force myself to push past the lingering unease as I head into the café. The comforting aroma of fresh coffee and pastries wraps around me, grounding me in the present. I place my order, my movements automatic, my mind still tangled in the strangeness of that encounter.

Outside, I settle at one of the small tables, hoping the crisp morning air will clear my head. I stare out at the street, the chatter of the town fading into the distant hum as I replay the woman's words, dissecting every inflection. The more I think about it, the more unsettled I feel.

Time blurs, and I barely notice my tea cooling on the table. When I finally lift the cut for a sip, the cold liquid makes me wince, and I set it back down with a sigh. Frustration simmers beneath my skin, and I absentmindedly stir the tea, debating whether I should get a new cup.

A faint wisp of steam curls from the surface, and my pulse stutters. I stare down into the swirling liquid. It wasn't warm before. I'm sure of it. A strange warmth lingers under my fingertips as I tighten my grip on the cup.

A hand lands on my shoulder, and I jerk, nearly sending the tea flying as my head snaps up. Mike stands above me, his expression a mix of amusement and apology.

"Didn't mean to scare you again, love." He raises both hands slightly, but the corner of his mouth curves into that charming grin I've come to expect. "I called your name, but you didn't seem to hear me. Everything alright?"

I force a smile, trying to steady my racing pulse. "Hey, Mike. Sorry, I must've been lost in my own world."

"Clearly," he teases, his grin widening into something more mischievous. "And here I thought you'd be harder to catch off guard. Guess I'll have to adjust my expectations." He leans in slightly, voice dropping to a low, velvety murmur. "Let me guess, you're replaying the ball in that head of yours?"

I arch a brow, refusing to let him see how much his tone gets under my skin. "It was an eventful night," I shrug, keeping my tone casual. "And for the record, I don't scare easily. You just have a talent for popping up at the worst possible moments. Must be your thing."

He laughs, the sound curls around me like smoke, and it sets me on edge. "I'll take that as a compliment," he smirks, amusement dancing in his eyes. "Seems like I'm exactly where I need to be. Especially when it involves you."

The blush creeping up my neck betrays me, but I manage a small smile, refusing to give him the satisfaction. "Well, you definitely excel at being in places where you're unexpected. Is that another one of your talents?"

He leans in, just enough to blur the line between playful and flirting. "Just looking out for people who might need it. Seems to me you fall into that category."

My lips twitch, but I maintain my composure. "You must be exhausted then, considering all the people out there are in need of a savior. That's practically a full-time job."

Mike's eyes flicker with challenge, his smile sharpening. "It's rewarding work." He straightens, but changes the subject. "Have you made it over to Skye yet?"

"Not yet," I shake my head. "But I think I'm planning to go tomorrow."

"Good," he says, his voice dropping slightly, the smooth timbre making it hard to look away. "Skye has a way of working its magic on people. You'll love it." His grin turns sly, lighting up his eyes. "Just promise me one thing. Don't let anything distract you while you're there."

I bite back the smile threatening to break free, heat rises to my cheeks despite myself. "It must be something if you're assuming there's enough out there that could hold my attention long enough to be considered a distraction."

His smile widens, a dangerous edge creeping into his expression. "You never know. Some distractions are worth the risk."

"I guess I'll have to see for myself," I keep my tone light. I'm honestly not sure what's even happening right now. Are we still talking about Skye?

He chuckles softly, "I like a challenge, love. I wouldn't be too quick to underestimate me."

Before I can think of anything to say, his phone buzzes, the sound slicing through the moment like a cold splash of water. His jaw tightens, and he glances down at the screen, muttering something under his breath. The flicker of irritation is small but telling. It's gone just as quickly as it appeared, replaced by his usual charm.

"Work," he says, his tone clipped despite his best efforts to sound polite. His gaze lingers on me for a moment longer, softening just slightly. "And just when I was starting to enjoy myself."

His lips curve into a regretful smile, as he answers his phone. "I'll talk to you later, Raven." He winks, turning on his heel.

I watch him go, but something tells me I'll need to keep an eye on Mike-n-ike.

The house is too quiet now, the kind of silence that lets your thoughts grow louder until they echo in your head like a challenge you can't ignore.

A sigh escapes me, and I let my head fall back against the cushion, staring up at the ceiling. My hands are tingling again. The warmth spreads through my palms like an itch I can't scratch. I press my hands together, trying to chase it away, but it lingers. I wish I could at least figure out how the hell I can get my hands to stop doing this.

The feeling pulls me back, triggering a memory I haven't thought about in years. My grandmother's voice guiding me as we sat cross-legged on the floor. "Focus on your heart, love," she'd say, her hands gently cupping mine. "Find your center. Balance is everything. If the heart is steady, the windows will open."

Every single time, without fail, I'd drift off mid-session and wake up snorting seconds later. I can almost hear her laughter now, "You'll get there." She'd whisper, brushing my wild curls back from my face.

The ache in my chest is immediate and bittersweet. Maybe she was right. Lately, I've been so on edge, the idea of balance feels laughable. But maybe meditation could help. If nothing else, it might keep me from spiraling into whatever hell this is.

I shift into a comfortable position, the crackle of the fireplace filling the room with a gentle rhythm that's almost hypnotic. Closing my eyes, I focus on my heart, letting the memory of her voice guide me. A familiar pressure builds in my chest, warmth radiating outward like a flickering flame. It's comforting and strange all at once.

The tingling in my hands pulses immediately, stronger this time, almost like the warmth is alive, responding to my thoughts.

No amount of Googling has helped me figure out why this keeps happening.

But just as I start to lean into the feeling, my thoughts drift to Kane. And that's when my attempt at mediation derails completely.

The image of him flashes through my mind like a scene from a movie I've watched too many times. It's a fan favorite, that's for sure. The memory of him kneeling between my legs, his mouth glistening as he licked me off his lips. A dangerous promise lingers in his eyes. Ugh. I need to get a grip.

A shiver races down my spine, and the memory sparks heat that spreads low and fast. Warmth pools in my belly, my thighs press together as the sensation builds. I squirm slightly, a quiet gasp slipping from my lips.

So much for balance.

My breath quickens, my chest rising and falling as I try to redirect my thoughts. Every time I push one memory aside, another takes its place.

"This is ridiculous." I don't need to be thinking about sex right now. *Who said anything about sex?* I groan internally, trying to shove the thought aside. This is why I can't be trusted to sit still for more than five minutes.

But who am I kidding? He's all I've been thinking about, and *that's* the real problem here.

Taking a deep breath, I focus on my hands again, willing the restless energy to settle. Slowly, the warmth subsides, and for the first time in days,

I feel a sliver of calm. It's refreshing, a rare moment of peace after endless sleepless nights. Maybe meditation *does* work.

Satisfied, I reach for my phone, planning to check the time and maybe indulge in a long bath before I leave. But the moment my eyes land on the screen, my stomach drops. *3:46 PM?!*

"You've got to be kidding me," I mutter, glaring at the time as if it's personally offended me. How did the entire day just vanish? I was *sure* I stayed awake during that meditation. Apparently not.

Panic slams through me, and I dart into the bathroom, splashing cold water on my face in a desperate attempt to snap out of the post-nap haze. It helps, but only a little. Time's ticking, and I need to pull myself together before he gets here.

Rummaging through my closet, I settle on a casual dress that's been begging to see the light of day. Why not? Dinner deserves something better than the endless rotation of sweats I've been living in lately.

I pull the dress over my head, smoothing the fabric as I glance in the mirror. My wild hair, as always, is doing its own thing. "Whatever, good enough," I mutter, rolling my eyes at my reflection. Snatching my coat from the hook by the door, and slipping on my Docs.

My chest tightens at the thought of seeing Kane again, and I shove the feeling aside. This is just dinner. Just dinner with a guy who practically burns holes through my soul every time he looks at me. No big deal.

Right on cue, a knock echoes through the house. My head snaps up, and my heart skips a beat. Of course, he'd be early. I grab my bag and head for the door.

"You should really keep your door locked if you're in here alone."

The words hit me like a challenge, stirring a flutter of something between nerves and defiance. I glance up at him, a sarcastic retort already on my lips, but the way he's looking at me stops me cold. His gaze sweeps over me with an intensity that makes my cheeks burn and my pulse race.

I shift under the weight of his attention, folding my arms across my chest in a defiant attempt to hold my ground. "What?" I challenge, tilting my head as if his staring is unwarranted, like my heart isn't trying to climb out of my chest.

"You look stunning." The words curl through the air. The corner of his mouth lifts into a confident smile, and all I want to do is punch him. I honestly don't know where I stand with him right now. I'm still annoyed, but I know I have no leg to stand on.

I scoff, forcing a smile of my own even though the warmth in his voice is unraveling my defenses faster than I'd like. "Thanks."

His smile deepens, dark amusement flickering in his eyes. "Remind me to do that more often."

"Do what?" I narrow my eyes, curiosity winning out despite myself. "State the obvious?"

"No," he smirks, taking a step closer, his presence pressing in around me. "Make you smile."

The air between us shifts, growing warmer and more dangerous. It's like standing on the edge of something I don't fully understand, and I can't decide if I want to step back or dive in headfirst.

"Don't get used to it." I'm trying to hold onto my anger toward him, but he's making that impossible.

His eyes narrow slightly, a challenge lurking behind that confident gaze. "Too late, Princess."

He breaks the tension with an easy grin, stepping back to let me pass. "Come on, let's get going."

I follow him, rolling my eyes even as a reluctant smile tugs at my lips. "Bossy as ever, I see."

He holds the car door open for me, his gaze lingering just long enough to send another jolt of heat through me. *Ugh.*

Once we're settled in the car, and we are on the road, he smiles, "I have a confession."

I arch an eyebrow, leaning back against the seat. "Should I be worried?"

He shakes his head slightly, the look in his eyes not giving anything away. "Cam isn't coming."

I blink, going into full panic mode. "Why not?"

"He's following up on a lead. Once he's locked onto something, there's no pulling him away until he's turned over every rock." His explanation makes sense, but a flicker of disappointment flares before I can shove it aside. Now what am I going to do?

I lift a brow, "So... what's the plan, then?"

Kane's lips curve into a smile as he shifts his focus back to the road. "I have a surprise for you."

"A surprise?" I repeat, skepticism heavy in my tone. "Now, I'm worried."

"Don't be. Unless you're afraid you'll like it too much."

I scoff, crossing my legs as I give him a sidelong look. "Please, you'll have to try harder than that."

"Is that a challenge?" he asks, glancing over at me, his gaze burning with something dark.

I match his stare, but my insides are mush. "You'd know if it was."

The tension between us hums, charged and alive, and for a moment I wonder if we're about to drive off a cliff just to see who flinches first.

But luckily, as we drive, the tension eases into something more comfortable, and the conversation shifts to lighter topics. He asks about what Rachel and I have been up to, and before I know it, I'm telling him everything about the little adventures, the quirky people, and the breathtaking sights we explored.

He listens intently, occasionally throwing in a question or comment, his attention flickering between me and the road. There's something disarming about the way he seems so genuinely interested.

It's nice talking about something other than the chaos that's been hanging over me lately. For a while, I let myself forget about the unanswered questions, the strange events, and the ever-present weight of uncertainty.

Kane mentions a few spots I haven't seen yet, places we hadn't thought to explore. The longer we drive, the more my curiosity nags at me. My question sits on the tip of my tongue, but I bite it back, letting the anticipation simmer instead.

Just when I think I can't take it anymore, the car begins to slow, and my eyes snap to the window. My breath catches as we approach the towering set of gates, their wrought-iron curves sending a jolt of surprise through me.

I whip my head toward him, eyes wide with disbelief. "Are you serious?"

A teasing smirk tugs at the corner of his mouth, his gaze steady as we pull through the gates. "You'll see."

The moment the car comes to a stop, I reach for the door handle, but his sharp, playful glare halts me mid-motion. "Don't."

I freeze, my hand hovering over the handle, biting back the grin tugging at my lips. "What? I'm perfectly capable..."

Kane shakes his head, a soft laugh rumbling in his chest as he steps out and circles the car with deliberate ease. He opens my door, extending his hand toward me with that effortless confidence that always sets me on edge.

I take it, letting him help me out, though my focus immediately shifts to the scene in front of me. The sunset paints the castle in fiery golds and warm ambers, colors that seem to glow around the towering castle. I'll never get over how beautiful it is here.

"Thank you," I murmur, my voice quieter than I intend, as my gaze sweeps over the view. "What are we doing here?"

He doesn't answer immediately, guiding me inside instead, his faint smile cryptic enough to make my pulse quicken.

When we step into the ballroom, I come to an abrupt halt, my breath catching in my throat. In the center of the room is a beautifully set table, glowing softly under the warm, golden light of the dimly lit chandeliers. In the corner, there's a small band playing a gentle, melodic tune that weaves through the air, creating an intimate, enchanting atmosphere.

"You really don't do anything halfway, do you?" I murmur, glancing at him beneath my lashes. There's a teasing edge to my voice, but I'm not sure who I'm trying to convince. Him or me.

His smile sharpens as he leans in. "Not when it comes to things that matter."

I swallow, heat rising in my chest, making it impossible to look away. "Careful, Kane. You might make me think you actually like me."

He steps closer, the space between us shrinking to nothing. "Maybe I'm just hoping you'll let me have a redo."

The weight of his words makes my heart hammer. There's no hiding the flush that creeps up my neck, and then he winks, my pulse goes into a full-on sprint. I take in the room again, needing a second to steady myself. When I look back at him, there's a softness in his expression that nearly stops me in my tracks. Something real. Something that feels dangerously close to feelings.

We make our way to the table, and he pulls out my chair with a grace that feels almost unfair.

"I was going to make you wear your mask," he teases, the corner of his mouth curling up into a devilish smile. "But I'd rather see your whole face."

"Oh, is that so?" I manage to reply, struggling to keep my voice steady.

He sits down and leans back in his chair, "I know you're a bit of a picky eater, but I have a feeling you'll approve of this..."

He nods and someone in an apron appears to my right. "What toppings would you like on your salad, miss?" The man asks, while filling our glasses with water.

I blink, momentarily caught off guard by how orchestrated this all feels, and glance between Kane and what I assume is the cook. "Um," I hesitate, feeling slightly ridiculous. "I'm not sure. Maybe cucumbers? Tomatoes? Or, I don't know, whatever you think. I'm sure it will taste amazing. Thank you."

The cook nods, and steps away.

Kane's grin widens, amusement dancing in his eyes as he crosses his arms over his chest. "Hold on, you're leaving this decision to someone else? A mystery order? Who are you, and what have you done with the girl I met at the bar?"

I roll my eyes, leaning back in my chair as a laugh slips out. "Something you should know about me is that I don't do well with decisions. Winging it is way less stressful. And if it's terrible, I can just blame you. Win-win."

He chuckles, shaking his head slowly. "Good to know. We'll make sure to avoid life-altering choices. Though, for the record, you don't strike me as much of a winger. You seem more like the type who quietly obsesses over every detail and pretends not to."

I narrow my eyes at him, "Well, you don't know me as well as you think, Kane."

He leans in, resting his elbows on the table, his gaze dropping to my lips before meeting my eyes. "Is that a challenge, Princess? Because I think I've got you pretty much figured out."

"Is that so?" I arch a brow, refusing to back down. "Guess we'll see."

His expression darkens slightly, something raw flickering behind that carefully constructed confidence. "Don't pretend I don't know exactly what makes you tick."

I can't decide if I want to push him away or drag him closer by that stupidly perfect shirt of his.

"Careful, *Kane.*" I let my voice drop a little lower, one corner of my mouth curling up. "I'd hate for you to bite off more than you can chew. Wouldn't want you choking."

His lips twitch into a smile that promises all kinds of trouble. The kind that sends warmth flooding through my chest and leaves my thoughts scrambling for coherence. I shift in my seat, pretending to adjust my dress, desperate for a moment to breathe.

I look over at the band in the corner, letting the soothing melody of their music distract me from whatever they hell Kane is trying to do. The tune shifts, and the melody begins to shift into a song I know all too well.

This night was clearly designed to test my self-control, and it's really not looking good for me.

The familiar notes wind through the room, wrapping themselves around me like a spell. My eyes snap back to Kane, my heart stuttering when I find him staring at me.

He doesn't look away. Instead, he stands slowly, the chair scraping softly against the floor. The sound is barely audible over the music, but it feels deafening. He extends his hand, his expression unreadable but his intent crystal clear. "Dance with me."

His voice is a little rough, and it sends a thrill curling down my spine. I blink, my heart skips another beat. At this rate, I should probably go see a doctor.

"Right now?" I ask, my voice coming out quieter than I intended. *Smooth.*

"Always," he replies simply, and there's something in the way he says it that unravels me completely, making it impossible to say no.

I swallow, placing my hand in his. "Fine. But don't step on my toes."

He laughs, pulling me in further. His smile alone could probably level me if I wasn't already halfway there. "I'll do my best, Princess."

The warmth of his palm against mine sends an involuntary shiver up my spine. Any chance I had at holding onto my anger about him lying to me, is quickly dissolving.

He helps me to my feet with a gentleness that feels out of place against his usual sharp-edged confidence. It's disarming, and it sets every nerve in my body on alert as he leads me toward the open space. *What is he up to?*

I drag in a deep breath, silently reminding myself that this is just a dance. I've faced life-or-death situations, a ball, and some psycho who elbowed me in the face, this week alone. Dancing with Kane shouldn't be that hard. Right?

We reach the center of the room as he pulls me closer, his hand settling on the small of my back with a confidence that makes my pulse stutter. His other hand wraps around mine, firm but strangely gentle all at once. "Relax," he murmurs, his breath warm against my ear. "You look like you're preparing for battle."

It takes everything I have not to laugh out loud. He's not entirely wrong, my fight-or-flight instincts are on high alert.

The romantic notes of *Enchanted* weave through the air, and for a second, I let myself be pulled into the moment. His hand rests firmly against my back, guiding me effortlessly. There's power in the way he moves, a precision that feels entirely too intoxicating for my own good.

When I glance up, his eyes are dark with a heat that threatens to burn straight through me. "Hi, I'm Kane." His tone is playful, like I don't already know exactly who he is and what he's capable of doing to me.

I roll my eyes, a giggle slipping out before I can stop it. "Hi. Raven. Welcome to my nightmare."

His smile deepens, "Raven huh?" His voice drops, "I'm enchanted to meet you."

The laugh that bubbles up is unrestrained. "You're ridiculous," I say, shaking my head, but my pulse betrays me with its frantic rhythm.

His grip tightens, pulling me closer until there's barely an inch of space between us. His hand slides lower, settling on my waist, firm and unapologetically possessive. "Welcome to my house."

I raise an eyebrow, trying to ignore the heat coursing through me. "You must be delusional," I laugh, "because only someone who actually lives here would call this a house and not a castle."

My gaze sweeps over the ballroom, taking in the grand, intricate details of the space. He chuckles, before spinning me around effortlessly. A laugh escapes me, like I've shed a weight I didn't even realize I was carrying.

As he pulls me back into his arms, he slows our movements to a soft, unhurried sway. His hand remains steady on my waist, and I can feel the heat of his touch through my dress. My heart feels like it's caught in a freefall, spiraling somewhere between panic and desire.

"Tell me, Raven," he murmurs, his voice is soft, but somehow commanding at the same time. "How are ye liking Scotland so far?"

The way he says my name sends another shiver through me. Heat pools between my thighs, and I need to keep it together or I'm going to end up slipping in the puddle I'm going to make on the floor. I meet his gaze, realizing just how close we've gotten. His intensity holds me captive, his presence overwhelming. "I really love it, actually," I admit. "I wish I could describe how it feels."

"Try," he urges, like he's daring me to bare more of myself than I'm ready to.

I hesitate, my thoughts a tangled mess. "It feels like home," I begin softly. "Like everything's alive. It feels like magic. The trees, the air... even the animals. It's like the whole place is whispering secrets, and I can't explain it. It just feels different. You know?"

A soft, nervous laugh escapes me, and I lower my gaze, feeling like I sound ridiculous. He grabs my chin and tilts my chin up to look at him and his eyes have softened. There's a flicker of something raw there that steals the air from my lungs.

"Aye," a faint smile tugs at his lips. "I know exactly what ye mean. Scotland has a way of weaving itself into your soul. It's not just a place, it's a feeling. The magic is real, even if most people can't see it."

His words sink into me, wrapping around my heart and squeezing tight. A shiver runs down my spine, and suddenly I'm all too aware of how exposed I feel. Everything feels too raw, too open, and I'm not sure what I want to do about it.

The door creaks open, breaking the moment as two staff members enter, their quiet movements shifting the energy in the room. The soft clinking of dishes fills the space, but my pulse still hasn't settled. I take a slow breath, willing my nerves to calm, but then I notice Kane reach into his coat pocket.

My stomach flips and my eyes lock onto his, my body on high alert as he pulls out an envelope.

"You can read it whenever you're ready," he tells me as his eyes search mine. "Or do you want me to tell you what it says?"

I hesitate, feeling like that envelope is a ticking time bomb. If I open it now, it'll shatter whatever spell this moment is. "Can we... can we do this a little later? Is that okay?"

A flicker of something crosses his face, but it's quickly replaced with a smile that makes my chest tighten for a whole different reason. "As you wish."

I let out a breath I didn't realize I was holding as my shoulders relax slightly. I can't help the way my chest tightens at his words, at the sincerity in his tone. "You know, growing up here wasn't what you think. Don't get me wrong, it had its moments. But it also came with its own challenges." His voice carries a quiet weight, and I find myself leaning in, drawn to the honesty behind his words. "My parents were always gone, handling their stuff. So, most of the time, it was just me, Cam, and my sister. We made our own fun, but trouble had a habit of finding us."

"What kind of trouble?" I ask, my curiosity clear despite my best efforts to keep it casual.

A smile tugs at his lips, and the warmth in his eyes is so unexpected it almost makes my heart ache. "We'd spend hours playing hide and seek, trying to outdo each other with the best spots. The place is full of hidden passageways, forgotten rooms, old journals, and trinkets left behind. It was like a treasure hunt every day. We were always snooping in places we shouldn't have."

He chuckles, the sound unguarded, and it makes him seem less like the force of nature I've come to know and more... human.

I can't help but smile, picturing a younger version of Kane tearing through this place, all mischief and curiosity. It's a side of him I never would have imagined. "Sounds like quite the adventure," I giggle softly. "Why do I get the feeling you were the reigning champ of hide and seek, too?"

His eyes glint with amusement as he leans back slightly, his grin widening. "Champion? That's putting it lightly. No one could ever find me. I was basically a ghost." I roll my eyes, fighting the grin that threatens to break free. *Of course he would say that.*

"Wait," I lean in slightly, my curiosity piqued. "Are there really secret rooms and passages here? Or are you just messing with me?"

"Of course," he replies smoothly, his tone light but carrying a note of challenge. "Wouldn't be much of a castle without them."

A thrill of excitement rushes through me at the idea, my mind spinning with possibilities. "I knew it." Then, just to make myself feel better, I slap his arm. "You're holding out on me. You could be hiding a dragon in one of those secret rooms, and I'd never know.

He laughs. "Dragons? No, sadly, it's mostly dusty books, old furniture, and occasionally a few ghosts."

My eyes narrow playfully. "You had me at ghosts."

He chuckles again, but then my brain catches up with everything he just shared. "Hold up... a sister?"

He raises an eyebrow, clearly amused by my surprise. "Yes, I have a sister. She's the blonde who came out to speak at the ball."

My jaw drops as realization hits. "Oh my God, she's stunning!" I feel a pang of embarrassment thinking about my assumption at the ball. *Okay, more than just a little embarrassed about that. Tiny misunderstanding.* "Do you two get along? Does she live here too?"

"Aye, we get along. She's the reason I haven't lost my mind running this place," he admits, a faint smile touching his lips. "But no, she doesn't live here. She's got her own life, though she's here often enough that it feels like she does."

I nod, "Sounds like she keeps you in line."

Kane's gaze flickers with amusement. "She tries. But no one really keeps me in line, Princess."

His words send a shiver down my spine, and I can't tell if it's a challenge or a warning. Maybe both. "Good to know."

He leans back in his chair, and there's a shift in his demeanor, something looser, like he's peeling back a layer just for me. "What else do you want to know?" His lips curve into a playful grin. "I love long walks on the beach, reading, I run six companies. One of which is a rental company." His eyes glint with humor. "And I inherited this estate from my parents, which keeps me busy enough. Wouldn't have it any other way."

He glances around the ballroom, and for a brief moment, pride laces his voice.

I let the easy rhythm of his words wash over me, but when he mentioned the rental company, something clicked in my brain. I pause, tilting my head. "Wait... rental company?"

He leans forward slightly, his gaze narrowing with amusement, like he's savoring my reaction. "Aye, I've got a few properties, mostly estates and townhomes. Very exclusive, though. Not the kind of thing you'd find on your average booking site."

His words land with an unexpected blow. I think back to the night we first met, his friend who drove us home like he knew exactly where to go and the way Kane seemed so familiar with the area. My curiosity sharpens, and I glance at him, piecing it together.

"The house we are staying at..." I begin slowly, my voice trailing off as the realization sinks in.

He holds my gaze, a knowing smile tugs at the corner of his lips. "Aye," he says softly. "It's mine."

The confirmation feels like a puzzle piece sliding into place, and I'm torn between annoyance and something much warmer. "You didn't know we were staying there?" I press, narrowing my eyes slightly, suspicion creeping in despite myself.

"I didn't," he replies without hesitation. "Not until you showed me the address."

His tone is calm, but there's a weight to his words that makes my pulse quicken. The fact that I've unknowingly been staying at one of his properties feels significant, like yet another layer to this unraveling story. It's unsettling how deep this connection between us seems to run, no matter how hard I try to keep my guard up. I made that reservation because it was one of the places my grandfather suggested when we talked about going together.

I open my mouth to respond, but the look in his eyes steals whatever I was about to say. There's a softness there, an openness I haven't seen before. I feel like I'm teetering on the edge of something I can't name, and it terrifies me just as much as it thrills me.

Kane stands, extending a hand toward me. His eyes hold that unmistakable glint, the one that's currently setting me on edge in the best way. "Come with me. There's something I want to show you."

Curiosity flares, and I take his hand. The contact sends a faint spark up my arm, and I have to remind myself to breathe. He leads me through the castle's now familiar hallways, the echoes of our footsteps soft against the stone floor. This space suddenly feels oddly intimate.

As soon as we get to the hallway with all the paintings I remember from the tour, it feels like stepping back in time, though that day seems like a lifetime ago. My eyes are drawn to the painting that first caught my attention.

"These are my great-who-knows-how-many grandparents," Kane says quietly, his voice carrying a reverence I've never heard from him before. "They built this place. Or so I'm told." He adds the last part with a hint of a shy smile that's so unexpected it nearly knocks me off balance.

I take a step closer, letting his words sink in. This isn't just a piece of history he's sharing, it's a piece of himself. He's peeling back layers he's kept hidden, letting me glimpse something deeper.

This isn't just a romantic dinner or a casual tour. It's deliberate, thoughtful, and sincere. It feels like he's trying to make up for all the times he could have let me in before.

I glance at him, noticing the slight tension in his shoulders, like he's bracing for my reaction. My chest tightens, and a warmth spreads through me, leaving me feeling unsteady. "It's beautiful," I smile softly, but the words carry more weight than I intended. Because I'm not just talking about the painting.

unravel

RAVEN

I take a deep breath, gathering my thoughts. Part of me is still fighting myself to be annoyed that he wasn't upfront with me, but another part knows I want to meet him halfway.

"I can't imagine growing up in a place like this," I glance around. "It sounds like it would've been... an adventure." My lips curve into a small grin as my gaze drifts back to him. "Not that I can complain, though, I loved where I grew up. My grandparents took care of me, they loved me, and taught me everything I know."

Kane chuckles softly, there's something about the way he's looking at me that makes it impossible to stop now, even if I wanted to.

"My grandmother is the one I have to thank for my love of all things magic." I pause, catching the faintest flicker of amusement in his expression. "But you probably guessed that part already." My grin widens a little, trying to keep the mood light despite the twinge of nostalgia creeping in.

He gives me a small nod, and I almost forget the tension I felt a minute ago. "She sounds like a remarkable woman."

"She was." I smile, letting the memory settle over me. "My grandpa, on the other hand, was not as soft. He was more about teaching me how to defend myself. At the time, it was mostly against bullies." A quiet laugh slips out.

When I look at Kane again, he's watching me with an intensity that nearly makes me lose my train of thought. It's like he's hanging onto every word, afraid to say anything that might make me stop.

Heat prickles up my neck, and I shift my weight, feeling strangely exposed. "My grandma would always save her best stories for the harder days. She'd sit beside me, playing with my hair while she retold them." A

531

bittersweet smile tugs at my lips, and I let out a small laugh. "Honestly, I secretly looked forward to those days, just for that."

Kane's expression softens with an understanding that catches me off guard.

"What does a *hard day* mean?"

My feet stop moving before I even realize it, I hadn't meant to let that slip. My throat tightens, my breath catching as I realize how dangerously close I came to opening a door I'm not sure I'm ready to walk through.

"Oh, um..." The words stumble out, clumsy and unsure, caught somewhere between the instinct to retreat and the strange pull to share. My hands twitch at my sides, unsure of where to go.

Kane stops, turning to face me fully. He notices my hesitation immediately. "You don't have to tell me," he says softly, like he's trying not to spook me.

I take a deep breath, the tension in my chest loosening slightly. I nod, grateful for the out he's giving me, though I don't need it.

Before I can say more, we step into the library, and the sight of it steals my breath all over again. No matter how many times I see this place, it never loses its magic. The towering shelves, filled with stories and secrets makes this room feel like the safest place in the world.

Which is why when I glance back at Kane, a part of me knows that just maybe, opening up wouldn't be the worst thing.

I let out a sigh, tucking a strand of hair behind my ear. "No, it's okay. I want to." My voice is stronger than I expect as the words come tumbling out. "My grandpa wasn't the type to go easy on me. He spoiled me rotten in almost every way, but when it came to life lessons, he was all business." Fondness and exasperation crossing my features, as the memories flood back. "He always said he wanted me to be strong. Mentally, physically, emotionally, and that he didn't believe in shortcuts."

Kane snorts, the sound catching me off guard. My eyes narrow, my lips twitching as I fight the urge to smile. "What's so funny?"

He shakes his head, failing miserably to suppress his smile. "Let me guess, you're a perfectionist? The type who gets worked up when things don't go exactly the way you planned?"

I roll my eyes, but a soft laugh escapes anyway. "Maybe," I admit, "That's probably why I loved it so much in the end. It taught me how to be honest with myself and everyone else. Because, really, what's the point if you're not?"

His expression shifts slightly, like he's seeing a glimpse of something he wasn't expecting. It's disarming, more dangerous than anything sarcastic he's thrown my way before.

"Sounds like your grandparents knew exactly what they were doing," he says quietly, and there's a weight to his words that lingers.

I pause for a moment, gathering my thoughts before continuing. "I mean they did teach me some important things. But my favorite thing was that life is going to be hard, but the only way to make life easier is to figure out how to get through it."

I expect him to throw in a teasing remark, but he stays quiet, his expression intent and focused, so I keep going.

"But to answer your question, my grandpa always switched things up to keep me on my toes, to make sure I never got too comfortable," I explain. "But there was one thing I hated more than anything and that was swimming in the lake. He would make me swim all the way across and back, no matter how cold it was. And trust me, it was always freezing. I'd be shivering like a leaf by the time I got out."

And cursing the very existence of lakes. Honestly, who decided *swimming* should be a life skill? If I ever have a future as a mermaid, at least I'll be prepared.

I shake my head, a small laugh escaping me. "Needless to say, I became a really good swimmer. But I also developed a deep-seated hatred for the cold. Unless, of course, it's followed by a hot bath, my favorite fairy tale, and someone playing with my hair."

Priorities.

Kane raises an eyebrow, amusement glinting in his dark eyes. "High standards you've got there, *Princess.*"

"It's strange," I admit, smiling. "I've never really talked about this with anyone before. It's just not... something that's ever really come up."

His lips curve into a genuine smile, and there's a warmth in his eyes that makes me feel too much. "I'm glad you're sharing it with me," his voice sounding sincere. Then his lips twitch, and that familiar cocky spark flashes back. "But if you keep sharing stories like that, I might have to start recording them. You know, just to have evidence that I didn't imagine the whole thing."

I roll my eyes, laughing despite myself. "Too bad you didn't think of that sooner," my eyes narrow. "This never happened."

Kane leans in slightly, "Can I ask you something else?"

I glance at my wrist. "Oh, yeah, look at that. Question time is over. Guess I better be heading back home now. My new friends are waiting for me." I say, desperate to deflect.

He tilts his head, one brow arching skeptically. "Friends?"

I shrug, glancing away, trying to hide my laugh. "All the animals that hang around the house," I mumble, lifting my chin and meeting his gaze head-on, "don't be an ass and assume that you and Cam are the only friends I've made since being here."

His laugh rings out, softening the sharpness of his features. God, he doesn't laugh like that enough.

"I'll answer your question," I narrow my eyes. "But only if you stop laughing at me."

The laughter fades, and his expression shifts, the teasing softening into something far more dangerous. He reaches out, his fingers brushing against the necklace at my collarbone. The touch sends a jolt through me, and I forget how to breathe.

"This," he murmurs, his voice low and threaded with something I can't place. "It suits you." His fingers linger just a second longer before pulling back. "Where did you get it?"

I hesitate, my hand instinctively lifting to touch it. "I'm not really sure where it's from," I admit, my voice softening. "It was in the box I got after my grandpa passed. I haven't really taken it off since. I'm assuming it belonged to my grandmother, but no one ever told me."

His eyes lift from the necklace to meet mine, and it's like he's not just listening but dissecting every word.

"Sounds special." His tone is gentle in a way that feels entirely too intimate.

Desperate to regain some control of my thoughts, I turn to the nearest bookshelf, my fingers grazing over the spine of a book. I force myself to look at him, lifting my chin, a defiant edge to my voice. "So, do you even have time to read? What kind of books does a guy with six jobs even like?"

Kane leans against the bookshelf, his posture deceptively casual, but there's a heat there. His eyes track my every move.

He tilts his head, that wicked smile deepening as he corrects me. "First of all, I don't have six jobs," he drawls. "I own six companies."

I huff out a laugh, despite myself. "Of course, you'd say that."

His hand reaches out to tilt my chin up. His other hand rests on the bookshelf behind me, blocking me in. My breath catches at the sudden shift in his expression. The teasing warmth is gone, replaced by something darker, something that steals the air from my lungs.

"Princess," the word rolls off his tongue like a secret meant just for me. It wraps around me, making my thoughts scatter.

"Hmmm?" The sound barely escapes my lips, my body leaning closer despite my better judgement.

"You can argue with me in a minute," he smirks, his voice dropping lower. "I'll even remind you. But right now..." He steps in, the space between us evaporating, his gaze darkening. "I'm going to kiss you."

My heart lurches into a full on sprint, my body buzzes with anticipation. His words hang in the air, heavy and impossible to ignore. Then he leans in so fucking slowly, and my heart stops altogether.

When his lips finally meet mine, it's like the world shifts. The kiss is firm but achingly tender. His restraint only makes the thrill sharper, igniting every nerve in my body. I melt into him, my fingers curling against his chest right as he pulls away.

He takes the book from my hand with a lazy confidence, setting it on the table with deliberate ease before leaning back against the shelf across from me, arms folded over his chest. His eyes hold a glint of challenge that makes my pulse race all over again.

"Was that so hard?"

I fold my arms, arching a brow. "Why do you keep calling me *Princess*?"

"Because you like pretending you're untouchable. It's cute."

My jaw tightens, heat flaring in my chest as I take a step closer, tilting my chin up to meet his infuriatingly steady gaze. "The only thing cute here is your inflated ego. Although, I can admit, tonight you've been rather charming."

His grin is entirely too confident. "Admit that you like it."

"I'd rather choke," I snap, but my voice betrays me.

Kane pushes off the shelf, closing the distance in two slow strides. He's so close now, I can feel the heat radiating off him, his presence swallowing up all the air in the room.

"You keep looking at me like that, and I might think you're asking for trouble."

I swallow hard, my heart pounding so loudly I'm sure he can hear it. "Maybe I am." The words slip out before I can stop them, and his predatory grin sharpens.

His hand comes up, his fingers brushing along my jaw before tilting my chin up. My breath catches as his thumb skims the corner of my mouth, the touch searing. "You're playing a dangerous game, Princess," his voice is soft but laced with warning.

"And what if I like danger?" I challenge, my voice barely more than a whisper.

His eyes darken, the teasing edge vanishing, replaced by raw intent. "Then you'd better be ready to lose."

Before I can respond his lips are on mine. The kiss is rough and consuming. His hands grip my waist, pulling me flush against him, and my body arches instinctively, heat flooding through me.

My fingers tangle in his shirt, pulling him closer as his tongue slides against mine. This kiss is utterly consuming, and I feel like I'm drowning in him.

Kane doesn't hesitate, his hands slip lower, gripping my thighs as he lifts me effortlessly onto the edge of the table. The movements are fluid, and it leaves me breathless.

His hands skim up the sides of my legs, bunching the fabric of my dress as he steps between my thighs. His mouth doesn't leave mine, not even for a second, as his grip tightens, his fingers dig into my skin in a way that's more intoxicating than it should be.

I gasp against his lips as his teeth graze my bottom lip, the slight sting sending sparks shooting down my spine. My legs tighten around him, locking him into place so he can't pull away this time, as his hands trail higher. His touch is rough and unapologetic, and I need him.

The sound of a book sliding off the table jolts me back to reality for half a second, but it doesn't break the hold he has on me. I pull back just enough to catch my breath, my forehead pressing against his as I struggle to steady myself.

"This is insane," I whisper, my voice trembling with a mixture of adrenaline and want.

"Completely," Kane agrees, his voice a low rumble that wraps around me like a vice. His lips curve into a grin that makes me realize I'm completely fucked. "But you started it."

"Are you going to finish it?" I challenge.

"Eventually," he growls, his lips claiming mine again with renewed urgency, leaving no room for argument.

The world narrows to the heat of his body, the relentless feel of his mouth, and the thunder of my own heart. I tilt my head, deepening the kiss, and a faint groan rumbles from his chest. It's like a shockwave that vibrates through me, igniting every nerve in its wake.

His hands side up my waist, pulling me closer until there's nothing left between us but the thin barrier of fabric and air. His palm drifts lower, pressing firmly against the small of my back, molding me to him as if daring me to break away.

God, how does he make breathing optional? His lips move with a deliberate slowness, savoring every second like he's got all the time in the world.

His tongue teases against my lips, and when a small, involuntary gasp escapes me, he seizes the moment. His control unravels just enough to send a jolt of heat straight to my pussy.

This is just a kiss, for fuck's sake.

Yeah, a kiss that's making me forget how to breathe.

His mouth curves against mine, and I can practically feel the smirk that follows. He knows exactly what he's doing. The bastard. His hands tighten on my hips, and my body reacts on instinct, arching closer, craving more.

Another low groan vibrates from his chest, and the sound of it unlocks something wild and reckless in me. My fingers dig into his shoulders, pulling him closer, feeling the solid strength of him beneath my hands.

Time slows, the world dissolves to nothing but the relentless heat of his body and the fire winding tighter inside me. As my eyes flutter shut, a sudden flash of light sears against my vision, cutting through the haze.

My eyelids fly open, and I catch the faintest glow from where my hands press against his chest.

The air around us shifts, charged with a strange, electric energy that wasn't there a moment ago. My breath catches, and the warmth in my palms flares hotter, buzzing like static under my skin.

I blink, my chest rising and falling as I try to make sense of the lingering sensation still tingling through my fingers. "What the hell..."

His eyes flicker with something dark and unreadable as he watches me, his breathing ragged. "Raven," he says with a hint of warning beneath the desire.

I swallow hard, fingers flexing against the heat radiating from my palms. I part my lips to respond, but before the words can form, I catch a flicker of hesitation shadowing his features. His laughter fades, replaced by something quieter, something that threatens to unravel me completely.

Before he can pull away, my fingers move on instinct, curling around the back of his neck and anchoring him to me. His muscles tense beneath my touch, the heat radiating like a flame begging to consume me.

"Not sorry," I whisper, breathlessly.

His grin returns, and his eyes drop to my lips. "Good. Because I'm not done with you."

There's no restraint this time, just a pure, reckless need.

Kane's hands slide into my hair, tangling in the strands as pulls me flush against him. Every inch of him presses into me, his arousal impossible to ignore. My hands grip his shirt tighter, holding onto him like he's the only thing keeping me upright.

My body arches against him, matching his intensity and I'm drowning in him.

Somewhere in the haze, the faint glow beneath my skin flares again, but I can't bring myself to care. All that matters is his touch, his heat, his lips claiming mine with unrelenting purpose.

I reach down, fingers brushing over the length of him, and he hisses, a rough sound that sends a thrill racing down my spine. His teeth graze my bottom lip, the slight sting sparking another wave of heat that leaves me trembling.

When he finally pulls back, it's with a ragged breath, his forehead pressed into mine. "You're playing with fire."

He looms over me, his presence consuming. "Now," he murmurs, his voice low and commanding, "you're going to sit right there." He gently guides me down onto the table. "And you're going to let me worship you. Understand?"

His words ripple through me, igniting something deep and raw that I can't name. Whatever it is, it's *hot as fuck,* and I feel my breath catch as I stare up at him, my heart pounding a wild rhythm against my ribs. My lips part, but all I manage is a nod.

He leans in, his dark eyes locking onto mine with intensity. "I need to hear you say it." He commands, his voice a velvety warning.

I roll my eyes, but there's no denying the thrill his tone sends coursing through me. "Yes."

Kane's eyes darken with satisfaction, a slow, predatory smile tugs at his lips. The way he towers over me, consuming every inch of space, makes me dizzy. "Good girl."

His hands find my jaw, his fingers brushing along its curve as he tilts my chin up. "Eyes on me," he murmurs softly, his tone leaving no room for argument. As if I could look anywhere else. His intensity pins me in place, his dark eyes dragging me deeper until I can't think of anything but him.

Kane kneels in front of me, his hands slide down the length of my thighs, sending sparks skittering across my skin. He's not rushing, and that deliberate control only makes me want him more.

His gaze holds mine, and for a moment I think he's going to pull me back into another kiss. But instead, he traces his fingers along the edge of my dress, his touch grazing my skin and leaving fire in its wake.

The sensation is intoxicating. It's as if he's writing a story across my skin, a story only he understands.

"You like this," he murmurs, his lips curling into a wicked grin as he presses a kiss to my overly sensitive skin. "You can't hide it, Princess."

A shiver races through me at his words, the dark confidence in his tone. "You're awfully smug for a man who's just getting started."

"You have no idea what I'm capable of." He leans in, teeth grazing my neck, sending a shockwave of pleasure straight through me. "But you will."

His hands slide down my sides with calculated precision. When he nips at the tender spot just below my ear, a soft moan escapes before I can stop it. The sound seems to fuel him, his teeth and lips dragging against my skin, his grip tightening just enough to hold me exactly where he wants me.

I want to touch him, but as my fingers reach for him, he freezes, lips hovering above my pulse.

"Don't," he murmurs, his breath warm and intoxicating. His command is velvet-wrapped steel, leaving no room for argument.

"You've got to be kidding," I whisper, my hands hovering, trembling with the need for contact.

His eyes lock onto mine, "If you touch me, I won't be able to do this. And right now, I want to take my time." He leans in, his mouth brushing against mine, his words a dark promise. "I want to show you what it means to truly be worshiped."

My hands falter, fingers curling against the edges of the table as I surrender to the weight of his command. His words are a slow-burning promise, igniting a fire that consumes me whole.

His mouth trails down my neck, each kiss deliberate, calculated to unravel me. My body responds instinctively, watching into him, every nerve alight with anticipation. His lips reach the edge of my dress, grazing the curve of my breasts, and I bite back a whimper as heat floods through me.

"Kane, please," I whimper. Unable to stay still and not touch him.

He pauses, his eyes drag up my body in a slow caress to meet mine. The intensity pins me in place, stealing my breath. He slowly gathers the fabric, inch by agonizing inch, revealing the sensitive skin beneath. His lips follow, each kiss sending a delicious shiver down my spine.

My hands twitch with the urge to reach for him, but his earlier command holds me captive. His hands slide further up my thighs, his fingers grazing the delicate fabric of my underwear. I gasp, my body arching into him, desperate for friction.

He pushes my legs further apart, and leans in, his mouth brushing against the inside of my thigh. "You smell so good," he murmurs, his voice dark and possessive. "Do you know how long I've wanted to do this?"

His words send a bolt of electricity straight through me, heat pooling between my thighs as my heart pounds wildly. My mind is a mess of need, the anticipation coiling tighter and tighter until I can barely breathe.

"Since the last time you did it?" I whisper, my voice trembling with the memory of that night. The words slip out before I can stop them, and his mouth curves into a wicked smile.

"Yeah, well," he murmurs, each word punctuated by a kiss that sets my nerves on fire. "I didn't get the chance to truly savor you the way I wanted." His lips skim higher, his breath a torment against my skin. "To make your body sing for me."

The flush spreading across my neck is impossible to hide, and I glance away, overwhelmed by the raw intensity in his eyes. But then his lips find the edge of lace, and all rational thought evaporates.

His hands slide to the delicate fabric, pushing it aside without hesitation, and his mouth claims me with a hunger that leaves me gasping. His tongue flattens, sweeping up my slit in one long, devastating stroke, like he's got nowhere else to be but buried between my legs. My head falls back against the table, surrendering completely to the sensation as he devours me like a man possessed.

His mouth moves with precision, his lips and tongue working together to unravel me, and I can't hold back the sounds that slip from my lips. His grip tightens on my thighs, leaving no room for escape.

My fingers tangle in his hair, pulling him closer, desperate for more of him. I'm lost and my body is arching into him as he drives me higher and higher. When his fingers tease my entrance, I'm left breathless with anticipation.

I gasp, my hand flying to cover my mouth and my hips lift toward him, silently begging for more. His response is devastating, his teeth grazing the edge of my thigh. "You don't get to do that. Let me hear you."

His command is like a brand, and I let my hand fall, surrendering to the moment. The sounds spilling from my lips are desperate and needy.

My thighs tremble, the pressure inside me coiling tighter, threatening to snap. He sucks harder, teasing the edge of my entrance, his fingers are coaxing me closer and closer to the breaking point.

The tension detonates, pleasure crashing over me in a tidal wave that obliterates everything else. "Kane," I gasp, his name ripped from my lips like a curse. My body bucks beneath him, my fingers tangling in his hair, clutching desperately to him as he pulls me under, consuming me completely.

My breath shatters into ragged gasps, chest heaving, as he slides a finger inside me. His tongue and lips devour me with a hunger that sets my nerves on fire all over again.

He curls his finger, finding that perfect spot, and my hips rock against him, chasing more, the need so consuming it leaves me raw and desperate. Then he adds another finger, the motion slick and the sound of it only amplifies the intoxicating pull.

"You like that?" His voice is a low, sinful growl that sends a shiver straight through me.

"Yes," I gasp, the word trembling on my lips, my body arching into him, offering myself up without a second thought.

A dark groan rumbles from him, reverberating through my body. His lips latch onto the inside of my thigh, teeth grazing, and the sharp bite sends pleasure rocketing through me. I'm coming undone, my hands fisting in his hair pulling him closer as I break apart beneath him, the orgasm tearing through me like a wildfire.

"That's it, Princess," his voice is rough and commanding. "Let me taste you." He doesn't stop, doesn't even slow down, drawing out every ripple of pleasure until I'm nothing but a trembling, breathless mess beneath him.

As the final waves subside, my first coherent thought is that I didn't know I could come this hard without him inside me. It's a revelation and a promise of what's to come.

He rises slowly, his wicked smirk dripping with dark satisfaction. He slides a finger into his mouth, his eyes locked onto mine as he sucks it clean with a deliberate, slowness. "You taste like sin," his voice is rough. "And I'm far from finished."

He leans in, his fingers graze the swell of my breast. Without breaking eye contact, he tugs my dress down, exposing my breasts to the cool air. My nipple hardens instantly, and a sharp thrill racing through me.

His hand returns between my legs, reigniting the fire curling deep inside me. His mouth descends, capturing my nipple in his mouth and I'm arching into him once again.

"Fuck," he mutters, his voice raw with hunger.

His hand trails up my body, leaving a burning path in its wake. His slick fingers brush against my lips and he pauses, his gaze locking onto mine, dark and predatory.

"Open."

It's not a request. My heart stutters, my pulse racing under the weight of his stare. Slowly, I part my lips, my breath catching as he pushes his finger inside. The taste of myself is heady, and his dark eyes never leave mine.

"Suck yourself off of me," he commands, his voice leaving no room for anything but obedience.

I wrap my lips around his fingers, my tongue swirling, tasting myself on him. His eyes burn with a possessive hunger.

He pulls his fingers out of my mouth and with one swift move, he pulls me off the table and onto his lap as he sits on the couch. His lips crash against mine, the kiss wild and consuming. His hands are everywhere, tearing my dress over my head and tossing it aside as if it's the only thing keeping him from devouring me.

"Look at you," he murmurs, his thumb brushing over my bottom lip. "You're perfect."

His lips are blazing a trail down my neck, across my chest, biting and marking as he goes. The need inside me is feral, and I'm desperate to be consumed. My fingers tear at his shirt, yanking it over his head, exposing hard muscle and ink that looks like shadows are carved into flesh. Lightning flashes through the room, illuminating him like a god of war, all lethal grace and power.

My breath catches as I take in his inked skin, rippling muscle, and scars that only make him look more untouchable. The way the ink curves and shifts with his muscles is mesmerizing, like it's daring me to trace it with my fingers. It's a declaration, a warning and an invitation all at once. He catches me staring, and the hunger in his eyes makes my pulse hammer against my ribs.

He chuckles and suddenly I'm on my back, the carpet soft against my skin.

Heat and muscle press me into the plush rug while his mouth moves lower. He's tearing me apart and putting me back together with every rough touch, every possessive graze of his lips. My nails rake down his back, and his muscles flex beneath me, a growl vibrating through him.

"Now," I gasp, my voice trembling with raw need. "Please."

His eyes lock onto mine, dark and wild. "Are you sure?"

"Please," I whisper, the word escaping as a plea.

With a dangerous smile, he pulls me flush against him, and with one swift motion, my panties are gone, discarded like they never mattered. The soft clink of his belt makes my breath hitch, and when he pushes his pants down, I'm incapable of looking anywhere else. He's all hard lines and impossible perfection, every inch of him is designed to ruin me.

He's huge. Like, *how-is-that-physically-possible* huge. My thoughts spin, struggling to comprehend how he could possibly fit. But my body seems to have other ideas. My gaze travels down, drinking in every inch of him.

But as he lines us up, the stretch is a blinding mix of pleasure and pain. An intoxicating burn as he fills me inch by inch. My body arches, welcoming him, even as I struggle to adjust. For a moment, I think I can't take all of him, but he doesn't stop. The sensation is overwhelming, a relentless pressure that leaves me gasping. His movements are intense, each thrust deeper, and more devastating.

His name spills from my lips, a broken cry as I cling to him, my body arching, meeting his rhythm. His hands grip my hips, fingers bruising as he pulls me closer, as if he can't get enough. His mouth crashes against mine, devouring me with a kiss that steals my breath and sets me on fire all at once.

"Kane," I gasp, breathless.

His pace quickens, each thrust hitting deeper, tearing me apart with ruthless precision. My legs tighten around his waist, dragging him even closer, the storm outside rages in tandem with the storm inside me.

"You're so close," his voice is a dark velvety command. "Let go for me."

My body shatters, pleasure crashing over me in violent waves, ripping a scream from my throat as I come undone beneath him. But he doesn't stop.

"Fuck," his grip tightens, his thrusts growing erratic. The sound sends another shiver through me, a final aftershock that leaves me trembling. Before I can catch my breath, heat spreads through my body all over again, and I'm suddenly desperate for more. He rolls, pulling me on top of him, his hands gripping my thighs, guiding my movements. "Ride me, Princess."

I roll my hips against him, feeling every thick inch of him stretching me. His eyes burn into mine, and his hands tighten while his fingers dig into my skin.

"That's it," he growls. "Take what you need."

My body moves on instinct, riding him desperately. My hips grind faster, chasing the pleasure that tightens, burning hotter with every movement. His body stretches me, making me dizzy with desire. He watches me for a second, but the control in his touch snaps, and he meets me thrust for thrust, his body just as desperate, just as insatiable as mine.

The pressure spirals, until I'm unraveling again, shattering around him. My body convulses, a wave of raw pleasure tearing through me as I come apart in his arms for the second time. I give myself over to it completely, feeling like I'm being consumed and set free all at once.

My body clenches, pleasure ripping through me like a force of nature, and I cry out, my nails digging into his shoulders, desperate to ground myself as I break apart. Stars dance behind my closed eyelids, the intensity of it leaving me lightheaded and utterly spent. But he doesn't stop. His hands guide my hips, dragging out every last ounce of sensation, pushing me higher, until I collapse against him, utterly undone and aching for more.

Before I can catch my breath, I'm on my knees and his hands steady me, positioning me exactly where he wants me. The heat of his body against mine is bliss, and I feel the hard length of him press against me. His fingers trace slow, deliberate patterns over my skin, and I swear I can feel myself dripping down my legs.

His rhythm is relentless, each thrust deeper, harder, more desperate. His grip tightens, flingers digging into my hips with enough force to leave bruises, and I love the way it feels. The raw sound that rips from his chest sends a final shiver through me, and with one last powerful thrust, he lets go completely, groaning my name as he finds his release.

The thunder crashes outside as lightning streaks across the windows. His weight presses against me with the heat of him sinking into my skin, it's everything I didn't know I needed.

We collapse and stay tangled together, the room is filled with the sounds of our ragged breathing and the faint hum of rain against the glass. His arm tightens around my waist, pulling me closer, like he's daring the world to interrupt this fleeting stillness. I don't want to move. My body is still tingling, the aftershocks of pleasure sparking under my skin.

It's reckless, and I don't know where it comes from, but I want more. The thought alone has me questioning my sanity. I want him to ruin me again and again until I'm nothing but a breathless, trembling mess beneath him. How could *that* just happen, and yet my body is telling me it wants more?

He shifts, rolling onto his side, his gaze locking onto mine. There's an openness there that feels raw and dangerous. His fingers trace lazy circles on my skin, and it's such a simple touch, but it's utterly disarming. The heat between us flares again, and I can feel the pulse of desire burning again.

How does he have this power over me? How does he make me want him even more when I just had him? It's infuriating, and I know I'm not walking away from this unscathed.

"Still with me, Princess?" his chuckle breaking the silence.

A smile tugs at my lips, and I arch a brow. "Well, I'm still breathing, so I'd say you didn't completely destroy me."

His lips curl into that signature smirk, which is equal parts infuriating and addictive. He leans in, fingers brushing a stray curl from my face, his touch deliberate. "If I wanted to destroy you, you wouldn't be talking right now."

The challenge in his tone sets me on fire, and I can't resist firing back. "Oh? Maybe you need to work on your technique, then." My voice stays steady, but my heart's racing like it's trying to break free.

His smirk deepens, eyes darkening. "Keep pushing, and you'll be begging for me."

A shiver races down my spine, and I bite my lip, refusing to back down, even as the heat in his gaze makes my pulse thunder, making me wet all over again.

Kane moves, reaching for the edge of the couch, and my eyes track the motion as he picks up the envelope. The teasing edge evaporates, replaced by something heavier as his expression hardens.

"I know you don't want to," he murmurs, his tone turning serious. "But you're going to want to look at this."

CHAPTER 39

Screaming Color

KANE

I watch her intently, tracking every flicker of uncertainty in her eyes as she holds the envelope with trembling fingers. The air between us shifts, the afterglow of what we just shared now replaced with a weight that settles between us like an unspoken truth.

I know it was a little fucked up to do that, and then hand it to her, but she needs to know what's in there.

Her hesitation as she hovers over the seal, tugs at something deep in my chest. I hate seeing her unsure and vulnerable. But I also know she doesn't need me to swoop in and fix it.

"I can tell you what's in there if you'd rather not open it." I offer.

Her eyes snap up to meet mine, and I see the weight of a thousand thoughts swirling beneath the surface. I want to rip the damn thing from her hands and shield her from what's inside, but I force myself to hold back. She's stronger than I'm probably giving her credit for, and I'm not about to take that from her.

A brave smile tugs at her lips, though it doesn't quite reach her eyes. "No, I've got it," her voice is steady but threaded with that biting edge I've come to expect. "Wouldn't want to scar you for life if it turns out to be something spooky."

Despite the tension, her attempt at humor pulls a faint smirk from me. "Fair enough." I lean back, but my eyes don't leave her face. This woman, this maddening, stubborn woman, always tries to carry the weight of the world on her shoulders, laughing it off even when it's tearing her apart inside. It's frustrating as hell. And it's one of the things I admire most about her.

I watch as her hands finally pull the papers free. I can see the way her breath hitches, and the tension ripples through her shoulders. I knew what was in there wouldn't be easy, but watching her unravel in real time? It's a hell I wasn't prepared for.

"Princess?" I say softly, my voice cutting through the heavy silence.

She takes a shaky breath, blinking rapidly as her fingers tighten around the papers. She's trying to find that strength I know she has buried beneath the uncertainty. "It's... it's what Cam found on my family." Her voice trembles, but it's threaded with determination. "He dug up a lot more than I was expecting."

"Do you want to talk about it?" I already know what's written there. But if saying it out loud helps her, I'll listen to every word she says.

"Looks like he found some things after all." She huffs, but her gaze is fixed on the papers. "My parents... might not be my parents. And my grandparents were... royalty? Which is insane." A bitter laugh escapes her lips. "The names on my birth certificate belong to an elderly couple, who are 87 and 89 years old. My birthday isn't my birthday, but I knew that already from the other envelope."

Her voice breaks on the last word, and my jaw clenches, the fire inside me roaring to life. She deserves the truth, and a hell of a lot more than this mess is.

"Basically, we have more answers, yet somehow know less." She grips the papers like they might disappear if she lets go. "Cam left a note, though." Her lips quirk into a shaky smile. "With a smiley face, no less. He says it's *great news* because it means someone's hiding something. And, of course, he's convinced he'll have answers for me in no time."

When her gaze finally lifts to meet mine, those unspoken tears hit me hard. I reach for her, pulling her into my arms and holding her tightly. She doesn't resist, sinking against me, her breath is warm and unsteady against my chest.

She stays pressed against me, her heartbeat frantic against mine. I let her take what she needs, refusing to let go until she's ready.

But when a sharp, urgent knock echoes through the room, my instincts flare to life. I grab a blanket and adjust it over her, making sure she's covered, before setting her on the couch. Her wide, questioning eyes follow me as I stride to the door, grabbing another blanket and wrapping it around my hips.

When I open the door, Ren is standing there, his face tight with unease. He's bracing himself for whatever he's about to say. Whatever it is, has to be bad. He knows I didn't want to be bothered tonight. His eyes flicker to my bare chest, and I catch the flicker of discomfort before he locks his gaze back onto mine.

"What is it?" My tone is sharp, every punch of patience I had already frayed to the edge. I step into the doorway, blocking Raven from view, every instinct on high alert.

"Boss," his voice is tight. "There's something you need to see."

I sigh, "Just tell me." I hear Raven shift on the couch, trying to hear what's going on.

"Every light outside is broken. Again."

The words hit me, igniting a storm of adrenaline in my blood. My gaze snaps back to Raven. She's clutching the papers, knuckles white, eyes wide with fear and confusion. She looks so small, wrapped in the blanket, and it makes me want to rip the world apart for her.

I turn back to Ren, my jaw clenching. "Check every camera. I want a full sweep of the grounds and every second of footage reviewed. You find out how this happened and who's responsible. Now."

"Yes, sir." He's gone before I've even closed the door, the urgency in his step telling me he knows exactly what's at stake.

As the door clicks shut, I hear a soft giggle behind me. The sound is so unexpected that it cuts through the storm in my head like a blade. I turn, one brow arching as I catch Raven's stare. There's a hint of amusement flickering beneath the tension in her eyes, her lips twitching with the ghost of a smile.

"What's so funny?"

She shrugs, a smile breaking free. "You answered the door nearly naked."

A slow smirk curves my lips as I cross my arms, leaning against the doorframe. "Didn't exactly have time to grab a robe, now did I? Besides—" I let my voice drop lower, "you didn't seem to mind."

Her cheeks flush, and she bites her lip, shaking her head. The sight sends a rush of heat straight through me, my body tightening in response. My cock twitches, and I catch the way her eyes drop. I'm seconds away from pinning her to the couch when her giggle fades, swallowed up by the weight in the room.

I push off the door, my smirk fades as I move closer. Her smile has slipped into something more fragile, and her gaze drops back to the papers still clutched in her hands. I can see the battle playing out behind her eyes, and the war she's fighting with herself.

"Raven." I need to know where her mind is going. Need to pull her back if she starts to spiral.

She lifts her eyes to mine, wide and uncertain. Her lips part like she wants to say something, but nothing comes out. The silence stretches, until she takes a shaky breath.

"I... I don't know how to explain it," she whispers, her fingers gripping the blanket tighter. "But I think... I think that was me."

A flicker of something dark stirs in my chest, and I close the distance between us, narrowing my eyes as I study her face. "What do you mean, what was you?" My tone is calm, but there's an edge beneath it.

She swallows hard, her gaze dropping to her hands. She's fidgeting with the edge of the blanket, like she thinks the answers might be written somewhere in the fabric. "The lights..." Her voice trembles. "I think I... I might've done that."

Her confession hangs between us, fragile and raw. For a second, I almost can't think. I want to tell her that it's impossible, that it doesn't make sense, but the look in her eyes stops me cold. I've seen enough to know that not everything can be explained. But this can't be something she caused, but the look in her eyes says she fully believes she's responsible.

"Raven," I say softly, sitting beside her. "Look at me."

She lifts her eyes to mine, the fear and confusion swirling like a storm I can't control. And fuck, this isn't something I'm used to dealing with.

"We'll figure this out," I tell her.

Her lip trembles, and for a heartbeat, I think she might pull away, that she might break down right here. But then she nods, her breath coming in shaky gasps as she tries to steady herself.

"It's late," my hand cups her cheek, and I brush my thumb against her cheek. "I don't think you should be alone right now. If you want to go home, I'll take you, but I think you should stay."

Her gaze flickers, a war raging in those hazel eyes of hers. Finally, she whispers, "Okay." The word is so small, so fragile, it hits me harder than any goddamn punch. "I'll stay."

Relief twists through me, the tension easing as I pull her into my arms, and she melts against me. "Why don't we go to my office and see what they've found," I suggest, "Unless you'd rather go to your room."

She hesitates, her fingers lifting to touch the necklace at her throat, a gesture I've seen her make a hundred times. "I'd like to come with you."

"Okay." I nod, offering her a faint smile. "Let's go."

As she pulls herself together, I watch her closely, noting the way her chin lifts, her shoulders squaring as she steels herself. And fuck, if that doesn't make me want her even more.

When she's dressed and ready to go, we leave the room together. Her head held high, despite the weight pressing down on her. The hallway feels longer tonight, the shadows flicker and dance with the storm raging outside.

I reach for her hand, half-expecting her to pull away. But she doesn't. Her fingers curl around mine, and it feels like a small victory.

When we step into my office, two of my men are already there, tension written in every line of their bodies. They stand as we enter, nodding at Raven before gesturing to the laptop on the table.

"You'll want to see this." One of them says.

I keep Raven close, her hand still locked in mine. Her gaze locks onto the screen, determination flaring in her eyes.

The footage plays, showing the estate's exterior from multiple angles. At first, everything looks normal. The soft glow of lights, the faint crackle of the storm. Then a bolt of lightning streaks across the sky, illuminating the grounds in a blinding flash. The thunder that follows rips through the air, and every single light explodes outward in a burst of sparks and glass.

"They all shattered at the same time." He explains, his disbelief echoing through the room. "No movement. No one was outside. No animals tripping the sensors. Just thunder, lightning... and then this."

He gestures to the screen as the footage replays, and my jaw tightens. The chaos unfolds on the screen making it somehow more surreal. Raven's hand tightens around mine, her fingers digging in, and I welcome the pressure. It grounds me, even as the fire of protectiveness surges hotter inside me.

"I'm guessing it was some kind of electrical surge from the lightning," one of my men offers, but the doubt in his voice is almost laughable.

Raven stiffens beside me, her tension radiating through our joined hands. I squeeze her fingers back, even as my mind churns with questions. She thinks this was her, I can see it in the way she holds herself, the slight tremor in her fingers. But there's no way that's possible.

Why does she believe that? What's she not telling me?

I slide my eyes to her, trying to read her expression, but she's locked up tighter than a safe. The only clue to her turmoil is the shallow rise and fall of her chest.

"Raven," I murmur, my voice low enough for only her ears. "Talk to me."

She flicks her eyes up to meet mine and opens her mouth like she's about to speak, only to falter and look away.

I turn to my men, my tone dropping to a lethal calm. "Thank you. That's all for now. Clean up the mess outside, comb through the footage again, and find me answers. I don't care how long it takes. If there's something out there, I want to know about it."

"Yes, sir," they reply, both moving quickly, leaving us alone in the dim light of my office.

Raven's fingers lift to her necklace, again. She's on edge, and I need to get her out of her own head.

"Let's take a walk."

She blinks, startled out of her thoughts, and looks up at me. For a second, I think she might refuse, but then she nods. "Yeah... okay."

I guide her out of the room, my hand at the small of her back, a possessive touch I don't bother to hide. As we move down the hall, the house feels different, the shadows dancing along the walls feel darker.

Raven drifts slightly ahead, stopping in front of a series of paintings hanging along one wall. Her eyes are drawn to them, like she's searching for answers in the brushstrokes.

"Those were my mother's doing." I try to keep my tone casual. "She insisted they stay, no matter how much I might've wanted to redecorate."

A faint smile tugs at her lips. "Poor baby," she teases. "The old paintings didn't fit your bachelor pad aesthetic?"

I cross my arms over my chest. "I'll have you know, I'm very attached to these paintings. They add character."

Her eyes linger on mine, "They're awesome," she whispers, her voice quieter now. "I can see why she wanted you to keep them."

For a moment, silence stretches between us. She lifts a hand, fingers hovering near the edge of the frame, but she hesitates, pulling back like she's not sure if she should touch them.

"What's on your mind?"

She exhales slowly, her shoulders sinking under the weight of whatever she's caught in. "Everything that's been happening... it's just too much," she admits, her voice tight. "The lights, the storm, the things Cam found about my family. It's like... I'm starting to wonder if there's more to this than just bad luck."

Her voice trembles, and I catch the fear she's trying so damn hard to hide.

I take a step closer, feeling the tension roll off her in waves. "Part of me wants to believe it's just a fluke," she continues, her eyes flicking between the paintings and the floor. "But another part I've tried to ignore for so long... wonders if there's something more. Ya know? Do you ever wonder if there's any truth to fairy tales?"

Her question catches me off guard as she lifts her eyes to mine, searching for judgement.

A small grin tugs at my lips. "My sister and Cam believed in magic too. Every Solstice, we'd leave little gifts for the fairies, hoping they'd lead us to their camp."

A quiet laugh escapes her, light and unexpected. "Did it work?"

"Not exactly. But Cam swore once that he saw a fairy ring light up. I didn't have the heart to tell him it was just fireflies." I chuckle, the image of Cam running around the garden with a jar of cookies still vivid.

Her smile softens, but the weight in her expression doesn't fully lift. I can feel it pulsing between us like a heartbeat. *Let me in, Princess.*

"Sometimes, I think those old stories hold more truth than we give them credit for," I add, my tone softer.

Raven stops walking, turning to face me fully, her eyes searching mine like she's trying to decide whether or not I'm trustworthy or just another person that's going to disappoint her.

"Whatever's going on, we'll figure it out." I pause, "Might even be kinda fun."

She lets out a soft laugh, the tension in her shoulders easing slightly, but I can still see the weight behind her eyes. "I think..." she hesitates. "I think I need to sleep on all of it." Her voice drops to a whisper. "Maybe we can talk more in the morning?"

I nod, recognizing the exhaustion in her voice. "Probably a good idea. It's been one hell of a day."

When we reach the door to her room, I stop, turning to face her. "If you need anything, you know where to find me."

Her gaze lifts to mine, and for a heartbeat, she just stares at me. Then, she smiles. "Thanks, Kane. For... everything."

Before I can respond, she steps closer. Her hand rises, fingers brushing my face, and the warmth of her parm is like a brand, searing me to the core. The softness of her touch is enough to send a jolt of heat straight through my veins.

And then she leans up on her toes, her lips brushing against mine. It's slow at first, but then her hesitation disappears. The kiss deepens, raw hunger surging between us again. My hands move to her waist, pulling her closer until there's no space left.

The way her body melts against me is like a drug I didn't know I was craving. My hand slides into her hair, angling her head to deepen the kiss, and her fingers curl against my jaw, her nails scraping lightly. *God, this woman.*

I pull her tighter, my grip possessive as our breath mingles. My body reacts instantly, a relentless ache I know I need to control. Now's not the time.

She pulls back just enough, but I can still feel her breath against my skin. Her eyes are dark with heat, and she smiles. "You better go to bed before I change my mind and we end up in another... library situation."

Her words are a challenge, and the playful wink she throws at me makes my restraint hang by a thread. It takes everything in me not to pull her back, to let the night spiral out of control.

I chuckle softly, my thumb brushing over her lower lip, lingering there as I lean in. "Is that a threat or a promise, Princess?"

Her laugh is soft, but there's a wicked edge to it. "Guess you'll have to find out," she teases, but her eyes betray her.

"You're going to be the death of me," I murmur.

A flicker of satisfaction dances across her lips, her fingers brushing the doorknob. "Goodnight, Kane," she whispers. The sound sends another jolt straight to my cock.

Fuck.

I stay rooted in place, watching as she steps into her room and closes the door behind her. The quiet click of the latch feels louder than it should be, leaving me alone in the empty hallway with nothing but the memory of her kiss and the fire still burning under my skin.

I exhale slowly, running a hand through my hair as a grin tugs at my lips. She's trouble. All kinds of trouble. And yet, I can't seem to stop walking straight into the fire.

Instead of heading to bed, I find myself detouring to my office. The house is silent, the kind of silence that makes your thoughts louder. I step inside, closing the door behind me, the familiar weight of the room settling over me.

Sitting down at my desk, I pull up the footage again. The glow of the screen casts shadows on the walls as I let the video play on repeat, my eyes scanning every frame with growing frustration.

The sequence is the same every time. Thunder, lightning, and then the lights outside exploding all at once. Over and over, I watch it, searching for anything that might make sense of it. A shadow, a flicker of movement, something to explain it. But there's nothing.

The lights shattered at the exact moment we were in the library. My jaw tightens as I replay the memory in my head. *That's impossible.* She was *thoroughly* occupied.

Leaning back, I exhale slowly.

What the fuck is going on with the lights around here?

This wasn't the plan. I'd wanted to give her a perfect evening, show her I'm not the liar she thinks I am.

She's like a force of nature. A five-foot whirlwind who somehow managed to dismantle every ounce of self-control I thought I had. It's like

557

something inside me snapped. A switch flipped, and now there's no turning it off.

It took every shred of restraint to let her go. To not carry her straight to my bed and claim her. Even now, the memory of her is branded into me, every little detail replaying in my mind like a fucking addiction I can't shake. *I want more. I want all of her.*

My eyes drift back to the footage on the screen, tension coiling tighter with each replay. *How could she think this is her fault? What makes her believe she has anything to do with lights shattering across the estate?*

A memory of my mother surfaces, her voice soft yet resolute. *"There's always more out there, Kane. If you're trying to make sense of it, it'll always be confusing."*

I exhale deeply. Maybe she was right.

The idea would be laughable if I didn't see the fear in her eyes, or the doubt crawling beneath her skin like a living thing. She's holding back, and that's a problem I intend to solve.

A memory claws its way to the surface of my mother's favorite thing to say to me. *Question nothing, or you'll always be wrong.*

It was one of her favorite things to say, and right now, it's pissing me off. But there's a part of me that can't ignore the echo of her words. I've seen enough in this life to know that logic doesn't always have a seat at the table.

With a heavy sigh, I pull out my phone and type a quick message to Cam.

> Me: Can you be here in the morning? We need to talk. Something's not adding up.

I stare at the message, thumb hovering over the send button. The lights. The storm. Raven.

The screen goes dark, but my thoughts refuse to settle. I shove back from the desk, the silence of the house pressing in as I make my way to my room. Each step feels like a countdown to something I can't see.

Something isn't adding up. I can feel it in my gut, that instinct that's never steered me wrong.

CHAPTER 40

I'm Sorry What?

RAVEN

I close the door behind me, leaning against it for a moment as I exhale slowly. My heart is still racing, and not just from what happened with Kane, but from everything else that's been thrown at me lately. A small laugh escapes before I can stop it, the absurdity of it all hitting me like a bus.

I press my fingers to my lips, still tingling from the memory of his kiss. *God, that kiss.* A kiss that's going to haunt me in the best and worst ways. It's burned into my bones, and I hate how much I'm not fighting it anymore.

Kane is... *intoxicating*. It's not just his stupidly perfect body or that lethal smile.

Normally, I'd flip out on anyone trying to boss me around. Hell, I'd make them regret it. But with him, it's different. It's like he's rewired my brain without my permission, and I can't decide if I want to slap him or drag him back for another round. Maybe both. *Probably both.*

I was so adamant about swearing off men, so determined to declare my independence like some crusader for emotional freedom. And yet, Kane walks in and makes me question everything with a single glance. A single touch. *How did I let it get this far?*

But, of course, the moment of bliss can't last. My smile fades, replaced by the unease that's been creeping in since the light situation. The heat in my hands... the timing... could I have caused it? Is that even possible?

I push off the door and pace the room, running my fingers through my hair. It's ridiculous. I've never done anything like that before. *Obviously.* But the memory keeps looping in my mind, tugging at the edges of my resolve. My stomach twists at the idea that I might be connected to whatever the hell is happening around me.

No. I need answers.

I grab my phone, quickly dialing Rachel's number, my fingers trembling slightly as I wait for her to pick up. It only rings twice before her familiar voice comes through. "Hey girl!" she yawns.

"Hey," I try to keep my voice steady even though my emotions are all over the place. "You busy?"

"I miss you too, depends. Are we talking *emergency level gossip* or *I need to hide a body?*" Her tone shifts, more alert now. At least I can count on her unflinching loyalty.

"Somewhere between those two." I drop onto the edge of the bed, pressing my free hand to my forehead. "I think I might be losing my mind, and I need you to tell me I'm not."

She snorts. "You've always been crazy, babe. But tell me what's up, and I'll be the judge of what level we're talking."

"Well, tonight at Kane's—" is as far as I get.

"I *knew* it! Oh my God, tell me. His dick is huge isn't it?"

"Rachel, seriously?" I groan, rolling my eyes even though I can't fight the smile tugging on my lips, at the visual. "He's hot and I *might* like him, but that's not why I'm calling." I take a breath. "We were talking, and one of his guys came in to tell him that every single light outside shattered. Like, all of them. At once."

Rachel's tone shifts, serious now. "Okay, that sounds insane... but I don't think you're imagining things. Maybe Kane likes you, you like him, and the lights exploded because of all the sexual tension. I knew I was onto something that first night there."

"This is not about Kane," I sigh. Waiting for her to be done laughing. *I will not choose violence today.* I deliberately left out the library, the kiss, and... everything else. Not because I don't trust her, but because saying it out loud would make it even harder to ignore the mess I'm making.

There's a brief pause on her end, and I can practically hear her opening her mouth, deciding against it, and then changing her mind again. The silence stretches just long enough to make me nervous before she suddenly bursts out laughing again.

"Bitch, it's about time you woke the fuck up!" Her voice practically crackles with amusement. "I love you, but Kane has been drooling over you since you verbally assaulted him in the bar."

I open my mouth to respond, but she steamrolls right over me. "Please tell me you fucked that God of a man. Because I'm telling you, if you haven't—"

"Rachel!" I screech, my voice high enough to wake the dead. "Do not finish that sentence!"

She's laughing so hard I can barely hear her, and despite myself, I start laughing, too. It feels good, even if I'm mostly laughing at how stupid we sound.

"Okay, wow," she finally wheezes, her laughter tapering off. "That's... a lot. Like, *a lot* a lot. But seriously, do you think there's more to this witchy stuff than you're willing to admit? Because it's starting to sound less like a *maybe* and more like a *yeah.*"

I sigh, dragging a hand through my hair, my fingers catching in the curls like they always do. "I don't know," I admit, frustration simmering. "But I can't shake the feeling that I need to figure it out. One way or another. I need answers, no matter how ridiculous they sound."

Rachel hums thoughtfully, and I can practically see her smug smirk through the phone. "I've literally been telling you that this whole time, babe, but I'm glad you've finally come to the party."

I roll my eyes, steering the conversation to safer ground. Rachel fills me in on her trip home. As much as I want to laugh at her Bobby complaints, I bite my tongue and let her talk. It's nice to talk about normal things, even if only for a few minutes. We toss around a few dates for her to come back, and I'm already mentally circling them on an imaginary calendar, counting down the days. Then she tells me she's going out of town for work and she'll likely be in a dead zone, but she'll check in when she can.

"Oh! Wait," a thought strikes me. "Before you go, can you check the office at the house? Like, really check it. Look for anything that might help. Books, journals, dusty old heirlooms, anything that might scream *useful* or *witchy*. I don't know."

She yawns, and I can practically hear her rolling her eyes. "You got it, Nancy Drew. I'm going to crash. I'm tired. Anything else, just text me."

"Shit, I'm sorry. I completely forgot about the time difference."

Her laugh is quiet, heavy with exhaustion. "Of course you did. Go figure out your witchy shit, get some dick, and call me later."

"Hey, love you. Be careful, okay?" she adds before hanging up.

I toss my phone onto the nightstand with a heavy sigh. The room is quiet, but my mind is anything but. It's tangled in a never-ending spiral of questions, theories, and possibilities that feel just out of reach. We're not even going to touch on Kane. Stupid, frustrating, intoxicating, infuriatingly hot, Kane. The man is a walking, talking, trap, and I walked right into it with open arms.

After what feels like hours of tossing and turning, I finally give up. Letting out a frustrated huff, I slide out of bed and grab the blanket draped over the bottom of the bed. Wrapping it around my shoulders, I pad quietly to the door, my steps muffled against the plush rug.

I'm sure Kane's high-tech security system is all rigged up, but I step out anyway. If there's an alarm, I'll deal with the fallout later. I step outside, but no alarm goes off.

The cool night air hits me, and for a moment, I just stand there, letting it wash over me. The stars are scattered across the sky like shards of glass, glittering against the inky blackness. The garden feels impossibly still, the kind of quiet that soothes your nerves and sets them on edge at the same time.

Right now, I need the space, the calm, the chance to *breathe.* I wander through the garden, letting the chilled air brush against my skin. With the blanket wrapped tightly around my shoulders, I look up at the stars. They're mesmerizing, scattered like shards of shattered glass, and the faint rustle of leaves adds a steady rhythm to the night. Somewhere in the distance, an owl hoots, its haunting echo carrying on the breeze.

For once, my brain isn't on the never-ending hamster wheel. The thoughts are still messy, sure, but at least they're not drowning me anymore. The moon peeks out from behind the clouds, its silver light scattering across the ground. I take a deep breath, letting the crisp air fill my lungs, and it soothes more of the chaos swirling inside me.

My steps are unhurried, as my mind wanders back to my childhood. A smile tugs at my lips as I imagine what it would've been like to grow up in a place like this. A castle, the endless gardens, a magical forest right in my backyard? My imagination would've been running wild. Secret kingdoms by the lake, forbidden adventures in the trees. I would've claimed every inch of this place as my own.

I can almost see my grandmother here, the two of us planting flowers in the garden, her stories weaving magic into every corner of the grounds. And the woods? God, that would've been my favorite place. She used to tell me stories about the fairies hiding in the woods, her eyes sparkling like she'd seen them herself. *The boundaries are thinner in the trees*, she'd say. *Anything is possible there.*

Standing here now, surrounded by the trees, I feel her words settling into my chest. I believed her then, but now? There's no doubt in my mind. The magic feels real.

I realize I'm close to the spot where I left the offering that night. I can still hear his low, velvety voice in my ear, telling me to pick something special, something that mattered.

A glimmer catches my eye at the base of the tree. It's faint, almost like a trick of the light, but it's there. Something shiny, nestled in the roots, reflecting the soft glow of the moon, and my breath hitches. "No way," I whisper, disbelief threading through my voice. My pace quickens and my heart pounds as I close the distance.

I wasn't expecting to find anything here. Hell, I was sure the flowers I left would still be there. Maybe I imagined it, maybe it's just the moonlight flickering through the branches.

But as I get closer, my breath stops.

There, at the base of the tree, is a dagger. *My dagger.* The very one I left in my bag back at the house. The one I definitely didn't leave under this tree.

My voice is barely above a whisper. "Is this a joke?"

Slowly, I crouch down, my hands trembling as I reach for it. My fingers trace the familiar details, the weight, the engravings, everything, it's mine all right. There's no question about it.

But as I hold it, something strange happens. Heat spreads through my palms, like a slow-burning fire that starts to seep into my veins. The dagger itself feels warm too.

My mind scrambles for any logical explanation. Maybe I'm losing it. Or just maybe, there's something seriously messed up going on. Like, *Kane's messing with me* messed up? Yeah, no. That doesn't track. He'd gloat about it.

The faint rustling of leaves snaps me from my thoughts. My breath catches as a shiver races down my spine. The air suddenly feels different, charged with tension that makes my skin crawl.

I'm not alone.

I let out a sigh of relief as soon as I see a dog step into view. It circles the base of the tree nearby with an almost unnatural grace before stopping to watch me. Its head tilts, eyes glinting in the moonlight.

"Kane never mentioned having a pet," I mutter, gripping the dagger a little tighter. "Aren't you a surprise." My voice is low, as I study the dog. No collar. No visible markings. All shadow and curiosity.

I decide to get closer. Because obviously, that's what a sane person would do. "Hey there," I call softly, stepping carefully into the trees, hoping it doesn't run.

The deeper I go, the quieter everything gets. It's like there's a calm settling over me, unnatural but oddly comforting.

"It's okay, I just want to pet you," I whisper. "Come on, little shadow dog. Do you have a name?"

A soft laugh escapes me, and I shake my head. Here I am, dagger in hand, trudging through the woods to follow a random dog. *Snow White's got nothing on me.*

The dog stays just out of reach, weaving through the trees. Every time I think I'm getting closer, it slips further away. Part of me wonders if this is a terrible idea, but that's future-me's problem.

That's when my foot catches on something, and I stumble forward, my hand shooting out to grab the rough bark of a tree. I look down, expecting a root or a rock. Instead, there's... a stick.

"A stick? Really?" I mutter, shaking my head. "Startled by a twig. Truly, I've outdone myself."

When I look back up, the dog is gone, melted into the shadows without a trace. Typical.

Leaning back against the tree, I let out a long sigh, closing my eyes for a moment.

The dagger is still warm in my hand, the heat pulses faintly against my skin. It's unsettling, but there's a comfort in it too. It makes me feel like I'm not completely powerless.

Right now, I know with one hundred percent certainty that I'm being watched.

My breath quickens, each thud of my pulse pounding in my ears. The unease crawls over my skin, sinking deeper into my bones. *Please let it just be the dog.*

The cool earth beneath me should ground me, but instead, it amplifies everything. The heavy silence presses in and it's suffocating. I sit back against the tree, feeling the weight of everything pressing down. The envelope. The chaos. The fragments of a story that refuses to fit together.

I thought I was fine. I thought I could live without knowing the truth. But now? Now it's all I can think about. The need to understand my past, my family, my place in all of this, and the not knowing of it all, is clawing at me.

"Get it together, Raven." The words are harsh and jagged in the silence. "We're not doing this pity party bullshit."

Sitting here like this? It's pathetic. Like I'm waiting for someone else to save me. Screw that. If I've learned one thing in my life, it's that no one's coming, and I sure as hell can't afford to fall apart now.

Tears sting at the corners of my eyes, and I bite down hard on the inside of my cheek, determined not to let them fall. *I'm fine.*

But the words feel hollow. My breath comes faster, like I'm trying to outrun something. It's all pressing down on me, demanding to be felt, no matter how hard I try to shove them down.

I press my forehead to my knees, my thoughts drifting to my grandparents. Their faces flash in my memory, warm and achingly out of reach. A pang of regret grips my chest. All the questions I never asked, all the moments I took for granted, assuming there would always be more time.

"What am I missing?" I whisper, a desperate plea to the universe. "I just want to know who I am."

The words hang in the air, swallowed by the stillness of the woods. I hate feeling like this. Like a stranger in my own skin.

I close my eyes, forcing myself to breathe. In. Out. I focus on the way the dagger feels in my hand. Solid and real. A reminder that I can't let myself drown in the *what-ifs*. Not tonight.

When I finally open my eyes, I take a long, deliberate breath, the crisp night air fills my lungs. I tilt my head up, really taking in my surroundings for the first time. The moonlight filters through the trees, casting shadows that dance across the ground, their movement almost hypnotic.

I push off the tree, steadying myself. "Okay." I brush myself off. "Time to head back before I completely lose it out here."

But as I turn to leave, a sharp *crack* shatters the silence. A twig snapping somewhere in the distance. I freeze, and my grip on the dagger tightens. The adrenaline surging through my veins sharpens my senses. The night air feels cooler, the shadows darker, every sound feels amplified.

I scan the darkness, my pulse racing, every muscle in my body coiled and ready. I don't know what I'm preparing for, but whatever it is, I'm ready.

A figure steps into view, emerging from the shadows just beyond the tree line. My eyes narrow, locking onto the silhouette. For a heartbeat, relief flickers in my chest. Took him long enough to come find me.

I take a step forward, the edges of a smile starting to form.

But then the smile drops, and a chill runs down my spine.

It's not Kane.

CHAPTER 41

Treacherous

RAVEN

"Raven?" Cam's voice slices through the night, with an edge that makes my stomach drop. He stops dead in his tracks, eyes wide like he's seen a ghost. "What the hell are you doing out here?"

The urgency in his tone is unmistakable, and it sets every nerve in my body on edge. The way he's looking at me has all my instincts firing. My fingers tighten around the dagger, "What's wrong?" I ask cautiously, though the edge in my own voice betrays the unease twisting in my chest.

My brows knit together as I tilt my head, eyes narrowing. "Wait... what are *you* doing here?" My tone is clipped, but I'm not about to let him flip this on me without an explanation.

Before he can answer, another horrifying thought barrels into me, my stomach tightens with a sickening mix of embarrassment. My grip on the dagger falters slightly. "Oh no," I blurt out, my voice rising. "Have you been at the castle this whole time?"

His expression doesn't shift like I expect it to. No sheepish grin, no snide remark. Instead, he just stares at me like I've grown a second head, his features twisted into something unreadable. And that look makes my blood run cold.

His jaw tightens, and his eyes narrow as he takes a deliberate step closer, tension rippling through his frame. "Raven," he says again, his tone all sharp edges. "What the hell are you doing out here?" His gaze sweeps over my shoulder, his posture rigid, like he's bracing for something.

The intensity in his voice puts me instantly on edge, my defenses slamming into place. "I needed air, Cameron." I bite out, irritation bubbling to the surface. "I couldn't sleep, so I went for a walk. Is that a crime now?"

I cross my arms, dagger still clenched tightly in one hand as I take a step back, narrowing my eyes. "Why are you looking at me like that?" My voice sharpens, ice creeping into my tone. "What's your problem?"

571

His eyes dart to the dagger in my hand, and for a split second, I catch something flicker across his face. "This isn't just a nightly walk, Raven." His voice growing urgent. "You're out here, alone, in the middle of the woods, in the middle of the damn night, holding a knife. Don't you think that's a little... concerning?"

"Concerning?" I echo, my voice dripping with disbelief. The frustration I was barely holding back finally spills over. "I couldn't sleep, and this," I lift the dagger slightly. "Is for safety. Not that I owe you an explanation."

I square my shoulders, refusing to let him rattle me. "I didn't think I needed a babysitter," I add coldly, my tone daring him to say otherwise. Then I tilt my head, letting my irritation sharpen my words. "And what about you, huh? What are *you* doing sneaking around in the middle of the night?"

His eyes widen, and he takes another step closer, his tone dropping into something more serious. "Okay... this might require a sit-down," he says, gesturing in the direction he just came from. He runs a hand through his hair, clearly struggling to mask whatever is making him uneasy. "I need you to come with me."

I hesitate, my instincts screaming at me to hold my ground. But Cam's gaze flicks back to me, and there's something in his expression that makes me follow despite every nerve in my body telling me not to.

We step into the clearing, and my eyes widen when I see a man standing there with two horses, their reins loosely held in his hands. The horses are calm, their breath forms soft clouds in the cool night air, and there's a stillness to the scene that makes my skin prickle.

I glance at Cam, confusion written all over my face, but he doesn't offer any answers. The scene might not seem that out of place during the day, but out here, in the dead of night, it feels... wrong.

The man notices us approaching, his brows lifting in mild surprise when his eyes land on me. His eyes shift slightly between us, a silent question hanging in the air.

"Evening, lass," he says, nodding politely, his voice carrying the same quiet calm as the horses beside him. But there's something else, something assessing. The flicker of surprise on his face is brief, gone before I register it.

Cam's entire demeanor shifts, turning sharp, almost businesslike. "You can go ahead," he says, his tone curt. "And as for what we discussed, move it to the top of the list. Make sure the others know as soon as you get back. I'll join you when I can."

The man nods without a word, his movements efficient as he swings himself up onto one of the horses. Before he takes off, he glances at me again, his voice low and even. "Goodnight, miss."

And then he's gone, the sound of hoofbeats fading into the night, leaving the clearing thick with tension. It presses down on me like a weight I can't shake, and I turn to Cam. "Who the hell was that?"

I glare after the rider, my heart pounds in my chest, a swirl of confusion and unease coiling inside me. My gaze snaps back to Cam.

"When does the explanation start? Should I be worried for my life, is this some secret serial killer confession?" I try for sarcasm, but my voice wobbles, the edge of panic impossible to miss. My nerves are frayed, and I'm not sure if I want to laugh or scream.

Cam's jaw tightens, his gaze flicking to the spot where the man disappeared before coming back to me. "It's not what you think," he says finally, but the flatness in his tone offers zero comfort.

His face is set, serious in a way I've rarely seen, and a cold twist of anxiety takes over. "Okay, seriously, Cam," I snap, my tone sharper than I intend, "You're scaring me."

He doesn't respond right away, instead he leads me toward the two stumps in the clearing. He sits heavily on one and gestures for me to take the other. I hesitate, crossing my arms like it'll shield me from whatever bomb he's about to drop, but eventually, I sit, glaring at him. "This better be good."

Cam exhales sharply, dragging his hands through his hair like he's trying to steel himself. His jaw flexes, and for a moment, he looks away, scanning the dark woods before his eyes snap back to mine. "Fuck."

My patience is almost non-existent at this point. "Cam," I snap. "What's going on? Spit it out."

He rubs the back of his neck, stalling. Finally, he meets my eyes. "Look, I know this is going to sound weird. Hell, it's going to sound insane, but there's something... unique about you. And I think I might know what's happening."

I blink at him, thrown completely off balance. "What?"

He lets out a nervous laugh. "Honestly, I can't believe I didn't figure it out sooner. It's been right in front of me this whole time. I had suspicions, but damn."

"Cam," I snap, my patience snapping like an overstretched rubber band. "This isn't funny."

He holds up his hands in apology, his face sobering instantly. "I know. I swear, this is just as weird for me as it is for you. I promise."

The words tumble out of my mouth before I can stop them. "Are you in love with me?"

The second the question escapes, I freeze, my hand flying to my mouth as if I could somehow shove the embarrassing words back in.

Cam blinks, his eyebrows shooting up in surprise. He looks so stunned I almost feel bad. Then his expression softens, and a genuine, hearty laugh bursts out of him, echoing through the clearing. The sound is so unexpected that I just stare at him, blinking.

You could just say no, pal. It's not that funny.

He shakes his head, as his laughter gradually fades. "Raven, did you hit your head on the way out here? Of course I'm not in love with you," a grin spreads across his face. "Besides, I like my head right where it is, thanks."

I frown, caught off guard. "What does your head have to do with anything?"

He smirks, clearly enjoying my confusion way too much. "Let's just say getting involved with you that way would likely lead to... consequences. And none of them would end well for me."

I narrow my eyes, irritation bubbling to the surface. *I don't know what the fuck is going on here, but if he doesn't tell me soon, I might stab him.*

"Okay, first of all. Rude. Second, what are you talking about? You're being cryptic as hell, and I'm losing my patience. You said you know what's happening to me?"

Cam's expression shifts, the smirk vanishing as seriousness takes over. "Yeah, I think I do." His tone is measured. "And it's the only explanation for why you're even out here." He gestures vaguely to the forest around us.

"Uh-huh..." I cross my arms, my gaze fixed on him like a laser. "Care to elaborate on that, or are we playing *guess what Cam means* all night?"

He exhales sharply, eyes locking onto mine with an intensity that makes my stomach do another flip. "I don't know how else to say this," he pauses. "But I think you have magic."

The words hit me like a slap to the face. My brain stalls, trying to process what he just said without having a complete meltdown. "What do you mean, it's the only explanation for me being here?" I ask, confusion slamming into me like a truck. "Wait... magic! What the fuck are you talking about?!"

I jump to my feet without thinking. My voice echoes through the clearing, startling even me, and my pulse pounds loud in my ears.

Cam glances around immediately, eyes scanning the tree line like he's worried someone's going to hear us. "Hey, stay with me," he says quickly, holding his hands up like I'm about to bolt. "This is going to be a lot, so let's just rip off the Band-Aid, okay? I'll tell you everything, but you've got to stay calm."

I cross my arms and glare down at him. "You'd better start talking." I snap, though my voice betrays me with the slightest tremble. I don't know what to feel. Shock, anger, disbelief? I need the whole story because right now, I'm teetering somewhere between wanting to laugh hysterically and spring into the woods like a lunatic and never come back.

Slowly, I lower myself back onto the stump, forcing myself to focus. I count my breaths—*one, two, three, four, five*. Trying to steady my heartbeat that's two seconds away from a prison break.

Cam rubs the back of his neck like he's not sure where to start. "Okay, um," he begins, his voice careful, almost hesitant, "we aren't exactly in Scotland anymore."

My head snaps up, frustration bursting through like a dam breaking. "Cam!" I shoot to my feet. "Why would you start with *that*, of all things you could've started with."

I throw my hands up, pacing back and forth as my mind scrambles to make sense of what he means. It's like he dropped a grenade and walked away.

Cam winces, holding up his hands defensively. "Sorry! I've never had to do this before." His tone half-apologetic. "Can I... show you instead of trying to explain? That might be easier, and we can talk while I do."

575

I stop pacing and whip around to face him, narrowing my eyes as I try to gauge if he's serious or just screwing with me. "Cam, I'm seriously questioning my judgment in trusting you right now."

A not-so-subtle wave of emotions surges through me. Confusion, frustration, and a spark of curiosity, to name a few. But panic is strangely absent. My heart is pounding, but there's an unsettling calm spreading through me, like my brain has skipped the meltdown phase entirely. I wonder if this is what shock feels like.

Cam's expression softens, sincerity etched into every line of his face. "I get it, Raven. I really do," his voice full of quiet understanding. "I promise I'm not trying to make things harder. I'm trying to help you make sense of it all. I think if you see it for yourself, it'll start to click. You'll understand, hopefully."

His tone is calm, almost soothing, and it tempers my irritation just enough to keep me from snapping back. I search his face, looking for any sign of deception or hesitation, but all I see is honesty and maybe a hint of worry. That alone is enough to keep me listening.

Part of me wants to demand answers right now, to make him spill every detail before we take another step. But the bigger part of me is intrigued. Whatever he's hinting at feels like it could finally shed some light on everything that's been happening. At least it's something. *No matter how crazy it sounds.*

Cam exhales slowly, like he's trying to untangle a web of thoughts that's just as confusing for him as they are to me. "Let me try again," he says, standing and gesturing in the direction the horses disappeared.

Despite my need for answers, I decide to follow, hoping I don't regret this. I fall into step beside him, my eyes scanning our surroundings.

The trees sway gently in the night breeze, whispering secrets to each other, but there's something about it that just feels off.

I look at Cam, half-expecting him to be focused on the path ahead. Instead, I catch him looking over at me, like he's expecting something. For a moment, neither of us speaks. The only sound is the soft crunch of the leaves beneath our feet.

"I'm sorry," he says finally, breaking the silence. "This is just... not something I saw coming, and that's kinda my job." He shakes his head, a frustrated huff escaping him. "Where was I? Oh, right, you have magic. Abilities—unknown."

My fingers tighten around the dagger in my hand, the weight grounding me as my mind races to keep up. "Magic?" I echo flatly. "You realize how insane that sounds, right?"

Cam's eyes flick to the blade. "Why do you have a dagger?" He gestures toward the blade still clutched in my hand.

"To protect myself, obviously," I reply, lifting it slightly to emphasize my point. "Don't make me stab you, Cam," I add, smirking despite the tension. It doesn't entirely land, but it's better than nothing.

Cam laughs, the sound echoing softly through the trees. For a moment, the weight of the situation lifts, and I catch a glimpse of the Cam that Rachel's always drooling over. He looks like the same tall, dark, and handsome man I saw that first night at the bar. He's always been attractive, but something about him feels different.

"Did you bring it with you to the castle?" His tone turns more serious, snapping me out of my daze.

I hesitate, "No."

Cam's eyes widen slightly, flicking to the blade in my hand. He notices my hesitation and holds up his hands. "Look, I know you are questioning if you can trust me right now, and you should be. It means you're smart. If you don't want to tell me about the knife, that's okay. You don't have to."

I study him, weighing my options. He seems genuine, but I've been wrong about people before. Still, there's something about the way he's looking at me that makes me want to believe him, even if I don't fully understand why.

"I had my suspicions about your background, but this..." His gaze drifts back to the dagger, his voice trailing off as if he's putting pieces together in his head. "This might be the answer to so many questions."

"Cam, you keep saying things without actually saying anything. Enough with the cryptic bullshit. Just tell me what's going on."

The wind picks up, rustling the leaves around us, carrying a chill that brushes against my skin.

"What am I missing here?" I demand, narrowing my eyes. Skepticism fills my voice, but curiosity creeps in too, uninvited and insistent. Maybe that's why everything about my family feels like a puzzle missing too many pieces. Am I losing my mind for even entertaining this idea?

Is this how people get kidnapped? By thinking that insane things are somehow a good idea? Or maybe I'm having a complete breakdown. Hell, maybe I've fallen asleep somewhere and stumbled into the weirdest dream of my life or forgot that I followed a white rabbit down a dark hole.

Cam's voice cuts through my spiraling thoughts like a lifeline. "Okay, so…" he begins casually, like he's just thinking out loud, "there's the realm where you live. Where people have jobs, go to school, pay bills, and do all the normal, boring human things." He gestures around us, his tone shifting. "And then there's this one. Where magic is as real as the air you're breathing. People have jobs, go to school, and do fun magical things."

I blink, trying to wrap my head around what he's saying, but it feels like grasping at smoke. "You've read stories, haven't you? About other worlds, about magic and things most people don't believe in? Did you ever wonder where those stories come from?"

Of course, I've wondered. So many late nights were spent devouring tales of magic and other worlds, secretly hoping they were real. Hell, there was a time when all I did was fantasize about being kidnapped by pirates.

Cam smiles, and even though I'm in the middle of all this insanity. I can't help but notice how annoyingly good-looking he is. Why does he have such perfect cheekbones, his hair is even perfectly tousled. That's when I see his ears. His *pointed* ears.

His laugh snaps me out of whatever that was, and I narrow my eyes. "You think this is funny? What exactly is so amusing about any of this?"

"Relax, Raven," his smile still plastered on his face. "Yeah, the looks are a perk. That part of the stories are true."

"As if your ego needs more inflating." I stop dead in my tracks as a new, horrifying thought crashes into me. "Wait, is Kane…" The words catch in my throat, too heavy to say out loud. My stomach churns with a nauseating mix of dread and suspicion. Has Kane been keeping more secrets from me too?

Cam's face shifts, his amusement vanishing as he takes a deliberate step closer. "That's… a complicated question," he says carefully. "But the short version? No."

Relief washes over me, but it's brief. "Complicated? What the hell does that even mean?" My mind races. If Kane's not involved, then what is this? What am I in the middle of?

"Raven, I think everything is connected to you. To who you are."

The weight of his words hits me like a punch to the gut. "What do you mean?" I ask, hating the tremor in my voice.

He sighs, raking a hand through his hair. "Your family. The trail just... disappears. And then there's the fact that what I did find, said your grandparents were royalty." His voice is almost casual, as if he's ticking off items on a checklist. "There's so much we don't know about them or you."

I nod slowly, trying to process the words, but my thoughts spiral faster, the more he says, the more outrageous it all gets. Royalty. Magic. None of it feels real, but there's a part of me that can't dismiss it outright.

Cam takes another step closer, the smugness is gone, replaced by something serious. "Raven."

The way he says my name makes my heart stutter.

"I'm telling you everything I know," he continues, his voice steady but edged with caution. "But I don't want to overwhelm you. If you need a moment, say so. I just can't have you freaking out."

I raise an eyebrow, defiance flaring despite the unease in my chest. "You're not exactly filling me with confidence here."

His jaw ticks, but his expression softens slightly. "If something happens, I'll have to put a stop to it. And that's not because I don't trust you. It's because it's the safest option for everyone." His voice drops lower, carrying a weight that sends a chill through me. "I need you to trust me on that."

I freeze, his words settle over me like a heavy fog. *Stop what?*

Cam watches me carefully, his eyes searching mine. "I mean... if your magic starts reacting to you, it could be dangerous. For both of us."

My stomach tightens. I think I'm going to be sick.

"I need you to stay calm," he continues, his tone careful. "To stay in control. Can you do that?"

I swallow hard, nodding slowly. Breathe in. And out. "I'll try." I whisper.

Cam exhales, relief flickering across his face. "I know this is a lot, and I know it sounds insane, but I'm here to help."

The sincerity in his voice throws me. For the first time since this bizarre conversation began, I feel something other than fear. *Trust?* Or maybe I'm just desperate for some kind of anchor in all this madness, but right now, I don't have any other choice. Especially if I want answers.

I take a slow, deliberate breath, forcing my heartbeat to steady. "I'm fine, just keep talking."

He nods once, then turns on his heel. I follow, still trying to untangle the questions and fears that refuse to settle.

"Fae, witches, and other creatures with magic, live here. We have for a very long time. But that's a story for another day." He looks over at me. "Right now, what matters is figuring out how you got here."

"So..." I hesitate. "How did I get here?"

Cam's expression remains unreadable. "The short answer? You have magic, Raven. And somehow, you used it to cross the veil, the boundary between realms. There are very few ways to do that. If you don't possess the ability to exist here, you *can't*. Humans can't cross over unless they're escorted by someone who can."

My steps slow as his words sink in. *Magic. Veil. Other realms.* It sounds like something straight out of the bedtime stories my grandmother used to tell me. But the way Cam says it... it doesn't feel like a story.

He hesitates, like he's trying to decide how much to say. "I've had my suspicions about who you are, but..." He rolls his eyes, laughing as he continues. "That's more of a show-and-tell conversation, and honestly? I'm still trying to wrap my head around all this. Even for me, it's a bit much."

I narrow my eyes at him. "Oh, *is that all?*" I scoff, trying not to be annoyed at his non answers. "Everything that comes out of your mouth so far is *crazy.* I'm probably dreaming right now, and none of this is real. I don't think it could get any weirder."

Cam smiles like he *knows* something I don't. "You'd think so, wouldn't you?" His tone shifts, the humor fading just enough to put me on edge. He pauses, his expression darkening slightly. "The names on your birth certificate? They're fakes, which you figured out. Your birthday, though? I believe that's real. Minus the day, of course. That part, I'm still working on. But here's where it gets even crazier..."

Every word pulls me deeper into this impossible reality. My breath catches, the skepticism still warring with the gnawing curiosity rising inside me. "Crazier than all this?"

Cam's eyes lock onto mine, and for the first time, I see something new in his eyes and I can't place what it is.

"We have an old... *saying*... over here," he pauses. "One that I think might pertain to you."

A shiver runs down my spine. My fingers grip the dagger like it's the only thing keeping me sane. "What's the saying?"

He doesn't hesitate. The words slip from his lips like a prayer.

When the twins rise high in the heavens,
Leaving her wild, untamed and free,
On a night when summer greets the moon,
and the solstice whispers to the sea.
When the longest day meets the fullest night,
And the blood is spilled upon the ground,
The stars will align in their ancient dance,
And all the signs shall come around.
The ground,
the whispers,
the flames and the sea...

He exhales, tilting his head slightly. "Then it goes on about wars, fates, and soulmates. You know, the usual."

His tone is light, but his expression is anything but. Out of the corner of my eye, I catch him looking at me, then quickly back to the trail ahead. Like he's still watching my reaction without trying to make it obvious.

I let out a slow breath, rolling my shoulders back like I can physically shake off the weight pressing against me. *"I'm not going to freak out,"* I say, though my voice wobbles just enough to betray me. "At least, I hope not."

Cam smiles, and his dimple makes an appearance as he looks at me. "I really do like you, you're funny." His amusement lingers, but there's something else beneath it. Something unreadable.

I bite back the urge to push, even though it's clawing at me.

"There are still gaps we need to fill in." His jaw tightens slightly before he continues. "The only people who know the whole story are the Protectors. They keep it hidden because the witch is…" a pause. "Powerful."

My frown deepens. "Protected? From who? And why is she such a big deal?"

Cam's expression darkens. "Because if the hunters catch wind of her existence…" He trails off, his jaw clenching. "They won't stop until she's dead."

A slow, creeping unease curls through my stomach. My hands tingle at his words. "They've been searching for her for centuries, drawn to the scent of her magic." His voice is quieter now. "That's why the Protectors guard the details so fiercely. If the hunters even suspect she's out there, it's over."

I swallow hard, my throat dry. "Wait." My voice comes out cautious and unsure. "Are you saying they don't even *know* who she is?"

Cam shakes his head. "No. No one does. That's part of the problem. There are hints, but nothing definitive. Most people don't even believe she's real anymore. The protectors reveal just enough to keep people searching, while keeping the witch herself hidden."

His eyes flick back to me, something heavy settling between us. "Let's just say the hunters aren't the only ones afraid of what she's capable of."

His words slam into me. My mind spins, grasping at fragments I'm not sure I want to piece together. Special sayings. Myths. Wars. Witches. A witch so powerful that she's both hunted *and* protected?

I force myself to speak, my voice barely louder than the rustling leaves. "Why would anyone want to kill her?"

His jaw tightens. "Because there's a lot of people out there who want to *control* that power." His voice dips lower. "And she's a witch."

I narrow my eyes. "And what does *that* have to do with anything? Don't you all have magic?"

He holds my gaze, something like frustration flickering behind his eyes.

"Yeah, most Fae have magic," he admits. "Witches, though, are different. Their power doesn't come from within them. Not entirely, anyway. It's tied to something *bigger*. Something ancient. They're connected to the very fabric of this realm in ways the rest of us aren't."

He pauses, then adds. "Witches went into hiding centuries ago."

I blink, my thoughts struggling to catch up. "So, what? Because her magic's stronger, she's automatically a threat? That's a bit dramatic, don't you think?"

Cam chuckles, but there's no humor in it. "Raven, you'd be surprised what people will do out of fear. It's not just her magic, it's what she *represents*. For better or worse, she changes everything."

A slow chill creeps over my skin. "How? By making people uncomfortable?"

His lips press into a thin line. "By waking things that were meant to stay buried."

I exhale sharply, irritation flaring. "We're getting off track," I mutter, shaking my head. "But let me guess, no one knows where she is still?"

He nods. "Exactly. When they find out, she'll be easier to hunt." His gaze sharpens. "And because I know you'll just keep asking, the fear isn't just about what she could do."

His words are cold and suffocating. "So, they want her gone because they're afraid of what she *might* do?" I scoff. "Shocker."

Cam pauses, his mask slipping back into place. "When you asked us to help with your family, I tried to dig deeper."

A pit forms in my stomach.

"But I couldn't find anything." he continues, his brow furrowing. "It was like they vanished without a trace." His eyes lock onto mine. "And that's saying something, because *I* can find anything."

"Not just because of, you know..." He trails off, letting the implication hang in the air before adding with that familiar cocky swagger of his, "But because I'm really fucking good at what I do."

Despite myself, a small, nervous laugh escapes me. "Modest, too."

Cam doesn't miss a beat. "I came *here* because your grandparents were royalty." His tone shifts, and the teasing edge is gone. "Over here, we have people who deal exclusively with royal bloodlines. Bartering goods, managing alliances, maintaining the balance, that sort of thing. If anyone knows who your grandparents really were, they'll be in *this* realm."

My stomach knots. "Okay," I reply cautiously. "Let's say all of that lines up. What does any of this have to do with me?"

Cam stops abruptly, his expression tightening like he's at war with himself. His chest rises with a slow, measured breath before his eyes find mine.

"You fit the description." His voice is full of certainty.

I blink. "Except for one tiny little flaw in that theory, buddy. I *don't* have magic."

The air shifts, and a gust tears through the trees, rustling the leaves at our feet. They lift, swirling in an unnatural dance around us. In the distance, thunder rumbles low across the sky.

I look up, pulse hammering. The stars that had been so vivid moments ago are now swallowed by thick, rolling clouds.

And *something inside me responds to it.*

A deep foreign pull, hums beneath my skin, threading through my veins. The hairs on the back of my neck rise as heat prickles at my fingertips.

For the first time, I wonder if maybe he's right?

I don't realize I've stopped walking until I feel Cam's eyes on me, his expression hesitant.

"Raven." His voice is laced with concern. "Hey, stay with me."

I nod faintly, but my gaze stays locked on the sky. The distant flashes of light pulse through the darkness. The energy around us is thick. I can *feel* it getting closer.

"Raven!" Cam's voice sharpens, more urgent now. He moves into my line of sight, cutting through the haze. "Look at me." His tone dips into something close to panic. "I need you to calm down. *Right now.*"

"I'm not *doing* anything!" I snap, my voice cracking as panic rises, clawing at my throat.

I squeeze my eyes shut, forcing air into my lungs.

One, two, three... but it's useless. *Four, five, six...* the energy presses in, thick and suffocating. *Seven... eight... nine...* the numbers tumble through my mind, but they aren't working.

My hands tremble at my sides, my grip on the dagger tight as I force my eyes open, locking onto Cam's.

"This isn't me, Cam," I say again, my voice raw, breaking under the weight of desperation.

I stumble back, shaking my head, my breath ragged. "Please, I'm not who you think I am! I don't know what's happening, but I'm not—" The words pour out, a dam breaking.

Cam steps closer, his voice calm despite the storm raging around us.

"Raven, sweetheart, *listen to me.*"

His hands find mine, his grip firm and grounding.

"We'll figure this out," he murmurs, his voice steady. "But I need you to breathe."

I shake my head, trying to pull away, but his hands hold me in place. The air crackles, the static before a storm pressing against my skin like a vice.

Crack.

Lightning strikes.

A nearby tree splinters apart, the blinding flash carving stark white into the darkness. The deafening roar of thunder slams through my chest like a battering ram, and the force of it vibrates in my bones.

I flinch, a strangled gasp tearing from my throat as the storm shakes the ground beneath me.

"I can't," I whisper, my voice fractured, barely audible above the wind's relentless howl.

I can't stop it.

I can *feel* the storm inside me. Burning and freezing at the same time invading every nerve, an unrelenting force clawing to be unleashed. My hands tremble violently, but all I hear is the loud, endless ringing.

The wind screams through the trees, branches snapping like brittle bones. Leaves spiral through the sky, caught in the violent current. The ground pulses beneath me, charged with something wild and all wrong.

The energy is rising, climbing higher with every frantic beat of my heart.

"Raven."

Cam's voice slices through the storm. Louder this time.

His hands move to my face, gripping firmly, forcing me to meet his gaze.

"If you don't calm down, you'll burn out." His thumbs press against my jaw, anchoring me. "And that is *not good*. Do you hear me?"

The sky splits open, unleashing a torrential downpour.

Rain comes down in sheets, soaking us instantly. It slams against my skin, cold and punishing, but the storm inside me doesn't care. It rages, clawing for control. The world is unraveling, and I can't stop it.

Somewhere deep inside me I feel something stir. And the only sound I hear is a whisper.

Fight.

A choked sob escapes my lips, the sound swallowed by the roaring wind. My chest tightens, squeezing until I can't breathe.

Something shifts. A strange warmth spreads through me, a pulse beneath my ribs, foreign but calming. It radiates outward, grabbing hold of my limbs, pooling in my fingertips.

Cam's grip tightens.

I can feel something warm trailing down my face. My stomach drops and I force my eyes open, blinking through the rain, and my breath catches.

Blood. I can taste it. It mixes with the rain, dark rivulets sliding down my cheek and my nose.

Cam catches my wrist mid-air. The sight of him startles me, his sharp, familiar features illuminated by the lightning.

His eyes are glowing. A faint pulse of light flickers in their depths, electric and unnatural. My breath catches.

For the first time, Cam feels like a stranger.

"I'm so sorry, Raven."

His grip tightens but his voice remains calm. The power radiating off him intensifies.

All I hear through the ringing in my ears is, "... safe."

The words barely register before something settles over me, drowning me in a tide of unnatural stillness.

No.

It's him. I know it's him.

"No!..." I manage, the whisper slipping from my lips as my body surrenders. But a wild, unyielding force flares inside me, fighting back. And it's furious.

Fight.

I feel it snap like a whip. A last, desperate pulse of resistance and lightning strikes. So close I feel the heat sear the air between us. The deafening BOOM rattles through me, and the tree beside us explodes into splinters.

My knees buckle.

The fire inside me sputters as his magic presses stronger. It wraps around me like a weighted blanket I can't shake off.

"I've got you."

The words sink into me, pulling me deeper. Dragging me under.

The storm, the pain, the fire. All of it fades.

The darkness closes in, and his voice is the last thing I hear before everything goes quiet.

CHAPTER 42

Flashback

RAVEN

The sunlight dances on the surface of the lake, sparkling like a thousand tiny diamonds and casting shifting patterns across the rippling water. The frigid waves lap against my skin, sharp and biting at first, but their rhythm pulls me into a strange, focused calm.

I've done this enough times now, that the initial shock of the cold barely lingers.

The faster I steady my breathing, the quicker I can cross the lake and back. And then I can get out.

The freezing water claws at my skin but I push through it. My legs kick harder, propelling me forward as the cold steals my strength. Each inhale burns my chest, and every exhale hangs in the crisp morning air around me.

On the shore, my grandfather stands tall, his eyes fixed on me, watching my every move with that unwavering intensity that somehow feels both comforting and demanding. "Come on, Raven!" he shouts, his voice slicing through the cold air. "You're stronger than this."

My muscles scream in protest, my body begging me to stop, but I don't. I can't. He always said he'd teach me how to control myself. Not sure how that translates to hypothermia drills, but here we are.

Finally, my hand brushes against the icy gravel at the shore, and I drag myself out of the water. My body trembles violently, the cold burrowing deeper into my bones. My teeth chatter so hard I'm sure they'll crack.

My grandfather is right there, wrapping a thick blanket around my shoulders, pulling me close. His warmth is immediate. "Good job, Bird," he murmurs, his voice carrying that familiar warmth that somehow makes everything feel okay.

I nod, too breathless and frozen to respond.

"See? You're stronger than you think." His voice softens. "It's about control. You must keep trying."

The walk back home is quiet, the only sound is the crunch of gravel beneath our boots. Finally, he speaks, his tone thoughtful.

"You know, sometimes we have to face the things we fear most to figure out who we really are." He glances at me, eyes unwavering.

I drift in and out of consciousness, time losing all meaning. Minutes? Hours? It all bleeds together into something strange and surreal.

Voices hum in the background, muffled and indistinct, like I'm hearing them through water or a thick wall. Everything feels distant, my head is heavy, my body feels heavier, and reality? Well, that's nowhere to be found.

Cam's voice cuts through the haze, slicing through my sluggish thoughts. I force myself to grab them, but the words are slippery and disjointed. "... *dangerous... no... I don't know... witch...*"

I don't know how much time passes before I hear more voices, clearer now, like someone turned the dial on an old radio. "Stronger... he wouldn't... it has to be."

It has to be what? The weight of those words lodges in my chest, dragging something to the surface that I can't quite name. My gut twists in protest, but my body refuses to cooperate. My eyes stay stubbornly shut, no matter how much I fight.

I try again, but it's like my limbs are weighed down with lead. The room spins and it's a nauseating tilt.

Voices filter through again, bits and pieces catching on the edges of my awareness. "... she has it... training... if the veil drops... no?" The words slip by, impossible to grasp.

Another wave of dizziness slams into me, and then this time, I hear a female voice. "The King... not much time... lying... I hope so."

The mention of a king sends a cold ripple of unease down my spine, and for a second, I want to scream. I'm too weak, too lost in this swirling fog to grasp anything for long. My voice won't even work to scream. At least I don't think so. I can't hear it.

I can hear rain patter against the window, broken by the occasional rumble of thunder. Normally, I'd find it soothing, but now it's just another sound piling on top of the chaos in my head.

"Look outside," someone says, their tone cold and condescending. "Conscious enough..."

My limbs feel disconnected, like they belong to someone else entirely. I want to scream at them, demand answers, do something, but all I can do is float here, useless and powerless.

The voices fade again, leaving me stranded. My grandfather's voice pushes me forward. My grandmother's stories echo in my ears.

And behind it all, I can hear the storm, wild and furious. Everything spins together, a violent whirlwind I can't escape.

I open my eyes, the steam from the bath curls around me, and my grandmother stands in the doorway with that familiar smile that always made me feel safe. "Come on, Bird," she says, her voice rich with affection. "Ye can't sit in the bath forever. I've got one of your favorite stories planned for tonight. Come on then, here's ye a towel."

I reach for it, the corners of my mouth lifting into a small, content smile.

Wrapping the towel around myself, I step out of the bath, the cold tile is a sharp contrast to the warm water I was just in. She motions for me to follow her into the bedroom, patting the space next to her as she sits down on the bed.

Once I settle in, she tucks the blanket around me with the care only she could give. I lean into her, breathing in the comforting scent of lavender and fresh linen.

"Tonight, my love, is all about the Lightning Queen," she begins, her voice soft and melodic, weaving the story into the quiet of the room. "A woman born under twins. She's wild and has a spirit that could bend magic itself."

Her voice lowers slightly, drawing me closer. "She'll rise on the night of her birth, under the season that greets the rising moon."

I'm captivated, my small hands clutching the blanket as I hang on her every word. "With the power to walk between worlds, she restores the balance where there is none. When the planets and the fates and all the stars align, blood will spill, promises will bind, and souls will collide."

A shiver rolls down my spine, though I don't fully understand why. She pauses, her eyes turning distant, her expression momentarily unreadable.

"But," *she says, her voice softening,* "She's the key..."

Her eyes sharpen suddenly, locking onto mine with an intensity that steals my breath.

"She must die. Only then can she break the curse." *She whispers.*

Her lips curve into a small, bittersweet smile.

Suddenly, a shadow flickers at the edge of my vision, a figure lingering just beyond the doorway. My grandmother's smile falters for a heartbeat, her gaze shifts behind me. It's subtle, but the spark of warmth in her eyes dims, replaced by something cold.

I try to turn, to look, but my grandmother's grip tightens on my hand, her touch suddenly colder than it should be. "Don't," *she whispers, her eyes flickering with something like fear.* "Not yet. You're not ready."

The shadow moves into the room, and its presence is heavy. My heart pounds, and I feel a strange pull.

"Raven..." *The voice is soft, carrying a faint echo, like whispers overlapping.* "You don't belong here... not yet..."

I glance back at my grandmother, but something about her has changed. Her expression has gone cold, her grip tightening painfully around my arm. When her eyes meet mine again, there's a flicker or something.

Her lips curl into a smile that doesn't belong to her. "About time you came out to play." *Her voice is different.* "This should be fun."

A searing heat spreads from her touch, burning into my skin like a brand. Panic claws at my throat as I try to pull away, but her hold is unbreakable.

Suddenly, she blinks, her eyes widening in shock. Her mouth twists into a snarl. "WINDOWS. NOW!"

Slowly, I manage to pry my eyes open, and it feels like a goddamn marathon.

Everything around me is blurry, the edges softened by sleep or... whatever the hell this is. I blink a few times trying to clear my vision. Sunlight streams through the window, spilling across the room.

For a second, I wonder if the rain was just a dream. The rhythmic drumming on the glass is gone, leaving behind a suffocating silence that feels too loud.

Another blink, and I feel an ache so deep it practically burrows into my bones. My entire body feels like it's been hit by a freight train, reversed over, and hit again for good measure. Every muscle protests as I try to move, my limbs weighed down like someone swapped my bones with lead. The dull throb of exhaustion radiates from every inch of me.

"Raven!" Cam's voice slices through the room, yanking me out of my haze. He's right there, a blur of movement that reveals a very stressed-looking Cam. His brows are drawn so tightly together I'm surprised they haven't fused into a unibrow.

"You're awake." Relief flashes across his face for half a second before he leans down and pulls me into a quick hug. The kind that says *thank God you're not dead.* When he pulls back, he plops down beside me, his hand resting lightly on mine, like he's worried I might bolt or dissolve into a pile of dust.

"Hasn't anyone ever told you that telling a girl to calm down is a bad idea?" I croak out, my throat so dry it feels like I've swallowed sandpaper. "What... happened?"

Cam exhales, a humorless chuckles slipping out as his shoulders relax a fraction. "You... lost control." His tone is careful. "I had to do something. I'm sorry, but it was the only way to keep you safe." His gaze flicks down to where his hand still rests over mine before he meets my eyes again, something unspoken hovers in the air. "You've been out for... a bit."

"How long is *a bit*?" I already know I'm not going to like the answer.

"Three days."

"Three *days*?" The words hit me like a brick to the chest. Panic wells up, clawing at my lungs, making it hard to breathe. "Three days?" I echo, louder this time, my voice cracking as my brain scrambles to make sense of it. I've been gone for three whole days?

Adrenaline floods through me, and I try to sit up, but my body has other plans. My muscles scream, and before I can get far, Cam's hand is there, easing me back down.

"Easy, Raven." His voice is calm, but there's an edge to it. The *don't mess with me* vibe that Cam pulls off way too well.

"Kane," I blurt out, my panic spinning faster than I can catch it. "He's going to freak out. I have to call him." My hands fumble toward the bedside table, searching for my phone, but Cam doesn't let me get that far.

"Raven, stop." There's something in his eyes I can't read.

"Are you kidding me?" I snap, frustration and panic clawing at my chest. "Three days, Cam. He's probably losing his shit."

Cam clears his throat like he's bracing for impact. "Kane won't know you're gone. I promise."

I narrow my eyes at him, full of suspicion. "What do you mean he won't know?"

Cam hesitates for a second too long, and I don't like it. "Time doesn't work the same over here as it does over there."

I blink at him. "Time doesn't... what? Seriously? That's your explanation? *Time doesn't work the same?*" My voice rising, frustration mixes with the leftover panic.

He shrugs like this is no big deal, like *time differences* are just part of the daily grind. "It's true," he says, his tone annoyingly even.

I want to slap at him, demand answers, but my body is too wrung out to do more than glare. "You better start explaining," I rasp. "Because I swear, if you're about to give me more vague cryptic shit, I'm not in the mood."

His lips twitch like he wants to smile, but the concern in his eyes doesn't budge. He squeezes my hand gently. "There's a lot we need to cover," he says carefully. "A lot you need to understand."

He pauses, scanning my face like he's gauging how close I am to losing it. "But right now, you need to rest. Your body's been through more than it used to. You pushed your magic way too hard, and it took a toll on you. Burnout like this isn't uncommon when someone's just starting to tap into their abilities."

"Burnout?" I repeat, the word settling uneasily in my mind. Great. Magical burnout. Just what I needed on my bingo card of insanity.

"Magic is demanding. Think of it like using a muscle you've never worked out before, it takes time to strengthen. Push too hard, and you'll only hurt yourself."

I nod slowly, his words washing over me as exhaustion pulls at my limbs. "So... no one knows I'm gone?" My voice is shaky, caught between relief and unease.

Cam's expression remains calm. "No. You don't need to worry about that right now."

A shaky breath escapes me as I try to absorb it all. "Why do I feel like there's something you're not telling me?"

His gaze softens, "We'll talk about that soon," he says gently. "But only when you're strong enough to handle it. Right now, your body needs to heal. You've already pushed yourself too hard."

I study his face, searching for some kind of clarity, but all I find is quiet determination. He's holding back, but I'm too worn out to push. Besides, there's a tiny, annoying part of me that wants to believe he knows what he's doing. I'm still alive.

"Okay," I murmur, my eyelids growing heavy. "I trust you." *I think.*

He chuckles, and a reassuring smile flickers across his face. "Good," he says. "Just rest, Raven. You're safe here."

I exhale slowly, tension slipping from my body as I sink deeper into the bed. Whatever this is, whatever's happening, I let myself lean on the fact that Cam is here. That has to be enough.

The world fades as my eyes flutter shut, sleep pulling me under once more.

My body feels lighter, the crushing weight from earlier has subsided, though I'm still worn out, like I've just survived the world's longest nap. Carefully, I stretch, testing my limbs. They're stiff and reluctant to cooperate.

The thought of being out for days makes my stomach twist into knots as I sit up slowly, dragging a hand through my hair, which I'm pretty sure is a rat's nest at this point.

The sheets are cool against my skin, and the faint scent of lavender lingers in the air, a detail that feels too out of place.

I glance around, finally taking in the room. It's beautiful. The walls are painted in warm tones that remind me of a sunrise, casting the space in a cozy glow that screams *nothing bad happens here*. I thought my bed in Scotland was big. This bed is *massive*, a canopy draped in sheer, flowing fabric that sways with the breeze from an open window. It's like someone wanted me to forget everything outside of these walls.

Nice try. But I can't.

I swing my legs over the edge of the bed, my bare feet brushing against the cool floor. The air is crisp and fresh, carrying the faint scent of flowers and rain. A small reminder that the storm was real. I look down at the soft dress I'm wearing, it's different from the one I was wearing when I left the castle. I push that thought aside. I need to find the bathroom.

I spot a door tucked discreetly in the corner and make my way over, my legs steadying beneath me. My body feels stronger, even if my mind is hanging on by a thread. Pushing open the door, I freeze.

The bathroom is ridiculous. I thought the bedroom was insane. Gold accents gleam on every surface, natural light floods the space through oversized windows, and a circular bathtub sits in the center like some kind of throne. Dozens of candles surround it, casting a warm inviting glow. It's the kind of place that would make even the fanciest spa jealous.

For a second, I let myself be impressed. If this were my bathroom, I'd probably never leave. Deciding to take full advantage, I cross the room, turning the golden handles until steam curls into the air. My gaze lands on a collection of oils neatly arranged along the edge of the tub. Why not indulge? After the week I've had, I've earned it.

I pour a generous amount of oil into the water, the rich calming scent spreading through the room. I slip out of my clothes and step into the tub, sinking down until the warmth wraps around me. A soft sigh escapes me as I lean back letting my head rest on the edge. For the first time in what feels like forever, my body finally relaxes.

Taking a deep breath, I slide under the surface, the water closing over me. Everything goes silent. The only sound is the faint rush of water in my ears. It's almost like I've left the chaos behind, and it feels so nice. It's so quiet under here. Peaceful, even.

I break through the surface, gasping softly for air as I push my hair back from my face, blinking as the room comes back into focus.

"Raven!"

Cam's voice cuts through the stillness, and I whirl toward the door, sending ripples through the water, causing it to slosh all over the floor. My heart leaps into my throat as he stands in the doorway.

He freezes, eyes wide, alarm etched across his face. "Oh." His gaze sweeps over me, just a fraction too long. He snaps out of it quickly, his mouth opens and closes, like he doesn't know what to say.

"I... uh... I'm so sorry!" He looks up at the ceiling, words tumbling out faster than his brain can process. "I called your name, and I couldn't find you, then I heard you gasping in here, and—" He groans, flustered. "I wouldn't have just barged in if I knew you were... I mean—"

A small, breathless laugh escapes me, partly from the ridiculousness of the situation, partly because I'm still catching my breath. "Cam, relax. Didn't mean to scare you."

His cheeks turn a faint red as he rubs the back of his neck. "Right. Of course." He clears his throat, still looking anywhere but at me. "I just... thought something was wrong. I didn't mean to... you know."

"You're fine," I say, unable to keep the teasing smile off my face. "Trust me, you seeing me naked, is honestly the least of my problems right now."

His face goes an even deeper shade of red, and I catch the ghost of a smile threatening to break through his flustered exterior. "... I wasn't exactly expecting..." He gestures vaguely, then quickly averts his eyes again.

I lean back, crossing my arms along the edge of the tub. "Well, unless you're planning to join me, you might want to give me a few more minutes to enjoy this slice of heaven."

He lets out a strangled noise as he makes a swift retreat. "Yeah. I'll, uh... I'll wait outside."

As he closes the door behind him, I can't help but laugh softly to myself. If nothing else, at least I've got Cam to make me laugh.

I let myself sink deeper into the bath, closing my eyes as the warmth soaks in. The water's nothing short of divine, and I savor every last moment of calm, knowing it won't last.

Eventually the water cools, forcing me to leave my temporary paradise behind. I don't feel one bit guilty for staying in longer.

Wrapping myself in a towel, I step out of the bathroom, my feet padding softly against the floor as I make my way back into the bathroom. My eyes sweep the room, searching for Cam, but he's nowhere to be seen.

Instead, my gaze catches on the bed, where some clothes and boots have been neatly placed by the bed.

I run my fingers over the softness of the material, feeling the faintest hint of luxury. Did Cam pick this out? The thought makes me smile. I half expect him to pop out from some corner, fumbling through another awkward apology, but the room remains blissfully silent.

I let out a soft sigh, glancing toward the window where the sunlight dances across the floor. Part of me wants to stay in this quiet pocket of calm forever, but the other part knows I can't hide in here forever.

And I'm starving.

CHAPTER 43

Welcome to Nveri

RAVEN

I'm too hungry to be patient. Just as I'm about to venture out, the door swings open, nearly smacking me in the face.

A woman stands on the other side, all golden hair and flawless, doll-like features. Her effortless smile is the kind that makes you wonder if she's ever had a bad day in her life. "Oh, hello," she chirps, her smile catching me off guard. "I was coming to see if you wanted something to eat. You must be starving. I'm Elle."

I like her already. "Hi!" I mirror her energy with a grin of my own. "I was actually about to go looking for food. I'm Raven, and yes, I'm absolutely *starving*!"

"Perfect! We can stay in here if you'd like or I can take you down to the kitchens?"

"As gorgeous as this room is, I'd love to see *anything* else," I admit, maybe a little too eagerly.

She laughs, "I thought you might." Motioning for me to follow. "Come on, then. Let's get you fed."

I step into the hall, my eyes adjusting to the soft glow lighting the space. It's all understated elegance, with vaulted ceilings and dark-toned stone. I notice a man stationed at the far end of the hall. His stance is rigid, and his expression is unreadable. He nods as we pass, then resumes his statue impersonation.

It takes me a second, but then recognition hits. He's the man I saw with Cam in the woods. The one with the horses.

"Uh... why is he just standing there like that?" I nod back toward him, a little uneasy.

"He's guarding your room," she says matter-of-factly, like it's the most normal thing in the world. "Someone's been outside your door since you got

601

here. Sometimes more than one." She chuckles, shaking her head. "But now that you're awake, maybe they think you can handle yourself."

I narrow my eyes, "Handle myself with what?" *And who's they?* Though, I keep that part to myself for now.

She ignores my question and gives me that same warm smile, like I asked if the sky was blue. "Come on, you'll feel better once you've eaten."

Fine, I'll play along. For now. I'm too hungry to push, and she's probably not the type to spill information anyway.

Her easy chatter distracts me from the simmering unease creeping in. "So," she tilts her head, "what's your favorite food? Or your favorite color? What do you like to do for fun?"

Her curiosity is so genuine it's almost disarming. "Uh, favorite food? Probably pizza. Favorite color is black, but I guess it depends on my mood. And as for fun, I guess I like being outside or reading?" *Boy do I sound like a good time.*

Elle's eyes light up. "You'd love the woods here, then. They're incredible. You'd also really love the library, maybe I'll have to show it to you."

I arch an eyebrow, remembering just how *fun* those woods were the last time I was in there. The library on the other hand, "yeah, I'll take your word for it. The library *does* sound fun though, I'd love to see that."

The place is enormous, by the time we reach the kitchen, I'm positive the place is more castle than house.

The kitchen is warm and bustling with life. The smell of fresh bread hits me first, followed by something sweet that has my mouth watering.

Elle throws her arms out dramatically the second we walk in. "Lynn, take pity on us. We're starving over here!"

A short woman, who looks like she'd beat you with a spatula and the kindest eyes I've ever seen, looks over her shoulder from the stove. Her laugh fills the room. "Help yourselves, ladies. But I don't want to see a single dish left on the counter, Miss Elle."

I can't help but grin as Elle bounces toward the food. The chaos of the last few weeks slips away, replaced by this weird, fragile sense of normalcy.

"Thank you." My voice slips out before I can overthink it. "Everything smells amazing, I wish I knew how to cook like this."

Lynn's laughter is softer this time. "Stick around long enough, and you'll learn a thing or two." Her eyes linger on me for a second too long. They must get a lot of visitors here if she doesn't even bat an eyelash that we're in here.

Elle leans in, and whispers. "She doesn't like to get attached to anyone who might leave. She's a bit of a softy." She winks, handing me a plate. "But, once you're in her good graces? It's free butter cakes, and cinnamon rolls for life."

"Good to know. That's enough motivation to stick around."

Elle grins and nudges me toward the table. "See? You're catching on fast."

I hesitate for half a second before giving in to my overflowing curiosity. "Okay, but where *exactly* is here?" Finally letting the question slip. Maybe she'll actually tell me something useful instead of just tossing me into another round of cryptic bullshit.

"You're in Nveri." Her voice is bright with enthusiasm. "Welcome!" She flashes me another warm smile.

"Maybe while you're here, I can show you around." She continues scooping food onto her plate like we're just two normal people having breakfast. "It's beautiful, the people are amazing, and I really think you'd love it."

I nod slowly, because what else am I supposed to do? Freak out? Throw a plate? Demand an immediate return ticket to Scotland? Not exactly productive. I mean it does sound like a good idea to at least know my way around. Besides, Elle's smile is doing this weird thing where it makes me feel like everything is okay. And less like I should be sprinting the opposite direction.

We eat in silence for a few minutes while the kitchen buzzes around us. It's mesmerizing, honestly. Everyone moves like they're part of some well-oiled machine, seamlessly dodging each other, passing ingredients, handling pots and pans with ease. It's a weird kind of beautiful, watching them work.

CRASH.

The sharp shatter of glass slams through the kitchen, breaking the easy rhythm. I'm embarrassed by the scream that comes out of my mouth, as my head snaps toward the noise. A guy stands frozen over the mess, his hand

603

hovering mid-air, his expression looks like he's deep in concentration. A beat passes, and he *snaps his fingers.*

The broken shards lift from the floor, catching the light as they fly back together, fusing seamlessly into the cup he now holds.

I blink, gasping, as my fork slips from my fingers, only to hit my plate and cause everything to clatter to the floor. The sound is *deafening* in the now-dead-silent kitchen.

I look up and everyone in the kitchen is staring at me, like I'm the most fascinating thing they've seen all morning. *Great. Love that for me.*

Elle, bless her soul, breaks the moment with a perfectly timed distraction. "Lynn, this breakfast is *divine*." She grabs a cinnamon roll off the platter and takes a dramatic bite, sighing like it's the best thing she's ever eaten.

And just like that, the kitchen exhales. The noise resumes. People start moving again, and the moment is over.

I let out a quiet breath, standing so I can clean up the disaster I just made, only to see that there's no mess, like I totally didn't just lose my cool over a little casual magic. *No big deal. Just some casual magic.*

I look over at Elle, who leans in slightly, handing me another plate. Her voice lowers to a whisper. "You'll get used to it."

I give her a look, my pulse still hammering in my throat. "Will I?"

"You're doing great." She grins, but there's something reassuring beneath it. "This place is a whirlwind at first, but you'll find your rhythm."

I don't get the chance to respond before Cam *bursts* into the kitchen like a damn wrecking ball.

"Lynn! Why did I hear that there were cinnamon rolls, and no one told me. Do you even love me anymore?" He heads straight to the counter, snagging a cinnamon roll with the confidence of a man who's done it a thousand times.

"Raven, I was actually just coming to see if you wanted to eat, but it looks like you've already made a friend." He nods toward Elle with a raised brow. "Don't trust a word she says."

My eyes flick to Elle, who gasps, pretending to be offended.

"*Wait, why?*"

"The *real* person you shouldn't be listening to is *this* assface." Elle rips off a piece of her cinnamon roll and chucks it at Cam with expert precision.

He catches it mid-air, and pops it into his mouth without missing a beat, and smiles. "Jealousy doesn't look good on you Ell. But it's okay, most people are."

Lynn, who I've just decided is my favorite person here, waves her spoon in their direction without even turning from the stove. "Don't you make me yell at you in front of this nice girl and scare her off, she doesn't even know how to cook."

Elle and Cam exchange a look before mumbling, "Sorry, Lynn."

Lynn levels me with a look, nodding toward Cam like this is a serious problem. "He doesn't know how to cook either, don't worry."

Cam presses a hand to his chest, gasping like she just accused him of kicking her puppy. "Lynn, that was *one* time—"

"That *was not* one time," Elle cuts in, launching the rest of her cinnamon roll at him.

Cam catches it effortlessly. "You cannot keep throwing food at me and expecting it to solve your problems."

"That's exactly what I expect," she flashes him an innocent smile before turning back to me. "See, Raven? This is what I deal with. Daily."

I can't help the laugh that escapes me. "I like her." I give Cam my best glare, knowing I look anything but angry. "She actually got me food, which was more than I can say for you."

Elle claps, pointing her spoon at Cam like she just won. "Thank you! Can you believe he didn't even think to feed you?"

Cam rolls his eyes in defeat. "Great. Just what I needed."

Elle glances outside and suddenly jumps to her feet with a burst of energy. "I gotta run." She's already halfway to the door when she turns around, and is pulling me into a quick, tight hug. "We're going out later." She declares. "I'll find you."

Then, like a whirlwind, she's gone.

I blink at the now-empty space where she stood. "She's something else, I really like her."

"She's definitely *something*," he mutters, stealing another cinnamon roll. "Don't let her fool you though, she'll drag you into trouble faster than you can blink."

"I love her already."

Cam groans dramatically. "Of course you do. But be careful with her, though," he says casually, brushing crumbs from his hands.

I straighten. "What do you mean?"

He leans against the counter, watching me carefully. "She can read minds."

I freeze, staring at him. "She can *what?*"

Cam holds up a hand, clearly amused by my immediate *what the fuck* reaction. "Relax, she won't do it without your permission. And if she *had* gone digging around in your head, you'd know."

I narrow my eyes. "What do you mean I would know if she had? How do you know she wouldn't?"

Cam watches me carefully, but my mind is already off to the races. *How exactly would I know? Does it hurt? Would she say something? Would she know all the shit running through my head?*

He must see the look on my face because his voice drops into something calmer. "Because she's my sister." He pauses, like that alone should explain everything. "It also means you passed her test."

My stomach twists. "*Test?*" I echo. "Are we just *ignoring* how creepy that sounds?"

His lips twitch. "She'd call it an *evaluation.*"

"I'm not really sure if that makes it better."

I force a small smile, but it doesn't reach my eyes. The idea of someone poking around in my head, even with permission, makes my skin crawl.

"Seriously," he says. "You don't need to worry about it. If she didn't like you, you'd know. She can be terrifying when she wants to be. But you can trust her."

I nod slowly, still trying to process where this conversation went. "Good to know," I mutter, forcing out a half-laugh. "I'll, uh... do my best to stay on her good side."

My mind is spinning with a million questions. "Can everyone do that? Read minds?"

Cam shakes his head, leaning back against the counter, folding his arms. His whole stance shifts into something more casual. "Not necessarily. Everyone's gifts are different," he explains. "Some are more unique and rare. Everyone's level of power, I guess you could say, is different. Some gifts are stronger than others. But the abilities that most of us inherit are accelerated healing, sharper senses, enhanced speed, heightened instincts. It's like breathing for us, it's just second nature."

I arch a brow. "So, you're basically magical superheroes."

His smile returns. "Not quite. And it's not all sunshine and rainbows. Magic comes with its own challenges."

I stare at him, my brain short-circuiting for a solid second before I shove the freak-out to the back of the list. "What can *you* do?"

Cam chuckles, the corner of his mouth curling into a half-smile. "The only impressive one is shifting." He throws that out so casually, like he's telling me about the movie he just watched last night.

"Shifting? Like... full-on *turning* into something else?" My voice rises slightly, somewhere between disbelief and very real concern.

"Exactly." He replies, grinning. "Animals, mostly. People, if I focus. But animals are easier. Less complicated."

I cross my arms, narrowing my eyes. "Prove it."

His grin widens, and for a second, I'm both excited and nervous. "Oh, you want a demonstration?" He steps closer, his expression playful. "I *would*, but... you're not ready for that."

I roll my eyes so hard they practically leave my skull. "Oh, come on. You *cannot* just casually drop that you can *shapeshift* and not show me! That's a total dick move."

He laughs, holding up his hands. "Fine, maybe later."

I open my mouth to argue but snap it shut, still trying to process the absolute insanity of the last few days. I still have so many questions, and he seems to be answering some of them, so maybe I should test my luck.

"Who's the most powerful one here? The king?"

Cam nods, something unreadable flickering across his face. "Aye. He is," he says, but I can tell he's hesitant to answer. "The King's abilities are... unmatched."

I frown. "Why do you say it like that?"

Cam hesitates, his expression tightening. "It's hard to explain. But... powers like that always have a cost."

A chill prickles down my spine. "A cost?"

He nods, the teasing edge in his voice is gone. "That's why he's both revered and feared. People respect him, but they also..." He tilts his head slightly, voice dropping lower. "Tread lightly."

I chew on that for a second before asking the obvious. "So, does that mean he's *dangerous*?"

Cam gives a small, humorless smile. "Anyone with that much power can be dangerous, Raven. It's all about how they choose to wield it."

I exhale slowly. "And what are his powers, exactly?"

Cam's smirk returns, but it doesn't quite reach his eyes. "Anything and everything." He laughs, intentionally vague, yet again. *Well, that wasn't suspicious at all?* But before I can press him further, he smoothly pivots.

"Why don't we go for a walk? I'll show you around."

I arch a brow at the subject change but decide to let it slide. For now. "A walk sounds nice."

He looks at me for a beat, then starts walking down the hall, not waiting to see if I'll follow. "Look, until we know more about you, you're safe here as long as you're with someone. Especially in Nveri." He watches me closely. "The people here won't hurt you, but if you are who I think you are..." His voice trails off, his meaning clear. "It's better to play it safe."

I nod, even though I've only gotten half answers, and I still have so many unanswered questions. *And what the hell does that even mean? Who does he think I am?*

"Okay," is the only thing I can think of to say. Because if I stop moving, if I let myself think too hard, I might actually unravel. I haven't allowed myself to process everything yet, and I know I need to. But it's easier to compartmentalize than to unravel the shitstorm that is my life right now. Is that the healthiest option, probably not. But absolutely necessary for the time being. Until I find out more.

As we walk through the halls, I take in my surroundings, trying to commit everything to memory. The place is unlike anywhere I've ever been. And yet, there's something about it that feels oddly familiar. Not in a way I can place, more like a fragment of a dream, something just out of reach.

Cam's voice pulls me back to the present. "There's so much to tell you, but I'm not sure where to start," he says thoughtfully, his brow furrowing.

"You definitely have magic, that much is obvious. Even while you were asleep, we had a few storms."

I nod, remembering the thunder I heard when I was in and out of consciousness. There were voices too, hushed conversations I caught bits and pieces of. But I keep that to myself.

"Am I going to be allowed to leave?" My voice is barely above a whisper. The thought of being stuck here makes me want to throw up. And honestly, depending on his answer, I might have to come up with an escape plan.

Cam stops walking, turning to face me fully. His hands settle lightly on my shoulders. "Raven." The look on his face is all business. "Of course you can leave. You're not a prisoner here. I just want to make sure you're safe. And that you understand what's happening to you."

The tension in my chest loosens just a little. I know he's keeping things from me, but the sincerity in his tone makes me believe he's telling the truth. "Okay," I nod, but the nervous knot in my stomach lingers. "I just... I don't want to be trapped."

"You're not trapped," he says gently. "There's so much you need to know, Raven. So much you *deserve* to understand about yourself, and about your magic. I promise, I'm here to help you."

I search his face for any trace of deception, but all I find is quiet sincerity. The nervousness doesn't vanish, but something else settles in alongside it. There's a flicker of hope, but I don't want to give it life just yet.

"Alright," I sigh, inhaling deeply. "I'll stay. *For now.* But I need answers, Cam. I need to understand everything." My voice wavers, but I force a smile. "And I'll try my best not to freak out again."

Cam chuckles, giving my shoulders a light squeeze. "One step at a time, okay?" He winks before turning on his heel. "Come on."

I hesitate for a second before following, realizing I don't have much of a choice, since I have no idea where I am. I don't really feel like wandering aimlessly through a place I've never been. Especially since he said I'm safest with someone. I'll do my sneaking at night, when I can hide a little better.

So far, we've walked through endless hallways, turned a few corners, and much to my surprise, entered more hallways that look just as annoyingly gorgeous as the last. The entire place feels like something out of a fairytale, except this one doesn't stay neatly on the pages of a book. This one breathes. People live here.

Cam laughs so suddenly, I nearly jump out of my skin.

"What's so funny?"

"Nothing." He grins, "It's kind of *adorable*, watching you take it all in. It's... different."

I snort, unimpressed. "Oh, so I'm just your entertainment for the day? I guess you're welcome."

"Pretty much," he admits without hesitation, his grin widening.

I roll my eyes but can't stop the small smile tugging at my lips. "I can't believe you have *electricity* here."

He bursts out laughing, clutching his chest like I've just said the most hysterical thing he's ever heard.

"Raven," he wheezes between chuckles, "we aren't *cavemen*. We've actually had it longer, considering we were the ones who showed you guys how to use it."

I shoot him a look. That is definitely something I want to know more about. "I don't know what I expected, but I guess I imagined more... candles and ominous firelight."

"That's still the vibe in some places," he concedes with a shrug. "But no, we like to keep the best of both worlds."

The more we walk, the more questions I ask. And shockingly he answers most of them. We've talked about how Nveri functions, the food I have to try, and the town's marketplace. For a few minutes, it almost feels normal. Like we're just two people casually talking, no magic, no apocalyptic-level revelations hanging over my head, no abnormal storms, and no one is trying to kill me.

CHAPTER 44

I Do it All the Time

RAVEN

"**S**o," he glances at me like he's gauging my reaction. "I know you can fight. What else did your grandparents teach you?"

I pause mid-step, giving him a wide-eyed look.

He raises an eyebrow, smirking. "Oh, so you're *still* sticking to the story that you tripped the night of the ball?"

I open my mouth, ready to deny it, but honestly? I'm tired of hiding things. It's clear he already knows about it. How, I have no clue, but there's no point in pretending anymore if he knows.

With a sigh, I rub the back of my neck. "Umm... I know how to garden?" I start, my throat dry. "I know a lot about herbs and how to use them for pretty much everything." I glance at him, but his face gives nothing away, so I keep going. "I can defend myself with the basic stuff. Um... I know how to meditate, and... I'm really good at swimming."

Cam raises a brow and the look on his face is unreadable. "Well, that's a start." He exchanges a nod to a man walking by. "Listen, I don't know how else to say this, but I want to train you, or at least see what you do know and brush up on a few things, just in case." His voice turns more serious. "I know you might think it's unnecessary, but trust me, it's better to be safe than sorry. And I also want to help you understand your magic. How to use it, how to *control* it. The more we work with it, the easier it'll be to figure out what you're truly capable of. Especially while we're piecing everything together."

I blink, surprised by the offer. "Can we start today?" The words leave my mouth before I can second-guess them. Excitement and nerves hit at the same time. But the idea of sitting around all day, aimlessly waiting for everyone else to figure out what's happening to me... yeah, *not happening*.

Cam smiles, clearly pleased with my enthusiasm. "If you're up for it. How are you feeling? You should actually be back to normal by now."

I hesitate. *Am I ready for this?* Because once I start, once I actually *do* something with *magic*, it's going to make everything feel a hell of a lot more *real*. No more brushing it off as a fluke. No more pretending I can just wake up from this.

But then I think about everything that's happened in the last several months. The unanswered questions, the strange *pull* I've been feeling for weeks, the way I *knew* something was coming before I ever stepped foot here.

I can't keep avoiding it.

"Now that you mention it, I *do* feel good." I square my shoulders. "So yes. Let's do it."

Cam walks me back to my room, and I spot the same man stationed at the end of the hallway. He's still there, his posture solid and alert, standing like some kind of statue. A statue that could kill you.

"Hi, you're doing a great job. It's nice to see you again." I throw in an awkward wave for good measure before glancing at Cam. Lowering my voice, I ask, "Is that really necessary? I thought this place was supposed to be *safe*?"

"You *are* safe," he reassures me. "But that doesn't mean we shouldn't be cautious."

I nod, though the idea of needing a guard outside my room still feels like a lot. And unnecessary if you ask me. If I didn't think he was keeping secrets before, I for sure do now. Why else would I need someone outside of my room? Either they are trying to keep me in, or keep something else out.

"You can change, and I'll be out here when you're ready," Cam adds, catching my questioning look before I can even voice it. "In case you haven't snooped yet, there are clothes in your drawers and probably your closet now too. All courtesy of Elle." He pauses, smirking. "She also said I was a *dick* for not thinking of it earlier."

I snort. "I mean, she's not *wrong*."

He shakes his head, muttering something about how this is his worst nightmare as he starts to walk over to the statue of a man watching over my hallway. He pauses, turning back toward me. "Hurry up, trouble. We've got a long day ahead of us."

I roll my eyes, but a smile tugs at my lips as I step into the room, and head straight to the dresser. I pull the drawers open and find them stuffed with neatly folded clothes. A bit of everything I could possibly need... *and then some.*

Warmth spreads through my chest, catching me off guard. It's a small thing, but knowing someone thought about what I would possibly want and need feels really nice, and also a little unexpected.

I think Rachel and Elle would love each other. Just thinking about Rachel sends a pang of emotion through me. I really miss her, but I'm also relieved that Cam said no one will notice I'm gone. I know if Rachel couldn't get a hold of me she would show up with a pitchfork at Kane's front door.

I giggle at the thought as I grab a pair of leggings and a different top, opting for something easy to move in. I have *no* idea what Cam has planned, and I'm not about to show up unprepared. I throw a sweater over the top, just in case.

When I step back into the hallway, Cam gives me a quick once-over, his eyes flicking over my outfit before giving a short nod of approval. "Good." He turns on his heel, heading down the hallway.

Without a word, I fall into step beside him, the nervous energy buzzing beneath my skin stays quiet for once. My thoughts, however, are a different story. A million questions swirl in my head, tangling and twisting until they're impossible to sort.

We round a corner, and I spot Elle. Her face lights up, pulling me out of my thoughts.

"Hey!" I call, waving.

"I couldn't wait until our date later," she teases, her eyes sparking. Then she takes a second look at me and whistles. "Wait, damn. You look *good* in that."

I barely get the chance to respond before I clock Cam's expression. He's up to something.

"She's here for you," he says, catching my look. "I'm just observing."

My nerves shift into a more familiar territory. Sarcasm. "Oh, so you're afraid I'll hurt you?" I cross my arms, knowing damn well he could kick my ass if he wanted to.

Elle giggles, clapping her hands together. "I absolutely *love* her.

Cam rolls his eyes, but there's the ghost of a smile tugging at the corner of his mouth. "No, *Raven*," he corrects, his voice dropping into something edged with warning. "I'm afraid *I'm* going to hurt *you.*"

I laugh, shaking my head. "Sure. Whatever you say."

I turn back to Elle, about to say something, but before I can get a word out, she *lunges* right for me.

My body reacts on instinct. I twist out of the way just in time, her strike missing me by inches.

What the *fuck?*

She watches me, circling with calculated steps, her lips curling into a knowing smile. "Something you should know," her eyes lock onto mine like a predator sizing up her prey. "Things are different here. You have abilities. If you haven't picked up on that already, you should keep that in mind. Always."

She tilts her head slightly. "Your senses are sharper. Your reflexes are faster. But don't expect that to save you on its own."

Then her tone shifts, like a blade pressing against my skin. "And I'm *not* going to go easy on you. That won't help you in the long run. If someone genuinely wants to kill you, they *will*. They're not going to wait until you're ready."

I don't even have time to respond before she's lunging at me again.

Fuck. She's *fast.*

I throw myself back, barely dodging in time. But I'm off balance. I stumble and the second I do, her knee slams into my stomach.

Pain *explodes* through my ribs, stealing the air from my lungs. I double over, gasping, clutching my stomach as a sharp burn radiates outward.

Shit.

"Move." Elle commands, her voice cutting through the fog. "Get up."

I force myself to straighten, wincing through the ache. "Ow," I mutter, breathless, letting out a laugh.

What the hell am I thinking? My grandfather never went easy on me either. *Why would this be any different?*

I roll my shoulders, adjusting my stance, centering myself. *Your body's a weapon,* he'd always say.

I plant my feet, adjusting my stance. *Fuck it.*

616

Elle doesn't give me a moment more. She moves again, a blur of power and precision. But this time, I'm ready.

I dodge, barely, twisting on instinct. I go left, then strike.

She sidesteps, but not fast enough, my elbow connects with her ribs. Not as hard as I was hoping, but enough to make her *feel* it.

Enough to make her grin.

"Don't hesitate." Her tone is all fire. "Trust your instincts. They'll keep you alive."

And then she's on me again. We spar for what feels like hours, moving seamlessly through the halls, like we've done this forever. At some point, we've made it outside, leaving a *massive* mess in our wake. But now, it's just the two of us. A dance of movement and violence.

I land hits. *Good ones.* A hook to her ribs. A sharp jab to her cheek. A well-placed kick that sends her back a few steps.

But Elle isn't pulling her punches either. My lip splits, and the metallic tang of blood is sharp on my tongue. My brow throbs, and I know that's bleeding too. My ribs ache, my arms burn, and I know I'll have a black eye by morning.

And yet, I feel amazing. I feel alive in a way *I haven't felt in years.* I forgot what this feels like, instinct and skill taking over, letting my body do what I was trained to do. Turns out, all those years weren't wasted.

I shake out my arms, still buzzing on adrenaline, and glance over to see if Cam is there. He's been in and out all day.

Right now, he's standing there watching me. Arms crossed, shoulders tense, and his expression is unreadable. But it's not his usual smirk, not that cocky amusement I've come to expect. No, this is different. His gaze lingers, sharp and assessing, like he's *actually* seeing me for the first time.

"Not bad, bitch." Elle says, wiping a streak of sweat from her brow, her grin stretching from ear to ear. "You're stronger than you look."

Then her stance shifts, and I know she's not done with me yet. My body tenses in anticipation.

"But," she continues, cracking her knuckles, rolling her shoulders like she's just getting warmed up. "You could use some work."

She explodes forward. Faster than before.

I move, but she's already there. A first slams into my chin, a brutal, punishing strike that has my head whipping to the side, and I can taste blood in my mouth. Pain lances through me, as she twists, using the force of the first hit to drive her knee into my stomach.

Ow.

The impact knocks the wind from my lungs, and I'm on my back. Stars burst behind my eyelids as the cold dirt presses against my spine.

She drops down, pinning me in a second, her forearm pressing against my throat, hard enough to remind me that she could easily end it right here if she wanted to.

Her grin is still there, but it's calculated.

"This," she breathes, barely winded, "is why you need training."

I glare up at her, sucking in air between gritted teeth, my whole-body aches, but I don't break eye contact. I'm not sure if we're going to stop, but I'm sure as hell not going to be the one to tap out.

She studies me for a beat longer, and just like that, she's off of me.

I roll onto my side, coughing, trying to push myself upright. Cam, *the asshole*, is laughing now. He definitely enjoyed that.

Elle extends a hand, and after a second, I take it. She hauls me up easily, gripping my hand.

"You did good," she says. "But you hesitate a lot."

I scowl, running a hand over my jaw.

Tomorrow should be fun. Elle laughs, tossing an arm around my shoulder like she didn't just wreck me. "Tomorrow? Same time?"

I swallow hard, resisting the urge to ask if she was reading my thoughts. I trust her, at least, Cam says I should, but the way she looks at me makes me feel stripped down to the bone. Exposed.

Because she's *right*.

I have been holding back. Not just in this, but in everything. Always in control, always keeping myself contained, afraid of what might happen if I *let go*.

But now I'm starting to wonder if holding back is what's going to get me killed.

"And no, I don't need to read your mind to know that," Elle adds, laughing. "It's obvious in the way you move."

I arch a brow, turning to face Cam. "You good over there?"

"He's just surprised." She teases, sidestepping Cam as he throws her an annoyed glare. "Which, by the way, is *extremely* hard to accomplish. He didn't think you could do any of that. He thought you were just a *pretty face*."

Cam's head snaps toward her, eyes narrowing with warning. "Elle." His tone is lethal. "Get. Out. Of. My. Head."

"You let your walls down." She gins. "That's on you."

I cross my arms, giving Cam my best smile. "A *pretty face, huh*?"

His reaction is immediate. A muscle ticks in his jaw, but his expression remains blank. But his eyes flash with something dark for just a second before that mask slips right back into place.

"That's *not* exactly what I was thinking." He exhales, rolling his shoulders. "But I'll admit it, I *am* impressed. Not many people can go against Elle and walk away on their own."

There's a reluctant admiration in his tone. Not sure what that's about, but I don't have the capacity to care right now.

"Do you read people's minds during a fight?" I'm not even going to pretend I'm not dying to know.

She smiles, tossing her hair over her shoulder like she's in a damn commercial. "Not exactly," she says with a wink. "Well, yes and no." She shifts on her feet, energy crackling in the air. "In a real fight? *Absa-fucking-lutely* I'll use it. Survival over fairness, always. But training? Nah. That's boring." She winks. "I love proving I can win *without* it. It's so much more satisfying."

I nod, still reeling from the casual *yeah I could've read your thoughts, but I didn't.* She laughs. "But don't worry, I didn't peek inside your head during our little scuffle. I wanted to see what you could do without the advantage. And you, my dear, are *dangerously* underestimated."

Cam groans, dragging a hand down his face. "Elle, could you *not* inflate her ego any more than it already is?"

I grin, completely unfazed. "Oh you mean, *the ego that goes with my pretty face?*"

Elle cackles and Cam exhales slowly. He levels Elle with a look. "To answer your question, people don't beat Elle, because she's one of our *Commanding Officers,*" He says, voice edged with something close to pride. "And she's *nearly* impossible to beat."

My head snaps toward Elle, my stomach flipping. "Wait, *WHAT*?"

She nods, entirely unbothered. "Looks like I might have to train with you more often, since everyone else is too afraid to get hurt."

Then, like she didn't just casually ruin my day, she winks. "Anyway, good game. Raincheck for our night out. Trust me, you'll thank me later. Take a bath and use the hazy lavender bottle."

Then she turns and bounces down the walkway.

Beside me, Cam exhales, shaking his head. "You did good, Rae."

The nickname sends a flicker of warmth through my chest, curling around something fragile. A tingle rushes down my spine, and I swallow hard, blinking rapidly to push back the sudden swell of emotion.

I shift my gaze to the horizon, where the sun is dipping below the hills. Never in a million years did I picture my life turning out like this. Coming to Scotland, meeting these people, feeling this strange, undeniable pull toward a world I never knew existed.

And the wildest part is... I don't want to leave. For whatever reason, being here feels right.

I inhale deeply, forcing my voice into something lighter. "So when do I get to kick your ass?"

Cam chuckles, shaking his head. "Let's save that for another day." He picks up my sweater, handing it to me. "If you're up for it, we could try something different before dinner. Maybe a little magic?"

"Yes!" I blurt out, far too eager.

Cam laughs outright, shaking his head as he turns toward the castle. "Let's go, dork."

We've been sitting in his office for the last hour, and nothing has happened.

I exhale sharply, resisting the urge to bang my head against the desk.

First, we meditated. Then, Cam led me through some simple energy exercises. And still, nothing. No tingling hands. No sparks of power. *No inexplicable holy shit moments.*

Just... nothing.

And I *hate* that I'm this disappointed.

I was starting to warm up to the idea that maybe all of this was real. That maybe I was something more than I thought, and maybe I belonged here. I had hoped this would give me the answer I needed about what's been happening to me.

Cam did say I couldn't have entered this place if I didn't have magic. So where the hell is it?

"Rae."

Cam's voice cuts through my thoughts, sharp enough to snap me back into the moment.

I blink. "What? Sorry, I was just... thinking."

His eyes narrow slightly, but his voice stays even. "It's in there, don't worry, I can feel it."

I *want* to believe him. But right now, his reassurance doesn't do much to untangle the frustration knotting in my chest.

"You can sense it?" I pause, thinking. "Could you before?"

"If I hadn't been so shocked to see you that first night, I would've picked up on it then." His brows pull together slightly, like he's piecing it together in real-time. "But when you were sleeping, when the storms were happening, I felt it again. I could *smell* it. I knew it was your magic. So yeah, it's in there."

My stomach flips. A sharp, uneasy prickle runs down my spine.

I grab his arm before I realize what I'm doing, my grip tight. "*Smell* me?"

Cam frowns, clearly puzzled by my reaction. I can barely breathe.

The memory slams into me, a voice in the dark, low and mocking. *"I can smell you."* My heart stumbles, and my pulse spikes replaying the night of the attack on the street. The lights shattering. His scream. All of it coming back in vivid detail.

Cam's eyes widen. "He said he could *smell* you?" His tone turns razor-sharp, all casual amusement gone. "Why the *fuck* didn't that come up before?"

I blink, coming back to the present. "Wait, I thought you said you couldn't read minds?"

I stand up, the familiar buzz in my fingertips starts to spread up my arms.

621

His frown vanishes and is replaced by a smug grin. "I can smell you right now."

I recoil. "That's... ew. Wait, what the hell do you mean?"

"It means," Cam leans back, absolutely thriving off my confusion, " ... you did it!"

"I did what? What exactly did I do?"

He laughs, looking shocked. "I think you just showed me." He gestures between us. "With your thoughts." He shakes his head, eyes gleaming. "I have no clue how you managed to just do that, I'm not even sure you meant to..."

He trails off, his voice is filled with an excitement that I can't place. I didn't *do* anything.

"That's extremely rare, by the way. Not many people can do that. *Interesting*."

I barely hear him. My mind is spinning too fast. And then, I feel it. A strange, intense pull blooms in my chest, spreading like wildfire. The tingling spreads past my arms, and I can feel it in my whole body.

Cam notices the shift immediately. His amusement is replaced with something else.

"Talk to me, what's happening?" His voice drops lower, calmer now, but still all business.

"My whole body feels..." I hesitate, searching for the right words. "Tingly. And my hands are heating up. I feel this... pressure in my chest." I glance down at my hands, half-expecting them to glow. "But this kinda happens a lot."

He freezes and his entire demeanor shifts, and his voice dips into something darker. He leans forward, his full focus locking onto me. "Let's back up for just a second, the man who attacked you," he says slowly, each word carrying weight. "What exactly did he say? *Start to finish*."

I blink, thrown off by the intensity of his reaction.

"Uh, he said..." my throat tightens, the memory too real. "He could smell me. Called me reckless. Sounded... disgusted." My pulse thrums in my ears. "And that I was exactly who they've been looking for."

Cam doesn't move. Doesn't blink. The silence that follows is deafening. He launches to his feet so fast his chair scrapes back across the floor, hard enough to shake the desk.

My stomach plummets, because I already know that whatever he's about to say is not good. When he finally speaks it's calm, his usual mask securely back in place.

"And you didn't think to mention this *sooner*?" His tone isn't outright accusing, but there's an edge to it that's sharp enough to cut.

I wince, arms crossing automatically over my chest. "I didn't know it was important," I snap, defensively. "I just thought he was a creep who had me confused with someone else."

Cam exhales slowly through his nose. "That explains a lot, actually." His voice drops lower, talking more to himself now. "Explains why he said he could smell you. If your magic's spilling out of control, that's what he was picking up on."

His jaw tightens. "And if you're radiating like that..." He trails off, muttering a quiet, "*Shit.*"

A pit forms in my stomach. "What does that mean?"

Cam's shoulders set. When he looks at me again, there's a crack in his expression, and it looks a lot like worry. "It means," he sighs, "you've been using magic for longer than just today. And you've been lighting yourself up like a Christmas tree to anyone who knows what to look for."

His words land like a punch. I open my mouth, then shut it again. Because what the hell am I even supposed to say to that?

The heat flares in my hands, so suddenly, that I suck in a breath. A tingling sensation rolls under my skin, snaking through my fingertips like electricity searching for an exit.

The air around me shifts. The kind of heavy, expectant silence before a storm.

My pulse kicks up, fast and frantic. I glance at Cam, hoping for some kind of direction.

But he's already looking around. His entire stance is alert as he looks toward the windows. I can hear a low rumbling off in the distance.

I swallow hard, my throat suddenly tight.

"What do I do?" My voice is too high, panic licking at the edges of my control as the tingling spreads. My hands are on fire now, like I'm holding onto something that's desperate to escape.

And Cam chuckles. Actually *chuckles.*

623

I glare at him, not seeing how any of this is remotely funny.

"Close your eyes." His voice is annoyingly calm. "Focus on your breathing. Everything we just practiced. You've got this."

I try. I really do, but the sensation is too much.

A sharp prick stabs at my nose. I inhale quickly, reaching up on instinct and when I pull my hand away, my fingers come away streaked with red. A bloody nose is not what I need right now.

I snap my eyes to Cam, but my vision wavers. He's saying something, his lips are moving, and his eyes are locked on me. But I can't hear him.

The buzzing in my skull rises to a roar, drowning out everything.

Every window in the room shatters as glass explodes everywhere and papers whip through the air.

A strange, unnatural calm settles over me, and it feels wrong in a way I can't explain. It creeps into my limbs, curling through my veins like fog, thick and suffocating.

My body sways, the last shreds of energy draining from me and my lips twitch into something faintly like a smile.

Because I know this feeling. It's Cam's magic.

My head tilts slightly, the weight of exhaustion pulling me under.

Cam's voice is the only thing that cuts through the void. It's soft, and steady. Anchoring me in the chaos.

"I got you, Rae."

CHAPTER 45

Fortnight

RAVEN

I t's been a few days since my last incident.

There's been... several.

The days have turned into weeks, but Cam still assures me that no one knows I'm gone. It's always the same *'time works differently here'* excuse.

Training with Elle all day has left my muscles screaming in protest, a dull ache settles into every inch of me. Cam's been off doing something *important*. At least, that's what Elle said when she walked me to my room earlier. She also casually mentioned she had plans tonight she couldn't get out of, then added that dinner would be brought to me.

A quiet, relaxing evening alone is a miracle around here.

After spending far too long in the bath, probably pushing the limits of humans and magical tolerance, I finally drag myself out. The oil Elle recommended is laced with magic, literally, and it helps speed up the healing process, drastically. I call it the *lavender haze*.

The moment I'm done putting on comfortable clothes and settle in for what I hope will be an uneventful night, there's a knock at the door.

That must be dinner.

Except when I open it, it's not dinner. Tyler leans casually against the doorframe, looking like he's been waiting there forever.

"Hey, beautiful." He grins.

For a second, the memory of running into him here for the first time flashes through my mind. That day had been...a *shock*, to say the least.

It was the day after the incident in Cam's office, when I showed him my thoughts. Something I still can't get over, and haven't been able to do since. When I woke up, Tyler was sitting there, lounging like he was enjoying a day off. I hadn't seen him since that night at the bar when Rachel and I first played them in darts, so seeing him here was not what I was expecting. I accidentally almost punched him.

The first thing I heard was, *"Hey, beautiful."* Followed by, *"Cam's off doing Cam stuff, guess you're stuck with me today."* Stretching like he had all the time in the world.

Apparently, he'd been assigned as my babysitter for the day. And the several days that followed. I didn't mind, though, we had a lot of fun together. He actually answered my questions, and would come with me when I wanted to sneak around.

That whole first day, we just threw sharp things at each other. Which, honestly? Has been my favorite activity so far. Mostly because I hadn't thrown a knife since I was a kid.

He learned quickly not to underestimate me. His first attempt to *test my skills* ended with my knife sinking dead center in the target before he even started his *lesson* on how to throw a knife.

After that, things escalated quickly and he started to get creative.

Tyler learned the hard way, that I don't miss. He stood there, with an apple perched on his head, grinning like a damn fool. Overconfident and smug. I told him it was a terrible idea, and he told me that he was confident I would miss.

That image will haunt me forever. That was also the first time I saw firsthand how their fast healing worked.

One second the knife was sticking out of his forehead, blood everywhere. The next? Nothing but smooth skin and that same cocky smirk.

He had the audacity to laugh it off while I stood there, crying.

We spent hours like that, laughing, baiting each other, until the sky outside bled into deep purples and golds. Then we'd sit down to dinner, getting way too creative with ways to prank Cam and inevitably getting scolded for the mess.

So the fact that he's standing in my doorway now, tells me all I need to know.

"Babysitting duty?" I tease, raising an eyebrow as Tyler strolls in like he's got nothing better to do.

"No way." He shoots back with a grin. "Besides, you know you'd rather hang out with me than be alone. Don't lie." He tugs a cart behind him, fully loaded with food. "Dinner? And I brought the Fae wine, in case I needed to bribe you."

"You convinced me."

We settle into our comfortable rhythm while we eat. Then out of nowhere, he asks, "Do you ever miss being over there?"

I pause, swirling my drink, considering.

"You know," I say finally, "I've never really loved being glued to my phone all the time. It's nice here. No alarms, no bills to pay, no schedules, no emails telling me what I should be doing. I don't have to care what time it is or live by someone else's expectations. It's just... me. Doing my own thing. On *my* time."

Tyler watches me, something unreadable flickering behind his eyes. Then, he slowly nods.

"It suits you." His voice suddenly sincere. "You look free, I guess. Happier."

His lips twitch into a smile, the kind that makes it impossible to tell if he's being serious or setting up for another joke. "It looks good on you, Bird."

I roll my eyes, but warmth pools in my chest despite my best efforts.

"Don't start," I warn, but he just laughs, leaning back in his chair with entirely too much charm for someone who's just sitting.

I'm not going to lie, it took me a few days to get used to how good-looking everyone is around here. You get used to it, but every once in a while, I still get caught staring. Which everyone finds hilarious—especially when it's at Tyler. Tall, and built like he was carved from stone, with that effortless, cocky charm and dark blonde hair that's always messy. Tattoos wind down his arms, cutting over muscle in a way that I really don't want to notice. He's a walking distraction. And yeah, maybe I stared a little too long once or twice. It was enough to earn teasing that I will never live down.

"I still don't know how humans do it every day," he continues, shaking his head. "Wake up, eat, work, come home, *Netflix and chill*, repeat. Sounds like torture."

He pauses, tilting his head as if reconsidering. "Some things over there *are* quite amazing, though." He admits.

He's been calling me *Bird* since the moment I woke up that day, and the first time, I'd nearly choked on my drink, which, of course, only made him double over in laughter. Turns out, he was the one who called me that the night of the ball. Something he confessed with zero remorse.

He still swears he knew I had magic from day one.

I still don't believe him.

Tyler never had to worm his way into my heart, he just strolled right in like he belonged there. And now I can't imagine him not being here.

His usual playful demeanor shifts, and he straightens, his warm hand closing around mine. "You know I'm here for you, right?"

I meet his eyes, the sincerity in them makes my breath catch.

"Always." The single word carrying a weight I didn't realize I needed to hear. A promise he makes without hesitation.

I open my mouth to respond, but the intensity of his gaze roots me to the spot. Instead, I nod, my throat too tight for words, and offer him a small smile. It's all I can manage, but from the way his expression softens slightly, he understands.

A comfortable silence stretches between us, while we finish eating.

I thought those tequila shots were strong. The Fae wine is next level. That will fuck you up if you have too much. I found that out the hard way the first time Tyler gave it to me. Everyone else got a kick out of it. Even though Cam forbade him to ever give me more than a glass. I will say, the taste is so much better than the liquor in Scotland. It tastes exactly like grape juice.

"You know what's wild?" He refills both our glasses with wine.

I blink at him, wary of the sudden shift. "What?"

He leans back in his chair, tilting it onto two legs. "As good as you are at stabbing things, you're the worst at sneaking around."

I snort. "We get caught, because you talk too much."

He gasps, clutching his chest like I wounded him. "I do *not* talk too much! I talk just the right amount. You just have commitment issues."

I roll my eyes. "Oh my God. What does that have to do with anything?"

"No, hear me out." He insists, grinning now. "You're one of those people who thinks they can just go through life solo, you're all... *I don't need anyone, I'm totally fine on my own,* but really, if you just learned how to trust people..."

I pause. "Tyler, I don't know if trusting people will make me better at sneaking around."

"My point is, you have all of us, even though you don't want to let us in. But I think you like us." He takes a big drink, then sets his glass down, wiping his mouth.

I open my mouth to argue, but...

Shit.

He's right. I've gotten really close to all of them since being here. Even Lynn has taught me some things in the kitchen during our morning breakfast routine together. Yet, I still find it hard to trust them with things. It's hard to let them in when I know they're all keeping secrets from me still. Despite that, I really do like them all.

Tyler grins, clearly reading my expression. "See? Told you."

I sigh, leaning my elbow on the table. "Fine. Maybe I do like *some* of you."

Tyler claps his hands together. "A win's a win."

The weight in my chest eases, the heaviness of the last few days shifting into something lighter. I don't know how he does it, but he has a knack for making things feel a little less impossible.

I stretch my legs out under the table, shooting him a knowing look. "You're a pain in the ass, you know that?"

He leans back in his chair with a smug grin. "A pain in the ass you can't live without."

I roll my eyes. "I take it back. I *hate* you."

He laughs, tipping his head back, but when he straightens, I can see the worry in his eyes. "You ever think about what comes next?"

I frown. "What do you mean?"

He exhales, running a hand through his hair. "I mean... all of this. The training, the magic, all the shit you've been looking for. You ever stop and think about what it actually means for you? You know, like if you're going to stick around?"

The question sits heavy between us, pressing into my ribs like a weight I don't know how to carry yet. I don't answer right away, because the truth is, I don't know the answer.

Instead, I swirl my drink, watching the liquid spin as I gather my thoughts. *I guess I've been trying not to think too far ahead.* "Everything's happening so fast, and it's easier to just focus on the step right in front of me instead of trying to piece together some grand, life-altering destiny I didn't ask for. Ya know? Besides, I doubt I'm the girl everyone thinks I am."

Tyler nods, his usual teasing nowhere to be found. His gaze flickers with something I can't place. "Fair enough."

There's something I've been dying to ask him, and he seems to be in a chatty mood. So here goes nothing. "Why haven't I met him yet?"

His brow furrows. "Who?"

I shrug, hoping he doesn't notice how casual I'm trying to be. "The King. Or the Queen?"

The air in the room tightens.

He sets his drink down, but the way his jaw ticks tells me I've hit a nerve. "What do you mean?"

"I mean... I've been here for weeks. I've met a bunch of people. I've been training, learning, figuring out whatever the hell is going on with me. But he's supposed to be the one in charge around here, right?" I tilt my head, still trying to piece it together, but coming up short. "Shouldn't he be involved in some way? Shouldn't I have seen him around by now?"

Tyler holds my stare for a long second before looking away, drumming his fingers against the table. "The King... doesn't get involved in things unless he *wants* to."

I narrow my eyes. "That's a vague non-answer. What the fuck Tyler?"

His lips twitch, but the amusement doesn't reach his eyes. "That's the only answer you're getting."

The Fae wine is making my brain slower, or maybe it's making me too aware, because something about his response doesn't sit right with me. He's usually pretty open when I ask him questions.

I lean forward, setting my drink down. "What aren't you telling me?"

Tyler exhales sharply through his nose, shaking his head like he's regretting even entertaining this conversation. "You should drop it, Bird." The nickname comes out as a warning this time.

Which only makes me more curious.

"Tyler." I fix him with a pointed stare. "You know something."

He hesitates. Just for a second, but that's all I needed to know. Just more secrets. More lying.

His eyes shoot to the window and my stomach is in knots. I can hear the thunder in the distance.

"Look," he says, his voice quieter now. "The King isn't just some guy sitting on a throne, making decisions about taxes and trade deals." He lifts his drink again but doesn't sip. "He's not someone you seek out. If he wants to see you, he'll find you."

My pulse picks up. "So why hasn't he?"

Tyler finally meets my eyes, and something dark flickers behind them. "Maybe, he already has."

A chill rolls down my spine as Tyler tips his drink back, the conversation apparently over.

Whatever he's not telling me, I'm going to find out.

The days pass, blending seamlessly into one another as I settle into a routine that's both exhausting and strangely satisfying.

I wake up to the soft glow of dawn filtering through my window, the air crisp with a promise of a new day. After a quick breakfast, it's straight to training with Elle.

Most days, she hands me my ass without breaking a sweat. Turns out, she really was going easy on me that first day, and hasn't let me forget. Her sessions are brutal, designed to push every limit I thought I had, and then push them further. Every punch, every dodge, every swing of a blade carves away at the weaker version of myself.

Despite the intensity, I can feel the difference. My reflexes are sharper, my movements more deliberate. I'm getting stronger, faster, more in tune with my instincts. It's not just physical though, there's something deeper, a connection beginning to hum beneath my skin, like my mind and body are finally on the same page.

Elle, of course, doesn't let me dwell on it for too long.

"Focus, Rae!" She shouts, and I barely dodge her next swing.

When training is finally over. Tyler joins us for a much-needed lunch break. It's the only time of day we're all together, and they're not trying to teach me something. Which mostly means they spend it teasing me about how much I still have to learn.

Once lunch is over, it's time for my daily session with Cam.

These moments are usually a lot quieter, and a lot less laughing. Which is ironic, because Cam is usually always the one cracking jokes.

He has a way of balancing his natural confidence with an impressive amount of patience. He walks me through exercises designed to help me tap into my abilities, guiding me step by step as I struggle to find that control.

"It's about intention," he reminds me as he watches my frustration grow. "You have to feel it, direct it, own it."

There are days when my frustration boils over, where nothing clicks, when I question everything. But Cam never wavers. He always stays calm. He's a damn good teacher.

Slowly, bit by bit, I've begun to see progress. Not massive breakthroughs, but small victories that felt monumental. It feels like a win, a flicker of control over something I barely understood weeks ago.

By dinner, I'm usually so exhausted I can barely lift my fork, but Cam always insists I eat. Either Cam or Lynn is scolding me for not eating enough.

"You won't make it through tomorrow if you don't fuel your body." His tone never leaves any room for argument. I honestly just laugh it off, because truthfully I'm always starving. Exhausted, but starving.

Most nights, I'm asleep before my head even hits the pillow, my body wrecked from the intensity of the day. But for the first time in a long time, the exhaustion feels earned.

I've been here for nearly eight weeks now, and while I've grown to love this place, the people, my routine, and all my progress, I can't shake the feeling that it might be time to go back.

Surely enough time has passed that Kane must be wondering where I've gone. I'm assuming even by now, I have messages from Rachel.

Cam, for the millionth time assured me that isn't the case, but still, the nagging thought lingers.

So last night, I decided to try sneaking out *again* to find answers, only this time without Tyler. Despite what he says about me needing to realize I have people, he does talk too much, and Kody always catches us because of it.

Just when I think we're about to find something, Kody appears. Like he's waiting for us, or he knows exactly where to look. I'm starting to think Tyler rats us out.

I know I'm good at sneaking around, considering I did it all the time with my grandparents, when they thought I wasn't listening.

I waited until the halls were empty, and Kody was looking the other way, sticking to the shadows. I want to try to find where the King and Queen stay. Maybe if I can just get a peak. I can't get what Tyler said out of my head. *He'll find me if he wants to? No thanks.*

Why let me stay here, leave me in the dark, then do absolutely nothing about it?

The castle is massive, an endless maze of hallways and shadowed alcoves. I moved carefully, keeping to the edges, pressing myself against the walls whenever I heard the faintest sound of movement. The air was heavy with the kind of silence that feels too still, like the entire place was holding its breath along with me. It was the longest I'd gone without getting caught.

Every door I tried was locked.

Every hallway stretched into more dimly lit nothing.

I somehow stumbled into a hallway I hadn't been down before, and at one point, I thought I heard something, voices echoing from somewhere beneath me. But the moment I turned the corner, they vanished.

I was just about to turn the knob of the *first* door that wasn't unlocked when I hear footsteps.

I pressed myself into the shadows, waiting, praying that it wasn't Kody.

The footsteps disappeared down the hall and I genuinely thought I was onto something. I opened the door and it was just an empty room with two doors in it. Both locked.

Except when I quietly closed the door, and turned around, I ran right into Kody.

He stood there with his arms crossed, like he'd been waiting for me.

"Are you serious?"

Kody didn't even flinch. Didn't even look surprised. He just shook his head slightly, like he'd expected to see me.

Then with a tired sigh, he said, "Come on, kid. I'm impressed you made it this far."

In quieter moments, usually in the mornings before Elle bursts into my room declaring I've had *more than enough beauty sleep*, my thoughts always seem to drift to Kane.

It's not intentional, but he's there, on the edge of my mind.

There are more times than I'll ever admit out loud, that I've sunk into the bath, the warm water loosening my muscles and my thoughts wandering straight to that night in the library.

I think about the way he looked at me, the way he touched me, the way his voice always sent a slow-burning heat through my veins. And it always leaves me both longing and incredibly sexually frustrated.

One particularly heated memory had me taking matters into my own hands, and even that hadn't been enough to satisfy the ache.

I don't know how it happened, but... I miss him.

Despite missing Kane, I've grown really close to everyone here. So most of the time when I think about Kane, I think about leaving here and I'm always torn. I've even grown close to Kody. The man who barely acknowledged me when I first got here. *He's just doing his job,* they told me. And yet, somehow, I wore him down. Turns out, he has a surprisingly witty sense of humor. *Guess sneaking out did some good after all.*

On nights when I can't sleep he's always there, leaning casually against the wall. With his arms crossed, ready with some dry remark that never fails to make me laugh.

Our late-night chats have become something I've come to love.

He pretends to be annoyed when I disturb his *work,* but I've caught the amusement in his eyes more than once, especially when we start talking about sports and *Aristotle,* which I find absolutely hilarious.

He'll insist I go back to bed, grumbling about how I'll regret being tired the next morning, but I can tell he secretly enjoys our talks. I know I do.

Most of our conversations fall into me teasing him about his overly serious demeanor, and him throwing it right back with a perfectly timed comment about how if I spent more time learning about magic than harassing him, I wouldn't be awake in the middle of the night.

But last night, when he caught me sneaking around again, something was different. I don't know what it is, but I know I'm getting closer to things they don't want me to know.

That's why, right now, while I'm sitting in Cam's office, Cam's empty office, the urge to snoop is *impossible* to ignore.

He's always here first, ready to start. The fact that he isn't here yet, feels like an opportunity I'm not going to miss.

I haven't seen much of this place beyond where Cam, Elle, and Tyler keep me confined with their relentless routine.

For all the space I assume this place must have, my world here feels... *small*.

Even the amount of people I interact with are limited.

So right now, standing alone, the need to know something outweighs common sense. I glance around the room and it's surprisingly sparse. No photographs. No trinkets. Nothing personal at all. Like the space is designed to give nothing away.

A thought creeps in, one I've had before but shoved aside.

Could Cam be the King?

I've never heard anyone mention the king by name. And every time Cam disappears, it's brushed off as him doing *Cam stuff*, which feels like a convenient excuse.

It would explain a lot. His authority. The way people defer to him. The way his responsibilities pull him away at the most unpredictable times.

I shake my head, laughing softly to myself, trying to shake the thought. Ridiculous. Right?

Except, nothing about this place has been normal. And if anyone could keep a secret like that, it'd be Cam.

I wander toward the nearest shelf, trailing my fingers along the spines of the books. Most are in languages I don't recognize, their titles written in intricate, looping scripts that look more decorative than practical.

Curiosity gets the better of me, and I pull one at random, flipping it open.

The text is dense, packed tightly into the pages. I don't understand a single word, and just skimming it makes my head spin. Hard pass. I turn the page to see if there's anything else and give myself a paper cut. I close the book and put it back on the shelf.

"Ow." I whisper, putting my finger in my mouth.

Still, the feeling lingers, knowing that there's so much I don't know about this place or the people in it. I keep snooping around, but the room itself is unhelpfully vague. *Shocker*. That seems to be the theme of my life lately.

I let out a slow breath, my fingers idly trace the spine of a book as my mind drifts back to Cam.

Could he really be hiding something that big?

There's a difference between being private and being calculated, and the longer I'm here, the more I wonder if there's more to Cam that he lets on.

It's not paranoia if the pieces fit, right?

The thought lingers, pressing in heavier the longer I stand here, piecing together fragments of conversations I've overheard and subtle shifts in the way people act around him. The way he disappears without warning.

The door swings open and I jump slightly, schooling my expression like I *wasn't* just blatantly snooping.

Cam strides in like he owns the place, because maybe he *actually* does.

He looks slightly out of breath, his usual composure just off enough to make my stomach flip. His hair is tousled, like he's been running his hands through it, and there's a faint flush on his cheeks that tells me he's been doing something that requires some effort.

"Raven."

The way he says my name like he knows exactly what I was up to makes my nerves spark. His gaze sweeps the room before settling fully on me. "Sorry I'm late. Got caught up in something."

I straighten, shoving down the nagging questions clawing at my throat. "No worries." I watch him closely, trying to read between imaginary lines. "Everything okay?"

He exhales, rolling his shoulders like he's shaking off whatever just happened. "Yeah, just had to... handle some things."

His voice is distant enough that it only makes me more suspicious. He's being intentionally vague, *again*.

His eyes dip to my necklace and come right back to mine. "Where did you get that necklace?"

"My grandparents gave it to me," I say, reaching up to touch it, the metal is warm beneath my fingers. A familiar comfort.

He studies it, fingers grazing his jaw as if working through something in his head. "Interesting."

I let out a soft chuckle, trying to ease the strange tension that's settled between us. "Is it?"

His eyes flicker back to mine. "It looks familiar, is all."

A prickle of unease slides down my spine. *Familiar?* How would this look familiar to him?

"Cam, I have something to ask..." I hesitate, then just say it. "Are you the King?"

He bursts out laughing, head tipping back like I just said the funniest shit he's ever heard. The tension evaporates in a single breath, his entire body shaking with amusement.

"Fuck no, I'm not."

That was a lot of laughter for what should've been a simple no. If he's telling the truth, then I'm right back to knowing nothing.

He shakes his head. "I'm the King's right hand, though. Have been since before he was even King. But no, I'm *definitely* not him."

That explains... something. Or at least, it *should*. But the relief I feel is almost drowned out by the dozen new questions flooding my brain.

"Then where are the King and Queen?" I ask, grasping at whatever scraps of information I *do* know, desperate to make sense of something in this place where everything feels just out of reach.

Cam's laughter fades, something guarded settling in its place. There's a flicker of something in his eyes but it's gone too fast to pin down.

"That's... a complicated question." His voice is quiet, and I almost step closer just so I can hear him. "The King is... handling business matters."

He hesitates, exhaling as his hand runs through his hair.

"And the Queen?"

Cam's jaw clenches just enough for me to notice.

"There is no Queen."

No Queen? "Why not? What happened to her?"

His posture goes rigid. The air in the room shifts, and it feels like something is sitting on my chest.

"It's a long story, Raven." He says it like he's done talking about it. "One that's not mine to tell. But I promise, when the time is right, you'll know what you need to."

That... sounds a hell of a lot like another non-answer.

A part of me wants to push past whatever wall he's clearly putting up, but the look in his eyes tells me it's pointless.

Don't get me wrong, I'm grateful for everything they've done for me, but I'm getting *really fucking* tired of all the secrets.

I see the way they exchange glances when they think I'm not looking. The silent conversations before I step into a room. The way Elle, who normally has no filter, suddenly chooses her words carefully around me.

They think I don't notice. But I do.

CHAPTER 46

You're Kidding Right?

RAVEN

"Are you ready to get started? We're heading outside today." Cam strolls into his office, setting down a stack of papers.

I take a deep breath. "Yeah. Let's do it."

Cam flashes me a reassuring smile before gesturing toward the open door.

The sunlight is warmer today, golden rays spilling through the canopy, streaking across the clearing in shifting patterns. The breeze carries hints of wildflowers, pine, and earth, grounding me even as my nerves hum with anticipation.

We step into the open space at the edge of the trees, and Cam stops turning to face me. "I want you to try to create a storm."

I blink. "*What?*"

"You heard me."

A breathless laugh escapes me before I can stop it. "Cam, I can't." I shake my head, I haven't been able to create a storm since the last incident in his office, when I broke all the windows.

"You've got to be kidding. I can't just... *summon a storm*."

He tilts his head, completely unfazed. "Of course you can," he says, like it's the most obvious thing in the world. "You've done it before, whether you meant to or not. Now, I want you to focus. To *try*."

My jaw tightens as I exhale through my nose. "That was different. I wasn't trying before. It just happened."

"And now I'm asking you to stop waiting for it to happen and own it." His voice doesn't waver, and the look in his eyes tells me he isn't going to back down without a fight. "You control your magic, Raven. Not the other way around. But you need to *believe* that."

643

I huff, rubbing my hands together, the familiar prickle of energy just beneath my skin. "Fine."

I close my eyes and do what I've been doing for weeks. Focus inward. I bring my attention to my hands, where the buzz of energy hums like an unspoken promise, waiting. Slowly, I coax it forward, imagining it spreading through my body like ripples across water.

The tingling sensation crawls up my arms, down to the tips of my toes.

But the harder I try to grab onto it, the more slippery it becomes. Frustration coils in my chest, winding itself around my ribs, tightening with every passing second.

The thread of energy I was holding onto slips away, dissolving into nothing. My eyes open, and I let out a sharp, irritated huff.

"See, I can't." My voice is tight with frustration. "It's not working."

Cam steps closer, crowding my space. "Take a breath," he says, scratching the back of his head. "You're overthinking it. Stop forcing it, Rae. Magic doesn't work like that. Let it come to you. You have to trust yourself."

His tone is exactly how I feel. He sounds frustrated with me, and honestly? I'm frustrated with myself.

"Easy for you to say." I shake out my hands, rolling my shoulders to release some of the tension curling through me.

Frustration simmers beneath my skin, but I force my eyes shut again, shutting out everything around me. Cam, the clearing, my doubt, all of it.

I focus on elements of a storm, the rolling thunder, the sharp crack of lightning when it splits the air, the weight of the clouds pressing down, thick with power.

I imagine that energy coursing through my veins, pooling in my core, waiting to be unleashed. I take a slow breath and sink into it. I let it wrap around me, letting it pull me under.

The tingling spreads, creeping up my arms, colliding in my chest. It feels like standing at the edge of a cliff, the energy urging me to jump.

The air shifts. A whisper of wind stirs the edges of my hair. My breath quickens, my focus narrowing to that building power.

And then, *I feel it*. A sudden rush, surging through me like a current. It's nothing like before, this isn't a flicker of magic or stray spark of energy.

This is raw.

The sky darkens. A distant rumble rolls through the air. The wind stirs around us, rustling the leaves on the branches.

My eyes fly open, and I see the clouds gather, the air charged with the promise of rain. My heart pounds, caught between exhilaration and fear.

"Good," Cam says, his voice steady, cutting through the rising storm. "Keep going."

I try to hold onto it. To stay in control, but I hear a faint whisper.

Then, all the sudden, it's louder, like someone was standing right behind me.

"Raven."

The storm lurches, a violent gust tearing through the clearing. My pulse spikes as my body tenses. "Did you hear that?"

Cam's eyes flicker with confusion. "Hear what?"

I swallow hard, the air is thick with static. My fingers tremble, power still surging, uncontained. "Nothing."

I feel a brush against my ear, the voice curling through the storm like a thread pulled loose from the fabric of the world.

Then I hear a slow chuckle.

I yank back, cutting off the connection. The wind dies instantly. The sky clears. My chest heaves as the power drains from me.

Cam exhales through his nose, studying me carefully.

"Why?" The word is out before I can stop it. "Why are you training me? Why not a witch?"

A muscle in Cam's jaw jumps.

I don't miss the shift in his stance, or the way his shoulders tighten ever so slightly. "That's complicated. I told you, they went into hiding."

I lick my lips, forcing my voice to stay even. "Why, though? I'm sick of the half answers."

Then, he sighs, running a hand down his face. "Because they had to."

Still not an answer.

I step closer. "Had to? Or were forced to?"

His golden eyes darken, the weight of something unsaid pressing between us. His next words come out slow.

"The witches weren't meant to survive, Raven."

The words sink like lead in my stomach. A cold, creeping dread curls around my ribs, tightening with each passing second. "What exactly does that mean?"

His jaw clenches, like he doesn't want to say anything. "They were hunted. It wasn't just about stopping witches, it was about making sure no one ever found... her."

A chill races down my spine. I shake my head. "That doesn't make any sense."

Cam exhales. "They started killing anyone who might fit the description of the prophesied witch." His voice turns grim, his eyes dark and serious. "Any bloodline remotely connected to the old magic, any coven that might have harbored or protected her, anyone who could have been *her*. They were marked for death."

The breath leaves my lungs. "You're saying they slaughtered every witch they could find that *maybe* fit a description, just to make sure they weren't a woman who *might* exist?"

He nods once. "That's exactly what I'm saying."

A sick feeling coils in my stomach, sinking through my veins like ice. "So where are the ones who survived?"

He hesitates. "Scattered. Some are still in hiding. Some found protection in other realms." His voice drops lower. "Most didn't make it."

The weight of his words hit me, stealing the breath from my lungs. My nails dig into my palms, my chest tightens with something too big to name.

For weeks, I've been grappling with the idea that I *might* be something more. That my magic, my past, my everything, is tangled in a history I never knew existed. But this? This is different. What if *this* is part of my history? Am I going to be hunted too?

The thought makes me nauseous, especially when I think about the old woman telling me I've been marked.

The wind howls. The sky booms with a deafening crack of thunder, and I barely hear it.

If all those witches died because I'm the *witch* he thinks I am...

My vision blurs at the edges, my entire body buzzing with unspent energy, fury, grief, all of it. A storm thrumming beneath my skin, desperate to be unleashed.

The energy slips from my grasp, vanishing like water through my fingers. The connection is gone, but the storm remains. This one's no longer mine.

Exhaustion slams into me, dragging at my limbs like dead weight. My legs wobble, and I have to force myself to stay upright.

"What if it's me?" The words rip out of me, frustration clawing up my chest. My hands clench into fists, nails biting into my palms, but it does nothing to stop the bitter weight of failure sinking deep into my bones.

Above us, the storm churns, chaotic and uncontrolled, just like me.

"Raven, one step at a time."

Cam steps closer like he's speaking to a wild animal that might bolt. "You've only been doing this for a few weeks. You're not going to be perfect right away. It takes time to learn how to control this kind of power."

I glance at him, irritation still buzzes under my skin. His words chip away at the edges of my anger, but not enough to soothe it.

"Yeah, well, *maybe* if my family didn't feel the need to keep me in the dark, I'd actually know what the hell I was doing." I snap.

But I don't want to stop. I want to be angry.

The wind picks up, whipping my hair around my face, but I barely register it. I hear the whisper again. *Fight.*

"Maybe we wouldn't be out here in the middle of fucking *nowhere*, and you wouldn't have to be my *babysitter*."

I know things are getting out of control, I can feel it. All the feelings I've kept bottled up are starting to bubble to the surface. If I don't push them back down, I won't be able to put the lid back on.

"Besides, not all of us get to grow up in a castle with parents who actually taught them things." The bitterness scrapes against my throat, but I can't stop. "You're just like everyone else here. Probably had magic tutors. I bet you even got to go to *Hogwarts. Lucky you.*"

Cam raises his eyebrow. He doesn't flinch. Doesn't react the way I want him to. If anything, he looks *amused.*

"Feel better now?" His voice is infuriatingly calm, carrying the barest hint of challenge.

I glare at him, arms crossing tightly over my chest. "No, actually, I don't."

The wind rips around us, tugging at my clothes. The storm is still there, raging, but I'm too caught up in my own to care.

Cam doesn't so much as blink. Instead, he steps closer, "Good. Let it out. All of it. Because holding it in isn't doing you any favors, Rae. You keep pushing all this shit down and it's going to consume you."

I scoff, rolling my eyes. I can't help it. "Oh, yeah, great advice. Just throw a tantrum, that'll definitely fix everything. Is that the advice you give the king too?

He tilts his head, the corners of his mouth twitching like he's fighting a smile. Which only makes me more mad. "It's not about throwing a tantrum." His voice is annoyingly patient. "It's about actually acknowledging what you're feeling, and not letting it control you."

He gestures upward. "Right now, you're not in control..."

I follow his gaze... *shit.*

The sky is black. Thunder rolls, like the growl of some ancient beast. The wind howls, clawing at my skin, my hair, my clothes. The air vibrates with raw electricity, pressing against my ribs, curling through my veins. I can feel it in my fingertips, but I can't reach it.

A flicker of guilt sparks beneath my frustration, but I'm not ready to back down.

"Maybe if anyone bothered to tell me about any of this before now, I wouldn't be standing here struggling to figure it out alone!"

My voice cracks at the end, betraying the exhaustion, the confusion, the weight of everything unraveling too fast. I don't even realize I'm crying until a tear slips down my cheek.

The air tightens.

Lightning strikes.

A blinding flash rips through the sky, slamming into the ground.

Right where Cam is standing.

A deafening boom detonates through the clearing, the shockwave slams into me, rattling my bones. The pressure crushes against my ribs, warping reality, and my vision tilts like the entire world just flipped upside down.

For a few terrifying seconds, I hear nothing but white noise.

Nothing but static and chaos.

Cam.

The name rips from my throat before I even register the scream.

As the haze begins to clear, my stomach plummets. He's still standing, but barely. His hands are braced on his knees, and his chest is heaving. A thin line of blood trickles from his nose, dark against his skin. His jacket is singed, the edges still smoking.

Oh. My. God.

Did I just kill him?

The thought slams into me like a gut punch, but before I can even process it, I'm already moving.

"Cam!" The words rip from my throat as I lunge toward him, hands gripping his arms, frantic, searching for damage I can't undo.

He tenses beneath my touch, his body is too warm. But I don't let go. I can't. What if I just melted his internal organs? What if he drops dead any second?

He should be pissed. He should be yelling at me. Hell, I'm yelling at me.

And then he laughs, like this is nothing. Like getting struck by actual lightning is just another Tuesday.

I jerk back, staring at him like he's lost his goddamn mind. "Are you seriously laughing right now?

He wipes the blood from his nose, shrugs like he didn't just almost die. "I'm fine."

I blink at him. *Fine*?

"Oh, right, sure, that's totally normal," I snap, the words tripping over themselves in disbelief. "You just got struck. *By fucking lightning.*"

He grins, the absolute lunatic. "Didn't hit me. Damn near did, though." He smirks, brushing dirt off his jacket like I didn't just nearly obliterate him. "Thank the Gods I have the reflexes of a cat."

What. The. Actual. Fuck. is going on right now?

I just almost killed him, and he's smug about it?

I stare at him, my pulse still hammering in my throat, while he casually acts like he just tripped over a rug instead of nearly being electrocuted to death.

"What the fuck is wrong with you?" I demand, my voice high with disbelief.

But Cam doesn't flinch. Instead, he meets my eyes. "You woke it up." Then he grins. "Great job!"

I blink. Did he just—?

"Great job?" I echo, somewhere between panic and hysteria. "Cam, I could've had a body count!"

His expression shifts slightly, and I can see the gears in his brain working, and the way his lips twitch like he's physically holding back laughter tells me he somehow made that dirty.

And for some reason, that makes me want to punch him even more.

"It's okay to be frustrated," he says after a beat, sounding infuriatingly calm for someone who was just almost reduced to ash. I honestly think I'm in shock.

"This is a lot to take in, but you're not alone, Rae. We're here to help you. Not because we have to, but because we want to."

And then he does the last thing I expect, he exhales, standing up slowly, and pulls me into a hug.

A real one.

And God help me, I let him.

I don't move. Don't breathe. Just stand there, wrapped in his arms, his heartbeat a steady drum against my ear.

And then I break. The tears hit before I can stop them, they slip past the walls I've spent years perfecting. I squeeze my eyes shut, furious at myself, but it doesn't stop my chest from shaking violently.

Cam doesn't let go, he just lets me cry.

When my sobs turn into sniffles, he slowly pulls away, his hands settle on my shoulders, steadying me. But I still can't meet his eyes.

"Needing people doesn't make you weak."

I want to scoff, to push him away. But I don't have the energy. Instead, I stay frozen as he steps back, just enough that the warmth of him disappears, leaving nothing but the cold air between us. His eyes search mine.

"You should do whatever you think is best," he says slowly. "You can leave if you want to. Stay if you'd like. I told you that you're free to make your own choices, and you are. But everyone needs—"

I cut him off before he can finish. Shutting the door so that he can't see me break any more than he already has.

"I don't need anyone."

The lie tastes bitter, but saying it feels like control.

650

Cam doesn't argue, doesn't push, he just waits.

And that's what breaks me.

I swallow hard, but it doesn't stop the words from spilling out.

"I'm just... so tired of not knowing who the hell I am." My voice barely scrapes above a whisper, and it's humiliating to admit it out loud. "And what I'm supposed to be doing." My breath shudders, and I shake my head, trying to stop the rest before it claws its way free.

"And I just accidentally struck you with lightning, Cam!"

My voice cracks again, but he doesn't even flinch.

"Fuck this."

The words rip out of me, my hands clenching into fists at my sides. But there's no real fight left in them.

I know it and he knows it.

"And on top of all of it?" My voice rises, frustration latching onto the only thing I do have control over. My own goddamn outrage.

"You tell me that you're here for me and that I'm not alone, but you're avoiding my questions. You're keeping secrets. Don't think I can't tell."

Silence. His expression falters. Just for a second. But it's there.

I don't give him the chance to respond.

I turn on my heel and storm off.

The momentum of my anger is the only thing keeping me together. The only thing that's keeping my walls up. Because if I stop moving, if I stop pretending I have any control over this, I might just break. And I don't want to be near anyone when that happens.

Cam says something behind me, but it's muffled. I don't know when it happened, but all I hear is ringing in my ears. My pulse pounds, my body still vibrating with unchecked energy, and all I know is that I need to get the hell away from him before I lose control again.

Before I hurt him for real this time.

Then, out of nowhere, ice cold water slams into me.

Shock explodes through every nerve in my body. My breath rips from my lungs, my muscles locking up as the freezing sensation shreds through me like a blade.

What the fuck!

For a split second, every nerve in my body goes numb, then comes back to life all at once.

I gasp, stumbling back, shivering violently.

"*What the fuck!*" I shriek, shoving my dripping hair out of my face as I spin around.

And there he is, standing there with a bucket. A fucking bucket and a smirk.

"Magic," he says smoothly, entirely too pleased with himself.

He's so lucky I'm not holding a weapon right now.

"Are you serious?" My voice pitches higher, as I wipe at the freezing water dripping down my arms. "What the hell was that for?"

Cam shrugs, completely unfazed. Which only pisses me off more.

"You were getting out of control," he says so simply. "Sometimes, you just need a cold shower to cool down." Then, the smirk widens, his voice dipping into something else. "Or, you know... something else. But I can't give you that." He taps his temple. "I like my head where it is, remember?"

Oh, for fuck's sake.

I glare daggers at him, torn between strangling him and laughing despite myself. Damn him. My body is still shaking, but the burning frustration from earlier has dulled significantly.

I shake my head, still shivering. "You could've just said *calm down,* you know."

Cam chuckles. "Would that have worked, *Princess*?"

My mouth snaps shut... damn it. I hate that he's right.

I also really don't want to end up unconscious for another three days. With an annoyed sigh, I mutter, "Fine. Point taken. But don't call me that."

His laughter deepens, his smirk pure trouble. "No promises."

I roll my eyes but don't bother hiding my smile. "Yeah, yeah. I'll try again," I say, rubbing my arms, covering up a shiver. "But if you dump water on me again, I swear—"

Cam grins wider. "It worked, didn't it?"

Smug bastard.

"You know," I say, narrowing my eyes. "My grandfather used to make me swim in freezing water, so I'm kinda used to it." I wring out my soaked sleeve, sighing dramatically. "But at least give a girl some warning next time, so I can, you know, dress for the occasion. Maybe bring a towel. A wetsuit. Emotionally prepare."

Cam chuckles, and for the first time today, I feel some of the tension eases from my body.

But then, just like that he's staring at me again.

The amusement vanishes. His entire posture changes, as his jaw tightens.

"Why would he have you do that?"

I hesitate, shifting on my feet, the lingering cold from the water nothing compared to the sudden chill crawling down my spine, with the way he's looking at me.

"When I was younger," I say carefully, testing the words as they leave my mouth, "he'd have me swim in this freezing-ass lake. Said it was part of training, but..." I shrug, forcing a lightness I don't feel. "Never got my gold medal for swimming."

He doesn't say anything.

A flicker of something dangerous flashes across his face before he exhales, dragging a hand through his hair.

"Fuck," he mutters under his breath, shaking his head. "*They knew.*"

"Umm hello?" I wave a hand in front of his face, trying to snap him out of whatever spiral he's just plummeted into. "They knew what? Care to share with the class?"

My tone is sharp, irritation creeping right back in. I am so fucking done being kept in the dark. His eyes snap to mine, like he's piecing together something I can't see.

"I'm assuming you were your usual charming self, back then, too."

His lips twitch, like he wants to laugh but wisely chooses not to.

Fucker.

"If your grandfather had you swimming in a freezing lake with no clear reason or pattern, then he must have known."

My stomach drops.

"Known what?" The words come out a question, but deep down I know exactly what he means. *There's no way.*

I'm soaked, I'm freezing, and I'm not in the mood for more cryptic bullshit.

"What are you talking about, Cam?"

Please tell me he's not about to say what I think he's going to say.

"Your grandparents must have known about your magic, Rae."

I freeze.

He exhales, watching me carefully. "Think about it, the cold water, it wasn't some random endurance test or training exercise. It was to help you manage your emotions. To keep your power in check. I'm sure of it."

The world narrows.

I blink, my heart skipping a beat. "You mean... he was training me to control my magic?"

The words feel foreign, like they don't belong to me.

He nods slowly, "It makes sense. They might not have told you outright, but they were preparing you in their own way. They knew, even if you didn't."

They knew. The realization crashes into me, knocking the breath from my lungs.

They *knew*. They *knew* this whole fucking time.

A storm rages in my chest.

Anger, frustration, grief, relief. *They knew.*

For the first time since all of this started, something actually makes sense.

I shake my head, "They should've told me." I whisper, the words raw and bitter. "They should have *trusted* me."

My voice cracks, and I hate how small it sounds.

"They did trust you."

Cam's voice is soft, pulling me back before I unravel completely. His grip on my arm is firm.

"Enough to prepare you." His voice lowers, something serious settling in his tone. "Enough to believe that when the time came, you'd figure it out. Or at least train you enough to watch your back."

The words hit something deep, something I'm not ready to look at.

And then he turns sharply, his usual easy going demeanor replaced by sheer focus. "Come on. This changes everything."

And just like that, he's walking away, already lost in thought, like this is just another problem to solve.

I stare after him, my pulse spiking, and my mind is spinning with a dozen questions, all fighting to be first.

654

"What do you mean this changes everything?" I practically jog to keep up, my breath coming faster, the energy beneath my skin crackling again.

He glances over his shoulder, his expression softening just enough to temper the storm building in my chest.

"I'll meet you for dinner."

I stop dead in my tracks.

"Dinner?" Disbelief cuts through my frustration. "That's all you're giving me?"

Cam finally pauses, turns to face me fully. His eyes lock onto mine.

"Rae, I need some time to sort this out." His voice is careful. "Hopefully, by dinner, I'll have answers for you."

He doesn't wait for my response. Doesn't explain anything, he doesn't even glance back. Just turns and walks away.

And for the hundredth time since stepping into this place, I'm left standing here, utterly pissed off, with more questions than answers. Only this time I'm soaking wet and freezing on top of it.

Unbelievable. My clothes cling to me like a second skin, cold settling into my bones now that the adrenaline is fading. The frustration is still burning, tangled with the lingering shock of Cam's sudden revelation.

My grandparents knew.

"Cam!" My voice rips through the clearing, but he doesn't stop. Doesn't even hesitate.

He's already gone.

I shake my head, muttering a stream of curses under my breath as I pace.

A faint sound catches my attention. Faint at first, like wind shifting through the trees. But then I hear it again.

I freeze, scanning the clearing. Empty.

But the whispering grows louder, curling through the air, slithering against my skin like a breath at the back of my neck.

A flicker of movement catches in the corner of my eye, a shadow slipping between the trees.

"Hello?" my voice wavers, and I curse to myself. I clear my throat, trying again.

"Helllooo..."

Silence.

Snap.

I whirl around, heart hammering so hard it nearly drowns out the wind.

Tyler.

Motherfucker.

"Hey beautiful," he greets, that signature grin stretching across his face like he didn't just almost send me into cardiac arrest.

I exhale sharply, pressing a hand on my chest like that'll stop my heart from trying to escape. "Tyler!" I snap. "Are you trying to get struck by lightning, too?"

His brows raise, amusement flickering behind his eyes. "You didn't?" He looks over my shoulder, and laughs. "Is he... alive?"

I punch his arm. "Not funny."

Tyler smirks. "I mean... it's kinda funny."

"Yes, he's fine. Completely fine, actually. Annoyingly fine."

He shrugs, entirely too smooth for someone who just got decked in the arm. "Calm down, you're fine." His tone is so casual I could scream. Like I'm the one being dramatic. "Besides, I figured I'd come find you before you wandered too far. Don't want anything... weird happening out here, do we?"

His grin falters slightly and I see something flash in his eyes.

I sigh, dragging it out. "Fine." Then, I shoot him a side glance. "But only because you scared the shit out of me back there."

He laughs softly, stepping closer, leaning in just enough that my pulse jumps again.

"Noted." His voice drops into that teasing tone of his. "I'll try not to be so charming next time."

"Charming?" I snort, shaking my head. "Not exactly the word I would've used. Idiot? Sure."

He smiles, putting his arm around my shoulder. "Come on, Bird. You never know what might be waiting in the shadows."

I roll my eyes. "Great bedtime story, *Frank*. But I'm not scared of the shadows."

Tyler stops mid-laugh. His brows pull together, pure offense flashing across his face. "Frank? The fuck for?"

I shrug, entirely unbothered. "Because you needed a nickname, too."

He blinks. Once. "And you landed on... Frank?"

"I didn't know what else to call you," I say, waving a hand like it's no big deal. "So Frank seemed like a solid filler name. When I come up with something better, I'll let you know."

He just stares at me, bewildered.

I grin, brushing past him, and head inside, laughing under my breath.

Raven -1. Tyler- Lost count.

CHAPTER 47

All Lies

RAVEN

*T*hey knew.

The realization tangles all of my emotions. Comfort and anger clashing together. Why didn't they ever tell me? Why keep something like this a secret?

The questions press against my ribs, as thick as the steam now curling around me.

I'm so distracted in my thoughts, the little lavender bottle falls into the bathtub. Well, guess I'm using the rest of the lavender haze tonight. I slip into the hot water, and the heat licks up my skin, chasing away the lingering chill in my bones. My muscles loosen, but my mind won't quiet. I exhale slowly, forcing myself to sink into the sensation, letting the warmth drown out the noise.

I slip under the surface, letting the water drown out any noise, quieting my mind. I hold my breath and try to calm the war in my mind. Once I feel the calm start to creep in, I sit back up, resting my head on the rim of the tub.

My eyelids grow heavy. My body melts into the heat. My thoughts begin to blur.

I wake up in a bed that's not mine.

The sheets are warm, tangled around my legs. The air smells like cedarwood and something darker.

My breath stills.

The room is still cloaked in shadows, but the warmth of another body beside me is unmistakable. I turn my head, and there he is.

Kane lies beside me, an arm draped lazily over his very naked stomach. His bare chest rises and falls, slow and steady. The hard lines of muscle cut deep under the low lighting.

My pulse stumbles.

The sharp angles of his jaw are softer in his sleep, his features relaxed in a way I've never seen before. Less guarded, no mask. The kind of peace he never allows himself when he's awake.

I can't look away, but I can feel heat pooling between my legs.

"You're staring."

His voice is thick with sleep, deeper, rasping over my skin like gravel and smoke. I swallow, but my throat is too dry. But everything else? Wet.

"Hi," I whisper, hating the way my voice betrays me, breathless and wrecked before he's even touched me.

Kane shifts, rolling to his side, and when his hand slides over my hip, my entire body reacts.

Heat spreads through me, deep and consuming. His thumb traces slow, lazy circles against my skin, a touch so simple yet so intimate it sends a chill racing over my body.

"How does it feel?"

A single touch and I'm already falling apart.

I hate him.

"How does what feel?" I whisper, my voice uneven, betraying me again.

His fingers still, lingering just long enough to drive me insane. I'm caught between melting into him and catching fire.

His eyes drag down my body, taking his time. Because he has all the power right now, and he fucking knows it.

Fucking unfair.

His smirk deepens like he can hear that thought, too. "I'd sleep better if you were closer," he murmurs, his voice full of intent.

His hand slides up my waist, like he has all the time in the world to make me fall apart.

The moment his hand cups my breast, a shiver rips through me, my body arching into his touch before I can stop myself.

His thumb drags over my nipple, slow and teasing, and my breath stutters, my fingers clutching at the sheets like they're the only thing keeping me here.

His touch doesn't just burn, it consumes me.

"Kane," I whisper.

I don't wait, I close the distance crashing into him, my lips meeting his in a kiss that's nothing short of a goddamn war.

It's reckless. A fight neither of us wants to lose.

His mouth is hungry, and when I slide my hands over his chest, I swear to God, this man feels bigger than he did last time.

A moan slips free, muffled against his lips, and his response is immediate.

His arm wraps around my back, pulling me on top of him in one fluid motion, never breaking the kiss.

The shift presses our bare skin together, and a jolt of pure electricity rips through me.

His hard length pressed into me, and I swear I might just get off right here.

I start grinding against him, desperate, chasing the friction I need like a woman starved.

He growls, low and rough.

Then his hands are everywhere.

They side down my back, dragging me exactly where he wants me.

His grip tightens and his fingers dig into my ass, holding me there, and this time I'm the one groaning. The vibration of it shoots straight through me, turning my bones liquid, making me ache in ways I can't even describe.

His mouth drops to my throat.

His teeth graze my neck, teasing, like he's fighting the urge to sink his teeth in.

But I need more. I need him to ruin me.

He drags his lips along my skin, his breath hot, his control unraveling, and fuck, I want him undone.

Then I hear his voice in my ear. A command.

"Eyes on me."

I barely have a second to obey before his fingers are exactly where I need them.

Slow at first, dragging through my slick folds, tormenting me. He doesn't make me wait long before he's pushing them deeper.

My breath shatters, and my back arches. My nails dig into his skin, but I don't care. I can't think, can't breathe.

His touch is fucking devastating.

I choke on a gasp, my entire body shattering beneath him, coming apart in his hands.

He groans, his voice rougher than usual.

"Fuck, Princess," he growls. "If you only knew what you did to me."

Oh, I know.

Because I can feel it. Everywhere. The heat rolling off him, the hunger in his touch, the way his cock presses against me.

I grind against him again, more deliberately, needing more of him. His grip tightens and he chuckles, his amusement tangled with something darker.

"Always so demanding," he teases, and fuck if that doesn't make me want to break him.

His hand slides into my hair, fisting at the roots, tugging just hard enough to send a sharp exquisite shock of pleasure straight through me.

My breath stutters as he pulls my head back, exposing me to him.

His teeth graze my neck and my pulse thunders beneath his lips, and when I whisper his name again, pleading, he groans.

"Kane, please."

His lips trail along my throat, leaving heat and devastation in their wake. Then his breath is at my ear, wrecking me from the inside out.

"Come again for me, and I'll give you what you want."

A shudder rolls through me so violently it might break me.

His hands grip my thighs, parting them further, his fingers working me, knowing exactly how close I am.

His fingers are pumping in and out, and he starts rubbing my clit with his other hand with precision.

A strangled moan tears out from me, and my entire body tightens. I'm seconds away from falling apart. But he's not done, not even fucking close.

The pleasure builds, it's almost unbearable. It coils inside me so violently it's too much and not enough all at once.

I gasp his name, begging, and he eats every sound I make, his lips claiming mine, drinking me in.

"Good girl," he murmurs against my lips.

My body trembles, my muscles locking tight as I hover on the edge. His pace doesn't falter, and his fingers don't stop.

"Come for me."

The words are my undoing.

Pleasure detonates, tearing me apart at the seams. My back arches, and I swear I see stars as my entire body shatters above him.

But he's not done.

His lips find mine again, swallowing my moans, kissing me through the aftershocks, like he's savoring every last tremor. His hands roam, keeping me right where he wants me.

And just as he's about to push inside me—

A knock. Loud and insistent.

No.

The world fractures.

I jolt, my eyes flying open. Only, I'm not in his bed.

The water has cooled. My breath is ragged and uneven. My body still hasn't realized we aren't about to get any dick, and my pussy is still throbbing.

The scent of cedarwood clings to me. It clings to my senses, wrapping around me, teasing me with a vividness that leaves me breathless.

Another knock at the door, only louder this time.

Then the door bursts open.

Elle stands in the doorway, eyes wide, panic all over her face.

"Raven?"

She stops dead, blinking at me still half-dazed in the tub, wrapped in nothing but the remnants of my dream.

"Oh." Her shoulders relax as she presses a hand to her chest. "Shit. Sorry. You didn't answer, and I thought—" She exhales sharply. "I dunno, maybe you drowned or something."

I blink at her, still fighting to separate my dream from reality. My skin still feels hypersensitive, and I'm still reeling from Kane's touch. Except it wasn't real.

Elle's nose wrinkles.

She sniffs. "What's that smell?"

I freeze.

"What smell?" My voice is too defensive.

Her eyes narrow, suspicion flaring as she sniffs again, this time more deliberately. I swear the entire room tilts as she levels me with a sharp stare. "Whatever bath salt you used, maybe don't use it again."

She stares at me, then her brows pull together, her lips parting slightly as she really looks at me. "Did you use the wrong oil or something?"

"Nope," I say, forcing my face into something resembling neutral, even as my entire body continues to betray me.

She doesn't buy it. Not for a second.

Her eyes flicker over me again, lingering slightly. Finally, she shrugs, waving a hand in front of her nose. "Well, whatever it is, it's strong."

I exhale a little too hard, relieved when she moves toward the mirror, fussing with her hair like she's already dismissed it.

"Anyway." She tosses me a towel, "I just wanted to check on you. You missed dinner."

I step out of the bath, wrapping the towel around myself, trying to gather what's left of my sanity. The scent of Kane still clings to my skin and his voice still lingers in my head.

I swallow hard, my voice softer now. "Elle?"

She looks at me in the mirror, eyebrows raised. "Yeah?"

I hesitate, still too caught between what was real and what wasn't. "Can I ask you something?"

Her hands still in her blonde hair, her eyes flicking to mine in the mirror once more, curious but patient. "Of course."

I shift under her stare, suddenly feeling ridiculous for even thinking this, let alone saying it out loud. But I've already started.

"Can you... smell me too?"

The words barely make it past my lips and she freezes, just for a second before her brows shoot up, her lips parting slightly in surprise before her cool and collected mask slips back into place.

"Smell you?" She echoes, turning to face me fully. Then, suddenly, she leans in and her nose twitches dramatically, sniffing the air near me. Then, just as fast, she recoils, wrinkling her nose.

"Ew." Her face twists in disgust before bursting into laughter.

I scowl, fully prepared to drown her in this bathtub.

She wipes a fake tear from her eye, still grinning. "Relax, I'm just messing with you." Then, her expression shifts. "But yeah, I can smell you."

My stomach tightens.

"Why?"

I don't know how much to say or how much I should admit. I know this whole trust thing works best with communication, but I still feel hesitant to share anything.

"It's just…" My fingers tighten around the towel. "Cam mentioned something about him being able to smell me."

Elle's playful smirk disappears. Her eyes go wide.

Oh. Her mouth forms the word without actually saying it, something unreadable flicking behind her gaze.

"Anyone can, really, if they're paying attention. Or if they know what they're looking for." She pauses, watching me closely. "Especially when you use magic."

The statement knocks the breath from my lungs. "What do you mean?"

I can barely control my abilities on a good day. Half the time, I don't even know when I'm using them. And now, apparently, I've been leaving a fucking breadcrumb trail for anyone with the right nose.

Elle leans against the sink, crossing her arms, her usual teasing nature nowhere to be found. "Think of it this way," her voice gets softer. "Your magic is tied to you, your thoughts, your memories, your emotions. When you feel something strongly, like anger, fear, love, joy, it seeps out. Whether you mean it to or not. And it leaves a mark. A scent."

I swallow hard, my pulse picking up. That's great to hear, I'm basically walking around broadcasting myself to anyone who knows what they're looking for.

"Can you hide the smell?" If I can hide it, maybe I should master that, just in case I don't figure out how to control it.

She hesitates. Her usual smile is replaced with something more careful. And that alone tells me she's hiding something.

"No," she says finally. "So you should probably learn to control it."

My stomach tightens. She's full of shit. But neither of us say anything.

Why lie? What the hell is she covering up?

Elle claps her hands together, like she didn't just dodge my question. "Get dressed. Come eat. I'll be waiting outside."

She winks before bouncing out the door, leaving me alone with this fresh new existential crisis. How am I supposed to be careful around people when I don't even know when I'm doing it?

The thought loops in my head, tightening its grip on my chest with every repetition. I need to somehow figure out what sets it off. See if I can pull it back when it happens.

That might explain why the attacker said I was being reckless. He must have sensed it. The magic I didn't even know I was using. Right?

How many of those storms were actually storms? Were the flickering lights me too?

The realization settles like a weight in my chest as the lights in the room start to flicker. Was that me?

I take a slow breath, trying to calm myself, but my heart is racing, my skin tingling with that now-familiar buzz of energy beneath the surface. I need to get a grip.

When I finally step out of my room, Elle's talking to Kody, who's laughing at something she said.

"Night." She gives him a casual wave before turning on her heel and falling into step beside me. Just like that, we're off.

We walk in comfortable silence, the soft hum of this place settling into the background.

The dining hall is warm and smells incredible. My stomach grows in anticipation. I spot Cam sitting at the end of the long table, nose buried in whatever he's reading. He doesn't even look up. Not until I'm practically standing over him.

"Raven, there yo—"

He stops mid-sentence, as his nose twitches. Then, like some kind of animal, he sniffs the air.

Oh, for the love of—

I groan internally, already regretting ever leaving my room. *Is this what my life is now? Everyone just sniffing me like some kind of scented candle?*

"What is that smell?"

And because the universe loves to make me suffer, Elle cackles.

"That's what I said!" She chimes in, way too amused at my expense. "Actually, it smelled worse in her room."

She raises both hands in defense as I shoot her a glare. "What? Just saying."

I swear to the Gods, I'm going to kill her. I roll my eyes, crossing my arms tightly over my chest. "Okay, seriously? I don't smell that bad. But if this is some magical side effect, I might need a warning label or something. I probably just used the wrong soap."

For a second, I swear something flashes in his eyes. It's there, then gone, so fast I almost think I imagined it.

"It just smells... weird."

His eyes go straight to Elle. Something unspoken passes between them, I'd bet my life on it.

I lift my own shirt, sniffing myself, half-expecting to catch some strange, overwhelming scent, but all I smell is the lavender haze oil that fell into the tub.

Elle chuckles, nudging me lightly with her elbow. "Could be worse, right?"

I let out a dry laugh, shaking my head. "Oh yeah, because smelling like an air freshener is all the rage."

I try to focus on my food, eating quietly, my mind still churning. Whatever they're thinking to each other, they're not going to say it out loud.

Cam sips his drink, his attention locked onto the book in front of him, but I can feel the occasional glance in my direction.

I'm trying to pretend not to notice the way Cam keeps looking at Elle. Then, finally, he breaks the silence.

"I don't want to sound like I'm kicking you out—" He sets his glass down. "You're welcome to come back right after, if you'd like. But if we're going to get you home without anyone noticing..."

His eyes flick to mine. I don't know why, but a slow, creeping unease coils in my stomach. I set my fork down, suddenly not hungry anymore.

"I was going to talk to you about it this afternoon, until..."

I exhale, leaning back in my chair. "Honestly? I was thinking the same thing." My fingers drum lightly against the table before I glance up. "Are you coming back, too?"

Cam's lips tug into a small, knowing smile. "Yeah." A glimmer of amusement flickering in his eyes. "I planned on coming back the night I ran into you, actually."

It's crazy because that feels like a lifetime ago. So much has happened in the past few weeks, it's like I've lived an entirely different life.

"When can I come back?" I try to sound casual, but my eagerness seeps through anyway.

"We'll talk about it on the way."

I nod. "Okay. When do you want to leave?"

"We can leave now if you're ready." He sets his book aside, waiting for my reply.

A spark of anticipation flickers in my chest. I take a deep breath, forcing myself to steady my nerves. "Alright. I didn't bring much, just my dagger. I'll grab it from my room, and we can go."

Just as I push my chair back, the door swings open, and Tyler strolls in, his usual carefree grin in place. "What'd I miss?"

Then he stops mid-step, brows knitting together, just standing there.

"What's going on?" His gaze sharpens, flicking between Elle and Cam.

"We're about to head back to Scotland." I smile.

He stiffens, and I can tell he's ready to argue, but before he can get a word out, Elle cuts in.

"Sorry we can't come with you, we're just a little busy here." Already waving a dismissive hand, like the entire realm is nothing more than a mild inconvenience. "I don't really care for it over there anyway. Besides, someone's gotta stay back and man the fort, ya know?"

Tyler's jaw ticks, but his smile slides back into place, smoothing over whatever he was about to say. "Guess that means it's just me and Cam, then. And you, of course, since you're the star of this little field trip."

I roll my eyes, but I can't stop the small smile tugging at my lips.

I don't even get the chance to say anything before Cam clears his throat, cutting through the moment like a blade.

"Actually," he says, his voice firm. "You're needed here, Tyler."

Tyler's amusement flickers. The grin stays, but something in his eyes sharpens. Another unspoken conversation. Another fucking secret.

Elle stands abruptly, turning to me with a warm hug that nearly knocks me off balance. "I'm gonna miss you, but I'll see you in a few days, I'm sure."

Before I can respond, she steps back, mischief dancing behind her eyes.

"Oh, and I made this for you."

She holds out a stunning holster, my dagger safely tucked inside.

I blink, caught completely off guard. "You... wait, when did you—?"

"Swiped it off your nightstand while you were getting dressed." Elle winks, completely unapologetic. "It straps around your thigh."

My fingers skim over the smooth leather, tracing the delicate, hand-etched designs. It's beautiful. And it's so... thoughtful.

"Elle..." I swallow hard. "This is incredible."

Her grin widens as she pulls me into another hug. "You're welcome," she whispers. "Just keep yourself safe, alright? Remember what I taught you."

I close my eyes briefly, soaking in the warmth of her embrace. "Thank you, Elle," I whisper back, meaning every word. "Really. I'll be back soon."

Cam clears his throat, slicing through the moment.

"We need to go."

I nod, reluctantly pulling away, tucking the holster close like it's already part of me.

Then, I turn to Tyler. "See you soon?"

I blink and his arms are around me, his hug is warm and entirely too much. "Obviously."

CHAPTER 48

Wildest Dream

KANE

My fingers curl into the space where she should be, my frown deepens as I blink against the remnants of sleep. I expected to find her tangled in my sheets, her wild hair a mess on my pillow, and her warm body pressed against mine.

But there's nothing except for the fucking hard-on straining beneath the sheets.

My cock is in full fucking denial. Clearly, it didn't get the memo that it was just a dream and that she's sleeping peacefully in her own room. Not here next to me.

I exhale slowly, dragging a hand down my face before gripping the back of my neck, my muscles tight with frustration.

What the fuck is wrong with me?

She's under my skin. Embedded. And I have no clue how to shake her loose.

Her scent has been haunting me since the moment she crashed into my life, challenging me with that sharp tongue and impossible fire in her eyes.

I grit my teeth, jaw tightening. This is getting ridiculous.

It's still early, and I'm not about to be the asshole who wakes her up. But if I don't do something about the situation between my legs, I'm going to regret it the second she walks out of her room.

If Cam were here, I'd drag his ass into the ring, making him give me something else to focus on. She's ignited a fire and left me to fucking burn.

The gym will have to do.

Two hours later, sweat clings to my skin as I take the stairs two at a time, my muscles burning, but my breathing is steady. Exhaustion should have set in by now, but it hasn't.

I walk past her door, but it's still closed. The kitchen is empty too, which means she's still either asleep or she left without saying a damn thing.

The thought irritates me more than it should.

By the time I've got a coffee in hand, a nagging feeling settles deep in my gut.

If she went outside, the alarms would've triggered. And she doesn't strike me as the type to slip away quietly. Not without some kind of sarcastic parting shot.

Before that thought even has time to take root, I'm already on my feet, moving toward her door. I knock firmly, the sound echoing in the quiet hallway.

"Hey, Princess. Rise and shine."

The teasing edge in my voice is light, but the weight in my chest digs its claws deeper. An unease I can't fucking shake.

No answer.

My jaw tightens. I knock again, a little harder. "Raven?"

Silence.

I reach for the handle, and the door creaks open slowly, her scent is the first thing that hits me and it's fucking distracting.

I inhale sharply, exhaling through my nose, forcing back the frustration already curling beneath my skin. I look over at the nightstand, where her phone sits untouched. A frown tugs at my lips.

She wouldn't go far without it.

"Raven, are you in there?" My voice is quieter now, scanning the space.

Still nothing.

The bathroom door is open, so I glance inside and it's also empty.

I take in the room, and it's a mess. Her bag is tossed onto the floor, her sweater is draped over the chair. There's a book perched on the edge of the nightstand like it might topple at any second. No sense of order, no real intention, just all her.

She's still here. She has to be. But when I move toward the back door, a sharp sense of unease wraps itself around me. The alarm system has been deactivated. And it's off.

That can't be right.

I don't ever forget to set the damn thing. Even last night, when my mind was clouded with thoughts of what I wanted to do to her, I would've set it out of habit.

And yet, here it is. Off.

My fingers flex at my sides as I exhale through my nose. Think. Where the fuck did she go?

I head outside and check the gardens first this time.

I half-expect to find her curled up on the stone bench, lost in thought, completely unaware of anything around her. The way she does when she drifts somewhere just out of reach.

Nothing.

Frustration sharpens at the edges of my patience, creeping into my blood like a slow burn. If she's not in the gardens, she might be in the woods.

My pace picks up, but before I reach the tree line, movement catches my eye.

And what do I see? None other than fucking Cam, walking side by side with Raven. Coming out of the woods like they went on a casual walk together.

Her laughter drifts through the air like a blade to the ribs and my jaw tightens. Cam spots me first, and the bastard grins, smug as ever.

"You really need to keep an eye on your house guests. Found this one wandering barefoot in the trees."

Of course he did.

A muscle ticks in my jaw, but I don't take my eyes off her. I try to keep my breathing even, but there's a weight pressing against my ribs, a dangerous heat curling where it shouldn't be.

I watch as Cam leans over and whispers something to her, and she hits his arm, her laughter spilling into the space between them, completely unguarded.

And then her gaze finds mine. And it's gone. Her laughter fades and her smile falters for a heartbeat, replaced by something darker, making my cock throb against my sweats.

It's there and gone in a flash, barely noticeable. If I weren't already so attuned to her every move. I would've missed it.

She clears her throat, pretending like she didn't just look at me like that.

"Kane." She smiles, her teeth catch on her bottom lip, and my thoughts are instantly fucking derailed.

That mouth of her has haunted me for weeks. I've pictured it doing a lot of things. But I can't think about any of those right now.

I force my voice to stay even and unaffected.

"Hey, Princess. How'd you sleep?"

She swallows, and my eyes track the movement. That delicate throat, the way her pulse picks up a little too fast. I can tell she's flustered. Good. Let her feel every bit of the way I do right now.

"Good!" She says too quickly. "I just wanted to get some fresh air."

I don't know what it is, but something about her looks different, yet exactly the same. Her hair's a mess, wild waves spilling over her shoulders, tangled from sleep. Her skin is flushed, and that damn dress clings to her body in ways that make my hands twitch with the need to touch her.

Fuck.

I should've never invited Cam over this early.

Scotland suits her. Too damn well.

"I was just coming to find you." My voice is neutral, but my thoughts? Not even fucking close. "Breakfast is ready if you want to eat."

I can see the heat flash in her eyes, as she shifts on her feet. Knowing that I'm getting to her is making it really hard to keep my dick in check.

The second we step into the castle, she pauses, looking up at me. Her fingers tuck her hair behind her ear. "I'm going to freshen up."

Her eyes linger a little too long, then she smirks. The kind of smirk that feels like a challenge, like she's daring me to break first. I don't move, I don't react. I just watch as she turns, hips swaying. She knows I'm still looking.

674

By the time she disappears around the corner, my blood is boiling, my body tense with a need I can't shake. A chuckle behind me yanks me back.

"All right there?"

The bastard is grinning.

I turn, pinning him with a sharp look. "Fine, thank you." The words come out clipped. He knows better than to push, but here he is, doing it anyway. "Why are you here so damn early?"

"You quite literally asked me to come this morning and personally cock-block you. Said it was to keep your head on straight, remember?"

Motherfucker.

I swear to the Gods...

"You're fucking lucky Raven is here, or I'd beat your ass right now." The growl rolls out before I can stop it, edged with warning.

Cam, smug as ever, dodges the swing I aim at him. How unfortunate, landing that would've made me feel a hell of a lot better.

"Okay, so those weren't your *exact* words, but close enough." He chuckles.

I exhale sharply, dragging a hand through my hair, shaking my head as we move into my office. He strolls right past me, dropping into the chair across from my desk.

I lean against the edge, arms crossed. "What the hell happened to you?" I give him a once-over, noticing how he looks like he went ten rounds with a wrecking ball.

He shrugs, brushing it off like it's nothing. "Just a job that didn't exactly go as planned. Had to... improvise. You know how it goes."

His tone is too casual, but something's off.

But before I can push, he changes the subject. "Anyway, how'd it go last night?"

I settle into my chair, as I fill him in about the lights, and how they shattered. His expression shifts just slightly as I pull up my laptop. He comes up behind me, leaning in to get a better look, and I can tell there's a stiffness in his posture, his usual easy-going nature cracking for just a second.

"Are you sure you're okay?" I ask, watching him closely.

Cam doesn't meet my eyes, which tells me everything I need to know. He's hiding something.

"Yes, Mom, I'm fine. Will you press play already?" His voice is easy, but his body is tense. Coiled tight like he's ready to bolt.

He watches in silence, and I can see his jaw tick. I can practically hear his brain working. But I don't fucking buy it. The dark circles under his eyes, the tight set of his jaw and the way he won't quite look at me. Yeah, something's definitely up.

I let it slide for now, considering we have shit to deal with, if he wanted to tell me something he would. I lean back in my chair, my fingers drumming against the desk before stilling. "Did you find anything else?"

His shoulders loosen, enough to make me more suspicious.

"I did, actually." He stretches his arms behind his head, like this is just another day at the office. Like he's not lying to my fucking face. "I found the usual. A few more rabbit holes. I'm confident one of them is going to lead us where we need to go."

"Good."

He shifts closer to the screen, closer to me. His focus locks onto it, but I see the way his fingers twitch, the way his jaw tightens, just barely. His brow furrows, a flicker or something before he smooths it out.

Then, like a switch flipping, he straightens abruptly.

"You got things handled here?" His tone is tight and rushed.

There it is again. That edge in his voice, like he's already halfway out the door, like something's pulling him away.

My eyes narrow, but I nod. "Yeah, go. Let me know what you find."

"Will do." He's already moving, barely waiting for my answer. Too fast and too eager. What the fuck is going on with him?

His footsteps echo as he disappears down the hall, a sharp contrast to the silence he leaves behind.

CHAPTER 49

So High School

RAVEN

E ver since that dream, I've been a wet, sopping mess. A slow-burning wreck of want, and every cell in my damn body is attuned to him. Every glance he's thrown my way is only making it worse.

It's pathetic, really. I've been practically drooling over him like some hormonal teenager. Like I'm starved. And maybe I am.

Something shifted while I was gone. It seems like something else woke up right along with my magic.

God, I missed him.

The banter. The glares. The way he looks at me like he's one second away from devouring me whole. Even those stupid fucking dimples that make it impossible to stay annoyed with him for long.

I still don't want a relationship, at least, that's what I keep telling myself. But I've let him walk right in the front door, and the worst part is, I don't hate it.

That's the terrifying part. I have no idea where he fits into this strange, new discovery that is my life. Everything is changing so fast. My magic, my identity, the lines I swore I wouldn't cross. Somewhere along the way, I've developed feelings for this annoyingly beautiful man. But I'm not staying here. So that's all it can be.

A long, scalding shower does absolutely nothing to clear my head. If anything, it makes it worse, because now I feel warm, and dangerously aware of what I really want.

Kane.

I yank a brush through my hair, throw my dress back on, because it's all I have, and head to the kitchen. The estate is too quiet and it's almost unsettling.

I get to the kitchen, but it's empty. No coffee cups, no half-finished breakfast, nothing.

I wander down the hall, checking the rooms I've already been in, but there's still no sign of him.

The library seems like a solid guess. If he's not in there, maybe I'll check the greenhouse. My footsteps echo softly, the quiet amplifying the restless energy buzzing under my skin. My phone vibrates in my hand, making me jump.

My heart kicks up a beat when I see Kane's name on the screen.

> Kane: You're getting warmer ...

I freeze, my breath hitching as my eyes flick up from my phone.

The hallway is empty. There's no sign of him, no sound other than the steady rhythm of my own pulse hammering in my ears. He's obviously here or he wouldn't know that I'm getting *warmer*. I feel it, the unmistakable weight of his presence pressing against my skin, winding around me like a predator circling its prey.

I exhale slowly, forcing my shoulders to stay loose, even as every nerve in my body tightens knowing he's watching me.

I roll my eyes. "Stalker."

Knowing him, he's close enough that he can probably hear me too.

I take a step forward, then another, my fingers curling tighter around my phone.

"Where are you?"

Silence.

My pulse ticks higher as I scan the hallway again, eyes flicking toward the archways that stretch into nothing. He could be anywhere.

"I do not like this game, just so you know." My words come sharper this time, laced with something that's close to irritation. I really hate hide and seek. But that doesn't stop me from taking another slow, deliberate step, forcing my pace steady even as the tension tightens in my stomach.

"When I find you," I add, my voice low, almost a whisper. "I'm going to punch you."

The second the words leave my mouth, my phone vibrates again, the sound unnervingly loud in the quiet hallway, making me jump again. My nerves are becoming more wound up with every step I take.

I glance down at the screen, my stomach flipping dangerously at his reply.

> Kane: Don't tease me with a good time, Princess.

Fuck.

Heat floods through me, a slow drip pools between my thighs. My fingers tighten around my phone, pulse hammering in my throat. That one message, that one fucking message, has my body reacting so fast.

I don't have time for this.

I need to find him, not stand here like an idiot, burning from the inside out. But damn it, he knows exactly how to wind me up, exactly where to push, and exactly how to pull the thread as tight as can be without ever snapping it.

I move down the hall, forcing my steps to stay even, and my breathing steady.

Another buzz.

I roll my eyes, but my stomach flips as I glance at the screen.

> Kane: Left or right, sweetheart? Choose wisely.

My lips part, and my head snaps up. I twist, scanning the empty hallway. My heart kicks up another notch. Well, if I wasn't sure he was watching, I am now. I can feel the weight of his stare like a physical touch. My fingers flex against my phone, my skin tingling.

That arrogant, smug, infuriating—

Another buzz.

> Kane: Tick Tock.

I can feel the heat curling through my veins, unraveling whatever logic I was hoping to take with me going into the conversation I planned on having with him. He's enjoying every second of this. If only he knew how worked up I was getting over nothing.

Two hallways stretch before me, one leads deeper into the estate, the other toward the library. Since I was already heading that direction, that's the way I choose to go. My stomach flips at the memory of the last time we were in there. That feels like a lifetime ago.

I exhale sharply, already moving.

The second I step inside, the smell of leather and something familiar wraps around me. My gaze flicks to the shelves, to the darkened corners where the shadows stretch deep. *Okay, Raven, think. There's only so many places he could be if he's in here.*

Another buzz.

Kane: Warmer.

I swear under my breath, scanning the space. "You're enjoying this way too much." I mutter, knowing damn well he can hear me.

Silence.

Then I hear a whisper of movement, and my head snaps to the left, heart hammering. A flicker of something out of the corner of my eye and gone before I can catch it.

I suck in a breath, fingers curling at my sides. My heart is hammering. If only he knew how much I truly hate this game. I might actually end up punching him in the face, and it's going to be his own fault.

But, alright, fine. If he wants to play, I'll fucking play. I school my expression and straighten my spine.

"You know, if you're trying to scare me," I say, dragging my fingers along the edge of the nearest bookshelf, trailing them over the spines of old leather-bound books, "You'll have to do better than this."

Still nothing.

But I feel him.

The heat of his presence pressing in, the air practically vibrating with it. Slowly, I turn, looking over the shelves. "I really don't like hide and seek," I continue, my voice hiding any nerves I might be feeling. "Never have."

I pause, letting the silence stretch.

My phone buzzes again, the vibration against my palm sending a jolt through me. My pulse jumps.

Kane is typing...

I glare at the dots on my screen like they personally offended me.

Kane: "..."

That's it? Oh, fuck no.

I exhale slowly, "What are you, in high school? Where the fuck are you?" My voice echoes through the library, swallowed by the rows of books towering around me. "I mean it, if you jump out and scare me, I'll hit you, and I won't even feel bad. Consider yourself warned."

Another buzz.

Kane: You're beautiful when you're angry. Did you know that?

I stop breathing.

My fingers tighten around my phone, heat rushes through me again. That smug, insufferable fuck.

Sure, it's obvious he wants me. The way he watches me, the way his eyes track my movements like he's memorizing all the ways he's going to ruin me. The barely concealed smirks, the tension cracking between, he's not exactly subtle. Well, not anymore. Not since our little date.

I'm not sure how to respond. Ignore him or call him out? Pretend like my body isn't currently throbbing in places it shouldn't be just from a goddamn text? Nope.

"Flattery won't save you when I find you."

A beat of silence and then... another buzz.

> *Kane: Who said I wanted saving?*

Jesus. I clench my jaw, my thighs pressing together on instinct. Damn him.

I tuck my phone away, determined to find him. To end this stupid game before my body reacts anymore to him than it already has. My body is tingling, lighting up like a Christmas tree. I sure hope magic doesn't work the same over here.

But before I take another step. There's another buzz.

I curse under my breath.

> *Kane: I think… you want me to drag you into the shadows. My hands in your hair, my mouth on your throat, my fingers pumping…*

I slap a hand over my mouth, a strangled noise breaking from my throat. Holy. Fucking. Hell.

Another wave of heat slams through me, sharp and unforgiving. My grip tightens around my phone again, and I'm surprised it hasn't cracked yet. My breath is coming too fast.

I should not be this affected by him texting me.

I absolutely should not consider ducking into one of these goodman alcoves just to get myself under control.

> *Kane: What's wrong, Princess? Can't handle the thought of me between your thighs?*

My heart fucking stops and I squeeze my eyes shut, willing my pulse to calm the fuck down. I hate him. I fucking hate him right now. My body doesn't ever seem to be on the same page when it comes to him.

"You're so fucking lucky I don't have a knife on me right now."

His response is instant.

> *Kane: Am I?*

> *Kane: Or will you finally admit how badly you want me when you're on your knees, blade in hand, waiting for my permission to use it?*

My breath stills. Is he for real?? "Permission? Please." Motherfucker.

> *Kane: Or maybe you'd rather I use it on you. Have you trembling and dripping, so desperate to be filled you'd beg me for it.*

"Jesus fucking Christ, Kane. Are we still talking about the knife?" I say out loud, looking around another corner. A hot, pulsing ache settles between my legs, and I don't know if I should be horrified by that. I clench my jaw, grinding my teeth so hard my head throbs. I can feel the tingly warmth spreading up my arms, and it's all I can do just to breathe, hoping that will stop it from spreading any further.

> *Kane: No, Princess. I'm talking about you.*

> *Kane: Your legs, shaking, while I drag the blade over your skin, teasing you...*

> *Kane: ... see, I think... you like it a little rough?*

A violent shudder rolls through me, I have to stop walking. My thighs clench so hard my muscles ache. I feel him everywhere. My pulse is pounding in my ears, my nipples tightening against my dress, my clit throbbing, desperate for friction.

Fuck. Fuck. Fuck.

I'm desperate for any type of control, but there isn't any. Not when it comes to him. Not when his words seep into my skin like a toxin, spreading through my veins, unraveling me from the inside out.

I take a slow, steadying breath and push deeper into the back corner of the library. Maybe if I stick to the shadows he can't see me. I know he has to be close if he can see my reactions. It means he's watching me, and I'm just going to not acknowledge the thrill that seems to go through me knowing that.

My eyes drift upward to the loft and there he is. The smug looking bastard leaning against the railing, one hip cocked, arms resting lazily on the wooden beam.

His eyes lock onto mine and his lips curl into that goddamn smirk that makes me want to either slap him or drop to my knees. Maybe both.

He doesn't move. He doesn't fucking have to. At this point I'd crawl up the stairs if it meant this ache would go away.

My breath is shallow, my chest rising and falling too fast, my body coming alive under the weight of his stare. And the bastard knows it.

He tilts his head, dragging his eyes over me like he's peeling me apart layer by layer, stripping me down with just a look. *As if I wasn't already unraveled.*

I should move, but I don't. I'm rooted to the spot, caught in his stare like a moth to a flame.

The tingling is back, or maybe it never left. I honestly can't tell if it's my magic or if it's just him? Hell, if I know, but I shove it down, force myself to focus.

Not that it helps.

His dark hair falls around his face, framing those sharp cheekbones in a way that makes my mouth go dry. I swallow hard, searching for *anything* else to focus on.

And Failing. Miserably.

The heat in my hands intensifies, a buzzing that refuses to be ignored. And then he moves. His eyes lock onto mine as he begins his slow descent down the staircase, one slow, stupid step at a time.

I'm still openly staring when his smirk deepens.

"Like what you see, Princess?"

And then he fucking *winks*. Followed by a low chuckle, that rolls over me like a caress. My whole body tightens, heat threatening to consume me whole. All I can do is breathe.

I blink, desperate to reboot my brain, but it's fried beyond repair.

"What? No. I mean, yes, but that's—"

Jesus. The words tumble out in a frantic mess, and I want to throw myself into the sun. *What the actual fuck was that?*

Kane's grin widens like I just handed him a gift. "It's okay," he murmurs, voice dipping, and I can tell he's trying to bait me. *And it's working.*

"I know you want me."

Fucker.

My mouth parts, my brain scrambling for a response. "No! I don't, actually!"

Too defensive. Way too defensive.

His brow lifts, all smug amusement, his silence dragging out just long enough to let me bury myself deeper.

Instinct kicks in, and I step back.

Right into the edge of the table. My breath catches, and he sees it. His smirk sharpens, like he enjoys every second of watching me squirm.

I lift my hands, intending to shove him away, but the second my palms land on his chest, he leans in instead.

Oh Shit.

Heat radiates off him, burning through the thin fabric of his T-shirt, searing into my fingers. Into me.

"Are you sure about that?"

Okay, fine. I can admit that I missed his arrogant ass... a little. Not that he needs to know that.

My heart pounds as he holds my stare, and the heat in his eyes is impossible to look away from.

Talk about a literal wet dream.

It doesn't help that I've been on edge since that fucking dream in the tub.

When he steps closer, the table digs into my legs, giving me nowhere to go. I perch on the edge, meeting his gaze, watching as his hands grip the surface on either side of me. Caging me in. Then his voice drops low enough to steal the air from my lungs.

"I've wanted to do this all morning."

His lips crash into mine. The kiss is searing, it's like holding back has been its own kind of torture, and now that he has me here, he's not wasting another second.

And fuck, if I'm going to be completely honest with myself. Neither am I. After the last few weeks, I'm done pretending.

I want him.

I meet him with equal fire, my tongue teasing his, coaxing and demanding all at once. He nips at my bottom lip, a delicious sting that sends a jolt of heat through me. When his hand slides up, gripping the back of my neck. He tilts me just enough to give him the access he wants. Kissing me like he owns me.

And, Gods help me, I let him.

I suck at his tongue just to see if he's imagining the same filthy things I am. And judging by the low, rumbling growl vibrating in his chest, he is.

His grip tightens. One hand slides up my waist, burning in its wake, before threading into my hair. He tugs just tight enough to make me gasp.

A deep, satisfied sound escapes him.

"Careful, Princess," he murmurs, against my lips. The heat in his voice alone could get me off. "You're already testing my self-control."

His words ignite something reckless inside me. But the second his teeth graze my jaw, I smirk.

"Maybe that was the point."

If he's going to push, then I'm pushing him just as much.

"Do your worst." His words are silk and gravel, pure fucking sin.

My pulse pounds between my legs, the heat tightening, and I know whatever comes next is going to ruin me.

But I don't hesitate.

I slide off the table and sink to my knees.

A deep guttural sound rumbles in his chest, his body tensing. He cups my face, his thumb brushing just beneath my ear, deceptively gentle. But I see it for what it is, a warning.

But I don't stop. I grip the waistband of his sweats, my fingers curling around the fabric, my intentions clear. His hand closes over mine, stopping me.

Our eyes lock and there's something flickering there. But I don't give him the chance to speak because if he talks, I might lose my nerve.

So I tug.

The fabric slides over hard muscle, smooth skin, and oh fuck. A rush of liquid heat slams into me, my pulse hammering like a war drum.

My thighs clench, that familiar, throbbing ache between my legs is begging me for any type of friction. Demanding relief I don't have time to chase. Because right now, I have other plans.

I lift my gaze, lips parting slightly, my breath shallow, every muscle wound so fucking tight I might snap.

Kane watches me with the kind of expression that should be illegal. Head tilted in a silent dare. He licks his bottom lip, his smirk deepening as my thighs press together on instinct.

"Something caught your attention, sweetheart?"

Oh he's enjoying this. And if I'm being honest, so am I. Having this much control over him is intoxicating.

As soon as his cock springs free, thick and heavy in his grip, my mouth waters. I shouldn't be this surprised. I've seen him before, but fuck. Nothing prepares me for him. He's thick. Massive. And perfect.

I can feel my nipples harden, rubbing against the fabric of my dress, and at this point my whole body is tingling. I haven't heard any thunder in the distance, so I think it's safe to say it's all him influencing my body's reaction.

I flatten my palms against his thighs, nails digging in slightly, dragging down slowly. I watch as his breath shudders, his jaw flexes.

His fingers sink into my hair, tightening his grip enough to make it sting. And then he leans down, his breath hot on my ear.

"Open that pretty mouth of yours."

The words are a command, dripping with authority, and fuck if I don't want to obey.

But I make him wait.

I press a slow, lingering kiss to his inner thigh, feeling the way his muscles flex beneath my lips, his control fracturing with every second that passes. The power I hold is thrumming through my veins like fire.

So I take my time, kissing my way up his leg, inch by inch, intentionally cruel. I love seeing the way his body is reacting to me, as much as mine is reacting to him.

His cock twitches, waiting, but I hover just shy of his swollen tip, letting my breath fan over him. A single bead of precum glistens, and before he can get out another order, I flick my tongue out, catching it, savoring the salty taste of him.

A sharp inhale leaves his lips. His grip tightens in my hair, his fingers threading deeper, another warning.

But I'm not giving him what he wants. Not yet.

I drag my lips along his length, placing slow, featherlight kisses along his shaft. My breath teasing the places I know he's aching to have touched. I take him in my hand, stroking him softly, but refusing to give him more.

The frustration rolling off him is thick, and it only feeds the thrill buzzing under my skin. His right hand wraps around his cock, stroking slowly as he watches me, his gaze dark with intent.

And when he brushes the tip against my lips, my breath catches. My stomach tightens and every muscle in my body locks up. Molten heat pools between my thighs, and I'm sure I'm dripping at this point. I don't know how much longer I can tease him before he snaps.

"Be a good girl and open your mouth."

Fuck. Me.

My control is slipping, fast. That tone is laced with authority and promise, and my entire body is seconds away from going up in flames. It shouldn't be this hot. It shouldn't have me this fucking wet before he's even really touched me.

I part my lips, my tongue flicks out, teasing just the tip before taking him, inch by inch, stretching my lips around him, hollowing my cheeks as I suck him deeper.

His sharp inhale is immediate, his grip in my hair tightening like he's seconds away from losing his control.

I work him, in slow, teasing strokes. My tongue swirling around the head before I take him all the way in, pressing my palms to his thighs for leverage, determined to hear more of the sounds that were making my pussy throb a second ago.

690

His fingers flex, tightening in my hair.

But then he pulls out.

Before I have time to object, his hand grips my throat, fingers curling around the delicate skin. He lifts me effortlessly, the movement is so swift, it knocks the air from my lungs. Control is all his.

My back hits the table, and before I can even fucking think. A sharp gasp rips from my throat as he yanks my dress up, spreading my thighs wide, no hesitation. He drops down. Then his mouth is on me. Devouring me.

A low groan rumbles through him as his tongue flicks against my clit, slow at first, teasing, then his pace turns relentless, his lips closing around me, sucking deep.

My hips jerk, and my legs are shaking as I arch into him, a broken moan spilling from my lips.

The sounds alone are bringing me closer to the edge. The way his mouth works me, is like it's his damn right to make me fall apart on his tongue. It's almost too much.

His grip on my thighs tightens, holding me in place, refusing to let me get away. His tongue circles, dragging me to the brink of insanity. I'm already so fucking close.

His teeth graze my clit and it's enough to have my entire body locked in place. I grip his hair, begging without words, needing him to finish what he started. I'm so close.

And then he's gone.

His heat disappears, his hands leave my body, and his mouth is no longer between my legs.

My choked gasp is instant. My body clenches around nothing, desperate, and my head snaps up just in time to see him rising from between my legs, his chin glistening and his eyes are dark.

He licks his lips, and a shudder racks through me.

My chest heaves, rage and need tangled together so tight I could scream.

Just as I open my mouth to protest, his mouth is on mine. I can taste myself on his tongue, feeling every thick, hard inch of him pressing right where I want it.

His kiss is devastating.

He moves with purpose, his grip is bruising as he pins me against him, the rough drag of his hands on my thighs sends sparks skittering under my skin.

I barely register the shift in his movement before my back slams flat against the table. Not a second later, he grips the edge and clears it in one swift motion. Papers, books, everything crashing to the floor as I gasp.

His mouth is back on mine, his hands push up my dress. And I hear the low rasp of fabric tearing before I even realize what's happening. *Did he just...*

Then he's on his knees and my back arches off the table, fingers twisting into his hair as his mouth closes over me, sucking hard, licking like he has something to prove.

"Fuck. Kane," I gasp, my magic flares, heat buzzing under my skin, crackling at the edges.

He groans into me, sending me right to the edge, about to spiral. Then he stops.

No.

A furious whimper leaves me as he rises to his full height, licking his lips, smirking like the asshole he is.

His fingers skim up my thigh, leaving fire in their wake. His other hand wraps around my throat, his thumb drawing circles on my skin.

"Relax, Princess." His voice is thick. "You'll get what you need."

My legs tighten around his waist, dragging him closer, my nails biting into his skin.

"Kane," I pant, my hands moving to his waist, suddenly his fingers are on my wrist, trapping me.

My spine hits the wood and my thighs spread wide. His hands grip my knees, forcing them farther apart, and my body arches. The lights flicker in time with the pounding in my veins, almost like my magic is as desperate for him as I am.

Is that a thing?

I suck in a sharp breath, forcing it down, trying to calm myself, to contain the wildfire crackling beneath my skin. But Kane doesn't let me.

He leans down, pressing his forehead against mine, his cock thick and heavy between us, rubbing right where I need him most.

"Is this what you want?"

My breath stutters, my entire body trembling, wound so tight I might implode.

Then he's kissing me. Tasting me. Consuming me. His tongue claims mine, his grip tightens on my waist as he pulls me to the edge of the table, lining himself up, sliding back and forth against my soaked entrance, refusing to give me what I want.

I hate him.

I bite his bottom lip, sucking it between my teeth, and he groans, grinding against me.

"Kane, if—"

But I don't get the words out, he thrusts inside me, and the world shatters.

My back bows, a choked moan ripped from my throat as he fills me in one, deep, brutal stroke. The lights flicker again, I feel it surging through my veins, spreading like a pulse. I need to rein it in, but I'm seconds away from exploding.

His head drops against my shoulder, a low curse leaving his lips, and his hands tighten on my hips.

The table shakes, rocking against the floor, every devastating movement sending pleasure licking up my spine.

I can't think. I can't fucking breathe.

Kane shifts, hooks my legs over his arms, angling me, hitting that spot that makes my vision go white.

"Fuck, Raven." His voice is all gravel. "You feel so fucking good."

I clench around him, my body trembling and my control on my magic is dangerously close to snapping.

He drops his hand between us, finding my clit. He circles once, twice...

And I come so hard that my entire body shudders. Pleasure crashes through me, violent and all-consuming. My body locks up, every muscle pulling tight as I shatter, his name rips from my throat. Somewhere outside the door, a light bursts, the sharp pop barely registering over the rush that's dragging my under.

Kane doesn't stop, not until his own control snaps, until he's lost to it and gives in following me over the edge.

Then silence.

Just panting breaths, the quiet hum of my buzzing skin, and Kane.

He leans in, his forehead brushing mine, lips brushing over my cheek, my jaw, my mouth. "... that was a good start."

He presses one last kiss on my jaw, then my lips, lingering enough to make me heat up all over again, before he pulls back entirely.

He adjusts his sweats, muscles flexing as he steps away.

I blink, my hazy mind snapping into sharp focus. "Wait, where are you going?" The words tumble out before I can stop them.

He glances back over his shoulder, that devastating smirk still in place. "I'll be right back. Don't move." His voice is firm, and it settles into my skin before I can analyze it.

I watch him as he walks over to the counter. My body is still humming, still entirely too aware of the fact that I just let Kane absolutely ruin me.

Holy shit.

My legs are still a little shaky, but I grip the edge of the table, pulling myself upright. Before I can move, he's back. A glass of water in one hand, a damp cloth in the other.

He doesn't say a word as he kneels between my legs, his touch is gentle as he presses the cloth against my skin, cleaning up the mess we made.

My breath catches, and a full-on war breaks out inside me.

I feel like I'm standing at the edge of something I won't survive if I fall. Especially since I'm not sure when I'll be coming back to Scotland. That thought alone has me sobering up real quick. I know this can't be anything but casual, since I'm leaving.

I swat at his hand, my cheeks burning. "I'll get it myself."

His eyes flick to mine, amusement flickering there. "Easy, killer."

I glare, but my body softens. I should hate this. I know if I don't get the fuck out of here, I won't get anything done and it will just be harder to leave with Cam.

"I have to go back to my house to get some stuff." The words come out too fast.

Kane's expression doesn't shift, his usual composed mask slipping neatly back into place. But there's something in the way he nods that tells me he's reading me like an open book.

"I'll have my driver ready in ten." He pauses, studying me, and something about the moment makes my stomach twist.

Then, as if testing the waters, he adds, "Would you like to come back later? Cam will be here, and we could go over some things over dinner? Maybe he'll have more answers for you when he comes back."

My breath catches.

For half a second, he's not the cocky, insufferable man I can't stop thinking about.

He's just... Kane.

God. What is this man doing to me?

I swallow, braving eye contact even though it's a mistake. "Yeah, that sounds fun."

That sounds fun? Really? That's the best you could do?

His smirk deepens, his eyes flickering with something unreadable, but no less heated.

"Come on, let's get you home."

I watch the landscape blur past, my thoughts just as tangled as the winding roads.

The last few weeks have been nothing short of insane. Magic, secrets, an entire history I didn't even know belonged to me. And yet, here I am, scrolling through my emails like my life is still normal. I know I have to think about all this, process it. But I just need to get everything here sorted first. Then I can breathe and make a plan.

A dry laugh escapes me.

I just found out I have actual magic, and I'm supposed to care about business details? The thought alone feels surreal, like I'm playing a part in a life that isn't mine. *But maybe it always has been? I just clearly was the only one who didn't know about it?*

All those years of training with my grandfather suddenly make sense. Each lesson meticulously crafted to prepare me for something I didn't even know existed. And the way he always seemed to know more than he let on... is now starting to click into place. How could they have not told me?

The thought tightens in my chest. A dull, deep ache beneath my ribs. Not now.

I shove that emotion down too, before it can take root. I have enough to process without opening that door.

My phone pings, pulling me back.

Shocker. Mike-n-ike.

A quiet giggle escapes me at the nickname. Sometimes it's the small things in life. My thumb hovers over the screen before I open it.

> Miss Taylor,
>
> I wanted to reach out, though I figured you might not respond until you're back from Skye. If you're still in town, I'd like to meet up to go over a few final details with you. It would be an opportunity to iron out the remaining specifics and discuss the proposal in person.
>
> Additionally, I think I'd very much like to work with you and your team, and perhaps we could even celebrate this next step together.
>
> Today works best, as I'll be leaving tomorrow. I can arrange a driver to pick you up this afternoon. I promise not to take up too much of your time, but I do believe this discussion warrants an in-person meeting.
>
> What do you think?
>
> Talk soon,
> Mike

I reread the email, my eyes narrowing slightly. *Celebrate this next step together?*

A chuckle escapes me as I roll my eyes. *Mike Wazowski strikes again.* Who does this guy think he is, casually summoning me? But honestly... I respect it. He's direct, and he runs his company like a damn fortress.

And tying up this last loose end might be exactly what I need before heading back to Nveri.

The thought of leaving tugs at something inside me, though, and my mind goes straight to Kane. I don't know where this leaves us. I know we are never going to be anything serious, because I have no clue how long I'm going to be gone. Even though the sex is amazing. But I also know one thing for certain, I have much bigger things to deal with right now.

I need to figure out who I am. What this magic means. What it means for my family, for my life. No matter how intense things with Kane have been, I can't let myself get lost in him.

Maybe that's why I let this morning happen, because deep down, I know I need answers more than I need distractions.

Even if those distractions come with dimples and an orgasm-inducing smirk.

I huff out a breath and type out a quick response to Mike, letting him know I'll be ready in a couple of hours. Daylight feels like a safer bet for this meeting. That, and it gives me enough time to get back to Kane's and make plans with Cam for the trip back to Nveri.

A flush creeps up my neck, and heat starts to spread under my skin just thinking about this morning.

I shake it off, marching straight to the bathroom. Like rinsing him off me will somehow fix whatever the hell is happening in my head. The hot water does wonders for my muscles, but it does absolutely nothing to quiet my mind. I secretly wish I had my lavender bath oil, and enough time to take a bath right now.

I scrub my hands over my face and go through my shower on autopilot. There's too much to do to be thinking about Kane and bath oils.

I towel off quickly, tossing my hair over one shoulder as I move through the house, grabbing the last few things I have scattered around that I need to pack. I grab my necklace off the nightstand, I'm about to put it on, but something in me hesitates. Instead, I slip it into the small pocket in my bag. I'll put it on later.

I move to the dresser, grabbing my crystals, rolling them in my fingers, and tossing those into my bag too. I scan the room, wondering where the hell that book could be. I definitely need to find that before I leave. My brows knit together as I check the drawers, the bedside table, I even check under the bed.

Nothing.

Frustration prickles at the back of my neck, my gut twisting as I scan the room again. *I know I brought it with me.*

I sigh, pushing a hand through my damp hair. If I don't find it now, I'm going to have to figure it out later, but I would rather not have to worry about it. It has to be somewhere. At least when I get back to Nveri, I'll have more time to explore and check out the library Elle said she'd show me.

I pick up my dagger that's still in the holster Elle made me, admiring the detail she put into this, before tucking it securely into my bag. I still have one last thing to check.

I grab my phone, already typing out a message.

> Me: Hey! I miss you so much, how are things? I need a favor. Can you check the study to see if that book is in there? I could've sworn I brought it, but it's not here.

Her reply comes almost instantly, and I'm already grinning before I open it.

> Rachel: Girl, I hope you're getting dicked down real good. Make sure you give that fucker the ride of his life so he doesn't think of anyone but you ;)

> I don't want to hear from you unless I get details!

> I'll check for the book... before I head out of town.

I huff out a laugh, rolling my eyes. Of course that's her first response. I'm not even going to justify that with a response. I move into the next room, my thoughts still circling back to the missing book.

"Where the hell are you?" I mutter, scanning every possible place it could be. Maybe Rachel accidentally put it in her bag?

I pause, putting my hands on my hips, exhaling slowly. *Okay, little book, you need to be here.* I'm not even sure this book is going to have any answers, maybe it's just a journal or a fairytale book, but whatever it is, I still need to find it regardless, it belonged to my grandparents.

After combing through every drawer, cabinet, and shadowed corner, I drop into the chair with a frustrated sigh. My phone is already in hand, typing out a message to Rachel, asking her to double check her bags.

My fingers hover over the send button, when I look up and there it is. Sitting right there on the coffee table, exactly where I could've sworn I already looked.

I knew I brought it.

"Are you kidding me?"

I just tore this place apart, and it's sitting right here on the table? I set my phone down reaching for the book, and my pulse thrums, my skin prickling, and that tingling sensation is back again. I really wish I could figure out what triggers the tingling, and what it means. Does that mean I'm using magic? Or something else?

I have some time before Mike's driver arrives, so I sink a little deeper into the chair, flipping the book open. The pages whisper as they turn, and then something stops me cold.

My pulse quickens.

Shifters:

Among the rarest of creatures, shifters walk the line between worlds, able to transition seamlessly between their human and animal forms. Though scarce, they are revered for their unwavering loyalty, and their ability to disappear.

But there is one other kind of shifter. The True Shifter:

A being unbound by the limitations of flesh and bone. One who can shift into anything they desire. Animal. Human. And the strongest can shift into objects.

Not a single confirmed record of them exists. At least, not anymore.

The last known mention of True Shifters dates back to before the rise of the Shadow Queen. Before Fae divided. Before the bloodlines fractured.

Some say they vanished. Some say they were hunted. Others believe they were never real to begin with.

Shifters served the Shadow Queen, their abilities shackled by spells so ancient that not even death could break them. They were soldiers. Pawns. Shadows bound to her will.

But a True shifter could never be bound. They're loyal to the bloodline. They also choose their loyalty and when they do, it's for life. It is for this reason that some scholars speculate the Shadow Queen herself was the one to eradicate them.

Yet the question remains. Did they ever exist?

I skim through a few other entries, some intriguing, but not immediately relevant. Blood magic, elemental affinities, telepathy.

Then my eyes land on a passage that makes my breath catch.

There are many forms of power. However, the strongest Fae to date is the Shadow King. No full record of his capabilities exists, but those documented include:
-Strength
-Healing
-Mind Manipulation
-Shapeshifting
-Shadow control.

My heart skips a beat.

I reread the words, letting them settle over me. Shapeshifting.

The mention of True Shifters already had me spinning, but this? Who is the King of Nveri? Cam mentioned the witches finding refuge in other realms, which means there has to be more than one king, right?

My thoughts flash to Cam. He said he could shift. Could he be a True Shifter? I know he laughed it off when I asked him if he was the king, but it says right here that the Shadow King can shift.

I shake my head, my fingers tightening around the book. The more I learn, the deeper the questions go. My only option is to just go back and find out as much as I can, and hope it leads to answers about my family.

The sharp buzz of my phone yanks me back to reality, jolting me from my thoughts, letting me know the driver will be here shortly.

I sigh, snapping the book shut before tucking it carefully into my bag. I slip in a few other things I plan to take to Kane's, but the uneasy feeling lingers, threading itself through my spine like a warning.

There's more to this, I can feel it.

I don't want to take my bag to my meeting, but I also don't know if it's just safe to leave out in the open. I'm sure the house is safe, especially if it belongs to Kane, but I decide to slide my bag under the bed anyway, you can never be too careful. I smooth my hand over my leggings, exhaling slowly, trying to calm the restless energy crackling beneath my skin.

I need air.

The driver will be here shortly, so I step outside and sink into one of the porch chairs, letting the warmth of the sunlight chase away the chill in my thoughts. I close my eyes and listen to the soft breeze, it should be calming, but my mind is now tangled in the words I just read.

True shifters. The Shadow King. The rise of the Shadow Queen. Who are these people?

CHAPTER 50

I Wish You Would...

RAVEN

T his place is different from the last restaurant Mike took me to. It seems cozier, more intimate. The kind of place where whispered conversations feel like secrets.

I step out just as Mike gets out of his own car, walking toward me with that signature confident ease. His suit is crisp, his hair is perfectly styled, and his smile is just the right mix of polished and warm.

"You look lovely today, Raven."

His tone is easy, but I don't miss the way his gaze flickers over to me, taking in every detail.

"Thank you." I offer a polite smile. "I have to admit, I wasn't expecting this meeting so soon. You work fast."

He chuckles, holding the door open for me as we step inside. "When I see something worth pursuing, I don't waste time."

It takes everything in me not to roll my eyes. I'm not sure if he's talking about the deal or me.

The restaurant is quiet but alive, the atmosphere is refined without being stuffy. We're led to a booth tucked into the corner, and it's just secluded enough to feel deliberate. I wouldn't be surprised if he totally planned this.

Once we're settled in, and the moment our menus are set aside, Mike launches into business.

His pitch is polished, every detail meticulously tailored, and, if I'm being honest, it's solid. I nod along, asking a few clarifying questions, but the more he talks, the more I realize he's already accounted for most of my concerns.

He's good. I'll give him that.

When he finally leans back, his expression remains unreadable, but I know he's watching me carefully. Waiting for my approval or waiting to see if I'll challenge him.

"What do you think?" His tone is all casual, but his body language is anything but.

"It's good," I admit, meeting his gaze.

His lips curve, but I don't miss the flicker of something sharper when I suggest a slight revision.

For a second, something flashes in his eyes that looks an awful lot like annoyance. He schools his features quickly, nodding like my suggestion doesn't bother him at all. "I'll have my team make the adjustment and send over the revision as soon as possible."

Mike is undeniably attractive, and for the most part, he's thoughtful and polite. But something about him is just too polished. There are moments where he seems almost sweet, but then the mask slips just enough for me to catch it.

And that interests me far more than his proposal could.

I don't even need to be here. I'm not the one signing the contract, Steven is. I'm just the one who knows what he will and won't go for. And this? This little power play won't fly.

I keep my tone polite. "As long as that revision is handled, we should be good to go."

Mike's smile returns, but it's not quite as relaxed as before. "Of course," he replies smoothly. "I'll send the updated version over soon."

Our food arrives just as I'm debating whether or not I actually want to keep entertaining this little game he's trying to play. Luckily I don't have to decide, because I'm starving. I want to eat.

"I'm actually heading to Skye soon," I swirl my fork through my plate. "Then, I'll probably head home after. If I'm gone too long, Steven might replace me."

But Mike's smile tightens.

"Well," he smiles. "I hope you're not leaving too soon. I'd love to take you out to dinner before you go."

Ah. There it is.

I'm not surprised by the invitation itself, but I am surprised by the sudden shift in his demeanor. I debate telling him I'm not interested, but maybe I'll just take the easy way out on this one, and once the contracts are signed, I can gracefully back out of the date he's wanting. I tap my fork against my plate, watching him for a beat longer than necessary. Then, finally, I offer a slow smile.

"Let me figure out when I'll be back from Skye, and I'll let you know!"

His smile widens slightly, the tension in his shoulders easing, but that satisfaction is still there.

"I would love that."

I take a real look at him. The sharp lines of his jaw, the effortless way his suit fits, the sheer confidence in his every movement. He dresses like a man who knows exactly what he wants. Yet, I don't feel the same spark with him like I do with Kane.

Mike leans back, his tone shifting to something more playful. "Well, Raven, darling, I'm off to work, but we'll be in touch."

"I'll get everything sent over to Steven for him to review, and in the meantime, I'll be on the edge of my seat waiting for you to let me know when I can take you out."

He chuckles, leaning in slightly as if sharing a secret.

"I know a few places you'd absolutely love, but the rest? That's a surprise." A confident smirk tugs at his lips. "If you want to know what it is, you'll just have to come and see for yourself."

There's an effortless charm in the way he says it, and I hate that it almost works on me. Despite myself, my lips twitch into a smile. But I shut it down just as fast. He doesn't need any more encouragement, and I refuse to be another name on his list. If he wants to impress me, he's going to have to do a hell of a lot better than a smirk and a little charm.

He stands, pulling a sleek wallet from his pocket and tossing more than enough cash onto the table. "Please, don't feel the need to rush on my account, your driver should be outside whenever you're ready."

I nod. "Thanks, Mike. This has been really nice." And I mean that. Despite the business aspect of our meeting, it's been surprisingly nice. "I'll let you know once I figure out my schedule."

He motions for me to stay seated as he adjusts the cuff of his suit, the movement is effortless. "Always a pleasure, Raven." His voice is warm and composed. "I look forward to hearing from you."

And just like that, he turns and walks out of the restaurant, his presence lingering even after he disappears through the door.

I can't shake the feeling that something feels a little off.

I sip the last of my drink, allowing him to have enough time to leave, so that I don't run into him outside. My fingers drum lightly against the glass as I let my thoughts settle. The meeting went well, I think Steven will like him. The deal is nearly finalized, and my part is done. I *should* feel good about this.

I shake it off as I push out of the booth and head outside, the late afternoon sun is still warm against my skin. I scan the lot for my ride, expecting to see the same driver who dropped me off. But the car isn't there.

My brows knit together as I step forward, scanning the rows of parked cars. But with each step, my body feels heavier, like something is pressing down on me, tightening around my chest.

What the hell?

A wave of dizziness crashes over me, the edges of my vision flickering. My breath quickens, shallow and uneven. I blink hard, trying to steady myself, but the ground tilts beneath me. My legs wobble, refusing to hold my weight.

No, no, no.

The asphalt shifts beneath me, my knees giving out.

A shadow moves nearby. I try to turn and react, but darkness rushes in before I can.

I blink, my mind sluggish, the haze lifting in slow, uneven waves. My body feels heavy, and my limbs feel useless, like they don't belong to me. There's something soft beneath me. A couch maybe?

Not good.

I've seen enough horror movies to know this isn't how I plan to go out. *Not today.*

A shadow moves to my right. My muscles tense, or at least they try to. Then, Mike steps into view. His expression is careful but not panicked.

"Raven." His voice is slightly hurried. "Thank God, you're awake."

I push myself up on my elbows, but the second I do, the world tilts and my stomach lurches

"What the fuck..." I mutter, blinking hard. Forcing myself to focus.

Mike lifts his hands, palms up. "Easy. You passed out in the parking lot. I was finishing a call when I saw you go down. Figured it was faster to bring you here than wait for an ambulance. I called for a doctor, he should be here soon to check you out."

I stare at him, letting his words sink in. There's a calmness in his tone, but it's doing nothing for my nerves. I guess if he was lying, he'd be twitchy and defensive.

I shift again, testing my strength. My body protests, sluggish and uncooperative, but deep in my core, there's something—weak, but still there. A flicker of power, waiting. But not gone.

That's good at least.

I exhale slowly, forcing my shoulders to relax, trying not to look like I'm mentally calculating every possible exit. I'm not in any shape to move yet, not that I even understand what the hell is going on.

Mike is watching me, his expression carefully balanced, just concerned enough without tipping me into panic. Nothing about his body language suggests a threat. If he wanted to hurt me, he had plenty of chances.

And yet, my instincts haven't stopped screaming since I woke up.

I force a slow, easy breath, schooling my features into something softer, keeping my tone even. "I'm glad you were there to help."

His posture remains steady, but his shoulders ease, just a fraction.

"Can I, by chance, get a glass of water?"

His smile is reassuring. "Of course. Just stay put and rest. I'll be right back."

I nod, keeping my expression neutral as he moves toward the kitchen. My heart hammers against my ribs. Something isn't right.

Muffled voices drift in and out, distant and warped, like I'm listening through thick glass. Someone is calling my name.

I try to respond, but it's like my lips aren't mine, like my body isn't mine. Why can't I move?

The voices fade as darkness pulls me under again, deeper this time. I don't know how long I drift suspended in a place between waking and unconsciousness. Like something is keeping me under, forcing me back down every time I get close to the surface.

My heart pounds sluggishly, each beat slow. My magic is there, but it's dulled. I try to reach for it, but it's like grasping at smoke.

The world sharpens like a blade, suddenly I hear the hum of traffic, the scent of asphalt, and see the glow of streetlights.

Is this a memory? A dream?

I'm stepping out of the restaurant, phone in hand. I press it to my ear, my pulse thrumming, as my voice shakes. "Kane?"

Static.

A harsh crackle distorts the line, his voice breaks apart, shifting between something familiar and something wrong.

"I think I need a favor," I manage. "Something's wrong, and I need you to come get me."

The static deepens, swallowing his response.

Then, nothing.

A sharp inhale rips through my lungs as I jolt awake. My heart is slamming against my ribs, my pulse feels erratic.

The storm rages outside, rain hammering against the windows, wind tearing through the trees with a howling I can't place.

I'm still on the couch. I'm still here, wherever here is. My heart sinks.

The air in the room is thick, heavy in a way that has nothing to do with my own exhaustion. I close my eyes, reaching for the storm, trying to feel it, to pull at its power like I've been practicing for weeks. But it's too distant. It feels like it's miles away. Like I'm buried underwater.

Every breath I take sends a wave of nausea rolling through me. Muffled voices drift from somewhere beyond the walls. It's too quiet to catch anything, but just loud enough to set me on edge.

I force my eyes to stay open, my thoughts slowly untangling as I take in my surroundings. The room is dimly lit, with the faint scent of leather and cologne lingering in the air. I'm on the couch, in what seems to be his living room.

My chest tightens, a desperate urge to leave crawls under my skin like a living thing. I need to get out of here, I need to be anywhere but here, in a stranger's house, feeling like my body isn't mine.

A cool breeze filters in through an open window, cutting through the thick haze in my mind. It's a small comfort, but one that I latch onto, trying to steady myself. This doesn't feel the same as what happened in Nveri. This is very different.

I need to leave. Now.

What I need to do is call Kane. No matter how smooth or accommodating Mike may seem, being here feels wrong.

As if summoned by my thoughts, Mike steps into the room, a glass of water in his hand. His expression is calm.

"Hey, you're awake," his voice smooth. "I brought you water earlier, but you were already asleep."

He holds the glass out to me, his movements slow. "Here, you should drink this. Just take it slow."

I take it, the cool condensation grounding me slightly. But a flicker of hesitation stays at the back of my mind, I keep my grip careful and my sips small.

"Thanks." My voice is hoarse. I clear my throat, pushing for casual. "Did you mention something about a doctor earlier?"

Mike nods, his face is unreadable. "Yeah, he's in the other room. He'd like to ask you a few questions, just to make sure you're okay."

My pulse kicks up a notch, and my eyes sweep the room. *Where is my stuff?*

I shift slightly, trying not to move too much or I might actually throw up. "You didn't happen to grab my bag, did you?" I force a small laugh, hoping it sounds effortless. "I had it with me when I left the restaurant, but it's not here. I need my phone, I should probably call my friend."

Mike tilts his head, a thoughtful look flickers across his face. "I don't recall you having a bag," he says after a moment. "But I'll check the car. Maybe it's in the backseat. If not, I can have my driver head back to the restaurant to retrieve it."

I nod, forcing an easy smile despite the tension tightening in my chest. "That would be great. Thanks."

His lips curve into a reassuring smile, but there's something practiced about it. He lingers a moment too long before finally turning away, his footsteps fading down the hall.

The second he's gone, I exhale, sinking deeper into the couch.

On the surface, Mike is a picture of charm and hospitality, polite, even thoughtful, checking all the right boxes. But no matter how hard I try to convince myself of that, unease curls in my stomach.

None of this makes sense.

I barely have time to process before someone else steps into the room.

He's older, tall, and dressed casually. Too casually for a doctor. A button-down, slacks, wire-rimmed glasses that catch the light as he adjusts them.

I don't like this.

"Hello, Raven," the man greets, his tone warm. "I heard you passed out. I'm here to check on a few things, and make sure you're alright. Mike said you weren't feeling well."

I swallow, keeping my expression neutral. "Yeah, I think I feel a little better now." I lift the glass of water slightly, as if that somehow proves my point. "Not sure what happened. One second, I was fine. The next, I felt dizzy, then... nothing."

My voice is steady, but my pulse isn't.

I reach for my necklace, but my fingers meet bare skin. My stomach plummets. Right, it's in my bag. The bag I don't have. Realizing I didn't actually bring my bag to our meeting makes me feel a little better. But I still need my phone, and I need to get the fuck out of here. Now.

The man smiles politely, but his eyes are elsewhere.

"I see." He tilts his head slightly, like he's trying to piece something together. Then, after a beat, he asks, "I have to ask, because it's surprisingly common in cases like this, but is there a chance you might be pregnant?"

I snort before I can stop myself. "No. Absolutely not."

The answer comes out sharper than I intend, but seriously? *That's what you're leading with?*

He chuckles, unfazed. "Had to ask."

His expression shifts, something more thoughtful settling over his features. "Have you experienced anything else before this? Dizziness? Warmth? Tingling in your hands? Memory issues? Anything... unusual like that?"

My pulse spikes. I open my mouth then stop.

A warning instinct flares in my gut. *Don't tell him anything.*

Something about the way he asked, the way his gaze sharpens just slightly, makes me feel like he's fishing.

I force a shrug, keeping my expression neutral. "Not really, I mean... I didn't feel great a few days ago, but I think it was just something I ate."

The lie feels shaky even to me.

His stare lingers before he hums thoughtfully. "Hmm. Maybe it was just low blood sugar." He leans forward a bit. "When did you last eat before the diner?"

I think. "Breakfast I guess?"

His brows lift, and I realize how long I've actually gone without eating. Could that really be it? Before he can ask another question, Mike walks back in, his presence shifting the air instantly.

The doctor barely acknowledges him, holding up a single finger before stepping aside and speaking in hushed tones.

I can't make out the words, but Mike glances at me. Just for a second.

The doctor's gestures seem casual, probably telling him I'm fine. That it was nothing.

And yet, the hairs on the back of my neck refuse to settle.

CHAPTER 51

theMOMENTIknew

KANE

I knew she was wild. Knew she had that fire barely contained beneath the surface. But this was something else. Like striking a match to gasoline and standing there, watching the flames lick higher, knowing damn well I should walk away. But not wanting to. Not being able to.

It should unnerve me, make me step back. But instead, the memory of her only fuels the fire. I run a hand through my hair, exhaling sharply, savoring the thought of her

I rush through the rest of my shower, knowing Cam is on his way. Today, I finally get to hit him, and for once, I might even go easy on him. It's hard to be in a bad mood when I feel this fucking good.

By the time I'm dressed in sweats and a shirt, I toss my phone onto the dresser and head downstairs, feet moving on autopilot toward my office.

But then silence surrounds me.

When I open my eyes, I'm not in my office.

I'm in the woods.

The shift doesn't startle me, not at first. The air smells like pine and damp earth, the distant rustle of leaves filling the silence. A deep, rich wilderness stretches out before me, familiar in a way it shouldn't be.

I tilt my head back. Birds cut through the treetops, dark shapes against the pale morning light. Then a raven dips low, circling me.

I let out a dry chuckle. If my mind was going to conjure something, it would be her.

But something is wrong.

The air shifts as the trees grow taller, their trunks stretching into the sky, branches knotting like skeletal hands overhead as shadows thicken around me.

713

A single caw pierces the stillness commanding attention. The raven doesn't land, it just hovers. Waiting.

A shiver creeps down my spine.

Then comes the storm. Lightning shatters the sky, bathing the forest in white for a single, blinding moment, I see her.

Darkness descends. Thunder rolls through the trees with a low, earth-shattering growl. Rain slams into the ground, soaking through the dirt in seconds, filling the air with its sharp, electric scent. I can't see through it, but I know what I saw.

"Raven?"

I step forward, cutting through the relentless downpour. She doesn't move or react. Every muscle in my body coils tight as she just stands there, silent. Her lips parted like she wants to speak but can't. The fire in her eyes is gone, replaced by something hollow and haunted. Something is very wrong.

I step forward, my pulse hammering in my ears, rain soaking through my clothes, and my body is tense with an unease I can't shake.

"What are you doing out here, Princess?"

She doesn't answer. She just stands there, drenched, and pale. Just staring right through me.

My gut twists.

"Princess." Urgency threading through my tone. "What's wrong, what happened?"

She finally looks at me, and the raw unfiltered fear in her eyes sends a bolt of unease straight through my chest.

Her lips part, her voice barely more than a breath, "Something's wrong."

My spine locks.

"I can feel it," she continues, her brows knitting together like she's fighting to grasp something just out of reach. "I don't know what's happening to me..." She trails off, her throat working around the words that never come. Then, her hand flies to her head.

She winces, her entire body tenses.

"Raven."

I reach for her, instinct taking over, my hands finding her waist just as she sways. The second my fingers touch her, the storm doesn't just surround us. It's everywhere.

And I have no fucking clue what to do. The wind shifts, slamming into us with a force that has the trees thrashing like they're fighting against something unseen. The air hums, charged with something unnatural.

Lightning tears across the sky, a brilliant white streak cuts through the blackness, illuminating her.

The sight of her terrifies me. She's shaking, her entire body is rigid with something I can't see.

"It's not safe," she whispers. Her voice is so soft, I almost don't hear it over the storm. "I feel stuck. Like I can't move. I'm sca—"

Her words cut off. A sharp, visceral gasp ripping from her throat, her body seizing violently.

"Raven!"

I lunge forward, grabbing her as she screams. A sound so gut-wrenching, it tears through my ribs like a blade. She clutches her chest, fingers digging into the fabric like she's being ripped apart from the inside.

Panic claws at my ribs. "Raven, sweetheart, talk to me."

Her fingers latch onto my bicep, tight enough to bruise, and sharp enough to break skin. The second she touches me I feel a surge of energy explodes between us, like a fucking strike of lightning straight through my veins.

I stagger as she convulses, my fingers press into her clammy skin, forcing her to look at me.

"Raven, you have to wake up."

She doesn't move. Doesn't blink. I shake her once, then harder.

"Raven. NOW."

My voice cracks through the storm like a command, for a second, the world pauses and there's a beat of stillness. Then everything goes dark. And just like that, I'm awake. Slamming back into reality so hard my vision tilts, my lungs drag in air like I've been drowning.

Pain explodes behind my temples, sharp and unrelenting, like my skull is cracking open.

Everything hits me at once. A flood so fast, so violent, it nearly drops me to my knees. The weight of it is unbearable.

I stumble forward, my hands gripping the desk like it's the only thing keeping me upright.

"FUCK."

The roar rips from my throat, and before I can stop myself, I shove everything off the desk, sending books, papers, and glass shattering to the floor. The chair topples over, crashing into the shelves behind me.

I can't fucking breath, the air is too thick. My hands tremble at my sides, curling into fists as rage boils over. She's in trouble, I know it.

I slam my fist onto the desk, the sound splitting through the room like a gunshot. Then the door bursts open a second later, Cam storming inside, his eyes wild and frantic.

"Where is she?" His voice is tight with urgency.

I swallow hard, forcing down the fire clawing at my throat, pushing past the chaos raging inside me. Only the words that matter make it out.

"Raven's in trouble."

The second the words leave my mouth, Cam goes still. The air shifts, heavy with something unspoken. His jaw tightens, a muscle ticking as his entire body locks up. But it's not just shock that flickers across his face, it's something deeper.

And beneath it, just barely visible, is a sliver of fear.

Slowly, he lowers himself to one knee and bows his head.

"My Lord."

Acknowledgments

First off, I just want to thank God. I honestly never could've imagined where this journey would take me, and I'm so beyond grateful for everything it's become.

A huge thank you to my husband, Trevor, for being the best inspiration a girl could ask for and the ultimate real-life book boyfriend. For the endless support, the late-night encouragement, and for all the times you sat in my office for "date night" just to hang out so I could write. Thank you for holding down the fort with the kids, for believing in me when I doubted myself, and for always reminding me why I started. Thank you to my three incredible kids—you teach me more than I could ever hope to teach you. Your sticky notes, your encouragement, and your unwavering belief in me mean more than words can say. You guys will always be my reason.

To Bri, Audrey, Ani, Nicole, Amanda, Rachel, and Brette—thank you for being my ride-or-dies through every chapter of this chaos. You read this story when it was nothing but messy, unfiltered word vomit and still cheered me on like it was gold. You dragged me out of my writing cave when I needed it, reminded me to breathe, checked in when I went quiet, and kept me going when I wanted to quit. I wish I could name every single person who helped bring this book to life, but there's not enough paper in the world. Just know—I see you, I love you, and I couldn't have done this without you.

And finally, I'm circling back to my amazing husband once again—you've stood by me through every high and low, supporting me no matter what life threw our way. You are, and always will be, my number one—and my forever book boyfriend.

Sneak Peek
of

NIGHTSHADE

A Shadow Series Book II

NIGHTSHADE

RAVEN

S omehow, I feel even worse than I did the last time I woke up. Which is saying something, considering I was already miserable.

My body feels like it's been put through a meat grinder, every muscle feels weighed down, every nerve sparking with dull, aching protest. My mind is thick with fog, like it's stuck buffering.

It's dark outside now. Shit.

My pulse spikes. *How long have I been out for?*

And I still don't have my phone. *Double shit.*

My throat feels like I've been stranded in the desert for days, and I swear my tongue might just crumble to dust. I reach for the glass of water sitting on the table, but even that tiny movement sends a fresh wave of pain rolling through me.

This is not great. Not great at all.

Before I can force myself to move any further, I hear something. Soft footsteps coming from the other room. My spine stiffens, but before I can decide whether to play dead or throw hands, Mike walks in.

Right. Mike.

I blink, caught off guard as he offers an easy, practiced smile. "Raven, how are you feeling?"

Like I got hit by a truck, thrown into a blender, and set on fire.

I clear my throat. "Much better, thanks." Lies. All lies. "But I really should be going. I had plans, and I'm afraid I might've missed them. Did you find my phone by any chance?"

His expression doesn't shift. But it still sets off every instinct screaming at me to get the hell out of here.

"Of course." He crosses the room, picks up my phone, and hands it to me.

I press the button. Dead of course.

Really? You couldn't have plugged it in? I bite my tongue, swallowing down the irritation clawing up my throat.

He watches me carefully, his gaze lingering a second too long. "Are you sure you're up for leaving? You can stay, really. Head out in the morning."

He chuckles, "This isn't exactly how I pictured our first date going."

I force out a little laugh, even as my body screams at me for it. Everything about this feels wrong. The timing. The words. Everything.

"Don't worry, this doesn't count as a date," I say, plastering on a half-smile.

"I should hope not." He grins, pulling out his phone. "I'll have the car brought around."

My instincts are screaming at me.

Maybe it's the fact that I've spent an entire day knocked out in a stranger's house with zero contact with the outside world. Maybe it's the lingering nausea, or the way my limbs feel like they're on fire. Or maybe it's the fact that every single moment since I woke up has been dripping in wrongness.

Either way, I'll feel a hell of a lot better once I'm anywhere but here.

I push myself up, still a little unsteady, and Mike is instantly there.

"Are you sure you're okay, love?"

I nod quickly, forcing a chuckle. "Yeah, my leg was just asleep." I shake it out, hoping he buys it. Hoping he doesn't notice the way I have to fight to stay upright as the nausea claws up my throat.

By the time we make it outside, the car is already waiting. Thank God.

I exhale, as relief washes over me. "Thanks again, for everything." I climb into the car as fast as I can without actually making it look like I'm running

Mike holds my gaze a second too long before shutting the door. "Feel better."

The car pulls away, and the knot in my stomach tightens. The house disappears behind a veil of rain, swallowed by rolling hills and endless, stretching blackness.

Where the hell even am I?

I squint past the sheets of rain battering the glass, trying to make sense of the landscape. But all I catch are glimpses of trees bending under the wind's wrath. No buildings. No lights. No signs of civilization.

How was this place closer than a hospital? That logic makes no damn sense.

The farther we drive, the heavier the exhaustion drags at my bones.

At first I chalked it up to low blood sugar. Maybe dehydration. Hell, maybe I just had food poisoning. But now? Now I'm not really sure anymore.

My thoughts race through every possibility. Magic shouldn't feel like this. Cam never mentioned anything about side effects, aside from *burn out*. And I didn't even use any magic. Not since I got back. So why does it feel like my body is shutting down?

The rain intensifies, pounding against the windshield in relentless waves as the wipers struggle to keep up, their frantic rhythm slicing through the silence.

My fingers tighten against my thighs. Something isn't right. The storm feels... off. Like it knows something I don't.

It's not just the storm, or the way the trees blur past in a dizzying streak of darkness. It's not even the exhaustion dragging at my limbs. It's more than that.

I reach for my magic, searching for that familiar pulse, the constant hum that has always been there even when I ignored it. It slips through my grasp like smoke. Every time I try, it feels further away, like something is dragging it beyond my reach.

I don't know how long we've been driving when suddenly–everything stops.

Tires shriek against the pavement, the sound tearing through the storm like a scream. Then all I see is a blinding flash that sears my vision. The world narrows to a single, deafening instant before it implodes.

Impact.

Metal contorts around me, twisting with a sharp, earsplitting shriek. Glass explodes in a violent spray, slicing through the air. The car lurches, gravity surrendering to chaos as we spin. My stomach drops, a sickening freefall that sends my head snapping forward, then back, the seatbelt locking like a vice against my ribs.

The world tumbles, a disorienting blur of darkness and motion. A rush of sound—metal grinding, glass shattering, my own breath torn from my lungs. The force of it all drowns out thought, replacing it with pure, unrelenting sensation.

Then there's nothing but stillness.

A sharp, high-pitched ringing fills my ears, relentless and all consuming, swallowing the fractured remains of the night. Distantly, a horn blares, muffled, almost unreal. For a moment, I might as well be underwater.

I inhale, shallow and pained. My ribs protest with a sharp, searing ache. Cold presses in from all sides, the sting of shattered glass embedded in my skin. My head pounds with a brutal, unrelenting rhythm, drowning out reason, making it hard to tell if I'm even fully conscious.

We're upside down.

The realization drags through my mind, slow and thick like honey. My limbs feel disconnected, heavy with exhaustion. The seatbelt keeps me suspended, its tight grip biting deep, it's the only thing keeping me from collapsing into the wreckage below.

A sharp metallic taste coats my tongue. Something warm snakes down my temple. My fingers tremble as I reach up, sluggish and uncoordinated, and the second they press against my skin, they come back slick and sticky, covered in blood.

I'm alive. For now.

The thought barely registers before urgency claws at my chest, pushing through the haze. Every muscle screams at me in protest as I force my hands toward the seatbelt. My fingers slip against the buckle, shaking too much to get a grip. *Come on.* Another attempt, *come on, damn it.*

Click.

Gravity takes hold, and I drop.

Pain flares through my side as I slam against the crumpled roof, the jagged remains of the windshield biting into my palms. The sharp sting barely registers beneath the deeper, pulsing ache spreading through my body. The air is thick with the scent of gasoline and scorched rubber. But beneath it, something else lingers.

My pulse stumbles, the world is swimming as I force myself to turn. The wreckage tilts in my vision, though I know it's not moving.

The driver is slumped against the wheel, his body eerily still and his face is turned just enough for me to see the gash splitting across his forehead. Blood seeps down his skin in slow, deliberate lines, pooling on the roof. The sight cuts through the numbness, sinking straight into my gut.

A new kind of fear grips me, one that has nothing to do with the wreckage around us.

The ringing in my ears fades, but the silence left in its wake is worse. A sound filters in, one that doesn't belong to the wreckage or the storm. Footsteps. Slow and heavy crunching on the glass.

My breath stills. Someone is out there. Every instinct I have screams that whoever is out there isn't here to help.

I don't know how I know that, but I just do.

A cold, primal fear coils through my body, but I can't move. Panic grips me, my limbs trapped under the weight of exhaustion and pain, my muscles refusing to cooperate. My fingers twitch against the jagged shards of glass beneath the weight of exhaustion and pain.

A shadow stretches through the wreckage, and my pulse stumbles. Maybe I'm wrong. Maybe help has found me. Maybe this nightmare is over.

I part my lips, ready to call out, to beg for help...

But nothing comes.

My voice lodges in my throat, as if my body already knows what my mind refuses to accept.

A gunshot shatters the night.

The driver's body jerks violently as blood sprays across the interior, streaking the shattered glass. The warmth splatters across my face, coating my arms and soaking into my clothes. My stomach lurches, the world tilting as my vision darkens at the edges.

Oh. My. God.

A scream claws up my throat, but when I open my mouth, nothing comes out.

Only silence.

Then a rough grip clamps around my arm, and before I can react, I'm yanked through the shattered window. The jagged glass slicing into my skin as I'm dragged from the wreckage like I weigh nothing at all.

Pain detonates through my body, sharp at first, then dulling to something distant, blurred at the edges, just out of reach. My limbs feel wrong, disconnected, as if they belong to someone else. My strength is a flickering candle, struggling against the wind, threatening to snuff out entirely.

My feet barely touch the ground before my legs give out. The earth tilts and my stomach heaves as I collapse beneath the weight of exhaustion and shock.

But I don't get the chance to fall.

Fingers grab my hair, tangling at the roots before wrenching me upright with a viscous unforgiving yank.

A sharp cry tears from my throat, pain exploding along my scalp as my head snaps back. White-hot, searing through every nerve. My knees barely hold me, my body screaming in protest, but the grip in my hair doesn't falter.

A low chuckle hums in my ear, dark and amused. "Looks like we found you." The words slither down my spine, slick with something cold and hungry. "Can't wait to have our fun first, though."

A rush of ice floods my veins.

No.

My body reacts, and instincts override my pain. I twist, lashing out, but I might as well be fighting through water. My movements are slow and uncoordinated. He laughs again, tightening his grip, yanking me closer until I can feel his breath against my cheek.

I will not die like this.

Fight.

The whisper slithers through the chaos, slipping beneath the raw terror clawing at my mind. A voice I haven't heard since Nveri.

I slam my elbow into his ribs with everything I have left. It's not much, but it's enough to make him grunt. His grip doesn't break, so I twist again, my nail raking across any part of him I can reach. His grip loosens just a fraction of a second, but it's all I need. I try to slip free, my body twisting in desperation.

"Bitch," he spits.

I don't wait.

I turn, a breath from running, when the crack of gunfire splits the night. The pain is immediate. A fire that tears through my arm, and my vision swims, black creeping in at the edges. The storm rages around me, the wind like a thousand icy knives slicing into my skin. Blood soaks through my sleeve, thick and warm, clinging to my arm like tar.

Just get to the trees.

The thought anchors me, the only solid thing in the chaos swallowing me whole.

Behind me, I hear a voice–angry and vicious. "*Stupid bitch!*"

Another gunshot.

A scream wrenches from my throat as I lurch forward, my legs nearly giving out beneath me. The ground tilts, but I don't stop. I can't. I have to keep moving.

Thunder splits the sky wide open, a deafening crack that shakes the earth. Rain hammers down, relentless and blinding, turning the world into a drowning blur. Water slams into my face and into my eyes, burning like ice.

Another gunshot–closer this time.

Then, something slams into me from behind, knocking the breath from my lungs. The world flips. Sky, ground, sky again. My body crashes into the earth, pain detonating through my ribs, my spine, and my skull. The air vanishes from my lungs in a brutal, strangled gasp.

Hot breath ghosts against my ear, thick with the scent of sweat and something rancid, seeping into my lungs like poison.

"Where are you running off to?" The voice sneers, coated with amusement, but there's something else lurking beneath it. Something colder.

The weight pressing me into the ground is suffocating, pinning my limbs beneath him like dead weight. My breath comes in shallow, frantic bursts, my body caught between exhaustion and terror. Fingers dig into my skin, bruising, his lips hovering too close.

"Don't worry, sweetheart," he murmurs, his voice thick with mockery. "We won't hurt you... too much."

My pulse hammers and my body locks up for a single, breathless moment. *Fear is a slow death, Raven.* My grandfather's words cut through the panic clawing at my chest. *Pain is a lesson. Use it.*

Panic ignites something wild inside me. I twist, ignoring the fire in my muscles, forcing my arm free. With every last ounce of strength I have left, I drive my elbow back–hard.

Bone meets bone and I hear the sickening crunch. His grunt of pain is a jagged, furious thing.

His grip loosens just enough. But that's all I need.

I rip free, scrambling to my feet. My body screams in protest, the wound in my arm blazing as my vision swims at the edges. My breath is ragged but I do not fall.

He staggers back, but not for long.

Fury twists his face into something else, his rage spilling over, snapping free like a beast finally off its leash.

"You little—" he snarls and lunges, his rage snapping free like an unchained beast.

I step back, raising my hands, my smirk razor sharp despite the exhaustion dragging at my limbs. Let him be angry. Let him be reckless. "Aw, did that hurt?" My voice comes out a little breathless. "My bad. Maybe next time, that'll teach you to get consent."

The fury in his eyes burns hotter, turning into something deadly. He moves faster this time, barreling toward me, his intent clear.

CRACK.

Lightning rips through the sky, blinding and violent. For a single, suspended heartbeat, the world turns white.

I see his face, frozen in wide-eyed terror, the light swallowing his hesitation whole. Then the electricity engulfs him, a blinding arc of raw power.

I don't stop to see what happens next. I run.

Rain slams down in sheets, drowning out everything–gunshots, shouting, the frantic pounding of my own heart. I push forward, mud slick beneath my feet, my body screaming in protest, but I don't stop.

The tree line is just ahead, and I run into it, the shadows swallowing me whole.

Branches lash at my skin, tearing at my clothes. The wind howls through the trees, screaming in my ears. The rain is relentless, turning the world into a blurred, shifting void, making every step treacherous. My lungs burn, my veins are on fire and my body pulses with fresh agony. I want to stop, but I can't.

Not yet.

Only when I'm sure I've gone far enough do I risk stopping.

I press my back against the rough trunk of an ancient tree, its bark is solid beneath my fingertips, an anchor to reality. My body trembles, but I force myself to lower, crouching against the roots, pulling my knees in tight.

One hand clamps over my mouth, muffling my breaths, silencing the terror clawing its way up my throat. My ears strain against the storm, searching for any sign of movement. Footsteps. Voices. Anything.

Every nerve in my body remains on edge, stretched so thin I feel like I might snap. My muscles are rigid with adrenaline, trembling with the effort to stay still. Pain pulses through my arm in sharp, unforgiving waves, the bullet wound is a searing ache that refuses to be ignored. My sleeve is soaked, whether from blood or rain, I can't tell anymore. My entire body is wrecked, not just from the crash or the fight, but from everything that happened since the diner.

And to top it all off, my phone is gone. Not that it would have helped, considering it was dead before any of this started.

A bitter laugh threatens to slip free, but I choke it down, pressing the heels of my palms against my eyes. *Hold it together.* I will not break here. Not now. Not when I still have a chance to get out of this.

But my body has other ideas.

The adrenaline that's kept me moving and alive, is wearing off. Fast.

A strange, creeping cold seeps into my limbs. My fingers tingle, my legs feel numb, and the fire in my arm dulls–not in relief, but in a way that feels wrong. Too much blood loss maybe? The storm rages on, but everything around me starts to feel distant, as if I'm slipping away, the sounds are muffled, my vision is starting to blur at the edges.

I was supposed to be on vacation. I was supposed to be living a normal life, exploring Scotland, drinking too much tea, making bad decisions that didn't involve running for my life. But then came the dreams. The journal. The flickering lights. The magic I still don't fully understand. And now? Now I'm being hunted?

A shuddering breath escapes before I can stop it. My fingers drag down my face, damp with sweat, rain, blood, and who knows what else. I barely register the single tear that slips past my defenses before I swipe it away.

Not yet.

The air around me feels heavier, the weight of the storm pressing against my skin, humming with energy. I don't know how long I've been sitting here, swallowed by darkness. Minutes? Hours?

My heartbeat stumbles. The trees blur.

No.

I try to move, but my limbs won't cooperate. The darkness pressing at the edges of my vision inches closer. My body feels disconnected and weightless. Somewhere in the haze, I know what's happening.

I'm in shock, and I've lost a lot of blood.

I blink, my eyelids are heavy, my body is so cold. I need to get up. I need to move.

I don't.

The last thing I register is the storm whispering through the trees, the rain tapping against my skin before darkness takes me whole.

Want to know more about the Shadow Series or me?
Stay connected here for all the updates!

TikTok

Instagram

Spotify Playlist

Made in the USA
Monee, IL
17 May 2025

17529805R00410